the Indigo Spell

the Indigo Spell

A *Bloodlines* NOVEL

RICHELLE MEAD

razOr
bill

An Imprint of Penguin Group (USA)

razOr
bill

A division of Penguin Young Readers Group
Published by the Penguin Group
Penguin Group (USA)
345 Hudson Street
New York, New York 10014, U.S.A.

USA / Canada / UK / Ireland / Australia /
New Zealand / India / South Africa / China
Penguin Books Ltd, Registered Offices: 80 Strand, London WC2R 0RL, England
For more information about the Penguin Group visit penguin.com

Published simultaneously in Canada

ISBN: 978-1-59514-613-7

Printed in the United States of America

5 7 9 10 8 6

For Heather Osborn,

Malachi Wolfe's biggest fan.

CHAPTER 1

THIS WASN'T THE FIRST TIME I'd been pulled out of bed for a crucial mission. It was, however, the first time I'd been subjected to such a personal line of questioning.

"Are you a virgin?"

"Huh?" I rubbed my sleepy eyes, just in case this was all some sort of bizarre dream that would disappear. An urgent phone call had dragged me out of bed five minutes ago, and I was having a little trouble adjusting.

My history teacher, Ms. Terwilliger, leaned closer and repeated the question in a stage whisper: "I said, are you a virgin?"

"Um, yes. . ."

I was fully awake now and glanced uneasily around my dorm's lobby, making sure no one was around to witness this crazy exchange. I didn't have to worry. Aside from a bored-looking desk attendant on the far side of the room, the lobby was empty, probably because no sane person would be up at

1

this time of night. When Ms. Terwilliger's call had woken me, she'd demanded I meet her here for a "life-or-death" matter. Getting interrogated about my personal life wasn't quite what I'd expected.

She stepped back and sighed in relief. "Yes, of course. Of course you're a virgin."

I narrowed my eyes, unsure if I should be offended or not. "Of course? What's that supposed to mean? What's going on?"

She immediately snapped back to attention and pushed her wire-rimmed glasses up the bridge of her nose. They were always slipping down. "No time to explain. We have to go." She grabbed hold of my arm, but I resisted and stayed where I was.

"Ma'am, it's three in the morning!" And then, just so she'd understand the severity of the situation: "On a school night."

"Never mind that." She turned in the direction of the desk attendant and called across the room, "I'm taking Sydney Melrose with me. Mrs. Weathers can argue with me about the curfew tomorrow."

The attendant looked startled, but she was just some college student who'd been hired to sit there overnight. She was no match for the formidable Ms. Terwilliger, with her tall, gangly stature and birdlike face. The real authority keeping girls in my dorm was the security guard outside, but he simply nodded in a friendly way when Ms. Terwilliger dragged me past. It made me wonder just how many girls she'd abducted in the middle of the night.

"I'm in my pajamas," I told her. It was the last protest I could offer as we reached her car, which was parked in a fire lane. She drove a red Volkswagen Beetle with flowers painted on the sides. Somehow, this didn't surprise me in the least.

"You'll be fine," she said, fishing car keys out of her massive velvet purse.

Around us, the desert night was cool and silent. Tall palm trees created dark, spiderlike shapes against the sky. Beyond them, a full moon and smattering of stars glittered. I wrapped my arms around myself, touching the soft fabric of my micro-fleece robe. Underneath it, I had on full-length striped pajamas paired with fluffy beige slippers. The ensemble worked well in my cozy dorm room but wasn't exactly practical for a Palm Springs night. But then, going out in pajamas wasn't really practical in any place.

She unlocked the car, and I stepped gingerly inside, having to dodge empty paper coffee cups and old issues of *Utne Reader*. My neat sensibilities cringed at that kind of mess, but it was the least of my worries right now.

"Ms. Terwilliger," I said, once we were driving through the suburban streets. "What's going on?" Now that we were out of the dorm, I hoped she'd start talking sense. I hadn't forgotten her "life-or-death" comment and was beginning to grow nervous.

Her eyes were on the road ahead of us, and lines of worry marked her angular face. "I need you to cast a spell."

I froze as I tried to process her words. Not long ago, this proclamation would've sent me into protests and fits of revulsion. Not that I was comfortable with it now. Magic still freaked me out. Ms. Terwilliger taught at my private high school, Amberwood Prep, by day and was a witch at night. She said I, too, possessed a natural affinity for magic and had managed to teach me some spells, despite my best efforts to resist. I actually had a few good reasons for wanting to avoid anything arcane.

Aside from inborn beliefs about magic being wrong, I simply didn't want to get caught up in any more supernatural affairs than I had to. I already spent my days as part of a secret society that kept vampires secret from the human world. That and my schoolwork were enough to keep anyone busy.

Nonetheless, her magical training had gotten me out of some dangerous situations recently, and I was no longer so quick to dismiss it. So, her suggesting I perform magic wasn't the weirdest thing going on here.

"Why would you need me for that?" I asked. There were few cars out, but occasionally, passing headlights would cast a ghostly light over us. "You're a million times more powerful. I can't cast a fraction of the things you can."

"Power is one thing," she admitted. "But there are other limitations and factors at work here. I can't cast this particular spell."

I crossed my arms and slouched back in the seat. If I kept focusing on the practical aspects, I could ignore how worried I was growing. "And it couldn't have waited until morning?"

"No," she said gravely. "It could not."

Something about the tone of her voice sent chills down my spine, and I fell silent as we continued our drive. We were headed outside of the city and suburbs, into the wilds of the true desert. The farther we drove from civilization, the darker it became. Once we were off the freeway, there were no street-lights or houses in sight. Spiky desert shrubs created dark shapes along the side of the road that put me in mind of crouching animals, ready to pounce. *There's no one out here,* I thought. *And no one back at Amberwood knows you're here either.*

I shifted uneasily as I recalled her virgin question. Was I

going to be a sacrifice in some unholy ritual? I wished that I'd thought to bring my cell phone—not that I could have told my organization, the Alchemists, that I was spending so much time with a magic user. And not just any magic user—one who was teaching *me* to become one too. Better to risk being sacrificed than face the Alchemists' wrath.

Twenty minutes later, Ms. Terwilliger finally pulled to a stop along the side of a dusty one-lane road that seemed to be a direct route to nowhere. She got out of the car and motioned for me to do the same. It was colder here than it had been back at Amberwood. Looking up into the night sky, I caught my breath. Free of the city lights, the stars were now out in full force. I could see the Milky Way and a dozen constellations usually hidden to the naked eye.

"Stargaze later," she said curtly. "We need to hurry, before the moon progresses much further."

A moonlight ritual, a barren desert, virgin sacrifice . . . what had I just foolishly walked into? The way Ms. Terwilliger pushed me into magic always annoyed me, but I never thought she posed a threat. Now I berated myself for being so naive.

She tossed a duffel bag over one shoulder and headed off into a desolate stretch of land, dotted with rocks and scraggly vegetation. Even with the brilliant celestial display there wasn't much light out here, yet she walked purposefully, as though she knew exactly where she was going. I dutifully followed, wincing as I crossed the rocky ground. My fuzzy slippers had never been intended for this sort of terrain.

"Here," she said when we reached a small clearing. She carefully set down the duffel bag and knelt to rifle through it. "This'll do."

The desert that was so mercilessly hot in the day became cold at night, but I was still sweating. Probably my own anxiety had more to do with that than the temperature or heavy pajamas. I retied my robe more tightly, making a perfect knot. I found that kind of detail and routine soothing.

Ms. Terwilliger produced a large oval mirror with a scalloped silver frame. She set it down in the middle of the clearing, glanced up at the sky, and then shifted the mirror over a little. "Come here, Miss Melbourne." She pointed to a spot opposite her, on the other side of the mirror. "Sit there and make yourself comfortable."

At Amberwood, I went by the name of Sydney Melrose, rather than my true one, Sydney Sage. Ms. Terwilliger had gotten my made-up name wrong on the first day of class, and it, unfortunately, stuck. I followed her directions, not that I could really get all that comfortable out here. I was pretty sure I could hear some large animal scuffling out in the brush and added "coyotes" to my mental list of dangers I faced out here, right below "magic use" and "lack of coffee."

"Now then. Let's get started." Ms. Terwilliger peered at me with eyes that were dark and frightening in the desert night. "Are you wearing anything metal? You need to take it off."

"No, I—oh. Wait."

I reached around my neck and unfastened a delicate gold chain that held a small cross. I'd had the necklace for years but had recently given it to someone else, for comfort. He'd given it back to me recently, by way of our mutual friend Jill Mastrano Dragomir. Even now, I could picture the angry look on her face as she'd stormed up to me at school and thrust the cross into my hand without a word.

I stared at the cross now as it gleamed in the moonlight. A queasy feeling welled up in the pit of my stomach as I thought about Adrian, the guy I'd given it to. I'd done so before he professed his love for me, something that had caught me totally off guard a few weeks ago. But maybe I shouldn't have been so surprised. The more I looked back—and I did so all the time—the more I began to recall telltale signs that should have tipped me off to his feelings. I'd just been too blind to notice at the time.

Of course, it wouldn't have mattered if I'd seen it coming or not. Adrian was totally unsuitable for me, and it had nothing to do with his many vices or potential descent into insanity. Adrian was a vampire. True, he was a Moroi—one of the good, living vampires—but it made no difference. Humans and vampires couldn't be together. This was one point the Moroi and Alchemists stood firmly together on. It was still amazing to me that Adrian had voiced those feelings to me. It was amazing that he could even have them or that he'd had the nerve to kiss me, even if it was a kiss that had left me dizzy and breathless.

I'd had to reject him, of course. My training would allow nothing less. Our situation here in Palm Springs forced the two of us to constantly be together in social situations, and it had been rough since his declaration. For me, it wasn't just the awkwardness of our new relationship. I . . . well, I missed him. Before this debacle, he and I had been friends and spent a lot of time together. I'd gotten used to his smirky smile and the quick banter that always flowed between us. Until those things were gone, I hadn't realized how much I relied on them. How much I needed them. I felt empty inside . . . which was ridiculous, of course. Why should I care so much about one vampire?

Sometimes it made me angry. Why had he ruined such a

7

good thing between us? Why had he made me miss him so much? And what had he expected me to do? He had to have known it was impossible for us to be together. I couldn't have feelings for him. I *couldn't*. If we'd lived among the Keepers—a group of uncivilized vampires, humans, and dhampirs—maybe he and I could have . . . no. Even if I had feelings for him—and I firmly told myself I didn't—it was wrong for us to even consider such a relationship.

Now Adrian spoke to me as little as possible. And always, always, he watched me with a haunted look in his green eyes, one that made my heart ache and—

"Ah! What is that?"

I squirmed as Ms. Terwilliger dumped a bowl full of dried leaves and flowers over my head. I'd been so fixated on the cross and my memories that I hadn't seen her coming.

"Rosemary," she said matter-of-factly. "Hyssop. Anise. Don't do that." I'd reached up to pull some of the leaves out of my hair. "You need that for the spell."

"Right," I said, getting back to business. I set the cross carefully on the ground, trying to clear my mind of green, green eyes. "The spell that only I can do. Why is that again?"

"Because it has to be done by a virgin," she explained. I tried not to grimace. Her words implied that she was not a virgin, and even if that made sense for a forty-year-old woman, it still wasn't a thought I wanted to spend a lot of time on. "That, and the person we're looking for has shielded herself from me. But you? You she won't expect."

I looked down at the shining mirror and understood. "This is a scrying spell. Why aren't we doing the one I did before?"

Not that I was eager to repeat that spell. I'd used it to find someone, and it had involved me staring into a bowl of water for hours. Still, now that I knew how to do it, I knew I could perform it again. Besides, I didn't like the idea of walking into a spell I knew nothing about. Words and herbs were one thing, but what else might she ask of me? Endanger my soul? Give up my blood?

"That spell only works for someone you know," she explained. "This one will help you find someone you've never met before."

I frowned. As much as I didn't like magic, I did like problem solving—and the puzzles magic often presented intrigued me. "How will I know who to look for, then?"

Ms. Terwilliger handed me a photograph. My eyes had adjusted to the darkness, and I looked into the face of a pretty young woman. There was a striking resemblance between her and my teacher, though it wasn't initially obvious. Rather than Ms. Terwilliger's dull brown hair, this woman's was dark, nearly black. She was also much more glamorous, dressed in a black satin evening gown that was a far cry from Ms. Terwilliger's usual hippie attire. Despite those ostensible differences, the two women shared the same high cheekbones and aquiline eyes.

I glanced back up. "She's related to you."

"She's my older sister," Ms. Terwilliger confirmed, her voice remarkably flat. Older? I would've guessed this woman was at least ten years younger.

"Is she missing?" I asked. When I'd scried before, it had been to find a kidnapped friend.

Ms. Terwilliger's lips twitched. "Not in the way you're thinking." From the never-ending duffel bag, she produced a small leather book and opened it to a marked page. Squinting at where she indicated, I could make out handwritten Latin words describing the mirror and herbal concoction she'd dumped on me. Following that were directions on how to use the spell. No bloodletting, thankfully.

"It sounds too simple," I said suspiciously. I'd learned that spells that only had a few steps and components usually required a lot of mental energy. I'd passed out from the other scrying spell.

She nodded, guessing my thoughts. "It takes a lot of focus— more than the last one. But, as much as you don't want to hear this, your strength has grown enough that you'll probably have an easier time than before."

I scowled. She was right. I didn't want to hear that.

Or did I?

Part of me knew I should refuse to go along with this mad- ness. Another part of me worried she'd abandon me in the desert if I didn't help. And still another part was insanely curious to see how this would all work.

Taking a deep breath, I recited the book's incantation and then set the picture in the middle of the mirror. I repeated the incantation and removed the picture. Leaning forward, I stared into the shining surface, trying to clear my mind and let myself become one with the darkness and moonlight. A hum of energy coursed through me, much more quickly than I expected. Nothing changed in the mirror right away, though. Only my reflection peered back at me, the poor lighting dulling my blond hair, which looked terrible both from sleeping on it and having a bunch of dried plants hanging in its strands.

The energy continued to build in me, growing surprisingly warm and exhilarating. I closed my eyes and sank into it. I felt like I was floating in the moonlight, like I *was* the moonlight. I could've stayed that way forever.

"Do you see anything?"

Ms. Terwilliger's voice was an unwelcome interruption to my blissful state, but I obediently opened my eyes and looked into the mirror. My reflection was gone. A silvery gray mist hung in front of a building, but I knew the mist wasn't physical. It was magically produced, a mental barrier to keep me from seeing the image that lay beyond it. Strengthening my will, I pushed my mind passed that barrier, and after a few moments, the mist shattered.

"I see a building." My voice echoed oddly in the night. "An old Victorian house. Dark red, with a traditional covered porch. There are hydrangea bushes in front of it. There's a sign too, but I can't read it."

"Can you tell where the house is?" My teacher's voice seemed very far away. "Look around it."

I tried to pull back, to extend my vision beyond the house. It took a few moments, but slowly, the image panned out as though I were watching a movie, revealing a neighborhood of similar houses, all Victorian with wide porches and creeping vines. They were a beautiful, perfect piece of history set in the modern world.

"Nothing exact," I told her. "Just some quaint residential street."

"Go back further. See the larger picture."

I did, and it was like I drifted up into the sky, looking down upon the neighborhood the way some soaring bird would. The houses extended into more neighborhoods, which eventually gave way to industrial and commercial areas. I continued moving back. The businesses became more and more densely packed. More streets crisscrossed between them. The buildings grew taller and taller, eventually materializing into a familiar skyline.

"Los Angeles," I said. "The house is on the outskirts of Los Angeles."

I heard a sharp intake of breath, followed by: "Thank you, Miss Melbourne. That will be all."

A hand suddenly waved across my field of vision, shattering the city image. Also shattered was that state of euphoria. I was no longer floating, no longer made of light. I came crashing down to reality, down to the rocky desert landscape and my stuffy pajamas. I felt exhausted and shaky, like I might faint. Ms. Terwilliger handed me a thermos full of orange juice, which I drank greedily. As the nutrients hit my system and strengthened me, I began to feel a little better. Intense magic use depleted blood sugar.

"Does that help?" I asked, once I'd downed the thermos. A nagging voice inside me started to chastise about how many calories were in orange juice, but I ignored it. "Was that what you wanted to know?"

Ms. Terwilliger gave me a smile that didn't extend to her eyes. "It helps, yes. Was it what I wanted?" She stared off into the distance. "No, not exactly. I was hoping you'd name some other city. Some city far, far away."

I picked up my cross and refastened it around my neck. The familiar object brought on a sense of normality after what I'd just done. It also made me feel guilty, looking back on the euphoric high the magic had given me. Humans weren't supposed to wield magic—and they certainly weren't supposed to enjoy it. Running my fingers over the cross's surface, I found myself thinking of Adrian again. Had he ever worn it? Or had he just kept it around for luck? Had his fingers traced the cross's shape like mine often did?

Ms. Terwilliger began gathering her things. When she stood up, I followed suit. "What does it mean exactly, ma'am?" I asked. "That I saw Los Angeles?"

I followed her back toward the car, and she didn't answer right away. When she did, her voice was uncharacteristically grim. "It means that she's much closer than I would like. It also means, whether you want to or not, you're going to have to work on improving your magical skills very, very quickly."

I came to a halt. Suddenly, I felt angry. Enough was enough. I was exhausted and ached all over. She'd dragged me out here in the middle of the night and now had the presumption to make a statement like that when she knew how I felt about magic? Worse, her words frightened me. What did I have to do with this? This was her spell, her cause. Yet, she'd given the directive with such force, such certainty, that it almost seemed as though *I* was the reason we'd come out here to this wasteland.

"Ma'am—" I began.

Ms. Terwilliger spun around and leaned toward me so that there were only a few inches between us. I gulped, swallowing whatever outraged words I'd been about to utter. I'd never seen her look like this. She wasn't scary, not exactly, but there was an intensity I'd never seen before, far different from the usual scattered teacher I knew. She also looked . . . frightened. *Life or death.*

"Sydney," she said, in a rare use of my first name. "Let me assure you that this is not some trick on my part. You *will* improve upon your skills, whether you like it or not. And it's not because I'm cruel, not because I'm trying to fulfill some selfish desire. It's not even because I hate seeing you waste your ability."

"Then why?" I asked in a small voice. "Why do I need to learn more?"

The wind whispered around us, blowing some of the dried leaves and flowers from my hair. The shadows we cast took on an ominous feel, and the moonlight and starlight that had seemed so divine earlier now felt cold and harsh.

"Because," Ms. Terwilliger said. "It's for your own protection."

CHAPTER 2

MS. TERWILLIGER REFUSED to say much more after that. She drove us back to Amberwood and hardly seemed to know I was there. She just kept muttering things to herself like, "Not enough time" and "Need more proof." When she finally dropped me off, I tried pressing her for more information.

"What was all that about protecting myself?" I asked. "Protection from what?"

We were parked in the fire lane again, and she still wore that distracted look. "I'll explain later, in our session tomorrow."

"I can't," I reminded her. "I'm leaving right after my regular classes. Remember? I have a flight to catch. I told you about it last week. And yesterday. And earlier today."

That brought her back to attention. "Did you? Well, then. I suppose we'll make do with what we must. I'll see what I can have for you in the morning."

I left her for my bed after that, not that I could get much sleep. And when I showed up to her history class the next morning, she was true to her word. Before the bell rang, she walked up to my desk and handed me an old book with a cracked red leather cover. The title was in Latin and translated to *Elements of Battle*, which sent a chill down my spine. Spells to create light and invisibility were one thing. There was a practicality to them that I could *almost* rationalize. But battle spells? Something told me I might have a little trouble with those.

"Reading material for the plane," she said. She spoke in her usual, addled scholar voice, but I could see a glint of that anxiety from last night in her eyes. "Focus only on the first section. I trust you'll do your usual thorough job—and then some."

None of the other arriving students paid any attention to us. My last class of the day was an independent study session on late-antique history, which she served as my mentor for. More often than not, she used the session as a passive-aggressive way to teach me magic. So, her giving me books like this was nothing out of the ordinary.

"And," she added, "if you could find out where that neighborhood is, it would be extremely useful."

I was speechless for a few moments. Locate one neighborhood in the greater Los Angeles metropolitan area? "That's . . . a very large area to cover," I said at last, choosing my words carefully with witnesses around.

She nodded and pushed her glasses up her nose. "I know. Most people probably couldn't do it." And on that semi-complimentary note, she returned to her desk at the front of the classroom.

"What neighborhood?" asked a new voice.

Eddie Castile had just arrived and slid into a neighboring desk. Eddie was a dhampir—possessing a mix of human and vampire DNA that had been passed down from days when the two races mixed. For all intents and purposes, though, he was indistinguishable from an ordinary human. With his sandy-colored hair and brown eyes, he also bore enough resemblance to me to support our cover story that we were twins. In reality, Eddie was here at Amberwood as a bodyguard for Jill. Dissidents among her own kind, the Moroi, were hunting her, and even though we'd seen no sign of them since coming to Palm Springs, Eddie was always vigilant and ready to pounce.

I slipped the red leather book into my messenger bag. "Don't ask. Another of her wacky assignments." None of my friends—save Adrian—knew about my involvement with Ms. Terwilliger's magic use. Well, and Jill by default. All Moroi possessed some sort of elemental magic. Adrian's was a rare and powerful one called spirit, which could work miracles of healing. He'd used that magic to bring Jill back from the dead when assassins had killed her. Doing so had made Jill "shadow-kissed"—that is, it created a psychic bond between them, one that allowed Jill to feel his emotions and sometimes see through his eyes. As a result, Jill knew more about what went on between Adrian and me than I liked.

I took my car keys out of my bag and reluctantly handed them over to Eddie. He was the only one I trusted to drive my car, and I always let him borrow it when I left town, in case he needed to run errands for our group. "Here you go. I better get it back in one piece. Do *not* let Angeline near the driver's seat."

He grinned. "Do I look suicidal? I probably won't even use it. Are you sure you don't want me to drive you to the airport later?"

"You'd miss class," I said. The only reason I was able to cut school early was because of the unusual nature of my independent study.

"I wouldn't mind, believe me. I've got a science test." He grimaced and lowered his voice. "I hated physics the first time, you know."

I couldn't help a smile. Both Eddie and I were eighteen and had graduated high school, me through homeschooling and him through an elite Moroi and dhampir academy. We couldn't pose as students without going through the motions of class, however. While I didn't mind the extra work, Eddie wasn't as taken with a love of learning as I was.

"No thanks," I told him. "A cab will be fine."

The bell rang, and Eddie straightened up in his desk. As Ms. Terwilliger called the class to order, he whispered to me, "Jill's really bummed she can't go."

"I know," I murmured back. "But we all know why she can't."

"Yeah," he agreed. "What I don't know is why she's mad at you."

I turned toward the front of the classroom and pointedly ignored him. Jill was the only one who knew about Adrian's declaration of love, thanks to that bond. It was another one of those things I wished hadn't been shared, but Adrian couldn't help it. Although Jill knew vampire-human romances were wrong, she couldn't forgive me for hurting Adrian so badly. To make things worse, she was probably personally experiencing some of his pain.

Even if our other friends didn't know what had occurred, it was obvious that something wasn't right with Jill and me. Eddie had picked up on it right away and immediately interrogated me. I'd given him a vague excuse about Jill not liking some rules I'd instated for her here at school. Eddie hadn't bought that, but Jill had been just as close-mouthed on the matter, leaving him clueless and frustrated.

The school day zipped by, and before long, I was in a taxi and on my way to the airport. I'd packed light and only had one small suitcase and my messenger bag, both of which could be carried on. For what seemed like the hundredth time, I took out a small silver and white gift bag and examined its contents. Inside was an expensive crystal sun catcher, the kind meant to be hung on a porch or in a window. It depicted two doves in flight, facing each other. Wrapping it back in its tissue paper, I returned it to its gift bag and then my own bag. I hoped it would be an acceptable gift for the upcoming event.

I was going to a vampire wedding.

I'd never been to one before. Probably no Alchemist had. Although we worked with the Moroi to protect their existence, the Alchemists made it clear they wanted no involvement that went beyond business contact. After recent events, however, both groups had decided it would be good to improve our professional relations. Since this wedding was a big deal, a few other Alchemists and I had been invited.

I knew the couple, and in theory, I was excited to see them married. It was the rest of the event that made me nervous: a huge social gathering of Moroi and dhampirs. Even with other Alchemists there, we'd be hopelessly outnumbered. Being in Palm Springs with Eddie, Jill, and the others had gone a long way in improving my feelings toward their kind. I got along with that little group well and now considered them friends. But even as liberal as I was in such matters, I still possessed a lot of the anxiety other Alchemists had inside the vampiric world. Maybe Moroi and dhampirs weren't creatures of evil, like I'd once believed, but they certainly weren't human.

I kind of wished my Palm Springs friends were coming with me, but that had been out of the question. The whole point of Jill and the rest of us being in Palm Springs was to hide her away and keep her safe from those trying to kill her. Both Moroi and Strigoi tended to avoid sunny, desert regions. If she suddenly showed up at a major Moroi function, it would defeat the whole purpose. Eddie and Angeline, another dhampir protecting her at Amberwood, had to stay behind as well. Only Adrian and I had been invited to the wedding, and we were thankfully on separate flights. If anyone had noticed that he and I were traveling together, it could attract attention back in Palm Springs, which could then expose Jill. Adrian's flight wasn't even leaving from Palm Springs. He was flying out by way of Los Angeles, two hours west, just to make sure we weren't linked together.

I had to connect through a different flight in Los Angeles, which reminded me of Ms. Terwilliger's task. Find one neighborhood in all of Los Angeles's greater metropolitan area. Sure, no problem. The only thing I had going for me was that the Victorian houses were so distinct. If I could find some historical society, there was a good chance they could direct me toward areas matching that description. It would narrow my search considerably.

I reached my gate at LAX an hour before the scheduled flight. I'd just gotten cozy with Ms. Terwilliger's book when an overhead announcement declared, "Paging passenger Melrose. Please come see a customer service agent."

I felt a sinking feeling in the pit of my stomach. Gathering up my things, I approached the desk and was greeted by a cheery airline representative.

"I'm sad to tell you this flight has been overbooked," she said. From her peppy voice and big smile, she didn't seem sad at all.

"What's that mean for me, exactly?" I asked, my dread growing. "I have a confirmed seat." I dealt with bureaucracy and red tape all the time, but overbooking flights was something I'd never understood. How did that even happen? It wasn't like the number of seats was a surprise to them.

"It means that you're no longer on the flight," she explained. "You and a couple other volunteers gave up your seats to accommodate that family. Otherwise, they would've had to be split up."

"Volunteers?" I repeated, following her gesture. Off to the side of the seating area, a family with seven children smiled back at me. The children were tiny and adorable, with big eyes and the kind of cuteness you saw in musicals about orphans finding new homes. Outraged, I turned back toward the agent. "How can you do that? I checked in way ahead of time! I have a wedding to get to. I can't miss it."

The woman produced a boarding pass. "We've more than made up for it. We've booked you on another flight, to Philadelphia—one that's leaving sooner. And you've even been upgraded to first class for your inconvenience."

"That's something," I said. I was still annoyed at this, simply out of principle. I liked order and procedure. Altering those threw off my world. I looked down at the boarding pass and then did a double take. "It's leaving now!"

She nodded. "Like I said, sooner. I'd hurry up if I were you."

Then, on cue, I heard a last-call announcement for my new flight, saying all passengers need to be on board now, as they were about to shut the cabin doors. I wasn't the swearing type, but I almost was then—especially when I saw that my new gate was on the opposite side of the terminal. Without another word, I grabbed my things and sprinted toward the gate as quickly as I could, making a mental note to write a letter of complaint to the airline. Through some miracle, I made it just before my new flight was closed to passengers, though the agent working that gate sternly told me that next time, I should plan ahead and allow more time.

I ignored her and headed into the airplane, where I was greeted by a much nicer flight attendant—especially when she saw my first class ticket. "You're right here, Miss Melrose," she said, pointing to the third row of the cabin. "We're so glad you could join us."

She helped me put my suitcase in the overhead bin, which proved to be pretty difficult since other, earlier passengers had taken up most of the space. It required some creative knowledge of spatial relations, and when we finally managed it, I practically passed out into my seat, exhausted from this unexpected flurry of excitement. So much for a relaxing trip. I had just enough time to fasten my seat belt before the plane began backing up. Feeling a little steadier, I plucked the safety card from its pocket so that I could follow along with the attendant's presentation. No matter how many times I flew, I always thought it was important to be up to speed on procedures. I was watching the attendant fasten an oxygen mask when a familiar and intoxicating scent washed over me. In all of the chaos of making this flight, I hadn't even bothered to pay attention to my seatmate.

Adrian.

I stared in disbelief. He was watching me with amusement and had no doubt been waiting to see how long it would take me to notice him. I didn't even bother asking what he was doing here. I'd known he was flying out of LAX, and through some wacky twist of happenstance, I'd been bumped to his flight.

"This is impossible," I exclaimed. The scientist in me was too amazed to fully realize the uncomfortable nature of the situation I now found myself in. "It's one thing for me to get moved to a new flight. But to end up next to you? Do you know what the odds of that are? It's incredible."

"Some might call it fate," he said. "Or maybe there just aren't that many flights to Philadelphia." He raised a glass of clear liquid to me in a toast. Since I'd never seen Adrian drink water, I had to assume it was vodka. "Nice to see you, by the way."

"Um, you too."

The engines roared to life around us, momentarily sparing me from conversation. Reality began sinking in. I was trapped on a five-hour flight with Adrian Ivashkov. *Five hours.* Five hours sitting only a few inches from him, smelling his overpriced cologne and looking into those knowing eyes. What was I going to do? Nothing, of course. There was nowhere to go, nowhere to escape since even first-class passengers weren't allowed parachutes. My heart began to race as I frantically groped for something to say. He was watching me in silence, still with that small smirk, waiting for me to lead the conversation.

"So," I said at last, staring at my hands. "How's, uh, your car?"

"I left it out on the street. Figured it'll be fine there while I'm gone."

I jerked my head up, jaw dropping. "You did *what*? They'll tow it if it's left there overnight!"

Adrian was laughing before I even finished. "So that's what it takes to get a passionate reaction, huh?" He shook his head. "Don't worry, Sage. I was just kidding. It's tucked away safely in my building's parking lot."

I felt my cheeks burn. I hated that I'd fallen into his joke and was even a little embarrassed that I'd just flipped out over a car. Admittedly, it wasn't just any car. It was a beautiful, classic Mustang that Adrian had recently purchased. In fact, he'd bought it to impress me, pretending he couldn't drive manual transmission in order to spend more time with me while I taught him. I thought the car was amazing, but it still astonished me that he would have gone to that much trouble for us to be together.

We reached our cruising altitude, and the flight attendant returned to get Adrian another drink. "Anything for you, miss?" she asked.

"Diet Coke," I said automatically.

Adrian tsked once she was gone. "You could've gotten that for free back in coach."

I rolled my eyes. "Do I have to spend the next five hours being harassed? If so, I'll go back in coach and let some lucky person 'upgrade' to my seat."

Adrian held up his hands in a placating gesture. "No, no. Carry on. I'll entertain myself."

Entertaining himself turned out to be doing a crossword puzzle in one of the in-flight magazines. I took out Ms. Terwilliger's book and tried to read, but it was hard to focus with him beside me. I kept sneaking glances out of the corner of my eye, partly to see if he was looking at me and partly just to study his features. He was the same Adrian as ever, annoyingly good looking with his tousled brown hair and sculpted face. I vowed I wouldn't speak to him, but when I noticed he hadn't written anything in a while and was tapping his pen loudly on the tray, I couldn't help myself.

"What is it?" I asked.

"Seven-letter word for 'cotton gin pioneer.'"

"*Whitney,*" I replied.

He leaned over and wrote in the letters. "'Dominates the Mohs' scale.' Also seven letters."

"*Diamond.*"

Five words later, I realized what was happening. "Hey," I told him. "I am *not* doing this."

He looked up at me with angelic eyes. "Doing what?"

"You know what. You're luring me in. You know I can't resist—"

"Me?" he suggested.

I pointed at the magazine. "Random trivia." I angled my body away from him and made a big show of opening my book. "I have work to do."

I felt Adrian look over my shoulder, and I tried to ignore how aware of his proximity I was. "Looks like Jackie's still got you working hard in her class." Adrian had met Ms. Terwilliger recently and had somehow charmed his way into a first-name basis.

"This one's more like an extracurricular activity," I explained.

"Really? I thought you were pretty against doing any more with this stuff than you had to."

I shut the book in frustration. "I am! But then she said—" I bit off the words, reminding myself that I shouldn't engage with Adrian any more than I had to. It was just too easy to slip back into old, friendly behaviors with him. It felt right when, obviously, it was wrong.

"Then what?" he prompted, voice gentle.

I looked up at him and saw no smugness or mockery. I didn't even see any of the burning hurt that had plagued me these last few weeks. He actually looked concerned, which momentarily distracted me from Ms. Terwilliger's task. Seeing him this way contrasted drastically with what had followed in the wake of our kiss. I'd been so nervous at the thought of sitting with him on this flight, and yet, here he was, ready to support me. Why the change?

I hesitated, unsure what to do. Since last night, I'd been turning her words and the vision over and over in my head, trying to figure out what they meant. Adrian was the only person who knew about my involvement with her and magic (aside from Jill), and until this moment, I hadn't realized how badly I was dying to discuss this with someone. So, I cracked and told him the whole story of my desert adventure.

When I finished, I was surprised to see how dark his expression had become. "It's one thing for her to try to get you to learn spells here and there. But it's a totally different thing for her to drag you into something dangerous."

His ardent concern surprised me a little—but maybe it shouldn't have. "From the way she talked, though, it wasn't like it was her doing. She seemed pretty upset about . . . well, whatever all this means."

Adrian pointed at the book. "And that'll help somehow?"

"I guess." I ran my fingers over the cover and embossed Latin words. "It has protection and attack spells—things that are a bit more hard core than what I've ever done. I don't like it, and these aren't even the really advanced ones. She told me to skip those."

"You don't like magic, period," he reminded me. "But if these can keep you safe, then maybe you shouldn't ignore them."

I hated admitting when he was right. It only encouraged him. "Yeah, but I just wish I knew what I was trying to stay safe from—no. No. We can't do this."

Without even realizing it, I'd slipped into the way things used to be, talking to Adrian in that easy, comfortable way we had. In fact, I'd even been confiding in him. He looked startled.

"Do what? I stopped asking you for crossword help, didn't I?"

I took a deep breath, bracing myself. I'd known this moment was coming, no matter how much I wanted to put it off. I just hadn't expected it to come while on a plane ride.

"Adrian, we have to talk about what happened. Between you and me," I declared.

He took a moment to consider my words. "Well . . . last I knew, *nothing* was happening between you and me."

I dared a look at him. "Exactly. I'm sorry for what happened . . . what I said, but it was all true. We have to move past this and go on with our lives in a normal way. It's for the good of our group in Palm Springs."

"Funny, I *have* moved past it," he said. "*You're* the one bringing it up."

I blushed again. "But it's because of you! You've spent the last few weeks all moody and sulking, hardly ever talking to me.

And when you do, there's usually some nasty barb in it." While recently having dinner at Clarence Donahue's, I'd seen one of the most terrifying spiders ever come crawling into the living room. Mustering all my courage, I'd caught the creepy little beast and set him free. Adrian's comment on my brave act had been, "Wow, I didn't know you actually faced down things that scared you. I thought your normal response was to run kicking and screaming from them and pretend they don't exist."

"You're right about the attitude," he said now, nodding along with my words. Once again, he looked remarkably serious. "And I'm sorry."

"You . . . are?" I could only stare. "So . . . you're done with all of that . . . stuff? Done with, uh, feeling that way?" I couldn't bring myself to elaborate. *Done with being in love with me.*

"Oh, no," he said cheerfully. "Not at all."

"But you just said—"

"I'm done with the pouting," he said. "Done with being moody—well, I mean, I'm always a little moody. That's what Adrian Ivashkov's all about. But I'm done with the excessive stuff. That didn't get me anywhere with Rose. It won't get me anywhere with you."

"*Nothing* will get you anywhere with me," I exclaimed.

"I don't know about that." He put on an introspective look that was both unexpected and intriguing. "You're not as much of a lost cause as she was. I mean, with her, I had to overcome her deep, epic love with a Russian warlord. You and I just have to overcome hundreds of years' worth of deeply ingrained prejudice and taboo between our two races. Easy."

"Adrian!" I felt my temper beginning to flare. "This isn't a joke."

"I know. It's certainly not to me. And that's why I'm not going to give you a hard time." He paused dramatically. "I'll just love you whether you want me to or not."

The attendant came by with hot towels, putting our conversation on hold and allowing his slightly disturbing words to hang in the air between us. I was dumbfounded and couldn't muster a response until after she came back to collect the cloths.

"Whether I want you to or not? What on earth does that mean?"

Adrian grimaced. "Sorry. That came off creepier than I intended. I just mean, I don't care if you say we can't be together. I don't care if you think I'm the most evil, unnatural creature walking the earth."

For the briefest of moments, his choice of words threw me back in time, to when he'd told me I was the most beautiful creature walking the earth. Those words haunted me now, just as they had then. We'd been sitting in a dark, candlelit room, and he'd looked at me in a way that no one ever had—

Stop it, Sydney. Focus.

"You can think whatever you want, do whatever you want," Adrian continued, unaware of my traitorous thoughts. There was a remarkable calm about him. "I'm going to just go on loving you, even if it's hopeless."

I don't know why that shocked me as much as it did. I glanced around to make sure no one was listening. "I . . . what? No. You can't!"

He tilted his head to the side as he regarded me carefully. "Why? It doesn't hurt you or anything. I told you I won't bother you if you don't want me to. And if you do, well, I'm all about that. So what's it matter if I just love you from afar?"

I didn't entirely know. "Because . . . because you can't!"

"Why not?"

"You . . . you need to move on," I managed. Yes, that was a sound reason. "You need to find someone else. You know I don't—that I can't. Well, you know. You're wasting your time with me."

He remained firm. "It's my time to waste."

"But it's crazy! Why would you do that?"

"Because I can't help doing it," he said with a shrug. "And hey, if I keep loving you, maybe you'll eventually crack and love me too. Hell, I'm pretty sure you're already half in love with me."

"I am not! And everything you just said is ridiculous. That's terrible logic."

Adrian returned to his crossword puzzle. "Well, you can think what you want, so long as you remember—no matter how ordinary things seem between us—I'm still here, still in love with you, and care about you more than any other guy, evil or otherwise, ever will."

"I don't think you're evil."

"See? Things are already looking promising." He tapped the magazine with his pen again. "'Romantic Victorian poetess.' Eight letters."

I didn't answer. I had been rendered speechless. Adrian never mentioned that dangerous topic again for the rest of the flight. Most of the time, he kept to himself, and when he did speak, it was about perfectly safe topics, like our dinner and the upcoming wedding. Anyone sitting with us would never have known there was anything weird between us.

But *I* knew.

That knowledge ate me up. It was all-consuming. And as the flight progressed, and eventually landed, I could no longer look at Adrian the same way. Each time we made eye contact, I just kept thinking of his words: *I'm still here, still in love with you, and care about you more than any other guy ever will.* Part of me felt offended. How dare he? How dare he love me whether I wanted him to or not? I had told him not to! He had no right to.

And the rest of me? The rest of me was scared.

If I keep loving you, maybe you'll eventually crack and love me too.

It was ludicrous. You couldn't make someone love you just by loving them. It didn't matter how charming he was, how good looking, or how funny. An Alchemist and a Moroi could never be together. It was impossible.

I'm pretty sure you're already half in love with me.

Very impossible.

CHAPTER 3

TRUE TO HIS WORD, Adrian made no other mention of the relationship—or lack thereof—between us. Every once in a while, though, I could swear I saw something in his eyes, something that brought back an echo of his proclamation about continuing to love me. Or maybe it was just his typical impertinence.

A connecting flight and an hour-long car ride later, it was night by the time we finally reached the small resort town in the Pocono Mountains. Getting out of the car was a shock. December in Pennsylvania was very, very different from December in Palm Springs. Crisp, frigid air hit me, the kind that freezes your mouth and nose. A layer of fresh snow covered everything, glittering in the light of the same full moon that Ms. Terwilliger and I had worked magic by. The stars were out here in just as much force as the stark desert, though the cold air made them glitter in a sharper way.

Adrian stayed in our hired car but leaned out as the driver

handed me my small suitcase. "Need any help with that?" Adrian asked. His breath made a frosty cloud in the air.

It was an uncharacteristic offer from him. "I'll be fine. Thanks, though. I take it you aren't staying here?" I nodded toward the bed-and-breakfast the car had stopped at.

Adrian pointed down the road, toward a large, lit-up hotel perched on a hill. "Up there. That's where all the parties will be, if you're interested. They're probably just getting started."

I shivered, and it had nothing to do with the cold. Moroi normally ran on a nocturnal schedule, starting their days around sunset. Those living among humans—like Adrian—had to adapt to a daytime schedule. But here, in a small town that must be bursting with Moroi guests, he'd have the chance to return to what was for him a more natural schedule.

"Noted," I said. A moment of awkwardness followed, but the temperature gave me an excuse for escape. "Well. I'd better get in where it's warm. Nice, uh, traveling with you."

He smiled. "You too, Sage. See you tomorrow."

The car door closed, and I suddenly felt lonely without him. They drove off toward the towering hotel. My bed-and-breakfast seemed tiny by comparison, but it was cute and in good shape. The Alchemists had booked me here precisely because they knew the Moroi guests would have other accommodations. Well, most of them.

"Are you here for the wedding, dear?" asked the innkeeper as she checked me in. "We have some other guests staying with us as well."

I nodded as I signed my credit card slip. It was no surprise that there'd be overflow to this inn, but there'd be a lot less here than the other hotel. I'd make sure to lock my door. I trusted my friends in Palm Springs, but all other Moroi and dhampirs were questionable.

Towns like this, and the inns within them, always seemed intended for couples on romantic getaways. My room was no exception. It had a California-king-size bed draped in a gauzy canopy, along with a heart-shaped Jacuzzi by the fireplace. It screamed love and romance, which brought Adrian back to my mind. I ignored it all as best I could and jotted out a quick text to Donna Stanton, a higher-ranking Alchemist who oversaw my assignment in Palm Springs.

Arrived in Pocono Hollow. Checked into inn.

Her response came quickly: *Excellent. See you tomorrow.* A second text followed a moment later: *Lock your door.*

Stanton and one other Alchemist were invited to the wedding as well. But they were already on the East Coast and could simply travel here tomorrow. I envied them.

Despite my uneasiness, I slept surprisingly well and dared to emerge for breakfast in the morning. I had no need to worry about Moroi, though. I was the only person eating in the sun-drenched dining room.

"How strange," remarked the innkeeper as she delivered my coffee and eggs. "I know many of the guests were out late, but I thought at least a few might be here to eat." Then, to emphasize the oddness of it all, she added, "After all, breakfast is complimentary."

The nocturnal Moroi, who were all still in bed, emboldened me to explore the town a little that day. Even though I'd prepared with boots and a heavy coat, the weather change was still a bit shocking. Palm Springs had made me soft. I soon called it an early day and spent the rest of the afternoon reading Ms.

Terwilliger's book by the fire. I flew through the first section and even went on to the advanced one she'd told me to skip. Maybe it was the fact that it was forbidden, but I couldn't stop reading. The scope of what the book described was so gripping and consuming that I nearly jumped a foot in the air when I heard a knock at the door. I froze, wondering if some confused Moroi had mistaken my room for a friend's. Or, worse, for a feeder's.

My phone suddenly chimed with a text message from Stanton: *We're at your door.*

Sure enough, when I opened it, I found Stanton standing there—with Ian Jansen, an Alchemist the same age as me. His presence was a surprise. I hadn't seen Ian since he, Stanton, and I had been detained by Moroi for questioning in the escape of a dhampir fugitive. Back then, Ian had had an unwelcome crush on me. Judging from the dopey smile on his face when he saw me, things hadn't changed. I gestured them inside, making sure to lock the door when I closed it. Like me, both Alchemists had golden lily tattoos on their left cheeks. It was the sign of our order, tattoos infused with vampire blood that gave us quick healing and were magically designed to stop us from discussing Alchemist affairs with those who didn't know about them.

Stanton arched an eyebrow at the heart-shaped tub and then settled into a chair by the fire. "No trouble getting here?"

Aside from traveling with a good-looking vampire who thinks he's in love with me?

"None," I replied. I regarded Ian with a frown. "I didn't expect you to be here. I mean, I'm glad you are, but after last time . . ." I paused as something hit me. I looked around. "It's all of us. All of us that were, uh, under house arrest."

Stanton nodded. "It was decided that if we're going to foster good relations between our groups, the Moroi would start by making amends to the three of us specifically."

Ian scowled and crossed his arms, leaning against a wall. He had brown eyes, with matching brown hair that he wore in a neat haircut. "I don't want any 'amends' from those monsters after what they did to us this summer. I can't even believe we're here! This place is crawling with them. Who knows what'll happen if one of them drinks too much champagne tonight and goes looking for a snack? Here we are, fresh humans."

I wanted to tell him that was ridiculous, but by Alchemist reasoning, it was a very legitimate concern. And, reminding myself that I didn't know most of the Moroi here, I realized perhaps his fears weren't that unfounded.

"I guess we'll have to stick together," I said. That was the wrong word choice, judging from Ian's happy smile.

The Alchemists rarely had social time, and this was no exception. Stanton soon got us down to business, going over our plans for the wedding and what our purpose was here. A file folder provided background on Sonya and Mikhail, as though I knew nothing about them. My mission and history with Sonya were secret from other Alchemists, so, for Ian's sake, I had to nod along with everything as if it was as new to me as it was to him.

"Festivities will probably last until almost sunrise," said Stanton, gathering up her papers once she'd finished the briefing. "Ian and I will be departing then and will drop you off at the airport on our way out. You won't have to spend another night here."

Ian's face grew darkly protective. "You shouldn't have stayed here alone last night. You should have had someone to look after you."

"I can look after myself," I snapped, a bit more harshly than I intended. Whether I liked it or not, Ms. Terwilliger's training had empowered me—literally and figuratively. That, and recent self-defense classes had taught me how to watch out for myself and my surroundings. Maybe Ian meant well, but I didn't like the idea of him—or anyone—thinking I needed coddling.

"Miss Sage is quite well as you can see," said Stanton dryly. Ian's crush had to be obvious to her, and it was equally obvious to me she had no use for such frivolity. Her gaze drifted to the window, which was glowing orange and red with the setting sun. "Well, then. It's nearly time. Shouldn't you be getting ready?"

They had arrived in their dress clothes, but I still needed to prepare. They talked together while I got ready in the bathroom, but each time I emerged—to get a hairbrush or earrings or something else—I'd see Ian watching me with that sappy look. Great. This was not what I needed.

The wedding was being held in the town's claim to fame: a huge, indoor garden that defied the wintry conditions outside. Sonya was a huge lover of plants and flowers, and this was pretty much her dream location for a wedding. The glass walls that composed the building were steamed from the drastic difference between inner and outer temperatures. The three of us stepped inside, into an entry area that was used to sell tickets during the greenhouse's normal operating hours. Here, at last, we found the Moroi that had been hidden to me in daylight.

There were about two dozen of them milling around in this entryway, dressed in rich clothing and eerily beautiful with their slim, pale features. Some were ushers and other attendants, helping organize the event and guide guests into the atrium farther into the building. Most Moroi were simply ordinary guests stopping to sign the guest book or chat with friends and family they hadn't seen in a long time. Around the sides, dhampirs in neat black and white suits stood sentry, watchful for any sign of danger. Their presence reminded me of a far, far greater threat than some drunken Moroi mistaking us for feeders.

Holding the event at night meant exposing us to attack by Strigoi. Strigoi were a very different type of vampire—so different, in fact, that I almost felt foolish being unnerved in this group. Strigoi were undead, made immortal by killing their victims, unlike the Moroi, who simply drank enough blood from human volunteers to sustain themselves. Strigoi were vicious, fast, and strong—and only came out at night. The sunlight that Moroi found simply uncomfortable was lethal to Strigoi. Strigoi made most of their kills on unwitting humans, but Moroi and dhampirs were their preferred food. An event like this—Moroi and dhampirs crammed into a small space—was practically like offering up a Strigoi buffet.

Eyeing the guardian dhampirs, however, I knew any Strigoi would have a difficult task breaking into this event. Guardians trained hard their entire lives, honing skills to fight Strigoi. Seeing as the Moroi queen was attending this event, I suspected the security I'd seen so far didn't even begin to scratch the surface.

A number of those gathered here stopped talking when they saw us. Not all Moroi knew about Alchemists or how we worked with their people. So, the attendance of three non-feeder humans was a bit of an oddity. Even those who knew about Alchemists were probably surprised to see us, given the formality of our relationship. Stanton was too experienced to let her unease show, but Ian openly made the Alchemist sign against evil as Moroi and dhampir eyes studied us. I did a pretty good job of keeping my cool but wished there was at least one familiar face in this crowd.

"Miss Stanton?"

A round-cheeked Moroi hurried forward. "I'm Colleen, the wedding coordinator. We spoke on the phone?" She extended a hand, and even tough Stanton hesitated before shaking it.

"Yes, of course," said Stanton, voice cool and proper. "Thank you for inviting us." She introduced Ian and me.

Colleen waved us toward the atrium's entry. "Come, come. We have your seats reserved. I'll take you there myself."

She swept us past the curious onlookers. As we entered the atrium, I stopped and momentarily forgot the vampires around us. The main greenhouse was magnificent. The ceiling was high and vaulted, made of that same steamed glass. A central area had been cleared and set with seats draped in flowers, very much like what you'd see at a human wedding. A dais at the front of the seating area was covered in more flowers and was obviously where the couple would take their vows.

But it was the rest of the room that took my breath away. It was like we'd stepped into some tropical jungle. Trees and other plants heavy with brightly colored flowers lined the sides, filling the humid air with a perfume that was almost dizzying. Since there was no sunlight to light up the greenhouse, torches and candles had been cleverly placed throughout the greenery, casting a mysterious—yet still romantic—light on everything. I felt as though I'd stepped into some secret Amazonian ritual space.

And of course, nearly hidden among the trees and bushes, black-clad guardians paced and kept watch on everything.

Colleen led us to three seats on the right side of the seating area, marked with a RESERVED sign. They were about halfway back—not as esteemed a spot as family would get, of course, but enough to show that the Moroi thought highly of us and really were trying to undo the strained relationship caused by our detainment.

"Can I get you anything?" Colleen asked. I realized now her exuberant energy was partially nervousness. We made her almost—but certainly not quite—as uneasy as she and the others made us. "Anything at all?"

"We're fine," said Stanton, speaking for all of us. "Thank you."

Colleen nodded eagerly. "Well, if you need anything—no matter how small—don't hesitate to ask. Simply grab one of the ushers, and they'll find me immediately." She stood there a moment longer, wringing her hands. "I'd best check on the others. Remember—call if you need anything."

"What I need is to get out of here," muttered Ian once she was gone. I said nothing, not trusting any response. If I reassured him we were safe, I'd be regarded with suspicion. Yet if I acted like our lives were in danger, I'd be lying. My views were somewhere in the middle of those extremes.

Someone handed me a program, and Ian leaned a bit more closely than I would've liked in order to read over my shoulder. The program detailed a list of songs and readings as well as the members of the wedding party. I could tell from Ian's face that he was expecting to see "Unholy Bloodletting" right after the Corinthians reading. His next words affirmed as much.

"They do a good job making it seem so normal, huh?" he asked, not bothering to hide the disgust in his voice. I was a bit surprised at how vicious his attitude was. I didn't remember him being quite this extreme last summer. "Like it's a real wedding or something."

He also wasn't regulating his volume, and I glanced around anxiously, making sure no one overheard. "So you're saying it's not a real wedding?" I whispered back.

Ian shrugged but at least took the hint and lowered his voice. "With them? It doesn't matter. They don't have real families or real love. They're monsters."

It was ironic that he mentioned "real love" just then because at that moment, Adrian and his father were ushered to the opposite side of the atrium. Adrian was always a nice dresser, but I'd never seen him in anything so formal. I hated to admit it, but the look was great on him: a navy suit and vest that was nearly black paired with a pale blue shirt and blue-and-white-striped tie. It stood out from the more somber black and gray suits most men here were wearing, but not in an outlandish or tacky way. As I was studying him, Adrian glanced up and caught my eye. He smiled and gave me a small nod. I almost smiled back, but Stanton snapped me back to reality. I allowed him one last, lingering look, and then I turned away.

"Mr. Jansen," Stanton said in a stern voice. "Please keep your opinions to yourself. Regardless of their validity, we are guests here and will behave in a civilized way."

Ian nodded grudgingly, flushing slightly as he glanced in my direction—as if being so openly chastised might ruin his chances with me. He didn't have to worry, seeing as he didn't have any chance to begin with.

Colleen sent an usher to check on us, and while he spoke to Stanton, Ian leaned toward me. "Am I the only one who thinks it's crazy that we're here?" He nodded toward Stanton. "She thinks this is okay, but come on. *They held us captive.* It's unforgivable. Doesn't that make you mad?"

I certainly hadn't liked it at the time, but I'd come to understand why it had happened. "I hate that they did that," I lied, hoping it sounded convincing. "I'm angry every time I think of it."

Ian actually looked relieved enough to drop the topic.

We sat in blessed silence as the atrium continued to fill up. By the time the ceremony was about ready to start, there must have been close to two hundred people in the room. I kept looking for familiar faces, but Adrian and his father were the only ones I knew. Then, at the last minute, a brightly clad figure came scurrying in. I groaned at the same time Stanton tsked with disapproval. Abe Mazur had just arrived.

Whereas Adrian had made color work with formal wear in a stylish way, Abe used color to offend the sensibilities. To be fair, this was one of the more subdued ensembles I'd ever seen Abe don: a white suit with a bright, kiwi green shirt and paisley ascot. He wore his usual gold earrings, and the sheen of his black hair made me think he'd been hitting some hair oil pretty voraciously. Abe was a dubiously moral Moroi and also the father of my friend—and Adrian's former dhampir love— Rose Hathaway. Abe made me nervous because I'd had some secret dealings with him in the past. He made Stanton nervous because he was a Moroi the Alchemists would never be able to control. Abe seated himself in the front row, earning a horrified look from Colleen the coordinator, who was supervising everything from the side of the room. My guess was that wasn't part of her seating chart.

I heard a trumpet sound, and those sitting in the back suddenly fell to their knees. Like a wave, those seated in the rest of the rows began following suit. Stanton, Ian, and I all exchanged confused looks. Then I understood.

"The queen," I whispered. "The queen is coming."

I could see from Stanton's face that was not something she had considered. She had a split second to decide on protocol for this situation and how to maintain our "civilized" guest status.

"We don't kneel," she whispered back. "Stay where you are."

It was a valid call, seeing as we owed no fealty to the Moroi queen. Still, I felt flustered and conspicuous at being one of the only people in the room not kneeling. A moment later, a ringing voice declared, "Her Royal Majesty, Queen Vasilisa, first of her name."

Even Ian caught his breath in admiration as she entered. Vasilisa—or Lissa, as Adrian and Rose continually insisted I call her—was a picture of ethereal beauty. It was hard to believe she was the same age as me. She carried herself with a poise and regality that seemed ageless. Her tall, willowy body was graceful even among Moroi, and her platinum blond hair fell around her pale face like some otherworldly veil. Although dressed in a very modern lavender cocktail dress, she managed to wear it as though it were some grand Victorian ball gown. A black-haired guy with piercing blue eyes walked at her side. Her boyfriend, Christian Ozera, was always easy to spot, providing a dark contrast that worked perfectly with her lightness.

Once the royal couple was seated in the front row—seeming very surprised to find Abe waiting for them there—the throng returned to their seats. An unseen cellist began to play, and everyone released a collective breath as we fell into the comfortable ritual of a wedding.

"Amazing, isn't it?" Ian murmured in my ear. "How fragile her throne is. One slip, and they'd fall into chaos."

It was true, and it was why Jill's safety was so important. An old Moroi law said that a monarch had to possess one living family member in order to hold the throne. Jill was the only one left in Lissa's line. Those who opposed Lissa because of her age and beliefs had realized killing Jill would be easier than going after a queen. Many opposed the law and were trying to change it. In the meantime, the political fallout from Jill's assassination would be monumental. The Alchemists, whose job it was to keep the Moroi world hidden and protected , needed to prevent their society from falling into chaos. And on a slightly more personal level, I needed to prevent Jill's death because against all odds, I'd grown to care about her in the short time we'd been together.

I shifted my mind from those grim thoughts and focused on the next stage of the wedding. Bridesmaids in deep green satin led the procession, and I wondered if Abe had been attempting to match them with his suit. If so, he'd failed.

And there, I spotted my first friendly face, aside from Adrian. Rose Hathaway. It was no surprise she'd be a brides-maid, seeing as she'd been responsible for the happy couple getting together. She'd inherited her father's dark hair and eyes and was the only dhampir among the bridesmaids. I didn't need to see the surprised looks of some of the guests to know that was pretty unorthodox. If Rose noticed or cared, she didn't show it. She walked proudly on, head held high and face glowing with happiness. With that humanlike dhampir appearance, she was shorter than her Moroi companions and had a more athletic build than the slender, small-chested Moroi.

Rose had what was a very normal, very healthy body among humans. Yet when I compared myself to Moroi, I felt enormous. I knew it was ridiculous—especially since I wore a smaller size than Rose—but it was a hard feeling to shake. Adrian recently had an unwelcome intervention with me, going so far as to claim I was on the verge of an eating disorder. I'd been outraged and told him to mind his own business . . . but ever since then, I'd taken a hard look at my behaviors. I now tried to eat more and had gained exactly one pound, something that had felt torturous and wrong until my friend Trey had recently commented that I was "looking pretty good these days." It had reinforced the idea that a few more pounds wouldn't kill me and *might* actually be good for me. Not that I'd admit any of that to Adrian.

We all stood when Sonya entered. She was glorious in ivory silk, with tiny white roses adorning her fiery hair. The queen had been magnificent, but there was a glow about Sonya that dwarfed even Lissa's beauty. Maybe it was just something inherent to brides. There was an air of love around Sonya that made her shine. I was surprised to feel a pang in my chest.

Ian was probably disappointed when no bloodletting followed, but the ceremony was sweet and filled with emotion. I couldn't believe how stone-faced my Alchemist companions looked—I was on the verge of tears as the couple recited their vows. Even if Sonya and Mikhail hadn't been through hell to be together, this was the kind of ceremony that couldn't help but pull at the heartstrings. As I listened to them swear they'd love each other forever, I found my gaze drifting to Adrian. He didn't see me looking at him, but I could tell the ceremony was having the same effect on him. He was enraptured.

It was a rare and sweet look for him, reminding me of the tortured artist that lived beneath the sarcasm. I liked that about Adrian—not the tortured part, but the way he could feel so deeply and then transform those emotions into art. I had feelings, just like anyone else, but that ability to express them into something creative was an area I would never, ever have expertise in. It wasn't in my nature. I sometimes gave him a hard time about his art, especially his more abstract pieces. Secretly, I regarded his skills with awe and loved the many facets of his personality.

Meanwhile, I had to fight to keep my face blank, to look as though I was a normal Alchemist with no concern for unholy vampire events. Neither of my companions questioned me, so apparently I pulled it off. Maybe I had a future in poker.

Sonya and Mikhail kissed, and the crowd erupted into cheers. They only got louder when he brazenly kissed her a second time—and then a third. The next stage of the festivities, the reception, was being held in the hotel where Adrian and most of the other Moroi were staying. Sonya and Mikhail left first, followed by the queen and other high-ranking royals. Stanton, Ian, and I waited patiently for our row to be dismissed so that we could line up for the limos that were ferrying guests the half mile to the hotel. It normally wouldn't have been that bad of a walk, even in heels, if not for the freezing temperature.

Our turn came, and the three of us got into the back of a limo. "Now we just have to get through the reception," said Ian as the driver shut our door. "At least we've got our own car."

Suddenly, the door opened, and Abe slid in beside me. "Room for one more?" He beamed at Stanton and me. "So nice to see you lovely ladies again. And you must be Ian. A pleasure." Abe extended his hand. At first, it looked as though Ian wouldn't shake it, but a sharp look from Stanton dictated otherwise. Afterward, Ian kept looking at his hand as though he expected it to start smoking.

The drive only took about five minutes, but I could tell from the other Alchemists' faces that it felt like five hours for them.

"I think it's wonderful that you three were invited," said Abe, perfectly at ease. "Considering how much we work together, we should have more of these pleasant interactions, don't you think? Perhaps you'll invite us to one of your weddings someday." He winked at me. "I'm sure you have young men lining up for you."

Even Stanton couldn't keep a straight face. The look of horror in her expression said there were few things more profane than a vampire coming to a human wedding. She looked visibly relieved when we reached the hotel, but we weren't free of Abe yet. Some thoughtful person—probably Colleen—had put us at his table, probably thinking it would be nice to be seated with a Moroi we knew. Abe seemed to take great delight in the awkwardness his presence provided, but I had to admit, it was kind of refreshing to have someone who openly acknowledged the strained relations between us rather than pretending everything was okay.

"There's no blood in that," Abe told us when dinner was served. The three of us were hesitating over cutting into our chicken marsala, even me. "The only blood is in the drinks, and you have to actually ask for those at the bar. No one's going to sneak you something, and the feeders are being kept in another room."

Ian and Stanton still looked unconvinced. I decided I would be the brave one and began eating without any more hesitation. Maybe vampires were unnatural creatures, but they certainly had excellent taste in caterers. A moment later, the other Alchemists joined me, and even they had to admit the food was pretty good.

When the plates were cleared, Ian bravely left for the bathroom, giving Stanton a brief opportunity to lean toward me for a hushed status report. "Everything was okay when you left?" Strained relationship or not, our mission to keep the Moroi stable hadn't changed.

"Fine," I said. "It's all quiet back there. No sign of trouble." She didn't need to know about my own interpersonal drama. Keeping my tone casual, I asked, "Any news about the Warriors? Or Marcus Finch?"

Stanton shook her head. "None. But I'll certainly let you know if we uncover anything."

I answered with a polite smile, seriously doubting her words. I hadn't always liked my Alchemist missions, but I'd spent most of my life following orders without question because I believed my superiors knew what was best and were acting for the greater good. Recent events now made me wonder about that. In thwarting some crazed vampire hunters who called themselves the Warriors of Light, Stanton had withheld information from me, citing that we were on a need-to-know basis. She had brushed it off, praising me for being a good Alchemist who understood such policy, but the incident had made me seethe with anger. I didn't want to be anyone's pawn. I could accept that fighting for a greater cause meant tough decisions, but I refused to be used or endangered because of "important" lies. I'd given my life over to the Alchemists, always believing what they did and told me was right. I'd thought I was important, that they would always look out for me. Now I didn't know.

And yet . . . what could I do? I was sworn and sealed to the Alchemists. Whether I liked what they'd done to me or not, there was no way out, no way to question them. . . .

At least, I'd thought that until I learned about Marcus Finch.

I'd only found about him recently, after discovering he'd once crossed the Warriors of Light by helping a Moroi named Clarence. Although the Warriors usually only went after Strigoi, a rebel group had once decided to target Clarence. Marcus had stepped up and defended Clarence against the Warriors, convincing them to leave him alone. I'd almost believed Clarence was making up the story until I saw a picture of Marcus.

And that was where things got *really* weird. Marcus seemed to have also crossed the Alchemists. In fact, Clarence and one of the Warriors had hinted that Marcus had at one time been an Alchemist—but was no longer. I hadn't believed it until I saw his picture. He didn't have a golden lily—but a large tribal-looking tattoo done in blue ink that was large enough to cover the golden one, if you were trying to hide it.

Seeing that was life changing. I'd had no idea it was possible to tattoo over something so powerful. I certainly hadn't thought anyone could leave the Alchemists or that anyone would even want to, not with the way our purpose was drilled into us practically from birth. How could someone consider abandoning our missions? How could someone go rogue and just walk away from the Alchemists? What had happened that would make him want to do that? Had he had experiences similar to mine? And would they let him go?

When I'd asked about him, Stanton claimed the Alchemists had no knowledge of Marcus, but I knew that was a lie. She didn't know I had his picture. His blue tattoo was big enough to cover a lily, and I'd seen metallic hints of one underneath, proving he had indeed once been one of us. And if he'd had the Alchemist mark, then they most certainly knew about him. They were covering him up, and that just intrigued me further. In fact, I was a little obsessed with him. Some instinct told me he was the key to my problems, that he could help me uncover the secrets and lies the Alchemists were telling me. Unfortunately, I had no clue how to find him.

"It's important no one here knows what you're doing, so remember to be discreet," Stanton added, like I needed to be reminded. A small crease appeared between her eyebrows. "I was particularly worried about that Ivashkov boy coming to this wedding. We can't let anyone know you two have more than a passing acquaintance. Little things like that could compromise our mission."

"Oh, no," I said quickly. "You don't need to worry about Adrian. He understands how important our work is. He'd never do anything to compromise it."

Ian returned, and our discussion ended there. Dinner soon gave way to dancing. With the atmosphere more relaxed, a number of Moroi came over to introduce themselves to us. I felt nearly as popular as the bride and groom. Ian shook so many hands that he eventually became immune to it. And as uncomfortable as it was for my companions, I could tell this event was actually accomplishing its goal of smoothing relations between

Alchemists and Moroi. Stanton and Ian were by no means ready to be best friends with any of them, but it was clear they were pleasantly surprised at how friendly and benign most of the guests seemed.

"I'm glad we got this chance to be together," Ian told me during a lull in our public relations. "It's so hard with our jobs, you know? I'm in St. Louis now, in the facility archives. Where do they have you?"

Secrecy was key in Jill's protection. "I'm in the field, but I can't say where. You know how it is."

"Right, right. But you know, if you ever wanted to visit . . . I'd show you around."

His desperation was almost cute. "Like for a vacation?"

"Well, yeah. Er, no." He knew as well as I did that Alchemists didn't get vacations easily. "But, I mean, they're doing all the holiday services, you know. If you decide to come to one, well, let me know."

Alchemist priests always conducted special services around Christmas in our main facilities. Some Alchemist families made a point of going to them every year. I hadn't been to any in a while, not with the way my missions kept jumping around.

"I'll keep that in mind."

There was a long pause, and his next words came haltingly. "I'd ask you to dance, you know. Except it wouldn't be right in this kind of unholy setting."

I gave him a stiff smile. "Of course. That, and we're here on business. We've got to focus on building good relationships with them."

Ian had started to respond when a familiar voice interrupted us. "Miss Sage?"

We looked up and found Adrian standing above us, dashing in his shades of blue. His face was the picture of perfect politeness and restraint, meaning something disastrous was probably about to happen.

"It's so nice to see you again," he said. He spoke as though it had been a while, and I nodded in agreement. As I'd assured Stanton, Adrian knew too much familiarity between us might create a trail back to Jill. "Did I just hear you two talking about building good relationships?"

I was tongue-tied, so Ian answered. "That's right. We're here to make things friendlier between our people." His voice, however, was most decidedly unfriendly.

Adrian nodded with all seriousness, like he hadn't noticed Ian's hostility. "I think it's a great idea. And I thought of something that would be an excellent gesture of our future together." Adrian's expression was innocent, but there was a mischievous sparkle in his eye that I knew all too well. He held out his hand to me. "Would you like to dance?"

CHAPTER 4

I FROZE. I didn't trust myself to respond.

What was Adrian thinking? Putting aside all the drama between us, it was absolutely unforgivable to ask this here, in front of other Moroi and Alchemists. Maybe in Palm Springs, where things were a little more casual with my friends, it might not be *that* crazy a request. But here? He risked exposing that we knew each other, which in turn risked Jill. Almost as bad, it could be a tip-off of his feelings for me. Even if I insisted that I had no matching feelings, the fact that things had progressed this far could get me in serious trouble with the Alchemists.

As all these thoughts raced through my mind, a more concerning one suddenly popped up. A good Alchemist shouldn't be worried about any of those things. A good Alchemist would have simply been horrified at the immediate problem: dancing with a Moroi. *Touching* a vampire. Realizing this, I quickly mustered an outraged expression, hoping I looked convincing.

Fortunately, everyone else was too shocked to pay much attention to me. Good relations only went so far. Stanton and Ian wore legitimate looks of disgust. The Moroi nearby, while not appalled, were astonished at the breach of etiquette. And yet . . . I also saw a couple exchange looks that said they weren't entirely surprised Adrian Ivashkov would suggest something so outrageous. This was an attitude I'd seen a lot with him. People often shrugged off his behavior with, "Well, that's Adrian."

Ian found his voice first. "She . . . no! She absolutely can't!"

"Why not?" Adrian glanced between all our faces, his expression still sunny and unassuming. "We *are* all friends, right?"

Abe, who was rarely shocked by anything, managed to shake off some of his surprise. "I'm sure it's not that big a deal." His tone was uncertain. He knew that Adrian wasn't a total stranger to me but undoubtedly assumed I had the usual Alchemist hang-ups. As tonight had demonstrated, most Alchemists still struggled with handshakes.

Stanton seemed to be waging a mental war. I knew she thought it was an outlandish request . . . yet she was still conscious of the need to keep things pleasant. She swallowed. "Perhaps . . . perhaps it would be a nice gesture." She shot me a sympathetic look that seemed to say, *Sometimes you have to take one for the team.*

Ian jerked his head toward her. "Are you crazy?"

"Mr. Jansen," she snapped, conveying a stern warning in just his name.

All eyes turned toward me as everyone realized that ultimately, it was my decision. At this point, I didn't know if I should be shocked or scared—and the thought of dancing with Adrian made me feel both. I met Stanton's eyes again and slowly gave a nod. "Sure. Okay. Good relations, right?"

Ian's face turned bright red, but another sharp look from Stanton kept him silent. As Adrian led me to the dance floor, I heard a few whispered comments from curious Moroi mentioning "that poor Alchemist girl" and "there's no predicting what he does sometimes."

Adrian put his arm around my waist, perfectly proper and distant. I tried not to think about the last time I'd been in his arms. Even with appropriate spacing between us, our hands were still clasped, our stances still intimate. I was hyperaware of every single place his fingers rested on my body. His touch was light and delicate but seemed to carry an extraordinary heat and intensity.

"What were you thinking?" I demanded once we were moving to the music. I was trying to ignore his hands. "Do you know how much trouble you may have gotten me in?"

Adrian grinned. "Nah. They all feel bad for you. You'll achieve martyrdom after dancing with a mean, wicked vampire. Job security with the Alchemists."

"I thought you weren't going to pressure me about . . . you know . . . that stuff. . . ."

The look of innocence returned. "Have I said a word about that? I just asked you to dance as a political gesture, that's all." He paused for impact. "Seems like *you're* the one who can't get 'that stuff' off your mind."

"Stop turning my words against me! That's not—no—that's not right at all."

"You should see that Stanton woman watching us," he remarked with amusement, glancing behind me.

"Everyone's watching us," I grumbled. It wasn't like the entire room had come to a standstill, but there were certainly a number of curious onlookers, gawking at the unlikely sight of a Moroi and a human—an Alchemist, at that—dancing.

He nodded and swept me into a turn. He was a good dancer, which wasn't entirely a surprise. Adrian might be brash and impertinent, but he knew how to move. Maybe dance lessons had been part of growing up in an elite tier of Moroi society. Or maybe he was just naturally skilled at using his body. That kiss had certainly show a fair amount of talent. . . .

Ugh. Adrian was right. I *was* the one who couldn't get over "that stuff."

Unaware of my thoughts, he glanced over at Stanton again. "She's got the look of a general who just sent her army on a suicide mission."

"Nice to know she cares," I said. For a moment, I forgot my dance floor woes as I thought angrily back to Stanton's "need to know" attitude.

"I can pull you closer, if you want," he said. "Just to see how much she cares. I'm always willing to help like that, you know."

"You're a real team player," I said. "If putting me in danger is for the greater good, then Stanton probably wouldn't do anything about you moving in on me."

Adrian's self-satisfied smirk faded. "Did she ever come clean about that guy you were trying to find? Martin?"

"Marcus," I corrected. I frowned. Her denial still bothered me. "She keeps claiming she doesn't know him, and I can't push too hard if I don't want her to get suspicious."

"I thought of a way you might find him," said Adrian. I would've thought he was joking if his face wasn't so serious.

"*You* did?" I asked. The Alchemists had vast information at our disposal, with hands in all sorts of agencies and organizations. I'd been scouring them these last few weeks and found it unlikely that Adrian would have access to something I didn't.

"Yup. You've got his picture, right? Couldn't you just do the same spell you did the other night? Locate him that way?"

I was so surprised, I nearly tripped. Adrian tightened his grip to keep me from falling. I shivered as that small gesture brought us closer. The tension between us kicked up a notch, and I realized that along with our bodies being nearer, so were our lips.

I had a little difficulty speaking, both because of how it felt to be so close to him and because I was still stunned by what he'd said. "That's . . . wow . . . that's not a bad idea. . . ."

"I know," he said. "I'm kind of amazed myself."

Really, the circumstances were no different from finding Ms. Terwilliger's sister. I needed to locate someone I'd never met. I had a picture, which was what the spell required. What was different was that I'd be initiating the spell myself. It was a difficult piece of magic, and I knew Ms. Terwilliger's coaching had helped me. There was also the moral dilemma of working that type of spell on my own. My conscience had an easier time handling magic when I felt coerced.

"I couldn't try until next month," I said, thinking back to the spell book. "I mean, I have the picture with me, but the spell's got to be done during a full moon. This is the last night for the current one, and I'd never be able to get the components in time."

"What do you need?"

I told him, and he nodded along, promising he could get them.

I scoffed. "Where are you going to get anise and hyssop at this time of night? In this town?"

"This town's full of quirky boutique shops. There's some herbal place that sells soaps and perfume made of anything you can imagine. I guarantee they've got what you need."

"And I guarantee they're closed." He swept me into another flourish-filled spin, and I kept up with him perfectly.

The song was wrapping up. The time had flown by faster than I'd thought. I'd forgotten about the onlookers. I'd even forgotten I was with a vampire. I was simply dancing with Adrian, which felt easy and natural, so long as I didn't think about our audience.

His roguish look returned. "Don't worry about that. I can find the owner and talk her into making an exception."

I groaned. "No. Not compulsion." Compulsion was an ability vampires had to force their wills on others. All vampires had it to a small extent, and spirit users had it in excess. Most Moroi considered it immoral. Alchemists considered it a sin.

The song ended, but Adrian didn't release me right away. He leaned a little closer. "Do you want to wait another month to find Marcus?"

"No," I admitted.

Adrian's lips were a breath away. "Then we'll meet in two hours by the hotel's service door." I gave a weak nod, and he stepped back, releasing my hands. "Here's one last sign of good relations." With a bow that could've come straight out of a Jane Austen novel, he gestured to the bar and spoke loudly. "Thank you for the dance. May I escort you to get a drink?"

I followed without a word, my head spinning with what I'd need to do in two hours. At the bar, Adrian astonished me by ordering ginger ale. "Nice restraint," I said, realizing he'd need to stay sober to work spirit. I hoped he hadn't indulged too much already. For him, the only thing better than an open bar would be a case of cigarettes showing up at his door.

"I'm a master of self-control," he declared.

I wasn't so sure of that but didn't contradict him. I sipped my Diet Coke, and we stood there in comfortable silence. Two Moroi men sidled up the bar near us, talking with the volume and exuberance of those who hadn't held back on sampling free liquor.

"Well, no matter how liberal that girl is, she's certainly easy on the eyes," one guy said. "I could look at her all day, especially in that dress."

His friend nodded. "Definitely an improvement over Tatiana. Too bad about what happened to her, but maybe a change of scenery was for the best. Did that woman ever smile?" They both laughed at the joke.

Beside me, Adrian's own smile vanished, and he went perfectly still. Tatiana, the former Moroi queen, had been Adrian's great-aunt. She'd been viciously murdered this summer, and though Adrian rarely spoke about her, I'd heard from a number of people that they'd been close. Adrian's lips twisted into a snarl, and he started to turn around. Without hesitation, I reached out and grabbed his free hand, holding it tightly.

"Adrian, don't," I said softly.

"Sydney, they can't say that." There was a dangerous look in his eyes, one I'd never seen.

I squeezed his hand harder. "They're drunk, and they're stupid. They're not worth your time. Please don't start a scene here—for Sonya's sake." I hesitated. "And for me."

His face was still filled with rage, and for a moment, I thought he would ignore me and throw a glass at one of those guys. Or worse. I'd seen angry spirit users, and they were terrifying. At last, that fury faded, and I felt his hand relax in mine. He closed his eyes briefly, and when he opened them again, they were dazed and unfocused.

"No one really knew her, Sydney." The sorrow in his voice broke my heart. "They all thought she was some draconian bitch. They never knew how funny she was, how sweet she could be. You can't . . . you can't imagine how much I miss her. She didn't deserve to die like that. She was the only one who understood me—even more than my own parents. She accepted me. She saw the good in my soul. She was the only one who believed in me."

He was standing in front of me, but he wasn't with me. I recognized the rambling, consuming nature of spirit. It messed with its users' minds. Sometimes it made them scattered and distant, like he was now. Sometimes it challenged people's grip on reality. And sometimes, it could create a despair with devastating consequences.

"She wasn't the only one," I told him. "I believe in you. She's at peace, and nothing they say can change who she was. Please come back to me."

He still stared off into someplace I couldn't follow. After a few frightening moments, he blinked and focused on me. His expression was still sad, but at least he was in control again. "I'm here, Sage." He removed his hand and glanced around to make sure no one had seen me holding it. Thankfully, the bride and groom had taken to the dance floor, and everyone was too mesmerized watching them. "Two hours."

He knocked back the rest of his drink and walked away. I watched him until he disappeared into the crowd, and then I returned to my own table, glancing at the clock along the way. Two hours.

Ian jumped out of his seat at my approach. "Are you okay?"

No Moroi well-wishers were around, so only Stanton was nearby to hear him. She seemed to share his concern. "I'm sorry you had to endure that, Miss Sage. As always, your dedication to our work is admirable."

"I do what I can to help, ma'am," I said. I was still worried about Adrian and hoped he wouldn't slip back into spirit's grip again.

"Did he hurt you?" asked Ian, pointing. "Your hands?"

I looked down and realized I'd been rubbing my hands together. They were warm from where Adrian had touched me. "Huh? Oh, no. Just, um, trying to rub the taint off. In fact . . . I should probably go wash up. Be right back."

They seemed to find this a perfectly reasonable idea and didn't stop me as I hurried to the restroom. Free of their concern, I breathed a sigh of relief. I'd dodged two bullets here, by not letting the Alchemists know that I was friendly with a vampire and also that I was plotting magic with him.

"Sydney?"

I was so distracted when walking out of the restroom that I hadn't noticed Rose standing nearby with Dimitri Belikov. They stood arm in arm, smiling at my surprise. I hadn't seen Dimitri tonight, and his black and white guardian attire told me why. He was on duty here and had undoubtedly been one of the shadows darting among the trees of the greenhouse, keeping a watch on everyone. He must be on a break now because there was no way he'd be standing so casually here, even with Rose, otherwise. And really, "casual" for Dimitri meant he could still leap into battle at any moment.

They were a striking couple. His dark-haired, dark-eyed looks matched hers, and they were both dazzlingly attractive. It was no wonder Adrian had fallen for her, and I felt surprised at how uncomfortable that memory made me. Like Sonya and Mikhail, there was a bond of love between Rose and Dimitri that was almost palpable.

"Are you okay?" asked Rose, eyes kind. "I can't believe Adrian did that to you." She reconsidered. "Then again, I kind of can believe it."

"I'm fine," I said. "I think the other Alchemists were more appalled than I was." I remembered belatedly that even if Rose and Dimitri knew I knew Adrian from Palm Springs, I still couldn't act too at ease here. I put on my earlier look of outrage. "It was still out of line, though."

"Propriety's never been Adrian's strong suit," Dimitri observed.

Rose laughed at the understatement. "If it makes you feel any better, you guys looked really good together out there. Made it hard to believe you're mortal enemies . . . or whatever it is Alchemists think." She gestured to my dress. "You even coordinated."

I'd totally forgotten what I was wearing. It was a short-sleeved silk dress, almost entirely black save for some splashes of royal blue on the skirt. That was a bolder color than I would normally wear, but the black tempered it. Thinking back to Adrian's shades of blue, I realized our palettes had indeed complemented each other.

You guys looked really good together

I don't know what expression I wore, but it made Rose laugh again.

"Don't look so panicked," Rose said, eyes shining. "It was nice seeing a human and a Moroi look like they belong together."

Belong together.

Why did she keep saying things like that? Her words were messing with the cool, logical demeanor I tried to maintain. I knew she was speaking in that friendly, diplomatic way that everyone was pushing so hard for. But as progressive as Rose and Dimitri were, I knew even they would be shocked if they knew the truth about Adrian's feelings and that monumental kiss.

I spent the rest of the reception with a knot of anxiety building within me. Fortunately, I didn't have to hide it. Moroi and Alchemist alike expected me to feel that way. In fact, Stanton soon got her own share of "diplomacy" when a middle-aged Moroi guy asked her to dance, obviously taking a cue from Adrian's display of goodwill. Apparently, as outrageous as Adrian's behavior had been, some Moroi thought it had been a smart move and decided to follow suit. Stanton could hardly refuse after encouraging me, so she took the dance floor with gritted teeth. No one asked Ian to dance, which was probably just as well. He didn't look at all disappointed.

Adrian stayed away, presumably to gather my spell components. Time ticked down, and as the two-hour mark approached, I realized that although I'd brought Marcus's picture with me on this trip (I rarely let it out of my sight), it was still in my room. I excused myself from Ian, telling him I needed to go back to the inn to change shoes and would take one of the cars that had been ferrying wedding guests around town.

Ian's face immediately grew protective. "Do you want me to go with you? It's not safe out there."

I shook my head. "No, you need to stay here. Stanton's in more danger." She was standing near the bar, speaking to two Moroi men. I wondered if she had another dance in her future. "Besides, it's early, so there's still more of them here than out there. At least the inn is run by humans."

Ian couldn't fault my Alchemist logic and reluctantly let me go. Catching a town car was easy, and I was able to make the round trip in almost the perfect amount of time. I even changed shoes so that I'd have proof for my story. Although I'd worn heels to the wedding, I'd packed flats in my suitcase, just in case. That was just smart planning for any occasion.

When I reached the service door, however, I realized my clever planning had failed. Filled with haste and anxiety, I'd left my warm, heavy shawl in the car, which was probably long gone. Now, waiting for Adrian in the bitter Pennsylvania cold, I wrapped my arms around myself and hoped I wouldn't freeze before he showed up.

He was good to his word, though, and arrived at exactly the appointed time with a tote bag over one shoulder. Even better, he was completely back to his normal self. "Ready to go," he told me.

"Seriously?" I asked, my teeth chattering. "You found everything?"

He patted the bag. "You ask, I deliver. Now where do we need to do this?"

"Somewhere remote." I scanned around. Beyond the hotel's parking lot was a vacant field that I hoped would suffice. "There."

Walking across the well-salted parking lot wasn't a problem, but once we "off-roaded" into the snowy field, even my practical flats were of no use. I was also so cold that I suspected my skin was as blue as my dress.

"Stop," said Adrian at one point.

"We need to go a little farther," I protested.

Adrian, who'd had the sense to put on a wool coat, was taking it off. "Here."

"You'll be cold," I protested, though I didn't stop him when he stepped forward and helped me put the coat on. He was taller than me, so the three-quarter length was mercifully full length on me. Its scent was a mix of smoke and cologne.

"There." He pulled the coat more tightly around me. "I've got long sleeves and the jacket. Now come on—let's hurry."

He didn't have to tell me twice. Aside from the temperature, we had to do this before we were caught by others. Even I wasn't going to be able to explain this away to the Alchemists.

The moon was still crisp and bright when we finally found an acceptable spot. I sifted through Adrian's bag, amazed that he'd come through with everything, from the mirror to the dried leaves and flowers. He stayed quiet as I set it all up, only speaking when I was just about ready to go.

"Is there anything I can do?" he asked gently.

"Just keep watch," I said. "And catch me if I pass out."

"Gladly."

I'd memorized the spell when Ms. Terwilliger and I had performed it. Still, I was nervous about going solo, especially since the environment was so distracting. It was kind of hard to find the mental focus I needed while kneeling in snow. Then I thought back to Stanton and the lies the Alchemists were telling me. A spark of anger flared in me, creating warmth of a different sort. I used that to direct my thoughts as I stared at Marcus's picture. He was Adrian's age, with shoulder-length blond hair and a pensive look in his blue eyes. The tattoo on his check was a tangle of indigo crescents. Slowly, I managed to sink into the spell.

I felt that same euphoria as the mirror shifted into a city image. No fog blocked me this time since presumably Marcus wasn't wielding the kind of protective magic that Ms. Terwilliger's sister had been using. The scene before me showed what looked like a very modest studio apartment. A mattress lay on the floor, and an ancient TV sat in one corner. I looked around for any identifying features but found nothing. The room's one window finally gave me a clue. Outside in the distance, I could see a Spanish-style building that looked like a church or monastery. It was made of white stucco, with red-roofed domed towers. I tried to get a closer look, to fly up like I had in the other spell, but suddenly, I became aware of the Pennsylvania cold seeping into me. The image shattered, and I was back to kneeling in the field.

"Ugh," I said, putting my hand to my forehead. "So close."

"Did you see anything?" Adrian asked.

"Nothing that'll help."

I stood and felt a little dizzy but managed to stay upright. I could see Adrian ready and waiting to catch me in case I did indeed keel over. "You okay?"

"I think so. Just a little light-headed from the blood sugar drop." I slowly gathered up the mirror and bag. "I should've had you get orange juice too."

"Maybe this'll help." Adrian produced a silver flask from his suit jacket's inner pocket and handed it toward me.

So typical, Adrian helpfully offering alcohol. "You know I don't drink," I said.

"A few sips won't get you drunk, Sage. And it's your lucky night—it's Kahlua. Packed with sugar *and* coffee-flavored. Trade me and try."

Grudgingly, I handed him the bag and then took the flask as we began walking back to the hotel. I took a tentative sip and grimaced. "That is *not* coffee-flavored." No matter how much people tried to dress up alcohol, it always tasted awful to me. I didn't understand how he could consume so much. But, I could taste the sugar, and after a few more sips, I felt steadier. That was all I drank since I didn't want to get dizzy for different reasons.

"What'd you see?" asked Adrian, once we reached the parking lot.

I described the spell's scene and sighed in frustration. "That could be any building in California. Or the Southwest. Or Mexico."

Adrian came to a halt and slung the bag over one shoulder. "Maybe. . . ." He took out his phone from his jacket and typed in a few things. I shivered and tried to be patient as he searched for what he needed. "Did it look like this?"

I peered at the screen and felt my jaw drop. I was looking at a picture of the building from my vision.

"Yes! What is it?"

"The Old Mission Santa Barbara." And then, just in case I needed help, he added, "It's in Santa Barbara."

"How did you know that?" I exclaimed. "What that building is, I mean."

He shrugged. "Because I've been to Santa Barbara. Does this help you?"

My earlier dismay transformed into excitement. "Yes! Based on the window's position, I can get a pretty good idea of where the apartment is. You may have found Marcus Finch." Caught up in my elation, I squeezed his arm.

Adrian rested a gloved hand on my cheek and smiled down at me. "And to think, Angeline said I was too pretty to be useful. Looks like I might have something to offer to the world after all."

"You're still pretty," I said, the words slipping out before I could stop them. Another of those intense moments hung between us, the moonlight illuminating his striking features. Then it was shattered by a voice in the darkness.

"Who's there?"

Both of us flinched and jerked back as a black-and-white-clad figure seemed to materialize out of the shadows. A guardian. It was no one I knew, but I realized I'd been foolish if I thought we could slip in and out of the hotel unseen. The grounds were probably crawling with guardians, keeping watch for Strigoi. They wouldn't have cared much about two people leaving, but our return would naturally be challenged.

"Hey, Pete," said Adrian, putting on that easygoing smile he excelled at. "Nice to see you. Hope you're not too cold out here."

The guardian seemed to relax a little upon recognizing Adrian, but he was still suspicious. "What are you two doing outside?"

"Just walking Miss Sage back," said Adrian. "She had to get something from her room."

I gave him a puzzled look. The inn wasn't in this direction. Pete looked dazed for a moment. Then he nodded in understanding. "I see. Well, you'd better get back inside before you freeze."

"Thanks," said Adrian, steering me away. "Make sure you get a break and try the canapés. They're amazing."

"You compelled him," I whispered, once we were safely out of earshot.

"Only a little," said Adrian. He sounded very proud of himself. "And being outside to walk you is a valid reason, one he won't think too much about later. Compelling someone into believing a story works best if there's a little truth—"

"Adrian? Sydney?"

We'd almost reached the back of the building now and were suddenly face-to-face with an ivory-clad figure. Sonya stood before us, a fur stole wrapped around her. Once again, I was struck by her beauty and the happy glow she seemed to radiate. She gave us a puzzled smile.

"What are you two doing out here?" she asked.

Both of us were speechless. Adrian had no brash words or tricks. Sonya was a spirit user too, and compulsion wouldn't work on her. Frantically, I groped for some excuse that wasn't: *We were out using illicit magic in a continuing effort to uncover secrets the Alchemists don't want me to know about.*

"You can't tell," I blurted out to her. I held up the flask. "Adrian was letting me sneak some of his Kahlua. Stanton'll kill me if she finds out."

Sonya looked understandably startled. "I didn't think you drank."

"Tonight's been kind of stressful," I said. It was hardly a lie.

"And it's coffee-flavored," Adrian pointed out, as though that might aid our cause.

69

I wasn't sure if Sonya was buying it, so I attempted a change in subject. "Congratulations, by the way. I didn't have a chance to talk to you earlier. You look beautiful."

Sonya let go of her inquisitiveness and offered me a smile. "Thank you. It's kind of unreal. Mikhail and I have been through so much . . . there were times I never thought we'd reach this moment. And now . . ." She glanced down at the diamond sparkling on her hand. "Well, here we are."

"What are *you* doing out here, Mrs. Tanner?" Adrian had recovered himself and was back to his outgoing self. "Shouldn't you be inside gazing adoringly at your husband?"

She chuckled. "Oh, we've got a lifetime of that ahead. Honestly, I just needed to get out of the crowd." Sonya took a deep breath of the crisp, cold air. "I should probably get back soon. We're about to throw the bouquet. You aren't going to miss your chance, are you?" That was to me.

I scoffed. "I think I'll sit this one out. I've already caused too much speculation tonight."

"Ah, yes. Your infamous dance." Sonya glanced between us, and a bit of her earlier puzzlement returned. "You two look very good together." Awkward silence fell for a few seconds, and then she cleared her throat. "Well, I'm getting in where it's warm. Hope you'll change your mind, Sydney."

She disappeared through the service door, and I resisted the urge to beat my head against the wall. "She knows we're lying. She can tell." Spirit users were good at reading subtle cues from people, with Sonya being one of the best.

"Probably," agreed Adrian. "But I doubt she's going to guess we were out working magic in a field."

A terrible thought came to me. "Oh God. She probably

thinks we were off doing—you know—romantic type, um, things—"

That amused Adrian far more than it should have. "See, there you go again. That's the first thought that comes to your mind." He shook his head melodramatically. "I can't believe you keep accusing me of being the obsessed one."

"I'm not obsessed!" I exclaimed. "I'm just pointing out the obvious conclusion."

"Maybe to you. But she's right about one thing: we need to get inside." He anxiously touched his hair. "I think my hair gel's frozen."

I handed him back the flask and opened the door. Just before stepping through, I hesitated and glanced back at him. "Adrian? Thanks for helping me."

"What are friends for?" He caught the door from me and motioned for me to go inside.

"Yeah, but you went above and beyond tonight for something that has nothing to do with you. I appreciate that. You didn't have to help. You don't have the same reasons I have for cracking open the Alchemists."

Not knowing what else to say, I gave him a small nod of thanks and went inside. As the warmth and noise of the crowd swallowed us, I thought I heard him say, "I have different reasons."

CHAPTER 5

I LEFT SHORTLY THEREAFTER with the Alchemists and didn't expect to see Adrian for a little while. He was staying on with the other Moroi a couple more days in Pennsylvania, so there was no chance of a repeat flight together. My trip back to California was quiet and uneventful, though my mind raced with all the developments of the last couple of days. Between Ms. Terwilliger's cryptic warning and my new lead on Marcus, I had plenty to occupy me.

A text message from Eddie greeted me when I hailed a cab at the Palm Springs airport: *We're eating at Marquee's. Wanna join us?* A follow-up message soon came: *You can drive us back.* I directed the driver to take me to a suburb on the far edge of the city rather than Amberwood's home in Vista Azul. I was hungry, seeing as there'd been no dinner served on the plane in coach, and besides, I wanted my car back in my own hands.

When I arrived at the restaurant, I found Eddie and

Angeline sitting on one side of a booth with Jill on the other. Immediately, I knew why they'd chosen to eat so far from our school. Being away meant Eddie and Angeline could go out as a couple. Back at Amberwood, everyone thought we were related. Eddie, Jill, and I passed ourselves off as siblings, while Angeline was our cousin. Eddie and Angeline had recently started dating, so they'd had to hide their relationship from our classmates to avoid raising suspicions. We already seemed to attract enough attention as it was.

Angeline was cuddled up in Eddie's arm. Even he looked like he was having a good time, which was nice to see. He took his responsibilities so seriously and was often so tense that it seemed as though it wouldn't take much to make him snap in two. Angeline—though uncouth, unpredictable, and often inappropriate—had proven remarkably good for him. That didn't make him any less diligent in his guardian duties, of course.

Things were a little different on the opposite side of the table. Jill looked miserable, slumped into the seat with her arms crossed. Her light brown hair hung forward, covering part of her face. After ill-fated romances with a guy who wanted to become a Strigoi and with Eddie's human roommate, Jill had come to realize that Eddie might very well be the guy for her. It was fitting, too, because for a long time, he'd harbored a secret crush on her, fiercely dedicated to her in the way a knight served his liege lady. He'd never believed he was worthy of Jill, and without any signs of her affection, he'd turned to Angeline—just when Jill had come around and wanted him. At times, it seemed like some sort of Shakespearean comedy . . . until I looked at Jill's face. Then I'd feel conflicted because I knew if Eddie returned her affection, Angeline would be the one with that sad, sad expression. It was kind of a mess and made me glad to be free of any romantic entanglements.

"Sydney!" Jill beamed when she saw me, brushing her hair away. Maybe it was because she needed the distraction, or maybe it was because Adrian's new attitude toward me had lifted some of her moodiness. Regardless, I welcomed a return to the old friendliness in her rather than the brooding and accusing looks she'd harbored since I rejected him.

"Hey, guys." I slid into the booth beside her. Immediately, I opened up my cell phone's picture album and handed it to her since I knew she'd want to know about the wedding right away. Despite all the intrigue that had gone down there, I had managed to take some pictures without the other Alchemists noticing. Even if she'd seen some of it through Adrian's eyes, Jill would still want to examine everything in detail.

She sighed with happiness as she scanned the pictures. "Look at Sonya. She's so pretty." Angeline and Eddie leaned across the table to get a look. "Oh. And there's Rose and Lissa. They look great too." There was an odd note in Jill's voice as she spoke. She was friends with Rose, but her half sister was still a bit of an enigma. Jill and Lissa hadn't even known they were sisters until recently, and the volatile political environment had forced Lissa to behave more as a queen than a sister toward Jill. It was a difficult relationship for both of them.

"Did you have a fun time?" Eddie asked me.

I considered my answer for several moments. "I had an interesting time. There's still a lot of tension between the Alchemists and your people, so some of it was a little weird."

"At least Adrian was there. Must have been nice to have

someone you know," said Angeline, in well-meaning ignorance. She pointed to a picture I'd taken of the reception hall. My intent had been to get a full shot of the venue for Jill, but Adrian had happened to walk into the shot, posed and perfect like some handsome spokesmodel hosting the event. "Always so pretty." Angeline shook her head in disapproval. "Everyone there is. I guess that means there weren't any celebratory wrestling matches?"

It was a sign of Angeline's progress that she'd deduced that so quickly. Her people, the Keepers, lived in the wilds of West Virginia, and their openness to romance between vampires, dhampirs, and humans was only one of their more bizarre customs. Friendly fights broke out often, and Angeline had had to learn that such behaviors weren't acceptable out here in mainstream America.

"Not while I was there," I said. "But hey, maybe something went down after I left." That brought grins to Jill's and Eddie's faces and a hopeful look to Angeline's.

A waitress came by, and I ordered Diet Coke and a salad. Maybe I'd loosened up in my tight calorie counting, but I swore I could still taste the sugar from all the wedding cake I'd eaten after the spell.

Angeline tightened her hold on Eddie's arm and smiled up at him. "If you ever get to see my home, you can fight my brother Josh to show that you're worthy of me."

I had to swallow a laugh. I'd seen the Keepers' community and knew she was absolutely serious. I worked to keep a straight face. "Aren't you breaking a lot of rules by being together without that having happened yet?"

Angeline nodded, looking a little glum. "My mom would be

so scandalized if she knew. But I guess this is a unique situation."

Eddie smiled indulgently at her. I think sometimes he thought we were exaggerating about the Keepers. He was going to be in for a shock if he ever did visit them. "Maybe I can fight a bunch of your relatives to make up for it," he said.

"You might have to," she said, not realizing he was joking.

It was hardly romantic banter, but Jill looked decidedly uncomfortable discussing their relationship. She turned to me, very obviously trying not to look at them. "Sydney, what are we going to do about Christmas?"

I shrugged, unsure what she was asking. "The usual, I guess. Give presents. Sing songs. Have Yuletide duels." Angeline lit up at that.

Jill rolled her eyes. "No, I mean, we're going to be on winter break in a few weeks. Is there any way . . . is there any way we can go home?"

There was a plaintive note in her voice, and even Eddie and Angeline broke their mutual admiration to stare at me. I shifted under their scrutiny. Angeline wasn't as concerned about visiting the Keepers, but I knew Eddie and Jill missed their friends and family. I wished I could give them the answer they wanted to hear.

"I'm sorry," I said. "You'll be staying at Clarence's for break. We can't risk . . . well, you know." I didn't need to emphasize the need for Jill's safety. We were all familiar with that refrain. Ian's comment about how fragile the throne was drove home the importance of what we did.

Jill's face fell. Even Eddie looked disappointed. "I figured," she said. "I just hoped . . . that is, I miss my mom so much."

"We can probably get a message to her," I said gently.

I knew that was no substitute for the real thing. I was able to make occasional phone calls to my own mom, and hearing her voice was a million times better than any email could be. I even got to talk to my older sister, Carly, sometimes, which always cheered me up since she was so bright and funny. My younger sister, Zoe . . . well, she was a different story. She wouldn't take my calls. She'd nearly been initiated into the Alchemists—to take on this mission, in fact—when I'd stolen it from her. I'd done it to protect her from committing to the Alchemists so young, but she'd seen it as an insult.

Looking at Jill's sad face, I felt my heart clench. She had been through so much. Her new royal status. Targeted by assassins. Fitting in to a human school. Her disastrous and deadly romances. And now enduring Eddie and Angeline. She handled it all with remarkable strength, always resolutely going through with what she *had* to do even if she didn't *want* to do it. Lissa was praised for being such an exemplary queen, but there was a regality and strength to Jill as well that many underestimated. Glancing up, I caught a spark in Eddie's eyes as he too seemed to recognize and admire that about her.

After dinner, I took them back to Amberwood and was pleased to see that my car was in perfect shape. I drove a brown Subaru named Latte, and Eddie was the only other person I trusted behind the wheel. I dropped him off at the boys' dorm and then took Angeline and Jill back to ours. As we were walking in the door, I caught sight of Mrs. Santos, a teacher I knew by reputation.

"You guys go ahead," I told Jill and Angeline. "I'll see you tomorrow."

They left, and I walked across the lobby, waiting patiently

for Mrs. Santos to finish a discussion with our dorm matron, Mrs. Weathers. When Mrs. Santos started to turn around and leave, I caught her attention.

"Mrs. Santos? I'm Sydney Melrose. I wondered if I could—"

"Oh, yes," she said. "I know who you are, dear. Ms. Terwilliger raves about you all the time at our department meetings." Mrs. Santos was a kindly-looking woman with silver and black hair. Rumor had it she'd be retiring soon.

I flushed a little at the praise. "Thank you, ma'am." She and Ms. Terwilliger were both history teachers, though Mrs. Santos's focus was on American history, not world. "Do you have a minute? I wanted to ask you something."

"Of course."

We stepped off to the side of the lobby, out of the incoming and outgoing dorm traffic. "You know a lot about local history, right? Southern California?"

Mrs. Santos nodded. "I was born and raised here."

"I'm interested in nontraditional architecture in the Los Angeles area," I told her, the lie rolling easily off my lips. I'd thought about this in advance. "That is, non-Southwest styles. Do you know any neighborhoods like that? I'd heard there were some Victorian ones."

She brightened. "Oh, yes. Absolutely. Fascinating subject. Victorian, Cape Cod, Colonial . . . there are all sorts. I don't have all the information on me, but I could email you when I get home tonight. There are several I know off the top of my head, and I know a historian who could help you with others."

"That'd be great, ma'am. Thank you so much."

"Always happy to help a star pupil." She winked as she

started to walk away. "Maybe next semester you'll do an independent study with me. Provided you can tear yourself away from Ms. Terwilliger."

"I'll keep it in mind," I said.

As soon as she was gone, I texted Ms. Terwilliger. *Mrs. Santos is going to tell me about historical neighborhoods.* The response came quickly: *Excellent. Come over right now.* I scowled as I typed back: *I just got here. Haven't even been in my room.* To which she replied: *Then you can get here that much faster.*

Maybe that was true, but I still took the time to put my suitcase back in my room and change out of my travel clothes. Ms. Terwilliger lived pretty close to the school and looked as though she'd been pacing in circles when I arrived at her house.

"Finally," she said.

I glanced at the time. "It's only been fifteen minutes."

She shook her head and again wore the same grim expression she'd had out in the desert. "Even that might be too much. Follow me."

Ms. Terwilliger's home was a little bungalow that could have doubled as a New Age store or possibly a cat shelter. The level of clutter set my teeth on edge. Spell books, incense, statues, crystals, and all sorts of other magical items sat in piles in all rooms of the house. Only her workshop, the room she led me to, was neat and orderly—even to levels I approved of. Everything was clean and organized, to the point of being labeled and alphabetized. A large worktable sat in the center of the room, completely cleared off, save for a stunning necklace I'd never seen before. The chain was made of intricate gold loops, and the pendant was a deep red cabochon stone in a lacy gold setting.

"Garnet?" I asked.

"Very good," she said, lifting the necklace. The candlelight in the room seemed to make every part of it glitter.

"It's lovely," I said.

She held it out to me. "It's for you."

I stepped back uneasily. "For . . . me? I . . . I mean, thank you, but I can't accept a gift like that."

"It's not a gift," she said. "It's a necessity. One that might save your life. Take it and put it on."

I refused to touch it. "It's magical, isn't it?"

"Yes," she said. "And don't give me that look. It's no different from any of the charms you've made for yourself."

"Except that anything you'd make . . ." I swallowed as I stared into the depths of that bloodred jewel. "It's going to be a lot more powerful than anything I can create."

"That's exactly the point. Now here." She thrust it so close to me that it nearly swung out and hit me in the face.

Steeling myself, I reached out and took it from her. Nothing happened. No smoke or sparks. No searing pain. Seeing her expectant look, I fastened it around my neck, letting the garnet lie next to my cross.

She sighed, her relief nearly palpable. "Just as I'd hoped."

"What?" I asked. Even if I sensed nothing special about it, the garnet felt heavy around my neck.

"It's masking your magical ability," she said. "No one who meets you should be able to tell that you're a magic user."

"I'm *not* a magic user," I reminded her sharply. "I'm an Alchemist."

A small flicker of a smile played over her lips. "Of course you are—one who uses magic. And to a particularly powerful person, that would be obvious. Magic leaves a mark on your blood that permeates your whole body."

"What?" I couldn't have been more shocked if she'd said I'd just contracted a deadly disease. "You never told me that before!"

"It wasn't important," she said with a small shrug. "Until now. I need you hidden. Do not take that off. Ever."

I put my hands on my hips. "Ma'am, I don't understand."

"All will be revealed in time—"

"No," I said. At that moment, I could have been talking to Stanton or any of the countless others who'd used me and fed me pieces of information throughout my life. "It will be revealed *now*. If you've gotten me into something dangerous, then you either need to get me out of it or tell me how to."

Ms. Terwilliger stared at me for several quiet moments. A gray tabby cat rubbed up against my legs, ruining the seriousness of the moment. "You're right," she said at last. "I do owe you an explanation. Have a seat."

I sat down on one of the stools by the table, and she sat opposite me. She clasped her hands together in front of her and seemed to be having a hard time gathering her thoughts. I had to force myself to stay calm and patient. Otherwise, the panic that had been gnawing at me since the desert would completely consume me.

"You remember that woman you saw in the picture?" she asked at last.

"Your sister."

Ms. Terwilliger nodded. "Veronica. She's ten years older than me and looks half my age, as you could undoubtedly tell. Now, it isn't difficult to create an illusion. If I wanted to appear young and beautiful, I could—emphasis on *appear*. But Veronica? She's actually managed to make her body young and vibrant. It's an advanced, insidious kind of magic. You can't defy age like that without making some sacrifices." She frowned, and my heart pounded. Creating youth made all my Alchemist sensibilities reel. It was nearly as bad as Strigoi immortality, maybe worse if she was talking about a *human* doing it. That kind of twisted magic had no place in this world. Her next words drove home the wrongness of it all. "Or, in her case, sacrificing others."

Sacrifice. The very word seemed to poison the air. She stood up and walked over to a shelf, producing a newspaper clipping. Wordlessly, she handed it to me. It was a recent article, from three days ago, talking about a nineteen-year-old UCLA student who'd been found comatose in her dorm room. No one knew what had caused it, and the girl was hospitalized with no indication of when or if she'd wake up.

"What is this?" I asked, not sure I wanted to know the answer.

I inspected the article more closely, especially the picture it contained. At first, I wondered why the paper would show a sleeping old woman. Then, reading the fine print, I learned that the coma victim also displayed some unexplained physical symptoms: gray-streaked hair and dry, cracked skin. Doctors were currently investigating rare diseases. I cringed, unable to believe what I saw. She was hideous, and I couldn't look at her for very long.

And just like that, I suddenly understood. Veronica wasn't sacrificing victims with knives and stone altars. She was conducting some kind of perverse magic on these girls that bent the rules of nature, putting them in this hideous state. My stomach twisted, and I gripped the table for support.

"This girl was one of Veronica's victims," confirmed Ms. Terwilliger. "That's how she maintains her youth and beauty—by taking it from others. When I read this, I thought—almost hoped—some other magic user was doing it. Not that I'd wish this on anyone. Your scrying spell confirmed she was in the area, however, which means it's my responsibility to deal with her."

I dared a look down at the article again and felt that nausea well up again. The girl was nineteen. What would it be like to have the life sucked out of you at so young an age? Maybe the coma was a blessing. And how corrupt and twisted would you have to be to do that to someone?

I didn't know how exactly Ms. Terwilliger would "deal with" her sister and wasn't sure I wanted to find out. And yet, if Veronica really was doing things like this to innocents, then yes, someone like Ms. Terwilliger needed to stop her. A magical attack of this magnitude was one of the most terrible things I could imagine. It brought back all my ingrained fears about the wrongness of magic. How could I justify using it when it was capable of such horror? Old Alchemist lessons came back to me: *Part of what makes the Moroi particularly dangerous is their ability to work magic. No one should be able to twist the world in that way. It's wrong and can easily run out of control.*

I tuned back into the present. "How do I fit into this, ma'am? I already figured out where she is. Why am I in danger?"

"Sydney," Mrs. Terwilliger said, looking at me strangely. "There are few young women out there with your abilities. Along with youth and beauty, she intends to suck someone's magic away and use it to make herself that much more power-ful. You, my dear, would be the ultimate coup for her."

"She's like Strigoi," I murmured, unable to repress a shiver. Although those undead vampires could feast on anyone, they preferred Moroi because they had magic in their blood. Drinking Moroi blood made Strigoi more powerful, and a chill-ing thought suddenly hit me. "Practically a human vampire."

"Something like that," Ms. Terwilliger agreed. "This amulet should hide your power, even from someone as strong as her. She shouldn't be able to find you."

A calico cat jumped up on the table, and I ran a hand over her sleek fur, taking comfort in the small contact. "The fact that you keep saying 'should' makes me a little nervous. Why would she even come looking in Palm Springs? Does she know about me yet?"

"No. But she knows *I'm* here, and she may check on me once in a while—so I need to hide you in case she does. I'm in a bind, however, because I need to find her but can't actively do the hunting. If she finds out I'm investigating, she'll know that I know she's here. I can't alert her. If I have the element of sur-prise on my side, I'm more likely to stop her." She frowned. "I'm honestly surprised she would come so close to me in California at all. Regardless, I need to keep a low profile until it's time to strike."

Ms. Terwilliger looked at me meaningfully, and I felt a sink-ing feeling in my stomach as I began to put together what she was saying. "You want me to hunt her."

"It's not hunting so much as gathering some data. You're the only one I can trust to do this. She and I can sense each other if we're close, no matter how much we try to hide our magic. I know this is going to sound shocking, but I actually think it'd be best if you hunted her—even if you're the one she's after. You're one of the few I can trust completely, and you're resourceful enough to pull something like this off."

"But I'd be putting myself out there. You just said I'd be a big catch for her." The twists and turns here were mindboggling.

"Yes. Which is why I gave you the amulet. She won't sense your magic, and if you're cautious in your investigation, she should have no reason to notice you."

I still wasn't following the logic here. "But why *me*? You have a coven. If you can't do it yourself, then there must be someone else—a stronger witch—who can do it."

"Two reasons," she said. "One is that you have excellent investigative skills—more so than others older than you. You're intelligent and resourceful. The other reason . . . well, if another witch goes after her, she might very well kill Veronica."

"Would that be such a bad thing?" I didn't like violence and killing by any means, but this might be a case where it was justified, if it could save other lives. "You said you were going to 'take care of her.'"

"If I have no choice . . . if I must kill her, then I will." She looked dejected, and I had a moment of empathy. I loved my two sisters. What would I do if I was ever in a deadly conflict with one of them? Of course, it was hard to imagine Zoe or Carly committing this kind of atrocity. "However, there are other ways of neutralizing and subduing a magic user. If there's any way—any way at all—I can do that, I will. My coven sisters won't feel that way, which is why I need your help."

"I can't." I pushed the stool back and stood up, nearly stepping on a cat in the process. "There must be some other way you can do this. You know I'm already bogged down in supernatural affairs." I actually couldn't bring myself to admit the real reason I wanted to dodge this. It was about more than just risking my life. So far, all my magical interactions had been with Ms. Terwilliger. If I signed on for this, I would be plunging into the world of witches, something I'd sworn I would never do.

Ms. Terwilliger tapped the article, and her voice was quiet when she spoke. "Could you let this happen to other girls, knowing there's a way you could stop it? I've never heard of any of her victims waking up. The way this spell works, Veronica needs to renew it every few years, and it requires five victims within one month. She did this once before, and it caught me off guard. This time, we have warning. Four more people could suffer this fate. Do you want that?"

There it was. She'd called me on the other part that had been nagging me because she knew me too well. I couldn't let innocents suffer, not even if it meant risking myself or facing the fears that haunted me. If I could stop this, I had to. No one deserved the fate of that girl in the paper. "Of course not."

"And let's not forget that you could soon be one of her victims."

I touched the garnet. "You said I'm hidden."

"You are, for now. And I hope against all hope you'll stay that way." I'd never seen her so grim before, and it was hard to watch. I was used to her prattling, bumbling, no-nonsense nature. "But here's something I've never told you about how magic users sense each other."

Something I'd learned over the years: it was never a good thing when people said, "Here's something I never told you. . . ." I braced myself.

"Untrained magic users have a particular feel that's unique from the more experienced," she explained. "There's a oh, wildness about the magic that surrounds you. It's easy for advanced witches to sense. My coven keeps track of novice magic users, but those are tightly guarded secrets. Veronica won't have access to those names, but there are spells she can use that can pick up on some of that untamed magic if it's near her. It's how she probably found this poor girl." Ms. Terwilliger nodded toward the article.

The idea of me having some "wild" magical aura was as shocking as her saying I had magic in my blood.

"When she absorbs a victim," Ms. Terwilliger continued, "she gets a burst of that wildness. It fades quickly, but when she possesses it, it can briefly enhance her ability to scry for another untrained victim. The more victims she takes, the stronger that ability will grow. There's a chance," Ms. Terwilliger said gravely, "that it could be enough to break apart the garnet. I don't know." She spread out her hands.

"So you're saying . . . with each victim she attacks, the chance that she'll find me increases."

"Yes."

"All right. I'll help you hunt for her." I shoved all my fears and doubts aside. The stakes were too high. My life, the other girls . . . Veronica had to be stopped for all our sakes. Someone like her couldn't be allowed to go on like this.

"There's more," added Ms. Terwilliger.

Really?

"More than hunting an evil witch who wants to drain me of my life and power?"

"If we can stop Veronica from finding less powerful victims, we can save their lives and limit her ability to find you." She produced a small velvet bag and emptied it out onto the table. Several small agate circles fell out. "These are charms that have some ability to mask magic. Not as strong as the garnet—that would take too long. But they're a quick fix that might save some of these other girls' lives."

I knew where this was going. "And you want me to deliver them."

"I'm sorry. I know I'm giving you some very difficult tasks here."

This was getting worse and worse. "Difficult? That's an understatement. And putting aside the fact that you want me to find a woman who could suck my life away, there's also the very small detail that the Alchemists would flip out if they knew I was involved with any of this."

Ms. Terwilliger didn't answer right away. She just watched me. A black cat jumped up beside her and joined in the staring. Its yellow-eyed gaze seemed to say, *Do the right thing.*

"Where do I start?" I asked finally. "Finding that neighborhood is part of it, right?"

"Yes. And I'll tell you where to find her potential victims, if you'll do the legwork of warning them. My coven keeps track of them. They'll be girls very much like you, ones with power who refuse to train and have no mentor to look after them. Once we have a clear fix on Veronica herself . . ." Ms. Terwilliger's eyes hardened. "Well, then. That's when I'll step in."

Once more, I wondered if I really wanted to know what that entailed.

A moment later, she added, "Oh, and I thought it would be a good idea to obscure your appearance as well."

I brightened. I couldn't explain it, but somehow, that made me feel immensely better. "There are a lot of spells for that, right?" I'd seen a number of them in my studies. Even if I had to use magic, it was better to at least look different.

"Yes. . . ." She drummed her fingers against the table. "But the amulet might not be able to hide you wearing an 'active' spell, which would then defeat the whole purpose. What I was actually hoping was that your 'brother' Adrian might be able to help."

My legs felt weak, and I sat back down. "Why on earth should Adrian be involved in this?"

"Well, he seems like he'd do anything for you." I eyed her, wondering if there was a double meaning in that. Her gaze was far away, her thoughts turned inward. She'd meant her words honestly. "Veronica wouldn't be able to detect vampire magic. His power . . . that spirit element he was telling me about . . . it can confuse the mind, right? Affect what others can see?"

"Yes. . . ."

She focused on me again, nodding in satisfaction. "If he could accompany you, help muddle whoever meets you . . . well, that would offer an extra level of protection."

I still didn't know what all I'd be doing to hunt Ms. Terwilliger's sister, but it sounded like, at the very least, there'd be a drive to Los Angeles in my future. Me, trapped in another small space with Adrian while he continued with that infuriating "loving from afar." I was so caught up in the emotional turmoil that idea caused that it took me a moment to realize the larger issue I was letting myself get sucked into.

"Do you realize what you're asking?" I said quietly. I touched the garnet again. "To be a part of this, you're asking me to expose myself to both human magic *and* vampire magic. Everything I try to avoid."

Ms. Terwilliger snorted, and for the first time tonight, I saw a return of her usual amused attitude. "Unless I'm mistaken, you've been exposing yourself to both kinds of magic for some time now. So, it can't go against your beliefs *that* much." She paused meaningfully. "If anything, it seems like it goes against the Alchemists' beliefs."

"The Alchemists' beliefs are my beliefs," I said quickly.

She arched an eyebrow. "Are they? I would hope your beliefs would be *your* beliefs."

I'd never thought about it that way before, but I suddenly hoped desperately that her words were true.

CHAPTER 6

I FOLLOWED MS. TERWILLIGER'S instructions diligently. I never took the garnet off, not even when I slept or showered. When school started the next morning, I wore it under my shirt to avoid any questions. It didn't exactly scream "magical amulet," but it was certainly conspicuous. To my surprise, Ms. Terwilliger wasn't in her first-period history class, making me wonder if she was doing some investigating of her own.

"Ms. T on some secret mission?"

I flinched and realized I'd been lost in my own thoughts. I turned and found Trey Juarez kneeling by my desk. Class hadn't started yet, and a confused-looking substitute teacher was trying to make sense of the chaos of Ms. Terwilliger's desk. Trey grinned at my surprise.

"Wh-what?" I asked. Had he somehow found out about Veronica? I tried to keep cool. "What makes you say that?"

"I was just joking," he said. "This is the second year I've had her, and she's never missed a day." He gave me a puzzled look.

"Unless you really do know something I don't?"

"No," I said quickly. "I'm just as surprised as you are."

Trey scrutinized me a few moments. We were good friends here at Amberwood, with only one teeny-tiny problem hanging between us.

His family was tied to the Warriors of Light.

Last month, the Warriors had tried to kill Sonya in a barbaric execution ritual. Trey had been one of the contenders for the "honor" of killing her, though he'd thrown the match at the last minute. I'd tried to appeal to the Warriors to release Sonya, but they hadn't listened. She and I were both saved when a raiding party of dhampirs showed up and defeated the Warriors. Stanton had helped orchestrate that raid—but hadn't bothered to fill me in that I was being used as a distraction. It was part of what had fueled my distrust of her and the Alchemists.

Trey had been blamed for getting me involved with the ritual, and the Warriors had ostracized his father and him. Just as I had been pressured by the Alchemists, Trey had had Warrior doctrine drilled into him his whole life. His father was so ashamed of the fallout that he would barely speak to Trey now. I knew how much Trey wanted his father's approval, so this silence was more painful to him than the Warriors' treatment.

Our allegiances made things difficult. When I'd once tentatively hinted to Trey that we still had unresolved issues between us, he'd responded with a bitter laugh. "You have nothing to worry about anymore," he'd told me. "I'm not hiding any secret plans from you—because I don't know any. They won't tell us anything. I'm not one of them, as far as they're concerned. I've been cut off forever, and it'd take a miracle for them to ever take us back." There'd been something in his dark eyes that told me if he ever could find that miracle, he'd jump on it. I'd tried asking about that, but he wouldn't discuss it any further. "I want to be your friend, Melbourne," he had said. "I like you. We're never going to resolve our differences. Might as well ignore them since we have to be together every day."

Amazingly, our friendship had managed to survive all that drama. The tension was always there, lurking between us, but we tried to ignore it. Although he knew about my involvement in the vampiric world, he had no idea I was taking behind-the-scenes magic lessons with our history teacher, of course.

If he thought I was lying about Ms. Terwilliger's absence today, he didn't push the matter. He nodded toward the sub. "This is going to be a blow-off day."

I dragged my mind away from magical intrigue. After being homeschooled for most of my life, some parts of the "normal" school world were a mystery. "What's that mean, exactly?"

"Usually teachers leave subs a lesson plan, telling them what to do. I saw the one Ms. Terwilliger left. It said, 'Distract them.'" Trey shook his head in mock sympathy. "I hope you can handle the wasted academic time. I mean, she'll probably say something like, 'Work on homework.' But no one will."

He was right. I wasn't sure if I could handle this. "Why wouldn't they?"

This seemed to amuse him immensely. "Melbourne, sometimes you're the only reason I come to class. I saw her sub plan for your independent study, by the way. It said you didn't even have to stick around. You're free to run wild."

Eddie, sitting nearby, overheard and scoffed. "To the library?"

This made both of them laugh, but my mind was already

spinning with possibilities. If I really didn't have to stay for my last class, I'd be free to leave campus early. I could go into Los Angeles to look for Veronica and—no. Adrian wasn't back. For a moment, I toyed with the idea of investigation without his spirit magic, but Ms. Terwilliger's warnings echoed through my mind. The hunt would have to wait.

But I could still look for Marcus Finch.

Santa Barbara was two hours away. That meant I had enough time to drive up there, do some investigating of Marcus, and still comfortably make it back by the school's curfew. I hadn't intended to go look for him until this weekend but realized now that I shouldn't waste this opportunity. Ms. Terwilliger's task weighed heavily on me as well, but I couldn't do anything about it until Adrian returned tonight.

Marcus Finch had been a mystery to me since the moment I'd discovered he was an ex-Alchemist. Realizing that I might actually get some answers *today* made my heart pound in overtime. It was one thing to suspect the Alchemists had been holding out on me. It was an entirely different matter to accept that I might be on the verge of having those suspicions confirmed. It was actually kind of terrifying.

As the day progressed, I became more and more resolved to make the drive. I had to face this sooner or later, and I might as well get it over with. For all I knew, Marcus had simply been sightseeing in Santa Barbara and could be gone already. I didn't want to repeat the scrying spell if I could help it.

Sure enough, when I showed up for what would normally be my independent study at the end of the day, the sub (looking extremely worn out after a day of following in Ms. Terwilliger's footsteps) told me I was free to go. I thanked her and hurried off to my dorm room, conscious of the clock that was now ticking. I didn't know exactly what I'd be facing in Santa Barbara, but I planned to be prepared for anything.

I changed out of my Amberwood uniform, opting for jeans and a plain black blouse. Kneeling by my bed, I pulled out a large metal box from underneath it. At first glance, the box looked like a makeup kit. However, it had an intricate lock that required both a key and combination. Inside was my Alchemist chemistry set, a collection of chemicals that would probably get me kicked out of school if found since it looked like it was capable of manufacturing illegal drugs. And really, some of the compounds probably were pretty questionable.

I selected some basics. One was a formula that was usually used to dissolve Strigoi bodies. I didn't expect to encounter any Strigoi in Santa Barbara, but the compound could also be used to disintegrate metal pretty handily. I chose a couple other mixtures—like one that could create a spy-worthy smoke screen—and carefully wrapped them all up before slipping them into my messenger bag. Then I locked the box again and slid it back under the bed.

After a little consideration, I took a deep breath and produced another hidden box. This was a new one in my collection. It contained various charms and potions I'd made under Ms. Terwilliger's instruction. Staring at its contents, I felt my stomach twist. Never in my wildest dreams had I imagined I'd have such a kit. When we'd first met, I'd only created charms under duress. Now I had several that I'd willingly made, and if what she'd said about her sister was true, I'd need to start making more. With great reluctance, I picked a variety of these as well and packed them up with the Alchemist chemicals. After a moment's consideration, I put a couple in my pocket for quick access.

The drive to Santa Barbara was easy this time of day. December had cooled off some of southern California's weather, but the sun was still out, making it seem warmer than it really was. And, as I drove up the coast, the desert gave way to more temperate conditions. Rain increased in the middle and northern parts of the state this time of year, making the landscape lush and green. I really did love Palm Springs and Amberwood, but there were times I wouldn't have minded if Jill's assignment had taken us up here.

Finding the Old Mission Santa Barbara wasn't difficult. It was a well-known tourist attraction and pretty easy to spot once you were nearby. The sprawling church looked exactly as it had in my vision save that it was lit by mid-afternoon sunshine rather than twilight. I pulled off to the side of the road in a residential neighborhood and gazed up at the beautiful stucco and terra-cotta masterpiece. I wished I had the time to go on a tour, but, as they so often did, my personal desires had to take a backseat to a larger goal.

Now came the more difficult part—having to figure out where the studio I'd seen might be. The neighborhood I parked in provided a view that was similar to the one I'd observed in the spell. The angles weren't exact, however, and this street only contained houses. I was almost certain the studio I'd seen had been in an apartment building. Keeping the mission in view, I drove a few more streets over and found what I'd hoped for: several blocks containing apartment complexes.

One looked too nice to have what I'd seen. The studio had seemed pretty bare bones and run down. The other two buildings on the street looked like more likely candidates. I drove to each one and walked around their grounds, trying to imagine what the angle might be when viewed from a higher window. I wished I'd had a chance to actually look down to the parking lot in the vision. It would have given me a better idea of the floor. After much thought, I finally deduced the studio had been on the third or fourth floor. Since one of the buildings only had two floors, that gave me a pretty positive hit on the correct place.

Stepping inside the building made me glad I'd packed hand sanitizer in my bag. The halls looked like they hadn't been swept in over a year. The walls were dirty, their paint chipped. Bits of trash sat on the floor. Cobwebs hung in some of the corners, and I prayed spiders were the only creepy-crawly inhabitants. If I saw a roach, I was probably going to bolt. The building had no front desk I could make inquiries at, so I flagged down a middle-aged woman as she was leaving. She paused, regarding me warily.

"Hi," I said, hoping I looked non-threatening. "I'm trying to find a friend of mine, but I don't know which apartment he lives in. Maybe you know him? His name is Marcus. He has a blue tattoo on his face." Seeing her blank look, I repeated the question in Spanish. Comprehension showed in her expression, but once she'd heard my entire question, her only response was a brief headshake. I didn't even have time to show her Marcus's picture.

I spent the next half hour doing the same thing whenever I saw residents going in or out. I stayed outside this time, preferring a brightly lit public area to the dingy interior. Some of the people I talked to were a little sketchy, and a couple of guys looked me over in a way I definitely didn't like. I was about to give up when a younger boy approached me. He appeared to be about ten and had been playing in the parking lot.

"I know the guy you're looking for," he told me in English. "But his name's not Marcus. It's Dave."

Considering how difficult Marcus had been to find, I wasn't entirely surprised he'd been using another name. "You're sure?" I asked the boy. I showed him the picture. "This is the guy?"

He nodded eagerly. "That's the one. He's real quiet. My mom says he's probably doing bad things."

Great. Just what I needed. "Do you know where he lives?"

The boy pointed upward. "At the top. 407."

I thanked him and went back inside, heading up to the fourth floor on stairs that creaked the entire way. The apartment was near the end of the hall, next to one that was blasting obnoxious music. I knocked on 407 and didn't get a response. Not sure if the occupant had heard me, I knocked more loudly and received the same result.

I eyed the doorknob, considering melting it with my Alchemist chemicals. Immediately, I dismissed the thought. Even in a disreputable building like this, a neighbor might be concerned to see me breaking into an apartment. I didn't want to attract any attention. This situation was getting increasingly frustrating, and I couldn't spend all day here.

I ran through my choices. Everyone said I was so smart. Surely there was some solution here that would work? Waiting around in the hall wasn't an option. There was no telling how long it could take for Marcus or "Dave" to show up. And honestly, the less time spent in the dirty hall, the better. If only there was some way to get inside that didn't involve actually destroying—

That's when the solution came to me. I groaned. It wasn't one I liked, but it would get the job done.

I went back outside and waved hello to the boy as he practiced jumping off the steps. "Was Dave home?" he asked.

"No."

The boy nodded. "He usually isn't."

That, at least, would be helpful for this next crazy plan. I left the boy and walked around the side of the building, which was mercifully deserted. There, clinging to the outer wall, was the most rickety fire escape I'd ever seen. Considering how rigid California safety standards were, I was astonished that this hadn't been reported. Of course, if it had, it didn't seem likely this building's owner would've been quick to act, judging from the rest of the conditions I'd seen.

Double checking that no one was around, I stood in the fire escape's shadow, hoping it more or less concealed me. From the messenger bag, I produced one of my charms: a necklace made of agate and crow feathers. I slipped it over my head and recited a Greek incantation. I felt the warmth of magic run through me but saw no ostensible changes. Theoretically, I should be invisible for those who didn't know to look for me. Whether that had actually happened, I couldn't say. I supposed I'd find out if someone came by and demanded to know why I was climbing into an apartment via the fire escape.

Once I stepped onto it, I nearly terminated the plan. The entire fire escape squeaked and swayed. The scaffolding was so rusty, I wouldn't have been surprised if it disintegrated beneath my feet. I stood frozen where I was, trying to work up the courage to go on. I reminded myself that this could be my one chance to find Marcus. The boy in the parking lot had confirmed he lived here. I couldn't waste this opportunity.

I gulped and kept going, gingerly moving from floor to floor. When I reached the fourth, I stared down in amazement, unable to believe the fire escape was still intact. Now I had a new problem. I'd figured out where Marcus's studio was, and it was one window over from the fire escape's landing. The distance wasn't that great, but on the narrow ledge between them would feel like miles. Equally daunting was the fact that I'd have to get through the window. It was shut, which made sense if he was in hiding. I had a couple magical amulets capable of melting glass, but I didn't trust myself to be able to use them on the narrow ledge—which meant I had to see just how good my aim had become in PE.

Still conscious of the precarious fire escape, I took out a small pouch of powder from my messenger bag. Sizing up the distance, I threw the pouch hard toward the window, reciting a spell—and missed. The pouch hit the side of the building, throwing up a dusty cloud, and began eating away at the stucco. I winced as the wall dissolved. The spell eventually burned itself out but left a noticeable hole behind. It hadn't gone all the way through, and I supposed given the state of the building, no one would probably even notice.

I had one pouch left and had to make it count. The pane was fairly big, and there was no way I could miss this time. I threw hard—and made contact. The powder smashed against the window. Immediately, a reaction spread out and began melting the glass. It dripped down like ice out in the sun. Now, watching anxiously, I wanted the reaction to go on for as long as possible. I needed a big enough hole to get through. Fortunately, when it stopped, I felt confident I could make it inside—if I could get over there.

I wasn't afraid of heights, but as I crept along the ledge, I felt like I was on top of a skyscraper. My heart was in my throat, and I pondered the logistics of surviving a four-floor drop. My palms began to sweat, and I ordered them to stop. I wasn't going to come all this way just to have my hands slip at the last minute.

As it turned out, it was my foot that slipped. The world spun, and I frantically flung my arms out, just barely grabbing the inside of the window. I pulled myself toward it, and with a surge of adrenaline-fueled effort managed to hook my other leg inside. I took a deep breath and tried to quiet my pounding heart. I was secure. I was going to make it. A moment later, I was able to pull myself up and swing my other leg around the ledge, tumbling into the room.

I landed on the floor, my legs weak and shaky as I worked to steady my frantic breathing. That was close. If my reflexes had been a little slower, I would've found out exactly what four floors could do to the human body. While I loved science, I wasn't sure that was an experiment I needed to try. Maybe being around dhampirs so much had helped improve my physical skills.

Once I'd recovered, I was able to assess my surroundings. Here I was, in the exact same studio I'd seen in my vision. Glancing behind me, I sized up the mission, verifying I had the same vantage. Yup. Exactly the same. Inside, I recognized the mattress on the floor and the same meager belongings. Across the room, the door leading out had a number of very new, very state-of-the-art locks. Dissolving the outer doorknob wouldn't have done any good.

"Now what?" I muttered. I'd made it inside. I didn't have Marcus, but I theoretically had his apartment. I was unsure what I was looking for but might as well start somewhere.

First, I examined the mattress, not that I expected much. It couldn't hide belongings like mine could. It could, however, hide rats and God only knew what else underneath it. I gingerly lifted a corner, knowing I must be grimacing, but there was nothing underneath—alive or otherwise. My next target was a small, disorderly pile of clothes. Going through someone's dirty laundry (because I assumed it was dirty, if it was sitting on the floor) wasn't much better than looking at the mattress. A whiff of fabric softener told me that these clothes were, in fact, recently washed. They were ordinary guy clothes, probably a young guy's clothes, which fit with Marcus's profile. Jeans. T-shirts. Boxers. As I sifted through the pile, I nearly started folding them and had to remind myself that I didn't want to leave any sign of my passing. Of course, the melted window was kind of a dead giveaway.

A couple of personal items sat nearby, a toothbrush and deodorant with a scent inexplicably called as "Ocean Fiesta." Aside from a rickety wooden chair and the ancient TV, there was only one other form of comfort and entertainment in the barren room: a battered copy of *The Catcher in the Rye*. "Great," I muttered, wondering what it said about a person who owned no other personal possessions. "Marcus Finch is pretentious and self-entitled."

The studio's bathroom was claustrophobic and barely had enough space for a single shower stall, toilet, and dripping sink. Judging from the mildew on the floor, a good deal of water sprayed out when the shower was used. A large black spider scurried down the drain, and I hastily backed out.

Defeated, I went to investigate a narrow closet door. After all my work, I'd found Marcus Finch but hadn't actually *found* him. My search had revealed nothing. I had limited time to wait for him, and honestly, if I were him and returned home to a melted window, I would promptly walk out the door and never return. If he ran, I'd have no choice but to keep scrying and—

"Ahh!"

Something jumped out at me as I opened the closet door— and it wasn't a rat or a roach.

It was a man.

The closet was tiny, so it was a miracle he had even fit inside. I had no time to process the spatial logistics, however, because his fist shot out and clipped me on the side of the face.

In my life, I'd been slammed up against brick walls and bitten by a Strigoi. I'd never been punched, however, and it wasn't an experience I wanted to repeat. I stumbled backward, so surprised that I couldn't even react right away. The guy lunged after me, grabbing my upper arms and shaking me as he leaned close.

"How did you guys find me?" he exclaimed. "How many more are coming?"

Pain radiated through the side of my face, but somehow, I managed to gather my senses. Last month, I'd taken a self-defense class with a slightly unstable Chihuahua breeder who looked like a pirate. Despite Malachi Wolfe's unorthodox behavior, he'd actually taught us some legitimate skills, and they came back to me now. I kneed my attacker in the stomach. His blue eyes went wide with shock as he released me and fell to the ground. It didn't keep him down for long, though. He scrambled back to his feet and came after me, but by then, I'd grabbed the chair and was using it to keep him at bay the way a lion tamer would.

"Back off," I said. "I just want to—"

Ignoring my threats, the guy pushed forward and grabbed one of the chair's legs, pulling it away from me. He had me backed into a corner, and despite some tricks Eddie had taught me, I wasn't confident in my own ability to throw a punch. Nonetheless, I put up a good fight when my attacker tried to grab me again. We struggled and fell to the floor. I kicked and clawed like crazy, making things as difficult as possible. It was only when he managed to pin me with his entire body that my flailing got stifled. I had enough freedom to reach a hand into my pocket, however.

"Who sent you?" he demanded. "Where are the others?"

I didn't answer. Instead, I pulled out a small vial and flipped the cap off with one hand. Immediately, noxious yellow vapor with the consistency of dry ice spilled out of it. I thrust it toward the guy's face. He recoiled in disgust, and tears sprang into his eyes. The substance itself was relatively harmless, but its fumes acted as a kind of pepper spray. He let go of me, and with strength I didn't even know I had, I managed to roll him over and hold him down. I drove my elbow into his wrist, and he made a small grunt of pain. With my other arm, I waved the vial with as much menace as I would a machete. This wouldn't fool him for long, but hopefully it'd buy me some time to reassess my situation. Now that he was still, I was finally able to get a good look at him and was relieved to see I'd at least achieved my goal. He had a young, handsome face with an indigo tattoo on his cheek. It was an abstract design that looked like a latticework of crescent moons. A faint silver gleam edged some of the blue lines.

"Nice to meet you, Marcus."

Then, the most astonishing thing happened. Through his watering eyes, he'd been trying to get a good look at me too. Recognition appeared on his face as he blinked me into focus.

"Sydney Sage," he gasped. "I've been looking for you."

I didn't have any time to be surprised because I suddenly heard the click of a gun, and a barrel touched the back of my head.

"Get off him," a voice demanded. "And drop the smoke bomb."

CHAPTER 7

I MIGHT HAVE BEEN DETERMINED to find Marcus, but I certainly wasn't going to argue against a gun.

I raised my hands in the air and slowly stood up, keeping my back to the newcomer. Just as carefully, I stepped away from Marcus and set the vial on the floor. Fumes still wafted out of it, but the reaction would burn itself out soon. Then I dared a peek behind me. When I saw the girl who stood there, I could barely believe my eyes.

"Are you okay?" she asked Marcus. He was unsteadily getting to his feet. "I left as soon as you called."

"You!" I couldn't quite manage anything more articulate.

The girl standing before me was close to my age, with long, tangled blond hair. She still had the gun on me, but a small smile appeared on her face.

"Nice to see you again."

The feeling wasn't mutual. I'd last seen this girl when I faced down the Warriors in their arena. She'd been toting a gun there as well and had had a perpetual snarl on her face. She'd pushed me around and threatened me, making no secret of how heretical she thought my defense of Sonya was. Although she seemed much calmer now than she had with those fanatics, I still couldn't dismiss what she was—or what the implications were. I turned to Marcus in disbelief. He was cradling the wrist I'd nailed with my elbow.

"You . . . you're one of them! One of the Warriors of Light!"

I don't think I'd ever been so let down in my life. I'd had so many hopes pinned on Marcus. He'd become larger than life in my mind, some rebel savior who was going to tell me all the secrets of the world and free me from being another cog in the machine of the Alchemists. But it was all a lie. Clarence had mentioned Marcus had convinced the Warriors to leave him alone. I'd assumed it was because Marcus had some incredible leverage he could use against the Warriors, but apparently, the key to his influence was that he was one of them.

He looked up from his wrist. "What? Those nuts? Hell, no."

I almost pointed at the girl but decided it would be best not to make any sudden moves. I settled for a nod in her direction and noticed all the locks on the door had been undone. I'd been so caught up in the struggle with Marcus that I hadn't heard them. "Really? Then how come one of them just saved you?"

"I'm not really one of them." She spoke almost casually, but the gun contradicted her tone. "I mean, I guess I kind of am. . . ."

"Sabrina's a spy," explained Marcus. He looked much more at ease too, now that I wasn't assaulting him. "A lovely one. She's been undercover with them for over a year. She's also the one who told me about you."

Once again, it was hard knowing how to respond to that. I

also wasn't sure if I bought this spy story. "What exactly did you tell him?"

He shot me a movie star smile. His teeth were so white that I wondered if he had veneers. It seemed out of character for a rogue who lived on the run, but nothing about this day was really turning out like I'd expected. "She told me about this Alchemist girl who defended a Moroi and then helped lead a dhampir raiding party."

Lead? Hardly. No one—notably Stanton—had felt the need to enlighten me about that raid until I was in the middle of it. I didn't want to tip my hand too early, though. "The Alchemists sanctioned that raid," I said.

"I saw the way you spoke," said Sabrina. Her eyes flicked between Marcus and me, fierce for me and admiring for him. "It was inspiring. And we watched you for a while, you know. You spent an awful lot of time with the Moroi and dhampirs in Palm Springs."

"It's my job," I said. She hadn't really seemed inspired at the time. Mostly she'd looked disappointed at not having a chance to use the gun on me.

Marcus's smile turned knowing. "From what I heard, you and those Moroi almost looked like friends. And then, here you are, looking for me. You're definitely the dissident we'd hoped for."

No, this was not turning out at all like I'd planned. In fact, it was pretty much the opposite of what I'd planned. I'd been so proud of my ability to track down Marcus, little knowing that he'd been watching me already. I didn't like that. It made me feel vulnerable, even if they were saying some of things I'd hoped to hear. Needing to feel like I was in control, I tried to play it cool and tough.

"Maybe there are other Alchemists about to show up," I said.

"They would've been here already," he said, calling my bluff. "They wouldn't have sent you alone . . . though I did panic when I first saw you. I didn't realize who you were and thought there were others right behind you." He paused, and that cocky attitude turned sheepish. "Sorry about, um, punching you. If it makes you feel better, you did something pretty serious to my wrist."

Sabrina's face filled with concern. "Oh, Marcus. Do you need to see a doctor?"

He tested the movement of his wrist and then shook his head. "You know we can't. Never know who might be watching at a hospital. Those places are too easy to monitor."

"You really are hiding from the Alchemists," I said in amazement.

His nodded, almost looking proud. "You doubted? I figured you'd know that."

"I suspected, but I didn't hear it from them. They deny you exist."

He seemed to find that funny. In fact, he seemed to find everything funny, which I found slightly irritating. "Yup. That's what I've heard from the others."

"What others?"

"Others like you." Those blue eyes held me for a moment, like they could see all my secrets. "Other Alchemists wanting to break free of the fold."

I knew my own eyes were wide. "There . . . there are others?"

Marcus settled on the floor, leaning against the wall and still cradling his wrist. "Let's get comfortable. Sabrina, put the gun away. I don't think Sydney's going to give us any trouble."

Sabrina didn't look so sure of that, but after several moments, she complied. She joined him on the floor, positioning herself protectively next to him. "I'd rather stand," I told them. No way would I willingly sit on that filth. After rolling around with Marcus, I wanted to go bathe myself in hand sanitizer.

He shrugged. "Suit yourself. You want some answers? You give me some first. Why'd you come looking for me off the Alchemist clock?"

I didn't like being interrogated, but what was the point of being here if I wasn't going to engage in a dialogue?

"Clarence told me about you," I said at last. "He showed me your picture, and I saw how you'd tattooed over the lily. I didn't even know that was possible." The tattoo never faded.

"Clarence Donahue?" Marcus looked genuinely pleased. "He's a good guy. I suppose you'd be friends with him if you're in Palm Springs, huh?"

I started to say we weren't friends but then reconsidered. What else were we?

"Getting this isn't easy," added Marcus, tapping the blue tattoo. "You'll have to do a lot of work if you want to do it."

I stepped backward. "Whoa, I never said that's what I wanted. And why in the world would I do it anyway?"

"Because it'll free you," he said simply. "It prevents you from discussing vampire affairs, right? You don't think that's all it does, do you? Think. What stops it from exerting other control?"

I pretty much had to just give up on any expectations for this conversation because every topic was crazier than the last. "I've never heard of anything like that. I've never felt anything like that. Aside from it protecting vampire information, I'm in control."

He nodded. "Probably. The initial tattoo usually only has the talking compulsion in it. They only start adding other components with re-inks if they've got a reason to worry about you. People can sometimes fight through those and if they do . . . well, then it's off to re-education."

His words sent a chill through me, and I rested a hand on my cheek as I flashbacked to the meeting I'd had when I was given the Palm Springs assignment. "I was re-inked recently . . . but it was routine." Routine. Normal. Nothing like what he was suggesting.

"Maybe." He tilted his head and gave me another piercing look. "You do anything bad before that, love?"

Like helping a dhampir fugitive? "Depends on your definition of bad."

Both of them laughed. Marcus's laugh was loud and rollicking and actually pretty infectious—but the situation was far too dire for me to join in.

"They may have reinforced your group loyalty then," he said, still chuckling. "But it either wasn't very strong or else you fought through it—otherwise you wouldn't be here." He glanced over at Sabrina. "What do you think?"

Sabrina studied me with a critical eye. I still had a hard time believing her role in all of this. "I think she'd be a good addition. And since she's still in, she could help us with that . . . other matter."

"I think so too," he said.

I crossed my arms over my chest. I didn't like being discussed as though I weren't there. "A good addition to what?"

"Our group." To Sabrina, he said, "We really need a name for it, you know." She snorted, and he returned his attention to me. "We're a mix. Some are former Warriors or double agents like Sabrina. Some are ex-Alchemists."

"And what do you do?" I gestured around us. "This doesn't exactly look like a high-tech base of operation for some covert team."

"Look at you. Pretty and funny," he said, looking delighted. "We do what you do—or what you want to do. We like the Moroi. We want to help them—on our own terms. The Alchemists theoretically want to help them too, but we all know that's based on a core of fear and dislike—not to mention a strict control of its members. So, we work in secret, seeing as the Alchemists aren't fans of those who break from the fold. They *really* aren't fans of me, which is why I end up in places like this."

"We keep an eye on the Warriors too," said Sabrina. She scowled. "I hate being around those nuts, having to play along with them. They claim they only want to destroy the Strigoi—but, well, the things I've heard them say against the Moroi too . . ."

I thought back to one of my more disturbing memories of the Warrior arena. I'd heard one of them make a mysterious comment about how someday, they'd deal with the Moroi too.

"But what do you guys actually *do*?" Talking about rebellions and covert operations was one thing, but actually effecting change was another. I'd visited my sister Carly at her college and seen a number of student groups who wanted to change the world. Most of them sat around drinking coffee, talking a lot and doing little.

Marcus and Sabrina exchanged glances. "I can't quite get

into our operations," he said. "Not until I know you're on board with breaking your tattoo."

Breaking your tattoo. There was something sinister—not to mention permanent—about those words, and I suddenly wondered what I was doing here. Who were these people, really? Why was I even humoring them? Then another, almost terrifying thought hit me: *Am I doubting them because of the tattoo's control? Is it making me skeptical around anyone who questions the Alchemists? Is Marcus telling the truth?*

"I don't really understand that either," I told them. "What it means to 'break' the tattoo. Do you just mean putting ink over it?"

Marcus stood up. "All in good time. Right now, we've got to get out of here. Even if you were discreet, I assume you used Alchemist resources to find me?"

I hesitated. Even if these guys were legitimate and had good intentions toward the Moroi, I certainly wasn't going to reveal my involvement with magic. "Something like that."

"I'm sure you're good, but we can't take the chance. This place has been compromised." He cast a wistful glance around the studio. Honestly, I thought he should be grateful I'd given him a reason to leave.

Sabrina rose as well, her face hardening. "I'll make sure the secondary location is ready."

"You're an angel, as always," he told her.

"Hey, how did you know I was coming?" I asked. "You had time to hide and call her." What I really wanted to know was how he'd seen me through the invisibility spell. I'd felt the magic fill me. I was certain I'd cast the spell correctly, but he'd discovered me. The spell wouldn't work if someone knew to look for you, so maybe he'd happened to glance out the window when I was scaling the fire escape? Worst timing ever.

"Tony warned me." Marcus flashed me another of those dazzling grins. I think he was trying to make me smile back. "Good kid."

Tony? Then I knew. The boy in the parking lot. He'd pretended to help me and then sold me out. He must have spoken to Marcus while I climbed the fire escape. Maybe Marcus only answered to some secret knock. At least I had the comfort of knowing I'd cast the spell correctly. It simply hadn't worked because Marcus had advance warning that some girl was coming after him.

He began packing up his meager belongings into a backpack. "*The Catcher in the Rye* is a great book, by the way." He winked. "Maybe someday we'll have a literary discussion."

I wasn't interested in that. Watching him, I saw that he kept favoring his uninjured wrist. I couldn't believe I'd caused damage like that and felt a little guilty, despite everything that had happened. "You should get that taken care of," I said. Sabrina nodded in agreement.

He sighed. "I can't. At least, not through conventional means. The Alchemists have eyes everywhere."

Conventional means.

"I, uh, might be able to help you get it healed through unconventional means," I said.

"You know some off-the-grid doctor?" asked Sabrina hopefully.

"No. But I know a Moroi spirit user."

Marcus froze, and I kind of liked that I'd thrown him off guard. "Seriously? We've heard of them but never met one.

That woman they had—Sonya? She was one, right? She was gone before we could find out more."

Talking about Adrian made me nervous, but Sabrina probably already knew he existed if they'd been watching me. "Yeah, she was one, and there's another in Palm Springs. I could take you to him and let him heal you."

Excitement lit Marcus's features. Sabrina looked at him in horror. "You can't just go off with her." Was that concern or jealousy in her voice?

"Why not?" he asked. "She's taking a leap of faith with us. We can't do any less. Besides, I'm dying to meet a spirit user. The safe house isn't that far from Palm Springs. You make sure everything's in order and then come pick me up later."

Sabrina didn't like that, not at all. Maybe I didn't understand the dynamics of their group yet, but it was obvious she regarded him as a leader and was insanely protective. In fact, I suspected her feelings for him were more than professional. They went back and forth on whether he'd be safe or not, and I listened without a word. All the while, I wondered if *I'd* be safe heading off with some unknown guy. *Clarence trusted him,* I reminded myself. *And he's pretty paranoid.* Besides, with Marcus's wrist out of commission, I could probably take him.

He finally convinced Sabrina to let him go but not before she snarled, "If anything happens to him, I'm coming after you." Apparently her hard-core character in the arena hadn't been entirely faked.

We parted ways from her, and before long, Marcus and I were on the road to Palm Springs. I tried to get more information out of him, but he wouldn't bite. Instead, he kept complimenting me and saying things that were only one step away from pickup lines. Judging from the way he'd bantered with Sabrina too, I didn't think there was anything particularly special about me. I thought he was just used to women fawning all over him. He *was* cute, I'd give him that, but it took a lot more than that to win me over.

It was sunset when we pulled up to Adrian's apartment, and I belatedly wondered if I should've given him some advance warning. Too late now.

We walked up to the door, and I knocked three times. "It's open," a voice called from within. I stepped inside, and Marcus followed.

Adrian was working on an abstract painting of what looked like a crystalline building from some fantasy world. "Unexpected treat," he said. His eyes fell on Marcus and widened. "I'll be damned. You found him."

"Thanks to you," I said.

Adrian glanced over at me. A smile started to form—and then instantly dried up. "What happened to your face?"

"Oh." I lightly touched the swollen spot. It still smarted but wasn't as painful as it had been earlier. I spoke my next words without thinking. "Marcus hit me."

I'd never seen Adrian move so fast. Marcus had no chance to react, probably because he was exhausted from our earlier encounter. Adrian shoved Marcus up against a wall and—to my complete and utter astonishment—punched Marcus. Adrian had once joked that he never dirtied his hands, so this was something I never could have prepared myself for. In fact, if Adrian was going to attack someone, I would've expected something magical and spirit-driven. Yet . . . as I watched him, I could see that anything as thoughtful as magic was far from

Adrian's mind. He had kicked into primal mode. See a threat. Go after it. It was yet another surprising—yet fascinating—side of the enigma that was Adrian Ivashkov.

Marcus quickly got his bearings and responded in kind. He pushed Adrian back, wincing a little. Even with his injury, he was still strong. "What the hell? Who are you?"

"The guy that's going to kick your ass for hurting her," said Adrian.

He tried another punch, but Marcus dodged and managed to land a hit that knocked Adrian back into one of his easels. When Marcus swung again, Adrian eluded him with a maneuver that was straight out of Wolfe's class. I would've applauded him if I wasn't so appalled by the situation. I knew some girls thought it was sexy to have men fight over them. Not me.

"You guys, stop!" I cried.

"No one's going to throw you around and get away with it," said Adrian.

"What happened with us has nothing to do with you," retorted Marcus.

"*Everything* about her has to do with me."

The two circled around each other, waiting for the other to pounce. "Adrian," I exclaimed. "It was an accident."

"Doesn't look like an accident," he replied, never taking his eyes off Marcus.

"You should listen to her," growled Marcus. The easygoing guy I'd met earlier was gone, but I guess being attacked would do that to you. "It might save you from getting your pretty face wrecked. How much styling did you have to do to get your hair like that?"

"At least I brush my hair," said Adrian.

Marcus lunged forward—but not directly at Adrian. He grabbed a painting off an easel and used it as a weapon. Adrian again managed a dodge, but the painting didn't fare so well. The canvas tore, and Marcus tossed it aside, ready for the next advance.

Adrian spared the canvas a brief glance. "Now you've really pissed me off."

"Enough!" Something told me they weren't going to listen to reason. This required direct intervention. I stalked across the room and pushed myself between them.

"Sydney, get out of the way," ordered Adrian.

"Yeah," agreed Marcus. "For once he's got something worthwhile to say."

"No!" I held out my hands to separate them. "Both of you back off—*now!*" My voice rang through the apartment, and I refused to budge. "Back. Off," I repeated.

"Sydney. . . ." Adrian's voice was a little more uncertain than when he'd told me to get out of the way.

I looked back and forth between them, giving each guy a healthy glare. "Adrian, it really was an accident. Marcus, this is the guy who's going to help you, so show some respect."

This, more than anything, seemed to derail them.

"Wait," said Adrian. "Did you say 'help'?"

Marcus was equally flabbergasted. "*This* asshole is the spirit user?"

"You're both acting like idiots," I scolded. The next time I had nothing to do, I'd have to get a book on testosterone-driven behavior. This was out of my league. "Adrian, can we talk somewhere in private? Like the bedroom?"

Adrian agreed, but not before giving Marcus one last

menacing look. I told Marcus to stay where he was and hoped he wouldn't take off or call in someone else with a gun. Adrian followed me to his bedroom and shut the door behind us.

"You know," he said, "under normal circumstances, you inviting me to the bedroom would be the highlight of my day."

I crossed my arms and sat on the bed. I did so out of simple fatigue, but a moment later, I was struck by what I was doing. *This is where Adrian sleeps. I'm touching the covers he's wrapped in every night. What does he wear? Does he wear anything?*

I jumped up.

"It really was an accident," I told him. "Marcus thought I was there to abduct him."

Adrian, having no such hang-ups with the bed, sat down. He winced, probably from the blow to the stomach. "If someone like you showed up to abduct me, I'd let you."

Even when he was in pain, it never stopped with him. "I'm serious. It was just instinct, and he apologized over and over in the car once he realized who I was."

That got his attention. "He knew you?"

I gave him a recap of my day in Santa Barbara. He listened avidly, nodding along, his expression shifting back and forth between intrigue and surprise.

"I didn't realize when I brought him back here that you'd inflict more damage," I said, once I'd finished the story.

"I was defending your honor." Adrian gave me that devil-may-care smile that always managed to both infuriate and captivate me. "Pretty manly, huh?"

"Very," I said dryly. I didn't like violence, but him doing something so out of character for me actually *was* kind of incredible. Not that I'd ever tell him that. "You did Wolfe proud. Do you think you can manage not to have any more 'manly' displays while he's here? Please?"

Adrian shook his head, still smiling. "I've said over and over, I'd do anything for you. I just keep hoping it'll be something like, 'Adrian, let's go hot tubbing' or 'Adrian, take me out for fondue.'"

"Well, sometimes we have to—did you say fondue?" Sometimes it was impossible to follow Adrian's train of thought. "Why in the world would I ever say that?"

He shrugged. "I like fondue."

I didn't even know what to say about that. This whole day was getting more and more exhausting. "I'm sorry I'm not asking for something as glamorous as melted cheese. But for now, I need to find out about Marcus and his group—and the tattoo."

Adrian recognized the situation's severity. He stood up and gently touched the lily on my cheek. "I don't trust him. He could be using you. But then . . . I don't like the idea of this controlling you either."

"That makes two of us," I admitted, losing some of my earlier toughness.

He traced the line of my cheek for a few breathless moments and then dropped his hand. "It might be worth helping him to get some answers."

"Will you promise not to get in any more fights? Please?"

"I promise," he said. "So long as he doesn't start one."

"I'll have him promise too." I just hoped their "manly" natures wouldn't get the better of them. As I ruminated on this, something I'd nearly forgotten about tumbled to the forefront of my mind. "Oh . . . Adrian, I've got one more favor to ask you. A big one."

"Fondue?" he asked hopefully.

"No. It's about Ms. Terwilliger's sister. . . ."

I told him what I'd learned. The amusement in his face faded and turned to disbelief. "You just mention this now?" he exclaimed when I finished. "That some soul-sucking witch might be after you?"

"She doesn't know I exist." I felt surprisingly defensive. "And I'm the only one who can help, at least according to Ms. Terwilliger. She thinks I'm some super-investigator."

"Well, you do have that Sherlock Holmes thing going for you," he said. His joking didn't last; he was too upset. "But you still should've told me! You could've called."

"I was kind of busy with Marcus."

"Then your priorities are off. This is a *lot* more important than his band of Merry Men. If we need to take out some evil sorceress before she gets to you, then of course I'll help." He hesitated. "With one condition."

I eyed him warily. "What's that?"

"Let me heal you too."

I jerked backward, almost more shocked than if he'd suggested hitting me again. "No! Absolutely not! I don't need it. I'm in better shape than him."

"You want to go back to Amberwood with that on your face? You're not going to be able to hide that, Sage. And if Castile sees it, he really will come after Marcus." Adrian crossed his arms defiantly. "That's my price."

He was bluffing, and I knew it. Maybe it was egotistical, but I knew he wasn't going to let me go into a dangerous situation without him. He did, however, have a point. I still hadn't seen the mark Marcus had left, but I didn't want to explain it back at school. And yes, there was a good chance Eddie would want to hunt down my assailant. Being beat up by an avenging dhampir might make working with Marcus difficult.

Yet . . . how could I agree? At least the magic I used was on my terms. And although my tattoo had trace amounts of vampire magic, I took comfort in knowing it was tied to the "normal" four elements, the ones we understood. Spirit was still an unknown entity, with abilities that continually surprised us. How could I subject myself to rogue vampire magic?

Guessing my inner turmoil, Adrian's face softened. "I do this all the time. It's an easy spell. No surprises."

"Maybe," I said reluctantly. "But each time you use spirit, you're more likely to go crazy."

"Already crazy about you, Sage."

At least this was familiar territory. "You said you wouldn't bring that up."

He simply regarded me without comment. Finally, I threw my arms up. "Fine," I said, with more boldness than I felt. "Just get it over with."

Adrian didn't waste any time. Stepping forward, he reached out and rested his hand on my cheek once more. My breath caught and my heart rate went up. It would be so, so easy for him to pull me to him and kiss me again. A tingling warmth spread over my skin, and for a moment, I thought it was just my normal reaction to him. No, I realized. It was the magic. His eyes locked onto mine, and for the space of a heartbeat, we were suspended in time. Then he removed his hand and stepped away.

"Done," he said. "Was that so bad?"

No, it hadn't been bad at all. The throbbing pain was gone. All that was left was the constant inner voice nagging me that what had just happened was wrong. That same voice tried to tell me that Adrian had left a taint behind . . . but that was hard to believe from him. I released the breath I'd been holding.

"Thank you," I said. "You didn't have to do that."

He gave me one of those small smiles. "Oh, believe me, I did."

A moment of awkward silence hung between us. I cleared my throat. "Well. We should get back out to Marcus. Maybe we'll have time for dinner before Sabrina shows up, and you guys can patch things over."

"I doubt even a moonlight stroll would fix things between us."

His words reminded me of something else I'd meant to bring up when he got back to town, something that had taken a very low priority. "Your coat—you never took it back after the wedding. It's in my car."

He waved dismissively. "Keep it. I've got others."

"What am I going to do with a wool coat?" I asked. "Especially here in Palm Springs?"

"Sleep with it," he suggested. "Think of me."

I put my hands on my hips and tried to stare him down, which wasn't easy since he was so tall. That, and because his words suddenly returned me to the disorienting feeling I'd had sitting on his bed. "You said you weren't going to bring up any romantic stuff around me."

"Was that romantic?" he asked. "I was just making the suggestion, since the coat's so heavy and warm. I figured you'd think of me since it was such a nice gesture. And yet, once again, you're the one who finds romantic subtext in everything I say."

"I do not. You know that's not what I meant."

He shook his head in mock sympathy. "I tell you, Sage. Sometimes I think I'm the one who needs to take out the restraining order on *you*."

"Adrian!"

But he was already out the door, knowing laughter echoing behind him.

CHAPTER 8

I THINK ADRIAN WOULD'VE gone hunting Ms. Terwilliger's sister with me then and there. Amberwood's curfew wouldn't allow it, and besides, it was something I wanted to do in daylight. To his credit, he did heal Marcus without them getting into a fistfight, so that was progress. Marcus lost a little of his animosity and tried to engage Adrian in conversation about what spirit could do. Adrian gave wary responses and looked relieved when Sabrina showed up to take Marcus away. He gave me a mysterious farewell, simply saying he'd text me soon about the "next stage." I was too tired to ask for more details and headed back to my dorm to sleep off what had been a pretty crazy day.

I was awakened at the crack of dawn by heavy pounding at my door. I squinted at the clock, grimacing when I saw that it was an hour earlier than I usually got up. I stayed in bed, hoping whoever it was would go away. If there was something really urgent happening, someone would've called me on my cell phone. The display showed no missed calls, however.

Unfortunately, the knocking didn't stop. With a feeling of dread, I finally dragged myself up, half-afraid of what I'd find outside my door.

It was Angeline.

"Finally," she said, inviting herself into my room. "I thought you'd never answer."

"Sorry," I said, shutting the door behind her. "I was busy sleeping."

She walked right up to my bed and sat down like she owned it. I really didn't know her schedule, but she always struck me as a late riser. Apparently not today. She was dressed in a school uniform, with her brilliant red hair pulled back in what was, for her, a rather tidy ponytail.

"I have a problem," she said.

My feeling of dread grew. I turned on my coffeemaker, which I always had ready with fresh grounds and water. Something told me I was going to need a cup to get through this. "What's going on?" I asked, settling into my desk chair. I made no attempt at even guessing. When it came to Angeline, her problems could range from throwing a desk in rage or accidentally spilling hydrochloric acid on another student. Both had happened recently.

"I'm failing math," she said.

This was unwelcome but not unexpected news. Angeline's mountain community, while still educating its children, didn't quite match the standards of Amberwood's elite curriculum. She struggled in a number of her classes but had managed to scrape by so far.

"I'm already in trouble in my Spanish class," she added. "But that piñata I made got me some extra credit, so I'm hanging in there okay for now."

I'd heard about the piñata. It had been for her class's cultural day, and she'd been so thorough with her papier-mâché that none of her classmates had been able to open it through normal means. Angeline had ended up beating it against a wall and had to be stopped by her teacher when she'd produced a lighter.

"But if I slip there *and* in math, I could get expelled."

That dragged me away from the flammable piñata and back to the present. "Ugh," I said, having no better way to articulate my thoughts. The problem with a school that had high standards was . . . well, it had high standards. Trouble in one class might be tolerated, but not two. And if Angeline got kicked out, we'd be down one level of security for Jill—not to mention the fact that I'd probably get blamed for it all.

"Ms. Hayward told me I need to get a tutor. She says I either need to get better or at least show I'm trying."

That was promising, I supposed. Even if a tutor couldn't help, hopefully the school would be lenient with her good faith effort.

"Okay," I said. "We'll get you a tutor."

She frowned. "Why can't you do it? You're smart. You're good at math."

Why couldn't I? Well, first I had to stop an evil sorceress from sucking the youth and power from innocent girls. Then I had to crack the secrets and lies that the organization I'd been born into was telling me.

Instead I said, "I'm busy."

"You have to do it. It'd be easy for you," she protested.

"Really busy," I said. "I'm surprised Eddie can't do it."

His name brought a smile to her face. "He offered, but his grades are just average. I need someone really good."

"Then I'll get you someone really good. I just can't do it myself right now."

Angeline didn't like that answer, but at least she didn't flip over my desk. "Okay. Fine. Just hurry up."

"Yes, your majesty," I muttered, watching her strut out of my room in a huff.

At least Angeline's academic problems were something a little easier to deal with than the other supernatural intrigues occupying my time. Since I was already awake and had coffee, I decided there was no point in going back to sleep. I showered and dressed, then caught up on some extra homework while I waited for breakfast. When the serving time started in our cafeteria, I headed downstairs and lingered near the entrance. It only took about five minutes before my friend Kristin Sawyer came by. She always went running before class started and was usually one of the first in line for breakfast afterward. She was also in AP calculus with me.

"Hey," I said, falling in step with her. "Good run?"

"Great run," she said. There was still a little sweat on her dark skin. "A lot nicer now that the weather's cooler." She eyed me curiously. "I don't usually see you here this early. I don't usually see you eat breakfast."

"It's the most important meal of the day, right?" I selected oatmeal and an apple. "Besides, I have a favor to ask you."

Kristin nearly dropped the plate of scrambled eggs one of the servers handed to her. Her brown eyes widened. "You have a favor to ask *me*?"

While I wasn't responsible for my human friends in the same way I was the Moroi and dhampirs, I still had a tendency to look after them. I'd helped Kristin a number of times.

"Yeah . . . my cousin Angeline needs a math tutor."

There was an expectant look on Kristin's face, like she was waiting for me to finish my story. Then understanding hit. "Who, me? No. No way."

"Oh, come on. It'd be easy." I followed her to a table, having to hurry to catch up. I think she thought that if she walked quickly enough, she might be able to escape my request. "She's in remedial math. You could tutor her in your sleep."

Kristin sat down and gave me a long, level look. "Sydney, I saw your cousin punch a grown man and throw a speaker at someone. Do you really think I'm going to sign on for a job that makes her do work she doesn't want to do? What if she gets frustrated at what I'm telling her? How do I know she won't stab me with a compass?"

"You don't," I admitted. "But I think it's unlikely. Probably. She really wants to improve her grade. Otherwise, she could get kicked out."

"Sorry." Kristin actually did look legitimately apologetic. "You know I'd do almost anything for you—but not this. You're going to have to find someone who's not afraid of her."

I thought about her words over and over as I headed off to history class. She was right. But the only people completely at ease around her were Eddie and Jill, and they were off the list as tutors. I wondered if maybe I should offer up money to someone when I went to calculus later.

"Miss Melbourne."

Ms. Terwilliger was back in her classroom, no doubt to the relief of yesterday's sub. She waved me up to her messy desk and handed me a single sheet of paper. "Here's the list we discussed."

I scanned it. It contained the names of six girls as well as their addresses. These must be the ones she'd mentioned, girls with known magical aptitude but no coven or teacher to look out for them. All the addresses were in the Los Angeles metropolitan area.

"I trust Mrs. Santos got you the other information you needed for your project?"

"Yes." Mrs. Santos had emailed me the historical neighborhoods she knew about, and I'd narrowed them down to a couple likely candidates. "I'll start working on the, uh, project this weekend."

Ms. Terwilliger arched an eyebrow. "Why are you putting it off? I've never known you to procrastinate on an assignment."

I was a little startled. "Well . . . normally I don't, ma'am. But this is going to take some extra time—travel time—and I don't have enough of it on school days."

"Ah," she said, realization hitting her. "Well, then, you may use your independent study for it. That'll give you extra time. And I'll tell Mrs. Weathers you may be coming in after curfew. I'll make sure that she's accommodating. This project is of the utmost importance."

There was no protest I could make. "I'll start today, then."

As I was walking back to my desk, a voice said, "Jeez, Melbourne. Just when I thought that independent study you had with her couldn't get any easier . . . now you don't even have to show up for class?"

I paused to give Trey a smile. He was Ms. Terwilliger's assistant during this class period, meaning he did a lot of filing and photocopying.

"It's a very important assignment," I said.

"I guess. What is it?"

"It'd bore you." I did a double take as I looked him over. I didn't even have to grope for a change in conversation. "What happened to you?"

His eyes were bloodshot, and the unkempt state of his black hair suggested he hadn't had a shower this morning. There was a sallow, almost sickly hue to his normally tan skin. He gave me a weak smile and lowered his voice. "Craig Lo's brother scored us some beer last night. It was from some microbrewery. I guess that's good."

I groaned. "Trey, I thought you were better than that."

Trey managed as much of an indignant look as he could in his hungover state. "Hey, some of us like to have a little fun now and then. You should give it a shot sometime. I already tried to help you with Brayden, but you messed that up."

"I didn't mess anything up!" Brayden was a barista who worked with Trey, one who rivaled me when it came to a love of academia and random knowledge. Our brief relationship had been full of facts and low on passion. "He broke up with *me*."

"You wouldn't guess it. Did you know he writes all this love-sick poetry about you on his breaks?"

I was taken aback. "He . . . he does?" The reason Brayden had broken up with me was because my various duties to my vampire family had constantly interfered with the two of us, forcing me to neglect him and cancel a lot. "I feel kind of bad he took it that hard. I'm surprised he'd have such a, I don't know, outburst of passion."

Trey snorted. "I don't know that it's that passionate. He's more concerned about form and sits around with books detailing iambic pentameter and sonnet analysis."

"Okay, that sounds more like him." The bell was about to ring, so I had started to return to my seat when I noticed something on Trey's desk. "You're not done with that?"

It was a big homework assignment we had for our chemistry class, involving a number of complicated acid and base problems. It was due in our next period, and it seemed unlikely Trey would finish in time since all he had on the paper so far was his name.

"Yeah . . . I was going to finish it last night, but . . ."

"Right. The beer. Having fun." I didn't even bother to hide my disapproval. "That's a huge part of our grade."

"I know, I know." He looked down at the papers with a sigh. "I'll finish as much as I can before then. Partial credit's better than no credit."

I studied him for a moment and then made a decision that went against many of my basic principles. I reached into my messenger bag and handed him my completed homework.

"Here," I said.

He took the pages with a frown. "Here what?"

"It's the assignment. Use my answers."

"I. . . ." His jaw dropped. "Do you know what you're doing?"

"Yes."

"I don't think you do. You're giving me your homework."

"Yes."

"And telling me to pass it off as my homework."

"Yes."

"But I didn't actually do the work."

"Do you want them or not?" I asked in frustration. I started to take the papers back, but he pulled them close.

"Oh, I want them," he said. "I just want to know what *you* want in return. Because this doesn't really make up for getting me ostracized from my family and friends." He kept his tone light, but I heard the edge of bitterness. There it was. No matter how friendly he and I were, our respective allegiances to the Warriors and the Alchemists would always be between us. Maybe it was a joke now . . . but someday it wouldn't be.

"I need a favor," I explained. "A small one, really. Has nothing to do with any of that . . . stuff."

Trey looked understandably wary. "Which is?"

The bell rang, so I spoke quickly. "Angeline needs a math tutor or else she'll fail. And if she fails, she'll get kicked out of school. It wouldn't be hard for you at all. And it'd look good on your college applications."

"Your cousin's a little unstable," he said. But he didn't say no, so I thought that was a good sign.

"You used to think she was hot," I reminded him.

"Yeah, that was before. . . ." He didn't finish, but I knew. Before he found out she was a dhampir. The Warriors had the same taboos the Alchemists did about relationships between the races.

"Okay," I said. "I understand. I'll just take my homework and go." I held out my hand, but he didn't give the papers back.

"Wait, I'll do it. But if she injures me, I hope you'll feel really bad. Basketball season just started, and the team will fall apart if I'm sidelined because of her."

I grinned. "I'll be devastated."

Angeline was not so thrilled when I told her at lunch. She flushed with rage and looked like she was about ready to throw her tray across the cafeteria.

"You expect me to work with that . . . that . . . vampire hunter?" she demanded. I wondered if she'd had another name in mind but had held back in some remarkable show of restraint. "Especially after what they tried to do to Sonya?"

"Trey's not like the rest of them," I said defensively. "He refused to kill her and even went through the trouble of getting me in to help her—which ended up severely messing up his life, I might add."

Eddie looked amused, despite the grim subject. "You should also add that he wants very, very badly to get back to that old life."

I pointed at Eddie with my fork. "Don't tell me you think Trey's a bad choice too."

"For tutoring?" He shook his head. "Nah, he's fine. I'm just saying you shouldn't be so quick to assume everything's happy and bright with him. It seems pretty likely his group's working against us."

"He's my friend," I said, hoping my firm tone would put an end to the discussion. After a few more assurances, Eddie convinced Angeline to work with Trey, reminding her she needed to keep her grades up. Still, Eddie's words haunted me. I believed absolutely that Trey was my friend but again wondered when that rift between us would rear its ugly head.

When Eddie and Angeline left to go to their afternoon classes, I asked Jill to hang back at the table for a minute. "What's Adrian doing right now?"

"He's in his painting class," she said promptly.

"The bond must be running strong today, huh?" I asked. Sometimes her view of his mind and experiences was clearer than others.

She shrugged. "No, but it's eleven on Tuesday."

"Right," I said, feeling foolish. I knew everyone's schedules;

it was necessary for my job. "I should've realized that. Do you think he'd be able to meet up with me after school?"

"To go on that witch hunt? Yeah, he'd probably leave right now."

Jill knew what Adrian knew, so she'd also been briefed about my search for Veronica. While I'd learned to accept Jill's knowledge as part of confiding in Adrian, it was still a little shocking for me to hear these forbidden topics discussed openly. Seeing my stunned reaction, Jill smiled a little.

"Don't worry," she said. "I keep Adrian's secrets. And yours." The bitterness in her voice also caught me off guard.

"Are you mad at me?" I asked, puzzled. "You're not . . . you're not still upset about what happened between Adrian and me, are you? I thought you'd eased up on that." Although Adrian's proclamation of loving me against the odds had been unsettling, his more relaxed attitude had come through in her until now.

"Adrian has," she said. "He doesn't see the danger of you running around with another guy."

I was lost. "Another guy? You don't mean . . . Marcus? That's crazy."

"Is it?" asked Jill. The bond was so strange at times. Jill was jealous on Adrian's behalf. "He's human, you're human. You've both got this rebel Alchemist thing going on. And I saw him. He's pretty cute. There's no telling what could happen."

"Well, I know what could happen: nothing," I said. Even through a psychic bond, Marcus could win over girls. "I just met him. I don't even know if I can entirely trust him, and I certainly don't have any feelings for him. Look, I get that you want to help Adrian, but you can't be mad at me about what happened. You know why I turned him down—especially after Micah." Micah was Eddie's human roommate, and even though she knew human-vampire relationships couldn't get serious, she'd still been surprised at just how complex and difficult the situation had been.

"Yeah. . . ." She frowned, no doubt conflicted over Adrian's feelings and what she knew was true. "But maybe with Adrian, I don't know. Maybe things could be different. Or maybe there's at least a way to make them less painful for him."

I looked away, unable to meet her eyes. I didn't like to think of Adrian in pain, but what else could I do? What did either of them expect me to do? We all knew the rules.

"I'm sorry," I said, picking up my tray and standing. "I never asked for any of this. Adrian will get over me."

"Do you really want him to get over you?" she asked.

"What? Why would you even ask something like that?"

She didn't answer and instead made a great show of stirring around her mashed potatoes. When I realized she wasn't going to elaborate, I shook my head and walked off toward the exit. All the while, I could feel her watching me as that question echoed in my mind: *Do you really want him to get over you?*

CHAPTER 9

AS JILL HAD SAID, Adrian was more than happy to begin our hunt that afternoon. In fact, when I finally got ahold of him, he offered to pick me up when classes ended, in order to maximize our time. I didn't mind this since it meant I'd get to ride in the Mustang. Admittedly, I would've preferred to drive it myself, but I'd take what I could get.

"When are you going to name the car?" I asked him once we were on the road to Los Angeles.

"It's an inanimate object," he said. "Names are for people and pets."

I patted the Mustang's dashboard. "Don't listen to him." To Adrian, I said, "They name boats all the time."

"I don't really understand that either, but maybe I would if my old man ever fronted me the money for a private yacht." He shot me a quick, amused look before returning his attention to the road. "How can someone as cold and logical as you be so obsessed with something as frivolous as this?"

I wasn't sure which part bothered me the most—being called cold or obsessed. "I'm just giving the proper respect to a beautiful machine."

"You named your car after coffee. That's a sign of respect?"

"The *highest* respect," I said.

He made a noise that sounded like a cross between a scoff and a laugh. "Okay, then. You name it. Whatever you want, I'll go along with."

"Really?" I asked, a bit startled. True, I'd been badgering him about naming the car, but I wasn't sure I wanted to be the one to wield that sort of power. "It's a big decision."

"Life or death," he said, deadpan. "Better choose carefully."

"Yeah, but you're the so-called creative one!"

"Then this'll be good practice for you."

I fell silent for a good part of the drive, struck by the gravity of the dilemma that lay before me. What should the name reflect? The car's sunny yellow color? Sleek lines? Powerful engine? The task was overwhelming.

Adrian pulled me out of my thoughts when we began nearing the outer Los Angeles suburbs. "We're not actually going into the city, are we?"

"Huh?" I'd been waging a mental debate between Summer Wind and Gold Dust. "Oh, no. We're heading north. Take the next exit."

Mrs. Santos had provided me with two neighborhoods known for their Victorian-style houses. I'd researched them extensively online, even going so far as to look at satellite pictures. I'd finally chosen one that most resembled my vision and crossed my fingers I'd have the same luck as I'd had in finding Marcus's apartment. Surely the universe owed me a few favors.

Unfortunately, things didn't look too promising when we finally reached the street I'd been given. It was a peaceful residential area, filled with those same distinctive houses, but nothing that quite matched the one I'd seen in my vision. We drove up and down the street as I scanned each side, hoping maybe I'd missed something.

"Ugh," I said, slouching back into my seat. No luck. The universe had apparently cut me off. "We'll have to check the other location, but seriously, it didn't look like a match."

"Well, it can't hurt to—" Adrian suddenly made an abrupt turn onto a side street we'd nearly driven past. I jerked upright as he clipped the curb.

"What are you doing? Think about your tires!"

"Look." He made another turn, putting us on a parallel street. Most of it was contemporary California housing . . . but one block had more Victorian houses. I gasped.

"There it is!"

Adrian came to a stop on the side of the street opposite from the house of my vision. Everything was there, from the wrapping porch to the hydrangea bush. And now, in the full light of day, I could make out the sign in the front yard: OLD WORLD BED-AND-BREAKFAST. Smaller print identified it as a historic site.

"Well, there we go." Adrian was clearly very pleased with his find, despite the risk to the car's tires. "Maybe Jackie's sister is staying here."

"Odd choice to run nefarious magical activities out of," I remarked.

"I don't know. Seeing as there aren't any ancient castles in the neighborhood, then why not a bed-and-breakfast?"

I took a deep breath. "Okay, then. Let's go make some inquiries. You sure you can muddle the minds of those who see me?"

"Easy," he said. "Easier still if you were wearing your wig."

"Oh, shoot. I forgot." I ducked down and retrieved a shoulder-length brown wig that Ms. Terwilliger had supplied me with. Even with Adrian's magic, we wanted to take extra precautions. While it would be good if people were visited by an unmemorable blonde, it'd be better still if they were visited by an unmemorable brunette. I tugged the wig on, hoping no one had seen my transformation. I lifted my head. "Does it look okay?"

Adrian's face showed approval. "It's cute. You look even brainier, which I didn't think was possible."

We left the car, and I wondered if I wanted to look brainier. A lot of people already thought I was boring. Blond hair might be the only exciting thing I had going for me. Then I thought for a minute about my recent experience scaling a fire escape, breaking and entering, and getting into a fistfight with a fugitive. Not to mention that I was now hunting a powerful evil witch alongside a vampire who could control people's minds.

Okay, maybe I wasn't so boring after all.

We stepped inside to find a cute little lobby with an ornate desk and a sitting area with wicker furniture. Stuffed rabbits dressed in ball gowns adorned the shelves, and the walls actually had oil paintings of Queen Victoria. The owners apparently took their theme very literally, though I wasn't sure how the rabbits fit in.

A girl my age sat at the desk and glanced up in surprise from a magazine. She had short platinum hair and hipster glasses. Tons of necklaces hung around her neck in a gaudy display that went against my minimalist sensibilities. Hot pink plastic beads, a sparkly green star, a gold and diamond locket, a dog tag . . . it was mind-boggling. Even worse, she was chewing gum loudly.

"Hi," she said. "Can I help you?"

We'd had a whole routine planned, but Adrian immediately went off script. He slung his arm around me. "Yeah, we're looking for a weekend getaway, and a friend of ours swears this is top-of-the-line romance." He pulled me closer. "Our anniversary's coming up. We've been dating for one year, but man, it hardly seems like it."

"That's for sure," I said, trying to keep my jaw from dropping. I forced what I hoped was a happy smile.

The girl glanced back and forth between us, her expression softening. "That's so sweet. Congratulations."

"Can we check the place out?" Adrian asked. "I mean, if there are any vacant rooms?"

"Sure," she said, standing up. She spit her gum into a trash can and walked over to us. "I'm Alicia. My aunt and uncle are the owners."

"Taylor," I said, shaking her hand.

"Jet," said Adrian. I nearly groaned. For inexplicable reasons, "Jet Steele" was a pseudonym Adrian really liked using. In our rehearsal today, he was supposed to be called Brian.

Alicia glanced back and forth between us, a small frown on her face that soon smoothed out. I had to guess it was Adrian's compulsion, confusing her perceptions of us a bit. "Follow me. We have a few vacant rooms you can see." With one last puzzled look at us, she turned and headed toward a stairway.

"Isn't this great, sweetie?" Adrian asked loudly as we walked up the creaking stairs. "I know how much you like rabbits.

Didn't you have one when you were little? What was his name, Hopper?"

"Yeah," I said, resisting the urge to punch him on the arm. Hopper? Really? "Best rabbit ever."

"Oh, neat," said Alicia. "Then I'll take you to the Bunny Suite first."

The Bunny Suite had more of those well-dressed stuffed rabbits as part of the decor. The quilt covering the king-size bed also had a border of alternating hearts and rabbits stitched in. Several books sat on the mantel above the wood-burning fireplace, including *The Tale of Peter Rabbit* and *Rabbit, Run*. Until that moment, I hadn't realized just how absurdly far a theme could be taken.

"Wow," said Adrian. He sat down on the bed and tested its bounciness, giving it a nod of approval. "This is amazing. What do you think, buttercup?"

"I have no words," I said honestly.

He patted the spot beside him. "Want to try it out?"

I answered with a look and felt relieved when he stood up. Adrian and beds stirred up too many conflicting feelings in me.

After that, Alicia showed us the Morning Glory Suite, the Velvet Suite, and the London Suite, all of which competed to outdo the others in tackiness. Nonetheless, despite the absurdity of Adrian's ruse, the tour had given me the opportunity to take note of the other labeled doors in the hallway. We followed Alicia back downstairs.

"We don't get to see the Sapphire Suite or the Prince Albert Suite?" I asked.

Alicia shook her head. "Sorry. Those are occupied. I can

give you a brochure with some pictures, if you want."

Adrian had his arm around me again. "Angel cake, wasn't the Prince Albert Suite where Veronica stayed? She's not still here, is she?"

"I'm not sure," I said. This, at least, was similar to what we'd rehearsed. I glanced over at Alicia. "You probably can't tell us that, huh? If our friend Veronica's here? She's really pretty, has long dark hair."

"Oh, yeah," said Alicia, brightening. "Of course I remember her. She was in the Velvet Suite, actually, and just checked out yesterday."

I resisted the urge to kick the desk. So close. We'd missed her by a day. Yes, the universe was definitely done giving me breaks. I wouldn't be able to cast the scrying spell until the next full moon, which was a month away.

"Oh, well," said Adrian, still with that easy smile. "We'll see her for Christmas anyway. Thanks for your help."

"Do you want to book a room?" Alicia asked hopefully.

"We'll get back to you on that," I said. I actually wouldn't have put it past Adrian to book one and then claim it was part of our cover. "We're checking out a few places. A one-year anniversary isn't something you want to make a hasty decision on."

"But," said Adrian, giving her a wink, "I've got a good feeling about the Bunny Suite."

Alicia walked us out, her eyes widening when she saw the Mustang. "Wow, nice car."

"It's an amazing car," I said.

"That's our baby—well, until we have real ones. Don't you think it needs a name?" asked Adrian. "I keep trying to convince

Taylor." Once again, I had to fight the urge to punch him.

"Oh, definitely," said Alicia. "That kind of car . . . it's like royalty."

"See?" Adrian shot me a triumphant look. "And Alicia's an expert on royalty. Didn't you see all those paintings?"

"Thanks for your help," I told her, steering him forward. "We'll be in touch."

We got in the car, and after waving goodbye to Alicia, Adrian drove away. I stared blankly ahead. "Much like with the Bunny Suite, I have no words to describe what just happened. I mean, really? Our anniversary? Jet?"

"I look more like a Jet than a Brian," he argued. "Besides, that was a much better story than the one about how we wanted to pay a surprise birthday visit to our 'friend' Veronica."

"I don't know about that. But it *did* give us the information we needed. Which isn't good."

Adrian grew serious. "Are you sure? Maybe Veronica left the area altogether. Maybe you and the other girls are out of danger."

"That would be good, I guess . . . except, it just means some other poor girl somewhere else would suffer instead, and we wouldn't have any way to stop it." From my purse, I pulled out Ms. Terwilliger's list of magic-using girls. "One of these addresses is in Pasadena. We can at least swing through on our way back and warn her."

The girl we sought was named Wendy Stone. She was a student at Cal Tech, which seemed like an odd vocation for a wannabe witch. Of course, Ms. Terwilliger had said these were girls who weren't actively studying the magical path. They simply possessed magical ability, and I supposed the fact that they had no mentors suggested that they might actually be resistant to their inborn abilities—kind of like me.

Wendy lived in an apartment near campus that was easy to find. It was a no-nonsense, primarily student residence, but it seemed like a luxury palace after Marcus's building. As we passed busy students carrying backpacks and talking about classes, I felt a pang of longing that I hadn't experienced in a while. Inheriting the Alchemist mantle meant I couldn't go to college. College was a dream I'd held on to for a long time, though enrolling at Amberwood had helped ease some of my longing. Now, in this buzz of academia, a surge of jealousy sprang up in me. What would it be like to have this kind of life? To have your days solely devoted to the pursuit of knowledge, with no intrigue or life-threatening situations? Even Adrian, with his part-time art classes, was able to have some sort of collegiate experience.

"Don't be so down," he said when we reached Wendy's floor. "You might get to college someday."

I looked over at him in wonder. "How did you know that's what I was thinking?"

"Because I know you," he said simply, no mockery in his eyes. "Your aura got sad, and I figured being on a college campus had something to do with it."

I couldn't meet his gaze and turned away. "I don't like that."

"What, that someone actually knows what's important in your life?"

Yes, that was exactly it. But why *did* it bother me? Because it was Adrian, I realized. Why was it that a vampire understood me so well? Why not one of my friends? Why not one of my *human* friends?

"You can be Jet if you want," I said brusquely, trying to get us back on track and cover up my troubled feelings. After all, this wasn't Sydney's Therapy Hour. "But we are *not* posing as a couple again."

"Are you sure?" he said. His tone was lighter now, turning him back into the Adrian I knew. "Because I've got a lot more terms of endearment to use. Honey pie. Sugarplum. Bread pudding."

"Why are they all high-calorie foods?" I asked. I didn't want to encourage him, but the question slipped out before I could stop it. "And bread pudding isn't really that romantic."

We had reached Wendy's door. "Do you want me to call you celery stick instead?" he asked. "It just doesn't inspire the same warm and fuzzy feelings."

"I want you to call me Sydney." I knocked on the door. "Er, Taylor."

A girl with freckles and frizzy red hair answered. Her eyes narrowed warily. "Yes?"

"We're looking for Wendy Stone," I said.

She scowled. "Are you from the registrar's office? Because I told them the check's on its way."

"No." I lowered my voice and made sure there were no witnesses. "My name's Taylor. We're here to talk to you about, um, magic."

The transformation was sudden and startling. She went from suspicious and cautious to shocked and outraged. "No. *No.* I've told you guys a hundred times I don't want to be involved! I can't believe you'd actually show up at my door to try to convert me to your little coven freak show."

She tried to shut the door, but Adrian managed to stick his

foot in and block it. Very manly. "Wait," he said. "That's not what this is about. Your life might be in danger."

Wendy turned incredulous. "So you guys are threatening me now?"

"No, nothing like that. Please," I pleaded. "Just let us talk to you for five minutes inside. Then we'll leave and never bother you again."

Wendy hesitated and then finally gave a nod of resignation. "Fine. But I'm getting my pepper spray."

Her apartment was neat and tidy, save for a pile of papers and engineering books scattered on the floor. We'd apparently interrupted her homework, which brought back my wistfulness. She made good on her promise to get the pepper spray and then stood before us with crossed arms.

"Talk," she ordered.

I showed her the picture of Veronica. "Have you ever seen this woman?"

"Nope."

"Good." Or was it? Did that mean Veronica might have Wendy tagged as a future hit and was waiting to pounce? "She's dangerous. I'm not exactly sure how to put it. . . ."

"She finds girls with magic and sucks away their souls," supplied Adrian helpfully.

Wendy did a double take. "I'm sorry, what did you say?"

"That's not exactly the case," I said. "But it's close enough. She seeks out girls with power and takes it for herself."

"But I don't use magic," Wendy countered. "Like I told you, I don't want anything to do with it. There's a witch who lives in Anaheim who's always telling me how much potential I have and how I should be her apprentice. I keep telling her no, and

I've never even tried any spells. This soul-sucking lady has no reason to come after me."

Ms. Terwilliger had warned me some of the girls might say this. In fact, she'd said most would have this argument.

"It doesn't matter," I said. "That won't stop her."

Wendy looked terrified now, and I didn't blame her. My reaction had been similar. It was frustrating to know the very thing you were trying to get away from might come after you.

"Then what should I do?" she asked.

"Well, avoid her if you can. If she comes to see you . . . I mean, don't let her in. Don't be alone with her." That was slightly lame advice, and we all knew it. "If you do see her, I'd tell that witch in Anaheim. In fact . . . I know you don't want to, but if I were you, I'd get in touch with that witch now and try to get her help. Maybe even learn a few defensive spells. I understand you don't want to—believe me, I really do—but it could save your life. Also . . . " I held out the agate charm. "You should take this and wear it at all times."

Wendy eyed the charm as though it were a poisonous snake. "Is this some trick to get me to learn magic after all? You come here with this whole act about how if I don't learn, I could get my soul sucked away?"

Again, I had to give her points. I would think exactly the same thing. "We're telling the truth," I insisted. "There's no proof I can offer—well, wait. Give me your email address, and I'll send you this article about another girl it happened to."

Wendy looked like she was on the verge of using the pepper spray. "I think I would've heard if some girl had her soul magically sucked away."

"It wasn't really obvious to those who don't know about the

magical world. Let me send it to you, and then you can make your own decisions. It's the best I can offer."

She reluctantly agreed and wrote down her email address. Adrian stepped forward to take it from her, but he must have moved too quickly because she suddenly thrust the can of pepper spray in his direction.

"Stay back!" she exclaimed. At the exact same moment, I sprang in front of him, terrified he was about to get a face full of pepper spray. I cast the first spell I could think of, a simple one that created a flashy—but harmless—show of colored light. A shielding spell would've been much more useful, but I hadn't practiced any yet. That would have to be rectified, in case our future errands involved more pepper spray.

"*You* back off," I warned.

As I'd hoped, the brilliant display was terrifying to someone anti-magic like Wendy. She retreated to the far side of her apartment and thankfully didn't use the spray.

"G-get out," she stammered, eyes full of fear.

"Please take precautions," I said. I set the charm on the floor. "And please wear this. I'll email you the article."

"Get out," she repeated, making no move toward the charm.

As Adrian and I walked out of her building and into the sun, I sighed loudly. I was dismayed enough that I didn't even have the chance to feel down about being at a college.

"That didn't go so well," I said.

He thought about it, then grinned. "I don't know, Sage. You threw yourself in the line of pepper spray for me. You must like me just a *little* bit."

"I—I figured it'd be a shame to ruin your pretty face," I stammered. In truth, I hadn't been thinking of anything that specific. All I'd known was that Adrian was in danger. Protecting him had been instinctual.

"Still, that spell was kind of badass."

I managed a small smile. "It was harmless, and that's the thing. Wendy didn't know any better. The reason Veronica goes after these girls is that they don't have any magical protection—and that's exactly why they probably can't stop her. I don't think pepper spray will help, but maybe the article will convince her. Oh, shoot. I'll have to make a fake email address for Taylor."

"No worries," said Adrian. "I already have a Jet Steele one you can use."

This actually made me laugh. "Of course you do. For all the online dating you do, right?"

Adrian didn't comment one way or the other, which bothered me more than it should have. I'd meant it as a joke . . . but was there truth to it? If rumors—and some of my own observations—were true, Adrian had experience with a lot of women. A *lot*. Thinking of him with others upset me, far more than it should have. How many other girls had he kissed with that same intensity? How many had been in his bed? How many had felt his hands upon their bodies? He couldn't have loved them all. Some—probably most—had been conquests, girls whose faces he forgot the next morning. For all I knew, I was just the ultimate conquest for him, a test for his skills. You probably couldn't find a greater challenge than a human with hang-ups about vampires.

And yet, thinking back on all the things said and unsaid between us, I was pretty sure that wasn't true. No matter how crazy this romantic entanglement was, he loved me—or thought he did. I was no superficial conquest. It'd probably be better if

I was, though. Without an emotional connection, he'd eventually give up and easily find comfort in someone else's arms. This would probably be a good time for me to suggest he do that anyway.

But I stayed silent.

CHAPTER 10

THE NEXT MORNING, I sought out Ms. Terwilliger before class to give her a recap of yesterday's adventures. She leaned against her desk, sipping a cappuccino as I spoke. Her expression grew darker as the story progressed, and she sighed when I finished.

"Well, that's unfortunate," she said. "I'm glad you were able to find the Stone girl, but that kills our lead on Veronica until the next full moon. It could be too late by then."

"You're sure there's no other scrying spell?" I asked.

She shook her head. "Most that I could attempt would alert her that I was looking for her. There is one that might mask me while I'm using it . . . but it also might not be able to penetrate any shielding she's using to hide herself."

"It's still worth a try, isn't it?" I asked. The warning bell rang, and students began trickling into the classroom. She shot me a smile as she straightened up.

"Why, Miss Melbourne, I never thought I'd hear you

suggesting such things. But you're right. We'll talk about it this afternoon. It's something I'd like you to see."

That anti-magic gut instinct started to rear its ugly head . . . and then stopped. Somewhere, against my wishes, I'd gotten caught up in all of this. I was too concerned now about Veronica's other victims to pay attention to my usual worries. In Alchemist eyes, using magic was bad. In my eyes, leaving innocents in danger was worse.

With no other critical situations to contend with, I found that the day flew by. When I rejoined Ms. Terwilliger for our independent study, I found her packed up and waiting for me to arrive. "Field trip," she told me. "We need to work on this at my place." A wistful look crossed her features. "Too bad we can't stop at Spencer's."

Caffeine and magic didn't mix, which was another good reason for staying away from the arcane. I started to point out that since I wasn't working any magic, I didn't have the same restrictions. A moment later, I decided that would be mean. Ms. Terwilliger had enough going on with a bloodthirsty sister on the loose. She didn't need to be taunted too.

The cats were waiting at the door when we arrived at her house, which was slightly terrifying. I'd never seen all of them at once and counted thirteen. I had to assume that number was by design.

"I have to feed them first," she told me as they swarmed at her feet. "Then we'll get to work."

I nodded wordlessly, thinking her plan was a good one. If those cats weren't fed soon, it seemed likely they would turn on us. I didn't like our odds.

Once they had food to distract them, Ms. Terwilliger and I

went to her workshop. There was little I could do except observe. Magic often required that the person doing the spell be the one to put in all the labor. I assisted with a little measuring, but that was about it. I'd seen her do a couple of quick, flashy spells in the past but never anything of this magnitude. It was clear to me that this was a very, very powerful feat. She had nothing to link her to Veronica, no hair or picture. The spell required the caster to use the image in her mind of the person being sought. Other components, herbs and oils, helped enhance the magic, but for the most part, the work was all on Ms. Terwilliger. Watching her prepare triggered a mix of emotions in me. Anxiety was one, of course, but it was paired with a secret fascination at seeing someone with her strength cast a spell.

When everything was in place, she spoke the incantation, and I nearly gasped as I felt power surge up in the room. I'd never sensed it from another person before, and the intensity nearly knocked me over. Ms. Terwilliger was staring at a spot a few feet in front of her. After several long moments, a glowing dot appeared in the air. It grew bigger and bigger, turning into a flat, shimmering disc, which hung there like a mirror. I stepped backward, half-afraid the disc would keep expanding and consume the room. Eventually, it stabilized. Tense silence surrounded us as she stared at that glowing surface. A minute passed, and then the oval began to shrink and shrink until it was gone. Ms. Terwilliger sank with exhaustion and caught the side of her table for support. She was sweating heavily, and I handed her some orange juice we'd had ready.

"Did you see anything?" I asked. There'd been nothing visible to me, but maybe only the caster could see what the spell revealed.

She shook her head. "No. The spell was unable to touch her mind. Her shielding must be too strong."

"Then we can't do anything until next month." I felt my stomach drop. I hadn't realized until that moment how much I'd been hoping this spell would work. So much of my life involved problem solving, and I felt lost when I ran out of options.

"You and Adrian can keep warning the other girls," said Ms. Terwilliger. Color was starting to return to her face. "At the very least, it might slow Veronica down."

I looked at the time on my cell phone. This spell had taken longer than I thought. "I don't think we can do a round trip to Los Angeles today. I'll get him tomorrow, and we'll see if we can finish off the list."

Once I was convinced she wouldn't pass out from magical exertion, I made motions to leave. She stopped me as I was about to walk out the door.

"Sydney?"

I glanced back, suddenly uneasy. The problem with having so many people call me by nicknames was that when someone called me by my actual name, it usually meant something serious was happening.

"Yes?"

"We keep talking about warning others, but don't forget to look after yourself as well. Keep studying the book. Learn to protect yourself. And keep the charm on."

I touched the garnet, hidden under my shirt. "Yes, ma'am. I will."

Marcus's promised text came as I was driving back to school, telling me to meet him at a nearby arcade. I knew the place and had actually been to its adjacent mini-golf course once before, so I had no difficulty heading over there. Marcus was waiting for me just inside the door, and thankfully, Sabrina wasn't around wielding a gun.

I hadn't spent a lot of time in arcades and didn't really understand them. They hardly meshed with my father's style of education. For me, it was a mass of sensory overload that I wasn't quite ready for. The smell of slightly burnt pizza filled the air. Excited children and teenagers darted back and forth between games. And everywhere, everything seemed to be flashing and beeping. I winced, thinking maybe my dad had been on to something in avoiding these places.

"This is where we're going to discuss covert activities?" I asked in disbelief.

He gave me one of his movie star smiles. "It's not an easy place for people to spy on you. Besides, I haven't played Skee-Ball in years. That game is awesome."

"I wouldn't know."

"What?" It was kind of nice to catch him by surprise again, even if it was for something so trivial. "You've been missing out. Spot me some money for tokens, and I'll show you." Apparently, being an on-the-run renegade leader didn't pay well.

He found the Skee-Ball machines instantly. I bought him a cupful of tokens and handed them over. "Have at it."

He promptly put a token in and threw his first ball. It landed completely outside of the rings, making him scowl. "You don't waste any time," I remarked.

His eyes were on the game as he made his second throw, which again missed. "It's a survival tactic. When you spend enough time on the run . . . hiding out all the time . . . well, you take advantage of these moments of freedom. And when pretty girls spirit you away."

"How do you know we're free? How can you be so sure the Alchemists haven't been watching me?" I asked. I was pretty sure I wasn't being watched and mostly wanted to test him.

"Because they would've showed up on that first day."

He had a point. I put my hands on my hips and tried to be patient. "How long are you going to play? When can we talk?"

"We can talk now." His next ball hit the ten-point ring, and he whooped with joy. "I can talk and throw. Ask away. I'll give you as many shocking secrets as I can."

"I'm not easily shocked." But I wasn't going to waste this opportunity. I glanced around, but he was right. No one was going to eavesdrop in this noisy place. We could barely hear each other as it was. "What'd you do to get kicked out of the Alchemists?"

"I didn't get kicked out. I left." This round ended, and he put in his next token. "Because of a Moroi girl."

I froze, unable to believe what I'd heard. Marcus Finch had started his great rebellion . . . because he'd been involved with a Moroi? It rang too close to my own situation. When I didn't say anything, he glanced over and took in my expression.

"Oh. *Oh*. No, nothing like that," he said, realizing my thoughts. "That's not a line even I would cross."

"Of course not," I said, hoping I was doing a good job at hiding my nervousness. "Who would?"

He returned to the game. "We were friends. I was assigned to Athens, and she lived there with her sister."

That derailed me. "Athens . . . you were in Athens? That was one of the places I wanted to be assigned. I went to St.

157

Petersburg instead, but I always kept hoping that, maybe, *maybe*, I'd get reassigned to Greece. Or even Italy." I was nearly babbling, but he didn't seem to notice.

"What's wrong with St. Petersburg? Aside from the high Strigoi count."

"What's wrong is that it wasn't Athens or Rome. My dad specifically requested that I *not* be assigned to either place. He thought it'd be too distracting."

Marcus paused again to give me a long, level look. There was sympathy in his expression, as though my entire history and family drama were playing before his eyes. I didn't want him to feel sorry for me and wished I hadn't said anything. I cleared my throat.

"So tell me about this girl in Athens."

He took the hint. "Like I said, she was a friend. So funny. Oh, man. She cracked me up. We used to hang out all the time—but you know how that's kind of frowned upon."

I almost laughed at his subtle joke. Kind of? That was an understatement. Field Alchemists weren't supposed to interact with Moroi unless it was absolutely necessary for some business matter or related to stopping and covering up Strigoi. My situation was a little unique, since my mission actually required me to talk to her on a daily basis.

"Anyway," he continued. "Someone noticed, and I got a lot of unwelcome attention for it. Around the same time, I started hearing all these rumors . . . like about Alchemists holding Moroi against their will. And even some Alchemists interacting with the Warriors."

"*What?* That's impossible. We would never work with those freaks." The idea of Moroi prisoners was outlandish, but it was that second part that truly stumped me. I couldn't even process it. He might as well have said the Alchemists were working with aliens.

"That's what I thought." He threw another ball, looking supremely pleased when it scored thirty points. "But I kept hearing whispers, so I started asking questions. A lot of questions. And, well, that's when things really went bad. Questions don't always go over so well—especially if you're a nuisance about them."

I thought about my own experience. "That's certainly true."

"So that's when I walked. Or, well, ran. I could see the signs. I'd crossed a line and knew it was only a matter of time before I had a one-way ticket to re-education." Another new round started, and he gestured me forward. "Want to give it a try?"

I was still stunned enough by his earlier words that I stepped forward and took a ball. The Alchemists were logical, organized, and reasonable. I knew there were Alchemists who wished we could do more to fight the Strigoi, but there was no way our group would work with trigger-happy zealots. "Stanton told me we only tolerate the Warriors. That we're just keeping an eye on them."

"That's what I was told too." He watched me line up a shot. "There's kind of a learning curve to this, by the way. It may take you a few—"

I threw and hit the fifty-point ring. Marcus could only stare for a few seconds, his earlier smirk vanishing.

"You said you'd never played!" he exclaimed.

"I haven't." I threw another fifty pointer.

"Then how are you doing that?"

"I don't know." Fifty points again. "You just base your force on the ball's weight and distance to the ring. It's not that hard. This is kind of a boring game, really."

Marcus was still dumbstruck. "Are you some kind of super-athlete?"

I nearly scoffed. "You don't need to be an athlete to play this."

"But . . . no . . ." He looked at the rings, then at me, and then back to the rings. "That's impossible. I've been playing this since I was a kid! My dad and I used to go to our town's carnival over and over in the summer, and I'd spend at least an hour playing this each time."

"Maybe you should have made it two hours." I tossed another ball. "Now tell me more about the Warriors and the Alchemists. Did you ever get any proof?"

It took him several moments to tune back into the conversation. "No. I tried. I even got cozy with the Warriors for a while—that's how I met Clarence. My group has found a few dark secrets about the Alchemists and saved other Moroi from the Warriors, but we were never able to make a connection between the two groups." He paused dramatically. "Until now."

I picked up the next ball. This mundane activity was helping me analyze his startling words. "What happened?"

"It was a fluke, really. We've got a guy working with us now who just left the Alchemists and broke his tattoo," he explained. He said it like it was no big deal, but I still couldn't shake how uneasy "breaking the tattoo" made me feel. "He'd overheard something that matched up to something Sabrina uncovered. Now we've just got to get the evidence linking it all."

"How are you going to pull that off?"

"Actually, *you're* going to pull it off."

He spoke just as I was releasing another ball. My shot went

wide, missed the rings and even the machine entirely. The ball bounced off the wall and landed at the feet of some startled girls. Marcus retrieved the ball and gave them an apologetic smile, which made them gush about how it was no problem at all. As soon as they were gone, I leaned toward Marcus.

"What did you say?"

"You heard me. You want to join our group? You want to break your tattoo?" He looked annoyingly smug. "Then this is all part of the process."

"I never said I wanted to do any of those things!" I hissed. "I just wanted to find out more about them."

"And I bet you'd really love to know if there are factions in the Alchemists working with the Warriors."

He was right. I did want to know that.

He caught hold of my hand. "Sydney, I know this is a lot to take in. I don't blame you for doubting, and that's exactly why we need you. You're smart. You're observant. You question. And just like me, those questions are going to get you in trouble—if they haven't already. Get out now while you can—on your own terms."

"I just met you! I'm not breaking away from the group that raised me." I pulled my hand back. "I was willing to hear you guys out, but now you've gone too far."

I turned and headed toward the door, unwilling to listen anymore. Yet as I walked away, his words crawled over me. Even though I'd been forgiven for my involvement with Rose, my record still probably had a black mark. And even though I hadn't pushed hard about Marcus Finch, had even bringing him up raised Stanton's suspicions? How long until little things added up?

I pushed open the doors and stepped out into bright

sunlight. It chased away the darkness of what I'd just heard. Marcus was right behind me and touched my shoulder.

"Sydney, I'm sorry. I'm not trying to scare you." That cocky attitude was gone. He was deadly earnest. "I just sense something about you . . . something that resonates with me. I think we're on the same side, that we want the same things. We've both gotten close to the Moroi. We want to help them—without being lied to or used."

I eyed him warily. "Go on."

"Please, hear us out."

"I thought I just did."

"You heard *me* out," he corrected. "I want you to meet the others and hear their stories. They'll tell you more about what they went through. They'll tell you about this." He tapped his tattoo. "And when you hear more about that task . . . well, I think you'll want to do it."

"Right. The big, mind-blowing thing that's going to unveil an Alchemist-Warrior conspiracy." He remained serious, which bothered me more than if he'd suddenly revealed this to be one big joke. "So, what? You're going to get the others, and we'll all have an arcade day?"

He shook his head. "Too dangerous. I'll gather them in some other place and then tell you where to meet us, but it's got to be last minute again. Can't risk detection."

"I can't go on some epic road trip," I warned. "No one cares much about LA trips, but traipsing all over the state is going to get that unwanted attention you were talking about."

"I know, I know. It'll be close. I just have to make sure it's secure." He was back to his excited, cheery self. "Will you do it? Come join us?"

In spite of myself, I *was* curious. Even though I refused to believe in any connection between the Warriors and the Alchemists, I wanted to find out what leads this group thought they had. I also just wanted to see this mysterious group of his, period. What had Adrian called them? Marcus's Merry Men? And, of course, there was the tattoo. Marcus kept alluding to its secrets but still hadn't given me the details.

"I'll do it," I said at last. "On one condition."

"Name it."

"I want to bring someone with me," I said. "You can trust him, I swear. But after Sabrina pulled a gun on me, you have to understand why I'd be a little nervous about walking into your clique."

Marcus looked like he might almost consider it but then suddenly recoiled. "Not Adrian?"

"No, no. This guy's a dhampir. No one who'd be interested in turning you over to the Alchemists, especially if you really are working to protect Moroi. You say you've got a good feeling about me? Then trust me that you have nothing to worry about with him. He'd just be there to make me feel a little safer."

"You have nothing to worry about with *us*," Marcus said. "We won't hurt you."

"I want to believe you. But I don't quite have that same good feeling you have yet."

He didn't say anything right away and then burst into laughter. "Fair enough. Bring your friend." He shook my hand, as though we were sealing some great bargain. "I'll be in touch later with the details. You won't regret it, Sydney. I swear it."

CHAPTER 11

MARCUS DISAPPEARED TO WHEREVER it was he was hiding out, and I drove home. What he'd said to me still seemed outlandish. I kept telling myself none of it could be true. It made things a lot easier to handle.

Back at Amberwood, I found the usual buzz of evening student activity. It felt comforting after my shocking outing, far removed from fanatics and cryptic spells. My phone buzzed with a text message the minute I stepped into my dorm room. It was from Jill: *Come see us when you're back.* I sighed. No rest for the wicked, it would seem. I left my purse in my room and then trudged down to the second floor, unsure of what I'd find.

Jill opened her door, looking immensely relieved to see me. "Thank God. We have a situation."

"We *always* have a situation," I said. I stepped inside and saw Angeline sitting on the floor, back against the wall and a miserable expression on her face. "What happened?"

She looked up quickly. "It wasn't my fault."

The sinking feeling in my stomach increased. "It never is, is it? I repeat: what happened?"

When Angeline refused to say, Jill spoke up. "She gave Trey a concussion with an algebra book."

Before I could even start to parse that, Angeline leapt to her feet. "The doctor said it wasn't a concussion!"

"Wait." I glanced between them, half hoping they'd burst into laughter at the joke they must be playing on me. "You did something to Trey that actually required medical attention?"

"I barely touched him," she insisted.

I sat down on Jill's bed and resisted the urge to crawl under its covers. "No. You can't do this. Not again. What did the principal say? Oh, God. Where are we going to send you?" After Angeline's brawl with a motivational group, it had been made very clear that further fighting would get her expelled.

"Eddie took the blame," said Jill. A small smile crossed her face as she spoke. "There weren't really many witnesses, so Eddie said they were playing around in the library and tossing the book back and forth. He claimed he got careless and threw the book too hard . . . and that it accidentally hit Trey on the head."

Angeline nodded. "That's kind of what really happened with us."

"No, it wasn't," protested Jill. "*I* saw it. You got mad when Trey told you it shouldn't be that hard to understand that *x* always has a different value."

"He implied that I was stupid!"

Variables didn't seem like too hard a concept to me, but I could tell under Angeline's bravado that she really was flustered. I always had the impression that back among the Keepers, Angeline had been a queen among her peers. Here she was constantly trying to keep up academically and socially, adrift in a world very different from the one she'd grown up in. That would make anyone insecure. And while I questioned if Trey had ever said she was stupid, I could understand how some of his snarky commentary could be perceived that way.

"Did Eddie get in any serious trouble?" I asked. I doubted he'd get expelled for something like this, but it would be just my luck that he'd get the punishment he'd saved Angeline from.

"Detention," said Jill.

"He accepted it very bravely," added Angeline.

"I'm sure he did," I said, wondering if either girl knew they were wearing mirror expressions of adoration. "Look, Angeline, I know the tutoring process must be frustrating, but you *have* to watch your temper, okay? Trey's just trying to help."

She looked skeptical. "He's got kind of an attitude sometimes."

"I know, but people aren't exactly lining up to fill his position. We need you here. Jill needs you here. Eddie needs you here." I saw some of her indignation fade at the mention of her friends and duty. "Please try to work with Trey."

She gave a weak nod, and I stood up to leave. Jill hurried after me into the hallway. "Hey, Sydney? How was your outing with Marcus?"

"It was fine," I said, certainly not about to dredge up Marcus's alarming revelations. "Informative. And I learned how to play Skee-Ball."

Jill almost looked offended. "You played Skee-Ball? I thought you were supposed to be learning about the Alchemists' secret history."

"We multitasked," I said, not liking her tone.

I left before she could comment further and texted Eddie when I reached my room. *I heard what happened. Sorry. And thanks.* His response was quick: *At least it wasn't a concussion.*

I braced myself for snark when I went to meet Adrian the next day. Jill had probably told him about my arcade trip, which would probably elicit a comment like, "Nice to know you're so dedicated to crack the Alchemists. Way to keep your eye on the ball."

When I pulled up in front of Adrian's apartment building, he was already waiting out front for me. As soon as I saw his grim face, my heart stopped. I jumped out of the car, just barely pausing to grab the keys as I went.

"What's wrong?" I exclaimed, jogging up to him.

He rested a hand on my shoulder, but I was too worried to care about the touch. "Sydney, I don't want you to freak out. There's no lasting damage."

I looked him over. "Are you okay? Were you hurt?"

For a moment, his somber expression turned puzzled. Then, he understood. "Oh, you think it's me? No, I'm fine. Come on."

He led me around the back of his building, to the private parking lot used by residents. I came to a halt, my jaw dropping as I took in the terrible, ghastly scene. A couple other residents were milling around, and a police officer stood nearby taking notes. Around us, seven parked cars had their tires slashed.

Including the Mustang.

"No!"

I ran over to its side, kneeling and examining the damage. I felt like I was in the middle of a war, kneeling by a fallen comrade on the battlefield. I was practically on the verge of shouting, "Don't you die on me!"

Adrian crouched beside me. "The tires can be replaced. I think my insurance will even cover it."

I was still horrified. "Who did this?"

He shrugged. "Some kids, I guess. They hit a few cars one block over yesterday."

"And you didn't think that was worth mentioning to me?"

"Well, I didn't know they were going to come here too. Besides, I knew you'd flip out and want to set up twenty-four-hour surveillance on this place."

"That's not a bad idea." I glanced up at his building. "You should talk to the landlord about it."

Adrian didn't seem nearly as concerned as he should have been. "I don't know that he'd go for it. I mean, this isn't really a dangerous neighborhood."

I pointed at the Mustang. "Then how come this happened?"

Even though we could take Latte to Los Angeles, we still had to wait around to finish up with the police and then get a tow truck. I made sure the tow truck driver knew that he better not get a scratch on the car, and then I watched mournfully as it was hauled away. Once that sunny splash of yellow disappeared around a corner, I turned to Adrian.

"Ready to go?"

"Do we have enough time?"

I looked at my cell phone and groaned. We'd burned up a lot of time handling the vandalism aftermath. And yet, I hated to wait until tomorrow, seeing as I'd already lost time yesterday while dealing with Marcus. I called Ms. Terwilliger and asked if she'd cover for me if I came in after curfew.

"Yes, yes, of course," she said, in a tone that suggested she couldn't understand why I'd even bothered calling her. "Just talk to more of those girls."

Ms. Terwilliger had given me six names. We'd already taken care of Wendy Stone. Three of the girls lived relatively close together, and they were our goal tonight. The last two were closer to the coast, and we hoped to reach them tomorrow. Adrian tried making conversation with me throughout the drive, but my mind was still on the Mustang.

"God, I'm an idiot," I said, once we'd almost reached our destination.

"That's never a term I'd use to describe you," he said promptly. "Articulate. Well dressed. Smart. Organized. Beautiful. I'd use those terms, but never 'idiot.'"

I nearly asked why "beautiful" had come after "organized" and then remembered the actual concern. "I'm obsessing about that car when girls' lives are on the line. It's stupid. My priorities are messed up."

My eyes were on the road, but I could tell he was smiling. "If your priorities were really messed up, you would've followed that tow truck. Yet here you are, off to help perfect strangers. That's a noble thing, Sage."

"Don't rule yourself out," I said. "You're pretty noble too, going on all these outings with me."

"Well, it's not the same as Skee-Ball, but it'll have to do. How was that anyway? Did you really learn anything?"

"I learned a lot—some pretty unbelievable stuff, actually. I'm still waiting to get some proof, though."

Luck was with us initially. The first two girls were home, though their reactions were similar to Wendy Stone's. This time, I'd had the foresight to bring the newspaper article, in the hopes it would make a stronger impression. That ghastly picture at least gave them pause, but I left not knowing if they'd really take me seriously or use the agate charms.

Our good fortune ran out when we reached the last name. She too was a college student, meaning we had another campus visit. Her name was Lynne Titus, and she lived in a sorority house. I admit, as I knocked on the door, I was fully prepared to find a group of girls dressed in pink, having a pillow fight in their living room. But when we were shown in, we discovered an orderly home not all that different from Wendy's building. Some girls were coming and going, while others sat around with textbooks and papers.

"Lynne?" asked the girl who'd let us inside. "You just missed her."

I knew this shouldn't be a surprise. These girls had lives. They wouldn't all be waiting around for me to come by and talk to them. I glanced uneasily at a window, taking note of the purpling sky. "Any idea when she'll be back?"

The girl shook her head. "No, sorry. I don't know where she went."

Adrian and I exchanged looks. "You're free from your curfew," he reminded me.

"I know. But that doesn't mean I want to spend all night waiting for Lynne." I did some mental calculations. "I suppose we could wait a couple of hours. Three at most."

Adrian seemed supremely delighted by this, and I couldn't help but wonder if he was more excited at hanging out on a college campus . . . or at spending time with me. "What's fun to do around here?" he asked our hostess. He glanced around at the quiet academic environment. "No raging parties here, huh?"

The girl put on a disapproving expression. "We're a very serious sorority. If you're looking for parties, I guarantee there's one going on just down the street. Those girls have one every night." Adrian shot me a hopeful look.

"Oh, come on," I said. "Can't we find some nice museum?"

"We want to stay close, in case Lynne comes back," Adrian said. Something told me if the party had been all the way across campus, he still would've pushed for it. "Besides, if you want to go to college so badly, you should see the full scope of what it has to offer. And aren't you a fan of Greek stuff?"

That was hardly what I had in mind, and he knew it. I reluctantly agreed but warned him he couldn't drink. I was sporting the brown wig and presumed he was using spirit to mask us further. Alcohol would diminish his ability to pull it all off. Plus, I just didn't want to see him drunk.

It was easy to find the party house because we could hear the music blasting from it. A guy and a girl openly drinking beer from plastic cups challenged us at the door. "This is Greek only," the girl said. She looked as though she might fall off her stool. "Who are you with?"

I pointed vaguely toward Lynne's sorority. "Um, them."

"Alpha Yam Ergo," said Adrian, without hesitation. I expected the door squad to point out that most of those weren't even Greek letters. Maybe it was because Adrian spoke so confidently—or because they'd had too much beer—but the guy waved us inside.

It was almost like being back at the arcade, an overwhelming flood of stimuli. The house was crowded and loud, with smoke hanging in the air and alcohol flowing freely. Several people offered us drinks, and some girl invited us—three times—to play beer pong, forgetting that she'd already spoken to us. I regarded it all in amazement, trying to keep the disgust off my face.

"What a waste of tuition. This is ruining all my collegiate dreams," I shouted to Adrian. "Isn't there anything to do that's not drinking or being stupid?"

He scanned around, able to see more of the room from his greater height. He brightened. "That looks promising." He caught hold of my hand. "Come on."

In a surprisingly nice and spacious kitchen, we found several girls sitting on the floor painting blank T-shirts. Judging from the sloppy job and paint spills, they too had been indulging in alcohol. One girl had a cup of beer next to an identical cup of paint, and I hoped she wouldn't mix them up.

"What are you doing?" I asked.

One of the girls glanced up and grinned. "Making shirts for the winter carnival. You want to help?"

Before I could say no, Adrian was already on the ground with them. "Do I ever." He helped himself to a white T-shirt and a brush with blue paint on it. "What are we putting on these?" The girls' shoddy work made that a valid question.

"Our names," said one girl.

"Winter stuff," said another.

That was good enough for Adrian. He set to work painting snowflakes on the shirt. Unable to help myself, I knelt down to get a better look. Whatever his faults, Adrian *was* a decent artist. He mixed in a few other colors, making the snowflakes intricate and stylized. At one point, he paused to light a clove cigarette, sharing one of the girls' ashtrays. It was a habit I didn't really like, but at least the rest of the smoke in this place masked his.

As he was finishing up the shirt and writing out the sorority's name, I noticed that all the other girls had stopped to stare.

"That's amazing," said one, her eyes wide. "Can I have it?"

"I want it," insisted another.

"I'll make each of you one," he assured them. The way they looked at him was an unwelcome reminder of the breadth of his experience with other women. I shifted a little closer to him, just so they wouldn't get any ideas.

He handed the white shirt to the first girl and then set to work on a blue shirt. Once he fulfilled his promise to each girl, he sifted through the T-shirt stack until he found a men's-size black one. "Gotta pay tribute to my fraternity."

"Right," I scoffed. "Alpha Yam Ergo."

Adrian nodded solemnly. "A very old and prestigious society."

"I've never heard of them," said the girl who'd claimed the first shirt.

"They don't let many people in," he said. In white paint, he wrote his fake fraternity's initials: AYE.

"Isn't that what pirates say?" asked one of the other girls.

"Well, the Alpha Yams have nautical origins," he explained. To my horror he began painting a pirate skeleton riding a motorcycle.

"Oh, no," I groaned. "Not the tattoo."

"It's our logo," he said. Adrian and I had once had to investigate a tattoo parlor, and to distract the owner, he'd gone in and pretended to be interested in a tattoo that sounded very much like what he was drawing now. At least, I assumed he'd been pretending. "Isn't it badass?"

"Badass" wasn't quite the word I would've used, but despite it being such a ridiculous image, he actually did a good job. I made myself comfortable, drawing my knees up to me and leaning against the wall. He soon stopped with his banter and grew completely absorbed in his work, meticulously painting the skeleton's bones as well as that of a skeleton parrot sitting on the pirate's shoulder. I studied his features as he worked, fascinated by the joy in his eyes. Art was one of the few things that seemed to anchor him and drive that darkness in him away. He seemed to glow with an inner light, one that enhanced his already handsome features. It was another rare and beautiful glimpse of the intense, passionate nature lying beneath the jokes. It came through in his art. It had come through when he kissed me.

Adrian suddenly glanced up at me. Our gazes locked, and I felt like he could read my mind. How often did he think about that kiss? And if he really was crazy about me, did he imagine more than just kissing? Did he fantasize about me? What kinds of things did he think about? His lips on my neck? His hand on my leg? And was that leg bare . . . ?

I was afraid of what my eyes might betray and quickly looked away. Desperately, I groped for some witty and nonsentimental comment. "Don't forget the ninja throwing stars."

"Right." I could feel Adrian's gaze on me a few moments longer. There was something tangible to it, a warmth that enveloped me. I didn't look back until I was certain his attention was again on the shirt. He added the stars and then sat back triumphantly. "Pretty cool, huh?"

"It's not bad," I said. In truth, it was kind of amazing.

"You want one too?" The smile he gave me stirred up those warm feelings again. I couldn't help but smile back.

"We don't have the time," I managed to say. "We've got to check on Lynne."

"I'll make you a fast one."

"Not the pirate," I warned. He found a small purple shirt and began painting on it in silver. "Purple?"

"It's your color," he insisted. A thrill ran through me at his words. Adrian could see auras, the light that surrounded all people and was tied into their personalities. He'd told me that mine was yellow, a color most intellectuals had. But he'd also said I had flares of purple, which indicated a passionate and spiritual nature. Those weren't qualities I usually thought I possessed . . . but sometimes, I wished I did.

I watched, enthralled, as he painted a large silver heart with flames edging one side. The whole design was Celtic in style. It was beautiful.

"Where did you get that from?" I asked in awe. I'd seen a lot of his work but never anything like this.

His eyes were on his heart, completely caught up in his work. "Just something kicking around in my head. Reminds me of you. Fiery and sweet, all at the same time. A flame in the dark, lighting my way." His voice . . . his words . . . I recognized one of his spirit-driven moments. It should've unnerved me, but there was something sensual about the way he spoke, something that made my breath catch. A flame in the dark.

He swapped out the silver paintbrush for a black one. Before I could stop him, he wrote over the heart: AYE. Underneath it, in smaller letters, he added: HONORARY MEMBER.

"What are you doing?" I cried. The spell had shattered. "You ruined it!"

Adrian regarded me with a mischievous look. "I figured you'd be flattered at being accepted as an honorary member."

"How can I get in?" asked one of the girls.

In spite of my outrage, I took the shirt when he offered it to me. I held it up gingerly, careful not to mess up the paint job. Even through the ridiculous words, the fiery heart was still stunning. It shone through, and I couldn't stop admiring it. How could someone so irreverent create something so beautiful? When I finally looked up again, I found Adrian watching me. That earlier thrall seized me, and I found myself unable to move.

"You haven't painted anything," he said softly.

"That's because I have zero creativity," I told him.

"Everyone's got *some* creativity," he insisted. He handed me the silver brush and slid over to join me against the wall. Our legs and arms touched. He laid out his own AYE shirt across his lap. "Go ahead. Add something, anything."

I shook my head in protest and tried to hand him the brush. "I can't draw or paint. I'll ruin it."

"Sydney." He pushed the brush back into my hand. "It's a pirate skeleton, not the *Mona Lisa*. You're not going to decrease its value."

Maybe not, but I had a hard time imagining what I could possibly add to this. I could do a lot of things, but this was out of my league—especially compared to his skill. Something in his expression drove me, however, and after a lot of thought, I gave my best shot at drawing a tie around the skeleton's neck. Adrian frowned.

"Is that a noose?"

"It's a tie!" I cried, trying not to feel offended.

He laughed, clearly delighted at this. "My mistake."

"He can go to a boardroom meeting," I added, feeling a need to defend my work. "He's very proper now."

Adrian seemed to like that even more. "Of course he is.

Proper and dangerous." A little of his mirth faded, and he grew pensive as he studied me, holding me in his gaze. "Just like you."

I'd been so worried about the artistic challenge that I wasn't aware of just how close he'd moved to me until now. So many details came into focus. The shape of his lips, the line of his neck. "I'm not dangerous," I breathed.

He brought his face toward mine. "You are to me."

And somehow, against all reason, we were kissing. I closed my eyes, and the world around me faded. The noise, the smoke . . . it was gone. All that mattered was the taste of his mouth, a mix of cloves and mints. There was a fierceness in his kiss, a desperation . . . and I answered, just as hungry for him. I didn't stop him when he pulled me closer, so that I almost sat on his lap. I'd never been wrapped around some-one's body like that, and I was shocked at how eagerly mine responded. His arm went around my waist, pulling me onto him further, and his other hand slid up the back of my neck, getting entangled in my hair. Amazingly, the wig stayed on. He took his lips away from my mouth, gently trailing kisses down to my neck. I tipped my head back, gasping when the intensity returned to his mouth. There was an animalistic quality that sent shock waves through the rest of my body. Some Alchemist voice warned me that this was exactly how a vampire would feed, but I had no fear. Adrian wouldn't hurt me, and I needed to know just how hard he could kiss me and—

"Oh my God!"

Adrian and I jerked apart as though someone had thrown cold water on us, though our legs stayed entangled. I glanced around in a panic, half expecting to see an outraged Stanton standing over us. Instead, I looked up into the terrified face of a girl I didn't know. She wasn't even looking at us.

"You guys won't believe what happened!" she exclaimed, directing her words to our fellow artists. She pointed vaguely behind her. "Over across the street at Kappa, they found one of their girls unconscious, and they can't wake her up. I don't know what happened, but it sounds like she was attacked. There's police out front and everything."

Adrian and I stared at each other for one shocked moment. Then, wordlessly, we both stood up. He held my hand to steady me until my trembling legs strengthened. *I'm weak because of this news,* I told myself. *Not because I was just making out with a vampire.*

But those dangerous and intoxicating kisses faded almost instantly when we returned to Lynne's sorority. It was busy with frightened people, and campus security moved in and out, allowing us to step right inside the open door.

"What happened?" I asked a brunette standing nearby.

"It's Lynne," she said, biting her lips. "They just found her in an empty auditorium."

Something in the way she spoke made me uneasy. "Is she . . . alive?"

The girl nodded. "I don't know . . . I think so, but they said there's something really wrong. She's unconscious and looks . . . well . . . *old.*"

I met Adrian's eyes and vaguely noticed he had silver paint in his hair. I'd still been holding the brush when I'd wrapped my arms around him. "Damn," he murmured. "Too late."

I wanted to scream in frustration. We'd been so close to warning her. She'd allegedly left just before we'd arrived. What if we'd come sooner? What if we'd visited her before the other two girls? I'd chosen the order randomly. Worse, what if we'd been able to find her instead of having art time with the drunken sorority girls?

What if I hadn't been all over Adrian? Or maybe he'd been all over me. Whatever you wanted to call it, I hadn't exactly resisted.

The more we learned, however, the more unlikely it seemed we would've been able to do anything if we'd stuck around Lynne's house and investigated. Nobody knew where she'd gone. Only one person had seen her leave, a girl with curly blond hair who frustrated the campus police with her vague answers.

"I'm sorry," she kept saying. "I just . . . I can't remember the girl she left with."

"Nothing?" asked one of the officers. "Height? Age? Hair color?"

The girl frowned, looking as though she was using every ounce of mental effort. At last, she sagged in defeat and shook her head. "I'm sorry."

"Did she have black hair?" I suggested.

The girl brightened a little. "Maybe. Er, wait. It might have been brown. No. Red, maybe?"

Adrian and I stepped away, knowing we could do no more. "That girl seems awfully confused," I said as we walked back to my car.

"She certainly does," he agreed. "Sound familiar?"

"Very," I muttered, recognizing the signs of magic.

No one could deny it. Veronica had been here. And we'd been too late to stop her.

CHAPTER 12

I FELT LIKE A FAILURE when I delivered Ms. Terwilliger the news before classes the next day.

She told me, her face pale and grim, that there was nothing I could've done. But I didn't know if I believed that. I still berated myself with the same questions as last night. What if I hadn't spent the previous day with Marcus? What if I hadn't spent so much time making sure the Mustang was taken care of? What if I hadn't been engaged in a massive public display of affection on the floor with Adrian? I'd let personal matters interfere, and now a girl had paid with her life. I wanted to skip school and warn the others immediately, but Ms. Terwilliger assured me that Veronica wouldn't be able to feed so quickly. She told me waiting until later in the day would be fine.

I gave a reluctant nod and returned to my desk, figuring I'd try to read until class started. I didn't expect to have much success. "Miss Melbourne?" she called. I glanced back and saw that her sad expression had lightened up a little. She almost looked amused, which seemed weird, given the situation.

"Yes, ma'am?"

"You might want to do something about your neck."

I was totally lost. "My neck?"

She reached into her purse and handed me a compact mirror. I opened it and surveyed my neck, still trying to figure out what she could be talking about. Then I saw it. A small, brownish purple bruise on the side of my neck.

"What on earth is that?" I exclaimed.

Ms. Terwilliger snorted. "Although it's been a while for me, I believe the technical term is a hickey." She paused and arched an eyebrow. "You do know what that is, don't you?"

"Of course I know!" I lowered the mirror. "But there's no way—I mean, we barely—that is—"

She held up a hand to silence me. "You don't have to justify your private life to me. But you might want to consider how you can actually keep it private in the next fifteen minutes."

I was practically out of my seat before she finished speaking. When I emerged from the building, I had the amazing fortune to find the campus shuttle just pulling up. I hurried onto it, and although the ride to my dorm only took a few minutes, it felt like forever. All the while, my mind reeled with what had happened.

I have a hickey. I let Adrian Ivashkov give me a hickey.

How in the world had that happened? The devastating news about Lynne had allowed me to ignore the full impact of my indiscretion, but there was no avoiding that now. Against every principle I possessed, I'd allowed myself to get drawn into kissing Adrian. And not just kissing. Thinking about the way our bodies had been pressed together made me feel as flushed as I had last night.

No, no, no! I couldn't think about that. I had to forget it had happened. I needed to make sure it didn't happen again. What had come over me? I didn't feel the way he felt about me. He was Moroi. And even if he hadn't been, he was undoubtedly the most unsuitable guy for me in the world. I needed someone serious, someone with the potential to get a job that had medical benefits. Someone like Brayden.

Yeah, how'd that work out for you, Sydney?

What happened with Adrian had been wrong. It had obviously been some twisted act of lust, probably brought on because he was so forbidden. That was it. Women fell for that kind of thing. When I'd researched relationship books, I'd seen one called *Bad Boys and the Women Who Love Them.* I'd ignored it because Brayden was pretty much the opposite of a bad boy. Maybe it would be worth getting that book now.

A flame in the dark. I needed to forget that Adrian had ever called me that. I had to.

We had another minute before we would reach my dorm, so I sent a quick text to Adrian: *I have a hickey! You can't ever kiss me again.* I honestly hadn't expected him to be awake this early, so I was surprised to get a response: *Okay. I won't kiss you on your neck again.*

So typical of him. *No! You can't ever kiss me ANYWHERE. You said you were going to keep your distance.*

I'm trying, he wrote back. *But you won't keep your distance from me.*

I didn't dignify that with a response.

When we reached my dorm, I asked the driver how long she'd wait before returning to main campus. "I'm leaving right now," she said.

"Please," I begged. "Wait sixty seconds. I'll pay you."

She looked offended. "I don't take bribes."

But when I sprinted back out of the dorm—in a scarf—she was still there. I made it back to Ms. Terwilliger's class just as the bell rang. She flashed me a knowing look but said nothing about my wardrobe change.

While I was in class, I received a text from Marcus. *Can you meet today? San Bernardino, 4 p.m.*

Well, he'd warned me about short notice. San Bernardino was an hour away. I'd given Eddie a heads-up about the meeting happening this week, and he'd agreed to go. I just hoped he didn't have anything planned this afternoon. I texted back that we'd be there, and Marcus sent me an address.

When class ended, a girl from my English class caught my attention and asked if she could borrow some notes since she'd been out sick yesterday. Eddie was gone by the time I finished with her, so I didn't get a chance to ask him about San Bernardino until lunch.

"Sure," he said, snapping into that fierce guardian mode.

Jill already knew about our errand because I'd told Adrian about it. I felt a little bad about taking Eddie from Jill. Okay, *really* bad. Removing Eddie was a serious risk, though I reminded myself that he wasn't always with her every single second. Sometimes it was impossible, which was why we'd acquired Angeline. Still, if anyone in the Alchemists found out I was using her main bodyguard for personal errands, I'd be in big trouble. Well, actually, I'd probably be in big trouble regardless, seeing as I was meeting with a group of rebels. I turned to Angeline, who was trying to decipher some notes about the quadratic equation.

"Angeline, you need to stay with Jill until we're back," I said. "And you should both actually just stay in your dorm, to be extra safe. Don't wander campus."

Jill accepted this, but Angeline looked up in dismay. "I'm supposed to meet Trey for math. How do you expect me to pass?"

I was helpless against an academic argument. "Study in the dorm lobby. That should be safe enough. Jill can just do homework with you."

Angeline didn't seem entirely pleased about that alternative, but she didn't protest it. She started to return to her notes and then did a double take. "Why are you wearing that scarf?" she asked. "It's so hot today." It was true. The unseasonable temperatures had returned.

Eddie, to my surprise, said, "I wondered the same thing."

"Oh, um . . . " *Please don't blush, please don't blush,* I ordered myself. "I've just been cold today."

"That's weird," said Jill, perfectly deadpan. "For someone who always seems to be so cold, you sure can warm up pretty fast."

It was straight out of Adrian's playbook. Jill knew perfectly well why I had on the scarf, and I gave her a warning look. Eddie and Angeline appeared completely mystified. I stood up, even though I'd barely touched my food. Probably none of them would find that weird.

"Well, I've got to go. I'll find you later, Eddie." I hurried off before any of them could question me further.

I'd been a little hesitant to let Eddie in on Marcus. Eddie certainly wasn't going to turn Marcus or me in to the Alchemists for sideline plotting. That being said, I also didn't want Eddie to think the Alchemists were involved in nefarious schemes against the Moroi. That might very well be something Eddie would relay back to his own people, which could in turn cause all sorts of diplomatic problems. Even this hint of the Alchemists potentially being in contact with the Warriors was dangerous. I decided that having Eddie as protection was worth the risk of him hearing something he shouldn't. He was my friend, and I trusted him. Still, I had to give him a little background information as we made the drive to San Bernardino.

"Who are these people exactly?" he asked.

"Ex-Alchemists," I said. "They don't like all the procedures and red tape and just want to interact with Moroi and dhampirs on their own terms."

"That doesn't sound so bad." I could hear caution in his voice. Eddie was no fool. "Why do you want me along?"

"I just don't know much about them. I think their intentions are good, but we'll see." I thought very carefully on how to phrase my next words. I had to give him a heads-up. "They've got a lot of conspiracy theories. Some even, um, think there might be Alchemists working with Warriors."

"What?" It was a wonder Eddie's jaw wasn't on the floor.

"They don't have any hard proof," I added quickly. "They've got a Warrior girl who spies for them. She thinks she overheard something . . . but it all sounds sketchy to me. They want me to help, but I don't think there's anything to uncover. I mean, the Alchemists helped raid the Warriors, right? Disrupting their crazy execution ritual wouldn't exactly foster good relations."

"I suppose not," he admitted, but it was clear he wasn't entirely at ease.

I decided to move on to safer territory. No need to worry

about Marcus and his Merry Men (I couldn't get Adrian's name out of my head) until we heard them out.

"How is everything?" I asked. "With Angeline? Jill? I've been so busy with, uh, stuff that I feel like we haven't talked much."

Eddie didn't answer right away. "Quiet with Jill, which is good. We want things to be as boring as possible for her. Things are better with her and Micah too. At first, a lot of his friends wouldn't talk to her after the breakup. But he's gotten over her enough that they can just be friends . . . so, the others have decided they can too."

"That's a relief."

When we'd first come to Amberwood, Jill had had trouble fitting in. Dating Micah had opened up a lot of social circles for her, and I'd worried about what would happen after they split up. Things had worsened when I'd forbidden her from modeling for a local and very assertive fashion designer, Lia DiStefano, who risked exposing Jill. Jill had felt like she'd lost everything, so I was glad to see things were coming together for her again.

"Jill's easy to like," I added. "I bet most of them were happy to stay friends with her."

"Yeah." It was all he said, but there was a lot of emotion in that one word. I glanced over and saw a dreamy look on his face. So. Micah might be over Jill, but Eddie wasn't. I wondered if he even knew it. "How's Angeline?"

The dreaminess became a frown. "Confusing."

I laughed. "That's pretty accurate."

"She goes from one extreme to another. When we first started going out, she, uh, couldn't stay away from me." I didn't entirely know what that entailed, and I really didn't want to think about it. "Now I can hardly get five minutes alone with her. She's started going to basketball games for some reason. I think she's just kind of dumbstruck at a game that's got so many rules, compared to whatever insanity the Keepers do for fun. And she's really into fixing that math grade too. I guess that's a good thing." He didn't sound too sure. I, however, was thrilled.

"I think the idea of getting kicked out really scared her. Despite all the tough adjustments she's had here, she doesn't want to go back home." When Rose had been on the run, I'd hidden Dimitri and her with the Keepers. That was where we'd first met Angeline, and even back then, she'd begged Rose to take her away from that rural world. "Give her time. This'll settle down, and her, uh, enthusiasm will come back."

We reached the address in San Bernardino, a hardware shop that seemed like a strange location for a secret meeting. I pulled into the parking lot and texted Marcus that we were here. No response came.

"That's weird," I said. "I hope he didn't change his mind."

Eddie was over his girl troubles and had that sharp guardian look in his eyes again. "I bet we're being watched. If they're as paranoid as you say, this probably isn't the place we're meeting. They've sent you here and are looking for signs to see if you were followed."

I turned to him in amazement. "I never would've thought of that."

"That's why you've got me along," he said with a smile.

Sure enough. Ten minutes later, Marcus texted with another address. We must have passed the test. This new location was in another loud, busy place: a family-friendly restaurant with actors walking around in giant animal costumes. It was, if possible, more absurd than the arcade.

"He picks the weirdest places," I said.

Eddie's eyes were everywhere. "It's brilliant actually. Too loud to be overheard. One exit in the back, one in the front. And if the Alchemists did show up, I'm guessing they wouldn't create a scene around this many children?"

"I guess."

Marcus met us in the lobby and waved us forward. "Hey, gorgeous. Come on, we've got a table." He paused to shake Eddie's hand. "Nice to meet you. We can always use more for the cause."

I'm not sure what I'd expected of the Merry Men. Maybe a bunch of rough-and-tumble outcasts with battle scars and eye patches, like Wolfe. Instead, what we found were a guy and girl sharing a plate of chicken fingers. They had golden lilies on their cheeks.

Marcus directed us to two chairs. "Sydney, Eddie. This is Amelia and Wade."

We shook hands. "Sabrina's not with you?" I asked.

"Oh, she's here," said Marcus, an enigmatic note in his voice.

I picked up on the subtext and glanced around. I wasn't the only one who'd brought protection. Sabrina was hidden somewhere in the crowd, watching and waiting. Maybe in an animal costume. I wondered if she'd brought her gun in here.

Amelia slid the plate toward us. "Want some? We've got mozzarella sticks on the way."

I declined. Even with my resolution to eat more, I drew the line at deep fryers. "Let's talk," I said. "You're supposed to tell me about the tattoos and this mysterious task you have for me."

Wade chuckled. "She gets down to business."

"That's my girl," said Marcus. I could almost hear an

unspoken *That's why we need her for the cause.* He waited for our waitress, who was dressed like a cat, to bring the mozzarella sticks and take our drink orders. At least, I think it was a waitress. Gender was a little hard to determine under the mask.

"The tattoo process is simple," Marcus said, once our privacy was back. "I told you that the Alchemists are able to put Moroi compulsion in it, right? To limit communication . . . and other things, if needed."

I still didn't know if I bought the idea of mind control in the tattoos, but I let him go on.

"When Moroi help make the blood ink, the earth users put in the compulsion that prevents you from discussing vampires. That earth magic is in harmony with the other three physical elements: air, water, and fire. That harmony gives the tattoo its power. Now, if you can get a hold of charmed ink and have a Moroi undo the earth magic in it, that'll shatter the bond with the other elements and kill any compulsion locked in. Inject that 'broken' ink into your tattoo, and it breaks the harmony of your elements as well—which in turn breaks any suggestions the Alchemists put in."

Eddie and I stared.

"That's 'all' I have to do?" I asked in disbelief.

"It's easier than you might think," said Amelia. "The hard part is . . . well, Marcus added another part to the process. Not technically necessary . . . but helpful."

We'd been here ten minutes, and I was already getting a headache. "You decided to do some improvisation?"

The laughter that elicited from Marcus was just as infectious as before . . . except, once again, the scene didn't really warrant laughing. He paused, like he was waiting for us to join in, and continued when we didn't. "That's one way of looking at it. But she's right—it's helpful. Before I'll let anyone do it, they have to perform a task. Some task that involves directly going against the Alchemists."

Eddie couldn't hold back anymore. "What, like an initiation ritual?"

"More than that," said Marcus. "I have a theory that doing something like that, something that challenges all the training you've had, will weaken the compulsion a little. Usually it's something that involves infiltration and helps our cause. That weakening makes it easier for the other ink to take effect. It's also a good test. Deactivating the tattoo doesn't mean you're ready to walk away. It doesn't undo years of mental conditioning. I try to find people who think they're ready to rebel, but sometimes, when they're faced with actually taking action, they crack. Better to know sooner rather than later, before we interfere with the tattoo."

I turned toward Amelia and Wade. "And you've both done this? You did some dare, and then your tattoos were deactivated?" They nodded in unison.

"We just have to seal it with indigo now." Seeing my confusion, Wade explained, "Even after breaking the elements in the tattoo, it can still be repaired. Someone could forcibly re-ink and compel you. Tattooing over it with indigo ink makes sure you can never be controlled again."

"And here I thought yours was just a style choice," I said to Marcus.

He absentmindedly traced the crescent pattern. "Oh, the design was. But the ink was mandatory. It's a special concoction that's hard to get a hold of, and I have to go down to a guy in

Mexico to get it. I'm taking Amelia and Wade there in a couple weeks to seal theirs. You could come too."

I didn't even acknowledge that crazy idea. "Seems like that blue ink would kind of be a tip-off to the other Alchemists that something's up."

"Oh, we ran away from the Alchemists," said Amelia. "We're not part of them anymore."

Once again, Eddie jumped in. "But you were just talking about infiltration. Why not keep doing other covert tasks once you've broken the elements? Especially if it frees you? Your tattoos look the same as Sydney's right now. If you really think there's something suspicious going on, then work from the inside and hold off on sealing with the indigo ink."

"Too risky," said Marcus. "You could slip up and say something that the tattoo wouldn't have let you before. Or, if you're not cautious, they might catch you going off to meet with others. Then you've got a date with re-education—where they could repair the tattoo."

"Seems like it'd be worth the risk for more information," I said. "If you're careful enough."

Marcus shook his head, no longer flippant. "I've known others who tried that. They thought no one was on to them. They were wrong. We don't make that mistake anymore." He touched his tattoo again. "This is the way we do it now. Complete your mission, break the tattoo, leave the Alchemists, and get sealed. Then we work from the outside. Also saves us from getting caught up in all the Alchemist routine and menial tasks."

"So there are others?" I asked, picking up on what he'd said.

"Of course." That amusement returned. "You didn't think it was just the three of us, did you?"

191

I honestly hadn't known. "So this is what you're offering me. A fairy tale about my tattoo, if I just complete some traitorous mission for you."

"I'm offering you freedom," Marcus corrected. "And the ability to help Moroi and dhampirs in a way that's not part of some larger conspiracy. You can do it on your own terms."

Eddie and I exchanged glances. "And speaking of conspiracy," I said. "I'm guessing this is the part where you tell me about the alleged Alchemist and Warrior connection—the one you need me to prove."

My sarcasm was lost on the threesome because they all grew excited. "Exactly," said Marcus. "Tell her, Wade."

Wade finished off a chicken finger covered in ranch dressing and then leaned toward us. "Just before I joined Marcus, I was assigned to the St. Louis facility. I worked in operations, handling a lot of visitor access, giving tours . . . not the most interesting work."

I nodded. This, at least, was familiar territory. Being in the Alchemists meant taking on all sorts of roles. Sometimes you destroyed Strigoi bodies. Sometimes you made coffee for visiting officials. It was all part of the greater cause.

"I saw a lot of things. I mean, you can probably guess." He looked troubled. "The harsh attitudes. The rigid rules. Moroi visited, you know. I liked them. I was glad we were helping them, even though everyone around me acted as though helping such 'evil' creatures was a terrible fate that we'd been forced into. I accepted this because, you know, I figured what we're told is true. Anyway, there was one week . . . I swear, it was just nonstop Strigoi attacks all over the country. Just one of those things. The guardians took out most of them, and field Alchemists were pretty busy covering up. Even though most of it was taken care of, I just kept wondering about why we were always dealing with the aftermath when we have so many resources. I mean, I didn't think we should start going after Strigoi, but it just seemed like there should be a way to help the Moroi and guardians be more proactive. So . . . I mentioned it to my supervisor."

Marcus and Amelia wore deadly earnest expressions, and even I was hooked. "What happened?" I asked softly.

Wade's gaze looked off into the past. "I was chastised pretty bad. Over and over, all my superiors kept telling me how wrong it was for me to even think things like that about the Moroi, let alone talk about them. They didn't send me to re-education, but they suspended me for two weeks, and each day, I had to listen to lectures about what a terrible person I was and how I was on the verge of corruption. By the end, I believed them . . . until I met Marcus. He made me realize I didn't have to be in that life anymore."

"So you left," I said, suddenly feeling a little more kindly toward Marcus.

"Yes. But not before completing the mission Marcus gave me. I got a hold of the classified visitor list."

That surprised me. The Alchemists were always hip deep in secrets. While most of our goings-on were recorded diligently, there were some things that our elite leaders didn't want the rest of the society to know about. Again, all for the greater good. The classified list would detail people allowed access—that the higher-ups wanted kept secret. It wasn't something the average Alchemist could see.

"You're young," I said. "You wouldn't be allowed access to something like that."

Wade snorted. "Of course not. That's what made the task so difficult. Marcus doesn't have us do easy assignments. I had to do a lot of dangerous things—things that made me glad to escape afterward. The list showed us the link to the Warriors."

"Did it say 'Top Secret Vampire Hunter Meeting'?" asked Eddie. Things like that, aside from his deadly protective skills, were why I liked having him along.

Wade flushed at the jibe. "No. It was all coded, kind of. It didn't list full names, just initials. Even I couldn't get the actual names. But one of the entries? Z. J."

Marcus and his Merry Men all looked at me expectantly, as though that were supposed to mean something to me. I glanced at Eddie again, but he was just as baffled.

"What's that stand for?" I asked.

"Zebulon Jameson," said Marcus. Once again, there was an expectation. When I didn't answer, Marcus turned disbelieving. "You were there with the Warriors. Don't you remember him? Master Jameson?"

I did, actually. He was one of the Warriors' high officials, an intimidating man with a salt-and-pepper beard who'd worn old-fashioned golden ceremonial robes.

"I never caught his first name," I said. "But isn't it kind of a leap to assume that's who Z. J. was? Maybe it was, I don't know, Zachary Johnson."

"Or Zeke Jones," supplied Eddie.

The cat came by with a refill for Marcus's lemonade, and I soon had proof that it was a woman. "Thanks, love," Marcus said, giving her a smile that nearly made her swoon and drop the tray. When he turned back to us, he was all business. "That's where Sabrina comes in. Not long before Wade got the list, she overheard Master Jameson talking to one of his cronies about an upcoming trip to St. Louis and how he was going to find out about leads on some missing girl. The timing lines up."

"It's an awfully big coincidence," I said. Yet even as I spoke, I was reminded of something Sonya Karp always said about the world of Moroi and Alchemists: *There are no coincidences.*

"What missing girl were they talking about?" asked Eddie carefully.

I met his eyes and immediately understood what he wasn't saying. A missing girl that the Warriors were interested in. There was one missing girl that the Moroi were very, very interested in as well. And whom the Alchemists were determined to keep safe. She was the reason I was stationed in Palm Springs in the first place. In fact, I was pretending to be her sister.

Jill.

I said nothing and focused on Marcus again.

He shrugged. "I don't know, just that finding her would create a lot of problems for the Moroi. The details aren't important yet. First we have to prove the connection."

Those details were immensely important to Eddie and me, but I wasn't sure how much Marcus and friends knew about Jill. I wasn't about to show too much interest.

"And that's what you want me to do?" I asked, recalling the arcade discussion. "How would you like me to do that? Go visit Master Jameson and ask him?"

"Every visitor is recorded on video if they're going through the secure access point," said Wade. "Even the top secret ones. All you have to do is steal a copy of that footage. They store it all in their computers."

These people had a very different idea than me of what "all you have to do" meant.

"I'm a field Alchemist in Palm Springs," I reminded them. "I'm not a computer hacker. I'm not even in St. Louis! How would I walk in and steal something?"

Marcus tilted his head to study me, allowing some of that golden hair to slip forward. "It's more of that resourceful vibe I get off you. Couldn't you find some way to get to St. Louis? Some reason to visit?"

"No! I'd have no . . ." I trailed off, flashing back to the wedding. Ian, with his lovesick eyes, had invited me to visit him in St. Louis. He'd had the audacity to use church services as a way to further his chances with me.

Marcus's eyes sparkled. "You've already thought of something, haven't you? Brilliant, just like I thought." Amelia looked mildly put out at hearing me complimented.

"It'd be a long shot," I said.

"That's kind of how we roll," said Marcus.

I still wasn't on board. "Look, I know someone there, but I'd have to get permission to even go, which wouldn't be easy." I stared at each of them in turn. "You know how it is. You were all in the Alchemists. You know we can't just take vacations whenever we want."

Wade and Amelia actually had the grace to look embarrassed, but Marcus was undaunted. "Can you let this chance pass? Even if you don't want to join us or alter your tattoo, just think about it. You saw the Warriors. You saw what they're capable of. Can you even imagine what could happen if they had access to Alchemist resources?"

"It's all circumstantial," argued the scientist in me.

"Sydney," said Eddie.

I turned to him and saw something in his eyes I'd never expected to see: pleading. He didn't care about Alchemist conspiracies or Marcus's Merry Men. What he cared about was Jill, and he'd heard something that made him think she was in danger. That was unacceptable in his world. He would do anything in his power to keep her safe, but even he knew stealing information from the Alchemists was out of his league. It was pretty much out of mine too, but he didn't know that. He believed in me, and he was silently begging me to help.

Marcus pushed his advantage. "You have nothing to lose—I mean, if you aren't caught. If you get the footage and we find nothing . . . well, so be it. False alarm. But if we get hard proof that Jameson was there, then I don't have to tell you how big that is. Either way, you should break your tattoo and join us. Besides, after a stunt like this, would you really want to stick around?" He eyed me. "But that part's up to you. Just help us for now."

Against my better judgment, my mind was starting to figure out how I could pull this off. "I'd need a lot more information about operations," I murmured.

"I can get you that," said Wade promptly.

I didn't answer. This was crazy—a crazy idea from a crazy group. But I looked at Marcus's tattoo and the way the others followed him—the way even Sabrina followed him. There was a dedication, an ardent belief that had nothing to do with Marcus's silly flirting. They might really be on to something.

"Sydney," said Eddie again. And this time: "Please."

I could feel my resolve weakening. A missing girl, who could cause lots of trouble if found. If they were really talking about Jill, how could I risk anything happening to her?

But what if I was caught?

Don't get caught, an inner voice said.

With a sigh, I looked back up at Wade. "All right," I said. "Give me the scoop."

CHAPTER 13

WADE TOLD ME EVERYTHING he knew. It was all useful, but I didn't know if it would be enough. First, I had to get to St. Louis . . . and that was going to be tricky. I braced myself for the phone calls I'd have to make, hoping I had enough Alchemist wiles to pull them off.

Before I took on that task, I just wanted the normality and comfort of my own room. Eddie and I drove back to Amberwood, analyzing every detail of our meeting. He was chomping at the bit to make progress, and I promised I'd keep him in the loop.

I had just reached my door when my phone rang. It was Ms. Terwilliger. I swear, sometimes I thought she had a sensor outside my room so that she'd know the instant I returned.

"Miss Melbourne," she said. "We need to meet."

My heart stopped. "There hasn't been another victim, has there? You said we have time."

"We do," she replied. "Which is why we need to meet sooner rather than later. Reading up on spells is one thing, but you require some hands-on practice. I refuse to let Veronica get to you."

Her words triggered a mix of emotions. Naturally, I had my knee-jerk reaction against practicing magic. It was quickly squashed by the realization that Ms. Terwilliger cared about me and was so concerned about keeping me safe. My own personal desire to not be in a coma was also a strong motivator.

"When do you want to meet, ma'am?" I asked.

"Tomorrow morning."

I realized tomorrow was Saturday. Already? Where had the week gone? I was driving Adrian to pick up his car in the morning, which hopefully wouldn't take a long time. "Could we meet at noon? I've got an errand to run."

"I suppose so," said Ms. Terwilliger, with some reluctance. "Meet me at my place, and then we'll go out to Lone Rock Park."

I was about to lie back on my bed and froze. "Why do we have to go out to the middle of the desert?" Lone Rock Park was remote and rarely saw many tourists. I hadn't forgotten how terrifying it was the last time she'd brought me out into the wilderness. At least this time we'd be in daylight.

"Well, we can hardly practice on school grounds," she pointed out

"True. . . ."

"Bring your book, and the components you've been working on."

We disconnected, and I jotted out a quick text to Adrian: *Need to be fast tomorrow. Meeting Ms. T at 12.* His response wasn't entirely unexpected: *Why?* Adrian naturally needed to know everything that was going on in my life. I texted back that Ms. Terwilliger wanted to work on magical protection. This time, he did surprise me: *Can I watch? Wanna know how she's protecting you.*

Wow, Adrian actually asked? He had a history of simply inviting himself along on outings. I hesitated, still confused after our heated moment at the sorority. He'd never mentioned it again, though, and his concern now touched me. I texted back that he could come along and was rewarded with a smiley face.

I didn't entirely know what to wear to "magical training," so I opted for comfortable layers the next morning. Adrian gave me a once-over when he got into Latte. "Casual mode, huh? Haven't seen that since the Wolfe days."

"I don't know what she has in mind," I explained, doing a U-turn on his street. "Figured this was best."

"You could have worn your AYE shirt."

"Wouldn't want to get it dirty," I said, grinning.

That was partially true. I still thought the fiery heart he'd painted was exquisite. But each time I looked at the shirt, too many memories seized me. What had I been thinking? That was a question I'd asked myself a hundred times, and every answer I came up with sounded fake. My preferred theory was that I'd simply been caught up in how serious Adrian had been about his art, how the emotion and passion had seized hold of him. Girls liked artists just as much as bad boys, right? Even now, something stirred in my chest when I thought about the enraptured look on his face. I loved that he possessed something so powerful in him.

But, as I told myself constantly, that was no excuse for climbing all over him and letting him kiss me—*on my neck.* I'd bought and downloaded the "bad boy" book online, but it had been completely useless in advising me. I finally decided the best way—if not the healthiest one—was to act like the moment had never happened. That didn't mean I forgot it. In fact, as I sat beside him in the car, I had a difficult time not thinking about how it had felt to be pressed up against him. Or how his fingers had felt entangled in my hair. Or how his lips had—

Sydney! Stop. Think of something else. Conjugate Latin verbs. Recite the periodic table.

None of those did any good. To Adrian's credit, he continued to withhold any commentary about that night. Finally, I found distraction in telling him about my trip to San Bernardino. Rehashing the conspiracy, rebel groups, and break-ins pretty much killed any passionate feelings I still had. Adrian didn't like the idea of Alchemists working with Warriors or of the tattoo controlling me. But he also didn't like me walking into danger. I tried to downplay the near impossibility of breaking into the St. Louis facility, but he clearly didn't believe me.

Ms. Terwilliger texted me twice not to be late to our meeting. I kept an eye on my watch, but the care of a Mustang was not something I took lightly, and I had to take my time at the mechanic's shop to make sure the Mustang was in pristine condition. Adrian had wanted to go with basic tires, but I'd urged him to upgrade, convincing him the extra cost would be worth it. And once I inspected them, I congratulated myself on the choice. Only after I was satisfied the car hadn't been unnecessarily scratched did I finally allow him to pay. We drove both cars back to Vista Azul, and I was pleased to see my timing was perfect. We weren't late, but Ms. Terwilliger was waiting on her porch for us.

We designated Adrian as our carpool driver. "Jeez," I said when she hurriedly got in the car. "Do you have somewhere to be after this?"

The smile she gave me was strained, and I couldn't help but notice how pale she looked. "No, but we do have a schedule to follow. I cast a large spell this morning that won't last forever. The countdown is on."

She wouldn't say any more until we reached the park, and that silence unnerved me. It gave me the opportunity to imagine all sorts of frightening outcomes. And although I trusted her, I suddenly felt relieved that Adrian was along as a chaperone.

Although it wasn't the busiest place, Lone Rock Park still had the occasional hiker. Ms. Terwilliger—who was actually in hiking boots—set off across the rocky terrain, searching for a suitably remote space to do whatever it was she had in mind. A few stratified rock formations dotted the landscape, but I couldn't really appreciate their beauty. Mostly I was aware that we were out here when the sun was at its fiercest. Even if it was almost winter, we'd still be feeling the heat.

I glanced over at Adrian as we walked and found him already looking at me. From his jacket pocket, he produced a bottle of sunscreen. "I knew you'd ask. I'm nearly as prepared as you are."

"Nearly," I said. He'd done it again, anticipating my thoughts. For half a heartbeat, I pretended it was just the two of us out on a pleasant afternoon hike. It seemed like most of the time we spent together was on some urgent mission. How nice would it be to just hang out without the weight of the world on us? Ms. Terwilliger soon brought us back to our grim reality.

"This should do," she said, surveying the land around her. She had managed to find one of the most desolate areas in the park. I wouldn't have been surprised to see vultures circling overhead. "Did you bring what I asked for?"

"Yes, ma'am." I knelt on the ground and rifled through my bag. In it was the spell book, along with some herbal and liquid compounds I'd mixed up at her request.

"Take out the fireball kindling," she instructed.

Adrian's eyes went wide. "Did you just say 'fireball'? That's badass."

"You see fire all the time," I reminded him. "From Moroi who can wield it."

"Yeah, but I've never seen a human do anything like that. I've never seen *you* do anything like that."

I wished he didn't look so awestruck because it kind of drove home the severity of what we were about to attempt. I would've felt better if he'd treated it like it was no big deal. But this spell? Yeah, it was kind of a big deal.

I'd once performed another spell that involved throwing a painstakingly made amulet and reciting words that made it burst into flames. That one had a huge physical component, however. This spell was another of those mental ones and essentially involved summoning fire out of thin air.

The kindling Ms. Terwilliger had referred to was a small drawstring bag filled with ashes made from burnt yew bark. She took the bag from me and examined its contents, murmuring in approval. "Yes, yes. Very nice. Excellent consistency. You burned it for exactly the right amount of time." She handed the bag back. "Now, eventually you won't need this. That's what makes this spell so powerful. It can be performed very quickly, with very little preparation. But you have to practice first before you can reach that point."

I nodded along and tried to stay in student mode. So far, what she was saying was similar to what the book had described. If I thought of all this as a classroom exercise, it was much less daunting. Not really scary at all.

Ms. Terwilliger tilted her head and looked past me. "Adrian? You might want to keep your distance. A considerable distance."

Okay. Maybe a little scary.

He obeyed and backed up. Ms. Terwilliger apparently had no such fear for herself because she stayed only a few feet away from me. "Now then," she said. "Apply the ashes, and hold out your hand."

I reached into the bag, touching the ashes with my thumb and forefinger. Then I lightly rubbed all my fingers together until my whole palm had a fine gray coating on it. I set the bag down and then held out my hand in front of me, palm up. I knew what came next but waited for her instruction.

"Summon your magic to call the flame back from the ashes. No incantation, just your will."

Magic surged within me. Calling an element from the world reminded me a little of what the Moroi did, which felt strange. My attempt started off as a red glimmer, hovering in the air above my palm. Slowly, it grew and grew until it was about the size of a tennis ball. The high of magic filled me. I held my breath, scarcely able to believe what I had just done. The red flames writhed and swirled, and although I could feel their heat, they didn't burn me.

Ms. Terwilliger gave a grunt that seemed to be equal parts amusement and surprise. "Remarkable. I forget sometimes what a natural you really are. It's only red, but something tells me, it won't take long before you can produce blue ones without the ashes. Calling elements out of the air is easier than trying to transform one substance into another."

I stared at the fireball, entranced, but soon found myself getting tired. The flames flickered, shrank, and then faded away altogether.

"The sooner you get rid of it, the better," she told me. "You'll just use up your own energy trying to sustain it. Best to throw it at your adversary and quickly summon another. Try again, and this time, throw it."

I called the fire once more and felt a small bit of satisfaction at seeing it take on more of an orange hue. I'd learned in my very first childhood chemistry lessons that the lighter a flame was, the hotter it burned. Getting to blue anytime soon still seemed like a long shot.

And speaking of long shots . . . I threw the fireball.

Or, well, I tried. My control of it faltered when I attempted to send it off toward a bare patch of ground. The fireball splintered apart, the flames disappearing into smoke that was carried off by the wind.

"It's hard," I said, knowing how lame that sounded. "Trying to hold it and throw it is just like an ordinary physical thing. I have to do that while still controlling the magic."

"Exactly." Ms. Terwilliger seemed very pleased. "And that's where the practice comes in."

Fortunately, it didn't take too many attempts before I figured out how to make it all work together. Adrian cheered me on when I successfully managed to throw my first fireball, resulting in a beautiful shot that perfectly hit the rock I'd been aiming for. I flashed Ms. Terwilliger a triumphant look and waited for the next spell we'd be moving on to. To my surprise, she didn't seem nearly as impressed as I expected her to be.

"Do it again," she said.

"But I've got it down," I protested. "We should try something else. I was reading the other part of the book—"

"You have no business doing that yet," she scolded. "You think this is exhausting? You'd pass out attempting one of the more advanced spells. Now." She pointed at the hard desert floor. "Again."

I wanted to tell her that it was impossible for me not to read ahead in a book. It was just how I operated with all my classes. Something told me now was not the best time to bring that up.

She made me practice the throw over and over. Once she was convinced I had it down, she had me work on increasing the fire's heat. I finally managed to get up to yellow but could go no farther. Then I had to work on casting the spell without the ashes. Once I reached that milestone, it was back to practicing the throws. She picked various targets for me, and I hit them all effortlessly.

"Just like Skee-Ball," I muttered. "Easy and boring."

"Yes," Ms. Terwilliger agreed. "It's easy hitting inanimate objects. But moving targets? Living targets? Not quite so easy. So, let's move on to that, shall we?"

The fireball I'd been holding above my hand vanished as shock shattered my control. "What do you mean?" If she expected me to start aiming at birds or rodents, she was in for a rude awakening. There was no way I was going to incinerate something *alive*. "What am I supposed to hit?"

Ms. Terwilliger pushed her glasses up her nose and backed up several feet. "Me."

I waited for the punch line or at least some further

explanation, but none came. I glanced behind me at Adrian, hoping perhaps he might shed some light on this, but he looked as astounded as I felt. I turned back to the singed ground where my earlier fireballs had struck.

"Ms. Terwilliger, you can't ask me to hit you."

Her lips twitched into a small half smile. "I assure you, I can. Go ahead, you can't hurt me."

I had to think a few moments for how to phrase my next response. "I'm a pretty good shot, ma'am. I can hit you."

This earned an outright laugh. "Hit, yes. Hurt, no. Go ahead and throw. Our time is running out."

I didn't know how much time had passed exactly, but the sun was definitely lower in the sky. I looked back at Adrian, silently asking for help in dealing with this insanity. His only response was a shrug.

"You're a witness to this," I told him. "You heard her tell me to do it."

He nodded. "You're totally blameless."

I took a deep breath and summoned my next fireball. I was so frazzled that it started off red, and I had to work to heat it up. Then I looked up at Ms. Terwilliger and braced myself for the shot. It was more difficult than I expected—and not just because I was worried about hurting her. Throwing something at the ground required almost no thought. The focus there was on aim and little else. But facing a person, seeing her eyes and the way her chest rose and fell while breathing . . . well, she was right. It was entirely different from hitting an inanimate object. I began to tremble, unsure if I could do it.

"You're wasting time," she warned. "You're sapping energy again. *Throw.*"

The command in her voice jolted me to action. I threw.

The fireball flew from my hand, straight at her—but it never made contact. I couldn't believe my eyes. About a foot in front of her, it hit some kind of invisible barrier, smashing apart into small flames, which quickly dissipated into smoke. My jaw dropped.

"What is that?" I exclaimed.

"A very, very powerful shielding spell," she said, clearly enjoying my reaction. She lifted up a pendant that had been hanging under her shirt. It didn't look like anything special, just a piece of unpolished carnelian wrapped in silver wire. "It took incredible effort to make this . . . and requires more effort still in order to maintain it. The result is an invisible shield—as you can see—that's impervious to most physical and magical attacks."

Adrian was by my side in a flash. "Hang on. There's a spell that makes you invulnerable to everything, and you only now just thought to mention it? You've been going on this whole time about how Sydney's in danger! Why don't you just teach her this one? Then your sister can't touch her." Although it didn't seem like Adrian was about to attack her as he had Marcus, he was almost just as upset. His face was flushed, his eyes hard. He had clenched his fists at his side, but I didn't even think he noticed. It was more of that primal instinct.

Ms. Terwilliger remained strong in the face of his outrage. "If it were that simple, then believe me, I would. Unfortunately, there are a number of problems. One is that Sydney, prodigy that she is, is nowhere near strong enough to cast this. *I'm* hardly strong enough. The other problem is that it has an extremely short time frame, which is why I've been so adamant about a schedule. It only lasts six hours and requires so much effort that you can't just cast it and permanently keep it on you at all times. I'm already worn out and will be even more so once it fades. I won't be able to cast it—or hardly any other magic—for at least another day. That's why I need Sydney to be prepared at all times."

Neither Adrian nor I said anything right away. I'd taken note of her weary state when she got in the car but hadn't thought much more about it. As we'd continued to practice out here, I'd observed her sweating and looking more fatigued, but I'd written it off to the heat. Only now could I fully appreciate the extent of what she had done.

"Why would you go to so much effort?" I asked.

"To keep you alive," she snapped. "Now, don't make this a waste. We've only got one more hour before it wears off, and you need to be able to aim at someone without thinking twice. You hesitate too much."

She was right. Even knowing that she was invulnerable, I still had a difficult time attacking her. Violence just wasn't something I embraced. I had to push down all my inner worries and treat it exactly like Skee-Ball. *Aim, throw. Aim, throw. Don't think.*

Soon, I was able to fight past my anxieties and throw without hesitation. She even tried moving around a little, just to give me a better feel for what it'd be like with a real foe, but I didn't find it to be much of a challenge. She was simply too tired and unable to run around or dodge me. I actually started to feel bad for her. She looked like she was about ready to pass out, and I felt guilty sizing up my next shot and—

"Ahh!"

Fire arced from Ms. Terwilliger's fingertips just as I released my fireball. My shot went wide, the ball disintegrating before it got anywhere near her. The fire she'd released passed me, about a foot away. With a weary grin, she sank to her knees and exhaled.

"Class dismissed," she said.

"What was that?" I asked. "I don't have a magic shield on me!"

She didn't display my same concern. "It was nowhere near you. I made sure of that. It was simply to prove that no matter how 'boring and easy' this seems, all bets are off when someone is actually attacking *you*. Now then. Adrian, would you be kind enough to bring me my bag? I have some dried dates in there that I think both Sydney and I would appreciate right about now."

She was right. I'd been so caught up in the lesson that I hadn't noticed how exhausted I had become. She was in worse shape, but the magic had definitely taken its toll on me. I'd never worked with amounts this big for so long, and my body felt weak and drained as the usual blood sugar drop occurred. I began to understand why she kept warning me away from the really difficult stuff. I practically inhaled the dried dates she'd brought for us, and although the sugar helped, I was desperate for more. Adrian gallantly helped us both walk back to the parking lot at the park's entrance, keeping one of us on each arm.

"Too bad we're out in the middle of nowhere," I grumbled, once we were all in Adrian's car. "I think you'd be amazed at how much I could eat right now. I'll probably faint before we're back to some civilization and restaurants."

"Actually," said Adrian. "You might be in luck. I think I saw a place not far from here when we were driving in."

I hadn't noticed anything, but I'd been too preoccupied worrying about Ms. Terwilliger's upcoming lesson. Five minutes after we were back on the highway, I saw that Adrian was right about a restaurant. He exited onto a drab little road, pulling into the gravel parking lot of a small but freshly painted white building.

I stared at the sign out front in disbelief.

"Pies and Stuff?"

"You wanted sugar," Adrian reminded me. The Mustang kicked up dust and gravel, and I winced on behalf of the car. "And at least it's not Pies and Bait or anything like that."

"Yeah, but the 'Stuff' part isn't exactly reassuring."

"I thought it was more the 'Pie' part that had you upset."

Despite my misgivings, Pies and Stuff was actually a cute and clean little establishment. Polka-dot curtains hung in the windows, and the display case was filled with every pie imaginable as well as "stuff" like carrot cake and brownies. We were the only people under sixty in the whole place.

We ordered our pie and sat down with it in a corner booth. I ordered peach, Adrian had French silk, and Ms. Terwilliger went with pecan. And of course, she and I had the waitress bring us coffee as soon as humanly possible since we'd had to abstain, painfully, for the magic. I took a sip and immediately felt better.

Adrian ate his slice at a reasonable rate, like a normal person, but Ms. Terwilliger and I dug in as though we hadn't eaten in a month. Conversation was irrelevant. Only pie mattered. Adrian regarded us both with delight and didn't try to interrupt until we'd practically licked the plates clean.

He nodded toward mine. "Another piece?"

"I'll take more coffee." I eyed the sparkling plate and couldn't help but notice that inner voice that used to nag me about calories was quiet these days. In fact, it didn't seem to be around anymore at all. I'd been so angry about Adrian's food "intervention," but his words had ended up having a bigger impact than I'd expected. Not that it had anything to do with him *personally*, of course. Lightening up my dieting restrictions was just a reasonable idea. That was it. "I feel pretty good now."

"I'll get you another cup," he told me. When he returned, he even had a mug for Ms. Terwilliger. "Figured you'd want one too."

She smiled in appreciation. "Thank you. You're very astute." As she drank, I couldn't help but notice she still looked tired, despite the fact that we'd just replenished with sugar. She no longer seemed in danger of passing out, but it was obvious she hadn't recovered as quickly as I had.

"Are you sure you're okay?" I asked her.

"Don't worry, I'll be fine." She sipped more coffee, her face lost in thought. "It's been years since I performed the shield spell. I forgot how much it takes out of me."

I was again struck by all the trouble she'd gone through for me. Ever since she'd identified me as a potential magic user, I'd done nothing but resist her and even be antagonistic.

"Thanks," I told her. "For everything . . . I wish there was a way I could make it up to you."

She set her cup down and stirred in more sugar. "I'm happy to do it. There's no need to reciprocate. Although . . . once this is all over, I'd like very much if you'd meet my coven. I'm not asking you to join," she added quickly. "Just to talk. I think you'd find the Stelle very interesting."

"Stelle," I repeated. She'd never called them by name before. "The stars."

Ms. Terwilliger nodded. "Yes. Our origins are Italian, though as you've seen already, the magic we use comes from a number of cultures."

I was at a loss for words. She'd gone to so much trouble for me . . . surely it wasn't a big deal just to *talk* to the other witches, right? But if it was such a small thing, then why was I terrified? The answer came to me a few moments later. Talking to others, seeing the larger organization, would kick my involvement with magic up to the next level. It had taken me a long time to come around to the magic I already used. I'd overcome many of my fears, but some part of me treated it as just some sideline activity. Like a hobby. Meeting other witches would change everything. I would have to accept that I was part of something so much bigger than just the occasional dabbling. Meeting a coven seemed official. And I didn't know if I was ready to be considered a witch.

"I'll think about it," I said at last. I wished I could give her more, but my protective instincts had seized me.

"I'll take what I can get," she said with a small smile. Her phone chimed, and she glanced down. "Speaking of the Stelle, I need to talk to one of my sisters. I'll meet you at the car." She finished her coffee and headed outside.

Adrian and I followed a few minutes later. I was still troubled about the coven and caught hold of his sleeve to keep him back. I spoke softly.

"Adrian, when did I reach this point? Trying to crack open the Alchemists and practicing magic in the desert?" Last summer, when I'd been with Rose in Russia, I couldn't even tolerate the idea of sleeping in the same room with her. I'd had too many Alchemist mantras running through my mind, warning me of vampire evils. And now, here I was, in league with vampires and questioning the Alchemists. That girl in Russia had nothing in common with the one in Palm Springs.

No, I'm still the same person at heart. I had to be . . . because if I wasn't, then who was I?

Adrian smiled at me sympathetically. "I think it's been a culmination of things. Your curious nature. Your need to do the right thing. It's all led you to this point. I know the Alchemists have taught you to think a certain way, but what you're doing now—it's not wrong."

I raked my hand through my hair. "And yet, despite all of that, I can't bring myself to have one tiny conversation with Ms. Terwilliger's coven."

"You have boundaries." He gently smoothed one of my wayward locks. "Nothing wrong with that."

"Marcus would say it's the tattoo holding me back."

Adrian dropped his hand. "Marcus says a lot of things."

"I don't think Marcus is trying to deceive me. He believes in his cause, and I'm still worried about mind control . . . but honestly, it's hard to believe I'm being held back when I'm out here doing stuff like this." I gestured outside, to where Ms. Terwilliger was. "Alchemist dogma says this magic is unnatural and wrong."

Adrian's smile returned. "If it makes you feel better, you actually looked natural out there—back in the park."

"Doing . . . what? Throwing fireballs?" I shook my head. "There's nothing natural about that."

"You wouldn't think so, but . . . well. You were . . . amazing, throwing that fire like some kind of ancient warrior goddess."

Annoyed, I turned away. "Stop making fun of me."

He caught my arm and pulled me back toward him. "I am absolutely serious."

I swallowed, speechless for a moment. All I was aware of was how close we were, that he was holding me to him with only a few inches between us. *Almost as close as at the sorority.* "I'm not a warrior or a goddess," I managed at last.

Adrian leaned closer. "As far as I'm concerned, you're both."

I knew that look in his eyes. I knew because I'd seen it before. I expected him to kiss me, but instead, he ran his finger along the side of my neck. "There it is, huh? Badge of honor."

It took me a moment to realize he was talking about the hickey. It had faded but wasn't entirely gone. I pulled away. "It is not! It was a mistake. You were out of line doing that to me."

His eyebrows rose. "Sage, I distinctly remember every part of that night. You didn't seem that unwilling. You were practically on top of me."

"I don't really remember the details," I lied.

He moved his hand from my neck and rested a fingertip on my lips. "But I'll stick to just kissing these if it makes you feel better. No mark." He started to lean toward me, and I jerked away.

"You will not! It's wrong."

"What, kissing you, or kissing you in Pies and Stuff?"

I glanced around, suddenly aware that we were creating a dinner show for the senior citizens, even if they couldn't hear us. I backed up.

"Both," I said, feeling my cheeks burn. "If you're going to attempt something inappropriate—something you said you wouldn't do anymore—then you could at least pick a better place."

He laughed softly, and the look in his eyes confused me further. "Okay," he said. "The next time I kiss you, I promise it'll be in a more romantic place."

"I—what? No! You shouldn't try at all!" I began moving toward the door, and he fell in step with me. "What happened to loving me from a distance? What happened to not, um, bringing up any of this stuff?" For someone who was allegedly just going to watch from afar, he wasn't doing a very good job. And I was doing an even worse job of being indifferent.

He moved in front of the door and blocked my way. "I said I wouldn't—if you don't want me to. But you're kind of giving me mixed signals, Sage."

"I am not," I said, amazed that I could even say that with a straight face. Even I didn't believe it. "You're presumptuous and arrogant and a whole lot of other things if you think I've changed my mind."

"You see, that's just it." There he was again, moving into my space. "I think you like the 'other things.'"

I shook off my daze and pulled away. "I like *humans*."

Another Alchemist lesson came to mind. *They look like us, but don't be deceived. The Moroi don't display the malice of the Strigoi, but creatures who drink blood and manipulate nature have no place in our world. Work with them only as you must. We are not the same. Keep your distance as much as possible. It's for the good of your soul.*

Adrian didn't look like he believed this either, but he stepped away and headed outside. I followed a few moments later, thinking I'd played with fire more than once today.

CHAPTER 14

SUNDAY ROLLED AROUND, and the day started off quietly. We were nearing the point when Veronica might strike again, and my stomach was in knots over what her next step would be . . . and how stuck we were on how to stop her. Then I received help from an unexpected source when my phone rang with an unknown number on the display.

Normally, I wouldn't answer something like that, but my life was hardly normal these days. Besides, it was a Los Angeles area code.

"Hello?"

"Hi! Is this Taylor?"

It took me a moment to remember my secret identity. I did not, however, recall giving my actual number to any of the girls we'd warned about Veronica.

"Yes," I said warily.

"This is Alicia, from Old World Bed-and-Breakfast."

"Hi," I said, still puzzled as to why and how she'd be calling me.

Her voice was as cheery and bright as when we'd met her. "I wanted to know if you'd thought any more about getting a room for your anniversary."

"Oh, well . . . that. We're still deciding. But, uh, probably we're going to go with something closer to the coast. You know, romantic beach walks and all that."

"I can totally understand," she said, though she sounded disappointed at the loss of a sale. "If you change your mind, just let me know. We're running a special this month, so you could get the Bunny Suite at a really good price. I remember you saying it reminded you of your pet rabbit. What was his name?"

"Hopper," I said flatly.

"Hopper! That's right. Such a sweet name."

"Yeah, awesome." I tried to think of a polite way to phrase my next question but simply chose directness. "Look, Alicia, how did you get this number?"

"Oh, Jet gave it to me."

"He did?"

"Yup." She'd apparently gotten over her disappointment and now sounded bright and chirpy again. "He filled out an info card while you guys were here and put down your number."

I nearly groaned. Typical.

"Good to know," I said. I wondered how often Adrian gave my number out. "Thanks for following up."

"Happy to. Oh!" She giggled. "I nearly forgot. Your friend is back."

I froze. "What?"

"Veronica. She checked back in yesterday."

219

My first reaction was excitement. My second one was panic. "Did you tell her we were asking about her?"

"Oh, no. I remembered you saying you wanted to surprise her."

I nearly sank in relief. "Thank you. We, uh, wouldn't to ruin that. We'll have to stop by and visit—but don't tell her."

"You can count on me!"

We disconnected, and I stared at the phone. Veronica was back. Just when we thought we'd lost all leads on her. I immediately called Ms. Terwilliger but was sent to voice mail. I left a message and then followed up with a text, saying I had urgent news. My phone rang again, just as I was about to call Adrian. I almost hoped Alicia had more to tell me, but then I saw that it was Stanton's number. After first taking a deep breath, I tried to answer in as calm a way as possible.

"Miss Sage," she said. "I received your message yesterday."

"Yes, ma'am. Thank you for calling me back."

I'd called her yesterday, just before meeting up with Adrian. Ms. Terwilliger's magical training had taken priority at the time, but I hadn't forgotten my deal with Marcus.

"I have a, um, favor to ask," I continued.

Stanton, who was rarely surprised, was clearly surprised now. "You're certainly entitled to ask . . . but you're just not usually the type who does."

"I know, and I feel bad. So, if you have to say no, I understand." In truth, if she said no, I would have a number of problems on my hands, but it was best not to sound too eager. "Well, I've been thinking about how I have to spend Christmas here—with the Moroi. And I definitely understand that, ma'am. It's part of the mission, but . . . well, I'd be lying if I said that didn't bother me. So, I was wondering if there's any way at all I'd be allowed to go to one of the big holiday services. It would make me feel . . . oh, I don't know. More connected. Purified, even. I'm just always surrounded by them here, by that taint, you know? I feel like I can't even breathe half the time. That probably sounds ridiculous."

I cut my rambling off. When Marcus had first suggested taking advantage of knowing someone in St. Louis, I'd immediately thought of Ian. Then I realized that wasn't enough. Alchemists on assignment couldn't just ask for casual time off to visit friends. Time off for something more spiritual and group-oriented—say, the Alchemists' annual holiday services—was a different matter. Lots of Alchemists were given clearance to travel and attend those services. They were tied to our faith and group unity. In fact, Ian had even brought it up at the wedding in the hopes of luring me to visit him. Little had he known his trick would pay off. Kind of.

"It doesn't sound that ridiculous," Stanton said. That was promising, and I tried to unclench my fist and relax.

"I was thinking maybe I could go before we're out for winter break," I added. "Jill can stay within the confines of the school, so there shouldn't be too much risk. And Eddie and Angeline are always with her. I could just hop over to St. Louis for a quick weekend trip."

"St. Louis?" I could almost see her frown through the phone. "There are services in Phoenix as well. That would be much closer."

"I know, ma'am. It's just. . . ." I hoped being genuinely nervous would help me sound convincing. "I, uh, was hoping I could also see Ian again."

"Ah. I see." There was a long pause. "I find that more sur-prising than you wanting to attend services. From what I saw at the wedding, you didn't seem to be that charmed by Mr. Jansen."

So. I'd been right that Stanton had noticed his crush on me. However, she'd also noticed I didn't return his affection. She was observant, even to little details, which brought Marcus's warnings back to me, about how the Alchemists paid attention to everything we did. I started to understand his fears and why he pulled his recruits out of the Alchemists so quickly. Was I already attracting attention? Were all the little things I did—even asking for this—slowly building a case against me?

Again, I hoped my anxiety simply made me sound like a flustered, love-struck girl, one Stanton would feel sorry for and shake her head over. St. Louis wasn't that much farther away by plane, and the end result was the same. "Well, that was busi-ness, ma'am. I didn't want to get distracted from our goal."

"Of course." Her next pause was only a few seconds long, but it felt like an hour. "Well, I see no reason why you can't go. You've done an admirable job in your work, and—from a personal point of view—I can understand why you'd want to be with familiar faces again. You've spent more time with the Moroi than many Alchemists ever will in their lives, and you didn't hesitate when that Ivashkov pushed himself onto you at the wedding."

I didn't really hesitate when he pushed himself onto me at the sorority, either. Or did I push myself on him?

"Thank you, ma'am."

She authorized me to go next weekend and said I could use Alchemist funds to book my travel arrangements. When we got off the phone, I contemplated calling Ian but then decided on a more impersonal approach. I jotted out a quick email telling him that I'd be in town and that I hoped we could meet up. After a few moments of thought, I then texted Marcus: *Arrangements made.*

Lunchtime came around, and Eddie texted to ask if I could meet Jill and him in my dorm's cafeteria. I headed downstairs at the appropriate time and found a glum Eddie sitting by himself at a table. I wondered where Angeline was and noted he hadn't mentioned her in his text. Rather than bring that up, I focused on who he had mentioned.

"Where's Jill?"

He nodded toward the opposite side of the cafeteria. I followed his gaze and saw Jill standing near a table, laughing and talking. She held a tray and looked as though she'd been stopped on her way back from the food line. Micah and some other guys were at the table, and I was happy to see he did indeed seem comfortable with being her friend again.

"That's nice," I said, turning back to my own food. "I'm glad she's getting along with everyone."

Eddie stared at me in amazement. "Don't you see what's going on?"

I'd been about to bite into an apple and stopped. I hated these kinds of loaded questions. They meant I'd missed out on some social subtlety—something that wasn't my strong suit. Glancing back at Jill, I tried to make my best guess.

"Is Micah trying to get back together with her?"

"Of course not," said Eddie, like I should've known. "He's going out with Claire Cipriano now."

"Sorry. I can't keep track of everyone's dating lives. I'll add it to my to-do list after, you know, busting Alchemist conspiracies and finding out whether the Warriors are after Jill."

Eddie's gaze was locked on Jill, and he nodded, making me think he hadn't actually heard a word I'd said. "Travis and Juan want to ask her out."

"So? She learned her lesson about human and vampire dating." I wished I had. "She'll tell them no."

"They still shouldn't be bothering her," he growled.

Jill didn't seem to be particularly bothered by their attention. In fact, I liked seeing her bright and smiling for a change. Confidence suited her and emphasized her royal status, and she clearly was enjoying whatever banter was going on. One thing I'd learned in my social education was that flirting wasn't the same thing as going out with someone. My friend Julia was an expert at the difference. If it made Jill happy, I certainly had no problems with it.

Honestly, it looked like the person who was most bothered by Jill's suitors was Eddie. He theoretically had the excuse of wanting to protect her, but this seemed pretty personal. I decided to bring him back to his own romantic life, the one he should actually be concerned about.

"Where's Angeline?"

Jill began walking toward us. Looking relieved, Eddie turned back to me. "Well, that's what we wanted to talk to you about."

Whenever anyone wanted to talk to me, it meant something weird was about to happen. Actual emergency issues were never given an introduction. They were just delivered immediately. This premeditated stuff was a wild card.

"What's going on?" I asked once Jill sat down. "With Angeline?"

She exchanged a knowing glance with Eddie. "We think Angeline's up to something," she said. A moment later, she clarified, "Something bad."

Not this again. I turned to Eddie. "Is she still being distant?"

"Yeah. She had lunch with us yesterday." He frowned. "But she was acting weird. She wouldn't explain why she's been so busy."

Jill concurred. "She actually got really upset the more we kept questioning her. It was strange. I think she's in some kind of trouble."

I leaned back in my chair. "The kind of trouble Angeline gets into is usually spontaneous and unexpected. You're talking like she's masterminding something in secret. That's not her style. At worst, she's harboring an illicit wardrobe."

Eddie looked like he wanted to smile but couldn't quite manage it. "True."

Jill apparently wasn't convinced. "You have to talk to her. Find out what's going on."

"Can't *you* talk to her?" I asked, looking between their faces. "You live with her."

"We tried," protested Jill. "I told you. She just got mad the more we talked."

"Well, I can understand that," I snapped. "Look, I'm sorry something weird is going on with her. And I don't want her in trouble, believe me. But there's only so much hand-holding I can do with her. I fixed her math problem. My job is to make sure she stays in school and doesn't blow your cover. Everything else is extraneous, and I just don't have time for that. And if she wouldn't talk to you, why on earth do you think she'd talk to me?"

I'd spoken a bit more harshly than I intended. I really did care about them all. I also didn't want trouble in the group. Nonetheless, it was always a little frustrating when they came to me with dramas like this, as though I were their mother. They were some of the smartest, most competent people I knew. They didn't need me, and Angeline was no criminal genius. Figuring out her motives couldn't be that difficult.

Neither one of them had an immediate response for me. "You just always seem to get through to people," Jill said at last. "You're good at communication."

That certainly wasn't a compliment I heard very often. "I don't do anything special. I'm just persistent. Keep trying, and maybe you'll get through." Seeing Jill start to protest, I added, "Please. Don't ask me to do this right now. You both know I've got a lot going on."

I gave each of them a meaningful look. Both knew about Marcus, and Jill also knew about Ms. Terwilliger's sister. After a few moments, that knowledge set in, and they both looked a little embarrassed.

Eddie gave Jill a gentle nudge. "She's right. We should keep working on Angeline ourselves."

"Okay," said Jill. My relief was short-lived. "We'll try a little more. Then, if it still doesn't work, Sydney can step in."

I groaned.

When I parted ways from them later, I couldn't help but think again about Marcus's comments in San Bernardino about how Alchemists got caught up in menial tasks. I tried to reassure myself that Jill and Eddie would take care of this on their own, meaning I wouldn't actually have to intervene. Presuming, of course, Angeline really wasn't planning something catastrophic.

Unfortunately, those doubts were soon shaken when I got on the shuttle that would take me to main campus. On weekends, there was only one bus that looped between all buildings, and this one had just picked up at the boys' dorm. I found Trey sitting in it, staring out the window with a happy expression. When he saw me, his smile vanished.

"Hey," I said, taking a seat beside him. He actually looked nervous. "Off to study?"

"Meeting with Angeline, actually."

There was no escaping her today, but at least if she was working on math, it seemed unlikely she'd be staging a coup or committing arson. His troubled expression concerned me, though.

"She . . . she didn't hit you again?" I didn't see any noticeable marks, but with her, you could never tell.

"Huh? No, no. Not recently." He hesitated before speaking again. "Melbourne, how long are you going to need me to do this?"

"I don't know." Mostly I'd been focusing on getting her through the present, not the future. One thing at a time. "She'll have her final coming up before break. If she passes, then I guess you're home free. Unless you want to keep up with it after break—I mean, provided she doesn't wear you out."

This startled him a lot more than I would have expected. "Okay. Good to know."

He looked so forlorn when he left to go to the library that I wondered if those chemistry answers had really been worth it. I liked Trey. I'd never thought inflicting Angeline on him would so radically alter his life. I guessed that was just the kind of effect she had on the world.

227

I watched him walk away for a few more seconds and then turned toward the science building. One of the teachers, Ms. Whittaker, was an amateur botanist who was always happy to supply Ms. Terwilliger with various plants and herbs. She thought Ms. Terwilliger used them for home craft projects, like potpourri and candles, and I frequently had to pick up the latest supplies. When I walked into her classroom today, Ms. Whittaker was grading exams at her desk.

"Hi, Sydney," she said, barely looking up. "I set it all over there, on the far counter."

"Thanks, ma'am."

I walked over and was surprised to practically find a spice cabinet. Ms. Terwilliger had requested all sorts of leaves, stems, and clippings. It was the most I'd ever had to pick up for her.

"She sure had a big order this time," Ms. Whittaker remarked, as though sensing my thoughts. "Is she really using garlic in potpourri?"

"Oh, that's for some, um, cooking she's doing. You know, holidays and all."

She nodded and returned to her work. One thing that often helped in Alchemist affairs (and witch ones) was that people rarely expected supernatural reasons for weird behaviors and phenomena.

I almost considered visiting Trey and Angeline at the library, just to assess her behavior myself, but decided it'd be better to not get involved. Eddie and Jill would handle it. With nothing else to do, I dared to hope I might actually just be able to stay inside and read today. But, when I returned to my dorm, I was greeted with the astonishing sight of Marcus sitting outside on a bench, playing an acoustic guitar. A group of four girls stood around, listening in awe. I walked up to the circle, my arms crossed over my chest.

"Really?" I asked.

Marcus glanced up and shot me a grin. One of the girls actually cooed.

"Hey, Sydney."

Four sets of eyes turned to me, displaying a mix of both disbelief and jealousy. "Hey," I said. "You're the last person I expected to see here."

"I never do what's predictable." He tossed his hair back and started to put his guitar back in its case. "Sorry, girls. Sydney and I have to talk."

I got more of those stares, which kind of annoyed me. Was it really that unbelievable that a good-looking guy would want to talk to me? His followers dispersed reluctantly, and Marcus and I strolled around the grounds.

"Aren't you supposed to be in hiding?" I asked. "Not panhandling with your guitar?"

"I never asked them for money. Besides, I'm incognito today." He tapped his cheek, and I noticed the tattoo was barely noticeable.

"Are you wearing makeup?" I asked.

"Don't judge," he said. "It lets me move around more freely. Sabrina helped color match me."

We came to a halt in a relatively private copse of trees. "So why are you here? Why didn't you call or text?"

"Because I have a delivery." He reached into his shirt pocket and handed me a folded piece of paper that looked like it had traveled around the world before reaching me. When I opened it and managed to smooth it out, I saw several painstakingly drawn diagrams. I jerked my gaze back to him.

"Wade's floor plans."

"As promised." A little of that self-satisfaction faded, and he actually looked impressed. "You've really got a way to get to St. Louis?"

"Sanctioned and everything," I said. "I mean, aside from the part where I break into their servers. But I've got a few ideas on how to pull that off."

He laughed. "Of course you do. I won't bother asking. Every girl's got her secrets. Maybe someday you'll share yours." From the tone of his voice, he might have been talking about non-professional secrets. "Once this is all over."

"Is it ever over?" I asked. I meant it as a joke, but it came out sounding a bit more melancholy than I would've liked.

He gave me a long, level look. "No, not really. But getting the tattoo sealed in Mexico is kind of fun. I hope you'll go with us. At the very least, we can take in some beaches and margaritas while undoing insidious magic. Do you own a bikini?"

"No. And I don't drink."

"Well, maybe one of these days we could go out for coffee. I know you drink that."

"I'm pretty busy," I said, thinking of everything weighing on me. "And you know, I also haven't decided if I'm going to do the first phase of tattoo breaking."

"You should, Sydney." He was all business again and tapped my cheek. "If nothing else, do that. Don't let them have any more control over you than they have to. I know you think we're a little out there, but this is one thing we're absolutely serious about."

"Hi, Sydney."

I glanced over and saw my friend Julia Cavendish carrying a huge stack of books. A couple seconds later, Marcus looked up at her too. Her eyes went wide, and she stumbled and dropped everything she was carrying. She flushed.

"Oh, God. I'm such an idiot."

I started to help her, but Marcus was by her side in a flash, his movie star grin firmly in place. "Happens to the best of us. I'm Dave."

"J-Julia," she said. In all the time I'd known her, I'd never seen her flustered around a guy. She usually ate them for breakfast.

"There we are." He handed her the books, all neatly stacked.

"Thank you. Thank you so much. You didn't have to do that. I mean, it was my own fault. I'm not usually that clumsy. And I'm sure you're busy. You must have lots to do. Obviously." I'd also never heard Julia ramble.

Marcus patted her on the back, and I thought she might pass out. "Always happy to help a beautiful damsel in distress." He nodded in my direction. "I've got to go. Sydney, I'll be in touch."

I nodded back. As soon as he walked away, Julia dropped the books again and hurried over to me. "Sydney, you have to tell me who that is."

"He already did. Dave."

"Yes, but *who is he*?" She gripped my arm and seemed on the verge of shaking answers out of me.

"Just a guy I know." I thought about it more. "A friend, I guess."

Her breath caught. "You guys aren't—I mean—"

"What? No! Why would you think that?"

"Well, he's gorgeous," she said, as though that were enough

to make us soul mates. "Don't you want to just rip his clothes off?"

"Whoa, no way."

"Really?" She scrutinized me, like I might be joking. "Not even a little?"

"Nope."

She stepped back and started picking up her books. "Jeez, Syd. I don't know what to think of you sometimes. I mean, I'm glad he's available—he is available, right?—but I'd be all over that if I were you."

Jill's words came back to me, about how he was human and had "that rebel Alchemist" thing going for him. Maybe I should start considering him or another ex-Alchemist as a romantic option. Having someone who wasn't a forbidden vampire in my life would make things a lot easier. I tried to dredge up the same reaction other girls had around Marcus, but nothing happened. No matter how hard I tried, I just didn't have that same attraction. His hair was too blond, I decided. And his eyes needed a little more green.

"Sorry," I told Julia. "Just not feeling it."

"If you say so. I still think you're crazy. That's the kind of guy you'd follow to hell and back."

All romantic musings disappeared, and I felt a sinking feeling in my stomach as we slowly headed back toward the dorm. Hell was a good analogy for what I would be walking into. "You actually might be closer to the truth on that than you realize."

She brightened. "See? I knew you couldn't resist."

CHAPTER 15

MS. TERWILLIGER WAS WAITING in the lobby when Julia and I returned to the dorm. "Seriously. Do you have a tracking device on me?" I asked. Julia took one look at our teacher's serious expression and quickly made an exit.

"Just excellent timing," Ms. Terwilliger replied. "I understand you have news."

"Surprisingly, yes."

Ms. Terwilliger's face was hard as she led me back outside to more privacy and yet another top secret outdoor meeting. These days, she hardly resembled the scattered, hippie teacher I'd met when I first started at Amberwood. "Tell me the news," she ordered.

I told her about Alicia's call, and her dismayed expression didn't really inspire me. I'd kind of hoped she'd reveal some amazing, foolproof plan she'd secretly been concocting.

"Well, then," she said once I'd finished. "I suppose I'll have to go out there."

"*I'll* go out there," I corrected.

She favored me with a small smile. "You've done more than enough. It's time I step up and deal with Veronica."

"But you sent me to that place before."

"When we weren't even sure where it was or what she was doing there. This time, we have an eyewitness confirming she's there right now. I can't waste this opportunity." She glanced at a clock near the door and sighed. "I'd go tonight if I could but haven't made the necessary preparations. I'll start working on them now and go in tomorrow evening. Hopefully I won't miss her again."

"No." The defiance in my voice surprised even me. I didn't contradict teachers—or any kind of authority—very often. Okay, never. "She eluded us before. Let us scout it out. You don't want to tip your hand yet, just in case something goes wrong. You'll be ready tomorrow night? Then let us go in the day . . . I mean, provided someone could get me out of school. . . ."

A little of that tension faded, and she laughed. "I suppose I could do that. I hate that I keep putting you in danger, though."

"We passed that point a long time ago."

She couldn't argue against that logic. I made arrangements for Adrian to pick me up the next day—after first scolding "Jet" for giving out "Taylor's" number. When morning came, Ms. Terwilliger was true to her word. I'd been excused from classes for a "research trip." The thing about being a star pupil was that none of my teachers had any problems with me skipping classes. They knew I'd get the work done. I probably could've taken the rest of the semester off.

During the drive, I told Adrian that I'd managed to score a trip to St. Louis in order to pursue Marcus's daunting task.

Adrian's expression grew darker and darker, but he stayed silent on the matter. I knew what a conflict it was for him. He didn't like Marcus. He didn't like me taking on this potentially dangerous mission. However, he also trusted me to make my own decisions. Contradicting me or telling me what to do wasn't in his nature—even though he secretly may have wanted to. His only comment was one of support.

"Be careful, Sage. For God's sake, be careful. I've seen you pull off some crazy shit, but this is extreme, even for you. You're probably the only one who can manage this, but still . . . don't let your guard down, even for a moment."

When I told him about how I was hoping to use Ian to get more in-depth access, Adrian's troubled look turned to one of incredulity.

"Hold on here. Let me make sure I'm following this. You're going to seduce some guy to help you with your espionage."

Seduce Ian? Ugh. "Don't jump to conclusions," I warned. "I'm just going to try to use his feelings for me to get what I want."

"Wow. Cold, Sage. Very cold."

"Hey, now." I felt a little indignant at the accusation. "I'm not going to promise to marry him or something and then dump him later. He wrote me about going to dinner when I'm there. We'll have a nice time, and I'll try to talk him into letting me tour the facility. That's it."

"And 'talking him into it' doesn't involve putting out?"

I glared at him and hoped he could see me in his periphery. "Adrian. Do I really seem like the kind of person who'd do that?"

"Well—" He stopped, and I suspected he'd held back from

RICHELLE MEAD

some snarky comment. "No, I suppose not. Certainly not with a guy like him. Did you get a dress?"

Here we were again, Adrian randomly jumping topics. "For dinner and the service? I've got plenty."

"I guess that answers my question." He seemed to wage a great mental battle. At last, he said, "I'm going to give you some advice."

"Oh no."

He looked over at me again. "Who knows more about male weakness: you or me?"

"Go on." I refused to directly answer the question.

"Get a new dress. One that shows a lot of skin. Short. Strapless. Maybe a push-up bra too." He actually had the audacity to do a quick assessment of my chest. "Eh, maybe not. But definitely some high heels."

"Adrian," I exclaimed. "You've seen how Alchemists dress. Do you think I can really wear something like that into a church service?"

He was unconcerned. "You'll make it work. You'll change clothes or something. But I'm telling you, if you want to get a guy to do something that might be difficult, then the best way is to distract him so that he can't devote his full brainpower to the consequences."

"You don't have a lot of faith in your own gender."

"Hey, I'm telling you the truth. I've been distracted by sexy dresses a lot."

I didn't really know if that was a valid argument, seeing as Adrian was distracted by a lot of things. Fondue. T-shirts. Kittens. "And so, what then? I show some skin, and the world is mine?"

"That'll help." Amazingly, I could tell he was dead serious.

"And you've gotta act confident the whole time, like it's already a done deal. Then make sure when you're actually asking for what you want that you tell him you'd be 'so, so grateful.' But don't elaborate. His imagination will do half the work for you. "

I shook my head, glad we'd almost reached our destination. I didn't know how much more I could listen to. "This is the most ridiculous advice I've ever heard. It's also kind of sexist too, but I can't decide who it offends more, men or women."

"Look, Sage. I don't know much about chemistry or computer hacking or photosynthery, but this is something I've got a lot of experience with." I think he meant *photosynthesis*, but I didn't correct him. "Use my knowledge. Don't let it go to waste."

He seemed so earnest that I finally told him I'd consider it, though I had a hard time imagining myself wearing anything like he'd described. My answer satisfied him, and he said no more.

When we reached the bed-and-breakfast, I put on the brown wig so that we could be Taylor and Jet again. I braced myself as we approached the door.

"Who knows what we're walking into?" I murmured. I'd been very brave while speaking to Ms. Terwilliger, but the reality that I might be going right up to an evil sorceress was sinking in. I had yet to develop the ability to sense magic in others, so I could very well be taken by surprise if she had a way to hide her appearance too. All I could do was have faith that Adrian's spirit and Ms. Terwilliger's charm would mask me. If Veronica was there, we'd just seem like an ordinary couple. I hoped.

Alicia was reading another magazine when we walked in. She still sported the same hipster glasses and clutter of gaudy necklaces. Her face lit up when she saw us. "You're back."

Adrian's arm immediately went around me. "Well, when we heard Veronica was in town again, we wanted to come see her right away. Right, honeydew?"

"Right," I said. At least he was going with healthier nicknames today.

"Oh." Alicia's sunny smile dimmed a little. "She just left."

"You have got to be kidding," I said. How could our luck be this bad? "So, she checked out?"

"No, she's still renting out the Velvet Suite. I think she was just running errands. But. . . ." She turned sheepish. "I may have, uh, ruined the surprise."

"Oh?" I asked very carefully. I felt Adrian's hold on me tense, but there was nothing romantic about it.

"I couldn't resist. I told her she might have some unexpected visitors soon. Good visitors," she added. "I wanted to make sure she didn't stay out too long."

"That's very nice of you," said Adrian. His smile looked as strained as mine felt. In trying to "help" us, Alicia might very well have ruined everything.

What did we do now? I was saved from an immediate decision when a middle-aged woman walked through the door.

"Hello," she told Alicia. "I wanted to get some information about hosting a wedding here. For my niece."

"Of course," said Alicia, glancing back and forth between all of us. She looked a little flustered over who to help, and I was quick to jump in.

"Hey," I said. "Since we're here, can we look at the Bunny Suite again? We can't stop talking about it."

Alicia frowned. "I thought you were going to the coast for your anniversary?"

"We were," said Adrian, following my lead. "But then Taylor was thinking about Cottontail the other night, and we thought we should reconsider." I had to give him credit for jumping in and going along with the story I was making up on the spot. Of course, you'd think he'd remember the name of the fake rabbit *he* had created.

"Hopper," I corrected.

"Is the Bunny Suite still vacant?" he asked. "We can just take a quick peek in while you help her."

Alicia hesitated only a moment before handing over a key. "Sure. Let me know if you have any questions."

I took the key and headed toward the stairs with Adrian. Behind us, I could hear the woman asking if it'd be okay to set up a tent in the backyard and how many hot plates the inn could hold before it became a fire hazard. Once we were on the second floor and out of earshot, Adrian spoke. "Let me guess. You want to go prowl through the Velvet Suite."

I rewarded him with a grin, pleased that he'd guessed my plan. "Yup. Pretty good idea, huh? Hopefully Alicia will be distracted for a while."

"I could have just compelled her," he reminded me.

"You're using too much spirit already."

I found the Velvet Suite and put the key in the lock, hoping Alicia had given us the master key and not one specifically for the Bunny Suite. When she had shown us around last time, she'd only used one key. A click told me we'd lucked out and wouldn't have to use any metal-burning chemicals today.

We'd seen the Velvet Suite during our last visit, and for the most part, it looked the same. Velvet bedding, velvet-covered furniture, and even velvet-textured wallpaper. Only, this time, the room wasn't in the pristine and unoccupied state as before. Signs around the room showed recent use. The bed was unmade, and the scent of shampoo from the bathroom indicated a shower not too long ago.

"Alicia might have been wrong about Veronica checking out," said Adrian. He opened drawer after drawer and found nothing. In the closet, he discovered high-heeled shoes tucked into a corner and a belt on a hanger—things that might be easily missed with frantic packing. "Someone left here in a hurry."

My hopes plummeted. In accidentally revealing our "surprise," Alicia had apparently scared Veronica into skipping out on the room. We found no sign that Veronica would actually return, and as Adrian had said, she seemed to have taken off quickly, based on the kinds of easy-to-forget things that were left behind: a razor in the shower, a bottle of perfume on the bathroom counter, and a stack of takeout menus on the nightstand.

I sat on the bed and sifted through the menus, not really convinced they'd tell me much. Chinese, Indian, Mexican. Veronica had diverse tastes, at least. I reached the bottom of the stack and threw them on the ground.

"She left," I said. I couldn't hide from the truth any longer. "That idiot Alicia tipped her off, and now we've lost her again."

Adrian sat down beside me, his face mirroring my dismay. "We'll find her. We've slowed her down by hiding the others. Maybe it'll buy us time until the next full moon so you can scry again."

"I hope so," I said, though I wasn't optimistic.

He brushed aside the wig's hair and turned my face toward him. "Everything's going to be okay. She doesn't know about you."

I knew he was right, but it was hollow comfort. I leaned my head against his shoulder, wishing I could fix everything. That was my job, right? "All that means is that someone else could suffer in my place. I don't want that. I need to stop her once and for all."

"So brave." He gave me a small smile. His fingertips slid down from my face, lightly stroking the line of my neck, down toward my shoulder. Everywhere he touched, a trail of goose bumps appeared. How did he keep doing this to me? Marcus— who made every girl in the world swoon—had zero effect on me. But one whisper of a touch from Adrian completely undid me. "You could give Castile a run for his money," he added.

"Stop that," I warned.

"Comparing you to Castile?"

"That's not what I'm talking about, and you know it." His hands were too dangerous, as was being with him on a bed. Terrified I might be kissed again, I jerked away, and the sudden movement caught him by surprise. His fingers got tangled in my hair, as well as in my two necklaces, which resulted in him snapping both chains and nearly pulling off the brown wig. I quickly caught the garnet before it could fall off, but the cross slipped away. Thank God I'd kept the important one on. "No more kissing," I warned. I refastened the charm and straightened the wig.

"You mean no more kissing unless it's a romantic place," he reminded me. "Are you saying this place doesn't scream romance?" He nodded around to our tacky velvet surroundings. He then picked up the small cross and held it in the air, growing thoughtful as he studied the way the light played off the gold surface. "You gave this to me once."

"And you gave it back."

"I was angry."

"And now?"

He shrugged. "Now I'm just determined."

"Adrian." I sighed. "Why do you keep doing this? The touching . . . the kissing . . . you know I don't want it."

"You don't act that way."

"Stop saying that. It's obnoxious. Next you'll be saying I'm 'asking for it.'" Why did he have to be so infuriating? Okay . . . I hadn't really sent a clear message back at the sorority. Or Pies and Stuff. But this time I'd done better. "I just pulled away. How much more direct do I have to be?"

"It's not your actions, exactly," he said. He still clutched the cross in his hand. "It's your aura."

I groaned. "No, no, not that. I don't want to hear about auras."

"But I'm serious." He shifted over and stretched out on the bed, lying on his side. He patted the bed near him. "Lie down."

"Adrian—"

"I won't kiss you," he said. "I promise."

"How stupid do you think I am?" I said. "I'm not falling for this."

He gave me a long, level look. "Do you really think I'd assault you or something?"

"No," I said quickly. "Of course not."

"Then humor me."

Warily, I lay down on my side as well, facing him with only a few powerful inches between us. An enraptured, slightly distracted look appeared in his eyes. He'd given himself over to spirit. "Do you know what I see in you now? The usual aura. A steady golden yellow, healthy and strong, with spikes of purple here and there. But when I do this. . . ."

He rested a hand on my hip, and my whole body tensed up. That hand moved around my hip, slipping under my shirt to rest on the small of my back. My skin burned where he touched me, and the places that were untouched longed for that heat.

"See?" he said. He was in the throes of spirit now, though with me at the same time. "Well, I guess you can't. But when I touch you, your aura . . . it *smolders*. The colors deepen, it burns more intensely, the purple increases. Why? Why, Sydney?" He used that hand on me to pull me closer. "Why do you react that way if I don't mean anything to you?" There was a desperation in his voice, and it was legitimate.

It was hard for me to talk. "It's instinct. Or something. You're a Moroi. I'm an Alchemist. Of course I'd have a response. You think I'd be indifferent?"

"Most Alchemist responses would involve disgust, revulsion, and holy water."

That was an excellent point. "Well . . . I'm a little more relaxed around Moroi than most Alchemists. Probably this is just some purely physical response driven by hormones and years of evolution. My body doesn't know any better. I'm as susceptible to lust as anyone else." There was probably a book about that or at least an article in *Cosmopolitan*.

The hint of a smile played over his lips. He was fully in tune with me again. "No, you aren't. I mean, you are, but not without reason. I know you well enough to realize that now. You're not the kind of person who's 'susceptible to lust' without some emotion to back it." He moved his hand back to my hip, sliding it down my leg. I shuddered, and his face moved closer to mine. There was so much in his eyes, so much desire and longing. "See? There it is again. My flame in the dark."

"Don't kiss me," I whispered. It was the only defense I could muster. If he kissed me, I'd be lost. I closed my eyes. "You said you wouldn't."

"I won't." His lips were only a breath away. "Unless you want me to."

I opened my eyes, ready to tell him no, that it didn't matter what my aura allegedly said . . . this couldn't keep happening. There was no emotion backing this desire, and I tried to cling to my earlier argument. I was so comfortable around Moroi now that clearly some primal part of me kept forgetting what he was. This was a base instinct. I was simply having a physical reaction to him, to his hands, to his lips, to his body. . . .

He caught hold of my arm and rolled me over. I closed my eyes again and wrapped my arms around his neck. I felt his lips touch mine, not quite a kiss, just the barest brush of—

The door opened, and I flinched. Alicia stepped inside, gasped, and put a hand up over her mouth to cover a shocked squeal. "O-oh," she stammered. "I'm so sorry . . . I . . . I didn't realize . . ."

Adrian and I jerked away and sat up. My heart was ready to beat out of my chest, and I knew I was blushing. I quickly patted my wig and was relieved to feel it was still in place. He recovered his voice more quickly.

"Sorry . . . we kind of got carried away. We started checking out the other rooms and decided to, uh, try them out." Despite his sheepish words, there was a smug look on his face, the kind you'd expect from a guy who'd just made a conquest. Was it part of the act, or did he really think he'd gotten away with something?

Alicia looked as uncomfortable as I felt. "I see. Well, this room's occupied. It's—" She frowned and did a double take. "It's Veronica's. It looks like she left."

I finally managed to speak. "That's why we thought it was empty," I said hastily. "There was nothing in here."

Alicia thankfully seemed to have forgotten about our compromising position. "That's weird. She didn't formally check out. I mean, she paid in advance in cash, but still. It's so strange."

We made a hurried escape of our own after that, once again feeding Alicia lines about how we'd be in touch. Neither of us spoke much when we got in the car. I was lost in my own thoughts, which were equal parts frustration over Veronica and confusion over Adrian. I refused to acknowledge the latter, though, and opted for my usual tactic. The sooner that moment was forgotten, the better. I was pretty sure I could keep telling myself that. Some part of me—nearly as snarky as Adrian—suggested I pick up a book on denial the next time I was in the self-help section.

"Another dead end," I said once we were on the road. I texted Ms. Terwilliger: *V's gone. No need for action.* Her response came a few minutes later: *We'll keep trying.* I could practically feel her disappointment through the display on my phone. She wasn't the only one. Adrian seemed particularly melancholy on the drive back. He responded whenever I spoke, but it was clear he was distracted.

When he dropped me off at Amberwood later that night, I found everything mercifully quiet. No crises, no dangerous missions. It felt like it had been ages since I had a moment to myself, and I curled up on my bed, taking solace in the ordinary tasks of homework and reading. I fell asleep with my face on my calculus book.

I experienced one of those nonsensical dreams that everyone has. In it, my family's cat could talk, and he was driving Adrian's Mustang. He asked me if I wanted to take a road trip to Birmingham. I told him I had a lot of homework to do but that if he wanted to go to Fargo, I'd consider it.

We were in the middle of negotiating who'd pay for gas when the dream suddenly dissolved to blackness. A cold feeling swept over me, followed by a feeling of dread that rivaled the time Adrian and I had faced down Strigoi in his apartment. A woman's laughter rolled around me, foul and sickening, like some sort of toxic smoke. A voice came out of the darkness, echoing in my mind.

She's kept you well hidden, but it can't stay that way forever. You can't conceal power like yours forever. I've caught your trail. I'll find you.

Hands suddenly reached out of the darkness for me, wrapping around my throat and cutting off my air. I screamed and woke up in my own bed, surrounded in books. I'd left the light on, and it chased some of the dream's terror away. But only some. Sweat poured off me, making my shirt stick to me. I touched my neck, but there was nothing wrong with it. The garnet hung in place but not my cross.

No need to fear a dream, I thought. It didn't mean anything, and really, with everything going on lately, it was a wonder I didn't have nightmares more often. But thinking back on it, I wasn't so sure. There had been something so terrible and real about it, a horror that seemed to reach into my very soul.

I didn't want to sleep after that, so I made a cup of coffee and tried to read again. It worked for a while, but somewhere around four, my body couldn't take it anymore. I fell asleep on my books again, but this time, my sleep stayed dream free.

CHAPTER 16

I GAVE MS. TERWILLIGER a full report on our trip to the inn the next morning. We met at Spencer's, and in a rare show of early rising, Adrian joined us. "I've got a study group meeting soon," he explained. His mood was a lot better, with no mention of yesterday's . . . indiscretion.

Even though there wasn't much to tell, lines of worry creased her face as she heard our story. The true panic came when I mentioned my dream. Ms. Terwilliger's eyes went wide, and she gripped her coffee cup so tightly, I thought it would break.

"She found out," she murmured. "Whether it was that Alicia girl or some other way, Veronica found out about you. I should never have sent you. I thought you'd slip underneath her radar if the other girls were charmed, but I was wrong. I was selfish and naive. It would've been better if she knew I was on to her from the very beginning. You're sure you were masking Sydney's appearance?" That was to Adrian.

"Positive," he said. "Everyone we talked to, all the girls and even Alicia . . . none of them would have a clear idea of what Sydney looks like."

"Maybe she's been spying on you," I suggested. "And saw us together. I haven't been in disguise around here."

"Maybe," Ms. Terwilliger conceded. "But we also know she was active in Los Angeles. She would have to spend considerable time stalking her victims, which wouldn't give her the chance to come here and watch me extensively. Even with her powers, she can't teleport." Her expression hardened with resolve. "Well, there's nothing to be done now but damage control. She doesn't seem to know exactly where you are yet or that you're even connected to me. I'll make you another charm to try to boost this one, but it may not work if she's found a way to reach out to you. And in the meantime, don't worry about offense anymore. You need to focus on defense—particularly invisibility spells. Your best protection against Veronica at this point is for her simply not to find you if she comes looking around Palm Springs."

I'd continued reading the advanced offense spells, despite her warnings. With this new development, though, I knew she was right about defense being more important. Still, I couldn't shake the worry that Veronica had discovered me by watching Ms. Terwilliger, which in turn made me fear for my teacher's safety. "You keep saying she's not after you . . . but are you really sure?"

"She'll avoid me if she can," said Ms. Terwilliger, sounding confident. "I have the power but not the youth and beauty she's after. And even she would draw the line at taking on her sister.

It's the only remnant of human decency she has left."

"Will she still have that attitude when you confront her?" asked Adrian.

Ms. Terwilliger shook her head. "No. Then anything goes. I'd like to meet with you tonight to practice a couple other defensive tactics."

I eyed her carefully. "Are you up for that? No offense, ma'am, but you already look exhausted."

"I'll be fine. Meet me at the park again around ten. I'll get Weathers to let you go. We must keep you safe." She stared off into space for several moments and then focused on me again. "In light of this development . . . it wouldn't be a bad idea for you to find some, ah, more basic means of defense as well."

"Basic?" I asked, puzzled.

"She means like a gun or a knife," supplied Adrian, catching on to what I hadn't.

Ms. Terwilliger nodded. "If you ever confront Veronica, it'll most likely come down to magic fighting magic . . . but, well, one can never say. Having something else for backup might prove invaluable."

I wasn't a fan of this idea. "I have no clue how to knife fight. And I don't like guns."

"Do you like being put into a coma and aging before your time?" asked Adrian.

I shot him a glare, surprised he'd be on board with this. "Of course not. But where would we even get one on such short notice?"

From the look on his face, he knew I had a point. Suddenly, he became enthusiastic again. "I think I know."

"I'm sure you two will figure it out," said Ms. Terwilliger, her mind already moving to something else. She glanced at her watch. "Almost time for classes."

We all stood up, preparing to go our own ways, but I held Adrian back. I couldn't imagine how in the world he would know where to get a gun on no notice. He wouldn't elaborate and simply said he'd meet me after school. Before he left, I remembered something I'd wanted to ask.

"Adrian, did you keep my cross?"

"Your—oh." Looking into his eyes, I could practically see yesterday's events playing through his mind—including us rolling around on the bed. "I dropped it when—ah, well, before we left. You didn't pick it up?"

I shook my head, and his face fell.

"Shit, I'm sorry, Sage."

"It's okay," I said automatically.

"It's *not* okay, and it's my fault. I know how much it means to you."

It did mean a lot to me, but I almost blamed myself as much as him. I should've thought of it before we left, but I'd been a little preoccupied. "It's just a necklace," I told him.

This didn't comfort him. He looked so dejected when we parted ways that I hoped he wouldn't forget about us meeting up later to visit his mysterious gun source. There was nothing to worry about, though. When classes ended, he was outside my dorm in the Mustang and looked much more upbeat, with no more mention of the necklace.

When he told me his gun plan, I was shocked, but after a few moments of thought, I realized he might be on to something. And so, a little less than an hour later, we found ourselves far outside the city, driving up to a forlorn-looking home on a large, barren piece of land. We had reached the Wolfe School of Defense.

"I never thought we'd be here again," I remarked.

Wolfe's house had no windows, and there were no cars in sight as we walked up to the door. "He may not even be home," I murmured to Adrian. "We probably should have called first."

"Wolfe never struck me as a guy who leaves the house very much," said Adrian. He knocked on the door, and almost instantly, we heard a flurry of barking and scampering feet. I grimaced. Wolfe, for reasons I would never be able to understand, kept a herd of Chihuahuas in his house. He'd once told us that they could kill a man upon a single command.

We waited a few minutes, but the barking was the only sign that there was any sort of life inside. Adrian knocked one more time (driving the dogs into an even greater frenzy) and then shrugged. "I guess you were—"

The door suddenly opened—just a slit—and one gray eye peered out at us from underneath a chain. "Oh," came a grizzled voice. "It's you two."

The door closed, and I heard the chain being unlocked. A moment later, Wolfe slipped outside, careful not to let any of the dogs out. He had a patch over his left eye, which was probably just as well since his other eye alone seemed to peer straight through me. "You should've called," he said. "I nearly turned the dogs on you."

Wolfe was dressed in his favorite pair of Bermuda shorts as well as a T-shirt showing a bald eagle riding on a monster truck. The eagle held an American flag in one set of talons and a samurai sword in the other. That seemed a weird weapon choice for such a patriotic shirt, but we'd long since learned not to question his wardrobe. That had come after he'd kicked a woman out of our class who'd dared to ask if he only had one pair of shorts or several identical ones.

"What do you kids need?" he asked. "Next classes don't start until after New Year's."

Adrian and I exchanged glances. "We, um, need a gun," I said. "I mean, just to borrow."

Wolfe scratched his beard. "I don't lend them out to students who haven't taken my gun class. Safety first." I found it promising, however, that he lent out guns at all. It was a sign of his character that he didn't even bother asking why we wanted one.

"I've already had training," I said. That was true. It was mandatory for all Alchemists. I'd done well in it, but as I'd mentioned to Adrian, I really didn't like guns at all. At least a knife had other uses. But a gun? It was only there to injure or kill.

Wolfe arched an eyebrow, the one over his good eye. Clearly, he didn't believe me. "Can you back that up?"

"Do you have a shooting range?" I returned coolly.

He almost looked offended. "Of course I do."

He led us to a building beyond the garage we'd trained in. I'd never been inside this building before, but like his house, it had no windows. The door was covered in enough locks to meet with Alchemist security standards. He let us inside, and I gaped when I saw not only a practice range but also a wall covered in various types of guns. Wolfe gave the small holding space a once-over.

"Earmuffs must be in the house. Be right back."

I continued staring at the wall, knowing my eyes were wide.

"There's no way those are all legal."

Adrian's response was unexpected. "Did you notice his eye patch?"

I dragged my gaze from the arsenal. "Um, yes. From the day we first met him."

"No, no. I mean, I swear it was on his other eye last time."

"It was not," I said immediately.

"Are you sure?" asked Adrian.

I wasn't, I realized. Words and numbers were easy for me to memorize. But other details, like clothing or hair—or eye patches—were sometimes easy for me to miss. "That doesn't make any sense," I finally said. "Why would he do that?"

"He's Malachi Wolfe," said Adrian. "Why *wouldn't* he do that?"

I couldn't argue against that.

Wolfe returned with ear protection. After examining his wall, he selected a small handgun and then unlocked a cabinet containing ammunition. At least he didn't leave a bunch of loaded guns around.

"I'll do that," I told him. I took the gun from him and effortlessly loaded it. He made a small grunt of approval. He gestured toward the far end of the range, to a large paper cutout showing a human silhouette with various targets marked on it.

"Now then," he said. "Don't worry about hitting the—"

I fired, perfectly emptying the clip into the most difficult targets. I handed the gun to him. He handed it back. Behind him, I could see Adrian staring at me with enormous eyes.

"Keep it," said Wolfe. "You passed. You've gotta buy your own ammunition, but as long as you fill out the rental agreement, you're good to go."

As it turned out, the "rental agreement" was a piece of paper where he wrote the gun type on one side and I put my initials on the other. "Really?" I asked. "That's all I need to do? I mean, I'm glad, but . . ." I didn't really know what else to say.

Wolfe waved off my protests. "You're a good kid. If you say you need a gun, I believe you. Someone giving you trouble?"

I slipped the gun into my messenger bag. "Something like that."

Wolfe glanced over at Adrian. "What about you? You need a gun too?"

"I'm good," said Adrian. "Besides, I haven't had the training. Safety first."

Wolfe opened up the ammunition cabinet again and produced a long wooden tube and a sandwich bag of what looked like small darts. "You want to borrow my blowgun? Not much of a learning curve on this. I mean, you'll never be able to match the skill and cunning of the Amazonian warriors that I stole this from, but it can get you out of a pinch."

"Thanks, but I'll take my chances," Adrian said after several long moments. He almost sounded as though he'd considered it.

I was still hung up on Wolfe's other words, not sure I believed what I'd heard. "You were in the Amazon?"

This time, Wolfe arched the eyebrow above his eye patch. "You don't believe me?"

"No, no, of course I do," I said quickly. "It's just, you've never mentioned it before."

Wolfe gazed off beyond us. "I've been trying for years to forget my time there. But some things, you just can't escape."

A very long and very uncomfortable silence followed. At

last, I cleared my throat. "Well, thank you, sir. We should get going. Hopefully I won't need the gun for very long."

"Keep it as long as you need," he said. "If I want it back, I'll find you."

And on that disturbing note, Adrian and I left. Although I understood Ms. Terwilliger's reasons for "old-fashioned" defense, I was in no way comfortable having a gun around. I'd have to keep it in my car in case school authorities ever did a search of my room and discovered it. My Alchemist and magical kits were already a liability. I was pretty sure there'd be no talking my way out of a gun.

Adrian returned me to Amberwood. I started to open the door and then paused to glance over at him. "Thanks," I said. "For everything. Going to the inn. Suggesting we see Wolfe."

"Hey, that was worth it just to know Wolfe owns a blowgun."

I laughed. "Actually, I'd be more surprised if he didn't. See you later."

Adrian nodded. "Sooner than you think."

"What's that mean?" I asked, suspicion rearing up in me.

He dodged the question and reached underneath his seat. "I called Alicia," he told me, producing a small box. "She couldn't find your cross. Her housekeeping service had already gone through and cleaned the room, but she says she'll check to see if it got caught up in the bedding. Oh, and I also asked about Veronica. She hasn't been back."

That was disheartening news, but I was touched he'd called. "Thanks for trying."

He opened the box and pulled out a necklace with a tiny wooden cross on it. "I got you a replacement. I mean, I know there's no real substitute, but I wanted to get you something.

And don't start about not being able to accept some fancy gift," he said, guessing the protest I was about to make. "It cost me five dollars from a street vendor, and I'm pretty sure the chain is brass."

I bit off my words and took the necklace from him. The cross barely weighed anything. Studying it more closely, I could see a tiny pattern of silver flowers painted on its surface. "The vendor didn't do that. That's your handiwork."

"Well . . . I know you're into simple stuff, but I've always got to have some embellishment."

I ran my finger over the cross's surface. "Why'd you choose morning glories?"

"Because I'm not the biggest fan of lilies."

I smiled at that.

When I returned to my dorm room, I laid the necklace out on my dresser. I gave it one last fond look and then tried to decide how best to spend the rest of my day. Our trip to Wolfe actually hadn't taken that long, so I had plenty of time to catch dinner and make sure I was up to date on my homework. I actually ate with Kristin and Julia for a change, which was kind of a nice break from the drama of my other friends. Of course, most of the meal consisted of Julia gushing about "Dave." By the end, both she and Kristin were demanding to know when I'd bring him by again.

As the evening pushed on, I began to prepare for my meeting with Ms. Terwilliger. I wasn't sure what kind of magic we'd be practicing outdoors but figured I should be ready for anything. I packed a wide variety of items from my kit and even had the foresight to bring a granola bar for post-magic fuel. Once everything was in order, I headed back downstairs. I was nearly out the dorm door when Mrs. Weathers called out to me.

"Sydney?"

I paused to glance back. "Yes, ma'am?"

"Where are you going? It's nearly curfew."

Frowning, I walked over to her desk. "I'm doing an assignment for Ms. Terwilliger."

Mrs. Weathers looked troubled. "Yes, I know you do that a lot for her . . . but I haven't received authorization from her to let you out after hours today." Her expression turned apologetic. "I'm sure this is all on the up-and-up, but, well, rules are rules."

"Of course," I said. "But she said she'd let you know. Are you sure you didn't get anything? A note? A phone call?"

She shook her head. "Nothing. I'm sorry."

"I understand," I murmured, though I wasn't sure I did. Despite her perpetually scattered nature, Ms. Terwilliger was usually good about this sort of thing. Mrs. Weathers assured me she'd let me go if Ms. Terwilliger gave the okay by phone, so I returned to my room and attempted to call her. I went straight to voice mail, and my text went unanswered. Had something happened to her? Had that magical confrontation I'd been dreading finally gone down?

I kicked around my dorm room for the next hour or so, letting all my worries eat at me. Veronica. Marcus. St. Louis. Ms. Terwilliger. The dream. Over and over, I kept imagining the worst outcome for all of them. Just when I thought I'd go crazy, Ms. Terwilliger finally returned my call.

"Why didn't you show up?" she asked as soon as I answered. I felt relieved. She'd gone to the park. That explained the lack of contact since there was no signal out there.

"I tried! Mrs. Weathers wouldn't let me out. You forgot to give me permission."

"I most certainly didn't. . . ." Her words trailed off uncertainly. "That is, I thought I did. . . ."

"It's okay," I said. "You've had a lot on your mind."

"It's *not* okay." She sounded angry, but it was at herself, not me. "I need to be on top of this."

"Well, you can call Mrs. Weathers now," I said.

"Too late. I'm already back home. We'll have to attempt this again another time."

"I'm sorry," I said. "I tried."

Ms. Terwilliger sighed. "I know you did. It's not your fault. It's mine. I'm letting all of this wear me down, and now I'm getting sloppy. I've already taken too many risks at your expense, and it's put Veronica on your trail. I can't let her get any farther."

A chill ran through me as I thought of those comatose girls—and the possibility of me joining them. I'd been able to stay cool and collected while investigating, but last night's dream had driven home the dangers I faced. That image of the girl in the newspaper hovered in my mind as I held the phone and paced my room. I stopped in front of a mirror and tried to picture myself like that, aged before my time. I squeezed my eyes shut and turned away. I couldn't let that happen to me. I just couldn't, and I needed Ms. Terwilliger if I was going to stay safe. Maybe I was a prodigy, but I was nowhere near being able to take on someone like her sister.

"Get some rest, ma'am," I said at last. "You sound like you need it."

"I'll try. And you be careful, Miss Melbourne."

"I will."

Being careful was the only thing I could do on my own for now. I just hoped it would be enough.

When we got off the phone, I didn't want to sleep again. I was afraid to, and it wasn't just because of the sheer terror I'd felt in last night's dream. Ms. Terwilliger had explained there was a type of searching spell that sought people in their sleep, and I worried that if Veronica reached out to me again, she might get a fix on my location. The problem was that after last night's sketchy sleep, I was now even more exhausted. My usual coffee and distraction tricks failed, and before I knew it, I was asleep.

I don't know how much time passed before I dreamed. One moment I was lost in the oblivion of sleep. The next, I found myself standing in the room that had hosted Sonya and Mikhail's reception. It looked exactly the same: flowers everywhere, tables covered in white linen and crystal glasses . . . The only difference was that the room was empty and silent. It was eerie, seeing all that richness and glamour with no one to enjoy it. I could've been in a ghost town. I looked down and saw that I wore the same dress from that evening as well.

"I could've made it red, you know. That's a better color for you—not that blue looks bad on you."

Adrian strode toward me, dressed in the same dark blue suit. Understanding hit me. I was in a spirit dream. It was another of that element's incredible feats, the ability for a spirit user to intrude on someone's dreams. No—not intrude. The user was actually able to create the dream itself, controlling every detail.

"It's been a long time since you pulled me into one of these," I said.

"And look at the progress you've made. Last time you were kicking and screaming." He held out a hand. "Want to dance?"

"No music," I said, not that I had any intention of dancing. He had a point about my reaction, though. I hadn't exactly been kicking and screaming, but I had kind of freaked out. I'd been in full possession of all my fears about vampires and magic, and being surrounded in a world completely constructed of that magic had left me frightened and unhinged. And now? Now I had apparently become so comfortable that my biggest concern was that he'd put me in this dress. I gestured to it.

"Can you change me out of this?"

"You can change yourself out of it," he said. "I'm letting go of the control. Just picture yourself the way you are in reality."

I did exactly that, and a moment later, I wore jeans and a pale blue knit top. This obviously disappointed him. "That's what you sleep in?"

"No." I laughed. "I was trying not to sleep at all. It didn't work. Why'd you bring me here?"

He strolled around and picked up one of the crystal goblets, nodding in approval as though he were some sort of glassmaking expert. "Exactly that reason. I saw how much that dream bothered you. I figured if I pulled you into one of these, it'd keep you from one of Veronica's."

I'd never thought of that. Vampire magic was certainly preferable to hers. Looking around, I gained a new appreciation for the room. It became a sanctuary, a place where she couldn't reach me. At least, I hoped not. We really didn't know how her magic would work against Adrian's. For all I knew, she might come walking through the door, carrying Sonya's bouquet.

"Thank you," I said. I sat down at one of the tables. "That was nice of you." It was another one of those incredible moments when Adrian had had the insight to guess my thoughts—or in this case, my fears.

"Well, it was also selfish. I wanted to see you in the dress." He reconsidered. "Actually, I wanted to see you in that red Halloween dress again, but I figured that would be pushing my luck."

I looked away as an image of that dress returned to me. Lia DiStefano had created the costume for me. She'd loosely based it on an ancient Greek dress and ended up with a gauzy confection of red and gold. That was when Adrian had said I was the most beautiful creature walking the earth. It had happened before he expressed his feelings for me, but even then, his words had undone me. I thought about what he was doing for me now and decided to give him a small compensation. I focused again on my clothes, and the blue dress returned.

"Better?" I asked.

His face lit up in a way that made me smile in return. "Yes."

Hoping I wasn't setting myself up for some suggestive answer, I asked, "So what are we going to do?"

"You sure you don't want to dance? I can make some music." My silence spoke for me. "Fine, fine. I don't know. We could play a game. Monopoly? Life? Battleship? Twister? Whatever we do, I am *not* playing Scrabble with you."

We warmed up with Battleship—I won—and then moved on to Monopoly. That took a little work to set up because Adrian could only create things that he could imagine. He couldn't remember all the streets and cards, so we made our best attempt to re-create them. Neither of us could remember one of the yellow streets, so he named it Jet Way.

We proved surprisingly well matched, and I became engrossed in the game. The power shifted back and forth between us. Just when one of us seemed to have all the control, the other would seize it back. I had no doubts about my ability to win—until I lost. I sat there, dumbstruck, staring at the board.

"Have you ever lost a game before?" he asked.

"I . . . yes, of course . . . I just didn't think . . ."

"That *I* could beat you?"

"No, I just . . . it doesn't happen very often." I looked up at him and shook my head. "Congratulations."

He leaned back in his chair and laughed. "I think beating you just improved your opinion of me more than anything else I've ever done."

"I've always had a high opinion of you." I stretched out, surprised to feel kinks in my body. It was strange how these dreams could have such a realistic physical component. "How long have we have been here?"

"I don't know. It's not morning yet." He appeared unconcerned. "What do you want to play next?"

"We shouldn't play anything," I said. I stood up. "It's been hours. I'm asleep, but you aren't. You can't stay up all night."

"I'm a vampire, Sage. A creature of the night, remember?"

"One who's on a human schedule," I chastised.

He still didn't seem worried. "Only one class tomorrow. I'll make it up."

"What about the spirit?" I began to pace restlessly as more of the implications hit me. "You have to be using a lot of it. That's not good for you."

"I'll take my chances." There was an unspoken *for you* at the end of his sentence.

I returned to the table and stood in front of his chair. "You have to be careful. Between this and the Veronica hunt. . . ." I suddenly felt bad. I hadn't thought twice about asking him to help with that. I'd forgotten the risks. "Once we've stopped her, you need to lay off the spirit."

"Don't worry." He grinned. "Once we've gotten rid of that bitch, I'll be celebrating so much that I won't be sober for days."

"Ugh. Not the healthiest way to do it. Have you ever thought about antidepressants?" I knew they helped some spirit users by blocking the magic.

His smile vanished. "I won't touch those things. Lissa took them and hated them. Being cut off from spirit nearly drove her crazy."

I crossed my arms and leaned against the table. "Yeah, but using it will drive you crazy too."

"No lectures tonight, Sage. It mars my stunning Monopoly victory."

He was far too casual for such a serious matter, but I knew him well enough to recognize when he wouldn't yield. "Fine. Then let's end on a high note. Send me back, and get some sleep."

"You sure you'll be okay?" His concern was so intense. I didn't think anyone had ever worried about me that much. Well, maybe Ms. Terwilliger.

"Probably she gave up for the night." I really didn't know, but I couldn't let him keep exerting himself. The thought of Veronica reaching out again terrified me . . . but the thought of Adrian endangering himself almost scared me more. He'd risked so much for me. Could I do any less? "You can check on me tomorrow night, though."

Adrian's face lit up as though I'd just accepted a date. "It's a deal, then."

And like that, the reception hall dissolved around me. I returned to peaceful sleep and just barely heard him say, "Sweet dreams, Sage."

CHAPTER 17

ALTHOUGH OUR MAGICAL PLANS had been derailed, Ms. Terwilliger had asked me to come by her room before classes started in the morning so that we could talk strategy and future assignments. I had just enough time to swing by the cafeteria for breakfast and found Jill, Eddie, and Angeline sitting together. It felt like it had been a long time since we'd all been together in some kind of normal setting, and I welcomed this small moment of bonding. It was a refuge in the storm that had been my life recently.

Jill was grinning about something that Eddie didn't seem to find so funny. "He didn't say anything about it to me," he said.

"Of course not." Jill laughed. "He's too embarrassed."

I sat down with my tray. "Who's too embarrassed?" I assumed any "he" they were talking about must be Adrian, though it was hard to imagine Adrian embarrassed about anything.

"Micah," said Jill. "I talked him into modeling for our sewing club again. And then he got Juan and Travis to do it too."

"How'd you manage that?" I asked. Jill had originally gotten involved with Lia through the school's sewing club. Back when Jill and Micah had dated, she'd convinced him to model some very badly made clothes. He'd done it out of adoration, though I wasn't sure he'd really enjoyed it.

Jill leaned forward, an excited sparkle in her eyes. "Claire guilted him into it! It was hilarious. But I don't know how he talked Juan and Travis into it. Maybe they owed him a favor."

"Maybe they have ulterior motives," said Eddie. His tone surprised me until I remembered his lesson about the latest social developments around here. What was it? Claire was Micah's new girlfriend. Juan and Travis were his friends, who liked Jill. Eddie didn't like that they liked her. Got it. Apparently, Eddie hadn't kept his opinions to himself because Jill rolled her eyes.

"Will you stop worrying about that?" she asked. She was still smiling but sounded just a *little* annoyed. "They're good guys. And I'm not going to do anything stupid. You don't have to lecture me about humans and Moroi. I get it."

Her jade eyes flicked over to me, and her smile faltered a little. She studied me for several long, troubled moments, and I wondered what she was thinking about. Was she still hoping for some romantic resolution between Adrian and me? Was she wondering why Adrian and I kept getting into intimate situations? I kind of wanted to know that too. She finally dragged her gaze away, letting her happy mood return.

"I'm just looking out for you," Eddie said obstinately.

"You look out for assassins. I can handle these guys. I'm not a child, and besides, these are the most male models we've ever had. It's great. If we could score a couple more, our club could do a whole project on men's clothing."

Eddie still looked way too serious for this discussion. "Maybe Eddie would volunteer," I suggested. "I bet guardian posture would be great on the catwalk."

He blushed, which even I had to admit was adorable. If Jill had been irritated by his earlier overprotectiveness, it was no longer obvious. From her dreamy expression, you'd think Eddie blushing was the most amazing thing she'd ever witnessed. I think he was too overwhelmed at the thought of strutting down a runway to notice.

Angeline had been completely silent so far. I glanced over at her, expecting her to have something funny to say about her boy-friend being encouraged to model. But to my surprise, she wasn't paying attention to the conversation at all. She had a geometry book open and was furiously trying to draw some circles freehand. It killed me to watch, but after Kristin's comment about Angeline stabbing someone with a compass, freehand might be best.

"What do you think, Angeline?" I asked, just to see how engrossed she was. "Do you think Eddie would make a good model?"

"Hmm?" She didn't look up. "Oh, yeah. You should let Jill try some clothes on you."

Now Jill blushed. Eddie's deepened.

Just when I thought this meal couldn't get any more sur-real, Trey stopped by. He nudged Angeline's chair with his toe. "Hey, McCormick." He nodded toward her graph paper. "Time to check out your curves."

Rather than answering with some biting response, she looked up instantly, a big smile on her face. "I've been working on them all morning," she said. "I think they're pretty good."

"They look good from where I'm standing," said Trey.

They were actually the worst circles I'd ever seen, but I guessed Trey wanted to encourage her. I was amazed at how seriously she was treating this math grade. It seemed to me that she was putting it above everything else, even her personal life. She gathered up all her things so that she and Trey could go to the library. Eddie looked disappointed but couldn't protest, lest it give away the truth about Angeline and him. Trey knew we weren't all actually related, but Eddie and Angeline's relationship was still kept secret.

I realized then that it was almost time to meet Ms. Terwilliger. I hurriedly finished a banana and told Eddie and Jill I'd see them later. Whether they would talk about male modeling or Jill's dating life, I couldn't guess.

I showed up right on the dot for my meeting but found Ms. Terwilliger's room locked and dark. Even in crisis mode, I supposed she was entitled to run a little late now and then, so I settled down on the hallway floor and read ahead for my English class.

I grew so absorbed that I didn't realize how much time had passed until I heard the warning bell ring and realized students were starting to fill the halls. I glanced up just as the same harried substitute teacher from before came scurrying up to the door with a set of keys. I scrambled to my feet.

"Ms. Terwilliger's out today?" I asked. "Is she okay?"

"They don't tell me the reasons," the sub said brusquely. "They just ask me to be here. I hope she left an assignment this time."

Knowing Ms. Terwilliger, I had a feeling it was going to be another "homework" day. I shuffled into the classroom after the sub, feeling a knot of anxiety in my stomach.

269

The next hour was agonizing. I barely heard as the sub told us to work on homework. Instead, I kept sneaking glances at my cell phone, hoping a text would come from Ms. Terwilliger. No such luck.

I went from class to class but was too distracted to give anything my full attention. I even shocked myself in English when I nearly mixed up *Henry IV* with *Henry VI* while answering an essay question. Thankfully, I caught myself before committing that embarrassing mistake to paper.

When I returned to Ms. Terwilliger's classroom for my independent study at the day's end, I was expecting the sub to tell me I could leave early again. Instead, I found Ms. Terwilliger herself, rifling through papers on her desk.

"You're back!" I exclaimed. "I thought something had happened to you."

"Not me," she said. Her face was pale and drawn. "But someone else wasn't so lucky."

"No. Not again." I sank into a chair, and all the fears I'd been carrying around today came crashing down on me. "I'd hoped we'd protected those girls."

Ms. Terwilliger sat down opposite me. "It wasn't one of them. Last night, Veronica targeted one of my coven members. Alana."

It took me several moments to truly process that. "Your coven . . . you mean, like a full-fledged witch?"

"Yes."

"Someone like *you*?"

Her face gave me the answer before she spoke. "Yes."

I was reeling. "But you said she only went after young girls."

"Normally she does. That way she can capture youth and

beauty along with power." Ms. Terwilliger didn't look like she had to worry about someone stealing her youth anytime soon. Fatigue and stress were taking their toll on her, making her look older than she was. "Now, some magic users who perform this spell are only concerned about power, not getting younger. That's never been Veronica's style, though. She's vain. She always wanted the superficial benefits—not to mention easier victims. Someone like my coven sister would be more difficult to take, so this is surprising behavior."

"It means *you* could be a target," I said. "You've been saying all this time that you're safe, but now everything's different."

Ms. Terwilliger shook her head, and a bit of steely resolve flashed in her eyes. "No. Maybe she did this to throw me off, to make me think it's someone else behind the spells. Or maybe to make me think she's not interested in you. Whatever the reason, she won't target me."

I admired Ms. Terwilliger for thinking so well of her sister, but I couldn't share her confidence that sisterly affection would overcome an evil quest for youth and power. "No offense, ma'am, but isn't there a slight chance you could be wrong about her coming for you? You said she'd only go after young novices, but obviously, that's not the case. She's already doing things you didn't expect."

Ms. Terwilliger refused to back down. "Veronica may do any number of terrible things, but she won't face me unless she's absolutely forced to." She handed over a new spell book and a small drawstring bag. "Just because she went after an older witch, it doesn't mean you're out of danger. I've marked some pages I want you to go over. There's a spell there I think will prove particularly useful. I've gathered some components for you, and you should be able to cast the rest yourself—just make sure you do it somewhere remote. Meanwhile, I still need to make you that secondary charm. There's just so much to do lately."

A mix of emotions swirled within me. Once again, I was amazed that Ms. Terwilliger would go to such lengths for me. Yet I couldn't shake my fear for her. "Maybe you should make one for yourself, just in case."

She gave me a wan smile. "Still pushing that, hmm? Well, once I've secured yours, I'll see about another. It may take a while, however. What I have in mind for you is particularly complex."

That made me feel even worse. She always looked so worn out lately, and all these things she was doing for me were only intensifying the situation. But no matter how many arguments I made, she refused to listen. I left her classroom feeling upset and confused. I needed to vent to someone. Obviously, my choices were limited in this matter. I texted Adrian: *V attacked a real witch last night. Ms. T won't protect herself. She's only worried about me.* As usual, I received a quick response: *Wanna talk about it?*

Did I? I wasn't the type to sit and analyze my feelings, but I did actually want company. I knew I shouldn't spend more time around Adrian than I had to when my feelings for him were already so mixed. But he was the only person I wanted to talk to. *I have to cast some spells for her now. Want to pick me up and come along?*

My answer was a smiley face.

She'd told me to go somewhere remote, so I picked Lone Rock Park again. When Adrian and I arrived, it was smoldering in the late-afternoon heat, and I found it hard to believe

Christmas was only a couple weeks away. I'd dressed in layers, just like before, and took off my Amberwood hoodie as Adrian and I trekked across the rocky terrain. He took off a coat as well, and I had to do a double take when I saw what he was wearing underneath.

"Really?" I asked. "Your AYE shirt?"

He shot me a grin. "Hey, it's a perfectly good shirt. I think I'm going to see if I can start a chapter on Carlton's campus." Carlton was the college he took art classes at. It was pretty small and didn't even have fraternities or sororities.

"A chapter?" I scoffed. "Don't you mean the *only* chapter?"

"Gotta start somewhere, Sage."

We reached the same spot where I'd practiced with Ms. Terwilliger, and I tried to ignore the scorch marks on the ground. Adrian had decided to turn this into a desert picnic and had brought along a basket containing a blanket and a thermos of lemonade. "I figured we could stop at Pies and Stuff on the way back since I know how much you like that place," he explained, deadpan, as he poured me a cup. "Hopefully this'll tide you over after the spell."

"I wish this was over," I said, running my hand over the weathered leather of Ms. Terwilliger's latest book. It was an old handwritten one called *Summonings and Conjurations*. "I hate living with the uncertainty, worrying that Veronica's lurking behind every corner. My life's already complicated enough without witches coming after me."

Adrian, face serious, stretched out on the blanket and propped his head up with his elbow. "If she's even coming after you."

I sat down cross-legged, careful to keep a lot more distance than in the Velvet Suite. "Ms. Terwilliger won't listen to me. She just keeps stressing over me."

"Let her," he suggested. "I mean, I totally get why you're worried about her. I am too. But we have to accept that she knows what she's talking about. She's been involved with this stuff a lot longer than we have."

I couldn't help but smile at that. "Since when are you involved with magic?"

"Since I started looking after you and being all manly and brave."

"Funny, I don't remember it that way." I worked to keep a straight face. "If you think about all the rides I gave you, me getting you into college . . . well, it kind of seems like I'm looking after you."

He leaned toward me. "I guess we look after each other."

We locked eyes and smiled, but there was nothing sensuous about it. There was no trick here, no sly move on Adrian's part to advance on me. And there was no fear on my part. We were just two people who cared about each other. It reminded me of what had initially drawn us together—before all the romantic complications. We connected. Against all reason, we understood each other, and—as he said—we looked out for each other. I'd never had a relationship quite like that with anyone and was surprised at how much I valued it.

"Well, then, I guess I'd better get to work." I glanced back down at the book. "I haven't had a chance to look at what she wants me to do. It doesn't sound like a defensive book."

"Maybe you're graduating from fireballs to lightning bolts," Adrian suggested. "I bet it'd be a lot like throwing ninja stars. Except, well, you could incinerate people."

When I found the page Ms. Terwilliger had marked, I read the title aloud: "Callistana Summoning."

"What's *callistana* mean?" asked Adrian.

I scrutinized the word, making sure I was deciphering the elaborate script correctly. "I don't know. It's kind of like the Greek word for 'beautiful,' but not quite. The spell's subtitle is 'For protection and advanced warning.'"

"Maybe it's some kind of shield, like the one Jackie had," suggested Adrian. "An easier one."

"Maybe," I agreed. I wouldn't mind a little bit of invulnerability.

I opened up the bag Ms. Terwilliger had given me. Inside, I found dragon's blood resin, a small bottle of gardenia oil, branches of juniper berries, and a glittering smoky quartz crystal, rutilated with lines of gold. Although she'd provided the ingredients, the spell's directions required that I use and measure them in a very specific way, which made sense. As usual, it was the caster's work that powered the magic. Adrian sat up and read over my shoulder.

"It doesn't really say what happens when you cast it," he pointed out.

"Yeah . . . I'm not really excited about that part." Presumably, the caster was supposed to just know what she was doing. If this was some kind of protective shield, then maybe the shield would materialize around me, just as it had for Ms. Terwilliger. "Well, no point in wasting time. We'll find out soon enough."

Adrian chuckled as he watched me walk over to a clear piece of land. "Am I the only one amazed that you now perform magic blindly?"

"No," I assured him. "You're not the only one."

I had to pluck the juniper berries off one by one and make a small ring with them, saying, "Fire and smoke," each time I placed one on the ground. When I finished, I anointed each berry with a drop of the oil and recited, "Breath and life." Inside the circle, I lit a small pile of the resin and rested the smoky quartz on top of it. Then I stepped back and reread the spell, committing the words and gestures to memory. Once I was satisfied I knew it, I handed it to Adrian and shot him a hopeful look.

"Wish me luck," I said.

"You make your own luck," he replied.

I tried not to roll my eyes and turned toward the circle. I recited the spell's complex Greek incantation, pointing in the four cardinal directions as I spoke, per the book's instructions. It was startling how quickly the magic welled up within me, filling me with that blissful power. I spoke the last words, pointing at the juniper circle as I did. I felt the magic pour from me and into the quartz. Then I waited for something to happen.

Nothing did.

I looked back at Adrian, hoping he noticed something I hadn't. He shrugged. "Maybe you did it wrong."

"It worked," I insisted. "I felt the magic."

"Maybe you just can't see it. At the expense of getting myself in trouble here, you should know how amazing you look when you do that stuff. All graceful and—" His eyes went wide. "Um, Sydney? That rock is smoking."

I glanced back at the circle. "That's just the resin that's—"

I stopped. He was right. Smoke was coming out of the quartz. I watched, fascinated, and then slowly, the quartz began to melt. Rather than dissipate into a puddle, though, the liquid began to re-form into a different shape, one that soon hardened into something new and unexpected: a crystalline dragon.

It was small, able to fit in a palm, and glittered just like the dark brown quartz had. The dragon looked more like the serpentine kind usually associated with Chinese culture rather than the winged types of European myth. Every detail was meticulously carved, from the tendrils of its mane to the scales on its hide. It was stunning.

Also, it was moving.

I screamed and backed up, running into Adrian. He put an arm around me and held me as protectively as he could, though it was clear he was just as freaked out. The dragon opened its crystal eyelids and peered at the two of us with tiny golden eyes. It elicited a small croak and then began walking toward us, its small claws scraping against the rocks.

"What the hell is that?" Adrian demanded.

"Do you really think I know?"

"You made it! Do something."

I started to ask what had happened to him looking out for me, but he had a point. I was the one who'd summoned this thing. No matter where we moved or backed up to, the dragon continued to follow and make a small, high-pitched screeching noise that sounded like nails on a chalkboard. I groped for my cell phone and tried to dial Ms. Terwilliger, but there was no reception out here. Darting over to the blanket, I grabbed the spell book and then hurried back to Adrian's side. I flipped to the index, looking up *callistana*. There I found two entries: *Callistana—Summoning* and *Callistana—Banishing*. You would've thought the two would be near each other in the book, but they were pages apart. I flipped to the latter and found the instructions brief and to the point: *Once your callistana has been fed and rested, you may summon and banish it at will for a year and a day.* A short incantation followed.

I looked up at Adrian. "It says we have to feed it."

"Will that make it shut up?" he asked. His arm was around me again.

"I honestly don't know."

"Maybe we can outrun it."

All my instincts about hiding the supernatural world kicked in. "We can't just leave it for some hiker to find! We have to get it some food." Not that I had any clue what to feed it. Hopefully humans and vampires weren't on the menu.

A look of determination crossed Adrian's features. In a great show of bravery, he lunged for the picnic basket and actually managed to scoop the dragon up in it. He slammed down the lid, and the mewling faded but didn't stop.

"Wow," I said. "Manly and brave."

Adrian regarded the basket with dismay. "I just hope that thing doesn't breathe fire. At least it's contained. Now what do we do?"

"Now we feed it." I made a decision. "We take it to Pies and Stuff."

I didn't know if dragons ate pie, but that was the closest food source we had. Besides, I was pretty sure I'd be able to get a cell phone signal there. So, Adrian drove us back to the little diner while I gingerly held the noisy basket. He went inside, and I stayed in the car and tried to call Ms. Terwilliger. I was sent to voice mail and didn't even bother with formalities. Was she never near her phone anymore?

"Call me now," I said through gritted teeth. The dragon's screeching was really starting to get to me.

Adrian returned in about ten minutes carrying two bags. I stared in amazement as he got in the car. "Did you buy out the store?"

"I didn't know what kind it wanted," he protested. Between the two bags, we had half a dozen slices of different kinds of pies. Each one's container was neatly labeled.

"I really don't know either," I said.

Adrian sifted through the bags and pulled out a slice of coconut cream. "If I were a dragon, this is what I'd go for."

I didn't argue, mainly because that statement had no logical argument. He took the lid off the pie and then looked at me expectantly. With a gulp, I opened the basket's lid and prayed the dragon wouldn't climb out and claw my face off. Adrian quickly set the pie down in the basket. Nervously, we both leaned forward to watch.

At first, the dragon looked as though it really would climb out after us. Then it noticed the pie. The little crystal creature sniffed at the slice, circled it a few times, and then began gnawing at the pie in teeny-tiny bites. Best of all, the screeching stopped. We watched in wonder as the dragon made its way through a third of the coconut cream pie. Then, without warning, it rolled over onto its back and began to snore. Adrian and I sat there, frozen, and then finally dared to look at each other.

"I guess you were right about the flavor," I said.

"Do you think you can banish it now?" he asked. "Is it fed and rested enough?"

I retrieved the spell book to double-check the incantation. "Time to find out."

I recited the words. Smoke fluttered from the dragon's body. He began to shimmer, and within moments, we were looking at an inert piece of smoky quartz. In another valiant display, Adrian picked it up but held it as far away as possible as he studied it. The ringing of my phone startled both of us, and he dropped the crystal back into the basket. I looked at the phone's screen and saw Ms. Terwilliger's name.

"You made me summon a dragon!" I exclaimed.

"I most certainly did not," she responded. "Callistanas are a type of demon."

I froze. "A demon."

"Well," she amended. "A very minor and generally benign kind." I didn't reply for a while. "Sydney? Are you still there?"

"You had me summon a demon," I replied, voice stiff. "You know how I feel about evil and the supernatural. You've spent all this time trying to convince me that the magic we do is all for some greater good in the battle against evil, and yet you made me summon a creature of hell."

"Creature of hell?" She snorted. "Hardly. You know nothing about demons. I told you it's benign, didn't I? Callistanas can be very useful. They'll warn you if dark magic is nearby and will even try to defend you if you're attacked—not that they can do much damage."

I wasn't buying it. "If they're so useful, then why don't you have one?"

"Oh, well, I'm at a level where I can sense dark magic on my own. That, and—if you'll forgive my language—callistanas are a real pain in the ass. They make the most irritating noise when they're hungry. Cats are more than adequate for my needs."

"Yeah," I said. "I kind of noticed the noise part. I fed it some pie and turned it back into a rock."

"There, you see?" She sounded happier than I'd heard her in days. "Look at the progress you've made already. No matter what comes of this mess we've found ourselves in, I'm more convinced than ever that I made the right choice in guiding you on the magical path."

I had too much going on to really appreciate the compliment. "So what do I do now?"

"It'll disappear on its own after a year and a day. Until then, you can call it when you need it. You can try to train it. And of course, you'll have to feed it. Whatever you choose to do, it will be loyal to you. It bonds with the first person it sees and will need to spend time with you . . . Sydney? Are you there?"

I'd gone silent again. "The first person it sees?" I finally managed to ask. "Not the caster?"

"Well, usually they're one and the same."

I glanced over at Adrian, who was eating a piece of blackberry pie while listening avidly to my side of the conversation. "What happens if there were two people there when it opened its eyes? Adrian was with me when I summoned it."

Now she paused. "Oh? Hmm, well, I probably should've said something before you cast the spell."

That had to be the understatement of the century. "You should've told me a lot of things before I cast it! What does it mean that the dragon—demon, whatever— saw both of us? Did it bond with both of us?"

"Look at it this way," Ms. Terwilliger said, after several moments of thought. "The callistana thinks of you two as its parents."

CHAPTER 18

I CERTAINLY HADN'T EXPECTED to walk away from today's trip with joint custody of a miniature dragon. (I refused to call it a demon). And, as it turned out, Adrian was already proving not to be the most dedicated of "fathers."

"You can take him for now," he told me when we got back to Amberwood. "I'll handle weekend visitations."

"You don't have anything going on. Besides, we're only a few days from the weekend," I protested. "And you don't know that it's a 'he.'"

"Well, I don't think he'll mind, and besides, I'm not going to investigate to find out the truth." Adrian put the quartz in the basket and closed the lid before handing it over to me. "You don't have to summon him back, you know."

I took the basket and opened the car door. "I know. But I feel kind of bad leaving him as a rock." Ms. Terwilliger had told me it'd be healthier for him if I let him out once in a while.

"See? Motherly instinct already. You're a natural, Sage."

Adrian grinned and handed me a bag of pie slices. He'd kept some for himself. "Look at you. You don't even need to break the tattoo. You think you would've been mothering a baby dragon a month ago?"

"I don't know." But he had a point. It seemed likely I would've run screaming from it back in the desert. Or maybe tried to exorcise it. "I'll take him for now, but you've got to pull your weight at some point. Ms. Terwilliger says the callistana needs to spend time with both of us. Hmm."

"Hmm, what?"

I shook my head. "Just getting ahead of myself. Wondering what I'd do with him if I did go to Mexico."

Adrian gave me a puzzled look. "What about Mexico?"

It had never come up, I realized. All Adrian had known about was Marcus's mission and the initial tattoo breaking, not the sealing. I hadn't been keeping the rest a secret, but suddenly, I felt uncomfortable telling Adrian about it.

"Oh. Well, Marcus says that after I perform this rebellious act, we can break the elements and free me from the tattoo's control. But to truly bind the spell and make sure the tattoo is never repaired, I need to tattoo over it—like he did. He calls it sealing. But it takes some special compound that's hard to find. He got his done in Mexico and is going to take some of his Merry Men there so they can do it."

"I see." Adrian's smile had vanished. "So. Are you joining them?"

I shrugged. "I don't know. Marcus wants me to."

"I'm sure he does."

I ignored the tone. "I've thought about it . . . but it's a big step. Not just for the tattoo, either. If I did that, there'd be no going back. I'd be turning my back on the Alchemists."

"And us," he said. "Unless you really are only helping Jill because of your orders."

"You know it's not about that anymore." Again, I didn't like his tone. "You know I care about her and . . . and the rest of you."

His face was hard. "And yet you'd run off with some guy you just met."

"It's not like that! We wouldn't be 'running off' together. I'd be coming back! And we'd be going for a specific reason."

"Beaches and margaritas?"

I was speechless for a few moments. It was so close to what Marcus had joked about. Was that all anyone associated with Mexico?

"I see how it is," I snapped. "You were all in favor of me breaking the tattoo and thinking on my own—but that's only okay if it's convenient for you, huh? Just like your 'loving from afar' only works if you don't have an opportunity to get your hands all over me. And your lips. And . . . stuff."

Adrian rarely got mad, and I wouldn't quite say he was now. But he was definitely exasperated. "Are you seriously in this much self-denial, Sydney? Like do you actually believe yourself when you say you don't feel anything? Especially after what's been happening between us?"

"Nothing's happening between us," I said automatically. "Physical attraction isn't the same as love. You of all people should know that."

"Ouch," he said. His expression hadn't changed, but I saw hurt in his eyes. I'd wounded him. "Is that what bothers you? My past? That maybe I'm an expert in an area you aren't?"

"One I'm sure you'd just love to educate me in. One more girl to add to your list of conquests."

He was speechless for a few moments and then held up one finger. "First, I don't have a list." Another finger. "Second, if I did have a list, I could find someone a hell of lot less frustrating to add to it." For the third finger, he leaned toward me. "And finally, I know that you know you're no conquest, so don't act like you seriously think that. You and I have been through too much together. We're too close, too connected. I wasn't that crazy on spirit when I said you're my flame in the dark. We chase away the shadows around each other. Our backgrounds don't matter. What we have is bigger than that. I love you, and beneath all that logic, calculation, and superstition, I know you love me too. Running away to Mexico and fleeing all your problems isn't going to change that. You're just going to end up scared and confused."

"I already feel that way," I said quietly.

Adrian moved back and leaned into his seat, looking tired. "Well, that's the most accurate thing you've said so far."

I grabbed the basket and jerked open the car door. Without another word, I stormed off toward the dorm, refusing to look back in case he saw the tears that had inexplicably appeared in my eyes. Only, I wasn't sure exactly which part of our conversation I was most upset about.

The tears seemed like they were going to stay put by the time I reached my room, but I still had to calm down. Even once my emotions were settled, it was hard to shake his words. *You're my flame in the dark. We chase away the shadows around each other.* What did that even mean?

At least smuggling a dragon into my room provided a pretty

good distraction. I brought the basket inside, hoping demonic dragons weren't contraband. No one stopped me when I went upstairs, and I was left wondering how I was going to confine him if I did summon him back. The basket didn't seem all that secure, and I certainly wasn't going to let him run loose in my dorm room. When I reached my door, I found Jill standing outside, her pale green eyes wide with excitement.

"I want to see him," she said. The bond was strongest in moments of high emotion, and judging from Adrian's face when the dragon had been chasing us, his emotions had been running pretty strong. I wondered if she'd witnessed our argument too or if that hadn't come through the bond. Maybe the tension between him and me was second nature to her now.

"I can't let him out yet," I said, letting her into my room. "I need something to keep him in. Like a birdcage. Maybe I can get one tomorrow."

Jill frowned in thought, then brightened. "I have an idea." She glanced at my alarm clock. "I hope it's not too late."

And without further explanation, she took off, promising to be back soon. I was still a little shaky from today's magic but hadn't had time to rectify the situation after all the other excitement. So, I sat at my desk with a spell book and ate the rest of the now-soft coconut cream pie, careful to first cut off the part where the dragon had eaten. I didn't know if callistanas had communicable germs, but I wasn't taking any chances.

Jill returned an hour later, bearing a rectangular glass aquarium, like the kind you'd keep fish or gerbils in.

"Where'd you get that?" I asked, moving a lamp off my desk.

"My biology teacher. Our guinea pig died a couple weeks ago, and she's been too sad to replace him."

"Didn't she ask what you needed it for?" I examined the tank and found it spotless, so someone had apparently cleaned it after the guinea pig's unfortunate passing. "We can't have pets."

"I told her I was building a diorama. She didn't question it." Jill eagerly brought the aquarium over to the desk. "We can give it back when you get your own."

I set the quartz crystal inside and slammed on the tank's lid, making sure it was securely attached. After more entreating from Jill, I spoke the summoning words. A bit of smoke appeared, and the quartz transformed back into the dragon. Mercifully, he didn't make any more of that screeching, so I guessed he was still full. Instead, he scampered around the tank, examining his new home. At one point, he tried to climb the side, but his tiny claws couldn't get traction on the glass.

"Well, that's a relief," I said.

Jill's face was filled with wonder. "I think he'll be bored in there. You should get him some toys."

"Toys for a demon? Isn't it enough that I give him pie?"

"He wants *you*," she insisted.

Sure enough, I glanced back at the tank and found the callistana regarding me adoringly. He was even wagging his tail.

"No," I said sternly. "This isn't a Disney movie where I have an adorable sidekick. You aren't coming out."

I cut off a piece of blueberry pie and put it in the tank in case he wanted a midnight snack. No way would I risk a late-night wakeup call. After a moment's thought, I added a stress ball and a scarf.

"There," I told Jill. "Food, a toy, and a bed. Happy?"

The callistana apparently was. He batted the ball around

a few times and then curled up on the nest I'd made with the scarf. He looked more or less content, aside from the fact that he kept watching me.

"Aww," she said. "Look how sweet he is. What are you going to name him?"

Like I needed something else to worry about. "His 'father' can name him. I'm already on the hook for the Mustang."

After a bit more swooning, Jill finally retired for the night. I made my own preparations for bed, always keeping one eye on the dragon. He did nothing threatening, however, and I even managed to fall asleep, though my sleep was restless. I kept imagining he'd find a way out and come get into bed with me. And of course, I had my usual fears about Veronica coming after me.

I did hit one stretch of sound sleep, during which Adrian pulled me into a spirit dream. After our earlier fight, I honestly hadn't expected to see him tonight, a thought that had saddened me. The reception hall materialized around us, but the image wavered and kept fading in and out.

"I didn't think you'd come," I told him.

No wedding clothes tonight. He wore what he'd had on earlier, jeans and the AYE shirt, though both looked a bit more wrinkled. He was dressed as he was in reality, I realized.

"You think I'd abandon you to Veronica?"

"No," I admitted. "What's wrong with the room?"

He looked a little embarrassed. "My control's not all it could be tonight."

I didn't understand . . . at first. "You're drunk."

"I've been drinking," he corrected, leaning against one of the tables. "If I was drunk, I wouldn't be here at all. And really, this is pretty good for four White Russians."

"White what?" I almost sat down but was afraid the chair might dematerialize beneath me.

"It's a drink," he said. "You'd think I wouldn't be into something named that—you know, considering my own personal experience with Russians. But they're surprisingly delicious. The drinks, not real Russians. They've got Kahlua. It might be the drink you've been waiting your whole life for."

"Kahlua does *not* taste like coffee," I said. "So don't start with that." I was insanely curious to know why he'd been drinking. Sometimes he did it to numb spirit, but he seemed to still want to access that magic tonight. And of course, half the time, he didn't even need a reason to drink. Deep inside me, I wondered if our fight had driven him to it. I didn't know whether to feel guilty or annoyed.

"I also had to come tonight to apologize," he said. He sat down, apparently not having the same fears about chairs.

For one inexplicably terrifying moment, I thought he was going to take back the part about me being his flame in the dark. Instead, he told me, "If you need to go to Mexico to finish this process off, then I understand. I was wrong to criticize you for it or even imply that I had some kind of say in it. One of the greatest things about you is that in the end, you always make smart decisions. Can't always say the same for myself. Whatever you need to do, I'll support you."

Those annoying tears almost returned, and I blinked them back. "Thank you. That means a lot . . . and to tell you the truth, right now, I still don't know what I'm going to do. I know Marcus is worried about me eventually getting in trouble and being under their control. Then again, staying part of the Alchemists seems like it'd give me more power, and besides . . . I don't want to leave you. Er, you guys."

He smiled, and it lit up his whole face. *Like a flame in the dark.* "Well, 'we' are certainly happy to hear that. Oh, and I'm also happy to watch our darling little love child dragon while you're in St. Louis."

I grinned back. "As a rock or in his real form?"

"Haven't decided yet. How's he doing right now?"

"He's locked in an aquarium. I'm guessing I'd wake up if he got into bed with me, so he must still be asleep." I hoped.

"Well, I'm sure getting into bed with you would be—" Adrian held back whatever comment he'd been about to utter. He instead gestured to the table, and a Monopoly board appeared. "Shall we play?"

I walked over and peered at the board. It apparently was also suffering from his drinking, seeing as half the streets were blank. The ones that were there had names like "Castile Causeway" and "Jailbait Avenue." "The board's a little incomplete," I said diplomatically.

Adrian didn't seem concerned. "Well, then, I guess that improves your odds."

I couldn't resist that and took a gamble on sitting in one of the chairs. I smiled at him and then began counting money, happy that all was (relatively) right in the world with us again.

CHAPTER 19

SOMEHOW, I STILL LOST.

If Adrian were capable of on-the-fly calculations, I'd swear he was using his powers to affect the way the dice rolled. Most likely, he either had some innate and inexplicable Monopoly skills I just couldn't understand—or he was very, very lucky. But through it all, I had fun, and losing to him was a lot better than having Veronica haunt me in my sleep. He continued the dream visits for the next few days, and although I never felt completely safe from her, I at least didn't have her occupying the forefront of my mind at all times. That honor was saved for my weekend trip to St. Louis, which came around more quickly than I expected.

Once I was on the plane, the reality of what I was about to attempt hit me. This was it, the point of no return. In the safety of Palm Springs, I'd been able to maintain a somewhat cool and collected attitude. St. Louis had seemed far away back then. Now the tasks ahead of me seemed daunting and kind of crazy. And *dangerous*. There was no part of this that wouldn't get me into serious trouble. Lying to Stanton. Breaking into top secret servers. Even charming information out of Ian could have repercussions.

And really, who was I to think I would have any ability to lure secrets from him? I wasn't like Rose or Julia. They had men fawning all over them. But me? I was socially awkward and pretty inept when it came to romance. Maybe Ian liked me, but that didn't mean I'd have some magical power over him. Of course, if that part of the plan with him failed, then I'd be free of my other tasks.

Every single part of this was overwhelming, and as I stared out the plane's window, watching St. Louis grow closer and closer, my feelings of dread grew. My palms were too sweaty to hold a book, and when I refused food, it was because of the queasiness in my stomach, not some obsession with calories.

I'd gone back and forth on whether to get a hotel room or stay at the facility itself, which provided guest housing for visiting Alchemists like me. In the end, I opted for the former. The less time I spent under the watchful eyes of my masters, the better.

It also meant I didn't have to worry about my outfit attracting attention. I hadn't exactly followed all of Adrian's suggestions, but the dress I'd purchased for this trip was a bit racier than my normal business casual wardrobe. Okay, a lot racier. It would have been completely out of place among the modest and neutral-colored attire Alchemists usually wore. But when Ian met me in the hotel's lobby for dinner, I knew I'd made the right choice.

"Wow," he said, eyes widening. "You look amazing."

Apparently, his Alchemists sensibilities weren't offended by my outfit. It was a form-fitting minidress that went about to my mid-thigh, with an open back and a disconcertingly low V-neck that gave me cleavage I hadn't even known was possible. Any demureness the dress's long sleeves might have offered was undone by the fabric combination: a beige underdress covered in black and maroon lace. It gave the illusion that I was wearing lace with nothing underneath. The saleswoman had assured me that every part of the dress was supposed to fit that snugly (for once in my life, I'd actually suggested a larger size) and that I needed at least four-inch black heels to make it all work. With the help of a lot of hairpins, I'd even managed to pull my hair up into a bun, which wasn't easy with my layered haircut.

I felt conspicuous walking through the lobby, but no one gave me any shocked looks. The few I did get were admiring ones. The hotel was pretty posh, and I was just one of a number of women dressed in holiday cocktail dresses. Nothing scandalous or out of the ordinary. *You can do this, Sydney.* And wearing a revealing dress wasn't nearly as difficult as breaking into a server, right?

Right?

I smiled as I approached Ian and gave him a quick hug, which was weird both because it was with Ian and because I felt naked in the dress. This femme fatale thing was harder than I'd thought it'd be.

"I'm glad I got to see you again," I said. "I know what an inconvenience this must be, with no notice."

Ian shook his head so adamantly that I almost expected to hear rattling. "N-no. No trouble at all."

Satisfied he'd gotten a look, I slipped on my coat, a

mid-length black trench, and gestured toward the exit. "Time to brave the elements?"

He hurried ahead of me to open the door. A scattering of snowflakes drifted down, resting on my coat and hair. My breath made a frosty cloud in the air, and I had a momentary flashback to traipsing across that field with Adrian. Little had I known that search for Marcus would lead to me running errands for him in a tight dress.

Ian had parked in the hotel's front circle drive. He drove a Toyota Corolla, which was made even more boring by the fact that he'd chosen it in white. A little air freshener shaped like a tree hung from the rearview mirror, but rather than the usual pine scent, a small label declared it to be "New Car Scent." Mostly it smelled like plastic. I put on a brave face. Marcus really owed me one.

"I made us a reservation at this really great seafood place," he told me. "It's close to the facility, so we can head on over to the service right away."

"Sounds great," I said. I never ate seafood in any landlocked state.

The restaurant was called Fresh Cache, which didn't improve my opinion of it. Still, I had to give it credit for attempts at a romantic atmosphere. Most of the lighting came from candles, and a pianist in the corner played covers of easy-listening songs. More well-dressed people filled the tables, laughing and chatting over wine and shrimp cocktails. The host showed us to a corner table, covered with burgundy linen and decorated with a scattering of green orchids. I'd never seen any up close and was actually quite taken with how exotic and sensual they were. If only I was here with anyone but Ian.

I was hesitant to take my coat off. It made me feel exposed, and I had to remind myself of the consequences of Alchemists and Warriors working together. As soon as the dress was unleashed again, I had the satisfaction of seeing Ian melt once more. I remembered Adrian's advice about confidence and put on a smug smile, hoping I gave the impression that I was doing Ian a great favor by allowing him to be in my presence. And, to my complete and utter amazement, it seemed to work. I even allowed myself to indulge in a dangerous thought: maybe it wasn't the dress wielding such power here.

Maybe it was *me*.

Opening the menu, I began skimming for a beef or poultry option. "What do you recommend?"

"The mahi mahi is great here," he said. "So is the swordfish."

The waiter stopped by, and I ordered a chicken Caesar salad. I figured they couldn't really mess up the anchovies in the dressing.

We were left alone to wait, with nothing to do now but move on to small talk. Ian picked up the ball. "I suppose you still can't tell me much about where you're at, huh?"

"Afraid not. You know how it is." I buttered a sourdough roll with what I was pretty sure was exactly half a tablespoon. I didn't want to go too crazy, but I could allow myself a little indulgence since I ordered a salad. "I can tell you I'm in the field. I just can't say much else."

Ian's attention shifted off my neckline as he stared into the candle's flame. "I miss that, you know. Being in the field."

"You used to be, right? What happened?" I hadn't thought much about it lately, but when Ian had accompanied Stanton and me to the Moroi court, he had been pulled from his post to make the trip. He'd been assigned somewhere in the south, Florida or Georgia, I thought.

"Those Moroi holding us prisoner is what happened." He shifted his gaze back to me, and I was startled at the fierceness I saw. "I didn't handle it very well."

"Well, none of us did."

He shook his head. "No, no. I really didn't handle it well. I kind of freaked out. They sent me to anger management training afterward."

I nearly dropped the roll. I had in no way expected that. If someone had asked me to name the top ten people who needed anger management, Ian wouldn't have even made the bottom of the list. My father, however, would have been near the top.

"How—how long were you there?" I stammered.

"Two weeks, and then I was good to go."

Admittedly, I didn't know the extent of the rage that had landed him in anger management, but I found it interesting that two weeks was good enough to deem him ready to work again. Meanwhile, Keith's scheme to use Moroi to make money had earned him at least two months in re-education—maybe more, since I hadn't heard any updates in a while.

"But they wouldn't let me work in the field," Ian added. "Figure I shouldn't be around Moroi for a while. So that's why I'm stuck here."

"In the archives."

"Yes."

"Doesn't sound so bad," I told him. I wasn't entirely lying. "Lots of books."

"Don't fool yourself, Sydney." He began tearing a pumpernickel roll into pieces. "I'm a glorified librarian."

Maybe so, but that wasn't my concern. What was my concern was Wade telling me that the archives were on a secure level, one floor up from the surveillance room that held security footage. He'd drawn me a map of each floor, making sure I memorized the layout and the best ways to get in and out.

"I'd still love to see them," I said. "I mean, the history they contain is amazing." Again, not entirely a lie. I leaned forward, resting my elbows on the table, and had the satisfaction of seeing his eyes drop to my plunging neckline again. This wasn't that difficult! Really, I didn't know why I hadn't been using my "womanly charms" a long time ago. Actually, I never really knew I had any, until now. "Could you get me in for a tour? Of the archives specifically. You seem like the kind of guy who could get access to . . . a lot of places."

Ian choked on his roll. After a bout of coughing, he glanced up at my face, then my cleavage (again), and then back to my face. "I'd, um, love to, but it's not really open to the public— I mean, even the Alchemist public. Only those with special scholar access are allowed in. We could look at the general access parts of the building, though."

"Oh. I see." I looked down at my plate, pouting slightly, but didn't say anything else. As the waiter arrived with our food, I hoped my silence was making him reconsider what he could be missing out on.

Eventually, Ian couldn't take it anymore. He cleared his throat, maybe because there was still bread stuck in it. "Well, I might be able to . . . you see, the problem is just getting you down to the secure levels. Once you're through that checkpoint, it's not hard to get you into the archives—especially if I'm working."

"But you can't do anything about the main checkpoint?" I coaxed, as if all real men should be able to do that.

"No, I mean . . . maybe. I've got a friend who works there. I don't know if he's got a shift tomorrow, but he still might be able to help. He owes me some money, so I can use this as a trade. I hope."

"Oh, Ian." I flashed him a smile that I hoped rivaled one of Marcus's. "That's amazing." I remembered what Adrian had said. "I'd be so, *so* grateful if you could pull it off."

My reaction clearly delighted Ian, and I wondered if Adrian had been right about how "so, so grateful" was translated. "I'll call him tonight after the service," Ian said. He looked determined now. "Hopefully we can make it happen before your flight tomorrow."

I rewarded him by hanging on his every word for the rest of dinner, as though I'd never heard anything quite so fascinating. All the while, my heart raced with the knowledge that I was now one step closer to fulfilling Marcus's task, one step closer to potentially proving a connection to a bunch of gun-toting zealots and the organization I'd served my whole life.

The salad was tiny, so I agreed to see the dessert menu after dinner. Ian suggested we share, but that was a little too intimate for me, not to mention unhygienic. So, I ate an entire lemon tart by myself, confident in the knowledge that I was still a long ways from the five-pound mark. When Adrian had told me I'd look healthier if I gained a little weight, he'd added that it would improve my bra size. I couldn't even imagine what that would do for this dress.

The Alchemist center in St. Louis was contained inside a giant, industrial building that went undercover as a manufacturing plant. Moroi facilities—the court and their schools—usually posed as universities. How ironic that "creatures of the night" would live among beautifully landscaped gardens while "servants of the light" like us skulked in ugly buildings with no windows.

Inside, however, everything was pristine, bright, and well-organized. A receptionist checked us in when we arrived at the main desk and buzzed us through, along with many others who arrived for the service. There were golden lilies everywhere. For many, this was a fun-filled family event, and lots of children trailed their Alchemist parents. It made me feel strange as I watched them, these kids who had been born into our profession. I wondered how they'd feel ten years from now. Would they be excited to step up to the plate? Or would they start questioning?

The center had three floors aboveground and five underneath. People off the street could hardly just come wandering in, but we still took precautions by keeping the more benign offices on the main floor. As we all walked down the corridor to the auditorium, we passed Payroll, Travel, and Maintenance. All the offices had clear windows looking into them from the hall, maintaining the Alchemist ideal that we had nothing to hide.

The secure offices belowground weren't quite so open, however.

I'd been in this facility once before for a training seminar, and it had actually taken place in the auditorium we entered for the service. Despite the spiritual theme of tonight's event, the room bore little resemblance to a church. Someone had gone to the effort of decorating the walls with red-bowed evergreen garlands and setting pots of poinsettias on the stage. The room had a state-of-the-art audio-visual system, including a giant screen that gave a larger-than-life look at whatever was happening onstage. The auditorium's seating was so efficient that even those in the farthest corners had a pretty clear view, so I think the screen was just for emphasis.

Ian and I found two seats near the middle of the auditorium. "Aren't you going to take off your coat?" he asked hopefully.

No way was I going to unleash the dress in this den of taupe and high collars. Besides, if I kept the coat on, it would just give him something to keep looking forward to. Adrian would be proud of my ability to manipulate the opposite sex . . . and I couldn't help but wonder just how well Adrian would be able to stand up to this dress. Clearly, I was getting overly confident with this new power.

"I'm cold," I said, pulling the coat tighter. It was kind of ridiculous since the lights from the stage and high number of bodies had already made the room stifling, but I figured since it was so cold outside, I could get away with it.

For someone who always seems to be so cold, you sure can warm up pretty fast.

"Sydney? Is that you?"

I froze, not from the shock of hearing my name, but from the voice that had said it. I'd know that voice anywhere. Slowly, I turned away from Ian and looked up into my father's face. He was standing in the aisle, wearing a heavy wool suit, with melted snowflakes in his graying dark blond hair.

"Hi, Dad," I said. Then I saw who was standing beside him. "Zoe?"

It was all I could do not to jump up and hug her. I hadn't seen or spoken to my younger sister since that night I'd been pulled out of bed and sent on my Palm Springs mission. That was the mission she believed I'd stolen from her, no matter my protests. It was the mission that had driven her away from me.

I eyed her now, trying to assess where we stood. She didn't wear the blatant hatred she had at our last meeting, which was a good sign. Unfortunately, she didn't look all that warm and friendly either. She was cautious, studying me carefully—almost warily. She did not, I noticed, have a golden lily on her cheek yet.

"I'm surprised to see you here," said my father.

His parting words to me had been "Don't embarrass me," so I wasn't really astonished by his low expectations. "It's the holidays," I said. Forcing a smile now was far more difficult than it had been with Ian. "It's important to be here with the group. Do you know Ian Jansen?"

Ian, wide-eyed, jumped up and shook my father's hand. Clearly, he hadn't expected a parental meeting so soon. "It's a pleasure to meet you, sir."

My father nodded gravely and looked back and forth between the two of us. Whatever surprise he'd had at seeing me here had just been trumped by me being here with a date. Glancing at Ian, I tried to guess how he'd appear to someone like my dad. Clean cut, respectful, an Alchemist. The fact that Ian tended to bore me was irrelevant. I doubted my father had ever thought much about me dating, but if so, he probably hadn't thought I'd get a catch like this.

"Would you like to join us, sir?" asked Ian. I had to give him credit; he'd overcome his initial shock and was now in proper suitor mode. "It would be an honor."

At first, I thought Ian was just laying it on thick. Then I

realized meeting my father might actually very well be an honor. Jared Sage wasn't a rock star, but he did have a reputation among the Alchemists that, by their standards, was outstanding. My father seemed to like the flattery and agreed. He took a seat beside Ian.

"Sit by your sister," he told Zoe, nodding in my direction.

Zoe obeyed and stared straight ahead. She was nervous too, I realized. Looking her over, I felt an ache from how much I'd missed her. We'd inherited the same brown eyes from our father, but she'd gotten Mom's brown hair, which made me a little jealous. Zoe also looked a lot more put together than the last time I'd seen her. She wore a pretty dark brown cashmere dress and didn't have a single hair out of place. Something about her appearance bothered me, and I couldn't quite put my finger on it at first. It soon hit me. She looked older. She looked like a young lady, like my peer. I supposed it was silly of me to feel sad, since she was fifteen, but I kind of wished she could stay a little kid forever.

"Zoe." I kept my voice low, not that I needed to worry about the men overhearing. My dad was interrogating Ian. "I've been wanting to talk to you for so long."

She nodded. "I know. Mom tells me each time you call." But there was no apology for dodging my calls.

"I'm sorry about the way we left things. I never meant to hurt you or one-up you. I thought I was doing you a favor, saving you from getting involved."

Her mouth tightened, and something hard flashed in her eyes. "I don't mind being involved. I *want* to be involved, you know. And it would've been great! Being in the field at fifteen. I could have a stellar career. Dad would be so proud."

I chose my next words very carefully so that she wouldn't

take offense. "Yeah, but another year with Dad will really be, um, stellar. He's got so much experience—and you want to get as much as you can, believe me. Even if you have to wait for an assignment at sixteen, you'll still be ahead of the rest of us."

Each word out of my mouth made me feel sick, but Zoe seemed to buy it. I wasn't bothered by her wanting to be part of the cause—but it killed me that she was clearly doing it to impress our dad. "I suppose. And I *am* learning a lot. I wish I could at least get some field experience—even if it's not my own post. It's all theory with Dad. I've never even seen a Moroi."

"I'm sure he'll fix that." I didn't like encouraging this, but at least she was speaking to me.

The lights dimmed, ending our conversation. Organ music filled the room, and the scent of frankincense drifted around us. Incense and resin were common components in magic, and my mind was instantly starting to make associations from the spell books I'd painstakingly copied. *Frankincense is used to heal burns. It can also be used when casting divining or purifying spells—*

I immediately stopped that train of thought. Even if I was keeping it to myself, thinking about magic in the middle of an Alchemist church service was pretty sacrilegious. I shifted uncomfortably, wondering what all these people would think if they knew the truth about me: that I practiced magic and had kissed a vampire. . . .

Alchemist priests were called hierophants. They performed blessings and offered moral advice, when needed. In day-to-day affairs, they wore suits, but for this occasion, the lead hierophant wore robes that reminded me uncomfortably of the robes some of the Warriors had donned. It was yet another reminder of our shared history—and maybe our shared future. Marcus had been right. This was a mystery I had to solve, regardless of where I stood on breaking the tattoo.

I'd attended services like this off and on throughout my life and knew the Latin prayers by heart. I chanted along with the rest of the congregation and listened avidly as the hierophant reaffirmed our goals, his voice echoing through the sound system. Even though the Alchemists' religion had loose connections to Christianity, there was very little mention of God or Jesus or even Christmas. Most of his sermon was about how we had to help protect humanity from the temptation of following Strigoi who offered unholy immortality. That warning, at least, wasn't exaggerated.

I'd heard stories and even seen for myself what happened when humans decided to serve Strigoi. Those Strigoi promised to turn their servants as a reward. Those humans helped Strigoi spread their evil and became monsters themselves, no turning needed. Keeping those dark vampires hidden was for the good of weak humans who couldn't protect themselves. I paid especially close attention when the hierophant mentioned the Moroi offhandedly in his sermon, as a means to an end in defeating the Strigoi. He didn't exactly inspire warm and fuzzy feelings about them, but at least he wasn't calling for Moroi and dhampir destruction either.

I agreed with a good part of the message, but it no longer filled me with the fire it once had. And when the hierophant started droning on and on about duty, obedience, and what was "natural," I really began feeling disconnected. I almost wished there was more talk of the divine, like you'd find at a normal church service. With everything going on in my life, I wouldn't have minded a connection to a higher power. Sometimes, when I listened to the hierophant, I wondered if everything he was saying had just been made up by a bunch of people sitting around in the Middle Ages. No holy mandate required.

I felt like a traitor when the service ended. Maybe Adrian's joke had been right: I didn't even need Marcus to break my tattoo and connection to the group. Glancing at my companions—and even the other Alchemists in the room—it was clear I was alone. All of them looked captivated by the sermon, devoted to the cause.

I was again eerily reminded of the Warriors and their fanatical devotion. *No, no, whatever else the Alchemists are guilty of, we have nothing to do with that kind of unhinged behavior.* And yet . . . it was more complicated than that, I realized. The Alchemists didn't shoot first and ask questions later or make our members battle each other. We were civilized and logical, but we did have a tendency to just do what we were told. That was the similarity, one that could be dangerous.

Zoe and my father walked out with Ian and me. "Isn't it amazing?" she asked. "Hearing that . . . well, it just makes me so glad Dad decided to raise another Alchemist in the family. It's good to boost our numbers."

Had that truly been his motivation? Or was it because he didn't trust me after I'd helped Rose?

It was infuriating that the only conversation I could have with Zoe centered around Alchemist rhetoric, but I'd take it over the silence of the last few months. In my heart, I longed to talk the way we used to. I wanted it back. Even though she'd warmed up a little, that old familiarity that had once existed between us was gone.

"I wish we had more time," I told her once our groups were ready to part in the parking lot. "There's so much I want to talk to you about."

She smiled, and there was a genuineness in it that warmed me. Maybe the distance between us wasn't irreparable. "Me too. I'm sorry about . . . well, the way things were. I hope we get some time together soon. I . . . I've missed you."

That nearly broke me down, as did her hug. "We'll be together soon, I promise."

Ian—whom my father now seemed to regard as a future son-in-law—drove me back to my hotel and couldn't stop gushing about how awesome it had been to meet Jared Sage. As for me, I could still feel where Zoe had hugged me.

Ian promised he'd get in touch with me in the morning about a tour of the archives. Then, weirdly, he closed his eyes and leaned forward. It took me a moment to realize that he expected a good-night kiss. Seriously? That was how he went about it? Had he ever even kissed anyone before? Even Brayden had displayed a little more passion. And, of course, neither guy measured up to Adrian.

When I did nothing, Ian finally opened his eyes. I gave him another hug—with the coat on—and told him how happy I was that he'd met my dad. That seemed to satisfy him.

Adrian made his nightly check-in with me once I was asleep later on. Naturally, he wanted to know about my dress. He also kept trying to find out how exactly I'd won Ian over and seemed amused at the few details I decided to give him. But mostly I couldn't stop talking about Zoe. Adrian soon gave up on the other topics and simply listened to me gush.

"She spoke to me, Adrian!" I paced around the reception hall, clasping my hands in excitement. "And she wasn't mad. By the end, she was happy to see me. Do you know what that's like? I mean, I know you don't have any brothers or sisters, but to have someone you haven't seen in a while welcome you back?"

"I don't know what it's like," he said quietly. "But I can imagine."

I was too caught up in my own joy at the time, but later, I wondered if he was talking about his incarcerated mother.

"It's nice to see you so happy," he added. "Not that you've been miserable lately, but you've had a lot to worry about."

I couldn't help but laugh at that and came to a halt. "Are you saying evil witches and espionage are stressful?"

"Nah." He walked over to me. "All in a day's work for us. But I'm going to make my way to bed now. You seem like you can get by without me tonight."

He'd visited me every night since Veronica's dream. Most of the trips were short now, but I still knew it was a lot of effort and spirit for him. "Thank you. I feel like I can't say that to you enough."

"You don't have to say it at all, Sage. Good luck tomorrow."

Right. Stealing top secret info from a highly secure facility.

"Thanks," I said again. A little of my mood dimmed, but not all of it. "No matter what happens, though, patching things up with Zoe makes me feel like this mission is already a success."

"That's because you haven't been caught." He cupped my face in his hands and leaned close. "See that you aren't. I don't want to have to dream visit you in prison . . . or wherever it is bad Alchemists go."

"Hey, at least I'd have you for company, right?"

He gave me a rueful headshake, and the dream vanished around me.

CHAPTER 20

IAN WOKE ME THE NEXT MORNING with a super-early phone call. At first, I thought maybe he hoped to sneak in before the other Alchemists woke up, but it turned out he just wanted to get breakfast beforehand. Seeing as he'd managed to get me access, I couldn't very well refuse. He'd originally wanted to go to the facility in the late morning, but I talked him into going closer to noon. It meant lingering longer over breakfast, but it was worth the sacrifice. However, I was strictly back to khakis and a linen top. Espionage aside, cocktail dresses and breakfast buffets just didn't mix. As a concession, however, I unbuttoned *two* buttons at the top of my shirt. Openly wearing that into the facility was practically R-rated, and Ian seemed thrilled by the "scandalous" act.

Sunday at the facility was much quieter than the previous night. Although Alchemists never really got a break from their duties, most of the center worked normal weekday business hours. I had no difficulties checking in through the main reception again, but as predicted, we had a small delay in getting to the secure area. The guy on duty wasn't the friend who owed Ian a favor. We had to wait for him to come out from the back room, and even then, it took Ian a bit of cajoling to convince his colleague to let me in. I think it was obvious to both of them that Ian was just trying to impress me, and finally, the first guy relented to what seemed like a harmless errand. After all, I was a fellow Alchemist, and I was only going on a tour of a library. What could possibly go wrong?

They searched my purse and made me walk through a metal detector. I had two spells in mind that I could perform without physical components, so at least I didn't have to explain any crystals or herbs. The trickiest part was a thumb drive I'd hidden in my bra. They might not have questioned me carrying one in my purse, but I hadn't wanted to risk it being called out. That being said, if the thumb drive did show up on the scan, I was going to have a much more difficult time explaining why I was hiding it. I tensed as I stepped under the scanner, bracing myself to either run or attempt a Wolfe move. But, as hoped, it was too small to find, and we were waved through. That was one obstacle down, though it didn't make me any less tense.

"Did you end up trading this for the money he owed you?" I asked once Ian and I were descending toward the archives.

"Yeah." He made a face. "I tried to just swap it out for half of what he owed, but it was all or nothing for him."

"So how much is this trip costing you?"

"Fifty dollars. It's worth it, though," he added quickly.

Dinner had cost about the same. This was turning into an expensive weekend for Ian, particularly since I was the only one truly reaping the rewards. I couldn't help but feel a bit guilty and had to remind myself again and again that this was for an important cause. I would've offered to pay him back for it all, but something told me that would counteract everything I'd been working to achieve with my "womanly charms."

The archives were sealed with electronic locks that opened when Ian scanned his card key. As we stepped inside, I nearly forgot that coming in here was just a cover for the larger plan. Books and books and books surrounded me as well as scrolls and documents written on parchment. Old and delicate items were sealed under glass, with notes and signs against a far wall on how to access digital copies of them on computers. A couple of Alchemists, young like us, worked at tables and were transcribing old books into their laptops. One of them looked excited about her job; the other guy looked bored. He seemed to welcome the distraction of us entering.

I must have worn an appropriately awed expression because when I turned to Ian, he was watching me with pride. "Pretty cool, huh?" Apparently being a glorified librarian had just become a much more exciting job for him. "Follow me."

He didn't have to tell me twice. We began by exploring the full extent of the archives room, which stretched back much farther than I initially realized. The Alchemists prized knowledge, and it was obvious from this collection, which dated back centuries. I lingered at the shelves, wanting to read every title. They came in different languages and covered a full range of topics useful to our trade: chemistry, history, mythology, the supernatural . . . it was dizzying.

"How do you organize it?" I asked. "How can you find anything?"

Ian pointed to small placards on the shelves that I hadn't

noticed. They bore alphanumeric codes that were part of no filing system I recognized. "These catalog it all. And here's the directory."

He led me to a touch screen panel embedded in the wall. I pressed it and was presented with a menu of options: AUTHOR, TIME PERIOD, SUBJECT, LANGUAGE. I touched SUBJECT and was led through a series of more and more specific topics until I finally realized I'd been searching for "Magic" in the supernatural section. It gave me a list of titles, each with its own code in the organizational system.

To my surprise, there were actually a number of books on magic, and I burned with curiosity. Did the Alchemists have records of witches? Or was it all speculation? Most likely these were moral books preaching the wrongness of humans even considering such feats.

"Can I browse some of the books?" I asked him. "I mean, I know I can't sit and read all afternoon, but there's so much history . . . I just kind of want to be a part of it. I'd be so, so grateful."

I really didn't think that would work twice, but it did.

"Okay." He pointed toward a small office in the back. "I need to catch up on a few things. Do you want to meet back here in an hour?"

I thanked him profusely and then returned to the touch screen. I yearned to investigate the magic books but had to remind myself why I was here. As long as I was in the archives, I might as well do some research that would help our cause. I flipped through the menus until I located the section on the Alchemists' early history. I'd hoped to find a reference to vampire hunters in general or the Warriors specifically. No luck.

The best I could do was follow the codes to shelves and shelves detailing our group's formation. Most of the books were dense and written in an antiquated style. The really old ones weren't even in English.

I skimmed a few and soon realized a task like this would take longer than an hour. The newer books had no mention of the Warriors, which didn't surprise me, seeing as that information was now covered up. If I was going to locate any references to vampire hunters, it would be in the oldest books. They didn't have much in the way of tables of contents or indices, and there was no way I could do a full read. Remembering my real mission here, I put the books away after about ten minutes and sought out Ian. That earlier tension returned, and I began to sweat.

"Hey, is there a restroom in here?"

I prayed there wasn't. I'd seen one down the hall when we'd come to this level. Part of my plan depended on getting out of the archives.

"Down the hall, by the stairs," he said. Some work issue had required his attention, and if my luck held, it would keep his eyes off the clock. "Knock on the door when you get back. I'll tell the scribes to let you in."

I'd had a knot of anxiety in my stomach all day that I'd been trying to ignore. Now there was no getting around it. It was time for the unthinkable.

Subtlety had no role in Alchemist security. The hallway contained cameras at each end. They faced each other, providing a long, continuous shot of the corridor. The restrooms were located at one end of the hall, almost directly under a camera. I went inside the ladies' room and verified there were no other people—or cameras—within. At least the Alchemists allowed some privacy.

Casting the invisibility spell was easy. Getting out was a little more difficult. The cameras' position made me think the restroom door was too flush with the wall for either camera to really get a good look at it. The door opened inward, so I was able to slip out and feel confident no camera had picked up a ghostly door opening. The door to the stairs was the real beast. It was in the range of one of the cameras. Ms. Terwilliger had told me the invisibility spell would protect me from video and film. So, I had no fear of being spotted. I simply had to take the risk of the camera recording the door opening by itself.

Although I knew security guards watched live feeds of the cameras, there were too many for them to scrutinize every second. If no sudden movement appeared on this one, I doubted any guard would notice. And if things stayed tame on this level, no one would have any reason to review the footage. But the operations level . . . well, if everything went according to plan, this sleepy Sunday was about to get a lot more exciting there.

I slipped in and out of the stairwell, opening the door with absolutely as little space as possible. The operations level was even more secure than the archives, with heavy, industrial-looking doors that required both key cards and codes. I had no illusions about cracking any of it. Entry into the security office, much like the rest of this task, relied on an odd mix of logic and luck. The one thing you could count on with Alchemists was reliability. I knew how schedules tended to work. Lunch breaks were taken on the hour at typical lunch times: eleven, twelve, and one. This was why I'd asked Ian to schedule our visit to this time, when I could be relatively certain workers would be moving in and out of the room. Noon was five minutes away, and I crossed my fingers someone would exit soon.

As it turned out, someone entered. A man came whistling down the hall. When he reached the door, the smell of fast-food hamburgers gave away his lunch choice. I held my breath as he scanned his card and punched in the numbers. The lock clicked, and he pushed the door open. I scurried in behind him and cleared the door without having to catch it or open it farther. Unfortunately, he came to a halt sooner than I expected, and I brushed against him. I immediately shrank away, and he scanned around, startled.

Please don't think there's an invisible person here. How terrible would that be to have made it this far, only to be detected now? Fortunately, magical subterfuge wasn't the first thing Alchemists turned to as a reason for anything. After a few more puzzled moments, he shrugged and called a greeting to one of his coworkers.

Wade had described the room perfectly. Monitors covered one wall, flipping back and forth between different camera views. A couple of guards kept an eye on the footage, while others worked away at computers. Wade had also told me which workstation contained the files I needed. I approached it—careful to avoid any other contact mishaps. A woman was already seated at the station.

"I was thinking of Thai carryout," she told one of her coworkers. "I've just got to finish this report."

No! She was about to take her lunch break. For my plan to work, that couldn't happen. If she left, she would lock her computer. I needed it accessible for this plan to work. She was running late on her lunch, which meant I had to act now.

This room wasn't exempt from surveillance. Even the watchers had watchers. Fortunately, there was only one camera. I selected an empty computer with a screen facing the camera and stood behind it. Wires and cords snaked out of the computer's panel, and the fans whirred steadily inside. I rested my hand on the panel and did one more quick assessment. The computer's back was out of the camera's view, but it would do no good if it was in the middle of someone else's line of vision. Everyone seemed preoccupied, though. It was time to act.

I created a fireball—a small one. I kept it in the palm of my hand and rested it right next to the panel. Despite its size, I summoned as much heat as I could. Not quite blue, but getting there. It took effect quickly, and within seconds, the cords and panel began to melt. The scent of burnt plastic rolled over me, and smoke drifted upward. It was enough. I let the fireball fade, and then I sprinted away from the computer just in time. Everyone had now noticed the burning computer. An alarm went off. There were cries of surprise, and someone yelled for a fire extinguisher. They all rose from their chairs to hurry over and look—including the woman who'd been at the computer I needed.

There was no time to waste. I sat immediately in her chair and plugged in the thumb drive. With gloved hands, I grabbed hold of the mouse and began clicking through directories. Wade hadn't been able to help much at this point. We'd just hoped finding the files would be intuitive. All the while, I was conscious of the time—and that someone might notice a mouse moving by itself. Even after they put out the fire, the Alchemists hovered around the smoking computer, trying to figure out what had happened. Overheating wasn't uncommon, but a fire happening that quickly definitely was. And these were computers that contained highly sensitive information.

I felt like there were a million directories. I checked a few likely candidates, only to hit a dead end. Each time I hit a dead end, I would silently swear at the wasted time. The other Alchemists weren't going to stay away forever! Finally, after more stressful searching, I found a directory of old surveillance footage. It contained folders linked to every camera in the building—including one marked MAIN CHECKPOINT. I clicked it open and found files named by date. Wade had told me that eventually these files were cleared and moved to archives, but the day I needed was still here. The cameras recorded one frame every second. Multiplied by twenty-four hours, that made for a huge file—but not nearly the size continuous filming would create. The file would fit on my thumb drive, and I began copying it over.

The connection was fast, but it was still a big transfer. The screen told me it had ten seconds to go. *Ten seconds.* The computer's owner could be back by then. I allowed myself another peek at the Alchemists. They were all still puzzling out the mystery. The thing about scientists like us was that a technological failure like this was fascinating. Also, it never occurred to any of them to look for a supernatural explanation. They tossed around theories with each other and started to take the melted computer apart. My file finished copying, and I sprang out of the chair, just as the woman began walking back toward it. I'd been fully prepared to risk another "ghost door" while they were distracted, but the fire alarm had summoned others in the hallway. People moved in and out with such frequency that I had no trouble holding the door open just long enough for me to sneak through.

I practically ran back to the archives level and had to calm myself when I reentered the restroom. I uncast the invisibility spell and waited for my breathing to slow. The thumb drive was back in my bra, the gloves back in my purse. Studying myself in the mirror, I decided that I looked innocent enough to return to the archives.

One of the scribes let me in. It was the engrossed girl, and she gave me a look that said opening the door was a waste of her time. Ian still appeared to be engulfed with work in the back, which was a relief. I'd been gone far longer than a bathroom trip would require and had worried he'd wonder where I was at. Things could've gone badly if he'd sent the girl to find me, both because I wasn't in the restroom and because she'd be *really* annoyed at the interruption. Over in the history section, I sat on the floor with a book picked at random, which I only pretended to read. I was too anxious and keyed up to parse the words, no matter how many times I tried to reassure myself. There was no reason for the Alchemists to suspect me of causing the fire. There was no reason for them to think I'd stolen data. There was no reason for them to think I was connected to any of this.

Ian found me when the hour was up, and I feigned disappointment at having to leave. In reality, I couldn't get out of this building fast enough. He drove me to the airport and chattered nonstop about the next time we'd get to see each other. I smiled and nodded appropriately but reminded him our work had to come first and that my post was particularly consuming. He was obviously disappointed but couldn't deny the logic. The Alchemist greater good came first. Even better, he didn't try one of those awful kisses again—though he did suggest we set up some times for video chatting. I told him to email me, secretly vowing I'd never open up any message from him.

I didn't relax until the plane took off, when the potential for an Alchemist raid seemed pretty low. The most paranoid part of me worried there could be a party waiting for me at the Palm Springs airport, but for now I had a few hours of peace.

I'd just assumed I'd deliver the drive to Marcus and leave it at that. But now, with it in my possession, my curiosity got the better of me. I had to get to the bottom of this mystery. Was the Z. J. who'd visited the Alchemists really Master Jameson?

With fresh coffee in hand, I opened the file on my laptop and began to watch.

Even with one frame per second, the footage went on forever. Most of it was nothing but a quiet checkpoint, with the most exciting parts being when the guards changed position or took breaks. Plenty of Alchemists passed in and out, but relative to the overall time span, they were few and far between. Ian actually showed up once, off to start his shift.

I wasn't even halfway through when the plane began its descent. Disheartened, I resigned myself to an evening of more of the same when I got back to the dorm. At least I'd be able to make some decent coffee to get me through. I was almost tempted just to push the file off on Marcus tomorrow and let him deal with reviewing it . . . but that nagging voice urging me to find out for myself won. It wasn't just because of my curiosity either. I didn't really think Marcus would fabricate anything, but if I could see for sure that—

There he was on the screen.

He wasn't in those over-the-top robes, but there was no mistaking Master Jameson's old-fashioned beard. He wore business casual clothing and seemed to be smiling at something a man beside him was saying. The man had a lily on his cheek but was no one I knew.

Master Jameson. With the Alchemists.

Marcus and his Merry Men's conspiracy had panned out. A suspicious part of me wanted to believe this was a setup, that maybe they'd altered and planted this. But, no. I'd taken it myself, off an Alchemist server. It was possible Marcus had more insiders running errands for him, but this hadn't been easy for me, even with magical assistance. Besides, why would Marcus go to so much trouble to make me believe this? If it was some twisted way to get me to join him, there were a million other ways he could have attempted it, with evidence much easier to fake.

Something in my gut told me this was real. I hadn't forgotten the similarities in our rituals or how the Warriors had wanted our groups to merge. Maybe the Alchemists and the Warriors weren't best friends yet, but someone had at least humored Master Jameson with a meeting. The question was, what had happened at that meeting? Had the Alchemist in the footage sent Jameson packing? Were the two of them together right now?

Regardless of the outcome, this was undeniable proof that the Alchemists and Warriors were still in contact. Stanton had told me we merely kept an eye on them and had no interest in hearing them out.

Once again, I had been lied to.

CHAPTER 21

SOME PART OF ME BEGGED FOR there to be a mistake. I watched the footage three more times, tossing crazy theories around in my head. Maybe Master Jameson had a twin who wasn't a fanatic who hated vampires. No. The video didn't lie. Only the Alchemists did.

I couldn't ignore this. I couldn't wait. I needed to resolve this immediately. If not sooner.

I sent Marcus a text as soon as my plane was on the ground: *We meet tonight. No games. No runaround. TONIGHT.*

There was no response from him by the time I got back to my dorm. What was he doing? Reading *Catcher in the Rye* again? If I'd known what dive he was holed up in, I would've marched over there right then. There was nothing I could do but wait, so I called Ms. Terwilliger both as a distraction and to buy some freedom.

"Nothing to report," she told me when she answered. "We're

still just watching and waiting—although, your extra charm is almost complete."

"That's not why I'm calling," I said. "I need you to get me a curfew extension tonight." I felt bad using her for something totally unrelated, but I had to do this.

"Oh? Are you paying me an unexpected visit?"

"Er—no. This is for something else."

She clearly thought that was funny. "Now you use my assistance for personal matters?"

"Don't you think I've earned it?" I countered.

She laughed, something I hadn't heard from her in a while. She agreed to my request and promised to call the dorm's front desk right away. As soon as we hung up, my phone chimed with the expected message from Marcus. All the text contained was an address that was a half hour away. Assuming he was ready for me now, I grabbed my messenger bag and got on the road.

In light of my past meetings with Marcus, I wouldn't have been surprised if he'd led me to a department store or karaoke bar. Instead, I arrived at a vintage music shop, the kind that sold vinyl records. A large CLOSED sign hung on the door, emphasized by dark windows and an empty parking lot. I got out of my car and double-checked the address, wondering if my GPS had led me astray. My earlier zeal gave way to nervousness. How careless was this? One of Wolfe's first lessons was to avoid sketchy situations, yet here I was, exposing myself.

Then, from the shadows, I heard my name whispered. I turned toward the sound and saw Sabrina materialize out of the darkness, carrying a gun as usual. Maybe if I showed her the one in my glove compartment, we could have a bonding moment.

"Go around back," she said. "Knock on the door." Without another word, she returned to the shadows.

The back of the building looked like the kind of place that screamed mugging, and I wondered if Sabrina would come to my aid if needed. I knocked on the door, half expecting some kind of speakeasy situation where I'd be asked for a password like "rusted iguana." Instead, Marcus opened the door, ready with one of those smiles he kept hoping would win me over. Strangely, tonight it put me at ease.

"Hey, gorgeous, come on in."

I stepped past him and found we were in the store's back room, which was filled with tables, shelves, and boxes of records and cassette tapes. Wade and Amelia stood against a wall in mirrored stances, their arms crossed over their chests.

Marcus shut the door behind me and locked it. "Glad to see you back in one piece. Judging from your text—and your face—you found something."

All the rage I'd been holding in since my discovery came bursting out. I retrieved my laptop from my bag and had to resist the urge to slam it against a table. "Yes! I can't believe it. You were right. Your insane, far-fetched theory was right. The Alchemists have been lying! Or, well, some of them. I don't know. Half of them don't know what the other half's doing."

I expected some smug remark from Marcus or at least an "I told you so." But that handsome face was drawn and sad, reminding me of the picture I'd seen of him and Clarence. "Damn," he said softly. "I was kind of hoping you'd come back with a bunch of boring video. Amelia, go swap with Sabrina. I want her to see this."

Amelia looked disappointed to be sent away, but she didn't

hesitate to obey his order. By the time Sabrina came back in, I had the video cued up to the correct time. They gathered around me. "Ready?" I asked. They nodded, and I could see a mix of emotions in all of them. Here it was, the conspiracy theory they'd all been waiting to prove. At the same time, the implications were staggering, and the three of them were well aware of how dangerous what they were about to see could be.

I played the video. It was only a few seconds long, but they were powerful ones as that bearded figure appeared on the screen. I heard an intake of breath from Sabrina.

"It's him. Master Jameson." She looked between all our faces. "That's really the Alchemist place? He's really there?"

"Yes," said Wade. "And that's Dale Hawthorne with him, one of the directors."

That triggered a memory. "I know that name. He's one of Stanton's peers, right?"

"Pretty much."

"Is it possible she wouldn't know about a visit like this?" I asked. "Even at her level?"

It was Marcus who answered. "Maybe. Although, walking him right in there—even to the secure level—is pretty ballsy. Even if she doesn't know about the meeting, it's a safe bet others do. If it were completely shady, Hawthorne would've met him off-site. Of course, the secure list means this wasn't out in the open either."

So, it was possible Stanton hadn't lied to me—well, at least not about the Alchemists being in contact with the Warriors. She'd certainly lied about the Alchemists knowing about Marcus since he'd said he was a notorious figure to most higher-ups. Even if she was ignorant about Master Jameson, it didn't change the fact that other Alchemists—important ones—were keeping some dangerous company. Maybe I didn't always like their procedures, but I'd desperately wanted to believe they were doing good in the world. Maybe they were. Maybe they weren't. I just didn't know anymore.

When I dragged my eyes from the frozen frame of Master Jameson, I found Marcus watching me. "Are you ready?" he asked.

"Ready for what?"

He walked over to another table and returned with a small case. When he opened it, I saw a small vial of silver liquid and a syringe.

"What is—oh." Realization hit me. "That's the blood that'll break the tattoo."

He nodded. "Pulling the elements out creates a reaction that turns it silver. It takes a few years, but eventually, the gold in your skin will fade to silver too."

All of them were looking at me expectantly, and I took a step back. "I don't know if I'm ready for this."

"Why wait?" asked Marcus. He pointed at the laptop. "You've seen this. You know what they're capable of. Can you keep lying to yourself? Don't you want to go forward with your eyes open?"

"Well . . . yes, but I don't know if I'm ready to have some strange substance injected into me."

Marcus filled the syringe with the silver liquid. "I can demonstrate on my tattoo if it'll make you feel better. It won't hurt me, and you can see that there aren't any dire side effects."

"We don't know for sure that they've done anything to me," I protested. He had a logical argument, but I was still terrified of taking this step. I could feel my hands shaking. "This could be a waste. There may be no group loyalty compulsion in me."

"But you also don't know for sure," he countered. "And there's always a *little* loyalty put in the initial tattoo. I mean, not enough to make you some slave robot, but still. Wouldn't you feel better knowing everything's gone?"

I couldn't take my eyes off the needle. "Will I feel any different?"

"No. Although you could walk up to someone on the street and start telling them about vampires." I couldn't tell if he was joking or not. "Then you'd just get thrown into a psych ward."

Was I ready for this? Was I really going to take the next step into becoming part of Marcus's Merry Men? I'd passed his test—which he'd been right about. Clearly, this group wasn't useless. They had eyes on the Alchemists and the Warriors. They also seemingly had the Moroi's best interests at heart.

The Moroi—or, more specifically, Jill. I hadn't forgotten Sabrina's offhand remark about the Warriors being interested in a missing girl. Who else could it be but Jill? And did this Hawthorne guy have access to her location? Had he passed it on to Master Jameson? And would this information put those around her at risk, like Adrian?

They were questions I didn't have the answers to, but I had to uncover them.

"Okay," I said. "Do it."

Marcus didn't waste any time. I think he was afraid I'd change my mind—which, perhaps, was not an unfounded fear. I sat down in one of the chairs and tipped my head to the side so that he'd have access to my cheek. Wade gently held my head with his hands. "Just to make sure you stay still," he told me apologetically.

Before Marcus started, I asked, "Where'd you learn to do this?"

His face had been solemn with the task ahead, but my question made him smile again. "I'm not technically tattooing you, if that's what you're worried about," he said. I was actually worried about *a lot* of things. "These are just some small injections, just like being re-inked."

"What about the process itself? How'd you find out about it?" It was probably a question I should have asked before I sat down in this chair. But I hadn't expected to be doing this so soon—or suddenly.

"A Moroi friend of mine theorized about it. I volunteered to be a guinea pig, and it worked." He switched to business mode again and held up the needle. "Ready?"

I took a deep breath, feeling like I was standing on the edge of a precipice.

Time to jump.

"Go ahead."

It hurt about as much as re-inking did, just a number of small pricks on my skin. Uncomfortable, but not really painful. In truth, it wasn't a long process, but it felt like it took forever. All the while, I kept asking myself, *What are you doing? What are you doing?* At last, Marcus stepped back and regarded me with shining eyes. Sabrina and Wade smiled too.

"There you go," Marcus said. "Welcome to the ranks, Sydney."

I took my compact out of my purse to check the tattoo. My skin was pink from the needle's piercing, but if this process continued to be like re-inking, that irritation would fade soon.

Otherwise, the lily looked unchanged.

I also didn't feel that changed on the inside. I didn't want to storm the Alchemist facility and demand justice or anything like that. Taking him up on his dare to tell an outsider about vampires was probably my best bet to see if my tattoo had been altered, but I didn't really feel like doing that either.

"That's it?" I asked.

"That's it," Marcus said. "Once we get it sealed, you won't have to worry about—"

"I'm not getting it sealed."

All those smiles vanished.

Marcus looked confused, as though he might have misheard. "You have to. We're going to Mexico next weekend. Once that's done, the Alchemists won't ever be able to get to you again."

"I'm not getting it sealed," I repeated. "And I'm not going to Mexico." I gestured toward my laptop. "Look what I was able to pull off! If I stay where I'm at, I can keep finding out more. I can find out what else the Alchemists and Warriors are doing together." *I can find out if Jill is in danger.* "Getting permanently marked and becoming an outcast kills all those opportunities for me. There's no going back after that."

I think Marcus almost always got his way, and this new development totally threw him off. Wade took up the argument. "There's no going back *now*. You're leaving a trail of bread crumbs. Look at what you've done. You already made inquiries about Marcus. Even if you haven't gotten super-friendly with the Moroi, the Alchemists still know you spend a lot of time with them. And one day, someone may realize you were there when the data was stolen."

"No one knows it was stolen," I said promptly.

"You hope they don't," corrected Wade. "These little things are enough to raise red flags. Keep doing more, and you'll make it worse. They'll finally notice you, and that's when it'll be over."

Marcus had recovered from his initial shock. "Exactly. Look, if you want to stay where you're at until we go to Mexico, that's fine. Make your peace with it or whatever. After that, you need to escape. We'll keep working from the outside."

"You can do whatever you want." I began packing up my laptop. "I'm going to work from the inside."

Marcus caught hold of my arm. "You're setting yourself up for a fall, Sydney!" he said sternly. "You're going to get caught."

I pulled away from him. "I'll be careful."

"Everyone makes mistakes," said Sabrina, speaking up for the first time in a while.

"I'll take that risk." I slung my bag over my shoulder. "Unless you guys are going to forcibly stop me?" None of them answered. "Then I'm going. I'm not afraid of the Alchemists. Thank you for everything you've done. I really do appreciate it."

"Thank you," said Marcus at last. He shook his head at Wade, who looked like he wanted to protest. "For getting the data. I honestly didn't think you'd be able to pull it off. I figured you'd return empty-handed, though I still would've broken the tattoo for you. A for effort, you know. Instead, you just proved what I'd thought before: you're remarkable. We could really use you."

"Well, you know how to get in touch with me."

"And you know how to get in touch with us," he said. "We'll be here all week if you change your mind."

I opened the door. "I won't. I'm not running away."

Amelia called goodbye to me when I got into my car, oblivious to the fact that I'd just defied her beloved leader. As I drove back to Amberwood, I was amazed at how free I felt—and it had nothing to do with the tattoo. It was the knowledge that I had defied everyone—the Alchemists, the Warriors, the Merry Men. I didn't answer to anyone, no matter the cause. I was my own person, able to take my own actions. It wasn't something I had a lot of experience with.

And I was about to do something drastic. I hadn't told Marcus and the gang because I'd been afraid they really would stop me. When I got back to Amberwood, I went straight to my room and dialed Stanton. She answered on the first ring, which I took as a divine sign that I was doing the right thing.

"Miss Sage, this is unexpected. Did you enjoy the services?"

"Yes," I said. "They were very enlightening. But that's not why I'm calling. We have a situation. The Warriors of Light are looking for Jill." I wasn't going to waste any time.

"Why on earth would they do that?" She sounded legitimately surprised, but if there was one thing in all of this that I believed wholeheartedly, it was that the Alchemists were exceptional liars.

"Because they know if Jill's whereabouts got out, it could throw the Moroi into chaos. Their focus is still on the Strigoi, but they wouldn't mind seeing thing go bad for the Moroi."

"I see." I always wondered if she paused to gather her thoughts or if it was simply for effect. "And how exactly did you learn this?"

"That guy I know who used to be with the Warriors. We're still friendly, and he's been having doubts about them. He mentioned hearing them talk about finding a missing girl that could

329

cause all sorts of trouble." Maybe it was wrong to drag Trey into this lie, but I seriously doubted Stanton would interrogate him anytime soon.

"And you assume this is Miss Dragomir?"

"Come on," I exclaimed. "Who else would it be? Do you know any other Moroi girls? Of course it's her!"

"Calm down, Miss Sage." Her voice was flat and untroubled. "There's no need for theatrics."

"There's a need for action! If they might be on to her, then we need to get out of Palm Springs immediately."

"That," she said crisply, "is not an option. A lot of planning went into getting her to her current location."

I didn't believe that argument for a second. Half our job was doing damage control and adapting to rapidly changing situations. "Yeah? Well, did you also plan on those psycho vampire hunters finding her?"

Stanton ignored the jab. "Do you have any evidence at all that the Warriors actually have concrete data about her? Did your friend supply you with details?"

"No," I admitted. "But we still need to do something."

"There's no 'we' here." Her voice had gone from flat to icy. "*You* do not decide what we do."

I nearly protested and then caught myself. Horror set in. What had I just done? My initial intent had been to either get Stanton to take legitimate action or else find out if she might accidentally reveal knowledge of a Warrior connection. I'd thought mentioning Trey would give me valid backup since I could hardly tell her the real reason I feared for Jill. Yet, somehow, I'd gone from a request to a demand. I'd practically yelled an order at her. That wasn't typical Sydney behavior. That wasn't typical Alchemist behavior. What had Wade said? *You're leaving a trail of bread crumbs.*

Was this because I'd broken the tattoo?

This was no crumb. This was a full loaf. I was on the verge of insubordination, and my mind could suddenly imagine that list Marcus kept warning about, the one that kept track of every suspicious thing I did. Was Stanton already updating that list right now?

I had to fix this, but how? How on earth did I take this back? My mind was racing frantically, and it took several moments for me to calm down and start thinking logically. The mission. Focus on the mission. Stanton would understand that.

"I'm sorry, ma'am," I said at last. *Be calm. Be deferential.* "I'm just . . . I'm just so worried about this mission. I saw my dad at the services, you know." That would be a fact she could check on. "You had to have seen how it was that night I left. How bad things are between us. I . . . I have to make him proud. If things fall apart here, he'll never forgive me."

She didn't respond, so I prayed that meant she was listening intently . . . and believing me.

"I want to do a good job here. I want to fulfill our goals and keep Jill hidden. But there have already been so many complications no one predicted—first Keith and then the Warriors. I just never feel like she's fully safe now, even with Eddie and Angeline. It eats at me. And—" I was no actress who could muster tears, but I did my best to make my voice crack. "And *I* never feel safe. I told you, when I asked to go to the services, how overwhelming it is with the Moroi. They're everywhere—and the dhampirs too. I eat with them. I'm in class with them. Being with other Alchemists this last weekend was a lifesaver. I mean, I'm not trying to dodge my duties, ma'am. I understand we have to make sacrifices. And I've gotten better around them, but sometimes the stress is just unbearable—and then when I heard this thing about the Warriors, I cracked. All I could think about was that I might fail. I'm sorry, ma'am. I shouldn't have flipped out on you. I was out of control, and it was unacceptable."

I cut off my rant and tensed as I waited for her response. Hopefully I'd given her enough to dismiss any thoughts of me being a dissident. Of course, I might have just come off as a totally weak and unstable Alchemist who needed to be pulled from this mission. If that happened . . . well, maybe I'd have to take Marcus up on Mexico.

Her characteristic pause was especially painful this time. "I see," she said. "Well, I'll take this all into consideration. This mission is of the utmost importance, believe me. My earlier questioning of your information was not some weakening of our resolve. Your concerns have been heard, and I will decide the best course of action."

It wasn't exactly what I wanted, but hopefully she would be true to her word. I really, really wanted to believe she was on the up-and-up. "Thank you, ma'am."

"Is there anything else, Miss Sage?"

"No, ma'am. And . . . and I'm sorry ma'am."

"Your apology is noted."

Click.

I'd paced while I'd talked and now stood staring at the phone. A gut instinct told me I really had driven Stanton to take some sort of action. The mystery was whether that action would prove beneficial or catastrophic for me.

Falling asleep was difficult after that, and it had nothing to do with Veronica for a change. I was too keyed up, too anxious about what had happened with Marcus and Stanton. I tried to seize that feeling of freedom again, using it to strengthen me. It was only a spark this time, flickering with my new uncertainties, but it was better than nothing.

I fell asleep sometime around three. I had a vague sense of a couple hours passing before I was swept into one of Adrian's dreams, back in the reception hall. "Finally," he said. "I almost gave up checking in. I thought you were going to pull an all-nighter." He'd stopped wearing his suit in these dreams, probably because I always showed up in jeans. Tonight he wore jeans also, along with a plain black T-shirt.

"Me too." I wrung my hands and began pacing here as well. The nervous energy from my waking self had carried over into the dream. "A lot of stuff's kind of happened tonight."

The dream felt real, solid. Adrian was sober. "Didn't you just get back? How much could've happened?"

When I told him, he shook his head in amazement. "Man, Sage. It's all or nothing with you. Never a dull moment."

I came to a halt in front of him and leaned against a table. "I know, I know. Do you think I just made a huge mistake? God, maybe Marcus was right, and there was some compulsion forcing me to be loyal in the tattoo. I'm free for one hour and completely go over the edge with my superior."

"It sounds like you covered your tracks," he said, though a small frown appeared on his face. "But I would be disappointed if they sent you somewhere less stressful. That seems like it might be the worst-case scenario from everything you said."

I started laughing, but it was the hysterical kind. "What in the world's happened to me? I was doing crazy stuff way before

Marcus broke the tattoo tonight. Meeting with rebels, chasing evil sorceresses, even buying that dress! Yelling at Stanton is just one more thing on a long list of insanity. It's just like I said at Pies and Stuff: I don't know who I am anymore."

Adrian smiled and clasped my hands, taking a few steps toward me. "Well, first off, *I'm* the expert in insanity, and this is nothing. And as for who you are, you're the same beautiful, brave, and ridiculously smart caffeinated fighter you've been since the day I met you." Finally, he put "beautiful" at the top of his list of adjectives. Not that I should have cared.

"Sweet talker," I scoffed. "You didn't know anything about me the first time we met."

"I knew you were beautiful," he said. "I just hoped for the rest."

He always got this glint in his eyes when he complimented my looks, like he was seeing so much more than just my actual appearance. It was disorienting and heady . . . but I didn't mind. And that wasn't the only thing I suddenly found overwhelming. How had he gotten so close to me without me even realizing it? It was like he had secret stealth abilities. His hands were warm on mine, our fingers locked together. I still had remnants of that earlier joy within me, and being connected to him amplified those feelings. The green of his eyes was as lovely as usual, and I wondered if mine had the same effect on him. There was a little amber mixed with the brown that he had once said looked like gold.

He's the only one who never tells me to do anything, I realized. Oh, sure, he asked me to do lots of things, often with cajoling and fast talking. But he made no demands on me, not like the Alchemists or Marcus. Even Jill and Angeline tended to preface their requests with, "You have to . . . ."

"Speaking of that dress," he added, "I still haven't seen it."

I laughed softly. "You couldn't handle it."

He raised an eyebrow at that. "Is that a challenge, Sage? I can handle a lot."

"Not if our history is any indication. Each time I wear some moderately attractive dress, you lose it."

"That's not exactly true," he said. "I lose it no matter what you're wearing. And that red dress was not 'moderately attractive.' It was like a piece of heaven here on earth. A red, silky piece of heaven."

I should've rolled my eyes. I should've told him I wasn't here for his personal entertainment. But there was something in the way he was looking at me and something in the way I felt tonight that made me want to see his reaction. Breaking the tattoo hadn't affected anything between us, but it—and the deeds I'd done this weekend—had left me feeling bold. For the first time, I wanted to take a risk with him, despite my usual set of logical arguments. Besides, there was nothing dangerous in letting him look.

I manipulated the dream the way he'd taught me. A few moments later, the lacy minidress replaced my jeans and blouse. I even summoned the heels, which bumped my height up. I was still nowhere near as tall as him, but the small boost brought our faces closer together.

His eyes widened. Still holding my hands, he took a step back so that he could take in the whole look. There was almost something tangible to the way his gaze swept my body. I could practically feel every place it touched. By the time his eyes reached mine again, my breathing was heavy, and I was acutely aware that there really wasn't that much clothing between the two of us. Maybe there was something dangerous in letting him look after all.

"A piece of heaven?" I managed to ask.

He slowly shook his head. "No. The other place. The one I'm going to burn in for thinking what I'm thinking."

He'd moved toward me again. His hands released mine and moved to my waist, and I noticed I wasn't the only one breathing heavily. He pulled me to him, bringing our bodies together. The world was all heat and electricity, thick with tension that was only one spark away from exploding around us. I was balancing on another precipice, which wasn't easy to do in heels.

I wrapped my arms around his neck, and this time I was the one who drew him closer. "Damn," he murmured.

"What?" I asked, never taking my eyes off his.

He ran his hands over my hips. "I'm not supposed to kiss you."

"It's okay."

"What is?"

"It's okay if I kiss you."

Adrian Ivashkov wasn't easy to surprise, but I surprised him then when I brought his mouth toward mine. I kissed him, and for a moment, he was too stunned to respond. That lasted for, oh, about a second. Then the intensity I'd come to know so well in him returned. He pushed me backward, lifting me so that I sat on the table. The tablecloth bunched up, knocking over some of the glasses. I heard what sounded like a china plate crash against the floor.

Whatever logic and reason I normally possessed had melted away. There was nothing but flesh and fire left, and I wasn't going to lie to myself—at least not tonight. I wanted him. I arched my back, fully aware of how vulnerable that made me and that I was giving him an invitation. He accepted it and laid me back against the table, bringing his body down on top of mine. That crushing kiss of his moved from my mouth to the nape of my neck. He pushed down the edge of my dress and the bra strap underneath, exposing my shoulder and giving his lips more skin to conquer. A glass rolled off and smashed, soon followed by another. Adrian broke off his kissing, and I opened my eyes. He had an exasperated look on his face.

"A table," he said. "A goddamned table."

A few moments later, the table was gone. I was in his apartment, on his bed, and was glad that I no longer had silverware underneath me. With the venue change complete, his lips found mine again. The urgency in the way I responded surprised even me. I never would've thought myself capable of a feeling so primal, so removed from the reason that usually governed my actions. My nails dug into his back, and he trailed his lips down the edge of my chin, down the center of my neck. He kept going until he reached the bottom of the dress's V-neck. I let out a small gasp, and he kissed all around the neckline, just enough to tease.

"Don't worry," he murmured. "The dress stays on."

"Oh? Is that your decision to make?"

"Yes," he said. "You're not losing your virginity in a dream. If that's even possible. I don't want to deal with the philosophical side of it. And besides, there's no need to rush anyway. Sometimes it's worth lingering on the journey for a while before getting to the destination."

Metaphors. This was the cost of making out with an artist.

I nearly said as much. Then his hand slid up my bare leg, and I was lost again. Maybe the dress was staying on, but he didn't mind taking liberties with it. That hand slipped under my dress, running along the side of my leg and up to my hip. I burned where he touched me, and everything within me became focused on that hand. It was moving far too slowly, and I grabbed it, ready to urge it on.

Adrian chuckled and caught hold of my wrist, pulling my hand away and pinning it down against the covers. "Never thought I'd be the one slowing you down."

I opened my eyes and met his. "I'm a quick study."

All that burning and animal need within me must have shone through because he caught his breath and lost the smile. He released my wrist and cupped my face in his hands, bringing his face down only a whisper away from mine. "Good God, Sydney. You are—" The passion in his eyes turned to surprise, and he suddenly looked up.

"What's wrong?" I asked, wondering if this was some weird part of "the journey."

He grimaced and began to fade away before my eyes. "You're being woken up."

CHAPTER 22

I OPENED MY EYES, groggy from the sudden shock of being pulled out of the dream. My body felt sluggish, and I squinted against the light. The lamp I'd left on last night was joined by sunlight streaming in through the window, but my phone's display still showed a freakishly early hour. Someone knocked at my door, and I realized that was what had woken me up. I ran a hand through my disheveled hair and rose unsteadily from the bed.

"If she needs a geography tutor now, I really am going to Mexico," I muttered. But when I opened the door, it wasn't Angeline standing outside my door. It was Jill.

"Something big just happened," she said, hurrying in.

"Not to me it didn't."

If she noticed my annoyance, she didn't show it. In fact, as I studied her more closely, I realized she probably had no idea (yet) about what had happened between Adrian and me. From what I'd learned, spirit dreams weren't shared through the bond unless the shadow-kissed person was directly brought into it.

I sighed and sat down on my bed again, wishing I could go back to sleep. The heat and excitement of the dream was fading, and mostly I felt tired now. "What's wrong?"

"Angeline and Trey."

I groaned. "Oh, lord. What's she done to him now?"

Jill settled into my desk chair and put on a steely look of resolve. Whatever was coming was bad. "She tried to get him to sneak into our dorm last night."

"What?" I really did need more sleep because my brain was having trouble understanding the reasoning behind that. "She's not *that* dedicated to her math grade . . . is she?"

Jill gave me a wry look. "Sydney, they weren't working on math."

"Then why were they—oh. Oh no." I fell backward onto the bed and stared up at the ceiling. "No. This can't be happening."

"I already tried saying that to myself," she told me. "It doesn't help."

I rolled over to my side so that I could look at her again. "Okay, assuming this is true, how long has it been going on?"

"I don't know." Jill sounded as tired as me—and a lot more exasperated. "You know how she is. I tried to get answers out of her, but she kept going on about how it wasn't her fault and how it just happened."

"What'd Trey say?" I asked.

"I never got a chance to talk to him. He got hauled away as soon as they were caught." She smiled, but there wasn't much humor in it. "On the bright side, he got in a lot more trouble than she did, so we don't have to worry about her getting expelled."

Oh no. "Do we have to worry about *him* getting expelled?"

"I don't think so. I heard about other people trying this, and they just get detention for life. Or something."

Small blessing. Angeline was in detention so much that they'd at least have bonding time. "Well, then I guess there isn't much to be done. I mean, the emotional fallout's going to be a mess, of course."

"Well . . ." Jill shifted nervously. "That's just it. You see, first Eddie needs to be told—"

I shot up out of my bed. "I am *not* doing that."

"Oh, of course not. No one would ever expect you to do that." I wasn't so sure but let her continue. "Angeline's going to. It's the right thing to do."

"Yes. . . ." I still wasn't letting down my guard.

"But someone still needs to talk to Eddie afterward," she explained. "It's going to be hard on him, you know? He shouldn't be left alone. He needs a friend."

"Aren't you his friend?" I asked.

She flushed. "Well, yeah, of course. But I don't know that it'd be right since . . . well, you know how I feel about him. Better to have someone more reasonable and objective. Besides, I don't know if I'd do a good job or not."

"Probably better than me."

"You're better at that stuff than you think. You're able to make things clear and—"

Jill suddenly froze. Her eyes widened a little, and for a moment, it was like she was watching something I couldn't see. No, I realized a moment later. There was no "like" about it. That was exactly what she was doing. She was having one of those moments where she was in sync with Adrian's mind. I saw her blink and slowly tune back into my room. Her eyes focused on me, and she paled. Just like that, I knew that she *knew*.

Rose had said that sometimes in the bond, you could sift through someone's recent memories even if you hadn't actually been tuned into the bond at that moment. As Jill looked at me, I could tell she'd seen it all, everything that had happened with Adrian last night. It was hard to say which of us was more horrified. I replayed everything I'd done and said, every compromising position I'd literally and figuratively put myself in. Jill had just "seen" me do things no one else ever had—well, except for Adrian, of course. And what had she actually felt? What it was like to kiss me? To run her—his?—hands over my body?

It was a situation I had in no way prepared for. My occasional indiscretions with Adrian had come through to Jill as well, but we'd all brushed those off—me in particular. Last night, however, had taken things to a whole new level, one that left both Jill and me stunned and speechless. I was mortified that she'd seen me so weak and exposed, and the protective part of me was worried that she'd seen anything like that at all, period.

She and I stared at each other, lost in our own thoughts, but Jill recovered first. She turned even redder than when she'd mentioned Eddie and practically leapt out of the chair. Turning her eyes away from mine, she hurried to the door. "Um, I should go, Sydney. Sorry to bother you so early. It probably could've waited. Angeline's going to talk to Eddie this morning, so whenever you get a chance to find him, you know, that'd be great." She took a deep breath and opened the door, still refusing to make eye contact. "I've gotta go. See you later. Sorry again."

"Jill—"

She shut the door, and I sank back into the bed, unable to stand. It was official. Whatever residual heat and lust I'd felt from being with Adrian last night had completely vanished in the wake of Jill's expression. Until that moment, I hadn't really and truly understood what it meant to be involved with someone who was bonded. Everything Adrian said to me, she heard. Every emotion he had for me, she experienced. Every time he kissed me, she felt it. . . .

I thought I might be sick. How had Rose and Lissa handled this? Somewhere in my addled mind, I recalled Rose saying she'd learned to block out a lot of Lissa's experiences—but it had taken a few years to figure it out. Adrian and Jill had only been bonded for a few months.

The shock of understanding what Jill had seen cast a shadow over everything that had been sensual and thrilling last night. I felt like I had been on display. I felt cheap and dirty, especially as I remembered my own role in instigating things. That sickening feeling in my stomach increased, and there was no stopping the avalanche of thoughts that soon followed.

I'd let myself spin out of control last night, carried away by desire. I shouldn't have done any of that—and not just because Adrian was a Moroi (though that was certainly problematic too). My life was about reason and logic, and I'd thrown all of that out the window. They were my strengths, and in casting them aside, I'd become weak. I'd been high on the freedom and risks I'd experienced last night, not to mention intoxicated by Adrian and how he'd said I was beautiful and brave and "ridiculously smart." I'd melted when he'd looked at me in that absurd dress. Knowing he'd wanted me had muddled my thoughts, making me want him too. . . .

There was no part of this that was okay.

With great effort, I dragged myself from the bed and managed to pick out some clothes for the day. I staggered to the shower like a zombie and stayed in for so long that I missed breakfast. It didn't matter. I couldn't have eaten anything anyway, not with all the emotions that were churning inside me. I barely spoke to anyone as I walked through the halls, and it wasn't until I sat down in Ms. Terwilliger's class that I finally remembered there were other people in the world with their own problems.

Specifically, Eddie and Trey.

I was certain there was no way they could be as traumatized as Jill and I were by last night's events. But it was obvious both guys had had a rough morning. Neither one spoke or made eye contact with others. I think it was the first time I'd ever seen Eddie neglect his surroundings. The bell cut me off before I had a chance to say anything, and I spent the rest of class watching them with concern. They didn't look like they were going to engage in any testosterone-driven madness, so that was a good sign. I felt bad for both of them—especially Eddie, who'd been wronged the most—and worrying on their behalf helped distract me from my own woes. A little.

When class ended, I wanted to talk to Eddie first, but Ms. Terwilliger intercepted me. She handed me a large yellow envelope that felt like it had a book inside. There was no end to the spells I had to learn. "Some of the things we discussed," she told me. "Tend to them as soon as you get the chance."

"I will, ma'am." I slipped the envelope into my bag and glanced around for Eddie. He was gone.

Trey was in my next class, and I took my usual seat beside

him. He gave me a sidelong look and then turned away.

"So," I said.

He shook his head. "Don't start."

"I'm not starting anything."

He stayed silent a few moments and then turned back to me, a frantic look in his eyes. "I didn't know, I swear. About her and Eddie. She never mentioned it, and obviously, they don't talk about it around here. I never would've done that to him. You have to believe that."

I did. No matter what Trey's other faults were, he was good-hearted and honest. If anyone was at fault for bad behavior here, it was Angeline.

"I'm actually more surprised that you'd get involved with someone like her, period." I didn't need to elaborate that "someone like her" referred to her being a dhampir.

Trey put his head on his desk. "I know, I know. It all just happened so fast. One day she's throwing a book at me. The next, we're making out behind the library."

"Ugh. That's a little more information than I needed." Glancing up, I saw that our chemistry teacher was still getting organized, giving Trey and me a little more time. "What are you going to do now?"

"What do you think? I have to end it. I shouldn't have let it get this far."

The Sydney from three months ago would have said of course he needed to end it. This one said, "Do you like her?"

"Yes, I—" He paused and then lowered his voice. "I think I love her. Is that nuts? After only a few weeks?"

"No—I don't know. I'm not really good at understanding that stuff." And by not really good, I actually meant terrible.

"But if you feel like that . . . maybe . . . maybe you shouldn't throw it away."

Trey's eyes widened, and surprise completely replaced his blue mood. "Are you serious? How can you say that? Especially you of all people. You know how it is. You've got the same rules as us."

I could hardly believe what I was saying. "Her people don't, and they seem to be fine."

For a moment, I thought I saw a flicker of hope in his eyes, but then he shook his head again. "I can't, Sydney. You know I can't. It would eventually end in disaster. There's a reason our kinds don't mix. And if my family ever found out . . . God. I can't even imagine. There'd be no way I'd ever get back in."

"Do you really want to?"

He didn't answer that. Instead, he just told me, "It can't work. It's over." I'd never seen him look so miserable.

Class started, and that ended the discussion.

Eddie wasn't in our cafeteria at lunch. Jill sat with Angeline at a corner table and looked as though she was delivering a stern lecture. Maybe Jill hadn't felt comfortable consoling Eddie, but she certainly had no problem speaking out on his behalf. I didn't really want to hear Angeline's excuses or meet Jill's eyes, so I grabbed a sandwich and ate outside. I didn't have enough time to check Eddie's cafeteria, so I sent him a text.

Want to go out for coffee later?

Don't feel sorry for me, he responded. I hadn't known if he'd answer at all, so that was something.

I just want to talk. Please.

His next text wasn't nearly so fast, and I could almost imagine his mental battle. *Okay, but after dinner. I have a study group*. A moment later, he added, *Not Spencer's*. Trey worked at Spencer's.

Now that the Angeline drama was on hold, I was able to return to my own messed-up love life. I couldn't shake that image of Jill's expression. I couldn't forgive myself for losing control. And now, I had Trey's words bouncing around my head. *It would eventually end in disaster. There's a reason our kinds don't mix.*

As though summoned by my thoughts, Adrian texted me. *You want to get the dragon today?*

I'd forgotten all about the callistana. He'd stayed with Adrian during my St. Louis trip, and now it was my turn. Since Adrian couldn't transform him back into quartz, the dragon had been in his true form all weekend.

Sure, I wrote back.

My stomach was in knots when I drove to Adrian's place later. I'd had the rest of the day to think about my options, and I'd finally reached an extreme one.

When he opened the door, his face was aglow—until he saw mine. His expression transformed to equal parts exasperation and sadness. "Oh no. Here it comes," he said.

I stepped inside. "Here what comes?"

"The part where you tell me last night was a mistake and that we can't ever do it again."

I looked away. That was exactly what I'd been going to say. "Adrian, you know this can't work."

"Because Moroi and humans can't be together? Because you don't feel the same way about me?"

"No," I said. "Well, not entirely. Adrian . . . Jill saw it all."

For a moment, he didn't seem to understand. "What do you—oh. Shit."

"Exactly."

"I never even think of that anymore." He sat down on the couch and stared off into space. The callistana came scurrying into the room and perched on the arm of the couch. "I mean, I know it happens. We even talked about it with other girls. She understands."

"Understands?" I exclaimed. "She's fifteen! You can't subject her to that."

"Maybe you were an innocent at fifteen, but Jill's not. She knows how the world works."

I couldn't believe what I was hearing. "Well, I'm not one of your other girls! I see her every day. Do you know how hard it was to face her? Do you know what it feels like to know she saw me doing that? And, God, what if there'd been more?"

"So, what's this mean exactly?" he asked. "You finally come around, and now you're going to just end things because of her?"

"Kissing you isn't exactly 'coming around.'"

He gave me a long, level look. "There was a lot more than kissing, Miss 'I'm a Quick Study.'"

I tried not to show how embarrassed I was about that now. "And that's exactly why this is all over. I'm not going to let Jill see that again."

"So you admit it could happen again?"

"Theoretically, yes. But I'm not going to give us the chance."

"You're going to avoid ever being alone with me again?"

"I'm going to avoid you, period." I took a deep breath. "I'm going to go with Marcus to Mexico."

"What?" Adrian jumped up and strode over to me. I immediately backed up. "What happened to you working undercover?"

"That only works if I can stay undercover! You think I can pull that off if I'm sneaking around with you?"

"You're with me half the time already!" I couldn't tell if he was angry or not, but he was clearly upset. "Nobody notices. We'll be careful."

"All it takes is one slipup," I said. "And I don't know if I can trust myself anymore. I can't risk the Alchemists finding out about you and me. I can't risk exposing Jill to what we'd do together. They'll send another Alchemist to look after her, and hopefully Stanton will take precautions against the Warriors."

"Jill knows I can't put my life on hold."

"You should," I snapped.

Now he *was* angry. "Well, you'd know all about that since you're an expert in denying yourself the things you want. And now you're going to leave the country to make sure you can deprive yourself even more."

"Yes, exactly." I walked over to the callistana and spoke the incantation that turned him back into his inert form. I put the crystal into my purse and summoned all my will to give Adrian the coldest look I could manage. It must have been a powerful one because he looked as though I'd slapped him. Seeing that pain on his face made my heart break. I didn't want to hurt him. I didn't want to leave him! But what choice did I have? There was too much at stake.

"This is done. I've made my choice, Adrian," I said. "I'm leaving this weekend, so please don't make it any more difficult than it has to be. I'd like us to be friends." The way I spoke made it sound like we were closing a business arrangement.

I walked toward the door, and Adrian hurried after me. I couldn't bear to face the agony in his eyes, and it took all my resolve not to avert my gaze. "Sydney, don't do this. You know it's wrong. Deep inside, you know it is."

I didn't answer. I couldn't answer. I walked away, forcing myself not to look back. I was too afraid my resolve would falter—and that was exactly why I needed to leave Palm Springs. I wasn't safe around him anymore. No one could be allowed to have that kind of power over me.

All I wanted to do after that was hide in my room and cry. For a week. But there was never any rest for me. It was always about others, with my feelings and dreams shoved off to the side. Consequently, I wasn't in the best position to give Eddie romantic advice when we met up that night. Fortunately, he was too caught up in his own emotions to notice mine.

"I should never have gotten involved with Angeline," he told me. We were at a coffee shop across town that was called Bean There, Done That. He'd ordered hot chocolate and had been stirring it for almost an hour.

"You didn't know," I said. It was hard maintaining my half of the conversation when I kept seeing the pain in Adrian's eyes. "You couldn't have known—especially with her. She's unpredictable."

"And that's *why* I shouldn't have done it." He finally set the spoon down on the table. "Relationships are dangerous enough without getting involved with someone like her. And I don't have time for that kind of distraction! I'm here for Jill, not me. I should never have let myself get caught up in this."

"There's nothing wrong with wanting to be with someone," I said diplomatically. *Unless that person turns your world upside down and makes you lose all self-control.*

"Maybe when I've retired, I'll have the time." I couldn't tell if he was serious or not. "But not right now. Jill's my priority."

I had no business playing matchmaker, but I had to try. "Have you ever thought about seriously being with Jill? I know you used to like her." And I was absolutely certain he still did.

"That's out of the question," he said fiercely. "And you know it. I can't think of her like that."

"She thinks about you like that." The words slipped out before I could stop them. After my own romantic disaster today, a part of me longed for at least someone to be happy. I didn't want anyone else hurting the way I did.

He froze. "She . . . no. There's no way."

"She does."

A whole range of emotions played through Eddie's eyes. Disbelief. Hope. Joy. And then . . . resignation. He picked up the spoon again and returned to his compulsive stirring.

"Sydney, you know I can't. You of all people know what it's like to have to focus on your work." This was the second time today someone had said "you of all people" to me. I guess everyone had a preconceived idea of who I was.

"You should at least think about it," I said. "Watch her the next time you're together. See how she reacts."

He looked as though he might consider it, which I took as a small victory. Suddenly, alarm flashed on his face. "Whatever happened with you and Marcus? The St. Louis trip? Did you find out anything about Jill?"

I chose my next words very carefully, both because I didn't want to alarm him and because I didn't want him taking some drastic action that could accidentally reveal my dealings with Marcus. "We found some evidence that the Warriors have talked to the Alchemists, but nothing that shows they're working together or have actual plans for her. I've also taken some steps to make sure she's protected."

I hadn't heard anything from Stanton today and wasn't sure if that last part would actually pan out. Eddie looked relieved, though, and I couldn't bear to stress him out any further today. His gaze shifted to something behind me, and he pushed the untouched hot chocolate away. "Time for us to go."

I looked back at a clock and saw he was right. We still had a comfortable window before curfew, but I didn't want to push it. I finished off the last of my coffee and followed him out. The sun was sinking into the horizon, coloring the sky red and purple. The temperature had finally cooled off to normal levels, but it still didn't feel like winter to me. There'd been a bunch of badly parked cars in the front of the lot, so I'd parked Latte in the back in case some careless person opened a door too fast.

"Thanks for the moral support," Eddie told me. "Sometimes it feels like you really are a sister—"

That was when my car exploded. Sort of.

I have to admit Eddie's response time was amazing. He threw me to the ground, shielding my body with his. The boom had been deafening, and I cried out as some sort of foam landed on the side of my face.

Foam?

Cautiously, Eddie rose, and I followed. My car hadn't exploded in flames or anything like that. Instead, it was filled with some sort of white substance that had blasted out with such force that it had blown the doors off and broken the windows. We both approached the mess, and behind us, I heard people coming out of the coffee shop.

"What the hell?" asked Eddie.

I touched some of the foam on my face and rubbed my fingertips together. "It's sort of like the stuff you'd find in a fire extinguisher," I said.

"How did it get in your car?" he asked. "And how did it get there so fast? I glanced over at it when we first walked out. You're the chemical expert. Could some reaction have happened that fast?"

"Maybe," I admitted. At the moment, I was too shocked to really run any formulas. I rested a hand against Latte's hood and wanted to burst into tears. My emotions were at a breaking point. "My poor car. First Adrian's, now mine. Why do people do stuff like this?"

"Vandals don't care," said a voice beside me. I glanced over and saw one of the baristas, an older man who I believed was the owner. "I've seen stuff like this before. Damn kids. I'll call the police for you." He took out his cell phone and backed away.

"I don't know if we'll make curfew now," I told Eddie.

He gave me a sympathetic pat on the back. "I think if you show a police report at the dorm, they'll be lenient with you."

"Yeah, I hope that—ugh. The police." I hurried over to the passenger side and stared bleakly at the wall of foam.

"What's wrong?" Eddie asked. "I mean, aside from the obvious."

"I have to get to the glove compartment." I lowered my voice. "There's a gun in there."

He did a double take. "A what?"

I said no more, and he helped me dig through the foam. Both of us ended up covered in it by the time I reached the compartment. Making sure no one was behind us, I quickly retrieved the gun and slipped it into my messenger bag. I was about to shut the lid when something shiny caught my eye.

"That's impossible," I said.

It was my cross, the gold one I'd lost. I grabbed it and then immediately dropped it, yelping in pain. The metal had burned me. Considering the foamy substance was cool, it didn't seem likely it had heated up the cross. I wrapped my sleeve around my hand and gingerly picked up the cross again.

Eddie peered over my shoulder. "You wear that all the time."

I nodded and continued staring at the cross. A terrible feeling began to spread over me. I found a tissue in my purse and wrapped the cross up before adding it to the bag. Then I retrieved my cell phone and dialed Ms. Terwilliger. Voice mail. I hung up without leaving a message.

"What's going on?" asked Eddie.

"I'm not sure," I said. "But I think it's bad."

I hadn't yet developed the ability to sense magical residue, but I was almost certain something had been done to the cross, something that had resulted in Latte's foamy demise. Alicia hadn't been able to find the cross. Had Veronica doubled back and taken it? If so, how had she located me? I knew personal items could be used to track back to a person, though the most common ones were hair and nails. As advanced as Veronica was, it was very likely an object—like this cross—would serve just as well.

Veronica might very well have found me. But if so, why vandalize my car instead of sucking out my life?

The police came soon thereafter and took our statements. They were followed by a tow truck. I could tell from the driver's face that it wasn't looking good for Latte. He hauled my poor car away, and then one of the officers was nice enough to return Eddie and me to Amberwood. Against all odds, we made it back just in time.

As soon as I got to my room, I tried Ms. Terwilliger again. Still no answer.

I emptied out my bag onto my bed and found it had gathered a number of items today. One of them was a donut I'd picked up at the coffee shop. I put it and the quartz crystal into the aquarium and summoned the callistana. He immediately went after the donut.

I found the cross and discovered it was now cool. Whatever spell it had been used in was gone. The gun was near it, and I quickly hid that back in the bag. That left Ms. Terwilliger's envelope, which I'd neglected all day. Maybe if I hadn't been so distracted by personal matters, I could have saved Latte.

I pulled the latest spell book out of the envelope and heard something jangle. I removed the book and then saw another, smaller envelope inside. I pulled it out and read a message Ms. Terwilliger had written on the side: *Here's another charm to mask your magical ability, just in case. It's one of the most powerful out there and took a lot of work, so be careful with it.*

That same guilt I always felt about her helping me returned. I opened the small envelope and found a silver star pendant set with peridots. I gasped.

I had seen this charm before, this powerful and painstakingly made charm that could allegedly hide strong magical ability.

I had seen it around Alicia's neck.

CHAPTER 23

FOR A MOMENT, I THOUGHT it had to be a coincidence. After all, what was so special about a peridot star? For all I knew, Alicia might have been born in August and was just sporting her birthstone among that mess of necklaces she always wore. And yet, if there was one thing I believed more than ever, it was Sonya's adage that there were no coincidences in the world of the supernatural.

I sank to the floor and tried to reason my way through things. If the charm Alicia had worn was like this one, then it meant she too was a strong magic user trying to mask her abilities. Did she know about Veronica? Was Alicia trying to protect herself? If so, then it seemed like she wouldn't have been so casual about Veronica staying at the inn. So, that meant either Alicia didn't know about Veronica's true nature—again, a suspicious coincidence—or that Alicia was covering for Veronica.

Could Alicia be in league with Veronica?

That seemed the likeliest answer to me. Although Veronica apparently sought out young, powerful magic users, it was totally possible that she'd seen the advantage of having one as an assistant. And, as we'd observed, Veronica had plenty of other victims to choose from. Alicia could therefore help and cover up Veronica's nefarious plans—like when a curious couple came asking questions.

I groaned. Alicia had been playing us from the beginning. From the instant we'd stepped through her door with stories about our anniversary and "friend" Veronica, she'd known we were lying. She'd known we weren't actually friends with Veronica, and she might have been strong enough to fight Adrian's compulsion a little. She'd gone along with everything—even being so helpful as to call me when Veronica had shown up again. I had no idea now what was true, if Veronica had ever left in the first place or returned from being gone. I did, however, have a sinking suspicion that my car wasn't the only one she'd incapacitated.

I could understand if she'd used the cross to find me, but how had she initially located the Mustang? I racked my brain for any identifying information. Adrian's spirit magic should have muddled our appearances, covering up any connection to us. Then I knew. Alicia had walked us out and admired the Mustang. A clever person—someone who was already on high alert because of our visit—could've made note of the license plate and used it to track down where Adrian lived.

But why slash the tires? *To delay us*, I realized. That was the night Lynne had been attacked. And we had arrived too late to warn her.

The more I began to sift through the events of the last few

weeks, the more I began to think we had been very, very care-less. We'd thought we were being so cautious about concealing ourselves from Veronica. No one, not even Ms. Terwilliger, had considered that she might have an accomplice we also had to watch out for. And the dreams . . . those had started the day Adrian and I had been on the velvet bed. The day my garnet had slipped and had possibly been enough for Alicia to sense a magic user in the inn.

Which brought me back to the present. Ms. Terwilliger. I had to tell her what I'd found. I called for a third time. Still no answer. Although I often had images of Ms. Terwilliger con-ducting late-night rituals, it was entirely reasonable that she'd be in bed right now. Was this the kind of thing that could wait until morning?

No, I decided on the spot. No, it wasn't. We were dealing with dangerous, violent magic users—and my car had just been attacked. Something might be happening as I stood there, try-ing to decide. I would have to wake her up . . . provided I could get to her.

It took only a moment to make my next decision. I called Adrian.

He answered on the first ring but sounded wary, which I couldn't blame him for after what I'd done earlier. "Hello?"

I prayed he was the noble guy I thought he was. "Adrian, I know things are bad between us, and maybe I have no right to ask, but I need a favor. It's about Veronica."

There was no hesitation. "What do you need?"

"Can you come over to Amberwood? I need you to help me break curfew and escape my dorm."

There were a few moments of silence. "Sage, I've been

waiting two months to hear you say those words. You want me to bring a ladder?"

The plan was already unfolding in my head. The security guards that patrolled at night would have eyes on the student parking lot, but the back property would be relatively unguarded.

"I'll get myself out of the building. If you come up the main road that leads to Amberwood and then go past the driveway, you'll see a little service road that runs up a hill and goes behind my dorm. Park there near the utility shed, and I'll meet you as soon as I get out."

When he spoke again, his earlier levity was gone. "I'd really like to believe this is some awesome midnight adventure, but it's not, is it? Something's gone really wrong."

"Very wrong," I agreed. "I'll explain in the car."

I quickly changed into clean jeans and a T-shirt, adding a light suede jacket against the evening chill. To be safe, I also decided to pack my bag with a few supplies and bring it along. If all went well, I'd simply be warning Ms. Terwilliger tonight. But with the way things had been going lately, I couldn't presume anything would be simple. Bringing the suitcase this time would be unwieldy, so I had to make a few quick decisions about chemicals and magical components. I tossed some in the bag and stuffed others in my jeans and coat pockets.

Once I was ready, I headed down to Julia and Kristin's room. They were dressed for bed but not asleep yet. When Julia saw me with my coat and bag, her eyes went wide.

"Sweet," she said.

"I know you've gotten out before," I said. "How'd you do it?"

Julia's many dates often occurred outside of sanctioned

school hours, and both she and Kristin had bragged about Julia's exploits in the past. I'd hoped perhaps Julia knew about a secret tunnel out of the school and that I wouldn't have to attempt some crazy feat of acrobatics. Unfortunately, that was exactly what I had to do. She and Kristin walked me to their window and pointed at a large tree growing outside it.

"This room has a view and easy access," said Kristin proudly.

I eyed the gnarled tree warily. "That's easy?"

"Half the dorm's used it," she said. "So can you."

"We should be charging people," mused Julia. She flashed me a smile. "Don't worry. We'll give you a freebie tonight. Just start on that big limb there, swing over there, and then use those branches for handholds."

I found it amazing that someone who'd claimed badminton in PE was too "dangerous" would have no qualms about scaling a tree from her third-floor room. Of course, Marcus's apartment had been on the fourth floor, and that fire escape had been a million times more unsafe than this tree. Thoughts of Alicia and Ms. Terwilliger snapped me back to the importance of my mission, and I gave Julia and Kristin a decisive nod.

"Let's do this," I said.

Julia cheered and opened the window for me. Kristin watched just as eagerly. "Please tell me you're running off to meet some breathtakingly handsome guy," she said.

I paused, just as I was about to climb out. "Yes, actually. But not in the way you're thinking."

Once I made it to the limb Julia had indicated, I discovered she was right. It was pretty simple—so simple, in fact, that I was surprised no school official had noticed this easy access escape route and chopped it down. Well, so much the better for those of us with late-night errands. I made it to the ground and waved goodbye to my watching friends.

The dorm's back property had some lights on it, exactly for the reason of deterring wayward students like me. It was also along the patrol route of one of the security guards but wasn't a spot he stayed regularly stationed at. He wasn't in sight, so I crossed my fingers that he was busy with another part of his beat. There were enough shadows on the lawn that I was able to stay within them the whole way—until I reached the back fence. It was lit up pretty well, and really, the only assets I had were that I was a fast climber and that the guard hadn't surfaced yet. Falling back on that hope that the universe owed me some favors—especially after tricking me about Alicia—I gulped and scrambled over. No one shouted at me when I landed on the other side, and I breathed a sigh of relief. I'd made it out. Getting back in would be harder, but that was a problem for later, hopefully one Ms. Terwilliger could help out with.

I found Adrian waiting for me in the Mustang, exactly where I'd indicated. He gave me a sidelong glance as he drove us away. "No black catsuit?"

"It's in the laundry."

He smiled. "Of course it is. Now, where are we going, and what's going on?"

"We're going to Ms. Terwilliger's," I said. "And what's going on is that we've been walking around in front of the enemy this entire time without even realizing it."

I watched Adrian as I related my revelations and saw his face go from disbelieving to dismayed the more I spoke. "Her aura was too perfect," he said once I finished. "Perfectly neutral, perfectly average. No one's is like that. I brushed it off, though. Figured maybe it was just a weird human one."

"Can someone influence how their aura looks?" I asked.

"Not to that extent," he said. "I don't know enough about these charms you guys use, but I'm guessing it was one of those that skewed the way her colors looked."

I slumped into the seat, still angry at not having figured this out sooner. "On the bright side, she doesn't know we're on to her and Veronica. That could give us an advantage."

When we reached Ms. Terwilliger's house, we found all the lights on, which was a surprise. I'd assumed she was in bed, though this certainly wouldn't be the first time she'd missed a phone call. Only, when we reached the house and knocked on the door, there was no answer. Adrian and I exchanged looks.

"Maybe she had to leave abruptly," he said. The tone of his voice conveyed what his words didn't. What if Ms. Terwilliger had already found out what we had and had taken off to fight Alicia and Veronica? I had no idea how powerful Alicia was, but the odds didn't seem promising.

When no answer came from my second knock, I nearly kicked the door in frustration. "Now what?"

Adrian turned the doorknob, and the door opened right up. "How about we wait for her?" he suggested.

I grimaced. "I don't know if I'm comfortable breaking into her place."

"She left the door unlocked. She's practically inviting us in." He pushed the door open farther and looked at me expectantly.

I didn't want to go back to Amberwood without speaking to her tonight, nor did I want to sit on her doorstep. Hoping she wouldn't mind us making ourselves at home, I gave a nod of resignation and followed Adrian inside. Her house was the same as ever, cluttered and redolent with the scent of incense. Suddenly, I came to a standstill.

"Wait. Something's different." It took me a moment to figure it out, and when I did, I couldn't believe I hadn't realized it immediately. "The cats are gone."

"Holy shit," said Adrian. "You're right."

At least one of them always came to greet visitors, and others were usually visible on furniture, under tables, or simply occupying the middle of the floor. But now, there were no cats in sight.

I stared around in disbelief. "What in the world could—"

An earsplitting shriek made me jump. I looked down toward my hip and found the dragon sticking his head out of my satchel and trying to claw his way up my side. Belatedly, I realized I'd forgotten to cover the aquarium. He'd apparently slipped inside the bag back in my room. The sound he was making now was similar to his hunger cry—except even more annoying. Then, impossibly, he nipped my leg. I bent over and tried to pull him off me.

"I don't have any pie! What are you trying to—ahh!"

Something zoomed over my head and smashed into the wall behind me with a loud splat. A couple wet drops of something landed on my cheek and began to burn. It was a wonder I didn't hear a sizzling sound.

"Sydney!" Adrian cried.

I turned toward where he was looking and saw Alicia standing in the doorway between the living room and the kitchen. Her palm was raised toward us, a shimmery and gooey substance cupped in it. Presumably it was the same substance that currently seared my skin. I almost wiped it away but feared I'd simply be spreading it to my fingers. I winced and tried to ignore it.

"Sydney," said Alicia pleasantly. "Or should I say, Taylor? I figured I'd be seeing you two again. Just not so soon. I guess your car trouble didn't delay you tonight."

"We know everything," I told her, keeping on an eye on that goo. "We know you're working for Veronica."

The smug look on her face momentarily shifted, overcome by surprise. "Working *for her*? I got rid of her ages ago."

"Got rid of. . . ." For a few seconds, I was at a loss. Then the rest of the puzzle pieces fell together. "*You're* the one who's been absorbing those girls. And that witch in San Diego. And . . . Veronica Terwilliger."

I'd been able to track Veronica back to the inn with the scrying spell. When Ms. Terwilliger had attempted a different locating spell, she'd come up blank. She'd assumed it was because Veronica had some sort of shielding. But the truth, I was suddenly certain, was that Veronica was already comatose. There was no active mind for Ms. Terwilliger to reach because Alicia had consumed Veronica.

Ms. Terwilliger . . .

"You're here for her," I said. "Ms. Terwilliger. Not me."

"The untrained do make easy targets," conceded Alicia. "But they don't have the same power as full-fledged witches, who can be just as easy to absorb if you break them down first. I don't need the youth like Veronica did, just the power. Once she showed me how the spell works, I was able to catch her in a weak moment. That other college girl tided me over until I wore down Alana Kale." Where had I heard that name? Alana . . . she was Ms. Terwilliger's comatose coven sister. "And finally I can take out the big hit: Jaclyn Terwilliger. I actually wasn't sure if I'd be able to break her, but it turns out she's done an awesome job of wearing herself out these last few weeks, all in the service of protecting her sweet little apprentice."

"I'm not her . . ." I couldn't finish. I'd been about to say I wasn't her apprentice, and yet . . . wasn't I? I wasn't just dabbling in magic anymore. I had joined the ranks. And now, I had to protect my mentor, just as she'd protected me. If it wasn't too late.

"Where is she?" I demanded.

"She's around," said Alicia, clearly delighting in having the upper hand here. "I wish you hadn't found out about all this. You would've made a good hit, once you'd learned a little bit more. You're just a small spark to Jaclyn's flame right now. She's the big score tonight."

"Tell us where she is," ordered Adrian, a powerful note in his voice that I recognized.

Alicia's gaze flicked from me to him. "Oh, please," she scoffed. "Stop wasting my time with your vampire compulsion. I realized what was going on after that first visit, when I kept having trouble remembering your faces." From her jumble of necklaces, she showed us a jade circle. "I acquired this afterward. Makes me impervious to your 'charms.'"

Something that resisted vampire magic? That would be a useful item to have in my bag of tricks. I'd have to look into it . . . provided I survived tonight.

I saw Alicia tense to throw again, and I managed to jump out of the way, pulling Adrian with me toward the living room. More of that goo splattered behind us with a hiss. I produced a dried thistle blossom and crumpled it toward Alicia, shouting a Greek incantation that would blind her. She made a small wave with her left hand and sneered at me.

"Really?" she asked. "That remedial blindness spell? Maybe you aren't a prodigy after all."

Adrian suddenly flipped open a small panel in the wall beside us. I hadn't even noticed it, largely because I'd been too distracted about having my face melted off. I saw a flurry of motion from his hand, and suddenly, we were plunged into darkness.

"Now *this* is remedial blindness," he muttered.

Alicia swore. I froze, immobilized by the blackness around me. As much as I appreciated any attempts to slow Alicia down, I was kind of at a loss myself.

I felt Adrian's hand grab hold of mine, and without a word, he tugged me farther into the living room. I followed quickly, relying on his superior vampire eyesight to guide us. I could already hear Alicia chanting and was sure some light-giving spell was coming soon. Either that or something that would magically fix a fuse box.

"Careful," Adrian murmured. "Stairs."

Sure enough, I felt my foot hit a wooden step. He and I hurried down as quietly and as quickly as we could, descending into a basement. My eyes still hadn't adjusted to the darkness, and I wondered if I'd just entered some secret dungeon. Yet as he wound us through stacks of boxes, I realized the basement was just used for ordinary storage. There was a lot of junk down here. After seeing Ms. Terwilliger's already messy house, I wondered what more she could possibly own.

Adrian finally stopped when we were in a far corner behind

some oblong boxes stacked nearly as high as me. He pulled me to him, keeping me in his arms so that he could speak softly in my ear. My head lay against his chest, and I could hear his rapid heartbeat, a mirror for my own.

"That was a good idea," I said in as low a voice as I could manage. "But now we're trapped down here. It would've been better if we could go outside."

"I know," he whispered back. "But she was too close to the door, and I didn't have time to mess with a window."

Above us, I could hear the floor creaking as Alicia walked through the house. "It's just a matter of time," I said.

"I was hoping it'd give you a chance to think of something to get us out of here. Can't you use that fireball? You were pretty good at it."

"Not inside. Especially not in a basement. I'd burn this place down around us. And we don't know where Ms. Terwilliger is yet." I racked my brain. The house was small enough that there weren't that many places Alicia could have stashed Ms. Terwilliger. And I had to assume she *was* stashed somewhere, if she hadn't come to our aid already. Alicia's language made it sound like she hadn't sucked away Ms. Terwilliger's power yet, so hopefully she was just incapacitated.

"You must be able to do something," said Adrian, tightening his hold on me. "You're brilliant, and you've been reading all those spell books."

It was true. I'd consumed tons of material these last couple of months—material I wasn't even supposed to have learned—but somehow, in this one terrified moment, my mind couldn't focus on any of it. "I've forgotten everything."

"No, you haven't." His voice in the darkness was calm and

reassuring. He smoothed back my hair and pressed one of those half kisses to my forehead. "Just relax and focus. Sooner or later, she'll be coming down those stairs after us. We need to take her out or at least slow her down so that we can escape."

His reasonable words centered me and allowed the gears of logic that ran my life to take over again. A little light was coming through from the basement's small, high windows, allowing my eyes to finally adjust and make out some of the dark shapes in the basement. I could still hear Alicia moving around upstairs, so I crept away from Adrian and walked over to the staircase. With a few graceful hand arcs, I chanted a spell over the steps and then hurried back to my corner with Adrian, slipping back under the shelter of his arm.

"Okay," I said. "I think I've got a minor delay ready."

"What is it?" he asked.

Just then, we heard the door at the top of the stairs open. Light spilled down, though we still remained in the shadows. "You're out of options," I heard Alicia say. "No place left to—ahh!"

There was a loud *thump-thump-thump-thump* as she went sliding down the stairs and hit the bottom with a crack.

"Invisible ice on the stairs," I told Adrian.

"I know I'm not supposed to say this," he said. "But I think I love you more than ever."

I took his hand and tried not to think about how happy his words made me, even in this life-or-death situation. "Come on."

We left our hiding spot and found Alicia sprawled ungracefully on the floor, trying to get to her feet. A silver orb of light hovered in the air near her, bobbing along faithfully with her movements. Seeing us, she snarled and waved her hands to cast at us. I'd anticipated this and had an amulet ready. I swung it on its silken cord and said a few quick words as we passed her. A brief, shimmering shield flared between us and her, just barely absorbing the small glowing darts she hurled our way. The shield was similar to the one Ms. Terwilliger had used at the park but had to be summoned on the spot and didn't last long.

I didn't know what Alicia planned on doing next, but obviously, something bad was coming. I cast a preemptive spell I'd never used before, one of the ones that Ms. Terwilliger had told me not to bother with. It took a lot of energy and was powerful if used correctly, yet was deceptively simple and elegant in its effects. I merely blasted Alicia across the room with a wave of power just as she was about to stand. She flew backward, into a stack of Christmas items. A box of ornaments fell down, shattering near her on the hard floor.

Casting the spell left me dizzy, but I managed to keep moving. I summoned a fireball when we reached the stairs but held it in my hand, keeping it low as though I were going to roll a Skee-Ball—though my intent was simply to carry it. I prayed it would melt the ice, and after my first few steps, I knew I was right. "Careful," I warned Adrian. "They're wet."

We made it to the top, but Alicia had already scrambled after us. From the bottom of the stairs, she used the same spell on me that I'd used on her, throwing a wave of invisible energy at Adrian and me that knocked us to the floor. I'd been holding on to the fireball, despite Ms. Terwilliger's warnings about how doing so would drain my own power. When Alicia knocked me down, the fireball flew from my hand and landed on Ms. Terwilliger's couch. Considering it looked as though it was covered in some cheap fabric from the 1970s, I wasn't entirely surprised that it lit up so fast.

On the bright side, the fire solved our darkness problem. On the downside, it meant the house was likely going to burn down around us after all. The callistana, who hadn't been fast enough to keep up with us when we'd gone downstairs, came scurrying over to my side. I had only half a heartbeat to make a decision.

"Go look in the rest of the house for Ms. Terwilliger," I told Adrian. "I'll stop Alicia."

The growing fire created weird shadows on his face, highlighting his anguish at this. "Sydney."

"This is one of those times you have to trust me without question," I said. "Hurry! Find her and get her out."

I saw a thousand emotions flash through his eyes before he obeyed and ran off toward the other wing of the house. The fire was spreading rapidly throughout the living room, in a way that had to be magical. The increasing smoke gave me an idea, and I cast a spell that enhanced it, creating a hazy wall at the entrance to the basement stairs. It allowed the dragon and me to make a short retreat before Alicia appeared, parting the smoke as cleanly as though she were opening curtains.

"That," she declared. "Hurt."

I cast a spell that should've encased her in spiderwebs, but they fell away before they even reached her. It was infuriating. I'd memorized so much, but these "remedial" spells weren't working. I understood now why Ms. Terwilliger's main strategy had been for me to lie low and hide my ability. How would I have ever been able to take on Veronica? True, Alicia had taken her out, but only after probably weakening her as she had Ms.

Terwilliger. I even understood now why Ms. Terwilliger had told me to get a gun—which, I realized now, I'd left in the car.

The ice spell had worked because Alicia hadn't seen it coming. The only other spell that had worked on her was the blast of power, an advanced one that had still left me weak. It was going to take another one of those, I realized. I had no idea if I had the ability to do a second one, but trying was the only chance I had of—

I screamed as what felt like a thousand volts of electricity shot through me. Alicia's hand movement had been so subtle, and she hadn't even spoken. I fell down again, writhing in pain as Alicia strode toward me, her face triumphant. The dragon bravely put himself between the two of us, and she simply kicked him aside. I heard him yelp as he skittered across the floor.

"Maybe I should absorb you," said Alicia. The shocks abated, and I could only sit there and gasp for breath. "You could be my fifth. I can come back for Jaclyn in a few years. You've turned out to be a lot more powerful than I thought—and annoyingly resourceful. You even made a good effort tonight."

"Who says I'm done?" I managed to say.

I cast the first of the advanced spells that came to mind. Maybe it was inspired by the broken Christmas ornaments, but suddenly, I had broken shards on the brain. The spell required no words or physical components and only the slightest of hand movements. The rest was taken from me—a draining of energy and power that hurt almost as much as the electrifying spell Alicia had just used.

But oh, the results were breathtaking.

On Ms. Terwilliger's coffee table (which was now on fire) sat a set of five perpetual motion balls. I used a transmutation spell on them, forcing them out of their spherical shape and breaking them apart into thin, sharp razor blades. They broke free of their strings and came at my command. That was the easy part.

The hard part was, as Ms. Terwilliger had told me, actually attacking someone. And not just making them slip and fall. That wasn't so bad. But an actual physical attack, one you knew would cause direct and terrible damage, was an entirely different issue. It didn't matter how terrible Alicia was, that she'd tried to kill me and wanted to victimize Ms. Terwilliger and countless others. Alicia was still a living person, and it was not in my nature to show violence or try to take another's life.

It was, however, in my nature to save my own life and those of my loved ones.

I braced myself and ordered the razors forward. They slammed into her face. She screamed and frantically tried to pull them out but in doing so lost her balance and went back down the stairs. I heard her shriek as she fell into the basement. Although I couldn't see her, her magical lantern orb merrily followed her all the way down.

My triumph was short-lived. I was more than dizzy. I was on the verge of passing out. The heat and light from the fire were overwhelming, yet my vision was going dark from the exhaustion of casting a spell I was in no way ready for. I suddenly just wanted to curl up there on the floor and close my eyes where it was comfortable and warm. . . .

"Sydney!"

Adrian's voice jolted me out of my haze, and I managed to peer up at him through heavy eyelids. He slipped an arm around me to help me up. When my legs didn't work, he simply scooped me up altogether and carried me. The dragon, who'd suffered no permanent damage from the kick, clung to my shirt and scurried into the bag that was still draped over my shoulder.

"Where . . . Ms. Terwilliger. . . ."

"Not here," Adrian said, heading swiftly toward the front door. The fire was spreading over the walls and ceiling now. Although it hadn't quite made it to the front of the house yet, our way was still thick with smoke and ash. We both were coughing, and tears ran out of my eyes. Adrian reached the door and turn the knob, yelping at how hot it was. Then he managed to kick the door open with his foot, and we were free, out into the clean night air.

Neighbors had gathered outside, and I could hear sirens in the distance. Some of the spectators watched us curiously, but most were transfixed by the inferno that was Ms. Terwilliger's bungalow. Adrian carried me over to his car and gently set me down so that I could lean against it, though he still kept an arm around me. We both stared in awe at the fire.

"I really did look, Sydney," he said. "I couldn't find Jackie in the house. Maybe she escaped." I prayed he was right. Otherwise, we had just abandoned my history teacher to a fiery death. "What happened to Alicia?"

"Last I saw, she was in the basement." A sickening feeling twisted in my stomach. "I don't know if she'll get out. Adrian, what have I just done?"

"You defended yourself. And me. And hopefully Jackie." His arm tightened around me. "Alicia was evil. Look what she did to those other witches—what she wanted to do to you guys."

"I never saw it coming," I said bleakly. "I thought I was so smart. And each time I talked to her, I dismissed her as some dumb, scattered girl. Meanwhile, she was laughing and countering my moves every step of the way. It's humbling. I don't meet many people like that."

"The Moriarty to your Holmes?" he suggested.

"Adrian," I said. It was all I needed to say.

He suddenly did a double take, noticing my attire for the first time tonight now that the jacket had come open. "You're wearing your AYE shirt?"

"Yeah, I never wage magical battles without—"

A small mewling noise suddenly caught my attention. I searched around until I spotted two green eyes peering at me from under a bush across the street. I managed to straighten up and found that my legs, though weak, could support my weight again. I took a few halting steps toward the bush, and Adrian immediately ran to my side.

"What are you doing? You need help," he said.

I pointed. "We have to follow that cat."

"Sydney—"

"Help me," I pleaded.

He couldn't resist. Supporting me with his arm again, he helped me walk across the street toward the cat. It ran ahead between two bushes, then glanced back at us.

"It wants us to follow," I told him.

So we did, cutting through houses and streets until when we were about four blocks from the bungalow, the cat dashed off into a park. Whatever energy I'd had when I started after the cat was long gone. I was panting and dizzy again and fighting hard to resist asking Adrian to carry me. Something in the center of the park caught my attention and gave me one last burst of adrenaline to run forward.

There, lying on the grass, was Ms. Terwilliger.

She was awake, thankfully, but looked nearly as exhausted as I felt. Tears and smudges suggested she'd been through quite an ordeal. She had managed to escape Alicia, but not without a fight. That was why we hadn't been able to find her in the house. Seeing me, she blinked in surprise.

"You're okay," she said. "And you found me."

"The cats led us," I said, pointing. All thirteen of them were sitting around in the park, surrounding their owner—making sure she was okay.

She glanced around at them and managed a weary smile. "See? I told you cats are useful."

"Callistanas aren't so bad either," I said, looking down at my satchel. "That 'pain in the ass' screeching saved me from a face full of acid."

Adrian put his hand to his heart in mock horror. "Sage, did you just swear?"

Glancing over, Ms. Terwilliger noticed him for the first time. "And you're here too? I'm so sorry you had to get dragged into this mess. I know you didn't ask for any of this trouble."

"It doesn't matter," said Adrian, smiling. He rested a hand on my shoulder. "Some things are worth the trouble."

CHAPTER 24

I FELT PRETTY BAD about burning down my teacher's house.

Ms. Terwilliger, for obvious reasons, seemed to think that was the least of her problems. She wasn't sure if her insurance would cover the damage, but her company was pretty speedy in sending someone out to investigate the cause. We were still waiting to hear their verdict on coverage, but one thing they didn't report finding was any sign of human remains. Part of me was relieved that I hadn't actually killed anyone. Another part of me feared we hadn't seen the last of Alicia. What silly comparison had Adrian made? *The Moriarty to your Holmes.* I had to imagine that being hit in the face with razor blades and then left in a burning building would make anyone hold a grudge.

A little investigation eventually turned up Veronica at a Los Angeles hospital, checked in as Jane Doe. Visiting her comatose sister became the greatest of Ms. Terwilliger's priorities, and she harbored hopes of possibly finding a way to undo the spell. Despite how busy she now was, my teacher still managed to urge me to meet her coven, and I agreed for a few different reasons. One was that it was kind of impossible for me to act like I didn't want to wield magic anymore.

The other reason was that I didn't plan on being around.

I was still resolved to go with Marcus to Mexico, and the week flew by. Winter finals were a breeze, and before I knew it, it was Friday, the day before our trip to Mexico. I took a risk by telling my friends goodbye. The safest thing would've been to disappear without a trace, but I trusted them all—even Angeline—to keep my secret and feign ignorance once the Alchemists discovered they had a runaway. I told Trey as well. No matter what had gone down between us, he was still my friend, and I would miss him.

As the day wore on, the dorm grew quieter and quieter—aside from unending Christmas music playing in the lobby. Not wanting to exclude other religions, Mrs. Weathers had also set out a menorah and "Happy Kwanzaa" banner. Tomorrow was officially the last day before everyone had to be out, and a number of people had already left for winter break. I'd finished my own packing, which was light. I didn't want to be burdened down with excess luggage since I really had no idea what to expect in Mexico.

I still had two people I needed to say goodbye to: Adrian and Jill. I'd avoided them both for very different reasons, but time was running out. I knew Jill was just a flight of stairs away, but Adrian was more difficult. We'd been in touch a couple times after the fire, simply to sort out some details, but he'd soon gone silent. No calls, no texts, no dreams. Maybe I should've been glad. Maybe I should've welcomed the chance to leave without any painful goodbyes . . . but I couldn't. My chest ached with the thought of not seeing him again. Even though he was the reason I was leaving, I still felt like I needed some closure.

It's not about closure, Sydney. You want to see him. You need to see him. And that's exactly why you have to leave.

Finally, I took the plunge and called him. It took me so long to work up the nerve that I could hardly believe it when he didn't answer. I resisted the urge to immediately try again. No. I could wait. There would still be time tomorrow, and surely . . . surely he wasn't avoiding me?

I decided to hold off on talking to Jill until the next day. Telling her goodbye was just as difficult—and not just because of what she saw through the bond. I knew she'd think I was abandoning her. In truth, if I stayed and ended up with Adrian, I'd possibly be caught and never be able to help her at all. At least if I was away and free, I could try to help her from the outside. I hoped she'd understand.

Waiting on her gave me the opportunity to take care of an unwelcome errand: returning Malachi Wolfe's gun. I'd never gone to his home without Adrian, and even though I knew I had nothing to fear from Wolfe, there was still something a little unsettling about going to the compound alone.

To my complete and utter astonishment, Wolfe let me into the house when I arrived. All was quiet. "Where are the dogs?" I asked.

"At training," he said. "I have a friend who's an expert dog trainer, and he's giving them some stealth lessons. He used to work for a local K-9 unit."

I didn't think it was in the Chihuahua genetic code to ever be stealthy. I kept that to myself and instead stared around in amazement at Wolfe's kitchen. I'd expected something like a ship's galley. Instead, I found an astonishingly cheery room, with blue-checkered wallpaper and a squirrel cookie jar. If someone had asked me to describe the most unlikely Wolfe kitchen out there, it would've looked something like this. No—wait. On the refrigerator, he had some magnets that looked like ninja throwing stars. That, at least, was in character.

Adrian's going to flip out when I tell him. Then I remembered I might not see Adrian for a very long time. That realization killed whatever amusement I'd just felt.

"So what do you need?" asked Wolfe. Peering at him, I suddenly had a strange feeling the eye patch really was on a different eye from last time. I should've paid more attention. "Another gun?"

I returned to the task at hand. "No, sir. I didn't even need the first one, but thanks for lending it to me." I removed it from the bag and handed it to him.

He gave the gun a once-over and then set it inside a drawer. "Fixed your problem? You can still hang on to it if you want."

"I'm leaving the country. Bringing it over the border might cause me some trouble."

"Fair enough," he said. He grabbed the cookie jar and took off the lid, leaning it toward me. An amazing scent drifted out. "Want one? I just made them."

I was really regretting not being able to tell Adrian about this. "No thanks, sir. I've had more than enough sugar these last few weeks." I felt like I should have a frequent customer card for Pies and Stuff.

"I thought you looked better. Not all skin and bones anymore." He nodded in approval, which felt really weird and slightly creepy. "So where are you two kids going?"

"Mexi—oh, Adrian's not going with me. I'm going with someone else."

"Really?" He slid the squirrel back across the counter. "I'm surprised. I always figured when you two left here, you went home and had your own private 'training sessions.'"

I felt myself turning bright red. "No! It's not like—I mean, we're just friends, sir."

"I had a friend like that once. Silver Tooth Sally." He got that faraway expression that always came on when he had an anecdote to share.

"I'm sorry, did you say—"

"Never met a woman like Sally," he interrupted. "We fought our way across Switzerland together, always watching each other's backs. We finally got out alive—just barely—and she wanted to come back to the States and settle down. Not me. I had dreams, you see. I was a young man then, drawn to danger and glory. I left her and went off to live with an Orcadian shaman. It took two years and a lot of vision quests to realize my mistake, but when I got back, I couldn't find her. When I close my eye at night, I can still see that tooth sparkle like a star. It haunts me, girl. It haunts me."

I frowned. "I don't think the Orcadians have vision quests, sir. Or shamans."

Wolfe leaned forward and shook a finger at me, his eye wide. "Learn from my mistakes, girl. Don't go to the Orkneys. You don't need some mystical vision to see what's in front of you, you hear me?"

I gulped. "Yes, sir."

I hurried out after that, thinking that being in a different country from Malachi Wolfe might be a good thing.

The next morning, I prepared to tell Jill goodbye, but she beat me to it and showed up at my door. It was the first time we'd truly spoken since the morning after that last dream with Adrian.

She walked into my room and frowned when she saw the suitcase. "You're really going?"

"Yes. And I'm sure you know why."

She crossed her arms and looked me straight in the eye, without any of the reservation she'd shown last time. I had trouble holding that stare. "Sydney, don't leave Adrian because of me."

"It's more complicated than that," I said automatically.

"It's really not," she said. "From everything I've seen and heard, you're just afraid. You've always controlled every detail of your life. When you couldn't—like with the Alchemists—you found a way to seize back that control."

"There's nothing wrong with wanting control," I snapped.

"Except that we can't always have it, and sometimes that's a good thing. A great thing, even," she added. "And that's how it is with Adrian. No matter how hard you try, you aren't going to be able to control your feelings for him. You can't help loving him, and so you're running away. I'm just an excuse."

Who was she to lecture me like this? "You think I'm lying about how awkward it is for you to see everything that happens between us? Every intimate detail is on display. I can't do that. I can't live like that."

"Adrian's learned to."

"Well, he's had to."

"Exactly." Some of her fierceness mellowed. "Sydney, he brought me back from the dead. It's the greatest thing anyone can or will do for me. I can't pay him back, but I can let him live his life the way he wants to. I don't expect him to shelter me because of the bond, and I'm not going to judge him—or you. Someday, he and I will learn to block each other."

"Someday," I reiterated.

"Yes. And until then, we do the best we can. All you're doing by leaving is making three people miserable."

"Three?" I frowned. "I'm helping you."

"Do you really think I'm happy when he's miserable? Do you think I like the darkness that crawls over him?" When I said nothing, she pushed forward. "Look, I don't have the same physical reaction to you that he does, but when he's with you, he's so full of joy . . . it radiates through to me, and it's one of the greatest experiences I've ever had. I've never been in love like you guys are."

"I'm not—" I couldn't say it, and she gave me a knowing look. I tried a different tactic. "Staying here is dangerous, especially with him. The Alchemists might find out about everything—him, my tattoo, Ms. Terwilliger, and God knows what else."

"And if they don't find out, look at what you get. Adrian. The rest of us. Magic. The chance to uncover their secrets. I know you love this life. Why would you give it up? You're too smart to get caught. We'll help you. Do you really think Marcus and his Merry Men can do that much fighting when they're always on the run?"

I shook my head. "They're like me. They understand me."

She was obstinate. "They aren't like you at all. They talk. You act."

It was so surprising to see her like this, so confident and so much wiser than her years. It was also a little irritating. If she was so wise, why couldn't she understand how much was at stake?

"Jill, staying is a big risk—in all ways."

"Of course it is!" she exclaimed, her eyes flashing with anger. "Any life worth living is going to have risks. If you go to Mexico, you'll regret it—and I think you know that."

My phone rang, cutting off my next response. It was Eddie. He rarely called, and panic seized me.

"What's wrong?" I demanded.

He sounded mystified. "I wouldn't say anything's wrong . . . just surprising. Is Jill with you? You guys should really come down. We're outside"

He hung up, and I was left totally confused. "What's up?" asked Jill.

"Something surprising, apparently."

She and I went down to the lobby, with no more mention of Adrian. When we stepped outside, we found Eddie and Angeline pointedly avoiding eye contact with each other. Standing near them was a tall, good-looking guy with neatly trimmed black hair and bright blue eyes. He wore a stern, serious expression and was scanning the area.

"He's a dhampir," Jill murmured to me.

His eyes locked onto us at our approach, and that fierce look relaxed.

"Jill, Sydney," said Eddie. "This is Neil Raymond. He's going to be joining us here."

Neil swept Jill a bow so low, it was a wonder he didn't hit the ground. "Princess Jillian," he said in a deep voice. "It's an honor to serve you, and I'll do so to the best of my abilities, even if it means sacrificing my own life."

Jill took a step back, her eyes wide as she took him in. "Th-thank you."

Eddie looked back and forth between them, a small frown appearing on his face. "Neil's been sent as backup. I guess you filed some complaint about Jill not having enough protection?" That was to me, and unless I was mistaken, there was an accusatory note in his voice.

"No—I. Oh. I guess I kind of did." When I'd been trying to do damage control with Stanton, one of my grievances had been that I never felt Jill was safe. I guess this was Stanton's response. It was surprising, just as Eddie had said, but more eyes on her couldn't hurt. From the way she was sizing Neil up, she certainly didn't seem to mind either.

I shook his hand. "Nice to have you around, Neil. Are they passing you off as another cousin?"

"Just a new student," he said. That was probably just as well. Our "family" was in danger of taking over Amberwood.

I would've liked to learn a little more about him, but my time was up. Marcus was picking me up soon to go to the train station, seeing as Latte had been declared totaled. I guess that was a different sort of closure, albeit a sad kind.

I told them all goodbye as I left to get my suitcase, acting as though I just had to run an errand. Eddie, Angeline, and Jill knew the truth, and I could see the hurt and regret in their eyes—especially Jill. I prayed they'd be okay without me. When I came back downstairs, I found Jill was the only one still there.

"I forgot to give you this," she said, handing over a small envelope. My name was on the outside, and I recognized the writing.

"I've been trying to get a hold of him and thought he might be avoiding me. This is his goodbye, huh?" I felt disappointed that I wouldn't be able to see Adrian in person one last time. Maybe a letter was better than nothing, but I wished I could have left with those beautiful eyes fresh in my mind. "Is he . . . is he really upset?" I couldn't stand the thought of him hurting.

"Read the letter," she said mysteriously. "And remember, Sydney. This isn't about me. This is about you guys. You can control everything else, but not this. Let go, and accept how you feel."

We left on that note, and I went outside to sit on the curb and wait for Marcus. I stared at the envelope, looking at the way Adrian had written my name. Three times I nearly opened it . . . but chickened out each time. Finally, I saw Marcus drive in, and the envelope disappeared into my purse.

As soon as he picked me up, he began talking excitedly about the big plans ahead. I barely heard. All I kept thinking about was Adrian and how empty my life was going to seem without him. Marcus and I were meeting Wade and Amelia at the train station, but I couldn't picture any of them understanding me like Adrian—even if they were human and shared the same background. None of them would have his dry wit or uncanny insight. And simmering beneath all those emotions were the more heated memories . . . the way we'd kissed, the way it had felt to be wrapped up in him. . . .

"Sydney? Are you even paying attention?"

I blinked and glanced over at Marcus. I think it was another of those moments where he couldn't believe someone wasn't hanging on to his every word. "Sorry," I said. "My mind's somewhere else."

He grinned. "Well, shift it to beaches and margaritas because your life's about to change."

It was always beaches and margaritas with him. "You left out the part about us sealing the tattoo. Unless your tattooist is also a bartender."

"There you go again, funny and beautiful." He laughed. "We're going to have a great time."

"How long will we be down there?"

"Well, we'll take care of the tattoos first. That's the most important thing." I was relieved to see him taking that seriously. "Then we'll lie low, enjoy the sights for a few weeks. After that, we'll come back and follow some leads on other dissatisfied Alchemists."

"And then you'll repeat the process?" I asked. In the rearview mirror, I could see the Palm Springs skyline disappearing as we drove north. I felt a pang of longing in my chest. "Get others to retrieve critical information and then free them?"

"Exactly."

We drove in silence for another minute as I processed his words. "Marcus, what do you do with that information you gather? I mean, what are you going to do about Master Jameson?"

"Keep finding more evidence," he said promptly. "This is the biggest lead we've ever had. Now we can really push forward in finding out more."

"It's more than a lead. Why not leak it to the Moroi?"

"The Alchemists would deny it. Besides, we don't want to be hasty."

"So what if they do deny it?" I demanded. "At least the Moroi will have a heads-up."

He glanced over at me with a look that reminded me of a parent trying to be patient with a child. Ahead of us, I saw a sign for the train station. "Sydney, I know you're eager, but trust me. This is the way we've always done things."

"I don't know that it's the right way, though."

"You have a lot of ideas for someone who just joined up." He chuckled. I wished he'd stop doing that. "Just wait, and then you'll understand."

I didn't like his condescending attitude. "I think I already understand. And you know what? I don't think you guys do anything. I mean, you've uncovered some amazing information . . . but then what? You keep waiting. You run away and skulk around. How is this really helping? Your intentions are good . . . but that's all they are." I could almost hear Jill's voice: *They talk. You act.*

Ironically, Marcus was speechless.

"You could do so much," I continued. "When I first found out about you, you seemed to hold all the potential in the world. Technically, you still do. But it's being wasted." He pulled into the train station's parking lot, still looking utterly stunned.

"Where the hell is this coming from?" he asked at last.

"Me," I said. "Because I'm not like you guys. I can't do nothing. I can't run away. And . . . I can't go with you."

It felt good to say that . . . and it also felt right. All week, my brain had been telling me the right thing to do was to walk away before things with Adrian and the Alchemists blew up. And yes, that probably was the smart thing. My heart had never entirely been on board, but I'd tried to ignore it. It wasn't until I'd listened to both Jill and Marcus that I realized just this once, my brain might have to opt for the less logical solution.

I had to give Marcus credit. He actually looked concerned and wasn't just put out at not getting his way. "Sydney, I know how attached you are to this place and these people, but it's not safe for you here. It's not safe for you anywhere, not as long as the Alchemists are watching. Not as long as your tattoo is vulnerable."

"Someone told me any life worth living has risks," I said, unable to hide a smile. I never thought I'd be quoting Jill.

Marcus slammed his fist against the dashboard. "That's sentimental bullshit! It sounds good in theory, but the reality is completely different."

"What kind of reality could you have created if you'd stayed with the Alchemists?" I asked. "How much could you have uncovered?"

"Nothing if I was caught," he said flatly. "And no matter how useless you think we are, I've freed dozens of Alchemists. I've helped Clarence and other Moroi."

"You aren't useless, Marcus. You do good work, but we're just not on the same path, that's all. I'm staying and doing things my way. Isn't that what you said when we first met? Helping the Moroi on our own terms? These are mine."

"You're wasting your time!"

"It's my time to waste," I said. Adrian had said exactly the same thing to me on the flight to the wedding, when I'd told him he couldn't keep loving me. I felt bad for Marcus. I really did, especially since he'd truly been counting on me to come with him.

He caught hold of my hand. "Sydney, please don't do this," he begged. "No matter how confident you feel, no matter how careful you think you are, things will spiral out of control."

"They already have," I said, opening the passenger door. "And I'm going to stop fighting them. Thank you for everything, Marcus. I mean it."

"Wait, Sydney," he called. "Just tell me one thing."

I glanced back and waited.

"Where did this come from? When you called me to tell me you were coming, you said you'd realized it was the smart thing to do. What made you change your mind?"

I gave him a smile that I hoped was as dazzling as one of his. "I realized I'm in love."

Marcus, startled, looked around as though he expected to see my *objet d'amour* in the car with us. "And you *just* realized that? Did you just have some sort of vision?"

"Didn't need to," I said, thinking of Wolfe's ill-fated trip to the Orkneys. "It's always been right in front of me."

CHAPTER 25

ONCE MARCUS FINALLY ACCEPTED that I wasn't going, he wished me well, though he still wore that stunned expression. He'd planned on abandoning the car at the station but handed the keys over to me as a parting gift. I watched him walk away and wondered if I'd made a mistake. Then I thought of green, green eyes and all the work Adrian and I had to do together. This was the right choice . . . I just hoped I wasn't too late.

He still wasn't answering my calls. Did he hate me? Or was he holed up somewhere, depressed and drinking away his sorrows? I fished his note out of my purse, wondering what I'd find. Knowing Adrian, I'd expected some long, flowery expression of love. Instead, all I found was a long series of numbers.

The numbers meant nothing to me. I studied them for a while in the car, applying a few common codes I knew. No answer appeared, though I wasn't entirely surprised. Codes and complex mathematics weren't exactly Adrian's style. But then, why had he left the note? Obviously, he assumed I could decipher it.

I held the note far away from me, hoping something visual would reveal itself. It did. As I looked at the numbers again, I saw a natural break in the middle of them, in a format that looked familiar. I entered the two sets of numbers into the latitude and longitude screen of my GPS. A moment later, it turned up an address in Malibu. Southern California. Was that a coincidence?

Without even thinking twice, I pulled out of the train station's parking lot and headed toward the coast. It was entirely possible I was about to waste two and a half hours (five, if you counted the round trip), but I didn't think so. *There are no coincidences.*

It felt like the longest drive of my life. My hands tightly clenched the wheel the entire time. I was eager yet terrified. When I was only a few miles from the address, I began to see signs for the Getty Villa. For a few seconds, I was confused. The Getty Center was a very famous museum, but it was closer to Los Angeles. I didn't understand the connection or why I had ended up in Malibu. Nonetheless, I dutifully followed the directions and ended up in the Villa's guest parking lot.

When I reached the entrance, I received my answers. The Villa was a sister museum to the Getty Center, one that specialized in ancient Greek and Roman art. In fact, a good part of the Getty Villa was set up like some ancient temple, complete with pillars surrounding courtyards filled with gardens, fountains, and statues. Admission was free but required a reservation. Things were slow today, and I quickly rectified the problem by making an online reservation on my phone.

When I stepped inside, I nearly forgot why I was there—but only for a heartbeat. The museum was a dream come true for a lover of classics like me. Room after room focusing on the ancient world. Jewelry, statues, clothes . . . it was as if I'd entered a time machine. The scholar in me longed to study and read about each exhibit in detail. The rest of me, with a racing heart and barely contained excitement, only briefly stopped in each room, just long enough to search and move on.

After looking in almost all the interior areas, I stepped into the outer peristyle. My breath caught. It was a huge outdoor garden built around a pool that had to be at least two hundred feet long. Statues and fountains dotted the pool's surface, and the whole space was surrounded in gorgeously manicured trees and other plants. The sun, warm despite the December day, shone down on everything, and the air hummed with birdsong, splashing water, and soft conversation. Tourists milled around, stopping to admire the sights or take pictures. None of them mattered, though—not when I finally found the person I was looking for.

He sat at the opposite end of the garden from where I'd entered, on the pool's far edge. His back was to me, but I would have known him anywhere. I approached with trepidation, still churning with that odd mix of fear and eagerness. The closer I got, the more detailed his features became. The tall, lean body. The chestnut glints that the sun brought out in his dark hair. When I finally reached the pool's end, I came to a stop just behind him, not daring to go farther.

"Sage," he said, without looking up. "Figured you'd be south of the border by now."

"No, you didn't," I said. "You never would've given me the

note or come all the way out here. You knew I wouldn't leave."

He looked up at me at last, squinting in the bright sun. "I was pretty sure you wouldn't leave. I *hoped* you wouldn't leave. Jill and I debated it forever. What'd you think of my sweet use of latitude and longitude? Pretty brilliant, huh?"

"Genius," I said, trying to hold back my smile. Some of my fear faded. We were back in familiar, easy territory again. Just Adrian and me. "You took a risk I'd know what those numbers meant. You could've been sitting out here all day."

"Nah." Adrian stood up and took a step toward me. "You're a smart girl. I knew you'd figure it out."

"Not that smart." The closer he came, the more my heart began to race again. "It took me a long time to figure some things out." I gestured around us. "And how is it possible that you knew this place existed, but I didn't?"

His fingertips traced the edge of my cheek, and suddenly, the warmth of the sunshine felt like nothing compared to the heat of that touch. "It was easy," he said, holding me in his gaze. "I had to start my search somewhere, so I typed 'ancient Rome' and 'California' into my phone. This was like the first hit."

"What search?" I asked.

He smiled. "The search for some place more romantic than Pies and Stuff."

Adrian tipped my face up toward his and kissed me. Like always, the world around me stopped moving. No, the world became Adrian, only Adrian. Kissing him was as mind-blowing as ever, full of that same passion and need I had never believed I'd feel. But today, there was even more to it. I no longer had any doubt about whether this was wrong or right. It was a culmination of a long journey . . . or maybe the beginning of one.

I wrapped my arms around his neck and pulled him closer. I didn't care that we were out in public. I didn't care that he was Moroi. All that mattered was that he was Adrian, my Adrian. My match. My partner in crime, in the long battle I'd just signed on for to right the wrongs in the Alchemist and Moroi worlds. Maybe Marcus was right that I'd also signed myself up for disaster, but I didn't care. In that moment, it seemed that as long as Adrian and I were together, there was no challenge too great for us.

I don't know how long we stood there kissing. Like I said, the world around me was gone. Time had stopped. I was awash in the feel of Adrian's body against mine, in his scent, and in the taste of his lips. That was all that mattered right now, and I found myself thinking of our unfinished business in the dream.

When we finally broke the kiss—much too soon, as far as I was concerned—we still stayed locked in an embrace. The sound of giggling caused me to glance to the side, where two small children were laughing and pointing at us. Seeing me watching them, they scurried away. I turned back to Adrian, wanting to melt away with happiness as I looked up into his eyes.

"This is a lot better than loving from afar," I told him.

He brushed some hair from my face and gazed into my eyes. "What changed your mind? I mean, I knew you'd never be able to stay away from me, but I won't lie . . . you had me scared there for a little while."

I leaned against his chest. "It was a combination of things, really. Some surprisingly good advice from Jill. One of Wolfe's charming anecdotes—I have to tell you about his kitchen, by the way. Plus, I kept thinking about when we were on the table."

Adrian shifted just enough so that we could look at each

other again. It was one of those rare moments where he was completely floored. "Let me get this straight. The future of our relationship hinged on advice from a fifteen-year-old girl, a probably untrue story from a one-eyed Chihuahua trainer, and me unromantically—yet skillfully—kissing you on top of silverware and china?"

"Yup," I said after a few moments of thought.

"That's all it took, huh? And here I thought winning you over was going to be hard." He grew serious again and pressed a light kiss to my forehead. "What happens now?"

"Now we check out this awesome museum you've lured me to. You're going to *love* Etruscan art."

That roguish smile I adored returned. "I'm sure I will. But what about the future? What are we going to do about us—about this?"

I caught hold of his hands, still keeping him close. "Since when are you worried about consequences or the future?"

"Me? Never." He considered. "Well, that is, as long as you're with me, I'm not worried. But I know *you* like to worry about those kinds of things."

"I wouldn't say I 'like' to," I corrected. A soft breeze ruffled his hair, and I resisted the urge to brush it back into place. If I did, I was pretty sure we'd start kissing again, and I supposed I should first be responsible and answer his questions.

"Are we going to run off to the Keepers?" he suggested.

"Of course not," I scoffed. "That'd be cowardly and immature. And you'd never survive without hair gel—though you might like their moonshine."

"Then what are we going to do?"

"We're going to keep all of this secret."

He chuckled. "That's not cowardly?"

"It's exciting and daring," I said. "Manly and brave, even. I figured you'd be into that."

"Sage." He laughed. "I'm into anything, so long as you're with me. But is it going to be enough? I'm not completely oblivious to consequences, you know. I get how dangerous this is for you, especially if you keep questioning the Alchemists. And I also know you're still worried about Jill watching us."

Right. Jill. Jill, who was probably witnessing all of this right now, whether she wanted to or not. Was she happy for his happiness? Was she filled with the joy of our love? Or was this excruciatingly uncomfortable for her?

"The three of us will find a way to cope," I said at last. I couldn't think much more about it right now or I probably would start freaking out. "And as for the Alchemists . . . we'll just have to be careful. They don't follow me everywhere, and like you said, I'm with you half the time anyway." I just hoped that was enough. It *had* to be.

And then the kissing started again. There was no avoiding it, not when we were together like this, far away from the real world of our normal lives. The setting was too perfect. He was too perfect, despite being one of the most imperfect people I knew. And honestly, we'd wasted far too much time with doubts and games. The one thing you learn from constantly having your life in danger is that you'd better not waste it. Even Marcus had admitted that in the arcade.

Adrian and I spent the rest of the day at the Villa, most of it kissing in the gardens, though I did convince him to check out some of the artifacts inside. Maybe I was in love, but I was still me, after all. When things finally closed down for the evening, we had dinner at a beachside fondue restaurant and lingered there for a long time afterward, keeping close to each other and watching the waxing moon shine on the ocean.

I was caught up in watching the crashing waves when I felt Adrian's lips brush my cheek. "Whatever happened to the dragon?"

I mustered my primmest tone. "He has a name, you know."

Adrian pulled back and gave me a curious look. "I didn't know, actually. What'd you decide on?"

"Hopper." When Adrian laughed, I added, "Best rabbit ever. He'd be proud to know his name is being passed on."

"Yes, I'm sure he would. Did you name the Mustang too?"

"I think you mean the Ivashkinator."

He stared at me in wonder. "I told you I loved you, right?"

"Yes," I assured him. "Many times."

"Good." Adrian pulled me closer. "Just making sure, Miss 'I'm a Quick Study.'"

I groaned. "I'm never going to live that down, am I?"

"Live it down? Hell, I'm going to hold you to it."

I suspected Marcus's car was stolen, so we left it in Malibu. Adrian drove me back to the dorm and kissed me goodbye, promising to call me first thing in the morning. It was hard to let him go, even though I knew I was being silly to think I couldn't go without him for twelve hours. I walked into my dorm like I was dancing on air, my lips still burning from his kisses.

It was crazy, I knew, attempting to have a relationship with him. Scratch that. It was going to be perilous—enough so that some of my euphoria dimmed as that realization hit me. I'd talked a good game with him, trying to ease his fears, but I knew the truth. Trying to figure out secrets within the Alchemists was going to be difficult enough, and my tattoo still wasn't secure. What I had going on with Adrian had raised the stakes exponentially, but that was one of those risks I gladly accepted.

"Miss Melrose."

Mrs. Weathers's cool voice snapped me back to reality with a jolt. I came to a halt in the middle of the dorm's lobby and looked over at her. She stood up from her desk and strolled over.

"Yes, ma'am?"

"It's midnight."

I looked at a clock, surprised to see she was right. "Yes, ma'am."

"Even though winter break is here, you're still registered in the dorm until tomorrow, which means you're still subject to the rules. It's after curfew."

The only thing I could manage was stating the obvious. "Yes, it is, ma'am."

Mrs. Weathers waited, as though she were hoping I'd say more. "Were you . . . doing another assignment for Ms. Terwilliger?" There was an almost comically desperate look on her face. "I didn't receive notification, but surely she can retroactively fix things."

I realized then that Mrs. Weathers didn't want me to be in trouble. She was hoping I had some reason for breaking the rules, some reason that I could avoid punishment. I knew I could've lied and said I'd been helping Ms. Terwilliger. I knew Ms. Terwilliger would even back me up. But I couldn't do it. It seemed wrong to taint my day with Adrian with a lie. And really, I *had* broken the rules.

"No," I told Mrs. Weathers. "I wasn't with her. I was just . . . out."

Mrs. Weathers waited a few moments more and then bit her lip with resignation. "Very well then. You know the rules. You'll have to serve a detention—once classes start again."

I nodded solemnly. "Yes, ma'am. I understand."

She looked as though she was still hoping I'd correct the situation. I had nothing to offer her and turned to walk away. "Oh, I nearly forgot!" she called. "I was too astonished by this . . . transgression." She turned back into the efficient dorm matron I knew. "Please let me know if your cousin will be staying with you in your room or if she needs her own."

I blinked in confusion. "Why would Angeline be staying with me?"

"Not her. Your *other* cousin."

I started to say I didn't have another cousin, but some warning voice inside me told me to neither deny nor confirm her words. I had no idea what was going on, but all my alarms were saying that *something* was definitely about to happen. Whatever it was, I needed to keep my options open.

"She had all the appropriate paperwork," explained Mrs. Weathers. "So I just let her into your room since it's only for the night."

I swallowed. "I see. Can I, um, let you know after break?"

"Certainly." After a moment's hesitation, she added, "And we'll discuss your detention then too."

"Yes, ma'am," I said.

I went upstairs, a feeling of dread in the pit of my stomach.

Who was waiting in my room? Who in the world was part of my imaginary family now?

As it turned out, it was someone from my real family.

When I unlocked the door, I found Zoe sitting on my bed.

Her face lit up when she saw me, and she sprang forward to grab me in a fierce embrace.

"Sydney!" she exclaimed. "I was so worried you weren't coming back tonight."

"Of course I was," I said stiffly. I was so shocked that I could barely return her hug. "What are you doing here?"

She pulled back and looked up at me with a big grin. There was no anger in her, not even the wariness she'd had in St. Louis. She was full of joy, truly happy to see me. I didn't know why she was here, but hope began to blossom within me that we'd finally get our reconciliation.

Until she spoke.

"They gave me a field position! I'm assigned here." She turned her face, showing me a golden lily tattoo on her cheek. My heart nearly stopped. "I'm officially an Alchemist now. Well, a junior one. I've got a lot to learn, so they thought it'd be best if I was with you."

"I see," I said. The room was spinning. Zoe. Zoe was here—and she was an Alchemist, one who would be staying with me.

Her exuberant expression became a little perplexed. "And I guess you were telling Stanton something about needing Alchemist backup? That it was really hard being around so many Moroi by yourself?"

I tried to smile but couldn't. "Something like that." I'd urged Stanton to take action, and she had. It just wasn't the kind I'd expected.

Zoe's enthusiasm returned. "Well, you aren't alone now. I'm here for you, not that you probably even need me. You don't ever get into any trouble."

No, I just had a romance going on with a vampire, was on

the verge of joining a coven, and was investigating secrets no one wanted me to know about. No trouble at all.

How in the world was I going to hide all that from her?

Zoe hugged me again. "Oh, Sydney! This is going to be great," she exclaimed. "We're going to be together all the time!"

Keep reading for
a sneak peek at the next

book . . .

CHAPTER 1

ADRIAN

I WON'T LIE. Walking into a room and seeing your girlfriend reading a baby-name book can kind of make your heart stop.

"I'm no expert," I began, choosing my words carefully. "Well—actually, I am. And I'm pretty sure there are certain things we have to do before you need to be reading that."

Sydney Sage, the aforementioned girlfriend and light of my life, didn't even look up, though a hint of a smile played at her lips. "It's for the initiation," she said matter-of-factly, as though she were talking about getting her nails done or picking up groceries instead of joining a coven of witches. "I have to have a 'magical' name they use during their gatherings."

"Right. Magical name, initiation. Just another day in the life, huh?" Not that I was one to talk, seeing as I was a vampire with the fantastic yet complicated abilities to heal and compel people.

This time, I got a full smile, and she lifted her gaze. Afternoon sunlight filtering through my bedroom window caught her eyes and brought out the amber glints within them. They widened in surprise when she noticed the three stacked boxes I was carrying. "What are those?"

"A revolution in music," I declared, reverently setting them on the floor. I opened the top one and unveiled a record player. "I saw a sign that some guy was selling them on campus." I opened a box full of records and lifted out *Rumours* by Fleetwood Mac. "Now I can listen to music in its purest form."

She didn't look impressed, surprising for someone who thought my 1967 Mustang—which she'd named the Ivashkinator—was some sort of holy shrine. "I'm pretty sure digital music is as pure as it gets. That was a waste of money, Adrian. I can fit all of the songs in those boxes on my phone."

"Can you fit the other six boxes that are in my car on your phone?"

She blinked in astonishment and then turned wary. "Adrian, how much did you pay for all that?"

I waved off the question. "Hey, I can still make the car payment. Barely." I at least didn't have to pay rent, since the place was prepaid, but I had plenty of other bills. "Besides, I've got a bigger budget for this kind of stuff, now that *someone* made me quit smoking and cut back on happy hour."

"More like happy day," she said archly. "I'm looking out for your health."

I sat down beside her on the bed. "Just like I'm looking out for you and your caffeine addiction." It was a deal we'd made, forming our own sort of support group. I quit smoking and cut back to one drink a day. She'd ousted her obsessive dieting for a healthy amount of calories and was down to only one cup of coffee a day. Surprisingly, she'd had a harder time with that than I'd had with alcohol. In those first few days, I thought I'd have to check her into caffeine rehab.

"It wasn't an addiction," she grumbled, still bitter. "More of a . . . lifestyle choice."

I laughed and drew her face to mine in a kiss, and just like that, the rest of the world vanished. There were no name books, no records, no habits. There was just her and the feel of her lips, the exquisite way they managed to be soft and fierce at the same time. The rest of the world thought she was stiff and cold. Only I knew the truth about the passion and hunger that was locked up within her—well, me and Jill, the girl who could see inside my mind because of a psychic bond we shared.

As I laid Sydney back on the bed, I had that faint, fleeting thought I always had, of how taboo what we were doing was. Humans and Moroi vampires had stopped intermingling when my race hid from the world in the Dark Ages. We'd done it for safety, deciding it was best if humans didn't know of our existence. Now, my people and hers (the ones who knew about Moroi) considered relationships like this wrong and, among some circles, dark and twisted. But I didn't care. I didn't care about anything except her and the way touching her drove me wild, even as her calm and steady presence soothed the storms that raged within me.

That didn't mean we flaunted this, though. In fact, our romance was a tightly guarded secret, one that required a lot of sneaking around and carefully calculated planning. Even now, the clock was ticking. This was our weekday pattern. She had an independent study for her last period of the day at school, one managed by a lenient teacher who let her take off early and race over here. We'd get one precious hour of making out or talking—usually making out, made more frantic by the pressure bearing down on us—and then she was back to her private school, just as her clingy and vampire-hating sister Zoe got out of class.

Somehow, Sydney had an internal clock that told her when time was up. I think it was part of her inherent ability to keep track of a hundred things at once. Not me. In these moments, my thoughts were usually focused on getting her shirt off and whether I'd get past the bra this time. So far, I hadn't.

She sat up, cheeks flushed and golden hair tousled. She was so beautiful that it made my soul ache. I always wished desperately that I could paint her in these moments and immortalize that look in her eyes. There was a softness in them that I rarely saw at other times, a total and complete vulnerability in someone who was normally so guarded and analytical in the rest of her life. But although I was a decent painter, capturing her on canvas was beyond my skill.

She collected her brown blouse and buttoned it up, hiding the brightness of turquoise lace with the conservative attire she liked to armor herself in. She'd done an overhaul of her bras in the last month, and though I was always sad to see them disappear, it made me happy to know they were there, those secret spots of color in her life.

As she walked over to the mirror at my dresser, I summoned some of the spirit magic within me to get a glimpse of her aura, the energy that surrounded all living things. The magic brought a brief surge of pleasure inside me, and then I saw it, that shining light around her. It was its typical self, a scholar's yellow balanced with the richer purple of passion and spirituality. A blink of the eye, and her aura faded away, as did the deadly exhilaration of spirit.

She finished smoothing her hair and looked down. "What's this?"

"Hmm?" I came to stand behind her and wrapped my arms around her waist. Then, I saw what she'd picked up and stiffened: sparkling cuff links set with rubies and diamonds. And just like that, the warmth and joy I'd just felt was replaced by a cold but familiar darkness. "They were a birthday present from Aunt Tatiana a few years ago."

Sydney held one up and studied it with an expert eye. She grinned. "You've got a fortune here. This is platinum. Sell these, and you'd have allowance for life. And all the records you want."

"I'd sleep in a cardboard box before I sold those."

She noticed the change in me and turned around, her expression filled with concern. "Hey, I was just joking." Her hand gently touched my face. "It's okay. Everything's okay."

But it wasn't okay. The world was suddenly a cruel, hopeless place, empty with the loss of my aunt, queen of the Moroi and the only relative who hadn't judged me. I felt a lump in my throat, and the walls seemed to close in on me as I remembered the way she'd been stabbed to death and how they'd paraded those bloody pictures around when trying to find her killer. It didn't matter that the killer was locked away and slated for execution. It wouldn't bring Aunt Tatiana back. She was gone, off to places I couldn't follow—at least not yet—and I was here, alone and insignificant and floundering . . .

"Adrian."

Sydney's voice was calm but firm, and slowly, I dredged myself out of the despair that could come on so quickly and heavily, a darkness that had increased over the years the more

I used spirit. It was the price for that kind of power, and these sudden shifts had become more and more frequent recently. I focused on her eyes, and the light returned to the world. I still ached for my aunt, but Sydney was here, my hope and my anchor. I wasn't alone. I wasn't misunderstood. Swallowing, I nodded and gave her a weak smile as spirit's dark hand released its hold on me. For now.

"I'm okay." Seeing the doubt in her face, I pressed a kiss to her forehead. "Really. You need to go, Sage. You'll make Zoe wonder, and be late for your witch meeting."

She stared at me with concern a few moments longer and then relaxed a little. "Okay. But if you need anything—"

"I know, I know. Call on the Love Phone."

That brought her smile back. We'd recently acquired secret prepaid cell phones that the Alchemists, the organization she worked for, wouldn't be able to track. Not that they regularly tracked her main phone—but they certainly could if they thought something suspicious was happening, and we didn't want a trail of texts and calls.

"And I'll come by tonight," I added.

At that, her features hardened again. "Adrian, no. It's too risky."

Another of spirit's benefits was the ability to visit people in their dreams. It was a handy way to talk since we didn't have a lot of time together in the waking world—and because we didn't spend much time talking in the waking world these days—but like any use of spirit, it was a continual risk to my sanity. It worried her a lot, but I considered it a small thing in order to be with her.

"No arguments," I warned. "I want to know how things go. And I know you'll want to know how things go for me."

"Adrian—"

"I'll keep it short," I promised.

She reluctantly agreed—not looking happy at all—and I walked her out to the door. As we cut through the living room, she paused at a small terrarium sitting near the window. Smiling, she knelt down and tapped the glass. Inside was a dragon.

No, really. Technically, it was called a callistana, but we rarely used that term. We usually called him Hopper. Sydney had summoned him from some demonic realm as a sort of helper. Mostly he seemed to want to help us out by eating all the junk food in my apartment. She and I were tied to him, and to maintain his health, we had to take turns hanging out with him. Since Zoe had moved in, however, my place had become his primary residence. Sydney lifted the lid of the tank and let the small golden-scaled creature scurry into her hand. He gazed up at her adoringly, and I couldn't blame him for that.

"He's been out for a while," she said. "You ready to take a break?" Hopper could exist in this living form or be transformed into a small statue, which helped avoid uncomfortable questions when people came by. Only she could transform him, though.

"Yeah. He keeps trying to eat my paints. And I don't want him to watch me kiss you goodbye."

She gave him a light tickle on the chin and spoke the words that turned him into a statue. Life was certainly easier that way, but again, his health required he come out now and then. That, and the little guy *had* grown on me.

"I'll take him for a while," she said, slipping him into her purse. Even if he was inert, he still benefited from being near her.

Free of his beady little gaze, I gave her a long kiss goodbye, one I was reluctant to let end. I cupped her face in my hands.

"Escape plan number seventeen," I told her. "Run away and open a juice stand in Fresno."

"Why Fresno?"

"Sounds like the kind of place people drink a lot of juice."

She grinned and kissed me again. The "escape plans" were a running joke with us, always far-fetched and numbered in no particular order. I usually made them up on the spot. What was sad, though, was that they were actually more thought-out than any real plans we had. Both of us were painfully aware that we were very much living in the now, with a future that was anything but clear.

Breaking that second kiss was difficult too, but she finally managed it, and I watched her walk away. My apartment seemed dimmer in her absence.

I brought in the rest of the boxes from my car and sifted through the treasures within. Most of the albums were from the sixties and seventies, with a little eighties here and there. They weren't organized, but I didn't make any attempts at that. Once Sydney got over her stance that they were a wasteful splurge, she wouldn't be able to help herself and would end up sorting them all by artist or genre or color. For now, I set up the record player in my living room and pulled out an album at random: *Machine Head* by Deep Purple.

I had a few more hours until dinner, so I crouched down in front of an easel, staring up at the blank canvas as I tried to decide how to deal with my current assignment in advanced oil painting: a self-portrait. It didn't have to be an exact likeness. It could be abstract. It could be anything, so long as it was representative of me. And I was stumped. I could've painted anyone else I knew. Maybe I couldn't capture that exact look of rapture Sydney had in my arms, but I could paint her aura or the color of her eyes. I could have painted the wistful, fragile face of my friend Jill Mastrano Dragomir, a young princess of the Moroi. I could have painted flaming roses in tribute to my ex-girlfriend, who'd torn my heart apart yet still managed to make me admire her.

But myself? I didn't know what to do for me. Maybe it was just an artistic block. Maybe I just didn't know myself. As I stared at the canvas, my frustration growing, I had to fight off the need to go to my neglected liquor cupboard and pour a drink. Alcohol didn't necessarily make for the best art, but it usually inspired something. I could practically taste the vodka already. I could mix it with orange juice and pretend I was being healthy. My fingers twitched, and my feet nearly carried me to the kitchen—but I resisted. The earnestness in Sydney's eyes burned through my mind, and I focused back on the canvas. I could do this—sober. I'd promised her I'd have only one drink a day, and I'd hold true to that. And for the time being, that one drink was needed for the end of the day, when I was ready for bed. I didn't sleep well. I never had in my entire life, so I had to use whatever help I could get.

My sober resolve didn't result in inspiration, though, and when five o'clock came around, the canvas remained bare. I stood up and stretched out the kinks in my body, feeling a return of that earlier darkness. It was more angry than sad, laced with the frustration of not being able to do this. My art teachers claimed I had talent, but in moments like this, I felt like the slacker most people had always said I was, destined for a lifetime of failure. It was especially depressing when I thought about Sydney, who knew everything about everything and could excel at any career she wanted. Putting aside the vampire-human problem, I had to wonder what I could possibly offer her. I couldn't even pronounce half the things that interested her, let alone discuss them. If we ever managed some normal life together, she'd be out paying the bills while I stayed home and cleaned. And I really wasn't good at that either. If she just wanted to come home at night to eye candy with good hair, I could probably do that reasonably well.

I knew these fears eating at me were being amped up by spirit. Not all of them were real, but they were hard to shake. I left the art behind and stepped outside my door, hoping to find distraction in the night to come. The sun was going down outside, and the Palm Springs winter evening barely required a light jacket. It was a favorite time of the evening for Moroi, when there was still light but not enough to be uncomfortable. We could handle some sunlight, not like Strigoi—the undead vampires who killed for their blood. Sunlight destroyed them, which was a perk for us. We needed all the help we could get in the fight against them.

I drove out to Vista Azul, a suburb only ten minutes away from downtown that housed Amberwood Prep, the private boarding school that Sydney and the rest of our motley crew attended. Sydney was normally the group's designated chauffeur, but that dubious honor had fallen on me tonight while she scurried off to her clandestine meeting with the coven. The gang was all waiting at the curb outside the girls' dorm as I pulled up. Leaning across the passenger seat, I opened up the door. "All aboard," I said.

They piled in. There were five of them now, plus me, bringing us up to a lucky seven, had Sydney been there. When we'd first come to Palm Springs, there'd just been four. Jill, the reason we were all here, scooted in beside me and flashed me a grin.

If Sydney was the main calming force in my life, Jill was the second. She was only fifteen, seven years younger than me, but there was a grace and wisdom that radiated from her already. Sydney might be the love of my life, but Jill understood me in a way no one else could. It was kind of hard not to, with that psychic bond. It had been forged when I used spirit to save her life last year—and when I say "save," I mean it. Jill had technically been dead, only for less than a minute, but dead nonetheless. I'd used spirit's power to perform a miraculous feat of healing and bring her back before the next world could claim her. That miracle had bonded us with a connection that allowed her to feel and see my thoughts—though not the other way around.

People brought back that way were called "shadow-kissed," and that alone would have been enough to mess up any kid. Jill had the added misfortune of being one of two people left in a dying line of Moroi royalty. This was recent news to her, and her sister, Lissa—the Moroi queen and a good friend of mine—needed Jill alive in order to hold on to her throne. Those who opposed Lissa's liberal rule consequently wanted Jill dead, in order to invoke an ancient family law requiring a monarch to have one other living family member. And so, someone had come up with the questionably brilliant idea to send Jill into hiding in the middle of a human city in the desert. Because seriously, what vampire would want to live here? It was certainly a question I asked myself a lot.

Jill's three bodyguards climbed into the backseat. They were all dhampirs, a race born of mixed vampire and human heritage from the time our races had shared in free love. They were stronger and faster than the rest of us, making ideal warriors in the battle against Strigoi and royal assassins. Eddie Castile was the de facto leader of the group, a dependable rock who'd been with Jill from the beginning. Angeline Dawes, the red-haired spitfire, was slightly less dependable. And by "less dependable," I mean, "not at all." She was a scrapper in a fight, though. The newest addition to the group was Neil Raymond, aka Tall, Proper, and Boring. For reasons I didn't understand, Jill and Angeline seemed to think his non-smiling demeanor was a sign of some kind of noble character. The fact that he'd gone to school in England and had picked up a faint British accent especially seemed to fire up their estrogen.

The last member of the party stood outside the car, refusing to get in. Zoe Sage, Sydney's sister.

She leaned forward and met my eyes with brown ones almost like Sydney's, but with less gold. "There's no room," she said. "Your car doesn't have enough seats."

"Not true," I told her. On cue, Jill moved closer to me. "This seat's meant to hold three. Last owner even fitted it with an extra seat belt." While that was safer for modern times, Sydney had nearly had a heart attack over altering the Mustang from its original state. "Besides, we're all family, right?" To give us easy access to one another, we'd made Amberwood believe we were all siblings or cousins. When Neil arrived, however, the Alchemists had finally given up on making him a relative since things were getting kind of ridiculous.

Zoe stared at the empty spot for several seconds. Even though the seat really was long, she'd still be getting cozy with

Jill. Zoe had been at Amberwood for a month but was in full possession of all the hang-ups and prejudices her people had around vampires and dhampirs. I knew them well because Sydney used to have all of them too. It was ironic because the Alchemists' mission was to keep the world of vampires and the supernatural hidden from their fellow humans, who they feared wouldn't be able to handle it. The Alchemists were driven by the belief that members of my kind were twisted parts of nature best ignored and kept separate from humans, lest we taint them with our evil. They helped us grudgingly and were useful in a situation like Jill's, when arrangements with human authorities and school officials needed to occur behind the scenes. Alchemists excelled at making things happen. That was how Sydney had originally been drafted, to smooth the way for Jill and her exile, since the Alchemists didn't want a Moroi civil war. Zoe had been sent recently as an apprentice and had become a huge pain in the ass for hiding our relationship.

"You don't have to go if you're afraid," I said. There was probably nothing else I could've said that would've motivated her more. She was driven to become a super Alchemist, largely to impress the Sage father, who, I'd concluded after many stories, was a major asshole.

Zoe took a deep breath and steeled herself. Without another word, she climbed in beside Jill and slammed the door, huddling as close to it as possible. "Sydney should've left the SUV," she muttered a little while later.

"Where is Sage, anyway? Er, Sage Senior," I amended, pulling out of the school's driveway. "Not that I don't like chauffeuring you guys around. You should've brought me a little black cap, Jailbait." I nudged Jill, who nudged me back. "You could whip up something like that in your sewing club."

"She's off doing some project for Ms. Terwilliger," said Zoe disapprovingly. "She's always doing something for her. I don't get why history research takes up so much time."

Little did Zoe know that said project involved Sydney being initiated into her teacher's coven. Human magic was still a strange and mysterious thing to me—and completely anathema to the Alchemists—but Sydney was apparently a natural. No surprise, seeing as she was a natural at everything. She'd overcome her fears of it, just as she had of me, and was now fully immersed in learning the trade from her zany yet loveable mentor, Jackie Terwilliger. To say the Alchemists wouldn't like that was an understatement. In fact, it was really a toss-up which would piss them off more: learning the arcane arts or making out with a vampire. It would almost be comical, if not for the fact that I worried the hard-core zealots among the Alchemists would do something terrible to Sydney if she was ever caught. It was why Zoe shadowing her had made everything so dangerous lately.

"Because it's Sydney," said Eddie from the backseat. In the rearview mirror, I could see an easy smile on his face, though there was a perpetual sharpness in his eyes as he scanned the world for danger. He and Neil had been trained by the guardians, the dhampir organization of badasses that protected the Moroi. "Giving one hundred percent to a task is slacking for her."

Zoe shook her head, not as amused as the rest of us. "It's just a stupid class. She only needs to pass."

No, I thought. *She needs to learn.* Sydney didn't just eat up knowledge for the sake of her vocation. She did it because she loved it. And what she would've loved more than anything was to lose herself in the academic throes of college, where she could learn anything she wanted. Instead, she'd been born into her family job, jumping when the Alchemists ordered her to new assignments. She'd already graduated from high school but treated this second senior year as seriously as the first, eager to learn whatever she could.

Someday, when this is all over, and Jill is safe, we'll run away from everything. I didn't know where, and I didn't know how, but Sydney would figure out those logistics. She'd escape the Alchemists' hold and become Dr. Sydney Sage, PhD, while I . . . well, did something.

I felt a small hand on my arm and glanced briefly down to see Jill looking sympathetically up at me, her jade-colored eyes shining. She knew what I was thinking, knew about the fantasies I often spun. I gave her a wan smile back.

We drove across town, then to the outskirts of Palm Springs to the home of Clarence Donahue, the only Moroi foolish enough to live in this desert until my friends and I had shown up last fall. Old Clarence was kind of a crackpot, but he was a nice enough one who'd welcomed a ragtag group of Moroi and dhampirs and allowed us to use his feeder/housekeeper. Moroi don't have to kill for blood like Strigoi did, but we did need it at least a couple times a week. Fortunately, there were plenty of humans in the world happy to provide it in exchange for a life spent on the endorphin high brought on by a vampire bite.

We found Clarence in the living room, sitting in his massive leather chair and using a magnifying glass to read some ancient book. He looked up at our entrance, startled. "Here on a Thursday! What a nice surprise."

"It's Friday, Mr. Donahue," said Jill gently, leaning down to kiss his cheek.

He regarded her fondly. "Is it? Weren't you just here yesterday? Well, no matter. Dorothy, I'm sure, will be happy to accommodate you."

Dorothy, his aging housekeeper, looked very accommodating. She'd hit the jackpot when Jill and I arrived in Palm Springs. Older Moroi didn't drink as much blood as young ones, and while Clarence could still provide an occasional high, frequent visits from Jill and me provided a near-constant one for her.

Jill hurried over to Dorothy. "Can I go now?" The older woman nodded eagerly, and the two of them left the room for more private accommodations. A look of distaste crossed Zoe's face, though she said nothing. Seeing her expression and the way she sat far away from everyone else was so like Sydney in the old days, I almost smiled.

Angeline was practically bouncing up and down on the couch. "What's for dinner?" She had an unusual southern accent from growing up in a rural mountain community of Moroi, dhampirs, and humans who were the only ones I knew of that freely lived together and intermarried. Everyone else in their respective races regarded them with a kind of mingled horror and fascination. As appealing as that openness was, living with them had never crossed my mind in my fantasies with Sydney. I hated camping.

No one answered. Angeline looked from face to face. "Well? Why isn't there food here?" Dhampirs didn't drink blood and could eat the regular kinds of food humans did. Moroi also needed that sort of food, though we didn't need it in nearly the same quantities. It took a lot of energy to keep that active dhampir metabolism fired up.

These regular gatherings had become kind of a family dinner affair, not just for blood but also for regular food. It was a nice way to pretend we led normal lives. "There's always food," she pointed out, in case we'd never noticed. "I liked that Indian food we had the other day. That masala or whatever stuff. But I don't know if we should go there any more until they start calling it Native American food. It's not very polite."

"Sydney usually takes care of food," said Eddie, ignoring Angeline's familiar and endearing tendency to stray into tangents.

"Not usually," I corrected. "Always."

Angeline's gaze swiveled to Zoe. "Why didn't you have us pick up something?"

"Because that's not my job!" Zoe lifted her head up high. "We're here to keep Jill's cover and make sure she stays off the radar. It's not my job to feed you guys."

"In which sense?" I asked. I knew perfectly well that was a mean thing to say to her but couldn't resist. It took her a moment to pick up the double meaning. First she paled; then she turned an angry red.

"Neither! I'm not your concierge. Neither is Sydney. I don't know why she always takes care of that stuff for you. She should only be dealing with things that are essential for your survival. Ordering pizza isn't one of them."

I faked a yawn and leaned back into the couch. "Maybe she figures if we're well fed, you two won't look that appetizing."

Zoe was too horrified to respond, and Eddie shot me a

withering look. "Enough. It's not that hard to order pizza. I'll do it."

Jill was back by the time he finished the call, an amused smile on her face. She'd apparently witnessed the exchange. The bond wasn't on all the time, but it appeared to be going strong today. With the food dilemma settled, we actually managed to fall into a surprising camaraderie—well, everyone except Zoe, who just watched and waited. Things were unexpectedly cordial between Angeline and Eddie, despite a recent and disastrous bout of dating. She'd moved on and now pretended to be obsessed with Neil. If Eddie was still hurt, he didn't show it, but that was typical of him. Sydney said he was secretly in love with Jill, something else he was good at hiding.

I could've approved of that, but Jill, like Angeline, kept pretending she was in love with Neil. It was all an act for both girls, but no one—not even Sydney—believed me.

"Are you okay with what we ordered?" Angeline asked him. "You didn't pipe up with any requests."

Neil shook his head, face stoic. He kept his dark hair in a painfully short and efficient haircut. It was the kind of no-nonsense thing the Alchemists would've loved. "I can't waste time quibbling over trivial things like pepperoni and mushrooms. If you'd gone to my school in Devonshire, you'd understand. For one of my sophomore classes, they left us alone on the moors to fend for ourselves and learn survival skills. Spend three days eating twigs and heather, and you'll learn not to argue about any food coming your way."

Angeline and Jill cooed as though that was the most rugged, manly thing they'd ever heard. Eddie wore an expression that reflected what I felt, puzzling over whether this guy was as serious as he seemed or just some genius with swoon-worthy lines.

Zoe's cell phone rang. She looked at the display and jumped up in alarm. "It's Dad." Without a backward glance, she answered and scurried out of the room.

I wasn't one for premonition, but a chill ran down my spine. The Sage dad wasn't the kind of warm and friendly guy who'd call to say hello during business hours, when he knew Zoe was doing her Alchemist thing. If something was up with her, something was up with Sydney. And that worried me.

I barely paid any attention to the rest of the conversation as I counted the moments until Zoe's return. When she did finally come back, her ashen face told me I was right. Something bad had happened.

"What is it?" I demanded. "Is Sydney okay?" Too late I realized I shouldn't have showed any special concern for Sydney. Not even our friends knew about me and her. Fortunately, all attention was on Zoe.

She slowly shook her head, eyes wide and disbelieving. "I . . . I don't know. It's my parents. They're getting divorced."

ONE

I FELT HER FEAR BEFORE I heard her screams.

Her nightmare pulsed into me, shaking me out of my own dream, which had had something to do with a beach and some hot guy rubbing suntan oil on me. Images—hers, not mine—tumbled through my mind: fire and blood, the smell of smoke, the twisted metal of a car. The pictures wrapped around me, suffocating me, until some rational part of my brain reminded me that this wasn't *my* dream.

I woke up, strands of long, dark hair sticking to my forehead.

Lissa lay in her bed, thrashing and screaming. I bolted out of mine, quickly crossing the few feet that separated us.

"Liss," I said, shaking her. "Liss, wake up."

Her screams dropped off, replaced by soft whimpers. "Andre," she moaned. "Oh God."

I helped her sit up. "Liss, you aren't there anymore. Wake up."

After a few moments, her eyes fluttered open, and in the dim lighting, I could see a flicker of consciousness start to take over. Her frantic breathing slowed, and she leaned into me, resting her head against my shoulder. I put an arm around her and ran a hand over her hair.

"It's okay," I told her gently. "Everything's okay."

"I had that dream."

"Yeah. I know."

We sat like that for several minutes, not saying anything else. When I felt her emotions calm down, I leaned over to the nightstand between our beds and turned on the lamp. It glowed dimly, but neither of us really needed much to see by. Attracted by the light, our housemate's cat, Oscar, leapt up onto the sill of the open window.

He gave me a wide berth—animals don't like dhampirs, for whatever reason—but jumped onto the bed and rubbed his head against Lissa, purring softly. Animals didn't have a problem with Moroi, and they all loved Lissa in particular. Smiling, she scratched his chin, and I felt her calm further.

"When did we last do a feeding?" I asked, studying her face. Her fair skin was paler than usual. Dark circles hung under her eyes, and there was an air of frailty about her. School had been hectic this week, and I couldn't remember the last time I'd given her blood. "It's been like . . . more than two days, hasn't it? Three? Why didn't you say anything?"

She shrugged and wouldn't meet my eyes. "You were busy. I didn't want to—"

"Screw that," I said, shifting into a better position. No wonder she seemed so weak. Oscar, not wanting me any closer, leapt down and returned to the window, where he could watch at a safe distance. "Come on. Let's do this."

"Rose—"

Her pale, jade-green eyes watched me with concern. Sh
stood up. "I'm going to get you something to eat."

My protests came awkwardly to my lips, and she left
before I could get out a sentence. The buzz from her bite had
lessened as soon as she broke the connection, but some of it
still lingered in my veins, and I felt a goofy smile cross my
lips. Turning my head, I glanced up at Oscar, still sitting in the
window.

"You don't know what you're missing," I told him.

His attention was on something outside. Hunkering down
into a crouch, he puffed out his jet-black fur. His tail started
twitching.

My smile faded, and I forced myself to sit up. The world
spun, and I waited for it to right itself before trying to stand.
When I managed it, the dizziness set in again and this time
refused to leave. Still, I felt okay enough to stumble to the
window and peer out with Oscar. He eyed me warily, scooted
over a little, and then returned to whatever had held his attention.

A warm breeze—unseasonably warm for a Portland fall—
played with my hair as I leaned out. The street was dark
and relatively quiet. It was three in the morning, just about
the only time a college campus settled down, at least somewhat. The house in which we'd rented a room for the past
eight months sat on a residential street with old, mismatched
houses. Across the road, a streetlight flickered, nearly ready
to burn out. It still cast enough light for me to make out the

"Come *on*. It'll make you feel better."

I tilted my head and tossed my hair back, baring my neck. I saw her hesitate, but the sight of my neck and what it offered proved too powerful. A hungry expression crossed her face, and her lips parted slightly, exposing the fangs she normally kept hidden while living among humans. Those fangs contrasted oddly with the rest of her features. With her pretty face and pale blond hair, she looked more like an angel than a vampire.

As her teeth neared my bare skin, I felt my heart race with a mix of fear and anticipation. I always hated feeling the latter, but it was nothing I could help, a weakness I couldn't shake.

Her fangs bit into me, hard, and I cried out at the brief flare of pain. Then it faded, replaced by a wonderful, golden joy that spread through my body. It was better than any of the times I'd been drunk or high. Better than sex—or so I imagined, since I'd never done it. It was a blanket of pure, refined pleasure, wrapping me up and promising everything would be right in the world. On and on it went. The chemicals in her saliva triggered an endorphin rush, and I lost track of the world, lost track of who I was.

Then, regretfully, it was over. It had taken less than a minute.

She pulled back, wiping her hand across her lips as she studied me. "You okay?"

"I . . . yeah." I lay back on the bed, dizzy from the blood loss. "I just need to sleep it off. I'm fine."

shapes of cars and buildings. In our own yard, I could see the silhouettes of trees and bushes.

And a man watching me.

I jerked back in surprise. A figure stood by a tree in the yard, about thirty feet away, where he could easily see through the window. He was close enough that I probably could have thrown something and hit him. He was certainly close enough that he could have seen what Lissa and I had just done.

The shadows covered him so well that even with my heightened sight, I couldn't make out any of his features, save for his height. He was tall. Really tall. He stood there for just a moment, barely discernible, and then stepped back, disappearing into the shadows cast by the trees on the far side of the yard. I was pretty sure I saw someone else move nearby and join him before the blackness swallowed them both.

Whoever these figures were, Oscar didn't like them. Not counting me, he usually got along with most people, growing upset only when someone posed an immediate danger. The guy outside hadn't done anything threatening to Oscar, but the cat had sensed something, something that put him on edge.

Something similar to what he always sensed in me.

Icy fear raced through me, almost—but not quite—eradicating the lovely bliss of Lissa's bite. Backing up from the window, I jerked on a pair of jeans that I found on the floor, nearly falling over in the process. Once they were on, I grabbed my coat and Lissa's, along with our wallets. Shoving my feet into the first shoes I saw, I headed out the door.

Downstairs, I found her in the cramped kitchen, rummaging through the refrigerator. One of our housemates, Jeremy, sat at the table, hand on his forehead as he stared sadly at a calculus book. Lissa regarded me with surprise.

"You shouldn't be up."

"We have to go. Now."

Her eyes widened, and then a moment later, understanding clicked in. "Are you . . . really? Are you sure?"

I nodded. I couldn't explain how I knew for sure. I just did.

Jeremy watched us curiously. "What's wrong?"

An idea came to mind. "Liss, get his car keys."

He looked back and forth between us. "What are you—"

Lissa unhesitatingly walked over to him. Her fear poured into me through our psychic bond, but there was something else too: her complete faith that I would take care of everything, that we would be safe. Like always, I hoped I was worthy of that kind of trust.

She smiled broadly and gazed directly into his eyes. For a moment, Jeremy just stared, still confused, and then I saw the thrall seize him. His eyes glazed over, and he regarded her adoringly.

"We need to borrow your car," she said in a gentle voice. "Where are your keys?"

He smiled, and I shivered. I had a high resistance to compulsion, but I could still feel its effects when it was directed at another person. That, and I'd been taught my entire life that using it was wrong. Reaching into his pocket, Jeremy handed over a set of keys hanging on a large red key chain.

"Thank you," said Lissa. "And where is it parked?"

"Down the street," he said dreamily. "At the corner. By Brown." Four blocks away.

"Thank you," she repeated, backing up. "As soon as we leave, I want you to go back to studying. Forget you ever saw us tonight."

He nodded obligingly. I got the impression he would have walked off a cliff for her right then if she'd asked. All humans were susceptible to compulsion, but Jeremy appeared weaker than most. That came in handy right now.

"Come on," I told her. "We've got to move."

We stepped outside, heading toward the corner he'd named. I was still dizzy from the bite and kept stumbling, unable to move as quickly as I wanted. Lissa had to catch hold of me a few times to stop me from falling. All the time, that anxiety rushed into me from her mind. I tried my best to ignore it; I had my own fears to deal with.

"Rose . . . what are we going to do if they catch us?" she whispered.

"They won't," I said fiercely. "I won't let them."

"But if they've found us—"

"They found us before. They didn't catch us then. We'll just drive over to the train station and go to L.A. They'll lose the trail."

I made it sound simple. I always did, even though there

was nothing simple about being on the run from the people we'd grown up with. We'd been doing it for two years, hiding wherever we could and just trying to finish high school. Our senior year had just started, and living on a college campus had seemed safe. We were so close to freedom.

She said nothing more, and I felt her faith in me surge up once more. This was the way it had always been between us. I was the one who took action, who made sure things happened—sometimes recklessly so. She was the more reasonable one, the one who thought things out and researched them extensively before acting. Both styles had their uses, but at the moment, recklessness was called for. We didn't have time to hesitate.

Lissa and I had been best friends ever since kindergarten, when our teacher had paired us together for writing lessons. Forcing five-year-olds to spell *Vasilisa Dragomir* and *Rosemarie Hathaway* was beyond cruel, and we'd—or rather, I'd—responded appropriately. I'd chucked my book at our teacher and called her a fascist bastard. I hadn't known what those words meant, but I'd known how to hit a moving target.

Lissa and I had been inseparable ever since.

"Do you hear that?" she asked suddenly.

It took me a few seconds to pick up what her sharper senses already had. Footsteps, moving fast. I grimaced. We had two more blocks to go.

"We've got to run for it," I said, catching hold of her arm.

"But you can't—"

decent standard of living, and the Silesian who sought asylum as a Pole, in order to secure his family a decent standard of living, there was, in truth, scant difference. They were both, as the popular joke had it, less *Volksdeutsche* than *Volkswagendeutsche*. But then, could not that equally well be said of most ordinary West Germans? And why not?

As a result of this unexpected and disconcerting development, the position of the German minorities became, like so many other aspects of German Ostpolitik, simultaneously an issue of domestic and of foreign policy. In domestic policy, a major debate began about the right of asylum. In foreign policy, the Kohl government began to give new emphasis and urgency to the second possible line of policy towards the Germans in the East: that of helping them to stay rather than helping them to leave. Beside the individual human right – to leave – the Bonn government increasingly placed the group rights of minorities.

People qualified as Germans under article 116 of the Basic Law should, it was argued in Bonn, be able to live as Germans in whatever state they now found themselves. They should have German-language teaching, cultural life, journals, church services etc, and equal opportunities. The unique culture of Central Europe had been made by the tense yet seminal co-existence of Slavs, Germans and Jews. The Jews could never be brought back, but the Germans might still play their part. This was thus, at its best, neither an illiberal nor an unattractive vision. But so long as the states of Eastern Europe remained communist, it remained just that: a vision.

Hungary was the exception that proved the rule. Here, in a state with a small German minority, relatively unburdened historic ties with Germany, and increasingly warm relations with Bonn, János Kádár's regime recognised the advantages that could accrue from an exemplary treatment of its Germans. On the first visit by a President of the Federal Republic, in 1986, Richard von Weizsäcker was entertained by schoolgirls from the so-called Swabians of the Danube, dancing folk-dances in colourful folk-costumes, singing folk-songs and reciting folk-poems. It was, said the President, 'an occasion that moves the heart'. The exemplary folk-treatment did not only move the heart-strings of the Federal President. It also moved the purse-strings of the Federal Government. In giving an untied DM 1 billion credit to the Hungarian government in 1987, Bonn made it very plain that this was partly in recognition of the good treatment of the German minority. On a visit to Hungary in 1988, the Christian Democrats' foreign affairs spokesman, Volker Rühe, went so far as to say that 'the treatment of minorities plays a dominant role in my present conversations with the Hungarian leadership and the Association of Hungary Germans'.

What is more, politicians and policymakers in Bonn made no secret of the fact that this credit was to be understood as a signal to other states in the Soviet bloc: if Poland, Czechoslovakia, Romania or even the Soviet

development of economic and industrial co-operation'? The problem with the 'jumbo credit' was precisely the cloudy mixture of motives and goals: moral and national, personal, political and economic. The one thing it certainly was not was good business – for either side. Between 1976 and 1980 the West German taxpayer paid DM 290.5 million in interest subsidies for this credit alone. Meanwhile, Gierek and his colleagues so misspent this and other Western credits that they not only ruined the Polish economy but also diminished rather than increased the country's chances of 'economic and industrial co-operation' with the West.

The only people who benefited (presumably) in the longer term were the more than 120,000 Polish Germans or German Poles thus 'bought free'. Yet the problem still would not go away. The more that left, the more there were who wanted to leave. The Germans in Poland multiplied like relics of the true cross: a development not unconnected with Poland's deepening economic crisis. At the end of 1983 the then Minister of State in the Foreign Ministry, Alois Mertes, observed that 'at least 120,000 Germans in the Oder-Neisse area and neighbouring areas of the People's Republic of Poland demonstrably desire to move permanently to the Federal Republic of Germany'. As we have seen this was not merely a practical problem. It was also a symbolic-political one.

In the same document which brought this answer – in the form of a long letter to a parliamentary colleague – Mertes estimated, on the basis of scrupulous calculations, that there were probably some 1.1 million people still living in Poland who were 'Germans' according to German law. He went on, however, to emphasise that 'over ninety per cent of the population' were Poles who 'now regard the Oder-Neisse area as their final *Heimat*'. And he concluded by recalling that liberal-conservative interpretation of Germany's position in international law which clearly indicated that a putative 'reunification' would include only the territory west of the Oder-Neisse line. His intentions were thus of the best. But they were misunderstood – in part deliberately so.

For the Polish authorities took this as a further ground for winding up, entirely in line with Soviet propaganda at that time, their own campaign against alleged West German 'revanchism': a campaign intended to mobilise the Polish population behind the Jaruzelski regime. It was a curious reward for the government which, of all major Western governments had shown most understanding for General Jaruzelski's attempts at 'normalisation' and 'stabilisation'. In this way, the German minorities issue, linked to the frontier question, once again blighted relations between the Polish and West German states.

Nor was it only the Jaruzelski regime. With that exquisite sensitivity to the feelings of other nations which he was later to display in his remarks on Polish-Jewish relations, Primate Glemp preached a sermon in which he said, in effect, that there were no Germans left in Poland, and they should anyway be glad to be Poles. Proudly he reported his retort to an old lady in West Germany who had asked him that no injury should be done to the Germans remaining in Poland. 'What Germans, what injury?' he had replied. This in turn provoked outrage in West Germany. And so, forty years after the end of the war, the bitter cycle of recrimination continued.

In the second half of the 1980s the remaining German minorities produced yet another problem for the Federal Republic. This time, it was a problem of success. For years, for decades, the Bonn government had urged and paid the authorities in Warsaw, Moscow and Bucharest (not to mention in East Berlin) to let their Germans go. And now, suddenly, they came, not just in their tens of thousands but in their hundreds of thousands. The total number of out-settlers from the Soviet Union and Eastern Europe soared from just over 40,000 in 1986 to nearly 80,000 in 1987, over 200,000 in 1988, a staggering 377,055 in 1989 and nearly 400,000 in 1990. The main reasons for this growth were twofold: a fundamentally altered emigration policy of the Soviet Union under Gorbachev, embodied in a new decree of January 1987; and the virtually free-for-all travel policy of the Polish government, combined with an economic situation that was a powerful incentive to take up the 'German option'.

Here, surely, was a great success for German Ostpolitik. Was not this precisely what Chancellor Kohl had demanded, with renewed emphasis, in his government declaration of 1983, referring to those concerned not merely as 'people of German origin' but simply as 'Germans'? Yet the result of this great flood of Germans 'coming home' was not an outpouring of national welcome and public delight but, on the contrary, a growing public resentment and resistance, reflected in election successes for the new party of the far right: the *Republikaner*. The *Republikaner* were a curious phenomenon: an extreme right-wing, populist nationalist party one of whose main sources of electoral support was resentment against newly arrived German nationals.

In vain did politicians from the President and Chancellor down argue that many of these Germans had suffered long and hard just for being Germans. In vain did they recall that a ruined Germany had after the war welcomed and integrated many times this number of Germans from the East. In vain did ministers and economists point out that these mainly young, often well-qualified, highly-motivated people would be a net economic gain to a country whose own native-born German population was shrinking and ageing. What disgruntled voters in the big cities like Berlin or Frankfurt or the poorer parts of rural Bavaria saw was housing, jobs, and extra social security payments going to newcomers, even in preference to the locals.

To understand this reaction one must understand that this large increase

in the number of out-settlers came at the same time, and partly for the same reasons, as a large increase in the number of Germans moving from East to West Germany, and of other East Europeans (for in the terms of Yalta Europe, the East Germans and the Germans in the East were also 'East Europeans') who came to visit, to stay illegally, or to seek political asylum. Here it is important to note that if in article 116 of its constitution, and the subsequent interpretation of that article in law and government practice, the Federal Republic had a remarkably generous definition of Germanity, then in article 16 of its constitution, and the subsequent interpretation of that article in law and government practice, the Federal Republic had a remarkably generous definition of asylum.

Mindful of the way in which Germans persecuted by the Nazis had been granted asylum in Scandinavia, America, Britain and other free countries, the drafters of the Basic Law said simply, sweepingly: 'Persons persecuted on political grounds shall enjoy the right of asylum.' In practice, even people with the barest claim to have been persecuted in Eastern Europe were not actually sent back. In the second half of the 1980s, the number of asylum-seekers from Eastern Europe, and particularly from Poland, soared, while, with the gradual *de facto* softening of the regime at home, the grounds on which they claimed asylum became ever thinner. Already in 1987, some eighty-five per cent of all those applying for asylum in the whole European Community were doing so in the Federal Republic. The total number of asylum-seekers topped the 100,000 mark in 1988, while at the end of that year some 200,000 Poles were registered as staying 'not just temporarily' in West Germany.

The cause for popular resentment was thus by no means only the Germans from the East, but rather a whole great influx of strangers of all shades and backgrounds. Even the Berliner who moved from one end of the Friedrichstrasse to the other was not immune to this resentment, and the tension between the so-called *Ossis* and *Wessis* – roughly, Easties and Westies – would become acute after the complete opening of the German-German frontier. But beyond this, opinion polls revealed a rough continuum of resentment from the (least resented) Germans from the GDR, through Germans from Romania or Russia, to Germans (or 'Germans') from Poland, to Poles, to the people known until the early 1990s as 'Yugoslavs', and thence to the (most despised) Gipsies, Africans and other lesser breeds without the D-mark. As one wit observed, the hostility was directed against everything beginning with A: *Asylanten, Ausländer, Aussiedler* (that is, asylum-seekers, foreigners, out-settlers).

Ironically, it was the Federal Republic's own interpretation of its own nationality and asylum laws which helped to create this continuum, especially by its treatment of that dubious middle ground represented above all by the inhabitants of Upper Silesia. For between the Silesian who suddenly rediscovered a German past, in order to secure his family a

Union conferred such rights on their Germans, they too could expect such rewards. Put very crudely, Bonn, having for years paid to get 'our compatriots' out of Eastern Europe and into West Germany, was now ready to pay to keep them (voluntarily) in Eastern Europe and out of West Germany. In a somewhat unguarded comment in a radio interview in August 1988, Chancellor Kohl, asked about the Bonn-Warsaw negotiations, replied: 'Both sides must move here. The Poles want economic support, we think of our compatriots . . . who live there.'

The theme was high on the agenda of German-Polish negotiations in the late 1980s, and in the round of German-Soviet negotiations in 1988-89. During Gorbachev's visit to Bonn in 1989, Kohl raised with him the subject of a possible separate republic for the Germans in the Soviet Union, either on the Volga, where many of them had originally been, or elsewhere. In both the Soviet and German press there was discussion of the suggestion, first raised by a leading German banker, of turning the Kaliningrad – that is, Königsberg – enclave into some sort of a special economic zone or autonomous region, with a major role for the Germans. Yet none of these discussions bore major fruit before the revolutions of 1989, while in Romania the position of the German (as of all other) minorities actually worsened in the last years of Ceauşescu.

The main effective thrust of West German policy right up to 1989 therefore continued to be in helping the Germans to leave rather than in helping them to stay. In sum, nearly a million people came to the Federal Republic as 'out-settlers' from the Soviet Union and Eastern Europe in the years 1950 to 1969, and more than 1.3 million in the years 1970 to 1989. This policy thus brought inestimable benefits to hundreds of thousands of individual human beings, who gained freedom and life-chances, albeit at the price of uprooting. There were also significant potential long-term benefits for the ageing West German population. The young out-settlers would, in time, help to pay their pensions.

Yet there were multiple ironies here. A general objective of Ostpolitik was to restore a traditional German presence in Central and Eastern Europe, in a constructive, peaceful, liberal form. But one effect, one 'success' of this Ostpolitik, was to deplete the remaining, permanent, settled German presence in the region. The slow death of centuries-old German communities in Transylvania or the Banat was, by any standards, a further Central European tragedy. It was the continuation of Potsdam by other means. Obviously the primary responsibility lay with the communist regimes in Bucharest, Warsaw or Moscow. Perhaps Bonn had no alternative. But the plain fact is that Bonn directly contributed to – and in part simply paid for – this depletion of the remaining German communities. What is more, the domestic impact of this deeply ambiguous foreign policy 'success' was to fuel popular resentments, bring votes to a new far-right party, and even increase criticism of the Ostpolitik.

Carrots and sticks

'Foreign trade,' said the architect of West Germany's *Wirtschaftswunder*, Ludwig Erhard, 'is quite simply the core and premiss of our economic and social order.' The Federal Republic was (and is) dependent on foreign trade to an extraordinary degree. In the 1980s, at least one third of its gross domestic product was derived from exports. About one in every five jobs depended directly on foreign trade. The Federal Republic was (and is) a 'trading state'.

Long before 1945, Walter Rathenau had adapted Napoleon's famous remark to Goethe that 'politics is our fate'. 'The economy', said Rathenau, 'is our fate.' The new phase of intensive industrial development after 1945 greatly increased Germany's overall dependence on foreign trade. But this was also exacerbated by the post-1945 truncation of Germany's territory. Whereas previously the country had obtained many of its raw materials and energy supplies from its own eastern territories – Silesian coal, for example – the diminished state(s) had now to import them, and to export more to pay for those imports.

For most of the post-war period there was in fact an obvious complementarity between the supply and demand profiles of West Germany and Eastern Europe. Not only was West Germany able to supply the manufactured goods and technology that Eastern Europe increasingly sought. West Germany was also able to take more of the primary goods that the Soviet Union and Eastern Europe had to offer in return: whether natural gas, basic chemicals, gherkins or geese.

This complementarity was not lost on Soviet leaders. Indeed they were inclined, on occasion, to build upon it grand hopes – and threats. 'You forget,' Khrushchev told the French Foreign Minister Christian Pineau, 'that [Germany's] economy is much less complementary with yours than with that of the USSR. When you begin to compete with German industry, it will turn towards the USSR where it will be able to find an appropriate area for expansion. That will be the time of a new Rapallo. Then you will be sorry that you didn't listen to us.' And the German ambassador to Moscow at the beginning of Brandt's Ostpolitik records Kosygin saying to him in 1971: 'We have all the raw materials in the world, you have the know-how. Let's get together, and we'll be autarkic.' As we have seen, Brezhnev also harboured visions of grandiose German-Soviet economic co-operation.

Though German leaders obviously took a far more sober view of what was possible, and knew that the balance of Germany's economic self-interest lay overwhelmingly in the West, they nonetheless had both an economic and a political interest in expanding trade with the East. In the circumstances it would have been a mark of extreme abnormality if West

Germany had not had a substantial trade with its neighbours to the east and south-east. In the late 1940s and early 1950s that was the deeply abnormal position. West Germany's trade with Eastern Europe grew strongly in the 1960s, and then, as we have seen, even more rapidly through the 1970s (see Table II), with the increase mainly being accounted for by the growth of German-Soviet trade. German politicians described this as a piece of 'normalisation', but what full 'normality' would be it was extraordinarily hard to say.

Throughout the 1970s and 1980s, the Federal Republic's trade with the Soviet Union and Eastern Europe, excluding the GDR, was never more than seven and a half per cent of the country's total foreign trade. If one included trade with the GDR, the figure reached a peak of more than nine per cent in 1975. However, while the actual volume of eastern trade continued to expand, the *proportion* of West Germany's total trade done with the European members of Comecon actually declined over the next decade. West German policymakers never tired of repeating that the Federal Republic's eastern trade was less than its trade with Switzerland. The repetition was made, however, with slightly different emphasis to different audiences. To worried Western allies, and especially to Americans, the statement was one of reassurance: don't worry, it said in effect, our trade is so small that there is no danger of our becoming dependent on the East. To their own businessmen, and to Soviet and East European partners, the statement was rather: look how ridiculously small this is, we must increase it!

Speaking to the Economic Association of the Iron-, Tin- and Metal-Processing Industry at the height of the debate about the ratification of the Eastern treaties in 1972, Walter Scheel declared that the figure for 1971 was 'not much, in the light of the importance of a neighbouring economic area with some 350 million inhabitants. It is only 3.8 per cent of our total foreign trade . . . Before the war it was twelve per cent for the German Reich.' Fifteen years later, addressing the World Economic Forum in Davos, his successor Hans-Dietrich Genscher formulated the same proposition in rather more cosmopolitan terms. 'At present, economic exchange between East and West is at an extraordinarily low level, if one considers the potential on both sides. For the Federal Republic, for example, the largest trading partner of Comecon, eastern trade is only four per cent of total foreign trade.' And then he made the by now almost ritual observation: 'to Switzerland alone we export one and a half times as much as to all the European Comecon countries put together'.

Scheel's comparison with the pre-war Reich would immediately spring to mind – and especially to East European minds – when discussing the return of a major German economic presence in the East. It was, however, impossible to make with any precision. In 1938 the German Reich did twelve per cent of its trade with just six countries of south-eastern Europe.

But this was a result of the distinctly abnormal German economic expansion after the depression. In 1929 the figure was only 4.5 per cent. So perhaps we should rather go back to before the First World War? But then trade with nearly half of post-1945 Poland would have counted as domestic trade, inside the frontiers of Germany!

In trade, as in other aspects of Germany's eastward relations, there simply was no 'normal' status quo ante, no historical moment to which one could reasonably aspire to 'get back'. Nor was there any generally accepted definition of 'normality' in relations between planned and market economies. Moreover, if one was making a comparison with the position of Germany before the war, one would surely have to include East Germany's trade with the Soviet Union and Eastern Europe. But that was measured in different and strictly in-comparable units of account. Only after the collapse of communism in Eastern Europe and the reunification of Germany would it become possible to make such comparisons properly again.

In the circumstances of 'Yalta' Europe, the real comparison was with the eastern trade of other Western states. What one can say with confidence is that by the mid-1980s West Germany had more trade with the Soviet Union and Eastern Europe than any other Western power: three times more than the United States or Japan in 1985, and nearly four times more if one included trade with the GDR. What was true of trade was also true of the other main aspects of economic relations. West Germany's banks lent more money, its firms transferred more technology. And when joint ventures became possible, Germany was again in the lead.

West Germany was not very dependent on this trade, but it was relatively more dependent on it than any other Western state – with the signal exceptions of Austria and Finland. Specific branches of West German industry, moreover, had a much higher direct dependence on eastern trade. In the mid-1970s as much as twenty per cent of the exports of the iron and steel industry went east. The leaders of these industries, and the banks that supported them while also lending directly to the east, had a significant voice in Bonn. They were an important lobby. Estimates of the number of jobs directly dependent on this trade varied from 100,000 to 300,000. As a result of successive pipeline deals, by 1989 West Germany depended on the Soviet Union for thirty per cent of its natural gas – some five per cent of its imported energy supplies. If the original interest in developing eastern trade was mainly political, the effect of this politically-driven expansion was nonetheless to increase the real economic interest as well.

As the comments by successive Foreign Ministers indicate, there was also a vague, unquantifiable sense that there should be a larger eastern market there in the future, as there had been in the past. It has been well observed that the discussion of Central Europe among European intellectuals in the early 1980s hovered between nostalgia and utopia. Yet even German businessmen had their nostalgias and utopias, even trade had its poetry. The leading German banker involved in eastern trade, F. Wilhelm Christians of the Deutsche Bank, paints in his memoirs a glowing vision of the special role that Germans could play in modernising the Russian/Soviet economy. He compares it with the relations of the dynamic ethnic German Ivan Stolz to the permanently recumbent Russian Oblomov, in Goncharov's famous novel.

'For centuries,' declared Walter Scheel, to the assembled masters of the Iron-, Tin- and Metal-Processing Industry in 1972, 'the German businessman in the East has realised our natural role as the mediator between the products and needs of West and Central Europe on the one side and of the Balkans and Eastern Europe on the other'. Referring to the Mannesmann pipes being supplied to the Soviet Union, he declared: 'I myself find it especially satisfying that these pipes are once again fulfilling the leading and connecting function given them by nature.'

Yet any real economic, political, or, so to speak, anticipatory West German dependency on eastern trade fades into insignificance beside the growing real dependency of Eastern Europe on West Germany. Throughout the period under review, virtually all the European members of Comecon looked increasingly to the West for trade, technology, finance and know-how, and their leading partner in the West was the Federal Republic. As indicated in the 1969 Budapest Appeal of the Warsaw Pact, this was an important original motive for their opening to the West, and specifically to West Germany.

By the mid-1980s, the Federal Republic accounted for between a quarter and one third of the western trade of all the East European states except Romania (for which the figure was lower) and the GDR (for which the real figure was still higher). An extreme case of dependency was Hungary. By the end of the 1980s, some forty per cent of its gross domestic product was created by exports. Because of the different units of exchange in the eastern and western markets it was impossible to say precisely what proportion of this trading state's total exports was taken by West Germany, but a quarter of all Hungary's exports to OECD countries went to the Federal Republic, which accounted for no less than half her total trade with the EC. According to the statistics, West Germany was second only to the Soviet Union as a trading partner. Qualitatively, it was second to none. By the end of 1989 about a third of the country's joint ventures were with German companies and another third with Austrian ones. Such figures are an important background to understanding the crucial foreign policy decisions of Hungary's still ostensibly socialist political leadership in 1989.

At the other extreme was the Soviet Union. In 1989 it was only dependent on trade for some eight per cent of its Gross Domestic Product, and trade with the West accounted for less than a quarter of its total foreign trade. Nonetheless, already in the late 1970s, more than a quarter of all the Western high technology supplied to the Soviet Union came from West Germany. By 1989 some eighteen per cent of its Western trade was with West Germany (and almost exactly the same proportion of its trade inside Comecon was with East Germany). German banks held the largest single portion of its hard currency debt, much of it in loans guaranteed by the Bonn government. As Gorbachev made crystal clear on his visit to West Germany in June 1989, once the Soviet Union embarked on economic perestroika, it was looking to West Germany above all for trade, technology and know-how in the vast enterprise of modernisation.

In sum, all the European states which had, or had had, a Soviet-type centrally planned economy faced a common general dilemma of growing relative economic backwardness. Western Europe was pulling further ahead. Both the revolution of high technology already engulfing the far West and Far East, and the progress towards a single West European market in 1992, threatened to widen the gap still farther and faster. In confronting this dilemma, they all, collectively, had to recast their relationship to the West in general and the European Community in particular. But of the individual states in the EC, they all looked in the first place to West Germany.

This growing dependency, and even greater expectation, once again recalled a central problem of Western policy towards Eastern Europe and the Soviet Union. From the very beginning, from even before the Federal Republic had any diplomatic relations with the East, it had been thought, in Bonn as in Washington, that the economic power of the West would be a major, perhaps *the* major instrument of achieving Western political goals in the East. From the very beginning, the question of how to use that economic power had been hotly disputed in the West. Increasingly, the line of hottest dispute tended to run between Bonn and Washington, with Paris, London and Rome taking up intermediate positions.

Of course this is to simplify a very complicated story. German leaders had not invariably been opposed to economic sanctions, nor were American leaders always averse to offering economic incentives. In 1963 it was Konrad Adenauer who embraced the idea of a grain embargo against the Soviet Union. As he told de Gaulle, the West should say to Moscow: 'If you want grain, show your goodwill and get rid of the Berlin Wall!' Such a grain embargo would, however, have hit the American economy harder than the German one. What actually happened in 1962/63 was an embargo on the export of large-diameter steel pipes to the Soviet Union, which hit the German economy harder than the American. The Federal Republic only reluctantly went along with this American-led embargo – but to the Americans' surprise, the British were even more recalcitrant. Moreover, although the phrase 'change through trade' – *Wandel durch Handel* – sounds particularly euphonious in German, some of its earliest advocates were actually American liberals.

Even in the 1970s, the most far-reaching statement of the case for 'change through trade' came not from a German but from a French-American of Polish-Jewish origin, Samuel Pisar. His influential book of 1970, *Coexistence and Commerce*, was enthusiastically hailed by Valéry Giscard d'Estaing as 'the bible on East-West economic relations'. At the same moment the veteran German practitioner of eastern trade, Otto Wolff von Amerongen, was warning against the 'romantics of eastern trade', and painting a much more sober picture of what might seriously be expected. It is true that some West German politicians – including Franz Josef Strauss – displayed what was almost a vulgar Marxism in their belief that the economic base would alter the political superstructure. But a naive faith in the automatic, transformative qualities of economic exchange and imported Western technology could be found on both sides of the Atlantic, and at both ends of the political spectrum.

American businessmen sometimes found themselves closer to the position of the German government than to that of their own on these issues. While still a businessman at the Bechtel corporation, George Shultz railed against what he called 'light-switch diplomacy': that is, the idea that business ties could be turned on and off at will for political purposes. Conversely, parts of the German defence establishment may sometimes have been closer to the Pentagon than to their own political leaders in their concern about the transfer of militarily usable technology to the Warsaw Pact. Any generalisation about American-German differences is, moreover, made doubly difficult by the fact that whereas there was one, largely consensual, German approach, there were many different American ones – successively and even simultaneously.

The Nixon-Kissinger team's cautious advocacy of trade liberalisation and economic inducements to the Soviet Union, broadly linked to Moscow's conduct in foreign policy, was itself soon curbed and distorted by the narrower restraints and linkages imposed by Congress through the Jackson-Vanik amendment (see page 238). With these still remaining in force, the Carter administration attempted a more closely calibrated 'economic diplomacy' of leverage and linkage, as advocated by Zbigniew Brzezinski and Samuel P Huntington. Here there was to be a direct linkage not only to the foreign policy but also to the domestic political conduct of the Soviet and East European regimes, and particularly to their record of respect or disrespect for the human rights of their more independent-minded citizens. One part of the Reagan administration then advocated an even harder-nosed punitive linkage, while another part – represented most visibly by the defence specialist Richard Perle – returned to a notion of economic warfare against the Soviet Union which was closer to the early

1950s than it was to the early 1970s. Each of those approaches was, however, directly affected and changed by Soviet actions on the one hand, and, perhaps even more, by the policies and reactions of the United States' West European allies on the other.

For all these caveats and complexities, the fact remains that there was, from the late 1970s until the late 1980s, a major argument within the Western alliance about the proper place and uses of economic instruments in Ostpolitik, and Bonn and Washington were the two main poles of that argument. The argument began, in a minor key, with a small set of sanctions – strictly speaking, vetting procedures on specified US exports to the Soviet Union – imposed by the Carter administration in 1978, with an explicit linkage to the treatment of prominent Soviet dissidents such as Alexander Ginzburg and Anatoly (Natan) Shcharansky. Of these measures the Schmidt government certainly did not approve, but nor was it directly affected by them. That could not be said of the second, much more significant round of sanctions, including both a (short-lived) grain embargo and a (partially observed) boycott of the 1980 Moscow Olympics, imposed – and demanded of West European allies – in response to the Soviet invasion of Afghanistan.

The largest crisis came, however, in 1982. Following General Jaruzelski's declaration of a 'state of war' in Poland, the Reagan administration imposed sanctions first on Poland and then on the Soviet Union, which it held responsible for the repression in Poland. The United States then tried to persuade its West European allies to join in, and specifically to stop a German-led consortium from going ahead with what had been billed as the 'deal of the century' – a massive pipeline system to supply Western Europe, and above all West Germany, with natural gas from the Siberian gas field of Urengoi. When the allies in general, and the Germans in particular, refused to be persuaded, the Reagan administration took the extraordinary step of banning US subsidiaries in Europe, and even European companies using US technology under licence, from exporting the necessary compressors and other parts to the Soviet Union. This was to burn a bridge too far, and, faced with a chorus of outrage in which Margaret Thatcher joined almost as vociferously as Helmut Schmidt, the Reagan administration was forced to retreat. Whereas in 1962 the United States had successfully leaned on West Germany to comply with its embargo, in 1982 it no longer could. Yet the controversy left a bitter after-taste, and American-German differences over economic relations with the East continued to smoulder through the decade.

Like all arguments within the Western alliance, this one was ostensibly about means not ends. We all want the same thing, was the polite assumption, the disagreement is only about how best to achieve it. The maverick West German commentator Josef Joffe would have none of this. 'With equal insistence,' he writes, 'Americans and Europeans claimed superior wisdom in their opposing analyses. The din of mutual recrimination merely helped to obscure the obvious: that an irreducible difference of interests lay at the roots of all their disputes. It was these interests that coloured their perceptions, not their perceptions that brought on the clash of American and European interests.'

The point is well taken, and an important corrective to official pieties. Yet the line between interests and perceptions is far from clear, particularly in the German case. Exports and jobs clearly were a hard interest of the Federal Republic. By Bonn's own definition, the benefits to be secured for the German minorities in Eastern Europe and the German majority in the GDR, by direct or indirect economic incentives, were also a basic national interest. If Germans suggested that there was a deeper harmony between the development of economic and political ties, between *Osthandel* and Ostpolitik, this also reflected German experience. Talks about trade were the first kind of talks that West Germany had directly, bilaterally, with the Soviet Union. Trading ties were the first sort of ties that West Germany developed with the East. Trade Missions were the first diplomatic representations the Federal Republic had in Eastern Europe. The flag followed trade. Then the establishment of full diplomatic relations at the beginning of the 1970s was followed by a sharp increase in the level of trade. Trade followed the flag.

In every case, the potential economic benefit to be gained from a closer relationship with West Germany was a crucial motive for the Soviet Union and East European states. Moreover, as several East European states got into deep difficulty about repaying the hard-currency loans originally granted to facilitate the expansion of East-West trade, so the capacity of the Bonn government to offer further government-guaranteed credits, or simply debt relief, became a very direct negotiating lever. It was a basic interest of the Federal Republic not to be constrained in playing its strongest cards.

From this point on, however, interests begin to shade into perceptions. Trade had a 'tension-reducing role,' wrote Otto Wolff von Amerongen. It was the lifeline along which political relations could be restored when they were otherwise in trouble. 'The Europeans have been trading with the Russians for centuries,' observed Helmut Schmidt. 'They believe trading with a close neighbour is politically and psychologically a good thing even if the volume of trade is small.' (For 'Europeans' read Germans).

When Franz Josef Strauss went to Moscow in 1987 he declared: 'Mars must leave and Mercury take the stage'. Now as the historian Harold James points out, Mercury has been a uniquely important god in the German pantheon since the early nineteenth century. Economic success in general, and export success in particular, have long been central pillars of national identity. And after all, Mercury, the god of commerce, is a peaceful god. Who could not prefer him to Mars, the god of war? Yet at the same time, the plain fact is that West Germany was, to use the crude vocabulary of the stockmarket, long in Mercury but still short (and uniquely constrained) in Mars, whereas the United States was uniquely long in Mars, but relatively much shorter (and arguably declining) in Mercury. If the central focus of East-West relations shifted from the security to the economic field, the unique importance of the superpower relationship would be diminished and the relative importance of the old-new economic power, Germany, would increase. Interest and perception were therefore hard to disentangle.

In a carefully worded treatment of this subject written in 1987, Jürgen Ruhfus, then the top-ranking West German diplomat, averred: 'In the West, East-West economic relations . . . are also considered to be of major political significance. Trade with the East is seen as a contribution to the long-term building of confidence between the blocs and to the stabilisation and reinforcement of East-West relations altogether. This should strengthen the part of the double strategy of the Atlantic Alliance directed at détente, dialogue, the interweaving (*Verflechtung*) of interests and partial interdependence.' No automatic change or convergence was to be expected. But economic co-operation had already encouraged 'reform beginnings' in Eastern Europe. Moreover, 'in the long-term the goal is to replace the condition of non-war [secured] by deterrence with a peace based on trust and co-operative security structures.' But if you had offered that as an unsigned statement, how many people in Washington, or, for that matter in London or Paris, would have agreed it was a definition of the West's common goals?

Yet in Washington, too, interests were mixed with perceptions. There was, for example, the hard interest of a military superpower in seeing that its main opponent did not gain militarily usable technological advantages. There was, on the other hand, the relative lack of positive economic interest, for eastern trade remained of strictly marginal importance to the US economy. But there was also the (albeit fitful) perception that a primary goal of Western policy should be to encourage greater respect for human rights and liberalisation in Eastern Europe and the Soviet Union, and that Western economic power should be applied directly to achieving that goal.

Of course West German policymakers also wished for political change and greater respect for human rights in Eastern Europe and the Soviet Union. But they had so many other reasons – state interests, national interests, perceptions of European and Western interests – for continuing with the development of economic ties that they were not prepared to consider cutting those ties on purely political or 'human rights' grounds. Even if there was no progress, indeed even if there was actual regress in those fields, economic co-operation had still to be pursued in the interests of the West German economy, the Germans in the East, stability, confidence-building, reconciliation, peace, and the web of interdependence that Bonn hoped to spin between East and West. In this last respect, the development of economic ties was not merely a means to an end. It was an end in itself.

The argument was thus neither just a difference of perceptions, nor simply a clash of interests. It had elements of both. In the second half of the 1980s the argument subsided, for two main reasons. Firstly, both American and West German policymakers made strenuous efforts to resolve it: although Jürgen Ruhfus's attempt to summarise the common position in 1987 actually reveals how far apart they still were in basic concepts and assumptions. The second, more important reason was that the changes introduced by Mikhail Gorbachev in the Soviet Union gradually transformed the overall agenda of East-West economic relations.

Even here, there were predictable differences of emphasis, with the West German Foreign Minister, Hans-Dietrich Genscher, being the first major advocate in the West of 'helping Gorbachev to succeed' by a broad offer of economic co-operation. Even now there were continued German-American differences on how far and how fast the West should respond to Soviet and East European appeals to trim the CoCom list of items that should not be exported to the East. Yet with the end of communism, first in Eastern Europe then in the Soviet Union, the terms of the argument were transformed out of recognition. In the new argument, about how best to assist the transition from planned to market economies, and who would foot how much of the bill, the German Mercury played a role second to none. To pursue that argument would, however, go beyond the bounds of this chapter.

Does the now finished history of East-West economic relations – in the context of 'Yalta' – allow us to make any more definite statements about the controversies that boiled or simmered for so long? Can we say, with benefit of hindsight, that one side of the argument about sanctions, eastern trade, credits and technology transfer was more right than the other? Are there any conclusions one can draw about what David Baldwin has called the 'economic statecraft' of the West? Here, as elsewhere, the difficulties of reaching any firm conculsions are still acute. As we have seen, there were often not just two but many sides to each argument. Quite different approaches were actually applied simultaneously – notably by the United States and the Federal Republic. Economic relations with the West were only part of a whole spectrum of factors affecting decisions and developments in the East.

The question of the efficacy of the strategic embargo on the export of military usable goods to the Warsaw Pact, and the extent to which it was undermined by illegal or third-country exports and the covert acquisition of know-how or technology by Eastern spies, we shall put aside here: not because it is uninteresting or unimportant, but because we do not have the specialised competence necessary to discuss it. The question of how far the Reagan administration's strategy (insofar as there was a strategy) of arms build-up as a form of economic warfare with the Soviet Union contributed to the change in Soviet foreign policy in the late 1980s has been considered in Chapter Four. The putative long-term positive contribution of economic ties and technological transfer to the opening of East European systems and societies, as part of an overall strategy of weaving (*Verflechtung*) between East and West in Europe, is considered in the next section.

What remains is the attempted use by Western governments of economic instruments to achieve changes in the foreign or domestic policies of Eastern states, in the short to medium term. 'The Americans,' Pierre Hassner once remarked, 'believe in sticks, the Germans believe in carrots and the French believe in words.' When all caveats have been entered, his *bon mot* contains a large kernel of truth. Bonn governments tended, from a mixture of interests and perceptions, to advocate a medium- to long-term economic incentive linkage. Washington administrations inclined, from a different mixture of interests and perceptions, to advocate a short- to medium-term economic deterrent linkage. As we have suggested earlier, in their pure forms both variants were premissed on questionable hypotheses of behavioural psychology: the former treating communist rulers as rabbits, the latter, as donkeys.

Both were further hamstrung by three structural problems. First, in states with market economies, governments find it both in principle dubious and in practice difficult to direct the behaviour of bankers, investors, traders and industrialists. Second, in modern parliamentary democracies – especially in 'television democracies' – governments cannot make and unmake such linkages at will. On this point the magisterial remarks of the American diplomatist George Kennan are germane.

'In the harsh realities of international life,' Kennan writes,

> a government influences another government through the dialectical interaction, in its own conduct, of measures favourable to the interests of the other government and measures that affect its interests adversely. Let us call these, for want of better description, favours and injury, respectively. Both are, at one point or another, necessary ingredients of any policy . . . But if these instruments of diplomacy are to be of any value, then whoever conducts policy must be in a position to manipulate them currently, fluidly and at will, as the situation may require . . . A favour which, to the certain knowledge of the other party, cannot be retracted, comes soon to be taken for granted and ceases to be regarded as a favour. An injury or hardship which, to the similar knowledge of the other party, cannot be removed, ceases to have any punitive effect . . .

Kennan wrote this with reference to a Congressional move to prevent the extension of Most Favored Nation status to Yugoslavia in 1962. But it could be applied to both American and German policies in the 1970s and 1980s. Kissinger argued, with some force, that the Jackson-Vanik amendment defeated its own purpose, because the prospect of its lifting became so remote that the Soviet Union ceased to respond to it. At the other extreme, with the tripartisan consensus on Deutschlandpolitik in the 1980s, West German financial transfers to the GDR came close to being favours that could not be retracted and therefore ceased to work as favours. In the one case the stick almost ceased to be a stick; in the other, the carrot almost ceased to be a carrot.

Thirdly, as we have seen, even the most powerful of free-trading liberal democracies could not simply compel other free-trading liberal democracies to behave as it thought fit. Indeed, in the West German view the impossibility of getting everyone to join in sanctions was one major reason why they never would 'work'. The readiness of Canadian and Argentinian producers to step into the breach left by the American grain embargo against the Soviet Union gave some force to this argument. Yet by themselves refusing to join in sanctions against the Soviet Union in 1982, West German policymakers made this a self-fulfilling prophecy.

Sanctions against the Soviet Union were thus never fully or consistently applied. In terms of the proclaimed goals, the record of the three main rounds of sanctions in American-Soviet relations could be construed as negative in the short term. If one considered the position in, say, 1985, then one could say: the Soviet dissidents have not been freed (or only in direct exchanges), the Red Army has not got out of Afghanistan, and Solidarity has not been restored in Poland. So the sanctions 'did not work'. But as Philip Hanson has argued, it is wrong to assess each 'sanctions episode' in isolation. One must also consider the cumulative effect. And the fact is that by the end of the 1980s the Soviet dissidents had been freed, the Red Army had got out of Afghanistan and Solidarity had been restored in Poland. Clearly, here as elsewhere, it is impermissible to say simply *post hoc ergo propter hoc*. Many other influences can be identified, including that of German-led incentive détente. Even with benefit of hindsight the causal reckoning remains highly speculative.

So far as direct sanctions against Poland are concerned, the story is also complex. But it would be quite wrong to suggest that support for sanctions was confined to government and newspaper offices in Washington DC. In the martial law period, many, probably most, Solidarity leaders and activists welcomed the Western economic sanctions against their own country. As late as November 1984 Adam Michnik, the opposition leader, told the author, for the record: '. . . it seems to me I have to thank the sanctions policy, among other things, for the fact that we can talk here today, that I'm sitting right here in my apartment and not in the prison on Rakowiecka Street. For this, my colleagues and I would like to thank all those who have helped us.' Of course, the Solidarity leadership then encouraged the gradual lifting of sanctions, when the time was judged right.

Looking back from 1989, Neal Ascherson, a highly experienced writer on Polish affairs, and very far from being a cold warrior of the ideological right, commented:

> . . . Poland provided one of the rare examples in which economic sanctions took spectacular and rapid effect. . . . There was a great bluster about how capitalist blackmail wouldn't deter Poles from doing what they thought right. However, one sweeping amnesty was soon followed by a second; the overwhelming need to obtain renewed Western economic assistance has nudged the Polish regime forward into one democratic concession after another, and that mechanism – long after formal sanctions have ended – functions to this day.

In other words, these 'sticks' were effective, but only because there was a realistic prospect of them turning into 'carrots' which the regime desperately needed.

Ascherson's verdict is supported by the researches of Zbigniew Pelczynski, who has attempted to reconstruct the Polish authorities' process of decision-making in the political opening of the late 1980s. Having talked at length to many of the key decision-makers, he concludes that the hard linkage made by the United States played a crucial part in propelling those decision-makers down the path to the Round Table. So in this case the balance of evidence is that sanctions, flexibly applied, actually did 'work', although greatly helped, of course, by many other factors beyond the West's control.

It is also interesting to ask the opposite question: not 'did the sticks work?' but 'did the carrots work?' An attempt has already been made to address this question so far as the GDR is concerned. The other two countries to which an advocate of 'change through trade' would have pointed in the 1970s were Poland under Gierek and Hungary under Kádár. Here generous Western engagement in the development of economic relations was, it was suggested, helping to open up the regime, to make the communist powerholders themselves more modern, Western, pragmatic, liberal. Once again, there were half-articulated assumptions of behavioural psychology. Trade would soften political hostilities: you were less likely to hate someone with whom you were regularly doing business. Seeing capitalism at first hand, the communist rulers would discover its attractions.

Now at the level of individual biography, some of this may have been true. Individual Polish or Hungarian powerholders were convinced, seduced or simply corrupted by the developing economic ties with the West. (In the case of the Gierek team in Poland one might add: 'and how!'.) But this was not what happened at the level of the economic and political system. Western trade, credits, and technology transfer were overwhelmingly channelled through organs under the central control of the party-state. They were used less to facilitate economic reform than as a substitute for such reform. As a result of this systemic misapplication, the Western 'carrots', far from setting these states on the path of sustained growth, with political modernisation following economic modernisation, instead helped them down the road to economic crisis.

Although Western loans were less badly used in Kádár's Hungary than in Gierek's Poland, in the Hungarian case too, albeit a few years later and somewhat less dramatically than in Poland, the soaring hard-currency debt contributed to an economic crisis which then became a political crisis. In effect, the carrots became sticks. Opponents of incentive détente never tired of repeating Lenin's quip that the capitalists would sell the Soviet Union the rope with which it could hang them. But what happened in this case was rather that the West sold Gierek and Kádár the rope with which they hanged themselves. Yet this was not what the sellers had intended.

By 1988, Poland had a net hard-currency debt of more than $35 billion. Hungary had more than $18 billion – that is, nearly $2,000 a head. For Gierek's and Kádár's successors, the hard-currency debt had become a kind of permanent Western sanction. To be sure, the 'linkage' was ostensibly economic. The pure economists of the IMF and World Bank would come in; on purely economic grounds they would grant a Western certificate of approval for the purely economic measures that the Polish or Hungarian governments proposed to take. But politics and economics in communist systems were more closely connected than Siamese twins. You could not operate on one without seriously affecting the other.

Thus in order to implement the 'purely' economic measures advocated by the IMF or World Bank, the Polish and Hungarian regimes felt impelled also to institute political reforms. This Western economic pressure therefore contributed to the retreat of the party not only from the economy but also from social control, and ultimately from the state itself. To be sure, it was only one among many causes: but a major one, nonetheless. Furthermore, although the criteria applied by the IMF and World Bank remained purely economic, those political changes marvellously increased the willingness of Western governments to approve IMF agreements, stand-by loans and the rest. (In the case of Poland, the political linkage in the 1980s was, of course, also explicit.)

The history of 'carrots and sticks' is thus rich in ironies. For both Poland and Hungary, the carrots of the 1970s became the sticks of the 1980s. For Poland after 1981, the sticks of sanctions were also carrots in disguise. Arguably, for the reasons already mentioned, neither the United States nor the Federal Republic achieved on their own that flexibility in the combined use of favours and injuries which George Kennan identified as the prerequisite for successful economic statecraft. Crudely put, the

Americans remained too hooked on sticks, while the Germans became too partial to offering carrots.

Insofar as this aspect of Western Ostpolitik contributed to the achievement of the desired results it was rather through the combination, as much by accident as by design, of the two contrasting approaches, in the overall policy of the West. Yet, to the very end, representatives of each approach fiercely denied the wisdom of the other; and, after the end, claimed that history had proved them right.

Weaving

It was not only economic ties that the Federal Republic consistently endeavoured to forge with the Soviet Union and Eastern Europe. The Bonn government declared itself interested in developing almost every possible sort of tie: political, social, cultural, touristic, sporting, academic, technological, scientific, environmental, road or rail, animal, vegetable or mineral. The stated object was to create a whole *Netz* or *Geflecht* – a net, network, mesh or web – of ties between Eastern and Western Europe. This idea of *Verflechtung* or *Vernetzung* – interlacing, networking, weaving – was another leitmotif of German Ostpolitik in the 1970s and 1980s.

The most tireless advocate and inexhaustible practitioner of *Verflechtung* was Hans-Dietrich Genscher. If the simile were not generally felt to be a little insulting, one might compare the veteran Foreign Minister to a spider, ceaselessly spinning his web across the face of Europe, today in Prague, tomorrow in Moscow, at the weekend in Paris. But the idea was by no means his alone. President Richard von Weizsäcker was an eloquent advocate of what he called 'system-opening co-operation'. A typical report from an East European visit by the Federal Chancellor consisted largely in a listing of new ties, new forms of 'co-operation', that the two sides had agreed to establish or at least to explore. Although this or that detail might occasionally give rise to party-political controversy, the general idea was part of the tripartisan consensus on Ostpolitik.

Like other elements of German Ostpolitik, this concept had both common Western and specific German roots. As early as August 1957, John F. Kennedy was advocating the development of trading, technical and humanitarian ties with Poland, and 'an increase of people-to-people contacts, of cultural, scientific, and educational exchanges representing every aspect of life in the two countries'. American ideas of 'peaceful engagement' and 'bridge-building', of moving 'from confrontation to co-operation', were essential background to the vision that Willy Brandt unfolded in the early 1960s.

Indeed, his first general statement of that vision was made in America – at Harvard in October 1962. 'We need,' Brandt said there, to seek forms which can overlay and penetrate (*durchdringen*) the blocs of today. We need as many points of contact and as much meaningful communication as possible. We have no need to fear the exchange of academics and students, of information, ideas and services. What should be decisive for us is that these are sensible enterprises in responsible forms. We should welcome common projects between East and West. So I am in favour of as many meaningful ties as can be achieved, also with the communist East.

Yet while speaking in Harvard Willy Brandt was still the Governing Mayor of Berlin. Not merely at the back but at the very front of his mind were the immediate problems of alleviating the unprecedented, unique and absolute division of his city. It would clearly be wrong to suggest that his large and vague vision was merely a magnified projection, on to the clouds, so to speak, of what he and his circle now saw as the immediate necessities in Berlin. But it would be even more wrong to suppose that what they started to do in Berlin (and then in Germany, and then in Europe . . .) was merely the local application of general Western and especially American ideas. It is worth noting that the idea of weaving was advanced with special emphasis by politicians who had at some point been Governing Mayors of Berlin: a list that includes not only Willy Brandt but also Richard von Weizsäcker and Brandt's successor as leader of the SPD, Hans-Jochen Vogel.

In advancing this overall approach, West German politicians and policymakers argued that they were implementing the 'détente half' of the Nato double strategy agreed in the 1967 Harmel report. But the framework in which the implementation was pursued was that of the so-called 'Helsinki process', which followed the signing in Helsinki in 1975 of the Final Act of the Conference on Security and Co-operation in Europe. The 'Helsinki process' had the unique advantage of including both the Soviet Union and the United States, both East and West European states, both East and West Germany. It was also particularly well-suited to West Germany's favoured foreign-policy style – discreet, multilateral, consensus-seeking and patiently attritional. Indeed, that characteristic West German policy style and the Helsinki process to some extent evolved together, each influencing the other. If Harmel was the Bible of the West German approach to East-West relations, then the Helsinki Final Act became its prayer book, and the successive Helsinki review documents its Corpus Juris Canonici.

Yet like the Bible, the prayer-book, and even canon law, 'Helsinki' was susceptible to very different interpretations. From the outset, there was not one but many ideas of Helsinki. There was Helsinki as the confirmation of 'Yalta' and Helsinki as the negation of 'Yalta'. There was the Helsinki of the persecuted and the Helsinki of the persecutors. There was Brezhnev's idea of Helsinki and Yuri Orlov's idea of Helsinki; Gustáv

Husák's idea and Charter 77's; Gierek's and KOR's. There was Erich Honecker's idea of Helsinki, and there was the idea that prompted tens of thousands of ordinary East Germans, following the publication of the Helsinki Final Act in *Neues Deutschland*, to apply to emigrate on the basis of its ceremonious and solemn undertakings. The differences in conception and interpretation were not only within the East and between East and West; they were also within the West.

Henry Kissinger, for example, agreed to the long-standing Soviet wish for a European security conference essentially as a diplomatic concession in return for Soviet agreement to proceed with Mutual Balanced Forced Reduction talks and the Quadripartite Agreement on Berlin. His then aide, Helmut Sonnenfeldt, boasted in 1975: 'We sold it for the German-Soviet treaty, we sold it for the Berlin agreement, and we sold it again for the opening of the MBFR.' Kissinger famously did not consider human rights to be an appropriate subject for discussions between states. In the initial phase of negotiating the Helsinki Final Act there was therefore a curious role-reversal, with Kissinger acting in the old European *Realpolitik* spirit of Metternich, while West European leaders acted more in the spirit of Woodrow Wilson. (This could not, however, fairly be said of the lower-level American diplomats directly involved in the Helsinki negotiations.)

Kissinger's attitude changed somewhat in the last months before the signature of the Helsinki Final Act. Following America's defeat in Vietnam, and facing growing domestic criticism of what had been called 'detente', he actually played a significant part in securing Soviet acceptance of the commitments to improve human contacts, information flows and cultural exchange in the so-called 'Basket 3' of Helsinki. With the arrival of the Carter administration, human rights came to the very top of the agenda of American foreign policy, partly in an attempt to rediscover the United States' sense of historic purpose after the trauma of Vietnam. This directly affected American Helsinki policy.

The change in emphasis was greatly assisted by pressure from the representatives of the substantial East European minorities inside the United States, and by both Congressional and independent initiatives to monitor implementation of the Helsinki accords. In this respect, Americans responded faster than West Europeans to the courageous initiatives of independent Soviet and East European citizens – the persecuted Helsinki monitors in their own countries. By the end of the 1970s, for most American politicians and policymakers 'Helsinki' had come to mean essentially 'human rights'. American newspapers referred to the 'Helsinki Human Rights Declaration', although human rights are mentioned as such only in one of the ten principles at the beginning of the Final Act. This understanding of Helsinki was clearly reflected in the American approach to the Helsinki review conferences in Belgrade, Madrid and Vienna.

At the other extreme there was the Soviet idea of Helsinki. Robert

Legvold has aptly observed that Soviet leaders saw Helsinki as a 'medium for healing Europe's economic division while sealing its political division'. Not only the territorial but also the political status quo would finally be 'recognised', with all the ambiguities of 'recognition' that we have already explored in West Germany's relationship to East Germany. Not only the 'Yalta' frontiers but also the permanence of Soviet domination and Soviet-type regimes – everything that Soviet writers summed up in the innocuous-sounding phrase 'post-war realities' – would be accepted by the West. At the same time, Soviet leaders were deeply interested in what came to be the second of the three 'baskets' of Helsinki: the section headed 'Co-operation in the field of economics, of science and technology and of the environment'. This was, as the historian Vojtech Mastny succinctly puts it, 'the favourite Soviet basket'. They were, to be sure, prepared to consider limited and selective 'Co-operation in humanitarian and other fields', as the third basket was headed. But charges about their lack of respect for the human rights of their own citizens were to be rejected as that 'interference in the internal affairs' of another state, which the signatories also solemnly renounced in the introductory list of principles.

This basic Soviet position changed very significantly after Gorbachev came to power in 1985. But in the first decade of the Helsinki process the lines between the Soviet idea of Helsinki and the American idea of Helsinki were starkly drawn. Now plainly the democratic oppositions in Eastern Europe were closer to the American than to the Soviet idea of Helsinki. That the party-states of Eastern Europe were closer to the Soviet than to the American position is also plain. This latter point does, however, require some qualification.

Like the Soviet ruling nomenklatura, the East European ruling nomen-klaturas were alarmed at those parts of the Helsinki process which threatened their domestic power monopoly. Like the Soviet Union, in fact even more so, they were interested in all those parts of 'basket two' that seemed to offer the possibility of modernising their economies and strengthening their states, while not undermining their own domestic political positions. Yet at the same time, the leaders of at least some East European states saw an opportunity to use the incremental multilateralism of the Helsinki process to increase their state's own international room for manoeuvre, and cautiously to test the limits of their autonomy from Moscow. This intention did not, however, go *pari passu* with domestic liberalisation: it was true of Kádár's Hungary and Gierek's Poland, but it was also true of Honecker's still comprehensively illiberal GDR and of Ceauşescu's increasingly repressive Romania.

Where did the Federal Republic fit into this complex picture? What was the West German idea of Helsinki? To attempt a fair characterisation of the German position one would have, for a start, to collate the whole vast forest of official West German statements on the Helsinki process, and compare them systematically with, say, American or French statements. One would then have to look into the countless stages of consultation that preceded and accompanied all Helsinki meetings, for many differences were already ground down by this intra-(West) European and intra-Western *engrenage* before they even reached paper. The first would be a mammoth, the second a virtually impossible task.

As we have noticed, the Federal Republic was particularly interested in, and became outstandingly adept at, *not* clearly articulating distinctive national positions, but rather feeding its own special German concerns and priorities into a common approach. It did this, first and foremost, in Western Europe, above all though European Political Co-operation, which really came to life in the Helsinki negotiations. It did this in the West, through Nato and through the 'Bonn Group' of the three Western Allies and West Germany. And it did this in a wider Europe, through working with the neutral and non-aligned countries, which played an unusually important part in the actual diplomacy of the Helsinki process, and through discreet, often tacit understandings with some East European states, including, on occasion, East Germany. The German use of Helsinki was altogether a classic and highly successful example of that 'attempt to cover (*abdecken*) our actions multilaterally' which Helmut Schmidt prescribed in his confidential Marbella paper of 1977. This was one of the essential ingredients of what would later become known as Genscherism.

The multilateral, multi-level, multi-stage nature of the Helsinki process, and the German approach to it, thus make firm generalisation very difficult. A few tentative statements may nonetheless be made.

A memorandum written for Chancellor Schmidt (probably in 1975) noted: 'The Federal Government had no original interest of its own in the CSCE.' Its first negotiating goal was therefore, as the memorandum put it, 'damage prevention'. The Soviet Union must not be allowed to turn this into a substitute peace treaty, binding in international law; nor to use it to close the door to the future possibility of German unification; nor to exclude Berlin. The most distinctive contributions of German diplomacy in the early stages of the Helsinki negotiations concerned these essentially defensive goals, all of which were achieved with the help of her Western allies.

The preamble to the Final Act declared it to apply to the participating states and 'throughout Europe' – a diplomatic phrase which specifically meant 'in West Berlin'. As we have seen, Henry Kissinger negotiated on Germany's behalf the crucial sentence allowing for the possibility of a 'peaceful change' of frontiers. This was placed in the list of principles before the affirmation of the inviolability of frontiers, and augmented by the commitment to the self-determination of peoples. It was these paragraphs, not those on human rights and fundamental freedoms, that Hans-Dietrich Genscher singled out for special mention when commending the Helsinki Final Act to the Bundestag in the summer of 1975.

Yet following intensive internal discussion, the Bonn government also decided earlier than most that this Soviet initiative might be turned to the West's advantage. By 1973, the head of the Foreign Ministry planning staff and leader of the German delegation to the Helsinki preparatory talks, Guido Brunner, could already write in very positive terms about the conference developing 'common rules of the game for peaceful co-operation and competition'. He went on to emphasise what would be a dominant theme in Bonn's approach to Helsinki. 'We intend,' he wrote, 'to establish contacts between people, contacts between professional groups, contacts from society to society, as autonomous factors in the process of detente.' And this theme of human contacts would be stressed again and again by German politicians and policymakers. This was something that Genscher did dwell on at length in commending the Final Act to the Bundestag. Détente, he said, using a formulation now common to the main Western participants, was a process which must directly benefit the people. The Final Act provided for a 'net of co-operation' and the increase of contacts. The subject of 'human alleviations', he went on, was now finally 'on the European agenda'. Progress, however, would be a matter of 'small steps'.

For anyone who had followed the evolution of West German policy towards the GDR over the previous decade, the code-words delivered a clear message. Here was the projection of Deutschlandpolitik onto a wider, European stage. The approach that had been adopted first in Berlin and then in Germany was now to be attempted 'throughout Europe' – which also meant, specifically, in Berlin! Of course the German approach had been combined with and modified by the attitudes and priorities of its negotiating partners. But the emphasis remained distinctive.

From the mid-1970s the United States saw the positive meaning and dynamic potential of Helsinki above all in its provisions for human rights. For the Federal Republic the positive meaning and dynamic potential lay above all in its provisions for co-operation and human contacts. Human contacts and human rights are closely related things. But they are not the same thing. American representatives would explicitly berate the Soviet Union and other East European states for their violations of human rights, pointing publicly to individual cases of persecuted dissidents, Christians and, not least, Helsinki monitors. German representatives tended to believe that this was misplaced energy, perhaps even counter-productive. 'Quiet diplomacy', Willy Brandt and others argued, actually did more for the persecuted individuals than American-style 'megaphone diplomacy'. Moreover, it was argued that by concentrating on these few spectacular cases one could block the path to more modest improvements – 'human alleviations' – for far more individual people. To increase contacts of all possible kinds between East and West in Europe, to knit the divided continent back together again by weaving and webbing: here was the real and larger meaning of Helsinki.

This West German approach was, in the short term at least, more congenial to East European rulers than it was to the small groups of human rights activists who pinned their colours to the Helsinki mast. While the 'quiet diplomacy' of Willy Brandt and others was of course appreciated, most persecuted human rights activists saw it as no alternative to, let alone a substitute for, the invaluable help of being loudly, publicly and individually mentioned by Western leaders, both in multilateral fora and in their bilateral dealings with the East. In Helsinki policy, as in other fields, the German-American difference was most acute in the months after the declaration of martial law in Poland, with the United States advocating a very hard Western line at the Madrid review conference, even at the risk of jeopardising it, while the Federal Republic advocated a softer line, emphasising the co-operative rather than the confrontational aspects of the Helsinki process.

The Federal Republic was also the major Western power which showed most demonstrative interest in pursuing the 'co-operation in the field of economics, of science and technology, and of the environment', mapped out in basket two. In these fields, the Federal Republic was the Western leader. And consciously so. 'Decisive is first of all basket two, co-operation,' wrote Richard von Weizsäcker in 1983. 'If we succeed in building up co-operation step by step in the fields of science, technology, nutrition, environment, transport, business, energy and development policy, then in the end arms control and even freedom of movement will move into the realm of the possible.' And 'to us Germans falls the task of making basket two a central focus of East-West relations.' Not accidentally, the first major Helsinki follow-on meeting to be held in Germany was on the subject of economic co-operation.

At the same time West Germany, like other Western states, hoped that all the multilateral and bilateral contacts permitted by the Helsinki process would enable East European rulers quietly to establish somewhat more autonomy from Moscow, while engaging more closely in all-European affairs. Helmut Schmidt sometimes presented himself, in Warsaw and Budapest, as the spokesman of the smaller and middle-sized states in Europe. In the 1980s, West Germany used these contacts, in a modest and cautious way, to push ahead the arms control and disarmament sides of the Helsinki process in ways which were not always wholly desired by the Soviet Union, but also, on occasion, by the United States. On these security and disarmament issues there was also some tacit co-operation with East Germany, sanctified by that famous mantra about 'only peace going out from German soil'.

While the cumulative, attritional effect on Soviet and East European leaders of all the countless rounds of talks involved in the Helsinki process should not be understated, it was only following the advent of 'new thinking' in Soviet foreign policy that a major step forward was taken from the provisions – so often honoured only in the breach – of the 1975 Final Act. Instead of hiding behind the 'interference in internal affairs' clause, the Soviet Union both curbed its own most obvious human rights abuses and engaged in a direct and spirited dialogue about respect for human rights in East and West. The Vienna review conference was finally wound up in January 1989, with a concluding document which established procedures for regular inquiry by member states into precisely those 'internal affairs' of other states, and with detailed provisions on such matters as freedom of movement, freedom of religion, freedom of information, the rights of national minorities and those of independent Helsinki monitors. For the West, this was certainly the greatest step forward since 1975.

Here, as in all the main Helsinki negotiations, there was a significant though complex linkage between the security and the human rights/contacts sides of the process – that is, in the jargon of Helsinki, between baskets one and three. This linkage evolved over time. As we have seen, at the outset Kissinger 'sold' the Conference for, among other things, the talks on Mutual Balanced Force Reductions (MBFR). While the MBFR talks got nowhere, the Helsinki talks proceeded with a series of broad trade-offs between the Soviet desire for recognition of frontiers and security in basket one and economic advantages from basket two, and the desire of the West – with varying national emphases – for advances above all in basket three. At the end of the Madrid follow-up meeting, the West secured modest improvements in the human rights field while agreeing to a Conference on Confidence- and Security-Building Measures and Disarmament in Europe held in Stockholm between 1984 and 1986. Yet this disarmament conference was also wanted by many European states – not least West Germany – and, with the change in Soviet foreign policy, its outcome was generally held to be highly acceptable to the West.

By the late 1980s, it was the Soviet Union which was looking for rapid progress in security talks, above all in the field of conventional arms reductions, while the West held out for more concessions at the Helsinki review conference in Vienna. This linkage was clearly spelled out at the time by the leader of the American delegation to the Vienna conference. The wheel had come full circle. Whereas in 1972, the United States would 'sell' the Helsinki conference in return for talks on conventional arms reductions, in 1988 the United States would 'sell' talks on conventional arms reductions in return for concessions at the Helsinki review conference in Vienna. The new round of conventional arms talks actually opened, also in Vienna, in March 1989, just a few weeks after the ceremonial conclusion of the Helsinki review conference.

It is, for the reasons already given, very difficult to establish what precisely was the German contribution to this outcome. The German Foreign Minister tried to push the Vienna review conference to an earlier conclusion in 1988, at a point when the Soviet (and some East European) delegations were still not prepared to concede some of the key detailed human rights provisions on which the American and British delegations were insisting, with active or tacit support from other Western, neutral, non-aligned, and even East Central European delegations. A senior American representative commented that while he spent his time talking about human rights, his German counterpart talked about town-twinning. This reinforces an impression one has from immersion in the relevant material, and from conversations with many policymakers, but it would be wrong to offer any firm conclusions without more detailed research.

There was, however, another remarkable document agreed in 1989 which perhaps gave a clearer idea of the German approach. This was the Joint Declaration signed by Helmut Kohl and Mikhail Gorbachev during the latter's visit to the Federal Republic in June 1989. The Bonn Declaration was a sort of bilateral Helsinki – although since the essence of Helsinki was multilateralism that may be a contradiction in terms. We have seen already its significance for the development of German-Soviet relations, and the novel statements it made about the right to self-determination. What should be noted here is the great emphasis that it placed on co-operation and, in a word, weaving.

Thus among the 'building elements' of a new 'Europe of peace and co-operation' it mentioned: a 'thick' dialogue on all themes, 'traditional as well as new', including regular meetings at the highest political level; 'the realisation of human rights and the advancement of the exchange of people and ideas' including 'town-twinning, transport and communication links, cultural contacts, tourist and sporting traffic, the encouragement of language teaching and also a benevolent treatment of humanitarian questions including family reunification and travel abroad'; the building of contacts between youth; comprehensive economic co-operation 'to mutual advantage, including new forms of co-operation'; 'the step-by-step construction of all-European co-operation in different areas, especially in transport, energy, health care, information and communication'; and 'intensive ecological co-operation'.

West Germany had come a long way from Brandt's Harvard speech in 1962. For here was a veritable weaver's charter – and signed by the Soviet leader.

What, then, was this network of contacts and co-operation supposed to achieve? What was the point of it all? Once again, there was a set of specific national grounds and a set of general ones. As Hans-Dietrich Genscher observed already in 1975, 'no one can have a greater interest than us Germans in the Conference achieving its goal, namely to improve the contacts between the states and people in Europe . . . I believe that no one would neglect their national duty more than us, were he to hesitate to use even the smallest chance for a development that could eventually ease the lot of the divided nation.' The divided nation could only be sewn back together again if the Europe around it was being sewn back together again. The closer the ties between Eastern and Western Europe as a whole, the closer could be the ties between Eastern and Western Germany. German-German, even Berlin-Berlin, contacts and 'co-operation' had to be embedded in European (including American)–European (including Soviet) contacts and co-operation. The basic thought was already there in Chancellor Kiesinger's speech on 17 June 1967.

All Western countries had a certain economic interest in expanded economic ties with the Soviet Union and Eastern Europe, but the truncated 'trading state' had a special interest in those ties. The vague but important goal of 'reconciliation' was another special national reason for wanting to develop ties – some of which, such as cultural or youth exchanges, were thought to contribute directly to 'reconciliation'. Rather as the physiotherapist will try to build up the muscles around an injured ligament, so West Germany – having some horribly torn ligaments with the East – tried to build up the muscles around them.

The idea of developing all-European ties in order to facilitate the growth of all-German ties was itself a multilateral version of what we have called the permissive function. But there were also more direct, bilateral versions. Even if no direct linkage was made, the development of a generous web of economic, technological, educational and other ties was thought likely to encourage Soviet and East European leaders to be slightly more 'co-operative' on those special German interests: the situation of the Germans in the GDR and the rest of Eastern Europe. For while this web of ties might politely be described as 'to mutual advantage', it was clear that in, say, science, technology, industry, or education West Germany would give more than it got. These ties were thus, in part, incentives: carrots from the second basket, in the hope of concessions on specifically German interests in basket three. But rather than talk of carrots it might be more accurate to talk of load-bearing structures. Having a special load in East-West European relations, the Federal Republic was especially interested in creating a strong framework: one that would bear the additional load and be resistant to shocks.

Now clearly these special functions overlapped. They also shaded into general considerations, such as would be discussed in other Western states. Naturally West German policymakers preferred the general Western or European formulation of this conception to the specific national one. In these formulations, too, several different ideas came glued together. 'The comprehensive extension of economic, technological and cultural co-operation,' said Hans-Dietrich Genscher in 1989, '. . . the networking of mutual interests, can make the détente process irreversible. We must create a web (*Verflechtung*) of interests and co-operations (*sic*) which no longer allows any country to get out of this association (*Verbund*) without severely damaging their own most vital interests. We need mutual dependencies in the good sense of the word.' The very difficulty of translating this off-the-cuff interview answer into English illustrates how specific the thinking was.

Earlier, in 1987, the Foreign Minister expressed it thus: 'through deepened co-operation, lying in the interests of both sides, an irreversible, system-opening process must be shaped. It must take account of mutual dependency but also of the indivisible responsibility for the survival of humanity. It must finally be an irreversible, inevitable process of co-operation.' 'Our policy,' he said in another speech in the same year, 'is today in harmony with the striving of Europeans, who can overcome the division of the continent by co-operation.'

It is perhaps helpful to try and separate out some of the ideas that came glued together in such portmanteau formulations. Firstly, there was the relatively simple idea that if you wanted to reduce the division of Europe you had to reduce the division of Europe. The division of Europe was not just a matter of political systems. It was also an economic, technological, scientific, educational and infrastructural division. As Genscher observed in a speech in 1985: 'We do not want a technological division of Europe. We want to hold open for our eastern neighbours the option of technological connection through co-operation.' Or as the then Governing Mayor of Berlin, Eberhard Diepgen, put it in 1988: 'Every jointly erected desulphurisation plant, every exchange of goods and services, every East-West traffic connection is to some extent a trust-building and division-reducing measure.'

Yet this was also the *reductio ad absurdum* of the idea. For it is plainly absurd to suggest that every exchange of goods and services between East and West was a 'trust-building and division-reducing measure'. Did the Siemens computers in the Polish Interior Ministry, or the American handcuffs with which the KGB held Vladimir Bukovsky, help to reduce the division of Europe? If so, how? Did the supply of Soviet or East European spies in the form of exchange scholars increase trust? If so, whose trust in whom? The examples are extreme. But they illustrate an important point. For there was indeed a tendency in German Ostpolitik to argue that all forms of tie and co-operation would help, in the long-run, to reduce the division. Yet in practice there were forms of tie and co-operation that reinforced the (political) division and reduced trust. It might reasonably be argued that these were unavoidable side-costs: if you supply a thousand computers it is hard to avoid one of them going to the secret police. The overall balance remained positive. But that argument had to be made concretely, and from case to case.

A second notion bundled up in the *Verflechtung* portmanteau was that of common problems, challenges or interests. We are all threatened by nuclear war or accident. Acid rain knows no frontiers. The pollutants put into the river in one country damage another. Drugs and disease endanger us all. We have only one world. This theme was announced by Genscher as early as 1971. 'We all have only one alternative,' he declared, 'namely to defuse the dangerous world-political tensions by together attempting to solve the great tasks of humanity in the last third of the twentieth century.' But it became a dominant motif only in the second half of the 1980s, with the emergence in the West of powerful Green and anti-nuclear movements, alarming reports of acid rain, dying forests and the greenhouse effect, the Chernobyl disaster, and Soviet 'new thinking' in foreign policy. Thus the Bonn Declaration began: 'The Federal Republic of Germany and the Union of Soviet Socialist Republics agree that on the eve of the third millennium humanity faces historic challenges. Problems that are of vital importance to all can only be resolved by all states and peoples together.'

Now at one level this was clearly true. Industrial and technological development meant that people in one part of the world were more directly affected by what people did in another part of the world. Chernobyl was one example of this; global warming another. There were (and are) new common problems. But it does not necessarily follow that there are common solutions. Pollution is a good example. Taken as a whole, Eastern Europe in the 1980s had less industrial production yet as bad or worse industrial pollution than Western Europe. Why? Because of the economic system which caused such wasteful, careless industrial practice, and because of the political system which did not allow popular discontent about life-threatening pollution to be translated into the appropriate corrective political-economic action.

To be sure, there were technical similarities between pollution in East and West: sulphur dioxide (East) was very similar to sulphur dioxide (West). To be sure, one might argue, as the Greens did argue, that the root of the problem in West as well as East was the common worship of economic growth. But the acuteness of the pollution problem in the Soviet Union and Eastern Europe was in large measure a result of the prevailing political-economic system. To take 'co-operative' steps, 'irrespective of system differences', was thus to treat the symptoms not the causes: a necessary, but by no means a sufficient, response.

The Chernobyl disaster well illustrated this distinction. The Chernobyl disaster was an accident. But it was not an accident that it happened in the Soviet Union, rather than in, say, West Germany. The West German response was, in effect, to say: 'we will help you to build safer nuclear power stations. In fact, if you like, we will build them for you' — common and self-interest happily coinciding. Now everyone, in East and West, would clearly breathe more easily if, given that the Soviet Union was determined to go on building nuclear power stations, those nuclear power stations were to be built by — or at least, with the advice of — West Germans. But this was not a common solution to a common problem. It was a Western panacea for a Soviet problem.

There is also the question of whether the growth in the prominence of such 'common problems' in East-West, and especially in (West) German-Soviet dialogue, was proportionate to the actual growth in the urgency of those common problems, or rather reflected a desire — essentially for other reasons — to find common ground. This would, after all, be nothing new. When John F Kennedy wished to signal his readiness to establish a better relationship with the Soviet Union, he said, in June 1963: '. . . let us also direct attention to our common interests . . . For, in the final analysis, our most basic common link is that we all inhabit this small planet. We all breathe the same air. We all cherish our children's future. And we are all mortal.' A remarkable discovery.

When two states wish to establish better relations they often reach for the highest common platitude. If there had been no 'common problems' for West Germany and the Soviet Union, it might have been necessary to invent them. Indeed it was curious to observe how hardened *Realpolitiker* on both sides suddenly developed a vibrant, tender concern for trees and plants, for 'all things bright and beautiful, all creatures great and small'. This is, of course, not to deny the reality or importance of these problems. It is merely to point out that their discovery and sudden prominence served a more traditional, instrumental function as well.

A third, related notion to be disentangled from the portmanteau is that of the desirability of interdependence. The argument from 'common problems' said, in effect: 'In the contemporary world we are increasingly interdependent, and our responses must therefore be multilateral and co-operative across the East-West divide.' But the Ostpolitik argument for *Verflechtung* went a stage further. It said not only that we are interdependent, but that we *should* be interdependent. This is a less obvious thing to say. Most states in modern history have wanted to be more independent, not less so. This remained true of the great majority of states in the world, in Africa, Asia or Latin America. Western Europe was a rare, partial exception, but even in Western Europe there were not so many French or British politicians who would have regarded increasing interdependence as a primary foreign policy goal. As for Eastern Europe, the central experience of this region in modern history was, precisely, dependency. For many, perhaps most people in Eastern Europe a primary meaning of 'freedom' continued to be the recovery of 'independence' for a nation in a state. The prospect of entering into new kinds of dependency — albeit 'mutual dependency' — before even sloughing off the old dependency (on the Soviet Union) was not instantly appealing.

So what was the case for interdependence? Insofar as any clear answer was offered to this question (and that is not very far) the underlying thought seems to be that the web of mutual dependencies would prevent any European state from striking at another, as they had done so often in the past. The *Verflechtung*, to recall Genscher's formulation, should no longer 'allow any country to get out ... without severely damaging their own most vital interests'. The model was the (West) European Community, and especially the Franco-German 'reconciliation', supposedly secured by precisely such a web of mutual dependencies. It was also linked to the notion of building trust and confidence between states. So in this respect, co-operation was primarily a means to achieving greater security between states in East and West, rather than to achieving change inside the states of Eastern Europe or the Soviet Union. There was more than an echo here of the Kissingerite notion of the 'Gulliverisation' of the Soviet Union. Interdependence was to be a pacifier.

Several caveats may be entered about this notion of interdependence as guarantee of international harmony. The first concerns the balance of dependence. The Franco-German interdependence functioned so well precisely because there was — in the Europe of 'Yalta' — a rough balance of mutual dependencies, political, economic and military, between the two countries. But there is no historical law that states this must be so. History offers far more examples of unequal dependencies: for example, the dependency of East Central Europe on Germany and/or Russia. Such unequal dependencies cannot be said to have diminished the likelihood of conflict between the states involved. Lenin's question — who, whom? — must therefore be applied to interdependence too: who becomes dependent on whom?

Secondly, there is the problem of third parties. If states A and B are 'interdependent' this may mean they are less likely to come into conflict with each other, but does it follow that state B is less likely to show aggression against state C? Only to the extent that state A chooses to make that a condition of its relationship with state B. Thus, for example, the Soviet invasion of Afghanistan did not directly threaten any Soviet-German interdependencies. It was a matter of choice — a calculation of interest — whether the Federal Republic responded by adjusting its own relationship to the Soviet Union. There was nothing 'inevitable', to recall Genscher's term, about that. In fact the Federal Republic's own perceived dependency on Moscow inclined it to react less strongly to Soviet aggression against a third party.

Now one German argument against imposing sanctions on the Soviet Union was that the Soviet Union was so relatively little dependent on economic ties with the West that it would not renounce what it saw as vital interests in order to preserve those ties. In other words, there was too little interdependence to pacify. There is some force in this argument. It is reasonable to suggest that interdependence must achieve, as it were, a critical mass, before it will affect the political behaviour of states. The necessary critical mass was, however, likely to be larger in the case of a Leninist party-state, because of the primacy of politics in such states. But how then might such a critical mass of interdependence be achieved? Was it possible to achieve such a critical mass without changing one or other system?

West Germany's own experience of trade, and more generally of economic, scientific and technical co-operation with the East, suggests that there are intrinsic limits to the number of ties that can be developed between two such different systems: between centrally planned and market economies, but also, more broadly, between dictatorships and democracies, between closed and open societies. Here was the problem. In order to affect the external conduct of the states in question, interdependence had to achieve a critical mass. In order to achieve that critical mass, however, there had to be change in the internal systems of the relevant states — of one system, or the other, or both.

West German politicians and policymakers did not fail to identify this problem. But here, too, they had an answer. To be sure, they said, an (unspecified) degree of systemic change is a precondition for achieving the peace-securing level of interdependence. But increasing interdependence is itself a means to promote systemic change! The favoured formula for this further golden harmony was 'system-opening co-operation'. Already in 1970 the influential policy intellectual, Klaus Ritter, had coined the phrase 'system-opening co-existence' as a response to the Soviet formula of 'peaceful co-existence'.

In June 1987 Ritter's friend and wartime comrade, Richard von Weiz-säcker, now Federal President, took up and popularised the phrase, in the post-Helsinki form of 'system-opening co-operation'. The purely military aspect of East-West relations had been overemphasised, he argued, during a speech to mark the fortieth anniversary of the Marshall Plan, delivered, like Willy Brandt's a quarter-century before, at Harvard University. 'We must,' he said, 'find other "currencies" of relations with each other than simply military power.' And rather as Brandt and Bahr had taken as their exemplar the American John F Kennedy, so now von Weizsäcker sum-moned up the spirits of James Fulbright and George Marshall. In a subsequent speech at an Aspen Institute conference in Berlin — paying tribute to another American European, Shepard Stone — he repeated his plea for 'system-opening co-operation' adding: 'under the sign of peres-troika'. Economic, scientific, technological, educational, environmental co-operation would, von Weizsäcker argued, not merely in itself reduce the economic, scientific and technological division of Europe, help to solve 'common problems', and increase the desirable 'interdependence'. It would also prove to be 'system-opening'.

What did this mean? One may safely assume that the 'system' referred to was primarily the Eastern system(s). The Gorbachev leadership, von Weizsäcker said in his Berlin speech, 'knows that it's a matter of reforming their system, not ours'. (Although there was some implication that the Western system needed a little 'opening' too: 'We too have our mistakes, we know the weaknesses of our virtues, we need to learn.') But what, in the context of the Soviet or Soviet-type system, was meant by 'opening'? Was this a polite euphemism for fundamental transformation, or did it just mean the same system made slightly more open — and if so, open for whom to do what? Again — as with the long-term definition of the 'European peace order' — the answers were vague and various.

Thus, in an intra-Western discussion devoted to precisely this subject, the then political director of the Foreign Ministry, Hermann von Richthofen, remarked: 'Through our policy we don't want to change the structures on the other side, just as we would not approve of an Eastern policy that aims to change the structures on our side . . .' 'For me,' said a German businessman in the same discussion, 'system-opening means above all people getting to know each other and the exchange of ideas and ways of thinking'. Soviet managers should be trained in West Germany, said the Federal President's press spokesman, 'that is then system-opening co-operation, because a Soviet manager who has been trained here will as a result later behave differently than he did before'.

The argument about the causal relationship between co-operation on the one side and systemic change (or 'opening') on the other was thus elusive and fragmentary. Sometimes the underlying thought seemed to be a modified version of convergence: the theory, most cautiously and precisely articulated by Raymond Aron, that advanced industrial societies would tend to become more like each other. 'I am inclined to believe,' Aron wrote, 'that advanced industrialisation, in Europe at least, favours an individualist rather than a collectivist civilisation . . . in the future perhaps Europe in this respect will extend as far as the Urals.' To encourage advanced industrialisation, by economic and technical modernisation, would therefore *ipso facto* encourage socio-political change.

At other times, the underlying thought seemed closer to that of subversion by example. The backwardness of the Soviet Union, said von Weizsäcker in Harvard, 'is the result of a closed system without participation (*Mitbestimmung*) and without incentives for the population, without free information . . . If there is now the chance of an opening, is that our risk?' By implication, to expose the Soviet population to Western habits, ideas, living standards was the risk of Soviet rulers. Again, the basic thought can be found already with Kennedy and Brandt in the early 1960s.

The new element linking these two notions was the nature of the latest phase of economic modernisation: the 'revolution of high technology', and, above all, information technology. The rapid, free flow of information, by computer, fax or satellite television, would be at once indispensable for economic modernisation and incompatible with the previously existing (or 'real existing') Soviet-type system, at whose very heart was the state's information monopoly — or, as Solzhenitsyn would put it, the Lie. The supposed magic of information technology would thus unite, as in a Hegelian synthesis, the two apparently opposed extremes of convergence and subversion.

Would an economic modernisation of the Soviet Union help the West? Hans-Dietrich Genscher rhetorically asked, in a spirited defence of developing Soviet-German economic ties in 1987. And he answered:

> whoever recognises the social developments which result from the new technologies in our free societies, towards more personal responsibility and smaller units, and whoever recognises that an opening of the Soviet Union quite automatically makes it necessary for it to move in this direction; they will also recognise that a Soviet Union which goes down the path of modernisation will in the end be a different one from that of today, a more open one, not a democracy in our sense, but a more open one compared with the Soviet Union of today.

Yet the claim for the system-opening effect of co-operation was not only made about the future. It was also made, albeit cautiously, about the past. 'The Conference on Security and Co-operation in Europe has, through its agreements in basket two, decisively contributed to the strengthening and deepening of East-West economic relations,' Richard von Weizsäcker observed in a further speech, in Hamburg in 1989. 'It has facilitated an economic, social and political change in Eastern Europe, one would like almost to say, it has made it in the long term unavoidable.' One might like almost to say this, but if one were to say it, then one would have to explain precisely how. Precisely what in economic, technical, scientific and environmental co-operation ('basket two') changed exactly what in Eastern polities?

'This attempt to cover the divided Europe again with a net of contacts, trade, exchange and co-operation, strengthens the reform forces in Eastern Europe,' said Horst Ehmke in a debate in January 1982, discussing the nature of Solidarity in Poland and the implications of martial law. Not that détente was the cause of reform movements. 'But the policy of détente, with its exchange and its contacts, has immensely increased the room for manoeuvre of this reform movement.' And again, 'détente policy naturally contributes indirectly to the setting free of ideas, forces, also productive forces, in Eastern Europe, which seek a new political expression'.

These hedged and fuzzy claims will be examined a little more closely later on. In particular we shall have to look at the balance between fostering an overall process which might indirectly encourage reforms, or 'system-opening', and, on the other hand, the direct encouragement (or discouragement) of people directly demanding respect for human rights and democracy. But before doing that it is worth briefly considering what sort of a web the Federal Republic did actually manage to spin with (around? over?) its Eastern neighbours in the twenty years from 1969 to 1989. How did the actual West German 'net' compare in quantity and quality with those of France, Britain, Italy or the United States?

The short answer is 'it was the thickest'. Starting from a position far behind its Western partners in everything except trade, the Federal Republic had by 1989, through the intensity and consistency of its efforts, built a more dense network of ties with all East European countries (not to mention East Germany) and even with the Soviet Union, than any other Western country. As we have seen, in all forms of economic tie, and not just in traditional Eastern trade, the Federal Republic far outstripped its main Western partners (see pages 244 f and Tables II and III).

In political relations, too, the sheer number of official visits and exchanges was unique. This included not just government ministers, officials and diplomats, but also senior and junior figures from all the main political parties, and from provincial as well as federal politics. There was not only a unique intensity of political contacts, but also a remarkable continuity on the West German side. In most East-West political contacts it was the Western partner who was constantly changing. In the case of West Germany it was almost the other way round. East European Foreign Ministers came and went, but the West German Foreign Minister remained the same. The same politicians, officials, commentators pursued the same business year in, year out. The only respect in which this political network was weak by comparison with, say, the American or British one, was in contacts with independent and oppositional political groups.

In cultural ties, the picture was more mixed. The Federal Republic gave a high priority to what in English would be called 'cultural diplomacy', in American sometimes also 'public diplomacy', and in German was described as *auswärtige Kulturpolitik* — that is 'external cultural policy'. The priority was emphasised by a new set of guide-lines in 1970, which also gave a more liberal and cosmopolitan definition of cultural policy, and remained so throughout the 1970s and 1980s, under the special care of a series of Free Democrat Ministers of State in the Foreign Ministry, but also under close parliamentary supervision. As much as one third of the budget of the Foreign Ministry went on cultural diplomacy, a proportion higher even than that of the traditional master of cultural diplomacy, France, and far higher than in the foreign affairs budgets of the United States or Britain. Roughly half this generous budget for external cultural policy was devoted to the teaching and promotion of the German language, called, in good German, *Sprachpolitik*.

Within this overall picture, Eastern Europe occupied a very special place. Cultural diplomacy in Eastern Europe was to serve as an important part of that overall Ostpolitik strategy of weaving a load-bearing web of ties. German culture, German scholarship, German enterprise had traditionally played a unique and even a leading role in much of the region now called Eastern Europe. But the last venture in the Ostpolitik of the German Reich, launched under the banner of *Kultur*, had delivered a terrible blow to the influence of the very culture in the name of which it claimed to act. The revulsion against everything German after 1945 was then swiftly reinforced by communist state policies in the conditions of the Cold War, and by the presence of a second German state which claimed alone to represent everything that was good, true and beautiful in German culture.

German, once the second language of many countries in the region (with French as that of the others), lost its place first to the officially imposed Russian and then to the unofficially triumphant English. French also lost out, but France fought a fierce semantic rearguard action, through well-endowed cultural institutes, often with a tradition dating back to before the war. The West German radio station broadcasting to the East — *Deutsche Welle* — achieved neither the audiences nor the impact of the BBC, Radio Free Europe or Voice of America.

These special difficulties remained remarkably persistent. If popular revulsion against all things German was gradually replaced, partly under the influence of the new Ostpolitik, by a more positive image of the new Germany, this did not necessarily endear the idea of expanding German cultural influence to the communist leaderships. In several East European states, the questions of German culture and language were also inextricably intertwined with the thorny issue of the German minorities. Last but not least, there was the dogged obstructionism of the GDR. Not the Goethe Institutes of West Germany but the Herder Institutes of East Germany should represent German culture in the East.

As a result, although the Federal Republic did negotiate framework cultural agreements with all East European states (except East Germany) in the 1970s, the responsible Foreign Ministry official, Barthold C Witte — himself, not accidentally, a Free Democrat — describes the years from 1975 to 1985 as a 'decade of stagnation' in West Germany's cultural relations with the East. He notes that official academic exchange with the Soviet Union, for example, remained at the ridiculous level of fifteen scholarships a year. Witte regards the Budapest Cultural Forum of 1985, the first major Helsinki follow-up meeting in this field, as the beginning of a breakthrough. But even in Hungary it was only in 1988 that West Germany was able to open an official cultural institute, and even then it was not formally called a Goethe Institute, due to the Hungarian authorities' residual concern about official East German sensibilities. (A Goethe Institute had, however, been established in maverick Romania in 1979, although it operated under increasing difficulties in the late Ceauşescu years.)

As late as mid-1989, the official map of German cultural establishments abroad shows an eloquent blank to Germany's east. So also with the statistics on German language-teaching — with the notable exception of the Soviet Union where, in another example of Russia's more sovereign approach to matters German, more than nine million schoolchildren officially learned German.

For most of Eastern Europe, in this as in other respects, 1989 marked the real breakthrough. Now official German cultural institutes were swiftly established in all the countries, and there was a veritable explosion of interest in learning German. While the objects of this cultural diplomacy continued to be stated in liberal and cosmopolitan terms, there were very clearly, as in British, French or American cultural diplomacy, goals of competitive national interest as well. German, wrote Barthold Witte in 1991, now had a chance to remain — by which he surely meant, to become again — a *lingua franca* in Central and Eastern Europe, although now 'beside English'. Elsewhere Witte would bluntly observe: 'Those who speak and understand German are also more likely to buy German . . .'

The special difficulties of official cultural diplomacy up to 1989 had, however, to some extent been circumvented by the very active programmes of what in English would be called 'quangos' (quasi-non-governmental organisations) such as the German Academic Exchange Service or the Alexander von Humboldt Foundation, which were largely or wholly financed from the public purse; by those of the party foundations, also partly financed from the public purse; and by those of major private foundations such as the Volkswagen Foundation, the Krupp Foundation, or the Robert Bosch Foundation, with its pioneering German-Polish projects.

Altogether, these public, semi-public and private West German institutions, including many individual universities, academies, cultural festivals and the like, managed to establish numerous links and to bring a large and increasing number of East European scholars, artists, intellectuals and students to work, study or perform in the Federal Republic, and sent a smaller (but also increasing) number to do the same in the other direction. By comparison with exchanges between West European nations, these remained very small, but the overall growth since the 1960s was impressive. Not a few members of the new governing élites of Central and Eastern Europe after 1989 had spent time in Germany on one or other of these programmes.

What was true at the level of the intelligentsia was even more true at the popular level: in both directions. No Western country sent more tourists into the East. But, in pursuit of its own special idea of Helsinki, the Helsinki of human contacts, the Federal Republic also let in far more ordinary, individual East Europeans than any other Western country. In 1988, the West German embassies in East Central Europe (taken here as Poland, Hungary and Czechoslovakia) issued a total of more than 1.3 million visas.

'It is important,' Kennedy had said at the Free University of West Berlin in 1963, 'that the people on the quiet streets in the East be kept in touch with Western society.' In the 1980s, few Western societies were more open to 'the people on the quiet streets' than West Germany. This brought benefits to the Federal Republic: for no one who actually visited West Germany could any more believe the Communist propaganda about an imperialist 'revanchist' German menace. But it also brought costs.

Many of these visitors worked illegally, to gain precious hard currency. A minority also sought political asylum, or simply remained in the country illegally. Due to the exceptionally liberal asylum clause in West Germany's Basic Law — and the generous interpretation of that clause — very few of them were actually sent back. If the generous interpretation of the nationality clause of the Basic Law meant that many East Europeans who were only dubiously Germans were accepted as such, the generous interpretation of the asylum clause meant that many East Europeans who were not even pretending to be Germans, but merely wanted to live in a free, prosperous country which happened to be called Germany, were allowed to do so. One way or the other, hundreds of thousands of East Europeans benefited directly from this policy of deliberate openness — and millions more benefited indirectly, through the hard curency, goods, and not least, experience that their relatives and friends sent or brought home.

Yet the numbers cannot tell the whole story. Beside the question of quantity there is the question of quality. And the quality of this web was uneven. We have mentioned already the weakness of the political ties to independent or opposition groups. In technology, in economics, and in the cultural and human exchanges, the interdependence was unequal. Genscher's offer of the 'technological connection' had a double-edge for East Europeans: the double-edge of recreating an historic dependency. Most East Europeans came to West Germany to learn or earn. Most Germans went East to spend or to teach. Most Germans in the East were holidaymakers, investors or employers. Most East Europeans in West Germany were impecunious shoppers, poorly paid *Gastarbeiter*, or, at best, poor relations. The small privileged crust of intellectuals, artists, and scholars was the exception which proved the rule.

This was not, of course, the West Germans' fault. They were not — or only in a very indirect, historical sense — responsible for the relative economic backwardness of Eastern Europe. They could not, as it were, help being rich. And ordinary men and women could hardly be expected to decline cheap labour or cheap pleasures out of some vague, elevated sense of moral or historical responsibility. Moreover, from the individual

East Europeans' point of view it was far better to earn a little hard currency — albeit on terms which for a West European would be considered exploitation — than to earn none. For the children at home, father's work as a window-cleaner in Dortmund, not his studies on Husserl at Warsaw University, made the difference between bearable austerity and sheer deprivation.

This was a lesser evil. But it was also a very long way from those elevated visions of mutually enriching European spiritual exchange to be found in the politicians' speeches. On the ground, the new 'interdependence' looked all too much like an old dependence. If East Europeans had become less dependent on the East they had become more dependent on the West. And if the East meant for them, as it had meant of old, Russia, the West increasingly meant, as it had meant of old, Germany. The phrase young Poles used for 'going to work in the West' was *na saksy*, a nineteenth-century slang phrase (containing the root 'Saxony') to describe the seasonal labour which, then as now, had been done primarily in Germany.

It must be stressed again that this situation was not of the Federal Republic's making and did not reflect its aims. But it was a reality which the Germans, as much as their eastern neighbours, would have to confront in the 1990s.

Stability before liberty

In October 1989 the prestigious Peace Prize of the German Book Trade was awarded to the Czech writer and opposition leader Václav Havel. Havel was prevented by the highest Czechoslovak authorities from travelling to Frankfurt to receive the prize. However, he sent an acceptance speech, which was read on his behalf at the ceremony in the Paulskirche in Frankfurt — where the assembly of German liberals and patriots had met in the revolution of 1848. President von Weizsäcker and Chancellor Kohl sat in the front row. Between them there was a symbolic empty seat. Havel's speech, entitled 'A Word about the Word', was a reflection both on the exceptional importance that words assume in a totalitarian system, and, beyond that, on the pitfalls, double-edges and multiple meanings of all the most important words: 'socialism', 'freedom', 'peace'.

'Your country,' Havel wrote at one point in his address,

has made a great contribution to modern European history: the first wave of détente, its well-known Ostpolitik. But even that word managed at times to be well and truly ambiguous. It signified, of course, the first glimmer of hope for a Europe without Cold War and iron curtain; yet at the same time — alas — it more than once signified the renunciation of freedom, and hence of a basic condition for any real peace. I still recall how at the beginning of the 1970s some of my West German friends and colleagues avoided me for fear that any sort of contact with me — someone out of favour with the authorities here — might needlessly provoke those authorities and thus threaten the fragile foundations of the nascent détente.

How was it possible that one of Czechoslovakia's most distinguished independent spokesmen could counterpose — albeit cautiously, personally, and in the past tense — the word 'Ostpolitik' to the word 'freedom'? Surely the highest representatives of the Federal Republic were sitting in the front row of the Paulskirche in Frankfurt to prove the opposite? To understand this one has to go back twenty years, to 1969, and notice again the ambiguities of another big word: 'normalisation'.

As we have seen, 'normalisation' was a key-term for the social-liberal architects of Ostpolitik in the early 1970s. For them it meant the restoration of a more 'normal' relationship of the Federal Republic with the Soviet Union and East European states, starting with the elementary 'normality' of diplomatic recognition. But 'normalisation' was also a key-word in Czechoslovakia at that time, and what it meant there was the attempt to return a European society, initially by the use of force, to Soviet norms. 'Normalisation' was what followed the Soviet invasion in August 1968. It was the crushing of the Prague Spring, the slow strangling of hard-won liberties, expulsions, sackings, censorship, repression.

These two kinds of 'normalisation' did not merely exist side-by-side. They were causally related. The Soviet invasion of Czechoslovakia was not the end of détente. It was not even, as the French Prime Minister Michel Debré memorably remarked, 'a traffic accident on the road to détente'. Rather it was the toll-gate on the highway to détente. 'That the Soviets found their way back to a more flexible diplomacy just at this time [i.e. early 1969],' writes Richard Löwenthal, 'was certainly in part a result of the fact that after the violent suppression of Czech reform communism they felt themselves more secure in their own sphere of influence: "Change through rapprochement" was no more to be feared.' 'Normalisation' à la Husák was thus a precondition for 'normalisation' à la Brandt.

Given this fateful connection, it became all the more important to ask what the effect might be in the other direction: that is, how East-West 'normalisation' might affect 'normalisation' inside the East. Would it facilitate 'normalisation' in the Brezhnev-Husák sense of a return, through repression, intimidation and *Gleichschaltung*, to Soviet norms? Or would it rather, albeit in the longer term, encourage a return to European, Western norms?

It must be said that this question — so crucial to the people of Czechoslovakia — was not high on the agenda of German Ostpolitik in the 1970s. West German politicians and policymakers were so preoccupied with addressing their own 'constitutive double conflict' with the East — the general Western and the special national — that they had little time to address the East Europeans' constitutive double conflict: that of states with the imperial centre, and of societies with (party-) states. The latter conflict was, indeed, barely recognised as such in the approach of social-liberal Ostpolitik.

In the speeches and writings of Helmut Schmidt, for example, the term 'East Europeans' seemed to apply almost exclusively to East European states, and those states were — a further highly questionable assumption — assumed to be represented by their communist rulers. So far as East Central Europe (apart from the GDR) is concerned, it is hard to disagree with the Polish writer Jacek Maziarski when he comments: 'of all the Western states, it is probably the Federal Republic of Germany which most weakly perceived the traps created by the disharmony between social aspirations and the policy of the official authorities . . .'

To the extent that West German policy did recognise the tension between party-state and society, it was argued that improvements could only be achieved *with* the authorities and not against them. Even 'human rights' it was said, could only be achieved with, not against the powers-that-be. These insights were born of one triumph of Soviet-backed force, the building of the Berlin Wall, and reinforced by another — the invasion of Czechoslovakia. To the limited extent that German Ostpolitik did have any notion of promoting domestic socio-political change in East Central Europe — that is, tackling the internal aspect of the division of Europe — it focussed on change in the party-state.

Insofar as there was any underlying concept, it remained that nostrum of behavioural psychology, originally articulated by Egon Bahr under the vague slogan 'change through rapprochement'; more precisely described by Josef Joffe as 'relaxation through reassurance'; and analysed earlier under the heading 'liberalisation through stabilisation'. With hindsight, we can see that it did not work like that: neither in East Germany nor anywhere else. But this is not just a matter of hindsight. For in Poland and Czechoslovakia there were already independent intellectuals in the 1970s who were saying that it would not work; and suggesting an alternative. One of them was called Václav Havel.

These independent East Central European intellectuals drew precisely the opposite conclusion to the West German social-liberal Ostpolitiker from the crushing of the Prague Spring. In the past some of them had believed — believed passionately — in so-called 'revisionism', in change from above following the growing progressive enlightenment of the leaders, in the possibility of Communism reforming itself voluntarily into democratic socialism. Indeed, as the Hungarian philosopher and social critic János Kis wrote, from the mid-1950s until the late 1960s the 'general idea of evolution in Eastern Europe was that of reforms generated from above and supported from below'. But this hope was crushed in 1968, under the Soviet tanks in Prague and the police batons in Warsaw. Those events reinforced the West German *Ostpolitiker* in their belief that change, or at least 'human alleviations', could only be achieved by dealing with the communist powers-that-be, in the hope of eventually starting the 'virtuous circle' of relaxation and reassurance, liberalisation through stabilisation.

But these independent East Central European intellectuals concluded: We have concentrated too much on the powers-that-be. These events have shown that they alone cannot bring lasting, meaningful change, even if (which is to be doubted) they really want change that will inevitably result in their loss of power and privilege. Let us instead work from the bottom up. Let us draw on 'the power of the powerless' — to use Havel's phrase of 1978. Let us concentrate on people organising themselves deliberately outside the structures of the party-state, in multifarious independent social groupings, working together and 'living in truth'. The operative goal will not be the reform of the party-state but the reconstitution of civil society. Yet of course, if the strategy is at all successful, the party-state will be compelled to adapt to these *faits accomplis*, if only by grudgingly accepting an incremental *de facto* reduction in the areas of its total control. But what is *de facto* today may eventually become *de jure* too. The *pays réel* will finally shape the *pays légal*.

This strategy of 'social self-organisation' was prefigured by Leszek Kołakowski's *Theses on Hope and Hopelessness* — published just six months after the Warsaw Treaty was signed. It was further developed by the veteran opposition leader, Jacek Kuroń, and by Adam Michnik, in his essay on 'the New Evolutionism', and guided the work not only of the Polish Workers' Defence Committee, KOR, founded in 1976, and in 1977 significantly renamed the Social Self-defence Committee-'KOR', but also of other opposition groups. Similar ideas were developed in Czechoslovakia — for example by Václav Benda in his 1978 essay 'The Parallel Polis' — and underpinned the work of Charter 77. The Solidarity movement in Poland was a piece of social self-organisation on a massive and unprecedented scale.

'Social self-organisation' was considered not only as a means to an end, but also as an end in itself. These autonomous social groupings and movements would, it was hoped, give the added push of 'pressure from below' to compel the ruling nomenklatura into making reforms. But even if those reforms did not come, the existence of these ligatures of autonomous association would be good in itself. For the totalitarian aspiration of a Soviet-type state was precisely to break all such autonomous ties: to rule over an atomised society. The essential bedrock of a liberal, democratic, Western, European state, by contrast, was a strong civil society, rich in intermediate layers of free and frank association. Every restored fragment of civil society was thus in itself a blow against 'normalisation' in the

Soviet sense, and for 'normalisation' in the sense of a return to Western, European norms.

Now it may justly be observed that the web of co-operation, communication and exchange — in a word, *Verflechtung* — that German Ostpolitik set out to spin did, in practice, facilitate the growth of these fragments of civil society. This is surely so. But if one looks at what West German Ostpolitiker said and did in the 1970s, then it is clear that this was not a primary intention. Building up civil society against the party-state was not what they thought they were doing. Not even in East Germany.

To be sure, here, unlike in the rest of East Central Europe, a distinction was made between helping 'the people' (*die Menschen*) and dealing with the party-state. But the notion of *die Menschen* is subtly but importantly different from that of civil society. For *die Menschen* means individual people, whereas civil society means people in free, self-conscious groups. The former exist in all societies, the latter are the ligaments of free societies. It was much easier for a Soviet-type party-state to accept 'humanitarian improvements' for individual people, even for hundreds of thousands of individual people, so long as they remained individual. Indeed, that was the Soviet understanding of Helsinki 'basket three'. *Die Menschen* may get humanitarian improvements; only civil societies secure human rights. The latter is a far more ambitious, more fundamental goal.

There was a curious asymmetry here. On the one side, a few seemingly powerless intellectuals said: Whatever the party-state wants, we will recreate civil society! We will win back human rights! On the other side, one of the most powerful and successful democratic states in Europe said: if we speak very gently to the party-state, and offer it bags of 'co-operation', perhaps we can win some humane improvements. The apparently powerless had a seemingly unfounded presumption of strength. The apparently powerful had almost as curious a presumption of weakness.

In part this presumption was explicable by the special German concerns that have been described above. In many respects, West Germany was the asking party in its relationship even with Poland or Czechoslovakia, let alone with the Soviet Union, in the 1970s. It had other fish to fry. Perhaps another part of the explanation for these very modest goals lies in the real experience of weakness after 13 August 1961. To some extent the Federal Republic in its whole relationship with Eastern Europe in the 1970s was a magnified projection of the West Berlin city government in its relationship with East Germany in the 1960s: Be thankful for every small mercy, since the other side has all the cards. 'Small steps are better than none.' Reassurance is the only hope of relaxation; stabilisation, of liberalisation.

In sum, therefore, it is not true to say that German Ostpolitik in the 1970s had no concept of fostering desirable socio-political change inside Eastern Europe. It had one, but it was a long-term strategy of deliberate indirection, based on the hope of modifying the behaviour of communist rulers by example, trust, co-operation and incentives. The dialectical principle developed by Brandt and Bahr in the 1960s stated that one must recognise the status quo in order to overcome it. A strong meaning of 'recognition' and a political definition of 'status quo' led to the more specific dialectical prescription that one must strengthen the party-state in order to weaken it. Since outspoken intellectuals and the would-be democratic opposition unsettled rather than reassured the communist rulers, and even seemed capable of 'destabilising' these states — so powerful are a few unfettered words! — this led logically to a third dialectical principle: one must ignore the democrats in order to support democracy.

The West would best serve the cause of liberty by not demanding it. Václav Havel might not appreciate this, but in the long run what those German visitors were doing was in his own best interest. Ultimately, it was better for him that they should not meet him. They knew best what was good for him.

This logic was, to say the least, patronising. But until the end of the 1970s it affected — and offended — only a small minority in East Central Europe, albeit a distinguished one. Their 'representativeness' could seriously be questioned. An argument could be made that the majority in the countries affected benefited more from Bonn's exclusive dealings with the powers-that-were. At the birth of Solidarity in Poland in August 1980, however, the clash of — what? analyses? aspirations? interests? — took on entirely new dimensions. For it now became a central issue in East-West relations.

The Polish revolution of 1980-81 both challenged the theory and threatened the practice of German Ostpolitik in a particularly acute form. The Soviet invasion of Afghanistan, the growing dispute about the deployment of new medium-range nuclear missiles in East and West, and the more general confrontation between the Soviet Union and the United States, all this already threatened to jeopardise the overall 'framework conditions' thought to be required for the successful pursuit of West German détente policy in general, and German-German relations in particular. Now the Polish crisis could be the last straw.

The Bonn government had done what it could to prevent the consequences of the Soviet invasion of Afghanistan — and of the American reaction to it — from adversely affecting its Ostpolitik. Because détente within Europe had to be indivisible, so violations of détente outside Europe had to be, so far as possible, minimised or disregarded. (A 'stabilisation' and 'normalisation' in Afghanistan was thus rather to be desired.) But détente could not survive another Afghanistan. And a Soviet invasion of Poland would be far worse than Afghanistan.

At the same time, Solidarity was, by its very nature, a frontal challenge to the concept of political change in Eastern Europe which, to the extent that there was any such concept, continued to underpin the social-liberal Ostpolitik. For Solidarity was a massive demonstration of the gulf between society and state, and the realisation — on an extraordinary scale — of the democratic opposition's vision of a self-organising society. Instead of reforms voluntarily conceded from above, in conditions of 'stability', there were concessions wrested by a (peaceful and self-limiting) revolution from below. Solidarity put liberty before stability: analytically as well as politically and morally. Instead of liberalisation through stabilisation it proposed stabilisation through liberalisation — with an inevitable period of transitional instabilities, and, of course, economic dislocation. And Solidarity was anything but dialectical. It said: if you want to change the status quo you must change the status quo; if you want to weaken the party dictatorship you must weaken the party dictatorship; if you want democracy you must demand democracy.

Throughout the sixteen months of Solidarity's overground existence (September 1980-December 1981) there was a deep ambivalence in the responses of West German politicians and policymakers. On the one hand, they proudly observed that without détente Solidarity would not have been possible. Marion Gräfin Dönhoff described Solidarity as a 'result' of détente. Like all assertions about causal connections between Western policies and Eastern politics, this proposition requires close and careful examination.

Thus it is, for example, plausible to argue that the Western credits made to the Gierek regime as part of Western détente policy contributed to the birth of Solidarity. But, as we have seen, they did so in ways that were not intended by those that made (or, strictly speaking, guaranteed) them. The credits, and associated increase of trade and technological transfers, were meant to facilitate a process of modernising through economic reform. In fact, they were used as a substitute for reform. They led first to a short-lived direct satisfaction of consumer desires through Western imports, and then to the downward spiral of an economy staggering under both the accumulated burden of a largely unreformed plan economy and the specific legacy of mismanagement and soaring hard currency debt from the détente period. This, and the consequent sharp disappointment of artificially raised consumer expectations, can with some confidence be identified as a cause of the crisis from which Solidarity emerged.

Somewhat more speculatively, one can argue that the sharp increase in the number of Poles travelling to the West, and particularly to West Germany, contributed to the popular discontent which fed into Solidarity. The annual tally of journeys made by Poles to the West passed the half million mark in 1977, with a grand total of some four million visits to the West in the course of the 1970s. Having seen the West at first hand, people were all the more sharply aware of the shortcomings of their own system — and not just, as many Westerners condescendingly assumed, in the area of consumer supplies. At the same time, they could no longer give any credence to the horror stories dished up by communist propaganda about life in the West. Specifically, they could no longer be frightened into support for the communist authorities by dark threats of German revanchism, and altogether by the German bogey which had served the communist regime so well for so many years. To remove the sense of a German threat, and replace it so far as possible by the attractions of the West German model, was a conscious purpose of Ostpolitik, and one which had already borne some fruit by 1980. Opinion polls on this issue are more than usually unreliable, but one independent survey indicated that in 1980 only 10.7 per cent of those asked saw a threat to Poland's independence from the Federal Republic, compared with 49.6 per cent who saw such a threat from the Soviet Union.

It can also be argued that the Helsinki Final Act provided an international charter to which the democratic opposition in Poland could appeal, while the Helsinki review process was an institutional goad to the Gierek regime to respect its provisions. The usefulness of Helsinki in this respect was recognised by Polish activists. But the bold claim that 'without Helsinki Solidarity would not have happened' must be qualified in three respects. Firstly, the causes of Solidarity are to be found above all inside Poland. When key participants come to write their memoirs, they make only passing reference to international influences in general, and Helsinki in particular.

Secondly, Helsinki was only one among many international treaties, charters or documents with which the opposition — in Poland and elsewhere — formally buttressed its claims. In opposition documents, it was often the human rights conventions of the UN that were first adduced. In the twenty-one demands of the Gdańsk strike, which gave birth to Solidarity, the specific reference was to 'convention 87 of the International Labour Organisation (ILO) . . . ratified by the Polish People's Republic'. And the influence of the human rights demands made by another international organisation, the Roman Catholic Church, can hardly be overstated. In terms of direct, demonstrable influence on the Polish people, Vatican II, as applied to Poland by the Polish Pope, was more important than the Helsinki Final Act.

Thirdly, insofar as it was the specific détente instrument of Helsinki which had a direct, positive influence on the evolution of the democratic opposition in Poland, it was above all Helsinki in the interpretation given it by the United States from 1977 on. As we have seen, it was the United States under Carter which made the direct linkage between human rights and new credits, a linkage which clearly influenced Gierek's tolerance of the fledgling democratic opposition. It was governmental, congressional, labour and human rights organisations from the United States which provided the most support, political, symbolic, moral and, not least, financial, to the predecessors of Solidarity — and then to Solidarity itself. While this story is of course a complex one, with notable exceptions, it is generally true to say that, as Havel indicated in his Frankfurt speech, West Germany was at the other extreme in this respect.

The approach of most leading practitioners of German Ostpolitik was characterised not merely by what are known in German as *Berührungsängste* (contact fears), but, as we have seen, by a conscious and deliberate avoidance of such potentially destabilising contacts. Klaus Reiff, a Social Democratic journalist who served as press attaché in the German embassy in Warsaw in the early 1980s, recalls that when Hans-Dietrich Genscher visited Warsaw in March 1981, talks with Solidarity were not on his programme. When Reiff tried merely to introduce a Solidarity journalist to him during a press briefing, the German Foreign Minister reacted with extreme irritation. And this at a time when Solidarity was a fully legal organisation, recognised as a 'partner' even by the communist authorities! The evidence on such issues is inevitably anecdotal: but there is no doubt in which direction the anecdotal evidence points.

One other aspect of Helsinki and the policy of interweaving was a deliberate effort to increase the free flow of information both between East and West and within the East. If one looks at the direct contribution of the increased flow of information to the Solidarity revolution, then it is probably true that the large presence of Western media (specifically sanctioned by Helsinki) and even, marginally, improved information technology, did help the birth and growth of the Solidarity movement. But much the most important direct contribution was made by purveyors of information which both organisationally and technologically preceded détente: the telephone, telex and television inside Poland, and Western radio stations from outside. The Polish-language services of Radio France Internationale, the BBC, Voice of America, and, second to none, Radio Free Europe, known to most Poles colloquially — and aptly — just as 'Free Europe' (*Wolna Europa*), were crucial in the spread of information inside Poland throughout the whole period under review.

Yet Radio Free Europe was an institution more closely identified with the Cold War than with détente. Willy Brandt's notes of his talks in Warsaw in December 1970 record a revealing exchange with the then party leader, Władysław Gomułka. Brandt records Gomułka asking: 'what would a German court say if we sued Radio Free Europe?' Brandt summarises his own response thus 'Reference to overall development [?], relations with USA, possible changes through passing of time.' This does not sound like a very vigorous defence of RFE. And then Gomułka: 'But you give the licence.'

The connections between détente and Solidarity are thus by no means clear or linear. Among the putative Western causes, some were not specifically 'détente' causes at all. One has to ask which version of détente, which Helsinki, contributed to the rise of Solidarity. The Eastern results of détente policies were often quite different from those intended. Arguably this was true of Solidarity altogether. For this kind of rapid, unstable, revolutionary movement for change from below was clearly not envisaged by the makers of Ostpolitik, who had hoped to contribute to a reduction, not a sharpening, of the tension between rulers and ruled in Eastern Europe. In a dialectical twist not anticipated by the dialecticians of détente, the policy of reducing tensions (*Entspannungspolitik*) had itself produced tensions (*Spannungen*). To be sure, the reduction of tensions and the growth of ties between East and West may have contributed to the restraint both of the Polish and of the Soviet regime in their response to the popular revolt. But the increase in tensions inside the East would now increase tensions between East and West. As one Western specialist pithily observed: détente was bad for détente.

Precisely because they saw this, the same West German politicians and policymakers who said 'without détente, no Solidarity', at the same time argued that this was the wrong way to go. The Poles organised in Solidarity were trying to go too far too fast. Only gradual change, controlled from above — as in Hungary — was feasible. This romantic Polish adventure would end in tears. And those tears would then also be German tears, because a Soviet invasion of Poland would finally bring down the house of détente in Europe, and jeopardise the small humane improvements that had so painstakingly been negotiated for the Germans in the East: for *die Menschen*. A judgment about the internal possibilities in Poland was thus mixed with a profound fear of the external repercussions for Germany.

It must be emphasised that the official, public position of the Bonn government in these sixteen months differed little from those of its major Western partners. Their positions were, indeed, very carefully co-ordinated in Nato, European Political Co-operation and bilateral consultations. Bonn, like Washington, Paris and London, emphasised the imperative of non-interference in Polish internal affairs, thus turning one of Moscow's favourite Helsinki formulae against the Soviet Union. Directly and indirectly it underlined how catastrophic would be the effects of a Soviet intervention. Maintaining a dialogue with the authorities and the Church, it also did more than most Western powers to ease the Polish government's immediate financial crisis. By Schmidt's own account, this financial help amounted to some half billion DM in the twelve months to October 1981. But significant differences of emphasis were apparent. Where American policymakers tended to laud the political gains in Poland, German policymakers tended to note the economic cost. Where the former stressed the opportunity, the latter stressed the risk.

The differences became acute with the declaration of martial law on 13 December 1981. This could not have come at a worse time for Chancellor

Schmidt, who found himself on the last day of his summit meeting with Erich Honecker in East Germany — a meeting that had already been postponed on account of the Polish crisis. Asked by a journalist for his first reaction to the declaration of the 'state of war' in Poland, Schmidt said: 'Herr Honecker was as dismayed as I, that *this has now proved necessary*. I very much hope that the Polish nation will succeed in solving their problems. They have already lasted a long time. And the economic and financial capacities of other states to help Poland are certainly not unlimited' (my italics). Klaus Bölling, who was with him at the time, suggests that Schmidt himself soon understood 'that it was a mistake to portray the Poles indirectly as an interference factor for German-German relations.' And five days later the Chancellor declared to the Bundestag: 'I stand with all my heart on the side of the [Polish] workers.'

Although the 'internal' military solution had been on the cards for some time — and some part of the Reagan administration had known about it more definitely from a high-level Polish defector — the major Western powers had not agreed a co-ordinated response to this contingency. As a result, the crisis of the Soviet bloc became a crisis of the Western Alliance. An internal East German assessment of the Schmidt-Honecker summit meeting, drafted for the Politburo at the end of December 1981, noted that Schmidt's attitude 'has contributed to the fact that so far there has been no unified front of the USA, Western Europe and Japan towards the PR [People's Republic of] Poland, the USSR and the socialist community; and this despite the repeated and intensified efforts of the USA . . . ' According to the East German assessment, the Schmidt-Honecker summit had thus 'given the Military Council of People's Poland a breathing-space which is not to be underestimated'.

The Reagan administration held the Soviet Union directly responsible for martial law in Poland, and therefore imposed sanctions on Moscow as well as on Warsaw. The Schmidt government insisted that this was still an internal Polish solution, and therefore refused to impose sanctions on Moscow, while also agreeing to receive in Bonn the Polish deputy prime minister, Mieczysław F Rakowski. Two arguments must be distinguished here: the narrow argument about sanctions and the broader argument about political change. The narrow argument has been considered above. It is the broader argument that concerns us here.

This issue of the proper response to martial law provoked a storm of political and publicistic argument both in and around West Germany. It is impossible to summarise all the arguments pro and contra, because they were so diverse, so fragmentary and so laden with emotion. But the main lines are roughly as follows. Leading Social Democrats and, to a lesser extent, Free Democrats, were criticised because they seemed almost to condone Jaruzelski's coup. They were charged with being chillingly indifferent to the cause of liberty — and especially to the plight of Polish social democrats fighting for the cause of liberty — in Central and Eastern Europe, by contrast with their enthusiasm — and active support for — those fighting for liberty in, say, Central and Southern America. Herbert Wehner, to take an extreme example, travelled to Warsaw in February 1982, there actually to embrace General Jaruzelski, while at the same time circulating to his parliamentary colleagues an appeal from the Bolivian 'consulate in resistance' in West Germany.

Leading Social Democrats were further accused of condoning repression in Poland out of a selfish concern for specifically national interests in the continuation of Ostpolitik in general, and Deutschlandpolitik in particular. They were thus charged with indifference to liberty, hypocrisy and national selfishness. Such criticism came not only from the United States and from the Christian Democratic opposition in Bonn, but also from French and Italian socialists, and finally, when at last they could speak, from Poles who had actually been locked up on 13 December 1981.

The case for the social-liberal line was also made in several different ways, and quite as emotionally as that against it. It was argued that the Polish state of war was a lesser evil. Helmut Schmidt recalls that he felt 'great relief' that it was not a direct Soviet intervention. (Schmidt's first response to martial law and Adenauer's first response to the building of the Berlin Wall had this in common. In each case the West German leader had feared a worse Soviet action, so his first reaction was of relief as much as outrage.) It was suggested that because of Germany's historical record in Poland, Germans could not be so outspoken in their denunciation of what Poles did to Poles. Schmidt himself cited the imperative of 'reconciliation' as a decisive motive for his own restraint. There was the related argument that external criticism — especially from Germany — would only strengthen the hand of the oppressors. There was also the argument that the food parcels which Germans sent in millions helped the Poles more than sanctions. Beyond this, three main reasons were given for, as Theo Sommer put it in *Die Zeit*, 'wishing success' to Jaruzelski's 'perfectly executed military coup'.

Firstly, the 'destabilisation' in Poland had threatened to upset the whole precarious equilibrium between East and West, possibly even spilling over into neighbouring countries. As Germans had renounced their claim to national unity, for the sake of peace, so the Poles would have to renounce their claim to freedom — in the name of 'the highest priority . . . keeping the peace', as Egon Bahr put it. Preserving world peace, wrote Bahr, was 'even more important than Poland'. So the state of war in Poland was needed to preserve the state of peace in the world.

Secondly, there was the familiar argument that 'stability' was a precondition for internal reform. Only when Poland's rulers felt themselves secure, could they again relax. The Polish leadership's goal, Bahr averred, was 'stability with a moderate continuation of the reform course'. What

Poland needed, said the vice-chairman of the Social Democrats, Hans-Jür-gen Wischnewski, was rather 'the Hungarian model'.

The third reason was: yes, we have to think of our own German interests too, and especially of the interests of the people in East Germany and West Berlin. 'In the GDR,' wrote Klaus Bölling, then Permanent Representative of the Federal Republic in East Berlin,

> people not only understood Schmidt's reticence [in relation to Poland], they were also grateful for the fact that he was among the minority in the West who thought ahead. The citizens in the GDR could easily imagine that after a bloodbath in Poland a long period of the peace of the graveyard would come in Eastern Europe and the GDR, that we, the Germans in both states, might perhaps have to wait a whole decade before we could talk to one another again.

One of the best West German journalistic observers of the GDR put the underlying compulsion very plainly: 'Bonn depends on the Soviet Union, so far as these 19 million compatriots are concerned.' (19 million being 17 million in the GDR plus 2 million in West Berlin.)

These three main reasons were all expressed in terms of one key-word: stability. As we have seen already in the discussion of Deutschlandpolitik, that word was used in several, different but conflated senses. Here we had stability as world peace; stability as precondition for reform; and stability as the permissive function for Deutschlandpolitik. Now anyone who followed the German political discussion in the early 1980s could be in no doubt that many West Germans believed that world peace was endangered. The high-point of Solidarity in Poland was also the high-point of the peace movement in Germany. And anyone who talked to German policy-makers at this time would have little doubt that they believed the 'Hungarian way' (or, indeed, the GDR way) was a better path to liberalisation in Eastern Europe. The genuineness of these opinions need not be doubted. But they were just that: opinions. Opinions differ.

Since the West had made it perfectly clear (since 1961, at the very latest) that it would not intervene militarily in Eastern Europe even if the Soviet Union did, 'world peace' was not directly threatened by developments in Poland. To be sure, these would increase tensions between the nuclear-armed superpowers. Yet it was the repression of Solidarity, not the 'instability' associated with its toleration, that most sharply increased those tensions. As for the judgement about the best path to internal liberalisa-tion: many people disagreed. Above all, most Poles disagreed. Did the Poles not know what was good for the Poles? These two claims thus turn out, on a little closer examination, to be highly questionable, analytically as well as morally.

There remains the third reason: national interest. This everyone could see: internees in Poland as well as policymakers in Paris, London and

Washington. Some at that time said that the first and second arguments were merely decorative wrapping for the third, that of hard national interest. But that was too simple a view. The problem lay deeper. So intrinsic and habitual was the conflation of European and, indeed, global interests with national interests in the language of Ostpolitik that many of its own advocates were scarcely capable of distinguishing the one from the other.

Take, for example, the argument that as the Germans had renounced their claim to unity in the interests of peace, so the Poles must renounce their claim to freedom in the higher interest of peace. If one looks at the history of German Ostpolitik in the 1960s and 1970s it is perfectly clear that the (West) Germans had not renounced their claim to unity. They had not done so at the formal-legal level. The Preamble to the Basic Law remained sacrosanct, and was reinforced by the Letter on German Unity. They had not done so at the political-operational level. The whole Deutschlandpolitik was an attempt to keep the nation and the people together, pending more favourable external circumstances. Much of Ostpolitik was an attempt to create those more favourable external circumstances. It was those favourable conditions, finally, which Solidarity was seen to threaten. The real logic of the third argument (stability as permissive function) was thus the opposite of the ostensible logic (or morality) of this first one. The real logic was rather: the Poles must curb their claim to freedom in order that the Germans might continue to pursue their claim to unity.

Polish and German interests therefore conflicted. This was hardly new. So long as there had been nations in Europe their interests had conflicted, especially those of neighbours, and nowhere more so than in Central Europe. This did not suddenly cease to be the case after 1945, although in Western Europe those conflicts were now mediated without the use of force.

The singular feature of this crisis was not the clash of Polish and German national interests. It was rather the reluctance to admit — or perhaps inability to see — that it was national interests that were clashing. This reluctance — or inability — took two forms. On the one hand, the German national interest (stability as permissive function) was conflated with a general human interest (stability as world peace), a European interest (stability as precondition for détente), and even an alleged Polish interest (stability as condition for reform). Political, analytical and moral arguments were rolled into one. On the other hand, Solidarity's claim to represent the Polish national interest was questioned. After all, Jaruzelski said he had imposed martial law in the national interest.

There was a genuine difficulty here. When all three main parties in the democratically elected Bundestag agreed that a continuation of the Deutschlandpolitik — as outlined above — was in the national interest, then it clearly was in the national interest. Nations define their own interests. But in Poland in 1981 there was fundamental disagreement between the main political forces about what was in the national interest. Who was right? Who was representative? Even the most sympathetic Social Democrats felt that at this moment General Jaruzelski and Deputy Prime Minister Rakowski could not simply be assumed to represent the Polish nation. So they called in aid . . . the Catholic Church. 'I shall very much follow the judgement of the Catholic Church and the Vatican,' said the Social Democrats' vice-chairman, Hans-Jürgen Wischnewski.

The disagreement about who 'spoke for Poland' and what was ultimately in the Polish 'national interest' could not, by definition, be finally 'resolved' one way or the other: although the fact that in 1981 Solidarity had ten million members, and the fact that in 1989 the Solidarity list won an overwhelming majority in free parliamentary elections, may be taken as important indicators. The point is simply to illustrate the difficulty — and the conflict.

Now it may be objected that this case was extreme. Indeed it was. The truth is also to be found by studying the extremes. One must, however, keep this extreme in perspective. Measured by the standard of conflict-free, harmonious co-operation that German Ostpolitik set itself, it was very grave. Measured by the pre-1945 standard of conflict between European nation-states, and above all by the pre-1945 standard of conflict between Germans and Poles, it was extraordinarily mild. It was, after all, essentially a matter of words. In actual deeds, the only substantial difference was over economic sanctions, and in that argument the country most outspoken in support of Solidarity — France — was on the side of the Federal Republic.

Words mattered — especially, as Havel reminded his audience in the Paulskirche in Frankfurt, in would-be totalitarian states, and most especially when such states were attempting 'normalisation'. Words were therefore important instruments of Western policy, not to be taken lightly. Yet even the muted and contorted assertions we have discussed were far from being unchallenged inside the West German body politic. Rather they were the subject of acute and agonised controversy.

In his response to Chancellor Schmidt in the Bundestag debate on 18 December 1981, the then opposition leader Helmut Kohl said:

> When a freely-founded union, a union movement that enjoys the broad sympathy of the country, is repressed by brutal terror, when tens of thousands, many tens of thousands, are put in concentration camps — let us use this term which God knows also through German guilt has become the word for such things — , when people are murdered and shot for their convictions — then, Mr Federal Chancellor, one must justify why one behaves this way rather than that . . . Surely you don't seriously believe that any Polish citizen would think

we were intervening in the internal affairs of the proud Poles, if we protest today against the injustice that is taking place there. They are waiting for the word of sympathy from us.

It would, however, be quite wrong to reduce this to a party-political difference. The main line of policy in this period was set by the Social Democrat, Helmut Schmidt, and he maintained it for the remaining few months of his Chancellorship. One strand of this broader line was then developed, indeed, taken to an extreme, by the foreign policy leadership of the Social Democrats in opposition (see Chapter Six). But the Foreign Minister in the new Kohl government as in the old Schmidt one was the Free Democrat, Hans-Dietrich Genscher. There was a profound continuity of policy through the change of government, reflecting much deeper, underlying national interests and perceptions. When Franz Josef Strauss visited Poland in the summer of 1983, his verdict on the Jaruzelski regime was of almost social-liberal politeness.

'Normalisation' à la Husák inside Czechoslovakia had been a precondition for 'normalisation' à la Brandt in West Germany's relations with the Soviet Union, Eastern Europe, and, especially, East Germany. Now 'normalisation' à la Jaruzelski in Poland was seen as a condition for the further 'normalisation' of West Germany's relations with the Soviet Union, Eastern Europe, and, above all, East Germany. To be sure, it was hoped that Jaruzelski's 'normalisation', or 'stabilisation', would be as civilised as possible, and would lead on to 'reform', but this was not the first reason for desiring it. In the spectrum of Western policies, and within the frameworks of Western policy co-ordination, the Federal Republic was the major power that showed most understanding of, and sympathy for, Jaruzelski's position and policies. As a German diplomat closely involved at that time observes, the Federal government led the way in the restoration of trade, in arguing for an early IMF membership for Poland (un-linked to political conditions), and in pushing for what he calls, in a characteristic phrase, 'the renormalisation of political contacts'.

If this policy did not bear more fruit for Polish-German inter-state relations in the mid-1980s, it was not for want of trying by the Bonn government. In the autumn of 1984 a planned visit by Hans-Dietrich Genscher was called off at twelve hours' notice. The reasons for the cancellation were instructive. On the one hand, Genscher had proposed to lay a wreath at the grave of the Solidarity priest, Father Jerzy Popiełuszko, murdered by secret police officers just a few weeks earlier. Following the precedent set by the British Foreign Office minister, Malcolm Rifkind, this was a clear symbolic gesture of recognition for Solidarity, agreed as part of a larger Western, and particularly West European, approach. On the other hand, he proposed to lay a wreath at the grave of a German soldier killed in one of the World Wars. The Polish authorities objected to both proposed gestures with almost equal vehemence.

The Foreign Minister's official visit did not then take place until January 1988. This initiated a round of very difficult negotiations, plagued by old-new conflicts about the frontier question, reparations, credits, and the position of the German minority. These difficulties stretched out the negotiations so long that, despite a real interest in an earlier date on the part of the Bonn government, Chancellor Kohl's first official visit took place only in November 1989. It was therefore more by good luck than by design that his partner for this meeting was the non-communist, Catholic, former Solidarity adviser, Tadeusz Mazowiecki, rather than the former communist, stalwart opponent of Solidarity, and co-architect of martial law, Mieczysław F Rakowski.

Poland was the most vivid, but by no means the sole example of these priorities. Equally serious efforts were made to improve ('normalise'?) relations with Husák's Czechoslovakia, despite the internal policy of the regime. With Hungary, it was easier to argue that support for government policy was also support for 'reform' and 'liberalisation'. Yet even here there was a considerable difference between the judgements made by West German — but not, of course, only West German — policymakers about the policies and intentions of those in power, and the judgements made by the small democratic opposition in the country itself, by independent intellectuals, and then by the majority of the people in free elections.

One notable example was the Bonn government's guarantee for a DM 1 billion loan to the Hungarian government, given on the occasion of a visit to Bonn by the then Prime Minister, the communist Károly Grósz, in October 1987. This loan helped ease an acute debt-service crisis for the Hungarian government. The Bonn government portrayed this as a contribution to further 'reform'. Not only Hungarian dissidents, not just respected reform economists, but even Grósz's successor as Prime Minister, Miklós Németh, would beg to differ. 'We spent two thirds of it on interest,' Németh subsequently noted, 'and the remainder importing consumer goods to ease the impression of economic crisis.' To import consumer goods to ease the impression of economic crisis was a political soft option which delayed the necessary economic (and political) reform rather than contributing to it.

The loan guarantee could, however, clearly be justified in terms of German national goals. In return, the Federal Republic was able to open a cultural institute (a Goethe Institute by another name), despite the fierce objections of the GDR, and the Hungarian government promised to treat the country's small German minority even better than it did already. As we have seen, this was also intended as a signal to other Soviet bloc states. What is more, this clearly contributed to that gradual change in the attitude of the Hungarian leadership which culminated in the crucial opening of the Hungarian-Austrian frontier for East Germans in September 1989. The direct contribution to desirable economic and political change inside Hungary was, however, at best minimal and at worst negative.

If one looks beyond governments to ask who in the West helped sustain the democratic opposition groups in Hungary and Czechoslovakia, and the broad Solidarity and post-Solidarity opposition movement in Poland, through the 1980s, the record is also complex — not least because such sustenance was necessarily discreet, and even conspiratorial, as well as coming from the most diverse sources. Often disproportionate amounts of help came from relatively marginal groups and eccentric individuals, by no means necessarily in the largest countries of the West. But of the major Western states, America was in the first place, and West Germany was still, in this particular respect, in the last.

This was true of those meetings of Western visitors with opposition leaders, so important in the symbolic politics of East Central Europe. Here the Americans and, to a lesser extent, the British led, others followed. (When the Christian Democrats' foreign policy spokesman Volker Rühe wanted to meet with opposition leaders in Hungary in 1988, the German embassy had to ask the American embassy for the right addresses.) It was true of the publicly proclaimed support for the democratic oppositions, their cause and their values, in the speeches and statements of Western politicians. In these two respects, as we shall see, the Social Democrats in opposition were not more bold than the Christian and Free Democrats in power, but actually more timid — indeed, programmatically so.

It was true of support for the Helsinki human rights monitors from Helsinki committees in the West. (The West German committee was established only in 1984 and remained largely decorative.) Last but by no means least, it was true also of finance. For obvious reasons, the financing of opposition activities in Eastern Europe was veiled in secrecy, disinformation and (not least) confusion. But the currency of that finance was dollars. No West European country had anything to compare with the American National Endowment for Democracy. While German companies and banks led the field in trade, credits, joint ventures, technology, while German foundations were second to none in financing official academic and cultural exchanges, they were nowhere when it came to supporting genuinely independent, let alone explicitly oppositional, activities. It is hard to say how far these would have survived without the dollars poured in, partly through Western Europe, by American foundations. One single American, George Soros, with his extraordinary network of foundations devoted to promoting the Popperian idea of an open society, probably put more money into sustaining the democratic opposition in Eastern Europe than all German sources together. And as Eduard Shevardnadze would later observe: 'you cannot have democracy without an opposition — an opposition that can take power in a democratic way'.

All this is not an indictment. As we have seen, Western Europe in general, and West Germany in particular, made a larger contribution in other ways. West Germany had special interests and special dependencies. But individual Germans and other West Europeans may ask themselves why they did not do more; why, four decades after the end of the war in Europe, so much that was crucial to overcoming the division of Europe was still done from America and by Americans, whether officially, semi-officially or unofficially. At the very least, it is a matter of historical justice to give credit where credit is due. Among the major Western countries, the largest part of the credit for the direct sustenance of those who actually led the revolutions of 1989 belongs to the United States of America.

Towards the end of the decade, leading German policymakers did begin to question, or at least to redefine, the 'stability commandment'. In 1988 Chancellery Minister Wolfgang Schäuble wrote of the need for 'a new stability' in the GDR. Speaking more generally of Soviet and East European reforms, the CDU's foreign policy spokesman, Volker Rühe, observed in November 1988 that stability could only be achieved through change, not vice versa.

Finally, even Hans-Dietrich Genscher declared in a speech to mark the opening of an office of the Free Democrats' party foundation, the Friedrich Naumann Foundation, in Budapest on 9 June 1989, that 'the process of reform demands the insight in East and West that frequently instabilities must be allowed for, to permit change towards a stability of higher value. A new stability, resting on democracy, freedom and justice, on openness and plurality in politics, the economy, culture and society.' Genscher went on, repeating a phrase that he had used so many times before: 'We do not want a destabilisation of our eastern neighbours'. This time, however, he added: 'we want them, through the rule of law, pluralism and co-determination (*Mitbestimmung*), to win, instead of forced stability, stability on the basis of trust . . .' But in that case, what kind of stability had he been talking about for the last fifteen years?

Writing at this same moment, in early summer 1989, the distinguished historian Hans-Peter Schwarz, himself a Christian Democrat, made the following very pertinent observation:

Not only Social Democrats have allowed themselves to be persuaded by the nomenklatura in Prague, Warsaw, Moscow and East Berlin, that peace in Europe is only secure when the inner order of these countries remains basically unchanged. To be sure, one declares reforms and liberalisation to be desirable, but one is neither courageous nor principled enough to recognise, and — albeit quietly — to work towards that fundamental change of system which must be the long-term goal — if only because the population in these countries increasingly want it.

One might perhaps argue about who persuaded whom that European peace depended on the continuation of the communist system in East Central Europe, external 'stabilisation' on internal 'stabilisation', 'normalisation' on 'normalisation': for German policymakers surely persuaded themselves as much as they were persuaded, and in some cases supplied this argument to Soviet and East European leaders rather than receiving it from them. One might marginally question the word 'increasingly': for it was not exactly for lack of wanting a fundamentally different system that the people of Poland or Czechoslovakia or Hungary or East Germany had not had it for forty years. But the basic point is very well taken.

'There are more things in heaven and earth, Horatio, than are dreamt of in your philosophy.' Like the unfinished Polish revolution of 1980-81, the revolutions of 1989 — including that in East Germany — were not dreamt of in the philosophy of Ostpolitik. These revolutions were dreamt of in the philosophy of that banned and persecuted writer who in October 1989 was prevented by the highest Czechoslovak authorities from travelling to Frankfurt to receive the Peace Prize of the German Book Trade, and in December 1989 became, himself, the highest Czechoslovak authority.

Reconciliation

Historic events are often fixed in our minds by one symbolic image, and in the late twentieth century that image is usually a photograph. The German invasion of Poland is those soldiers jovially lifting the frontier barrier. The Warsaw ghetto is that one terrified little boy being forced out of the cellars at gunpoint, with his hands in the air. The Hungarian revolution of 1956 is the boots from the toppled statue of Stalin. Prague 1968 is a tank in Wenceslaus Square. And German Ostpolitik? For many people around the world, Ostpolitik is Willy Brandt falling to his knees before the monument to the heroes of the Warsaw ghetto.

No one who has read the record of German Ostpolitik, watched and listened to its makers, can doubt for one moment that a genuine motive and goal of that policy was reconciliation. Making good past damage. Healing wounds. This was obviously, archetypically, true of Willy Brandt. But it was no less true, indeed at a deeper level it was perhaps even more true, of those like Helmut Schmidt and Richard von Weizsäcker who had actually fought on the eastern front. In a real sense, this was the mission of a generation. Helmut Kohl, although enjoying what he called 'the blessing of a late birth' — that is, being too young to have fought in the war — often stated his wish to achieve with Poland the kind of historic reconciliation that Adenauer had achieved with France.

The work of reconciliation with the East had not been pioneered by the politicians. In the so-called Tübingen Memorandum of 1962, a group of prominent Protestants declared themselves, for moral as much as political reasons, in favour of recognising the Oder-Neisse line. Richard von Weizsäcker recalls this as the moment at which he himself first became deeply engaged in discussions of Ostpolitik. The (then still all-German) organisation of the Protestant Church in Germany planted a further landmark with its 1965 report on 'the situation of the expellees and the relationship of the German nation to its eastern neighbours', as did the country's Catholic bishops with their response to a powerful letter from the Polish bishops in the same year.

'In spite of everything,' wrote the Polish bishops, 'in spite of this situation burdened almost hopelessly by the past, or rather just because of this situation . . . we cry out to you: let us try to forget! No polemics, no more Cold War . . .' And in a famous phrase, which earned them a torrent of abuse from the communist regime, the Polish bishops concluded: 'We forgive and ask for forgiveness.' 'We, too, ask to forget, yes, we ask to forgive,' replied the German bishops. Many individual writers, historians, young Christians in the so-called *Aktion Sühnezeichen*, young Social Democrats with their pioneering trips to Eastern Europe: all had prepared the way. But with Willy Brandt, those intellectual and moral impulses were taken up into the policy of the Federal government.

In this, he enjoyed the support of many of the country's best-known intellectuals, and perhaps most symbolically of Günter Grass, the great memorialist of German-Polish Danzig. At his own request, Grass actually accompanied the Chancellor to Warsaw in December 1970. In a letter written immediately afterwards, he thanked Willy Brandt for the privilege of being with him, and — in a striking and curious formulation — 'for the immediate gain of this journey: being allowed to be moved (*betroffen sein zu dürfen*)'.

'We must,' Brandt said in his television address from Warsaw, '. . . recognise morality as a political force.' A resonant formula, but, like all invocations of morality, not easy to translate into the practical policy of states. The problems of so doing were illustrated by the imprecise and shifting terms in which the makers of Ostpolitik defined this goal. The two German words for reconciliation — *Versöhnung* and *Aussöhnung* — are heavy with both emotional and religious overtones, containing in their root the word *Sühne*, meaning expiation, penance, atonement, and evoking the image, if not of 'God and sinners reconciled', then at least of two individual human beings falling tearfully into each others' arms. Yet German policymakers also used, in various combinations, and seemingly almost interchangeably, such terms as *Verständigung* (literally 'understanding' or 'coming to an understanding'), *gute Nachbarschaft* (good-neighbourliness), *friedliche Kooperation, friedliche Zusammenarbeit* (both meaning peaceful co-operation), *Ausgleich* (which implies a settlement based on the reconciliation or balancing of conflicting interests), *Entspannung* (for reconciliation might also be defined as the relaxation of historic tensions), and *Frieden* or *Friede* (peace), itself a term laden with emotional and religious overtones.

'We want to be a nation (*Volk*) of good neighbours', said Willy Brandt in his Government declaration in 1969. 'The social-liberal coalition,' said Helmut Schmidt in his farewell state of the nation address, 'has, with its treaty- and reconciliation-policy towards the eastern neighbours, created the second pillar, the necessary addition [to Adenauer's Western ties] for peaceful neighbourliness in all directions.'

The sentiments are admirable. The general message is clear. But the specific application was fraught with difficulties. For a start, there was the lapse of time: a quarter of a century between, as it were, the quarrel and the reconciliation. Of course one might argue that this passage of time was necessary for it to be possible at all. How could a German-Polish reconciliation, including a recognition of the Oder-Neisse line, possibly have been made in, say, 1950, when nearly one in every five citizens of the new Federal Republic had just fled or been expelled from the East? 'Time heals all wounds.' Yet clichés can mislead. For time also seals in old gunshot, which festers under the skin. It nurtures old grievances while repressing old guilt.

Were the psychological conditions for a reconciliation with Poland, Czechoslovakia or the Soviet Union actually so much worse in the 1950s than in the 1970s? To be sure, there was then the immediacy of bitter resentment among millions of expellees. Yet there was also the freshness of memory and the immediacy of shame. Freya von Moltke, widow of the German resistance hero Helmuth James von Moltke, recalls:

> We lived until 1945 in Kreisau, Kreis Schweidnitz, Silesia. Then we had to leave. That was not easy. But we knew already that the land would in future belong to the Poles . . . What I want to report is this: my husband, Helmuth James von Moltke, an active opponent of the Nazis for ages, and who lost his life in that struggle in January 1945 — he was condemned to death and executed — already foresaw in the middle of the war that the Germans would lose Silesia. 'The only question is, whether Silesia will go to Poland or the Czechoslovak Republic. For that we have to thank Hitler!' he said. It is very important for peace in Europe that the Germans have no illusions. That Silesia now belongs to the Poles is a direct result of Hitler's war and Hitler's rule of terror. One can not blame it on the allies. The blame is Hitler's.

And if that is put aside as the judgement of one highly untypical

German, consider the testimony of an anonymous German woman from Landeshut (now Kamienna Gora) in Lower Silesia. Writing in 1951, she recalls a day in 1946 when she was hauled off by the new Polish police to dig up the half-decomposed corpses of concentration camp victims. She describes in harrowing detail this appalling work; how she cried with horror and could not even wipe away the tears; and then suddenly she says: 'so stop crying, be brave and thus help in the work of atonement (*Sühneleistung*) for the crimes that had been done in our nation (*in unserem Volk*)'.

Of course there is no way of knowing whether the noble spirit of the Kreisau Moltkes, and the moving spirit of that one anonymous woman, personally mistreated, driven out of her homeland, yet still, in 1951, as it were mentally standing up for the work of atonement — whether those spirits might have made a reconciliation with Poland or Czechoslovakia subjectively possible for West Germany in the 1950s. For the Sovietisation of Eastern Europe and the Cold War made it objectively impossible.

What one can say, however, is that when the work of official reconciliation finally began twenty years later, it was now closely intertwined with the goals of perceived national interest on the one hand, and with domestic party-political controversy on the other. In agreeing large reparations payments to Israel in the early 1950s, Konrad Adenauer was restoring German 'honour', to use his own language, and seeking a 'purification of the soul'. He certainly expected — rightly — that this would also work to the general advantage of the Federal Republic in the world, but it was unthinkable that there should be any direct *quid pro quo*. While the moral and emotional elements were clearly important in the reconciliation with France in the late 1950s and early 1960s, the national interest — of both sides — was more plainly to the fore. In the relationship with Poland, as it developed in the late 1960s and early 1970s, the motif of reconciliation was from the outset entangled with the pursuit of other, direct German interests, in a context of domestic political controversy.

Here, for example, is Willy Brandt in his 1971 state of the nation address: 'In the relationship with Poland, too, we have in mind the German interest in the broadest sense, when we do what we can so that the German name can no longer be used as a symbol of injustice and horror, but rather counts as a sign for the hope of reconciliation and peaceful co-operation. That this hope is not in vain may also be seen by the number of Germans who will come to the Federal Republic over the next months.' Thus at home even Willy Brandt could equate 'reconciliation' with German emigration. We have seen already the same fateful entanglement in the 1975 package of agreements with Poland. Was it cash for Germans or a down-payment on forgiveness? And right through the 1980s the three elements — money, reconciliation, direct German interests

— were continually muddled up together in all official German-Polish dealings, and further confused by the domestic political context.

In an 'open letter to all Germans who wish to work for German-Polish reconciliation', written in 1982, the Polish critic Jan Józef Lipski observed that it would be 'favourable for a future reconciliation and friendship' if 'each should make the reckoning with their own guilt, and rather with their own than with the other's'. A familiar observation, you might think. 'Why beholdest thou the mote that is in thy brother's eye, but considerest not the beam that is in thine own eye?' as St Matthew had put it a few years earlier. Reconciliation consists in people saying 'I'm sorry for what I did' not 'I'm sorry for what *you* did'. But what might be feasible for individual human beings in relation to each other — although difficult enough even for them — was far more difficult for political leaders in the Federal Republic. They had to consider not only the unreconciled or unrepentant element in their electorate, but also the much larger number of Germans who considered that they were themselves in some sense victims of Hitler's (and Stalin's) crimes.

So again and again in official statements by the highest representatives of the Federal Republic, throughout the 1970s and 1980s, one finds the reference to Polish or Soviet or Czech suffering at German hands swiftly followed by the statement that of course the Germans suffered too. Thus, in a July 1989 declaration, Chancellor Kohl recalled that in the last war 'terrible things' (*Fürchterliches*) were done in the name of Germany and by German hands, especially to the Polish people. We neither wish nor may forget this,' he went on, 'but just as little may we forget that later bad things (*Schlimmes*) were done to Germans by Poles.'

President von Weizsäcker was widely regarded as more sensitive and adept in these matters, and his speech on the fortieth anniversary of the end of the war in Europe was a masterpiece of facing up to the German past in the spirit suggested by Lipski, and before him by the gospels. Yet even Richard von Weizsäcker did not entirely avoid the trope. In a message to the Polish President, General Jaruzelski, on the fiftieth anniversary of the German attack on Poland, the Federal President began by spelling out the terrible sufferings of Poland at German hands: 'The consequences of war and war crimes which the whole Polish nation has to bear are without parallel. But we Germans too,' he continued, 'were heavily marked by the war. We found that injustice and suffering struck back against our own nation, in whose name they had occurred. The heavy human losses, the destruction of Dresden and many other towns was followed by the expulsion of millions of Germans from their native homeland and, with the division of Europe, the division of our own nation and capital. Terrible wounds have been struck against each other . . .'

The President's and the Chancellor's words were chosen with painful care. Germans did *Fürchterliches* to Poles; Poles did only *Schlimmes* to

Germans. Injustice and suffering 'struck back'. Yet one is still moved to question. What had the Poles to do with the destruction of Dresden? Who suffered more from the division of Europe — the Germans or the Poles? Did the record of German-Polish relations really justify the symmetrical assertion 'terrible wounds have been struck against each other'? The point here is not to argue about any particular formulation. The point is that once the politician attempts to make such a summary historical reckoning — your suffering, our suffering, our guilt, your guilt — he is already lost. As the West German *Historikerstreit* (historians' dispute) around precisely such issues amply demonstrated, even independent scholars have difficulty in detaching comparative historical judgment from moral relativisation and hence at least implicit apologetics.

But a Federal President or Chancellor was in a far worse position than the independent scholar. He was compelled to simplify. He had to think all the time of preserving domestic political consensus as well: of, so to speak, internal reconciliation. And then — for even Federal Presidents are human — he too would have the personal need to be reconciled with his country's and his own past. Thus even with such a sensitive, thoughtful and liberal speaker as Richard von Weizsäcker, one did not ultimately know whether what was being sought was the reconciliation of Germans with Poles, of Germans with Germans, or of the speaker with himself. All three at once? But each reconciliation had slightly different requirements. As elsewhere in German Ostpolitik, so here in miniature, the attempt to pursue several divergent goals simultaneously — almost literally 'in the same breath' — resulted in dissonance rather than the longed-for harmony.

There was a further problem with the whole enterprise of, so to speak, governmental reconciliation. This was that governments had to deal with governments — which, in the case of the Soviet Union and Eastern Europe inevitably meant with communist rulers. But these communist rulers were not elected representatives of their peoples. Indeed they were generally in more or less acute conflict with the aspirations of their own peoples. If one sought reconciliation with these rulers, this did not necessarily help reconciliation with their subjects.

The most sensitive case in this respect was, once again, Poland. The problem of pursuing reconciliation with rulers to whom their own people did not wish to be reconciled was illustrated at the very outset. Brandt made the Warsaw Treaty with Gomułka — and within weeks the Polish people deposed that same Gomułka. Schmidt then pursued reconciliation with Gierek. His affection for, and grave misjudgement of, Edward Gierek are amply documented. He would, he said, 'take him straight into the cabinet'. When he sent Gierek a telegram congratulating him on the election of a Polish Pope, one might already detect a certain confusion. But when, on the evening before martial law was declared in Poland, we find

Schmidt asking Erich Honecker to use his good offices with the Polish authorities on behalf not of Solidarity but of Edward Gierek, then the confusion would have seemed to most Poles to go beyond a joke.

In defending his government's refusal to join in American-led sanctions against Poland and the Soviet Union, following the imposition of martial law, Schmidt directly confronts this issue. His 'specifically German motive' for not joining in these sanctions was, he writes in his memoirs, precisely the deep-seated desire for reconciliation. 'Reconciliation was a decisive motive for Willy Brandt's — and later my — Ostpolitik.' This meant dealing with the governments.

> 'Whoever as a German wanted to come to an understanding with Poland had to make treaties with the actual government in Warsaw — whether with Gomułka, Gierek, Kania or Jaruzelski. Any West German attempt to drive wedges between the Polish people and its (sic) government, to say friendly words to the former but to refuse help to the latter, was not only bound to fail; it would also supply the communist propagandists in Warsaw with arguments against the alleged 'German revanchism'.

Furthermore, sanctions would hurt the man in the street, not the rulers. Therefore he encouraged ordinary West Germans to send food parcels instead.

One cannot doubt the sincerity of his argument. The millions of food parcels sent by ordinary West Germans, with extraordinary speed, efficiency and generosity, were widely appreciated in Poland as gestures of humanitarian aid. As we have seen, Schmidt himself had declared in the Bundestag that he stood 'with all his heart' on the side of the Polish workers. Yet that was not the message that got through to the Polish workers and Solidarity activists in the internment camps. Quite the reverse. From the reported statements of leading West German politicians — and particularly of leading Social Democrats –, and from summaries of German commentaries, they got the impression rather of a sigh of relief. At least the Russians had not invaded. General Jaruzelski was probably a patriot. The German-German détente could continue. *L'ordre règne à Varsovie*.

A Catholic intellectual deeply committed to the Polish-German dialogue, Kazimierz Wóycicki, recalls his own experience in an internment camp at this time. High up in the corner of his cell was a loudspeaker, which could not be turned off. It spewed out official accounts of Western reactions to martial law in Poland. These praised especially the West German reactions: their good sense, their understanding of Polish realities, of the patriot Jaruzelski. 'We did not believe it,' writes Wóycicki,

> for we had other ways of keeping ourselves informed. In one of the cells there

was, as a hidden treasure, a transistor radio on which we could pick up more than just the official propaganda. But here was the confirmation. The Warsaw newspapers lied, but not entirely. In Germany people felt sorry for the Poles (this sympathy was later expressed in the large-scale sending of parcels) but in political circles one was of the opinion that reason was on the side of Jaruzelski; there would be no Soviet intervention, *so German Ostpolitik was saved.*

'We sat in the cell,' Wóycicki continues,

we were not radicals or professional revolutionaries but simple workers from Piaseczno and Ursus, farmers from the neighbourhood of Warsaw, also a few professors and journalists, and we discussed *at whose expense this German Ostpolitik was to be saved.* When you are in prison you have a lot of time and talk a lot. One of us, a young guy from the Ursus tractor factory, said: 'If they don't understand what our freedom is then they don't understand what their freedom is, and if they don't understand that, then they haven't changed, these *Hitlerowcy.*' We explained to him that one might have all sorts of objections to West German policy, but this last remark was stupid. So far as I can remember he was finally persuaded by the argument that if he described what was after all a democratic government in Bonn like this, he would be playing the tune of communist propaganda. (Emphasis added.)

Here is a circle of tragic irony. Helmut Schmidt believes that Germans should be reticent in their reaction to martial law, out of sense of historical responsibility for Hitlerite crimes, and in order not to furnish arguments for communist propaganda. The result: a simple worker in a prison cell feels the Germans haven't changed, and is only persuaded not to say this out loud by the reflection that this would furnish arguments for communist propaganda.

The misunderstanding was thus very deep. Among the factors that contributed to it on the German side was the previous failure to distinguish sharply enough between state and society in Eastern Europe; a general conviction (building out from the Bahr hypothesis about East Germany) that lasting change would come only 'from above'; and the mistaken belief that one could be friends with everyone, that is, in this case, with the gaoler and the prisoner. There was also one other element, which could not precisely be classed as a misunderstanding. For as the Polish prisoners rightly perceived, there was another 'special German motive' for welcoming the 'internal solution' in Poland. This was the belief that if the Soviets invaded 'everything would be *kaputt*' — where 'everything' meant the continuation of the German Ostpolitik, and especially of the policy towards the GDR, so painstakingly developed over so many years.

The dismay among those on the side of Solidarity in Poland extended also to the very symbol of German-Polish reconciliation: Willy Brandt. 'I must admit,' Adam Michnik wrote in 1984, 'that it made me angry that Willy Brandt had so quickly forgotten how bitter is the taste of that prison food, on which in his youth the German Social Democrats had been fed.' And he ended his article with an appeal to Willy Brandt to come to Poland, not just to shake the hands of 'our Generals and Party Secretaries' but to see the condition of political prisoners, to lay flowers on the memorial to the miners killed in December 1981. Willy Brandt did come to Poland in December 1985, to mark the fifteenth anniversary of the Warsaw Treaty. He shook the hands of the Generals and Party Secretaries. He spoke of reconciliation, peace, normalisation, stability. But he visited no prisons (in one of which he would have found Adam Michnik). He laid no flowers on the murdered workers' graves — nor on that of the martyred Father Popiełuszko. He declined an invitation to meet his fellow Nobel Peace Prize winner, Lech Wałęsa, in Solidarity's capital, Gdańsk.

The final irony of this focus on the Communist rulers was that it was they who were actually least interested in a reconciliation. They clung to the 'German bogey' as almost their last chance of winning popular support. It is, to be sure, far too simple to equate the internal divide — authorities/society — directly with attitudes to Germany. There were those in power who genuinely sought reconciliation and those in opposition who did not. As Primate Glemp demonstrated in his own person, the Church, too, contained elements of both. But as a rule, independent, Catholic and oppositional circles were far ahead of official circles in the quest for a genuine, lasting reconciliation.

It was the Polish Catholic bishops with their courageous message of 1965 — 'We forgive you and ask for your forgiveness' — who had paved the way, and been furiously attacked for it by the communist state. It was a Solidarity intellectual, Jan Józef Lipski, who wrote one of the most generous texts on the subject in 1981, and was again rewarded with a torrent of official abuse. West German historians exercised heroic patience in trying to come to terms with utterly unyielding communist-nationalist historians peddling the party line. Meanwhile, almost unnoticed in West Germany, there were independent scholars who offered far more common ground.

In an emotional message for a 'Day of Solidarity with Poland' on American television in January 1982, Helmut Schmidt declared: 'Germans and Poles have found their way to one another again, after a long history full of suffering. This belongs — like the reconciliation between Germany and France — among the great moral changes in Europe since the Second World War.' This noble statement contained, alas, a large measure of wishful thinking, about both the present and the past. For what did it mean to say that Germans and Poles had found their way to one another again? When were they together before? This implied a rose-tinted view of the German-Polish past worthy of the most nostalgic-utopian literary invocation of Central Europe. The 'normal, good-neighbourly' relations which West Germany had developed with France since the war were quite abnormal in European history: they were unprecedented. If Germany managed to do the same with Poland it would also be a first.

Nor did popular sentiments — of Poles about Germans and of Germans about Poles — entirely bear out this romantic contention, especially if one included among 'Germans' the population of the GDR. To be sure, many thousands of individual people on both sides had left the disputes of their leaders far behind. 'People are often ahead of politics,' as Richard von Weizsäcker wrote in his letter to General Jaruzelski on 1 September 1989, 'and level the path.' Introducing his new government to the Polish parliament later that same month, Poland's first non-communist Prime Minister for more than forty years, Tadeusz Mazowiecki, said almost exactly the same thing: 'We need a breakthrough in our relations with the Federal Republic of Germany. The societies of both countries have already gone much further than their governments.'

For all the complexities and contortions of the Bonn government's 'reconciliation policy', it must certainly be credited not only with permitting but with very substantially encouraging this popular rapprochement: in cultural, scholarly, youth exchanges, in tourism, in the large numbers of East Europeans allowed to visit and often to work in the Federal Republic, in everything that we have described as weaving. If in 1969 it was still possible for communist governments to win support by agitating against 'German revanchism', by 1989 such propaganda was almost entirely ineffective. Yet if the two peoples no longer saw each other as enemies, they were still far from seeing each other as friends. And not just in the older generation.

In a 1981 survey of Warsaw schoolchildren, fifty-six per cent of those asked said they did not like the Germans. Only the Russians, with sixty-five per cent, were more disliked. A majority of Poles and Germans asked in a major survey in 1991 expressed the view that a 'reconciliation was possible'. But this and other surveys also revealed that the two peoples still held a fairly low opinion of each other, by comparison with the view that each separately took of, say, the French or the Americans. Many incidents and conversations, especially in Berlin and the former GDR, revealed a high level of tension between Poles and Germans.

There was thus still a vast distance to travel before one could begin to talk of a (historically abnormal) normality such as prevailed between France and Germany. Some reasons for this have been indicated on both the West German and the Polish sides. The undemocratic nature of the Polish regime had also directly affected the attitudes of the younger generation, through the classroom. As one independent Polish writer put it, young Poles were brought up to believe that patriotism meant hatred of the Germans. In addition there was, even among those in outright opposition to the communist regime in Poland, the phenomenon that we have elsewhere described as the nationalism of the victim. Characteristic of the nationalism of the victim is a reluctance to acknowledge in just measure the sufferings of other peoples, and an inability to admit that the victim can also victimise. This naturally persists so long as the nation continues to be in some sense a victim: which post-Yalta Poland might reasonably consider itself to be.

It is also no accident that anti-Polish sentiments were more rife in the unfree than in the free part of Germany; indeed that national and ethnic resentments were altogether more acute in the unfree than in the free part of Europe. So in this respect, too, the internal aspect of the division of Europe was quite as important as the external aspect. By removing the credibility of the 'German bogey' the Federal Republic helped to facilitate internal change in Poland after 1970. But that internal change was then the *sine qua non* for a further, deeper rapprochement. Only the election in 1989 of a Solidarity prime minister, himself long committed to the work of Polish reconciliation with other nations, at last made that possible.

Shortly after Mazowiecki's election, Chancellor Kohl paid his long-delayed official visit to Poland. This visit was organised as a celebration of reconciliation, in a way that would have been impossible even a few months before. As Adenauer and de Gaulle had met for a High Mass in the cathedral of Rheims, so now the Polish and the German heads of government, Catholics both, would meet for an open-air Mass at the symbolic site of Kreisau — once an island of German resistance to Hitler, now Polish, as Helmuth James von Moltke had foreseen, but soon to be a joint Polish-German centre. After a sermon delivered partly in Polish, partly in German, by the Bishop of Opole (Oppeln), the two leaders would embrace in sign of peace.

Helmut Kohl's carefully prepared symbolic act did not achieve the historic radiation of Brandt's single, bleak, lone gesture. The Chancellor's trip was interrupted by his flying return to Berlin after the opening of the Berlin Wall, and marred by an ill-conceived plan to visit the St Anne Mountain in Silesia, the scene of bitter fighting between Germans and Poles after the First World War. For all that, it was a step forward. A state visit by Richard von Weizsäcker in the early summer of 1990 — the first time in 990 years that a German head of state visited Poland at the Poles' invitation! — reinforced the painful progress. Although negotiations about the frontier and the 'good neighbour' treaties remained fraught and long drawn-out, when both were finally signed and ready for ratification in 1991, Hans-Dietrich Genscher averred that they would break the vicious circle of injustice and new injustice 'once and for all'.

That bold claim reflected understandable but also double-edged sentiments. On the one hand, it expressed satisfaction that a long-pursued, high moral goal of West German policy could finally be said to have been achieved. After the reconciliation with Israel and France, here was the reconciliation with Poland. On the other hand, it signalled a hope that from now on Germans and Poles could talk less about this dark past and more about a brighter future, in peace, harmony and a united Europe. Intoning what was now officially the 'European anthem', Beethoven's choral setting of Schiller's Ode to Joy, they could sing:

> *Unser Schuldbuch sei vernichtet!*
> *Ausgesöhnt die ganze Welt!*

Let our book of guilt be destroyed — and the whole world reconciled!

The accepted pious wisdom was that to be reconciled did not mean in any way to forget that past. Quite the contrary. But when making up after a quarrel we say 'let's forgive and forget'. Forgiving and forgetting are, in real life, more intimately related than is quite comfortable for intellectuals, and especially for historians, to admit. As we have noticed, the Polish bishops in their letter of 1965 explicitly linked the offer to forgive with the offer to forget, a point taken up with what might almost be mistaken for eagerness in the German bishops' response.

The statement 'reconciliation sealed' — mission accomplished! — thus also contains an element of what Franz Josef Strauss once memorably described as Germany 'stepping out . . . from under the shadow of the Third Reich'. This, as liberal historians hasten to point out, is a risky step, because it carries the temptation of artificially shortening the shadow by, so to speak, pruning the history tree that casts the shadow. Yet perhaps in the mid-1990s, half a century after 1945, it would be morally permissible and politically sensible for leaders to talk somewhat less about the bitter past, and somewhat more about a better future? Perhaps at last the conditions had been created in which the past could begin to be past?

Against this hope, some notes of caution must be entered. The record of the two decades following Brandt's great symbolic gesture shows clearly the limits of what politics can achieve in the relations between peoples. Politics and true human reconciliation have quite different time-scales. A British prime minister famously observed that a week is a long time in politics. But in the work of reconciliation, twenty years is a short time. The true unit of measurement is the generation. Moreover, except in very exceptional circumstances — such as arguably did prevail between West Germany and Eastern Europe in the Europe of 'Yalta' — it is doubtful whether reconciliation as such is a credible explicit goal for the foreign policy of a state.

States may create the conditions in which reconciliation can occur. Politicians can give an example. As President von Weizsäcker and then, even more strikingly, President Havel of Czechoslovakia and President Göncz of Hungary demonstrated, there can be such a thing as moral leadership. But at the end of the day, peoples can only be reconciled if the individual people who make up those peoples wish so to be. The ripening of that wish is a very long process. It takes generations.

It is a process, moreover, rooted in freedom. As we have seen, the condition of unfreedom, whether in East Germany, Poland or elsewhere in Eastern Europe, both directly and indirectly hampered and distorted the process. The observation made by one commentator on the occasion of Chancellor Kohl's visit to Poland in November 1989, that reconciliation was 'only just beginning', might seem unduly depressing to those in the free part of Germany who had spent decades working to advance that goal. But it contained more than a grain of hard truth. It has famously been said that no free people can rule over another. One might also say that only free peoples can be truly reconciled.

Moreover, freedom is a necessary but not a sufficient condition. In those reconciliations that may be described as successful there has also been a rough equality, or at least a crude balance of mutual interest, between the partners. This is archetypically true of the Franco-German case. Not only were both states democracies. They also had economies at roughly the same level. Neither people had strong material reasons to look at the other with pronounced contempt or deep envy. Co-operation would be to mutual advantage. And in the 1950s and 1960s each state had a major political interest in the rapprochement. German economic power and political support would underpin France's aspiration to grandeur and a leading role in Europe. French forgiveness, blessing and political support would make a major contribution to Germany's recovery of its self-esteem and a respected place in the world. Together they could shape the European Community. One may argue, according to taste, as to whether reconciliation was the moral and emotional foundation and this the political and economic superstructure built upon it, or vice versa, but either way they were complementary.

In Germany's relations with Poland and Czechoslovakia this has never been so. In the case of the Soviet Union one could argue that in the 'Yalta' period there was a very crude equality or balance of mutual interest. Germany and Russia had indeed, to recall von Weizsäcker's phrase, inflicted terrible wounds upon each other. Each now wanted big things from the other. They could, as it were, say 'quits' and start cutting deals. But after the events of 1989-91, and the end of the Soviet Union, this ceased to be true for Russia as well.

Now all of Germany's neighbours to her east were poor and weak. Economically, the Oder-Neisse line threatened to become a North-South divide on the East-West axis, with all the potential for envy, resentment, tension and contempt that that implied. For Germany, the long-term promise of eastern markets was tempered by the immediate cost of assistance and opening western markets to eastern goods. Politically,

Poland, Czechoslovakia or the states of the former Soviet Union, could offer the new Germany the promise of stability and the threat of instability. But the promised political good was not as substantial as that offered by France in the 1950s and 1960s, while the threatened political bad, though more substantial, was still less so than the threat so coherently and consistently presented by the old Soviet Union.

Thus if one condition for reconciliation, freedom, was present at the beginning of the 1990s in a way it had not been throughout the 'Yalta' period, two others, rough economic equality and political mutuality, were not. To say that 'reconciliation was only just beginning' was plainly an overstatement; but scarcely more so than to say that reconciliation had been finally sealed. The truth lay, as so often, in-between. Some of the conditions for reconciliation had been created, partly as a direct result of the deliberate efforts of German Ostpolitik, partly as a consequence of developments to which it was only a contributory cause. Other, equally important, conditions had yet to be created. The chance to create those conditions lay partly, but again only partly, in the hands of the politicians and citizens of the Federal Republic.

VI

A Second Ostpolitik

Social Democrats in the 1980s

Thus far we have discussed the Ostpolitik of the Federal Republic of Germany. We have concentrated on what persons and parties in power actually did and said in the name of the government and the state. Our subject has been the policy of a state, not the views of groups or individuals. Yet we have found that in this area of policy, and above all when examining German-German relations, it is extremely difficult to draw a clear line between government policy and the wider penumbra of published and public opinion, of opposition parties, the media, academe and intellectuals. All were in some measure actors in Ostpolitik.

To analyse their parts systematically, however, requires other methods. Sweeping generalisations about 'the left', 'the right', 'the intellectuals', and, of course, 'the Germans', supported by selective quotation from a few allegedly typical authors, have their place on the op-ed pages and in the *feuilleton* sections of our leading national and international newspapers. There they contribute to the vigour of political debate, the sharpening of wits and the gaiety of nations. But a serious study of published opinion requires detailed literary criticism, for each individual author is a special case. Nothing is easier and more tempting than to quote a few striking results from public opinion surveys to underpin an argument. But the proper study of public opinion is a specialised craft.

The subject of this chapter — the Ostpolitik of the Social Democrats in opposition, from the autumn of 1982 to the autumn of 1989 — lies somewhere in between the hard reality of government policy and the more elusive realities of published and public opinion. The policy of a party in opposition can never be pinned down as firmly as that of a party in government, because it does not need to be definite, and, indeed, may benefit precisely from being indefinite. Politicians in power have to make real choices, keep promises or break them. Even their words are deeds. Politicians in opposition can — and regularly do — promise more than they can deliver and offer all things to all men. Moreover, except in the immediate discipline of an election campaign, the scope for internal diversity and discord is large. This is particularly true of a party in a federal state, and especially in an area of policy which many leading members of the party consider to be peculiarly theirs. Thus there are times when, and subjects on which, an opposition party does not have anything deserving the name of 'policy'. Even when it does, this policy is not comparable with the policy of a government.

All these reservations apply to the Ostpolitik of the Social Democrats in opposition. Yet for a number of reasons, a study of Ostpolitik cannot ignore it. Firstly, Ostpolitik was very closely identified with the Social Democrats, not just in West German politics but also in both states in Germany and abroad. 'Ostpolitik?' people from Moscow to Milwaukee would say, 'you mean Willy Brandt . . .' Secondly, Brandt, Bahr and their younger colleagues not only developed but actively pursued in their years in opposition what they called a 'second phase of Ostpolitik', a 'second phase of détente policy', or, more casually, a 'second Ostpolitik'.

This consisted not just of speeches and programmes, but of extensive talks with the leaders and ruling communist parties of the Soviet Union and Eastern Europe, resulting in joint communiqués, common papers and even draft treaties. Conceptually, this 'second Ostpolitik' built on and extended certain lines of their own first Ostpolitik, and thus also casts light back on to the earlier period. In operative terms, Brandt's meetings with Gorbachev or the Social Democrats' dialogue with the ruling Socialist Unity Party of East Germany in the 1980s had a real impact on the relations of the Federal Republic with the East.

The beginnings of this second Ostpolitik must be traced back to the last years of the social-liberal coalition, with the coming of what some called the 'second Cold War' and the great debate about 'peace' following Nato's double-track resolution of December 1979. Karsten Voigt, one of the Social Democrats' parliamentary spokesmen on foreign affairs, called for a 'second phase of Ostpolitik' as early as January 1980. Its first distinguishing feature was the focus on security policy. As we have seen, in the first phase of Social Democratic Ostpolitik Willy Brandt and his colleagues had, for a mixture of tactical and strategic reasons, deliberately refrained from making any of those initiatives on security policy which Egon Bahr, for one, considered theoretically desirable and even essential for the long-term realisation of the strategic goals of Ostpolitik.

After the election victory in 1972, Brandt and Bahr had hoped to push ahead first and foremost with conventional force reductions in the centre of Europe. But the talks that came to be known as MBFR got nowhere, while Chancellor Schmidt pursued his own, distinctive security policy based firmly on nuclear deterrence through the Nato alliance and classical precepts of the balance of power. Now, as differences with the Soviet

Union over precisely these issues seemed to be leading rapidly to the end of détente, the time had come to make good what Horst Ehmke would call the 'crucial deficit' of the first phase of Ostpolitik. With an echo of Clausewitz, Bahr would later characterise this second phase as 'the continuation of Ostpolitik in the military field'. Security, he would write, 'is the key to everything'.

The development of these new ideas was carried forward by a younger generation inside the party, with figures such as Karsten Voigt, Oskar Lafontaine, Andreas von Bülow and Hermann Scheer playing a prominent part. It was also clearly influenced by the growth of a large extra-parliamentary peace and ecological movement in West Germany. Here were hundreds of thousands of young people with voices that made headlines and votes that might be cast for the Social Democrats — or not, as the case might be. Yet the sharpest and arguably still the most potent formulation of the new security policy, or security Ostpolitik, came from an old man in a hurry.

Egon Bahr cast, or re-cast, his new-old ideas in his work for the Palme Commission in 1980–81. By his own account, it was in May 1981 that he first 'ventured' to formulate the view that 'security can now only be achieved in common. No longer against each other but only with each other shall we be secure.' This bold notion of 'common security' between East and West, to be achieved by means such as nuclear-weapon free zones, then became the leitmotif of the Palme Commission report, finally published in May 1982.

At about the same time, the Social Democrats — or at least, a very large number of them — parted company with their own Chancellor on the Nato missile issue, at the Munich party conference in April 1982. (Recalling the famous cartoon of Bismarck, on his resignation, as a pilot leaving the ship, wits observed that here the ship was leaving the pilot.) In attempting to defend his policy, Schmidt spoke in Munich of the need for a 'security partnership' with the Soviet Union, a term which he himself appears to have coined in 1978. Preserving a facade of unity, Egon Bahr, now appointed to chair a working group on 'New Strategies', respectfully referred to the Chancellor's formula of 'security partnership'. But a specialist close to Bahr clearly spells out the fundamental difference between 'security partnership' à la Schmidt and 'common security' à la Bahr. The former was a formula for arms control and arms reductions on the basis of deterrence. The latter was intended to replace deterrence, as Bahr himself wrote in a Festschrift for the Protestant peace philosopher (and brother of the President) Carl-Friedrich von Weizsäcker.

Like Bahr's own Conception C in his planning staff paper of 1968, the new notion of 'common security' clearly envisaged going beyond Nato and Warsaw Pact to a new European security system, called, of course, a 'European peace order'. Indeed, the new ideas on European security developed by leading Social Democrats in the 'peace debate' of the early 1980s contained substantial elements of earlier Social Democratic plans for European security from the 1950s — before the party's Godesberg programme and full acceptance of Adenauer's Western ties — , and more than a smidgen of the ideas of collective security popular on the left in the 1920s and 1930s. However, the superpowers' massive nuclear arsenals and split-second computer decisions gave a new apocalyptic backdrop, which some Protestant theologians would happily embroider.

By the time the Social Democrats were finally catapulted into opposition, in October 1982, their new thinking in this area was thus already far advanced. As not infrequently in the history of political parties (not just, though perhaps especially, those of the left, and by no means only in West Germany) the return to opposition — experienced at once as defeat and liberation — produced an explosion of critical debate and a quest for new ideas, with individual politicians jostling for position and competing for 'profile'. In such periods of ferment, the writings — or at least, the slogans — of political intellectuals are also more likely to be taken up, and so it was here.

This mixed crop was then sifted and ground through the mills of the party, to produce statements by the leadership, conference resolutions, and, for the 1983 and 1987 elections, two documents entitled 'government programme'. These documents were, of course, compromises between different tendencies inside the party, and between what party leaders themselves wanted and what they thought voters would vote for. While these programmatic papers were described as 'party policy' they contained commitments which would have been hard or impossible to reconcile in the real responsibility of government. Finally, there were the actual talks and dealings which leading figures in the party, more or less formally licensed by its leadership, conducted with political actors in Eastern Europe and the Soviet Union, and the documents that emerged from those encounters.

It is this last aspect which was most unusual, and most directly concerns us here. But before concentrating on this actual 'second Ostpolitik', a few words should be said about the prior and accompanying policy debate. The most reams of recycled paper were devoted to security issues. The basic idea of 'common security' was elaborated in the working group on 'new strategies'. The chairman of the party's commission on security policy, Andreas von Bülow, gave his name to a working paper (the so-called 'Bülow paper') which envisaged superpower disengagement from Central Europe by the year 2000, with a territorial militia left to defend West Germany from bunkers and woodland hideouts. Much thought was given to recasting conventional forces so they had a 'structural non-offensive capacity', thus giving 'defensive defence', as opposed to defence based on plans of attack. Two other members of the group profiled themselves with their own books: Hermann Scheer, with a volume entitled *Liberation from the Bomb*, and one of the party's rising stars, Oskar Lafontaine, with a little book revealingly entitled *Fear of the Friends*. The friends in this context meant above all the Americans.

The critical distance, to put it mildly, from the policies of the United States and its military presence in West Germany, found its positive counterpart in the neo-Gaullist concept of the *Selbstbehauptung Europas* — Europe's standing up for itself — or the 'Europeanisation of Europe'. The latter phrase appears to have been coined, or at least brought into wider circulation, by the commentator Peter Bender, who, like Egon Bahr, played an influential part in the formulation of the second as of the first Ostpolitik. In these writings there was a more or less explicit assumption that the past and present roots of Europe's (and, above all, Germany's) current problems lay in the hegemonial position and aspirations of both superpowers. Unless Europe stood up for itself, wrote Hermann Scheer, the European states would be pushed back to the status of 'relative vassals of the superpowers'.

It was in this general context that the slogan of Central Europe — *Mitteleuropa* — was taken up in the Social Democratic discussion. Initially revived by Czech, Hungarian and Polish intellectuals, in the debate about freedom in Eastern Europe rather than that about peace in Western Europe, the term was treated with understandable caution in Germany. If Brandt had initially thought that the word Ostpolitik was poisoned by pre-1945 German usage, then how much more so was the word *Mitteleuropa*, popularised by Friedrich Naumann in his book of 1915. The pioneer of the West German rediscovery of Central Europe as a cultural-historical concept, Karl Schlögel, was careful to disavow the political instrumentalisation of the concept, 'the proclamation of *Mitteleuropa* as goal'.

Peter Bender had fewer reservations. 'The renaissance of *Mitteleuropa*,' he wrote, 'is first a protest against the division of the continent, against the hegemony of Americans and Russians, against the totalitarianism of ideologies.' 'In the desire for détente,' he went on, speaking at a Social Democratic symposium on *Mitteleuropa* in early 1987, 'we have more in common with Belgrade and Stockholm, also with Warsaw and East Berlin, than we do with Paris and London'. Europe, he concluded 'was divided from the margins in; if it grows together again, then from the centre out'. (Some might argue that Europe was actually divided from the centre out: that is, starting with Hitler in Berlin.) Even more explicit and uninhibited was the then executive secretary of the SPD, Peter Glotz, himself born in the German part of Czechoslovakia before the war. 'We must win back *Mitteleuropa*,' he wrote, 'first as a concept, then as a reality.' 'Let us use the concept of *Mitteleuropa*,' he argued elsewhere, 'as an instrument in a second phase of détente policy.'

Going into detail, Glotz suggested a chemical-weapon-free zone embracing the Federal Republic, the GDR and Czechoslovakia; a nuclear-weapon-free corridor comprising the two German states; energy-sharing arrangements among Austria, Czechoslovakia and others; new kinds of tourist agreements; a more intensive *Wandel durch Handel* (change through trade), hindered as little as possible, he added, by 'Dick Perle's CoCom-ideology'; and even a modest Central European UNESCO for the systematic preservation of churches, market squares and houses, and for the restoration of communications inside this 'family of small nations'. (Was Germany small?.) The latter part of this agenda recalls the familiar Ostpolitik leitmotif of weaving.

Some of this would certainly have been acceptable and even attractive to some of those who were reviving the concept of Central Europe across the iron curtain, in Prague, Warsaw and Budapest. Yet a profound tension remained. For the immediate political thrust of the East European revival of the concept was clearly to get further away from the East — meaning above all the Soviet Union — and closer to the West. The political thrust of this German Social Democratic revival of the concept of *Mitteleuropa* was to pull away from the West — or at least, from the Western Alliance and the United States.

Now Social Democrats would immediately say that to distance themselves from what they saw as the mistaken security policy of the United States did not mean pulling away from the West *tout court*. Yet as the hard security discussion shaded into a larger geopolitical one, so the geopolitical shaded into an even more fundamental debate: about values. At just this time the chairman of the party's Commission on Basic Values, Erhard Eppler, was leading an extensive exercise to rewrite the party's basic programme, for after a quarter-century the Godesberg programme was felt to be in need of fundamental revision. Much of this revision concerned issues not directly connected with East-West relations: the position of women, for example, or the growing dangers to the eco-system which, in the view of Eppler and many other Social Democrats, required a fundamental reassessment of our attitude to economic growth. But over all this hung one commandment which was very directly related to Ostpolitik.

That commandment read: nothing is more important than peace. All other values and aspirations had to be subordinated to this. When Karl Kaiser criticised the seeming blindness of many of his fellow Social Democrats to violations of human rights in Eastern Europe, by contrast with their extreme alertness to such violations in, say, Central America, Egon Bahr charged Kaiser with 'lifting ideology on to the same level as peace'. The Social Democrats' new thinking demanded a 'de-ideologisation' of East-West relations, a notion eagerly taken up in Soviet new thinking. This demand was itself, of course, highly ideological. The ideology of de-ideologisation maintained that all the traditional differences of principles and values between West and East — for example, about human rights, the rule of law, freedom — must be subordinated to the requirements of the thing called peace. The authorised version of the new mantra, incorporated into the Social Democrats' 'government programme 1987–1990', ran: 'Peace is not everything, but without peace everything is nothing.' The word 'freedom' is not prominent in Social Democratic documents of this period.

This comprehensive relativisation of traditional Western values in the name of the supreme requirement of peace was, as we have noticed already, particularly apparent in relations with the GDR. The notion of the German-German 'community of responsibility' seems to have originated from the Social Democratic side. It was Social Democratic politicians and publicists who popularised the notion of a 'Peace of Augsburg' or 'Peace of Westphalia' between the two states in Germany, thus implying that the differences between Communism and democracy were little greater than those between Catholicism and Protestantism — just two versions of one faith. And it was, as we shall see, Social Democrats who went furthest in attempting to realise this singular peace.

Needless to say, none of this was undisputed inside the party. But if one looks at the official foreign policy resolutions of successive party conferences, and the two self-styled 'government programmes' of 1983 and 1987, then it is very clear that the trend was towards the increasing acceptance of this loose bundle of goals, mottoes, values and specific proposals. In the 'government programme' of 1983, after chapters on 'social peace' and 'peace with nature', the chapter on foreign policy was headed 'we want peace'. 'Humankind', it modestly began, 'wants peace. The highest goal of our whole policy is the preservation of peace. The SPD,' it went on, 'has never led Germany into a war.' (Had the Christian or Free Democrats?). It then reaffirmed the central importance of the Atlantic Alliance, although stressing the need for the Federal Republic to represent its own special interests within the alliance. ('In the German interest' was one of the party's 1983 election slogans.) The chapter went on to demand negotiations 'with the goal of a security partnership'.

If this still bore the clear imprint of Helmut Schmidt, the Cologne party conference in November 1983 saw the overwhelming rejection of the deployment of Cruise and Pershing II missiles, for which the conservative-liberal majority in the Bundestag was about to vote, and a ringing endorsement of the 'new strategies' proposed by the working group under Egon Bahr's chairmanship. By the 1986 Nuremberg conference, the new thinking was firmly established as party policy. 'The peoples in the East-West conflict will either survive together or perish together,' declared the main resolution on security policy. (That, while the Germans survived together, the people of Afghanistan were perishing separately was a detail too small to impinge on such a grandiose principle.) Consequently, 'the

Europeans in East and West can only survive in a security partnership'. (How they had survived for forty years without one remained mysterious.)

The need of the moment was to 'shape a security partnership in a second phase of détente policy', and for this the two German states had a special responsibility. 'Where the two German states give an example for the road to security partnership,' the resolution added, 'they are not treading a German special path (*Sonderweg*).' The long-term aim, as already affirmed at the 1984 Essen party conference, was 'to create, on the basis of a security partnership of the existing alliances, a European peace order which overcomes these blocs'.

In the 'government programme 1987–1990', prepared for the 1987 federal election with Johannes Rau as candidate for Chancellor, the chapter on foreign policy was headed 'securing peace'. Now, it said, the time had come to 'break the madness of the recently accelerated arms race and begin a second phase of détente policy'. This should include four elements: nuclear and chemical-weapon disarmament in Europe, the stabilisation of conventional forces at a lower level, increased economic ties between Eastern and Western Europe, and the promotion of cultural exchange to enhance the cultural identity of Europe. The aim was a European peace order 'which reaches over and eventually overcomes the power blocs'. The 'community of responsibility' between the two German states had a special part to play in developing this.

The programme went on to make a strong commitment to the further development of the European Community, which, among other things, 'should become a strong second pillar of the Atlantic bridge'. Within the Atlantic alliance, this chapter reiterated, the Federal Republic should be able to realise its own security interests, 'also our interest in common security'. Under the rubric of 'common security' it envisaged the revocation of the 1983 Bundestag resolution on the deployment of Cruise and Pershing II missiles, a chemical-weapon-free zone in Europe, and abrogation of the Kohl government's agreement with the United States on SDI. The Social Democrats' commitment to fight worldwide against violations of human rights was expressed in the concluding section. This, however, was devoted to the Third World.

Shadow policy

The Social Democrats' operative 'second Ostpolitik' consisted in high-level talks, the formation of joint working-groups and the drafting of common documents with the ruling communist parties of the East. This network had a basic geometry which both resembled and shadowed that of governmental Ostpolitik. The most important but not the most intensive contacts were those with the Communist Party of the Soviet Union. The

Moscow connection legitimised and facilitated the most intensive and special ties, with the ruling communist party in the GDR — the self-styled Socialist Unity Party of Germany. Relations with the Polish United Workers' Party, the Hungarian Socialist Workers' Party and the Communist Party of Czechoslovakia, played a secondary, supporting role — as did Bonn's relations with Warsaw, Budapest and Prague in governmental Ostpolitik.

The working groups with the Czechoslovak party, on ecological and subsequently on disarmament questions, with the Hungarian party, concentrating on the economic aspects of East-West relations, and with the Polish party, on 'confidence-building', produced ceremonious joint statements and communiqués, but without notable effect either in the countries concerned or in West Germany. That with the Soviet party produced vague joint proposals for redirecting the economic gains of disarmament to the benefit of the Third World. More important than this formal part, however, were the summit talks, notably between Brandt and Gorbachev, but also at a slightly lower level.

Reporting on one such set of talks to their East German comrades, the Soviet party leadership noted in October 1984 that 'many arguments that had previously been presented by us to the representatives of the SPD have now been taken over by them. This was especially apparent in the remarks of E. Bahr and K. Voigt'. Yet this complacent Soviet commentary can not simply be taken at face value. A cunning judo-player may seem to be yielding when in fact he is preparing to throw his opponent. Bahr, Voigt and others would maintain that after 1985 it was Soviet representatives who took over many of their ideas on security policy.

While Bahr's book of 1988, *Towards European Peace*, was sub-titled 'an answer to Gorbachev', it argued that Gorbachev had himself adopted many of the Palme Commission's recommendations. So, in a further triumph of Machiavellism, Bahr was actually answering himself! Although this claim was clearly exaggerated, it was not wholly without foundation. Social Democratic new thinking came before Soviet new thinking, and influenced it as well as being influenced by it.

Most intensive and most controversial were the contacts with the East German Socialist Unity Party. To older generations on both sides, this would have been like a true believer supping not just with the devil but — worse still — with heretics. Ever since the great schism in the German left, Communists and Social Democrats had been bitterly opposed. In the early 1930s the Communists described the Social Democrats as 'social fascists'. So deep was the enmity that even in Hitler's jails a Communist would tap furious polemics through the wall to the Social Democrat in the neighbouring cell. Many leftists from the generation of Willy Brandt and Erich Honecker held this fatal split to have been partly responsible for Hitler's triumph.

Yet if anything the old divide between Communists and Social Democrats had been made still deeper by the post-war, Stalinist attempt to overcome it. For the Socialist Unity Party of Germany (SED) was the product of the forced amalgamation, in 1946, of the Social Democrats in the Soviet occupation zone into a party of the Leninist-Stalinist type. Much of the Western, democratic identity of the West German Social Democrats, from Kurt Schumacher and Ernst Reuter to the younger Willy Brandt, had been forged in the furnace of opposition not just to Communism in general, but to this party in particular.

When Brandt launched a new phase of relations with the GDR, as Chancellor, the Social Democrats felt it necessary to pass a so-called 'demarcation resolution' defining their fundamental, irreconcilable differences with communism. The resolution was drafted by Richard Löwenthal, who had himself as a young man tried to bridge the differences between Communists and Social Democrats in order to fight Fascism. It was then amended by leading members of the party.

For its part, in the 1960s and early 1970s the Socialist Unity Party was if anything even more frightened of the influence of West German Social Democracy in the GDR than it was of that of the blackest reactionaries. The attempt to organise just an 'exchange of speakers' between the two parties in 1966, as part of the Social Democrats' vanguard role in Ostpolitik, had failed when the East German side cried off. Large areas of the GDR were traditional Social Democratic strongholds. The vision of democratic socialism had considerable appeal among the East German intelligentsia. In the 1970s, the most popular politician in East Germany was widely held to be Willy Brandt — and the reports of the Stasi's Central Evaluation and Information Group give some credence to this view.

Herbert Wehner, who had himself been a senior communist functionary in the 1930s, began his private message to Erich Honecker in December 1973 with the emphatic statement: 'In my view SED (Socialist Unity Party of Germany) and SPD (Social Democratic Party of Germany) are mutually exclusive.' (Wehner deliberately spelled out the full names of both parties.) Honecker agreed. Yet there was also, as we have noticed already in the particular case of Honecker and Wehner, a complex and profound fascination of each side with the other, as between brothers who have quarrelled or, indeed, between true believers and heretics. A close and sympathetic observer from a much younger generation talks in this connection of a 'love-hate relationship'.

Interestingly, the East German record of a conversation in 1979 between Honecker and Ponomaryev, the Soviet Central Committee Secretary responsible for relations with socialist countries, shows the East German leader gingerly raising the question of contacts with Social Democratic parties. After noting that Brandt had earlier proposed to establish inter-party relations, and that 'now Ehmke and Bahr pose the same question',

322 · *In Europe's Name*

Honecker averred that 'we don't want to establish relations with the SPD. The SPD has a hostile attitude to the GDR.' The time, he indicated, was not ripe. Ponomaryev replied that this was a matter for the East German party but, he added, the Soviet Union wouldn't mind if they didn't! Summing up, Honecker observed: 'we have relations with the SPD government and Schmidt telephones me more often than is necessary. The question of inter-party relations is something quite different.'

In fact, until 1982 there was little need for special direct relations between the two parties, since the Social Democrats were in government in Bonn while the communists commanded the government in East Berlin. As we have seen, Honecker also used direct and informal channels of communication. He and Schmidt telephoned and corresponded. The lawyer Wolfgang Vogel carried private messages to Herbert Wehner, whom Honecker also met privately in East Germany.

But when the Social Democrats fell from power, a new situation arose. Already on 2 November 1982, the East German Politburo minutes record a formal resolution: 'The request of the chairman of the board (*Parteivorstand*) of the SPD, Willy Brandt, to establish party-to-party relations between the SPD and the SED will be granted.' The director of the Central Committee's Academy of Social Sciences, Otto Reinhold, was charged with establishing the links. When he became leader of the Social Democratic parliamentary party in 1983, Hans-Jochen Vogel took over from Herbert Wehner the more or less regular contacts with Erich Honecker. In Vogel's case this took the form of an annual meeting with Honecker, in East Berlin or in the Hubertusstock hunting lodge. At their second such meeting, in March 1984, the two leaders agreed to set up a joint working-group on the subject of a chemical-weapon-free zone.

The SPD delegation, led by Karsten Voigt and including Egon Bahr and Hermann Scheer, and the SED delegation, led by Hermann Axen, the Central Committee Secretary for international relations, met six times and in June 1985 produced a remarkable document. Formally approved, as the Joint Communiqué noted, by the Presidium of the SPD and by the Politburo of the SED, it was headed 'Framework for an Agreement on the Formation of a Chemical-Weapon-Free Zone in Europe'. Replete with preamble, diplomatic terminology and notes, this was nothing less than a draft treaty for a chemical-weapon-free zone in, as it put it, *Mitteleuropa*. At a minimum, the zone was to include the Federal Republic, the GDR, and the Czechoslovak Socialist Republic. (But only in April 1988 were the two German parties formally joined in this initiative by the Communist Party of Czechoslovakia.) The working-group, said the Joint Communiqué, had felt itself inspired by the commitment expressed in Article 5 of the Basic Treaty (negotiator: E. Bahr), and by a sense of responsibility that (once again) 'no war should go out from German soil, that from German soil peace must go out'. The agreement provided 'a framework for government negotiations; it will encourage and advance, although it cannot supplant, inter-governmental negotiations'.

Following a cordial summit meeting between Brandt and Honecker in September 1985, the working-group was authorised to explore the subject of a nuclear-weapon-free-corridor in Europe, 'in accordance with the proposal of the Palme Commission'. These talks bore fruit in a set of 'basic principles', jointly presented in October 1986, for a corridor extending 150 kilometres each side of the iron curtain from the Baltic to Austria. Although not a draft treaty, this 'contribution from the centre of Europe' indicated, according to the Joint Communiqué, 'what can be achieved as the result of government negotiations'. Commenting on the results, Egon Bahr noted that, as with chemical weapons, the two sides had been discussing weapons which were not 'in German possession'. Nonetheless, the view of the SED was 'on account of its leading role in the GDR even more important than that of the oppositional SPD'. Moreover, one could assume that the East German side had consulted with Moscow.

East German sources confirm that this was very much the case. Manfred Uschner, a key member of the East German delegation, recalls that 'questions from the SPD negotiators were usually passed on directly to Moscow, and one often waited long and impatiently for the answer'. He himself would generally fly first to Moscow before proceeding (via Prague) to Bonn. The records of the Politburo and Central Committee also contain evidence of this very close consultation. Such progress in the SPD-SED talks was only possible because it accorded with the new thinking on Soviet foreign policy under Gorbachev.

The paper on a nuclear-free corridor therefore clearly had Moscow's approval. Whether it had Washington's was very much less clear. In his commentary, Bahr nonetheless went out of his way to argue that the proposal was entirely compatible with and indeed complementary to what had been agreed multilaterally at the Stockholm Conference on disarmament, and with the position recently taken by Ronald Reagan at his Reykjavik summit meeting with Mikhail Gorbachev. As with Kennedy back in 1963, the unexpected intervention of an American president came like a gift from heaven. Western and especially American détente license could again be claimed for German détente designs.

This series of talks on security issues was continued with the production in July 1988 of a joint proposal for a 'zone of trust and security' in what was now described as *Zentraleuropa*. Once again, East Berlin checked every detail with Moscow. Thus, for example, a document in the files of Hermann Axen's Central Committee department for international relations gives the Soviet answers to Egon Bahr's questions at a meeting of the joint working-group in January 1988. Commenting on the draft German-German statement on the trust zone, the Soviet response says: 'In point two there is mention of "decisive power centres". The mention of centres should be dropped.' This peremptory instruction nicely illustrates the point that Moscow was, indeed, the decisive power centre.

Before the trust zone proposals, however, the results of a quite different joint working-group were presented to the public. After nearly two years of discussions about possible exchanges between SPD and SED 'social scientists', a joint working-group composed of delegations from the Commission on Basic Values of the SPD, chaired by Erhard Eppler, and from the Academy of Social Sciences of the Central Committee of the SED, chaired by Otto Reinhold, was established in the summer of 1984. The diplomatic protocol was thus delicately pitched one degree below full, direct party-to-party talks. At a guest-house on the Scharmützelsee, outside East Berlin, the 'social scientists' began their arduous deliberations.

As the fortieth anniversary of the forced merger of the Social Democrats into the SED in 1946 approached, Willy Brandt lent his unique authority to this dialogue, in a statement rather portentously entitled 'six theses on the relations between social democrats and communists'. Reaffirming his view that 'the securing of peace is more important than the quarrel about theories', he went on to quote Kurt Schumacher to the effect that 'one can make the case for democratic socialism in different ways, and certainly a Marxist case also has its place in social democracy'. The SED, for its part, timed its party congress to coincide with the anniversary of the merger, which it celebrated as overcoming the fateful, historic division of the German left. For the first time, a representative of the SPD was an official observer at this congress. The SED 'social scientist', Otto Reinhold, writing in the party's authoritative ideological monthly *Horizont* on the occasion of the congress, made a small but significant revision. The Social Democrats, he suggested, were no longer to be identified as 'anti-communists'. They were now merely 'non-communists'.

In August 1987, on the eve of Honecker's visit to Bonn, Eppler and Reinhold finally presented their common paper. Entitled 'The Ideological Argument and Common Security', this was published not only in the West German press but also in the East German party daily, *Neues Deutschland*. It was a contorted text. The first section, entitled 'Securing peace through common security', began with the by now familiar assertion that 'our world-historically new position is that humankind can now only survive together or perish together'. It then spelled out principles which, it said, now underlay the concepts of both common security and peaceful co-existence (i.e. the Soviet concept).

The second section, entitled 'peaceful competition of the social systems', argued that this competition should be judged according to which system made the most effective contribution to the solution of 'the overarching problems of humankind' and which offered 'the most favourable social conditions for the unfolding of *Humanität*'. Above all, it said, what was at issue was the contribution of each social system to securing peace, to overcoming the ecological dangers and to the development of the third world. The conditions required for this included 'social control of scient-ific-technical progress' and 'the development of living democracy, the realisation and further development of human rights in their mutual interdependence of social, political and personal (individual) rights'.

The next part, on 'the need for a culture of political argument and dialogue', began with the ceremonious statement 'we, German communists and social democrats, agree that peace in our time cannot be achieved by arming against each other but can only be agreed and organised with each other'. After observing that both social democrats and communists felt themselving to be continuing the humanistic tradition of Europe, it went on to lay out, in alternating paragraphs, what Social Democrats and 'Marxist-Leninists' regarded as their basic values. The former began with the clear statement that 'the social democrats understand themselves as part of Western democracy', and stressed the importance of a division of powers, human rights and pluralism.

The paper then outlined 'approaches' and 'ground rules' for this 'culture of political argument'. 'No side can deny the other the right to exist', it said. The hope had to be that both sides were 'capable of reform' (*reformfähig*). Both sides had 'to consider each other capable of peace' (*friedensfähig*). And again, both systems 'must concede to each other the capacity to develop and the capacity to reform'. Before criticising, each side should try 'first to think into the logic of the other'. The ideological argument should not lead to an intervention in the internal affairs of other states, but even sharp criticism should not be rejected as 'interference in internal affairs'.

'Open discussion of the competition of the systems, their successes and failures, advantages and disadvantages, must be possible inside each sys-tem,' it said. 'That this discussion is promoted and has practical results is even a precondition for this true competition.' A 'comprehensive infor-medness' of citizens was also of increasing importance, and this required the circulation of 'periodically and not periodically appearing newspapers' (*sic*) in line with the Helsinki Final Act. Also of growing importance was the network of visits and cultural exchanges 'across the system-frontiers'. In the cause of securing peace, concluded the paper, the competition between the systems must be carried forward within mutually agreed rules and a 'culture of political argument'.

Unsurprisingly, this paper itself provoked lively political argument on both sides of the German-German frontier. Its critics in the West charged that Eppler and his colleagues had gone too far in conceding legitimacy to Communism in general and the SED in particular, while relativising the Western values still firmly upheld in the SPD's 'demarcation resolution' sixteen years before. Gesine Schwan, one of the best qualified Social

Democratic critics of the party's second Ostpolitik, argued that the paper's central concept of 'peace-capability' was itself radically flawed, because it ignored the vital dimension of internal peace. In the same way, she wrote, one could describe the Bismarckian Reich at the time when it persecuted Social Democrats as 'capable of peace', for after all, it prosecuted no external war. Was it really the Social Democratic view, she asked, that a dictatorship is just as 'capable of peace' as a democracy? Did the SPD really have to certify the communist one-party dictatorship a 'right to exist' because the Soviet Union had atomic bombs?

The paper was defended by its authors and supporters among the Social Democrats on two lines. Firstly, as in the earlier new thinking within the party, they suggested that the nuclear and environmental challenges had indeed changed and relativised the traditional priorities and values expressed in the Bad Godesberg programme. Reform was needed on both sides. 'If it really happens that one system is victor in the competition,' wrote Eppler in 1988, '... it will not be the system of today'. As for democracy, it could take many forms: 'there is, in the Third World for example, one-party rule which becomes tolerable because democracy occurs inside the party, that is, free discussion between intra-party trends and groups'. (One might ask: tolerable for whom?).

The second line of defence was different, and somewhat in tension with the first. This was to argue that the Social Democrats had in fact been spokespersons for Western democracy and Western values in this dialogue, and that the paper — even more than the Helsinki Final Act — provided a basis on which would-be democratic socialists or social democrats inside the SED, and even would-be democrats outside the Party, could justify their criticisms and demands. Here, after all, the Party leadership had subscribed to the necessity of 'open discussion . . . *inside* each system' (my italics). Even a critic like Gesine Schwan pointed to the positive opportunity in this passage. It appears to have been one of the reasons why Richard Löwenthal, the main author of the 1971 'demarcation resolution', also felt able to support the joint paper.

Now this argument is not without foundation. The joint paper produced a rare argument in the Politburo, with one member, Alfred Neumann, sharply attacking it. The SED's veteran ideologist, Kurt Hager, soon publicly qualified the paper's claims about the 'peace-capability' of imperialism. 'There were, if you like, social democrats inside the Party,' Kurt Hager told the author in a retrospective conversation in 1992, and he mentioned particularly the main SED author of the paper, Rolf Reissig. Reissig himself made a similar retrospective claim. Among some intellectuals inside the Party it almost certainly did help to activate (or reactivate) the democratic socialist or social democratic yeast. There are, however, sharply contrasting testimonies on how far this was actually reflected in open discussion inside the Party at the time.

A September 1987 report by the Stasi's central evaluation group on popular reactions to the paper dwelled at length on the extent to which Party members and 'progressive citizens' were unsettled and confused by what it said. The Stasi report emphasised rather the critical than the supportive voices. Thus the critics reportedly said that it would now be more difficult to maintain the 'defence-readiness' of the younger generation. Also 'the discussion on the competition of the systems, the comparison of their successes and failures, would set the GDR difficult tasks, in light of the difficult economic situation and in particular of difficulties with consumer supplies . . .' The Stasi went on to report that leading figures in the Liberal Democratic Party (one of the 'front' or 'bloc' parties in the East German system) took this as an occasion to hope for fundamental changes in the information policy of the GDR. Finally, 'hostile-negative persons' saw in the paper a positive chance for developing their activities.

This source has of course to be treated critically. It was the Stasi's business to identify and emphasise developments that were, from the viewpoint of state security, worrying rather than reassuring. Moreover, Mielke himself was hardly an enthusiastic supporter of the SPD-SED dialogue. Nonetheless, this contemporary testimony clearly buttresses the argument made for the unsettling and stimulating impact of the paper inside the GDR. It was also welcomed by leading figures in the Protestant Church. In general, the period following the publication of the joint paper was one of growing criticism from below in the GDR.

Yet once again we must beware of our old friend *post hoc, ergo propter hoc*. As we have seen, there were other, far larger and more immediate causes of that mounting criticism. In such subsequent central Stasi reports as the author has thus far been able to examine, the joint paper does not recur as a major cause of, or even pretext for, such criticism. Moreover, the period following the publication of the joint paper actually saw a sharp increase in the repression of criticism outside the Party, starting with the search of the 'environmental library' in the Zion Church and continuing with the arrest of independent demonstrators on the Luxemburg-Liebknecht march. The people whom the party-state thus attempted to gag were exercising peaceful criticism precisely in the terms of the 'culture of political argument' advocated by the common paper, and, indeed, sometimes with reference to it.

This glaring contradiction, combined with the criticism in West Germany, prompted a discussion within the parliamentary leadership of the Social Democrats. A small group had already been licensed to make cautious, informal contacts not only with the Protestant Church in the GDR (which was relatively unproblematic for the SED) but also with Church-protected peace activists. However, this activity was extremely low-key and fragmentary, and its leading protagonist, Gert Weisskirchen, himself says that the Social Democratic leadership continued to concentrate almost exclusively on contacts with the leaders of the East German party-state.

The talks on both security policy and ideological issues continued, although the latter were more difficult and tense than before. Erhard Eppler, in particular, seems to have been genuinely affronted by the failure of the SED to take seriously its own solemn commitment to internal dialogue. A balance of the dialogue with the SED drawn up by the Social Democrats' Commission on Basic Values in March 1989 contained, after some liberal self-criticism of unemployment and the erosion of social rights in West Germany, a sharp attack on the repressive policy of the GDR. 'Those who refuse internal dialogue,' it concluded, 'also endanger the external dialogue.' Eppler's counterpart, Otto Reinhold, found this criticism 'singular'.

Delivering the traditional 17 June speech in the Bundestag, Eppler then surprised many of his listeners with a dark warning about the future of the GDR. There was, he said, such a thing as a 'GDR-consciousness, a sometimes almost defiant feeling of belonging to this smaller, poorer German state'. If he was not mistaken, he said, this feeling had been stronger two years before (when the joint paper was published, in the summer of 1987) than it was now, in the summer of 1989. But there was probably, he averred, still a majority in the GDR which hoped 'not for the end but for the reform of their state. If, however,' he went on, 'the leadership of the SED continues to practice that blind self-satisfaction which we have seen in recent months, then in two years' time this majority could have become a minority.' As for the joint paper's concept of the right to exist, he wished now to add: 'neither side can stop the other from condemning itself to ruin'. Whether Eppler accurately characterised a change in the feelings of the GDR's citizens about their state may be doubted; but he certainly expressed a change in his own. Such plain public speaking about the internal condition of the GDR had not been heard from a leading Social Democrat for many a long moon.

Yet not all shared his public pessimism about the leadership of the SED. Receiving a delegation headed by Egon Krenz in Saarbrücken just ten days before, Oskar Lafontaine, the Social Democrats' next candidate for Chancellor, told his guests: 'We are pushing for the opening of official relations between the German Bundestag and the People's Chamber of the GDR. In this connection talks on youth policy and agriculture will be held. Erich Honecker and Hans-Jochen Vogel have agreed a working-group on environmental protection.' 'Let us use détente (*Entspannung*),' he declared, 'to get closer to each other. This,' he observed philosophically, 'is a dialectical process: the closer we get, the more relaxed (*entspannter*) we become.'

However, relaxing was what East Germany's leaders could not do, as the developments which had begun in Poland and Hungary now spread to the

GDR in the form of the emigration wave via Hungary, and increased opposition at home. The Social Democrats' reaction was extremely confused, some maintaining that caution and 'stability' were now more important than ever, others demanding a change in party policy.

Particularly noteworthy was the response of leading Social Democrats to an independent initiative to found a Social Democratic Party in East Germany. Walter Momper, then Governing Mayor of Berlin, was dismissive. 'Nothing can be changed by small groups founding parties in the GDR,' he said. 'What is important is that the pressure for reform in the population of the GDR and in parts of the SED finally gets through into the top of the state-party. For the SED has real power in the GDR, and will keep it for the foreseeable future.'

Then, in early September, the SPD leadership was shocked by a parliamentary broadside from the Christian Democrats' general secretary, Volker Rühe. Recalling Bahr's famous formula of *Wandel durch Annäherung* (change through rapprochement), Rühe accused the Social Democrats of attempting to achieve *Wandel durch Anbiederung* (roughly: change through sycophancy). Revealingly, it seems to have been this West German party-political attack more than anything that actually happened in East Germany, let alone Eastern Europe, which impelled the Social Democrats to change their line.

Soon the Social Democrat Norbert Gansel was advocating *Wandel durch Abstand* — change through keeping-our-distance. A planned visit by a Social Democratic parliamentary delegation to East Berlin was cancelled by the SED, after Horst Ehmke let it be known that he would demand reforms and meet privately with Bärbel Bohley, the best-known leader of the newly-founded New Forum opposition movement. The Social Democratic party leadership then announced that it was revising its policy. From now on, contacts with the Church and opposition groups would take priority over those with the SED.

As the demonstrations in East Germany grew, so did the Social Democrats' disarray. Of particular historical interest was the contrast between the two great veterans of Ostpolitik. As always following the intellectual logic of the chosen policy to an outspoken conclusion, Egon Bahr called for a stabilisation of the GDR, with reforms leading to a third way. What was needed was 'a different GDR'. The people of the GDR, he said, would not let their state be taken from them. As late as 8 October, he made a cautious defence of Erich Honecker, pointing to everything that had been achieved in German-German relations in his time. Honecker had, said Bahr, allowed 'homeopathic changes in his state', thus recalling an image from the Tutzing speech a quarter-century before. 'There have been, if you like, reforms.' And, just ten days before the East German leader was deposed, Bahr said 'there's a principle that applies in every system: you don't change horses in the middle of the stream'.

Willy Brandt also urged caution and restraint. But with his more intuitive sense of politics, he seems to have grasped earlier than his old intellectual *alter ego* the direction in which history was heading — towards that reunification of which Bahr even more than Brandt had dreamed all those years before. Already in the spring of 1989, Brandt was scenting the possibility, not of a *re*unification but of a *new* unification (*Neuvereinigung*), although he said he would not live to experience it. Following Gorbachev's visit to Bonn in June, he declared in the Bundestag that the time was approaching when 'that which arbitrarily divides the people (*die Menschen*), not least the people of one people (*Volk*), will have to be dismantled'.

By mid-September Brandt was writing, in the tabloid *Bild*, that, while it was an open question 'how and how far and in what form the people in both present states would come together', nonetheless 'what then, after all, belongs together, cannot for ever be kept apart'. It was then Brandt who, returning from a visit to Gorbachev, discreetly let it be known that Honecker's days were numbered. It was Brandt who found the right words to respond to the opening of the Berlin Wall: 'now what belongs together is growing together'. And it was around the grand old man and his famous phrase that the disoriented Social Democrats rallied at their party conference in Berlin in December 1989.

After the event

With elections to be fought, ranks were closed. But the history of the second Ostpolitik could not simply be forgotten. As past compromises and collaboration became a major theme not just in East German but in all-German politics, so the subject was constantly revived — often by Christian Democrats, themselves embarrassed by the past of the East German CDU that they had taken over, but also by former opposition activists and, not least, by Social Democrats from the East. The criticism focussed as much on what the Social Democrats had not said as on what they had said, as much on whom they had not talked to as on whom they had talked to.

A first line of defence was to say that leading Social Democrats had after all had discreet contacts with Church and opposition figures in East Germany and throughout Eastern Europe. Had not Willy Brandt met with Tadeusz Mazowiecki in 1985, and Hans-Jochen Vogel with Solidarity advisers in 1987? And what of Gert Weisskirchen's contacts with Church peace and opposition groups in the GDR?

This defence was not sustainable. For those same Solidarity leaders and advisers would testify that, so far as recognition and dialogue was concerned, West German politicians had in general been close to the rear of the Western pack, and the Social Democrats had been at the very back of the very rear. Precisely because of the moral and symbolic capital which the Social Democrats had built up with Willy Brandt, his visit in 1985 had been experienced as a slap in the face.

As for East Germany, Erich Mielke reported to the Politburo in September 1989 that from 1 August 1988 to 1 August 1989 SPD functionaries had thirty-seven contacts with Church figures in the GDR. But, even more than in the Polish case, contacts with the Church could by no means simply be equated with contacts with the opposition, as the case of Manfred Stolpe was to show. To be sure, the opposition in the GDR was much smaller and less easily identified than Solidarity in Poland. But Gerd Poppe of the long-established Initiative for Peace and Human Rights can recall no contacts with anyone who could be considered an official representative of the Social Democrats, except perhaps in the margins of a Church meeting. To be sure, nor did the Free or Christian Democrats make such contacts with any greater regularity. But they could at least argue that they had the governmental responsibility of keeping good relations with the East German authorities. As Egon Bahr himself observed: the Social Democrats, in opposition, might have risked more.

The second Ostpolitik of the Social Democrats consisted in an intensive dialogue with the ruling communist parties. Why? Egon Bahr, gave a first, simple answer: these were the contacts they already had. To continue them at the highest level, for Social Democratic leaders to be received by Gorbachev and Honecker, was also, in the 1980s, to gain credibility at home. The Social Democrats could say to the electors: You see, we are the people who can deal with the East. Ostpolitik is our speciality. Beyond this, many in the party itself pointed to the 'governmental' or 'statist' tradition in German Social Democracy, which, they suggested, gained the upper hand in these seven years. Bahr, in particular, was characterised as the Metternich of the left.

Yet there was also the hypothesis of behavioural psychology which, we have argued, underlay the concept of *Wandel durch Annäherung*, and subsequent relations with the GDR. Power lay with the powerholders, so change could only come from them. Cold War and confrontation had only hardened their posture. Détente should relax it. Only contacts, dialogue and reassurance would move them to reform. And it was no accident that the internal goal of the second Ostpolitik was defined precisely with that word: reform. 'As the external dimension of détente is called peace,' said Horst Ehmke, 'so the inner dimension is called reform.' Karsten Voigt pinned his hopes on reformers from the younger generation — his own generation! — within the SED. All these contacts were therefore meant to promote reform from above.

Finally, it was argued that this dialogue with the ruling Party expanded its tolerance of criticism, and the room for manoeuvre of Church and opposition groups. Quiet diplomacy did more than megaphone diplomacy or cheap gestures. To meet with those groups directly might have jeopardised the party talks. But, as Egon Bahr argued to Bärbel Bohley, on a television programme after unification: 'by our not having publicly demanded freedom of movement for the opposition, that became attainable'.

Particularly in the light of this last argument, it is important to enquire not only why the leaders of the Social Democrats chose the leaders of the SED as their partners, but also how they dealt with them. Part, but only part, of the answer is to be found in the published record discussed above. But what of the dealings out of the limelight, the private talks, the 'quiet diplomacy' to help the opposition? Here there is an obvious problem of sources. What is available at the time of writing is some reminiscences by participants in the talks, some remarkable original documents from the SED archives, but only a few from the SPD side. As more documents become available from these and other sources, we should get a more rounded picture.

One must stress once again that the original documents from the East German Party archives clearly have to be treated critically. Through most of the internal Party reports there is a tendency to tell superiors what they want to hear, and sometimes outright sycophancy. As in the case of the relations of churchmen and women inside the GDR with the party-state authorities, so also with the relations of West German politicians to those authorities, all generalisations are suspect and all collective judgements unjust. The policy of the SPD, like the policy of the Federation of the Protestant Churches in the GDR, can fairly be described, analyzed and judged from the formal documents and official statements of its elected leaders. But in the direct confrontation with the representatives of a dictatorship, each man and woman stands alone. Each therefore has a basic right to be judged on his or her own particular record, not on anyone else's.

Having said this, it must be admitted that some of what one finds in the files is even more peculiar than one might expect from the published record. Here we have, for example, the record of a conversation between Egon Bahr and Erich Honecker on 5 September 1986, at a time when German-German relations were fraught with the problem of thousands of East Asian asylum-seekers whom the GDR allowed to fly into East Germany and then to take the local train (*S-Bahn*) into West Berlin, where they became West Germany's problem. Bahr said, according to this East German record: 'It is clear that with this problem the GDR wins influence over the FRG as never before, above all for the first time to this extent over the domestic politics of the FRG. This could be very important if it would serve the cause of understanding.'

Of course, Bahr went on, he understood that the GDR had to deal with the present coalition government in Bonn, but — and here the record turns to direct quotation –

> the question arises: is there a chance of achieving a solution . . . which would also be favourable in relation to the election results on 25.1.1987. On instructions from W. Brandt I would like to say: we want to state quite authoritatively that if the SPD came to power the government of the FRG would fully respect the citizenship of the GDR, and thus this subject would be buried.

Even allowing for the possibility of a tendentious record, it seems quite clear that Bahr was not only (in consultation with Wolfgang Schäuble) looking for a solution to the asylum problem, but also looking for an electoral boost for the SPD.

To this end, he was boldly dangling — as was his wont — the fine-sounding (yet in fact still vague) prospect of a concession on one of Honecker's key 'Gera demands' in return. In reply, Honecker claimed that in 1985–86 he had not accepted the invitation to visit West Germany 'because I did not want to appear as election-helper of the CDU. We did not want the SPD to get, as we were told, six per cent fewer votes.' But why, Honecker went on, this being so, had Hans-Jochen Vogel made such critical remarks at the Nuremberg party conference about the GDR's conduct on the asylum question?

Following more detailed correspondence between Bahr and Axen, with Bahr proposing a joint communiqué signed by Honecker and the Social Democrats' candidate for Chancellor, Johannes Rau, it was proposed that Rau would make a separate statement in Bonn, announcing that the GDR would solve this problem following the talks with the SPD. The official notice to the Permanent Representative of the Federal Republic should be postponed to give Rau time to make his announcement first. A characteristic orderly annotation in Honecker's hand — 'Agreed, EH, 17. 9. 86' — sealed the decision.

Near the end of the file is the transcript of an interview with Bahr on West German evening television news the next day.

> Question: You're an old fox . . . wasn't this after all at this moment a bonbon for the SPD? Bahr: Well first of all we are of course pleased, there's no question about that. I will also tell you (name of interviewer) quite openly and honestly that I thought to myself yesterday evening, *Mensch*, what could one do if one were in government, on the basis of the experiences and on the basis of the credit which one has won, given that this was possible as an opposition.

The passage is underlined and marked with a large exclamation mark in pink felt-tip.

This theme of domestic party politics played across the German-

German border, linked to the Social Democrats' proclaimed readiness to make further concessions in German-German relations, and laced with flattery, runs through the files. In a conversation with Hermann Axen in April 1987, the SPD's leader in Schleswig-Holstein Björn Engholm is recorded as saying that 'the policy of the GDR deserved the label historic. It filled him, B. Engholm, with pride, that the SPD had helped to co-formulate this policy.' And further: 'The SPD would most emphatically press for the respecting of the citizenship of the GDR, for the regulation of the Elbe frontier along the middle of the river, and for the abolition of the so-called Registration Unit in Salzgitter' (that is, three of the four Gera demands).

In a conversation with Axen in the Central Committee building later that month, Bahr is recorded as saying that Wolfgang Schäuble had informed him about his talks with the GDR, that he welcomed the positive development of relations between the states, 'however it was the SPD's view, and especially also that of H.-J. Vogel, that one should not make things too easy for the CDU/CSU. The time had come "finally to haul them across the table on the central questions of security".' Yet Bahr was not only concerned about the Christian Democrats. 'E. Bahr requested that all visits of SPD politicians in the GDR should again be brought more firmly under control . . . One should distinguish clearly between private journeys and polit-tourism.'

Responding in this confidential spirit, 'H. Axen drew E. Bahr's attention internally (*sic*) to the fact that one had noted with dismay that of all the prominent interlocutors from the Bundestag parties of the FRG only H.-J. Vogel had raised questions about the frontier-regime and E. Honecker's possible participation in West Berlin [i.e. in the 750th anniversary celebrations.]' (Here was a criticism that, in retrospect, the Social Democrats' leader might read as high praise!) 'Also tactless,' Axen continued, 'was that Vogel posed with visitors from the GDR in front of a picture of the Wall.' In the light of his remarks at the Nuremberg party conference, the question arose whether Vogel did not thus 'support the progaganda of the Stahlhelm-fraction. He [Axen] asked for this to be brought home to H.-J. Vogel in relation to his forthcoming visit to the GDR.' According to this record, 'E. Bahr, who was most embarrassed and concerned, said H. Axen was right, and promised to talk with Vogel accordingly.'

Now was Vogel more 'tactful' as a result? At this point we have a valuable check on the East German records, because Hans-Jochen Vogel made available to the author the Social Democrats' own records of his annual conversations with Honecker, written by his note-taker, Dieter Schröder. These suggest a series of sober, business-like meetings, which followed a well-defined pattern. After long discussion of the international situation, focussing primarily on the great issues of war and peace, and the joint disarmament initiatives of the two parties, Vogel would turn to bilateral issues. After making encouraging noises about the development of economic relations, and perhaps referring to environmental problems, he would raise concrete issues of contacts between the two states — for example a request for a new frontier crossing — and then 'humanitarian questions', including cases of 'family reunification', emigration requests, and the wish of those who had left the GDR years before to be allowed back for a visit. Details of specific difficult cases would be handed over: seventeen pages of them at their last meeting, in May 1989.

Now obviously the line on security policy presented by Vogel was different from that of the Bonn government — although in the record of the 1983 meeting we actually find him, *mirabile dictu*, making a cautious defence of Ronald Reagan. And to be sure, there are moments when he, too, makes party-political points against Kohl. But in large measure he pursues, solidly and cautiously, the basic strategy of Bonn's GDR policy, as developed by the centre-left and continued by the centre-right governments. Putting to one side all the basic systemic differences, soft-pedalling the larger issues of human rights, he seeks to achieve concrete 'improvements for people'. One may criticise the strategy, but his personal conduct of it does not — on the evidence of these documents — merit reproach. He was no more sycophantic, to recall Rühe's term, than most Christian and Free Democrats were in their contacts with Honecker.

The record of their conversation in May 1987 shows that Vogel and Honecker quite openly, albeit in a conciliatory tone, continued the disagreement about the 750th anniversary celebrations, to which Axen had referred in talking to Bahr. 'Dr. Vogel replied,' it says at one point, '[that] Honecker would surely know what he [Vogel] thought about the Wall.' And near the end of the talk, Vogel objected to an East German Foreign Ministry warning to West German journalists. No one, he said, had objected to the East German media's reporting of the riots in Kreuzberg — that is, in West Berlin.

Now the East German record of this same conversation does not include that little barb. On the other hand, it does include more detail on what Honecker said in reply. It also suggests a slightly more confidential tone between the two men than one might gather from the West German record. But for the most part, the two records are very close. A comparison of the East and West German records of their meeting in 1988 also reveals no dramatic differences or distortions. However, here too it seems that the East German note-taker did somewhat downplay the more critical parts of what Vogel had to say. Thus there is in the West German record a passage about how he himself had learned in his dealings with young people in the student revolt of 1968 how, for example, in the Munich borough of Schwabing, 'the administration slipped unprepared into such situations'. Young people, in his experience, were best won over by dialogue. 'He had therefore observed the events of January 1988 very closely.' The reference was of course to the suppression of the alternative Luxemburg-Liebknecht demonstration, and subsequent reprisals.

Now the West German version of Vogel's immediately following comments is: 'The Social Democrats did not want any destabilisation of the GDR. But, based on the joint [i.e. ideology] paper, one must ask questions.' The East German version reads: 'So far as the events of 17 January in Berlin were concerned he [Vogel] wanted to say that nothing was less desired than to talk up a destabilisation, but on account of the joint paper it had been asked what the SPD's attitude was.' There is a small but far from insignificant difference here, because the point of Vogel's slightly oblique remarks was of course to ask what the SED's attitude was. Honecker replied indignantly that the disruption of the (official) demonstration was an outrage, for until 1933 this march had never been disturbed. But Vogel could rest assured about the young people of East Germany, who 'at the moment were above all preparing for the fortieth anniversary of the foundation of the GDR'!

These documents show how each individual politician must be judged on his or her own conduct. The differences, in style, to stay the least, were clearly great. They also show how cautiously the East German records must be treated, and how important it is to have the West German ones as well. However, the comparison does not suggest that the East German records are unusable. At the very least, they are to the truth as smoke is to fire.

Returning to the documents in the East German Party archive, we find the record of a meeting that Oskar Lafontaine, Klaus von Dohnanyi and Klaus Wedemaier had with the East German leader, on the occasion of the East German state celebrations to mark the 750th anniversary of Berlin. According to this record, Dohnanyi, after saying that Hamburg would have been delighted to do what Franz Josef Strauss had done in Munich — that is, to give Honecker the full honours due to a visiting head of state — pointed to the desirability of the SPD returning to power in the Bundestag elections of 1990. Honecker, for his part, said that talk of reunification raised fears also among West Germany's Western allies. 'For the beginning of 1988 he had an invitation to France . . . This too showed that the French would rather have two German states.'

Honecker's fellow Saarländer, Oskar Lafontaine, observed that 'in the FRG it has become the general consensus that the dual statehood is a reality which no one can ignore. Just as much desired, however, were fundamental improvements for the people (*die Menschen*). He therefore wanted to request that in 1988 they should discuss together what in the view of the GDR leadership was feasible and what not.' Honecker agreed, and said this should be pursued with Axen. Later, Lafontaine suggested that 'a stabilisation on one side must be coupled with a maximum liberalisation in the relations between the two German states'.

Some two months later, Lafontaine was visited in Saarbrücken by a Central Committee department head, Günter Rettner, who raised the issue of a critical statement Lafontaine had made about the police search at the Zion Church. 'Personally, Comrade Rettner continued, O. Lafontaine was in the process of losing credibility in the GDR. Visibly dismayed,' continues the note, 'O. Lafontaine replied that it had never been his intention to discredit the policy of E. Honecker. He had profound confidence in E. Honecker.' His statement about the Zion Church events, 'had been made in the first place for domestic political reasons. He had not considered the effects in the GDR.' Precisely because he was known to have such good relations with Honecker and the SED, people expected a commentary from him 'when people in the GDR have difficulties on account of their views'. When Rettner objected to this interpretation, Lafontaine replied that 'for domestic political reasons he could not wholly abstain in the face of developments deserving criticism. However, one would have to weigh more carefully in future when and where one did it. A timely hint from Berlin could be very helpful in this connection. O. Lafontaine said that he was always ready to come to Berlin to talk with Erich Honecker about this.'

Receiving Rettner again five months later, Lafontaine was worried that — according to Rettner's report — the SPD would have a problem if it

left it to the conservatives to support forces critical of the system in the socialist states. . . . In the party presidium there was agreement that support for forces in the socialist states which exercised criticism was for the SPD first of all a domestic political issue. At the same time there was full agreement that in their appearances in the GDR the Social Democrats must avoid everything that would mean a strengthening of those forces.

This last, very plain statement, is underlined in black, presumably by Axen.

In the same file there is a short memorandum which relates closely to this theme. Dated 8 July 1988, and entitled 'note on a confidential [piece of] information from K.D. Voigt', it refers to a lunchtime conversation the previous day between Voigt and two members of the SED delegation who were in Bonn for the joint press conference to announce the joint document on a 'zone of trust and security in Central Europe'. According to this note, Voigt informed his luncheon guests that he had been told that two leading opposition figures from the GDR, Wolfgang Templin and Bärbel Bohley, who had been allowed out on fixed-term visas, 'intended, on 6. 8. 1988, in collaboration with the media and secret services of the FRG, to test the promise of the GDR to allow them to return after expiry of the exit-permission'.

'In his [Voigt's] personal opinion,' the note continued, 'the happiest solution would be first to let them enter and then to pick them up and expel them during or on account of relevant activities. They themselves and the services behind them hoped and reckoned that the security organs of the GDR would prevent their entry. It was intended to use this against the co-operation on security policy of the SED and SPD. Only for this reason was K.D. Voigt informing Comrade Uschner and Comrade Wagner about it.' Unsurprisingly, the interpetation of this unsigned note is hotly disputed by those involved.

In August 1988, Lafontaine had his eagerly sought personal summit with Erich Honecker. 'The question was,' Lafontaine said, according to the East German record, 'what shall we do in Deutschlandpolitik if we come to power: A concept for that eventuality was desirable, something that went beyond the concepts used up till now. O. Lafontaine suggested coming to an understanding about this with the SED and mentioned as a concrete example the problem of low-level [military] flights, which exercised many people particularly in the FRG.'

A year later, in August 1989, there was a tense exchange of messages with Egon Bahr about the arrangements for publishing yet another joint paper, this time on 'structural non-offensive capability'. Somehow the time did not seem quite right for a glowing presentation of these results, and the Politburo agreed to go ahead with publishing the document, but without a press conference. On 24 August an urgent message came to Axen from the GDR's Permanent Representation in Bonn. Bahr wished to meet with Honecker or Axen: 'He is afraid relations between both states could get out of control'. As indeed they could.

Perhaps fittingly, the very last document in this file is a copy, courtesy of the Stasi, of the proposal, signed by Martin Gutzeit and Markus Meckel, to form an 'initiative group with the goal of creating a social democratic party in the GDR'.

Now it must be stressed yet again that these documents have to be handled with care. One reason for quoting from them at length is precisely to give the reader a chance to savour their peculiar language and to judge how far they 'ring true'. Each document has to be placed in context. More will, we hope, become available. As the Vogel-Honecker papers show, only the release of the SPD's own records will allow a full and fair account. The people concerned will have to add their own commentaries. One should avoid the temptations both of tabloid sensationalism and of retrospective hypocrisy. As we have already seen, scholars and journalists also frequently indulged in flattery and dissimulation in order to obtain information from communist powerholders, and often in competition with each other.

Yet when all this is said, these documents still raise serious questions about the conduct of at least some representatives of one of Europe's great democratic parties. Looking back in 1992, Erich Honecker described his conversations with the Social Democrats as 'comradely' (*kameradschaft-*

lich). Yet what the available records suggest is less a closet comradeship of the left than an unprincipled party-political opportunism. Or was it Machiavellism? For if the object was, with the cunning sometimes called dialectical, to embrace the opponent in order to suffocate him, or to move him to 'reform', or to preserve that peace without which 'everything was nothing', then perhaps the end justified the means? Could not Bahr, or Voigt or Lafontaine say, adapting Bertolt Brecht 'we who hoped for uprightness could not ourselves be upright'? What, finally, is wrong with sycophancy and appeasement, if it works?

To this there are two responses. First, Brecht was not expressing the morality which is supposed to underpin Western democracy, whether Social, Christian or Free. This insists that there are some means that no end justifies, some minimum standards of dignity, some moral limits which should never be overstepped. The question then becomes: did this or that individual politician overstep that line?

Secondly, even if one puts aside the moral issue, the policy did not work. The only definite, concrete success one can confidently point to is the release (usually to the West) of many individual men and women from the GDR whose names were on the lists handed over by Social Democrats. According to a note prepared for Hans-Jochen Vogel in 1990, of some 4,320 cases raised since 1983 by the Social Democrats' office for 'humanitarian help/GDR', 2,128 were resolved before the opening of the Wall. (Whether some of these would not have been released anyway through the usual unusual channels is another question.) One cannot seriously maintain that world peace was preserved by the dialogue between the SPD and the SED. As for reform, we have seen in an earlier chapter that it did not happen. To be sure, the dialogue helped to promote discussion and even dissent within the SED. But was that of any decisive importance?

In a retrospective statement on the fifth anniversary of the joint paper on ideology, the Basic Values Commission of the (now themselves reunited) Social Democrats argued that it was: 'There is much to be said for the arguments of Rolf Reissig and Manfred Uschner that the uncertainty which the paper caused in the SED contributed to breaking the dogmatic self-confidence of the state-party' so that it lacked the resolve to use force against protesters. And again 'a bloodbath would probably have been unavoidable if in 1989 there had only been a movement against the SED and not also inside the state-party.'

Like all counter-factual arguments, this cannot be proved or disproved. But persuasive it is not. There is no evidence that 'reformers' were in any key decision-making posts at the critical moments, whereas the old guard certainly were. Moreover, in 1989 all the very different communist parties of Eastern Europe conceded without violence, with the single, unique exception of Romania. Thus, for example, the Communist Party of Czechoslovakia, purged of reformers after 1968 and unaffected by any dialogue with Western social democrats, surrendered power to an entirely extra-party movement more swiftly, peacefully and completely than the SED. If history had happened otherwise, the reform debate inside the SED might have been significant. In normal weather conditions, wood-worm do weaken a fence. But if an avalanche sweeps away the fence, the woodworm's work makes little difference.

There were, in the event, two basic mistakes in the second Ostpolitik. The first was to believe that, as Bahr put it, 'security is the key to everything'. To be sure, the new thinking on security policy was a very important part of the first phase of new thinking in Soviet foreign policy, and the Social Democrats may rightly claim some credit for influencing it. To be sure, the nuclear disarmament agreements between the superpowers, and the conventional disarmament talks between all concerned, were an important precondition for the ending of the Cold War — although one should note that, to recall Bender's image, Europe was actually disarmed from the margins in, not from the centre out. Yet, as Havel and others had argued, it was political change, both from below and from above, in the Soviet Union and in Eastern Europe, that cut the path to the dissolution of the blocs, not vice versa.

When Bahr was asked early in 1990 'you expected everything from the government and little from the people?' he replied, with the clarity which was his hallmark, 'that's right. I thought: if we first provide for security, then social and political changes will follow over there. It happened precisely the other way round.' And two years later he observed:

> My real mistake was, as I see now, that in the last thirty-five years I have believed: since the heart of the matter is the security question, the power question, one must make sure that wars are no longer possible. Then politics and everything else will follow. Including German unity, including the over-coming of the East-West division in Europe. That was wrong. Politics have overtaken the security question.

The second basic mistake concerned politics. This was the belief that political change in Eastern Europe could only come from those who already held power, through reform from above — and the concomitant neglect of the individuals, groups and movements working for change from below. We have argued that, in the extreme form adopted by German Social Democrats in the early 1960s ('liberalisation through stabilisation'), this belief was always flawed. Nonetheless, in the 1960s it was a working hypothesis shared by many in Eastern Europe, and the opposition groups outside the Party scarcely existed. However, after the 1970s had demon-strated the limits of reform from above and the sixteen months of Solidarity in Poland had shown the possibilities of social self-organisation from below, it should no longer have been credible.

Yet it was a concept — or at least a word — that the key figures in the formulation of the second Ostpolitik clung to well into the autumn of 1989. Bahr's final defence of Honecker's GDR — 'there have been, if you like, reforms' — delivered on Sunday, 8 October 1989, just a day before the breakthrough of the Leipzig demonstration on Monday, 9 October, was the rather desperate *reductio ad absurdum* of this notion. For if what happened in the GDR in the 1980s was already reform, then how on earth should we describe what had happened in Hungary over the same period? The word was stretched to breaking-point, and then popped like a balloon.

The forlorn hope of reform in Eastern Europe, the idea that '89 could be '68 *bis*, was one which Social Democrats shared with Gorbachev. The illusions of the Prague Spring, long buried in East Central Europe, had a second life in Moscow — and in Bonn. As we have suggested already, these Russian illusions were, in the event, helpful illusions for the peoples of Eastern Europe. Inasmuch as the Social Democrats of the 1980s by their own illusions reinforced Gorbachev in his, while at the same time helping to reassure Erich Honecker that he did not really need to reform, one may argue that their second Ostpolitik also contributed to overcoming the division of Europe. But this was hardly the route intended.

These two basic mistakes are now matters of historical record. Theoretically it might have happened as the Social Democrats' second Ostpolitik anticipated and intended. In practice it did not. The whole issue of whom the Social Democrats did (or did not) deal with, and how, is also now a historical question — albeit still a live one. But the broader issue of the redefinition of values, concepts and priorities is not in the same sense a historical one.

At its Berlin party conference in December 1989, the party duly adopted the new basic programme over which Erhard Eppler and his colleagues had laboured so profoundly. Although hastily revised at a few points, the Berlin programme — still valid at the time of writing — contained much of the new thinking of the 1980s. 'We work for a world in which all peoples live in common security,' it said. 'Humankind can only survive together or perish together.' 'From German soil peace must go out.' A by now familiar litany. Of course, in its more than fifty pages this successor to the Bad Godesberg programme of 1959 made countless other commitments as well: also to freedom and human rights. But the contrast with the few, simple, old-fashioned principles which the peoples of Eastern Europe raised on their banners at this time was striking.

As we have noticed, the Social Democrats emphasised in the mid-1980s that what they were pursuing was not a new version of what has been called the German *Sonderweg*, or special historical path. And indeed it was not, if only because this particular path led nowhere. Yet German historians have also identified a more limited form of historical peculiarity: not a *Sonderweg* but a *Sonderbewusstsein*, a special consciousness. Taken all in all, and comparing the vocabulary and policies of the German Social Democrats with those of other West European parties of the left, there are at least traces of such a special consciousness, some of them still to be found in the Berlin programme of 1989.

One element of this special consciousness was the relativisation of what Social Democrats of an older generation had come, through bitter experience, to regard as basic values of the West. This relativisation did not result only from the specific version of détente known as Ostpolitik, but that was certainly one important cause. As Richard Löwenthal wrote in 1984, there was, 'in a large part of the young generation, a loss of the understanding that the conflict with the Soviet Union is not only a conflict between two great powers and their associates, but also a conflict between freedom and tyranny'.

The contemporaries of these West Germans on the other side of the 'Yalta' divide may indeed have been less alert to the new global challenges, to the problems of the Third World and the environment, or to feminist concerns. But this they had not forgotten. One of the founding fathers of the new Social Democratic party in the GDR, Martin Gutzeit, recalls meeting a representative of the West German Social Democrats in the summer of 1989. Gutzeit said to him: 'all we ask is that you should seek for us the same rights and freedoms that you yourselves enjoy'. And referring to the record of the SPD in the 1980s he said simply: 'how could you be so unprincipled?' 'Unprincipled?' a West German Social Democrat might reply. 'But look at the documents of our Commission on Basic Values. Look at our Berlin programme. There you will find tens, no, hundreds of principles. In fact, we have more principles than anyone else!' But perhaps these are two ways of saying the same thing.

VII

German Unification

Does the story of German unification belong to the history of Ostpolitik? Yes and no. No, because what followed the opening of the Berlin Wall on 9 November 1989 was fundamentally different from anything that West Germany had done, dealt with, envisaged or planned in its Ostpolitik. This unification was not the gradual coming closer of the people in the two states, not even the 'growing together' of which Brandt spoke, but a hurtling and hurling together, sanctioned by great-power negotiations. In many respects, what happened in the 329 days between the opening of the Wall and the 'day of German unity' was closer to Adenauer's hopes of the early 1950s than it was to Brandt's of the early 1970s. In this sense the Ostpolitik that began after the building of the Berlin Wall ended with the opening of the Berlin Wall. On the other hand, yes, it does belong, because unification came after Ostpolitik, many elements or legacies of Ostpolitik played an important part in the unification process, and Ostpolitik will now always be viewed through the prism of unification.

Yet it is clearly impossible to do justice to this story here. More happened in ten months than usually does in ten years. The whole map of Europe was — or began to be — redrawn. Even the basic headings are disputed. Was what happened in East Germany a revolution or merely *die Wende* (the turn)? When the two German states became one was that unification or reunification? New analyses are pouring from the presses. Many key witnesses have not yet given their accounts. Most documents are unavailable. Further years of research would be needed to collect the evidence, and more hundreds of pages to present it properly. And it may be that, as Peter Pulzer has suggested, the autumn of 1989 is one of those intense, pivotal historical moments — in this (and one hopes only in this) comparable to the summer of 1914 — the interpretation of which will forever be disputed.

What follows can be little more than a highly selective sketch, based on published sources, supplemented by personal observation, and concentrating on the external and especially the Eastern sides of the story. The next chapter then contains more analytical reflections on the contribution of German Ostpolitik to German unification, as compared with that of other putative causes.

Refolution and revolution

The word reunification, writes Michael Wolffsohn, should be spelt *H-u-n-g-a-r-y*; or at least, that is how it begins. By this he means that Hungary's decisions, first to dismantle what was literally an iron curtain along its frontier with Austria, beginning in May 1989, and then specifically to let East German refugees out to the West, starting on 11 September, were the immediate external causes of the collapse of the Honecker regime in East Germany. Such a claim is of course highly contestable. Some would maintain that, for a start, it was unification not reunification, and this should be spelt *G-o-r-b-a-c-h-e-v*. They would point to the whole background of perestroika, glasnost and the more permissive Soviet policy towards Eastern Europe, and then to the specific push to the Honecker regime that was delivered by Gorbachev's famous comment 'who comes too late is punished by life', and perhaps also by more direct and conspiratorial means.

Another spelling popular among German politicians after unification was *H-e-l-s-i-n-k-i*, while in America and Britain the alternative *N-a-t-o* was often preferred. Others again would write *E-u-r-o-p-e*, meaning primarily the (West) European Community which called itself that, or even *c-a-p-i-t-a-l-i-s-m*. Some in East Germany would still write *L-e-i-p-z-i-g*, referring to the great popular demonstrations in that city in the autumn of 1989. A few, mainly in Poland, would even suggest *S-o-l-i-d-a-r-i-t-y*, arguing that the Polish Solidarity movement had led the way both in the attempted, peaceful, self-limiting revolution of 1980–81 and in the negotiated transition from communism at the Round Table of early 1989. In any case, what is clearly wrong is to suggest, as Chancellor Kohl's former government spokesman Hans ('Johnny') Klein seems to in the title of his genial book on this subject, that 'It began in the Caucasus'. If 'it' means unification, then the crucial agreement between Kohl and Gorbachev in Moscow in mid-July 1990, consolidated at an obscure Caucasian hamlet, was not the beginning but almost the end of the historic process.

Without making any such apodictic claim about the 'real beginning', it is clearly true to say that in the summer of 1989 Hungary and Poland were making the running in Central Europe. Both were in the midst of what we have called a 'refolution', that is, a mixture of reform and revolution, with more of a revolutionary push from below in Poland and more of preemptive reform from above in Hungary. In August 1989, Poland became the first East European country to elect a non-communist prime minister,

Tadeusz Mazowiecki. Moscow's actual acceptance of this step was as important as any general declaratory statements about non-interference and free choice. However, Wolffsohn is right to suggest that the decisions of Hungary's still nominally socialist government had a greater direct impact on East Germany. The dismantling of the iron curtain encouraged a growing number of East German escapes, and attempts to get out by taking refuge in the West German embassies in Budapest, Prague and Warsaw. The formal opening of the Hungarian frontier for East Germans in mid-September turned the stream into a flood.

As we have seen, until the summer of 1989 emigration and opposition in the GDR were still more contradictory than they were complementary. To use Albert Hirschman's terms, 'exit' and 'voice' were both alternatives to 'loyalty', but they were alternative alternatives. The old quip that 'emigration is the German form of revolution' was actually a bitter one, implying as it did that Germans were not really capable of revolution. However, in the autumn of 1989, the quantity of emigration gave a new quality to the internal opposition. Now swelling crowds began to chant 'we're staying here'. Even if Gorbachev was mainly thinking of his own experience in the Soviet Union when he said 'who comes too late . . .', what mattered was not how the remark was meant but how it was understood.

The ninth of October, when security forces faced a massive crowd in Leipzig, but stepped back from a Tiananmen massacre, was the first crucial breakthrough in what many in East and West Germany would refer to at the time as a German revolution. The second crucial breakthrough came exactly a month later, on 9 November, when a mixture of common sense and bungling by the state's new communist leaders turned a planned opening of the German-German frontier and Berlin Wall into one of post-war Europe's most extraordinary and magical scenes. There followed, very swiftly, what German historians have called 'the turn within the turn'.

In East Germany's 'October Revolution', led by opposition groups drawn mainly from the intelligentsia, the chant had been 'we are the people' and the aim a truly democratic German Democratic Republic. In and after the 'November Revolution', the increasingly broad and popular protest turned the chant to 'we are one people', and the aim became, in the long unsung words of East Germany's own national anthem, 'Germany, united fatherland'. This change happened spontaneously, not at the instigation of Helmut Kohl or any other West German politician. But of course the response — and promises — of Kohl and others did subsequently encourage it.

When Kohl telephoned Erich Honecker's successor Egon Krenz on 26 October 1989 he was clearly still reckoning with the continued existence of the other German state, albeit with far-reaching reforms encouraged —

but also ultimately constrained — by the Kremlin. According to a transcript, he wished Krenz 'success' in the difficult task ahead of him and said the Bonn government was interested in 'a calm, sensible development'. In other words, the perspective for change was still within the horizons of Ostpolitik. When, just three and a half months later, Kohl coldly received in Bonn the Prime Minister of the GDR, Hans Modrow, one of Moscow's (and Bonn's) long-sought and cherished East German 'reformers', he did not even need to wish him failure. Modrow had already failed. Meanwhile, Kohl and Genscher had just got the go-ahead from Gorbachev to proceed with the internal unification of Germany, with no direct Soviet involvement. (The external aspects, concerning alliances, security arrangements and the like, were a different matter.) The cabinet in Bonn had formed a committee called 'German Unity', and decided to take the DM to East Germany.

The process of arriving at these decisions was more confused than it appears with hindsight. An important step was obviously Chancellor Kohl's '10 point programme' of 28 November, which sketched a path through the 'treaty community' already proposed by Prime Minister Modrow (and very much in the spirit of the earlier West German policy towards the GDR), through 'confederative structures' (of which East German leaders had also spoken in the past), to the final, but also the most distant point — full state unity. This programme was partly a response to developments inside East Germany, partly prompted by the questions of a Soviet emissary, and partly designed to improve the Christian Democrats' standing in the opinion polls and to regain the initiative in West German politics — all in all, a quite characteristic Bonn mixture. The real and very emotional breakthrough for the Chancellor was his visit to Dresden just before Christmas, where he was greeted by huge, patriotic crowds literally packing the rooftops and crying out for unity.

This cry from the people in East Germany, the continued flood of emigration and what can only be described as the collapse of the East German state were the three major factors which impelled the Bonn government to move from a measured 'calm and sensible development' to a headlong dash to unity. The East German Round Table(s), established following the Polish and Hungarian precedents, co-existed for a time with the Modrow government, in what Trotsky would have called 'dual power'. But by the end of January, it was rather dual impotence. Modrow was obliged to admit this collapse to Gorbachev in Moscow, and returned proclaiming his own commitment to 'Germany, united fatherland'. (Just three weeks earlier, Modrow had declared that unification was not on the agenda — one of many, many turns within the turn.)

Meanwhile, nearly 350,000 East Germans had gone west in 1989, and they were now leaving at the rate of 2,000 or more a day. The level of haemorrhage which in 1961 had led to the building of the Berlin Wall would now decisively hasten unification. To this challenge there seemed to be only two responses: to divide completely or to unite completely. *Tertium non datur!*

Yet while most West Germans might in principle dearly love their compatriots in the East they also dearly wished them to stay there — for their own good, of course. On the very evening of the opening of the Berlin Wall, the Free Democrat Wolfgang Mischnick concluded his welcoming speech in the Bundestag with a plangent plea to the East Germans to stay at home: *Bleibt daheim!* This from a man who had himself fled from East Germany forty-one years before, and enjoyed a successful career in the West. Whatever the degree of personal commitment which individual West Germans may or may not have had to the cause of unity, the single most important argument used to convince West German voters of the necessity of economic and monetary union was: if we don't take the DM to the people, the people will come to the DM.

The further steps to internal unification, intricate and fascinating as they are, cannot be our subject here. Vitally important was the resounding election victory won by the Christian Democrats and their allied parties in the 18 March elections in East Germany: a vote for rapid unification which cleared the way for a straight accession to the Federal Republic under article 23 of its Basic Law. With the introduction of the DM in the German economic and monetary union on 1 July 1990, the GDR effectively ceased to be a sovereign state. The details of the encyclopaedic Unification Treaty, negotiated by Wolfgang Schäuble, are more relevant to an understanding of what happened afterwards than to that of what went before.

Peace, agreement and Realpolitik

The story of external unification is much closer to our theme. As we have seen, it had been a consensual (though not wholly undisputed) maxim of West German policy up to 1989 that German unity could only be achieved by peaceful means and with the understanding/agreement/support of Germany's neighbours. After 1990 it became a commonplace of German politics to laud the fact that German unity had been achieved peacefully (in contrast to 1871) and with the understanding/agreement/support of her neighbours. But it did rather depend which neighbour one was talking about, which word one chose, and what meaning one gave to it.

All expressed their *understanding* and general approval at the Helsinki summit in Paris in November 1990; that is, after the event. Formal approval had obviously to be given by all the Federal Republic's EC partners to the arrangements for the European Community's incorporation of the former East Germany. *Agreement*, in a narrower and stronger sense, was given by just four non-German states, the Soviet Union, the United States, France and Britain, with the first being obviously the most important, the second very important, the last two somewhat less so. Of course linkages were also made to the interests of other states, notably Poland. Of course everyone in sight was wooed, reassured, sometimes informed and even occasionally consulted. But for all the polite words, probably only the Soviet Union and the United States had the power to stop it. As for *support*, in the autumn of 1989 the Bonn government's first tentative moves towards unification were actively supported by just one state: the United States. France and Britain became supportive only somewhat later, in the first half of 1990. Poland, as Bronisław Geremek frankly told a domestic readership, could not stop the unification of Germany and therefore had to get to like it.

The formula agreed in mid-February for negotiating the external aspects of unification was '2 + 4'. But of the two German states, the Eastern one was always a fraction of the Western one, and a rapidly disappearing fraction at that. France and Britain were a somewhat larger and more constant fraction of the American one. But the most important negotiations were between Bonn, Moscow and Washington — the Big Three at the end of the Cold War. Genscher would subsequently characterise the true mathematics of '2 + 4' to the author as 'perhaps two and a half', meaning that the central deal was between Bonn and Moscow, but with Washington playing a very important supporting role. Co-ordination between Bonn and Washington was exceptionally close and successful in this period, as was policy co-ordination inside the American government. Much remains to be told of the American side of this story, but some essentials are clear.

The American Ambassador to Bonn, Vernon Walters, and the American foreign policy planner, Francis Fukuyama, both guessed sooner than any leading German politician that unification really was back on the agenda. The Bush administration, having decided early in 1989 that the Federal Republic was to be its West European 'partner in leadership', backed Kohl unambiguously at the end of 1989. Even more important, it made this clear in direct talks with the Soviet Union. There were several possible ways of charting the path 'from Yalta to Malta', and it was by no means a foregone conclusion that Washington would chart it the same way as Bonn.

The American diplomatic team under James Baker was instrumental in winning French and above all Soviet agreement to the '2 + 4' formula, rather than a '4 + 0' peace conference of the victor powers of 1945 (Adenauer's nightmare called Potsdam!) or even a '4 + 2'. In close co-operation with Britain, it forged a common Western position on Nato membership for a united Germany, which was its own — and Britain's — central *sine qua non*. Yet at the same time, by pressing forward with summit, arms control and disarmament talks with the Soviet Union it gave Moscow an incentive which only the other nuclear superpower could offer. In the spring and early summer it brokered with Moscow the specific guarantees about united Germany's military and security position which enabled Gorbachev to accept Nato membership.

What American policymakers somewhat biblically described as the Nine Assurances were discussed by Baker with Shevardnadze in Moscow in mid-May, and then by Bush and Gorbachev at the Washington summit. The United States self-evidently took a leading role in the radical redefinition of Nato's role at the London summit, and in formulating the encouraging (if still vague) message delivered to the Soviet Union by the Houston summit of the Group of Seven leading industrial nations. These three summits formed the psychological take-off ramp for the Kohl-Gorbachev meeting in mid-July. Together, they contrived to suggest that the prize at which Gorbachev and Shevardnadze's whole foreign policy had been directed — a new co-operative relationship with the West which would permit the modernisation of the Soviet Union — was now within Moscow's reach. Just one more concession, and they could be there!

In the event, this was to prove yet another Gorbachevian illusion. But it was an extremely important, perhaps even a decisive illusion for the achievement of Soviet agreement to a united Germany within the Western alliance in the summer of 1990. Finally, the United States helped the Federal Republic through the last hoops at the 2 + 4 meeting in Moscow in mid-September, which saw the signature of the Treaty on the Final Settlement with Respect to Germany — the '2 + 4 Treaty', which was for the external unification what the Unification Treaty was for the internal.

In looking at the evolution of the Soviet position we have all the usual problems of incomplete sources and retrospective rationalisation. The story of the public positions taken by the Soviet leadership is that of a dramatic retreat. The Soviet leadership would 'see to it that no harm comes to the GDR', Gorbachev told his Central Committee in December 1989. It was 'quite impossible' that a united Germany should be in Nato, he said on West German television in March 1990. And so on. Of course these public statements cannot simply be taken at face value, since they were diplomatic bargaining positions and also intended for domestic political consumption. Private thinking was ahead of public speaking, although probably not so far ahead as some would fondly imagine with hindsight.

Three sets of factors seem to have determined the rapid evolution of the Soviet position. Firstly, there was the internal collapse of the GDR and the rapid emergence of non-communist states elsewhere in Eastern Europe. These developments meant that the near-impossibility of holding on to the outer empire became apparent to all but the most square-headed conservative and bull-necked marshal.

Secondly, there were developments inside the inner empire of the Soviet Union itself. With his acquisition of the powers of an executive president

in March and his hard-fought but successful defence of his policies —
including those towards Eastern Europe and Germany — at the 28th Party
congress in July, Gorbachev briefly established matchless supremacy over
the only partly reformed structures of the Soviet party-state. Yet at the
same time economic crisis and nationality conflicts were shaking the very
foundations of those structures, while in Russia itself his arch-rival Boris
Yeltsin returned to power. Gorbachev as it were secured his command of
the oil rig USSR, but the oil rig was itself being rocked by a gathering
storm.

This in turn made the third factor, the active policies of the West, all
the more important. Return to 'the civilised world' was the long-term goal
of Soviet westernisers in foreign policy. But by now the West, and above
all West Germany, was also the Soviet leader's last hope of help in an
immediate crisis. As we have seen, here were Bonn's strongest cards even
before the unification process began. During unification they were played
as trumps.

Much from the German side is also still to be revealed, and we await
the memoirs of Kohl, Genscher and others. Yet the published day-by-day
account of Kohl's chief foreign policy adviser, Horst Teltschik, gives a
vivid impression of the German-Soviet waltz danced inside the American-
German-Soviet threesome (itself inside the '2 + 4' reel, which in turn was
inside the multiple bilateral and multilateral, EC, Nato, Warsaw Pact, G7,
G24 and Helsinki *mêlée*). Thus, for example, Teltschik reveals that, as East
Germany imploded in early January 1990, a message came to the Chancellery from Shevardnadze. The message recalled Kohl's offer of help to
Gorbachev during their conversations in Bonn in June 1989 — an offer
made in response to Gorbachev's own account of his economic difficulties,
following Kohl's weighty plea for German unity (see page 117f). Shevardnadze asked: did the offer still stand?

Within hours, Kohl was discussing with his Agriculture Minister
arrangements for a huge delivery of meat. The Soviet Ambassador said
that these supplies were needed to remedy some temporary bottlenecks —
a familiar refrain! Naturally the Soviet Union wished to pay for them, but
a 'friendship price' would be welcome. Less than three weeks later, the
package was agreed: 52,000 tonnes of canned beef, 50,000 tonnes of pork,
20,000 tonnes of butter, 15,000 tonnes of milk powder, 5,000 tonnes of
cheese, at a 'friendship price' subsidised by the Federal Government to the
tune of DM 220 million. A mere bagatelle compared with what would
follow.

Now it would of course be quite absurd to suggest that German unity
was bought for 52,000 tonnes of beef. But this was an important and very
specific signal that the prospect of Germany being Gorbachev's greatest
helper in his embattled attempt to modernise the Soviet Union was made
not less but more real by the possibility of German unification. This was

of course a prospect which the Federal Republic had already skilfully painted in the years 1987 to 1989, and in a larger sense ever since 1969.

At the German-Soviet summit meeting in Moscow in mid-February, the first of the two external breakthroughs in the unification process, Kohl elaborated *fortissimo* on a theme that he had already played *basso profondo* at his meeting with Gorbachev in Bonn eight months earlier. By Telt-schik's account, he now told Gorbachev that Germany and the Soviet Union should shape the last decade of the twentieth century together. Gorbachev, in return, said the Germans had the right to decide whether they wanted to live in one state. According to Teltschik's Russian counterpart at these talks, Anatoly Chernyaev, Gorbachev said: 'On the point of departure there is agreement — the Germans should make their choice themselves. And they should know that this is our position.' When Kohl asked, 'You mean to say that the question of unity is the choice of the Germans themselves?', Gorbachev replied, 'yes . . . given the realities'. The path to internal unification was open.

In April, the theme of German-Soviet co-operation was further de-veloped, in theory and practice. Following a suggestion made by Boris Meissner, the Kohl government proposed to Moscow that they should already start negotiating a bilateral co-operation and 'friendship' treaty for the period after unification. This was a shrewd psychological move. According to Teltschik, the Soviet Ambassador to Bonn, Yuli Kvitsinsky, reacted almost euphorically. His dream since he came to Germany, he said, had been to build something 'in the Bismarckian spirit' between Germany and the Soviet Union. Two weeks later, Shevardnadze directly confirmed to Kohl the Soviet Union's delight at the proposal. At the same time, he asked for a loan.

Just ten days later, Teltschik was off on a secret mission to Moscow, with two leading German bankers in the plane. The Soviet side spoke frankly about their hard-currency debt, revealing that the Federal Repub-lic was by a clear head their biggest creditor (with Japan in second place, and, rather surprisingly, Italy in third). After discussing the possible loan and the bilateral treaty, Teltschik recalled the suggestion once made by Gorbachev that he should meet with Kohl in the Soviet leader's Caucasian homeland. While James Baker discussed with Shevardnadze possible security guarantees and military limitations for a united Germany in Nato, Kohl organised an immediate, untied, government-guaranteed loan of DM 5 billion. Writing to Gorbachev with the good news, he emphasised that this was to be seen as part of an overall solution to the questions that still remained open in connection with German unification. A hefty *quid*, but for a much larger *quo*.

Once again, it would clearly be absurd to suggest that Soviet assent to united Germany's membership of Nato was bought for DM 5 billion. This was but one of many Western signals, and Western policy but one of many factors. Like the beef, it was nonetheless an important and well-timed move. Talking to Kohl in Moscow in mid-July, at the beginning of the summit that would end in the Caucasus, the Soviet leader himself said that the five billion credit was a 'chess move' made at the right moment. He valued it highly. Despite the suffering of the war, Gorbachev said, according to the edited and then retranslated Russian record which he himself released for publication in 1993, 'we must turn to Europe, and go down the path of co-operation with the great German nation'. However, it should not be forgotten that 'some accuse us of selling for German Marks the victory that was bought at such a high price, with such great sacrifices'.

After exchanging 'non-paper' drafts for the German-Soviet friendship treaty prepared by Anatoly Chernyaev and Horst Teltschik respectively — and, according to the Russian record, Kohl stressed that he had involved neither his Foreign nor his Finance Ministry in its preparation! —, the two leaders got to the point. And already there in Moscow, Gorbachev made the key concession that united Germany could be a member of Nato, although with special conditions and reservations, especially so long as Soviet troops remained 'on the former territory of the GDR', as he himself put it. But, Gorbachev went on, according to the Russian record: 'The sovereignty of united Germany will thereby in no way be put in doubt.'

The security conditions, agreed with the help of vodka and cardigans in the Caucasian hamlet of Arkhyz, were then extraordinarily favourable for West Germany, and for the West as a whole. Soviet troops would withdraw from East Germany within four years. While 'Nato structures' would not be extended to that territory, articles 5 and 6 of the Nato treaty would immediately apply and Bundeswehr units not integrated into Nato could be stationed there straight after unification. In return, Germany would limit its armed forces to 370,000, and at the moment of unification would solemnly reaffirm the renunciation of atomic, biological and chemical weapons already made by the old Federal Republic.

Now whenever Germany and the Soviet Union seemed to be getting close, the spectre of Rapallo would invariably be raised somewhere in the West. It was therefore not surprising that, picking up the name of the nearest big town, Stavropol, the relentlessly punning *Economist* would christen this meeting 'Stavrapallo'. The comparison with Rapallo helped to highlight the fundamental differences, for this was not an arrangement made against the Western powers, nor even in substance behind their backs. Yet this was also a very long way from the new, post-national, multilateral style of international relations which the Federal Republic publicly preached, and which went by the name of 'Helsinki'. In style and content this was a great-power deal. As Gorbachev himself remarked at the concluding press conference: 'We [have] acted in the spirit of the well-known German expression *Realpolitik*.'

Indeed, in some ways the whole negotiation of German unification recalled the meeting that had been held in another scenic Soviet location, in the Crimea, forty-five years before. Here was, so to speak, a Yalta to undo Yalta. It was, to be sure, diplomacy in peace not war. It was diplomacy transformed by the new technologies of communication. But it was still élite, great-power diplomacy, the few deciding about the many. While thousands of diplomats, officials and experts were involved in the whole process, Stephen Szabo, who has made a close study of the diplomacy of unification, concludes that the most important decisions and deals were made by eleven men in three capitals. And even President Bush and James Baker were apparently surprised and just a little piqued by the German-Soviet deal in the Caucasus. The Federal Republic's closest and most important West European allies, France and Britain, were neither present nor intimately involved in the crucial negotiations. In this sense Britain now experienced what France had always most bitterly resented about Yalta — not being there.

As for the neighbour most directly affected in both cases: then as now, Polish politicians might repeat the old cry *nic o nas bez nas* ('nothing about us without us'), but then as now the strong would decide about the weak. As we have seen, Chancellor Kohl had long recognised that Germany would have to concede the Polish frontiers established after Yalta and Potsdam as the price for German unification — although he would deliberately prevaricate until all but the most dunderheaded expellee could see that this was so (see page 230). Here was one thing on which all Germany's neighbours and partners agreed.

Yet at the same time, the Federal Republic made quite sure that Poland would not be a full participant in the 2 + 4 negotiations. According to the published, edited and re-translated Russian version (which must clearly be treated with great caution), Kohl told Gorbachev in Moscow in mid-July that he did not quite understand why 'the Poles' were hesitating about his offer of negotiating a frontier treaty after unification, followed by a general political treaty. 'But,' he continued, according to this version, 'when Germany then concludes its treaty with the Soviet Union they will immediately wrinkle their noses, make a great rumpus and remember history. We should try to think how that can be avoided, how one can bring the Poles to reason.'

At the insistence of other participants in the 2 + 4 negotiations, the Polish Foreign Minister was invited to the meeting in Paris which dealt with the frontier issue, the day after the Caucasus summit. Teltschik has an extraordinary vignette of Genscher talking to Shevardnadze about the next day's 2 + 4 meeting, during a helicopter trip to the town of Mineralniye Vody (that is: Mineral Waters) for the concluding press conference of the Caucasus visit. 'Genscher is mainly concerned,' noted Teltschik, 'to get Shevardnadze's support against Poland.'

Now the word 'against' in this sentence refers to diplomatic tactics, not to fundamental content. As we have recorded above, in substance Genscher was clearly for the final recognition of the Polish western frontier. So this conversation was to earlier German-Soviet ones (Rapallo, Ribbentrop-Molotov) as mineral water is to vodka. But in the politics of unification, as in the whole preceding Ostpolitik, Bonn put Moscow first and Warsaw second. The frontier treaty with Poland was not signed until after German unification. It was not actually ratified by the Bundestag until a year later, in a package with a bilateral 'good neighbour' treaty in which the Bonn government entrenched its interest in the German minority in Poland.

What was true of Poland was even more true of a little country like Lithuania, at this time struggling to regain the independence it had lost in 1939/40, as the result of a German-Soviet pact. When President Bush told Chancellor Kohl that he would find it difficult to sell to Congress a large package of economic aid to the Soviet Union, because of Moscow's attitude to Lithuania, Kohl replied that the Lithuanians had his 'sympathy', but they could not be allowed to determine the policy of the West. Up to and even beyond the Soviet ratification of the 2 + 4 Treaty, the Federal Republic was among the least supportive of all Western states in relation to Lithuania's struggle for independence. As Bonn itself raced headlong to realise the Germans' 'right to self-determination', it sagely advised the Lithuanians to take things very slowly.

Now there were powerful arguments for this attitude from the point of view of German interests, even of Western interests altogether. Germany was by no means alone in its concern about Lithuania's stance. But it is clearly not the case that the national interests of all other European states and peoples, as they themselves defined those interests — and who else should define them? — were all equally respected in the process of unification. This was *Realpolitik* in a highly civilised form, with the telephone and the cheque book instead of blood and iron; but it was *Realpolitik* all the same.

The last treaty work

The veteran Soviet expert on Germany and head of the Central Committee's international department, Valentin Falin, would later describe the concessions made by Gorbachev in the Caucasus as the emotional decisions of an exhausted man. Shevardnadze's contribution he characterised witheringly as 'Georgian games'. The clear implication was that true Russian professionals — such as Falin — would have struck a harder deal.

Perhaps mindful of such criticism, Gorbachev haggled hard on the telephone with Kohl in early September, securing a round DM 12 billion plus a further DM 3 billion credit, to cover the costs of the Soviet troops in the (now hard-currency) territory of the former GDR and their relocation to the Soviet Union. This removed the last major obstacle to the conclusion of no fewer than four German-Soviet treaties, which had been negotiated in an extraordinary diplomatic sprint. The 2 + 4 Treaty could now be signed in Moscow, with a last-minute British objection brushed aside into an addendum.

Noting in the preamble 'the historic changes in Europe, which make it possible to overcome the division of the continent', the treaty gave united Germany 'full sovereignty over its internal and external affairs'. Thirty-five years after Adenauer celebrated the Federal Republic's day of sovereignty, the day of sovereignty had come.

The very next day, in Moscow, Genscher and Shevardnadze initialled their bilateral 'Treaty on good-neighbourliness, partnership and friendship'. A patchwork quilt of fragments from German-Soviet agreements and declarations over the twenty years since the Moscow Treaty, hastily sewn together with golden thread by Genscher's chief negotiator, Dieter Kastrup, this contained some remarkable statements. 'The Federal Republic of Germany and the Union of Soviet Socialist Republics,' said its preamble, 'wishing finally to have done with the past...' (Francis Fukuyama had recently declared the end of history, but perhaps only Germans and Russians could commit themselves in a treaty to have done with the past.) Yet, picking up a formula from the Bonn Declaration of June 1989, the preamble also said that the Federal Republic and the Soviet Union were 'determined to follow on from the good traditions of their centuries-long history'.

There followed a familiar catalogue of areas of co-operation and good intentions. This included, for example, the assertion that the two sides 'will never and under no circumstances be the first to use armed force against each other or against other states. They call upon all other states to join in this commitment to non-aggression.' Taken literally, this meant that Germany was joining the Soviet Union in calling upon, say, the United States not to use armed force against, say, Iraq. But of course it was not meant to be taken literally. It was meant to secure Soviet agreement to German unification. This was Machiavelli dressed as Luther.

On the third of October 1990, Germany celebrated, with fireworks, flags and champagne, what would henceforth replace the 17 June as the 'day of unity'. But two more detailed agreements remained to be signed: that on 'several transitional measures', meaning the agreed payments for the removal of Soviet troops, and that specifying the precise terms on which the Soviet troops would remain and withdraw by the end of 1994. On 9 November, the first anniversary of the opening of the Berlin Wall, Kohl and Gorbachev formally signed in Bonn the friendship treaty that Genscher and Shevardnadze had initialled in Moscow and yet another treaty — 'on the development of a comprehensive co-operation in the fields of eco-nomics, industry, science and technology'. Gorbachev concluded his speech with the modest words: 'Let the Soviet-German treaty signed for twenty years be transformed into the treatise "To Eternal Peace".' Kant as cant.

With this, the latest and in the event the last German-Soviet treaty work was complete. It was the most complex in form, the simplest in content. Yet the cautious diplomats said it was still not wholly secure. Ratification of the 2 + 4 Treaty by the Western signatories was a foregone conclusion. The complex arrangements with the EC had already been agreed. The frontier treaty with Poland would be signed by Genscher in Warsaw a week later. The blessing from the Helsinki summit in Paris was easy. But something could still go wrong in Moscow. Thus Genscher would argue that German unification was only definitely achieved when the Soviet Ambassador handed over the Soviet ratification document for the 2 + 4 Treaty, in the Foreign Ministry in Bonn on 15 March 1991. Only then was Germany finally united, again; or was it rather, anew?

In July 1987, Gorbachev had said to Weizsäcker that German unification might perhaps come 'in a hundred years'; generously reducing the period, on Weizsäcker's intervention, to a round fifty. In January 1989, Erich Honecker had declared that the Berlin Wall might survive for fifty or a hundred years, if the grounds for its existence were not removed. The hundred had happened in one.

Yet was Germany really united? Asked for his hopes on 'the day of unity', the writer Reiner Kunze, one of many free spirits driven out of Honecker's GDR, said he hoped that after this day the Germans would prepare themselves for it. The deep truth in that deceptively simple remark was to become apparent to everyone over the next two years. Economically, socially, culturally and pyschologically, the Germans were still very far from united. Nonetheless, Germany, the state, was united in a way that Europe, for example, was not. What is more, united Germany was, whether it liked it or not, once again a major power in the centre of a still disunited Europe.

VIII

Findings

German and European

An old truth: the more you know, the less you know. Politicians and commentators in happy possession of a little knowledge can make the most confident pronouncements about the certain future effects of a given policy on another country. After making a detailed study of what actually happened, one hesitates to make any positive statements at all. This applies not only to the tangled skein of cause and effect. It applies even to intentions.

If we return to the issue of the relationship between the German and the European questions, raised in Chapter One, then our first general finding is that German Ostpolitik was above all a German answer to the German question. However, from the 1960s onwards German politicians — not all German politicians, but politicians in all parties — concluded not only that this required seeking German answers to the European question, but also that these German answers must be built into a larger European answer to the European question. The way forward led not through reunification to détente but through détente to reunification. Bonn would work towards a European peace order, in which the Germans could achieve unity in free self-determination. West European integration or 'European Union' would be a contribution to the larger European unification. This in turn might be described as a European answer to the German question — indeed even, one German historian suggested, the most constructive answer to the German question since the Thirty Years' War.

Throughout, almost every aspect of Bonn's policy towards Europe (West) and Europe as a whole had (at least) two sides. The multilateral also facilitated the unilateral. The renunciation of sovereignty was also about the recovery of sovereignty. The transfer of power also served the (re)acquisition of power.

From Adenauer to Kohl, West German Chancellors asked the West and

especially Western Europe to place golden handcuffs upon Germany. Both
the Atlantic Alliance and the European Community were to save Europe
from itself — that is, from reverting to the bad old ways of warring nation
states —, to protect all of Western Europe from the Soviet Union and to
protect the rest of Western Europe against Germany. But they were also
to protect Germany against itself. However, it was precisely this German
readiness to transfer or share power and give up sovereignty which helped
to convince West Germany's neighbours that the Germans could be
trusted with restored sovereignty. In a feat worthy of Houdini, it was by
laying on the golden handcuffs that Germany set itself free.

Similarly with the East. In talking of and working for all-European
solutions, the Bonn government was also thinking of and working for
all-German ones. In being so comprehensively and demonstratively peaceful, co-operative and 'European', West Germany built up what Genscher
called *Vertrauenskapital* — literally trust-capital — in West and East.
These reserves of trust, as much as the reserves of DM — and the capital
of trust was also partly trust in German capital — were heavily and
successfully drawn upon to achieve German unification. When Genscher
said 'the more European our foreign policy is the more national it is' he
summarised the apparent paradox — and a real ambiguity.

There are strong echoes of Stresemann here. If one is looking for
parallels in the earlier history of German foreign policy, then the admix-
ture of the Adenauerian and Bismarckian traditions that Waldemar Besson
identified in 1970 actually came out in the 1980s closest to Stresemann —
a model whom both Kohl and Genscher would happily acknowledge. As
with Stresemann, there was the attempt to achieve national and revisionist goals through the patient but active rehabilitation of Germany in the
international community, peaceful negotiation, harmonising Europeanism
and all-round reconciliation — with, nonetheless, important qualitative
differences between the western and the eastern Locarnos. As with
Stresemann, there was the mixture, so difficult to analyse, of genuine
Europeanism and genuine nationalism, of more or less affected Europeanism for foreign audiences but also of more or less affected nationalism for
domestic audiences — such as Germans from lost territories to the east.

Yet such comparisons are useful also for the differences they point up,
starting with the fact that the Bonn government succeeded where Stresemann failed. The year of 1990 saw a triumph of peaceful, moderate
German revisionism of which Stresemann could only dream. The Federal
Republic, having in two great steps, the Western and the Eastern treaty
works, regained its (relative) freedom of action as a state in Europe, West
then East, had expanded its connections, attraction, good reputation and
power to the point where it could seize an extraordinary (and unexpected)
historic opportunity to achieve the maximum possible revision of the
post-war ('Yalta') map of Europe to Germany's advantage. But this was a

triumph within — and made possible by — a profoundly different domestic context.

The basic structures out of which West German foreign policy was made, the democratic polity, the modern, centrist character of stable parties of both left and right, the legal system, the economy, the social structure (with the remnants of the old agrarian, aristocratic élites from east of the Elbe now supporting neo-Stresemannesque policies from the leader columns of *Die Zeit* and the boardrooms of thoroughly modern banks), the subordinate and democratic character of the military (those model 'citizens in uniform'), the attitudes of writers, scholars, intellectuals, public opinion — all were quite different from those of Stresemann's day.

The question of the relationship between the German and the European can also be posed slightly differently, and more generally, in the terms of an ongoing debate about the nature of contemporary international relations. On the one side are those (sometimes loosely called Realists) who see these as still fundamentally about the immanently competitive relations between states, each struggling to maintain and increase its own power, in a great game that would in its innermost essentials be familiar to Metternich, to Machiavelli, to the Athenians of Thucydides' Melian debate. By no means only war belongs to this great game, but public and private diplomacy, economic statecraft, summitry, secret understandings and public alliances, including supposedly permanent ones, called Ententes, Empires, Treaty Organisations, Axes, Commonwealths or Communities.

On the other side there are those who emphasise the fundamentally new elements in post-1945 international relations, not only but perhaps especially in Europe: the degree of 'complex interdependence', the special attributes of the nuclear age in strategy, the global village in communications, the single world economy and ecology. All these, they argue, make today's international relations, Alliances and Communities qualitatively different from those analysed by historians from Thucydides to Lewis Namier.

Not only a large part of German scholarship but much of official German foreign policy consciously presented itself in the 1970s and 1980s as belonging to the latter school. Bonn's was the very model of a modern foreign policy: post-national, multilateral, acronymic, economistic, supremely peaceful in all respects, preaching interdependence in all directions, seeking friends everywhere, seeing enemies nowhere — only 'enemy-images' (*Feindbilder*) that had to be 'dismantled'. In this rhetorical world there were no conflicts, only 'irritations'; power was a dirty word, to be replaced by 'responsibility'; and national interests were always to be discreetly covered, like Victorian piano legs, by curtains marked 'Europe', 'peace', 'co-operation', 'stability', 'normality' or even 'humanity'.

Of course one should beware of caricature. As we have seen, there were notable exceptions in German scholarship and commentary, while German policymakers were themselves quite capable of thinking and even talking in terms of power and national interest, especially to domestic audiences and even more in internal discussions and private communications. In fact, we have found that the reality of German foreign policy in general, and German Ostpolitik in particular, was a great deal more national, power-oriented and, so to speak, hard-nosed and old-fashioned, than its public presentation.

German Ostpolitik gave a special twist to an analysts' term, by proclaiming 'interdependence' as a goal of foreign policy. Yet preaching interdependence helped to achieve full *in*dependence for the Germans who preached it, while contributing to a new (or new-old) dependence for many of those to whom interdependence was preached.

Now such a conclusion will naturally prompt the criticism that this merely reflects the general views of the author. The author, it will be said, has found what he set out to prove: his conclusion is actually his starting point. But this must be disputed in three very important respects. Firstly, these really are findings, not just opinions. We have carefully presented a mass of detailed evidence, drawing on sources often of unusually high quality, to show what German policymakers did actually say at the highest level, among themselves and to their key Eastern partners. Secondly, this is not what the author set out to find. This book started as a search for answers to the European question, as posed in the Prologue. Closer examination suggested that German answers would be the most important. Only still closer examination revealed the full extent to which these German answers were actually, first and last, answers to the German question.

Thirdly, and most importantly, it is by no means contended here that the German use of 'Europe' was merely instrumental. In fact, the sudden, unexpected achievement of German unification may not only reveal but also obscure what German policymakers themselves thought they were trying to do. As we have seen, German Ostpolitik was designed to clear away some heavy burdens of the past, to increase the Federal Republic's freedom of action, and to create European conditions in which the Germans in the two states could come closer together again, and eventually reunite. Inasmuch as one can talk of a basic 'logic' of a policy, irrespective of the understanding of the people practising it at a given moment, this remained the 'logic' of German Ostpolitik. But from the outset there was a wide range of different motives among policymakers. As different people came to the helm, and as things in Germany and Europe developed over the 1970s and 1980s, so different priorities, different intentionalities, different visions of a European peace order, would overlay that original and arguably always underlying logic.

Thus there is, for example, no doubt that Helmut Kohl was genuinely committed to a vision of European Union in the (then) boundaries of the European Community. In the early to mid-1980s his foreign policy was more concretely directed towards this goal than to that of German unification. If in the event he achieved German rather than (West) European unity, this does not mean that his commitment to the latter was any less genuine. It simply means that it did not happen.

In the 1980s, Willy Brandt may genuinely have thought as often and cared as deeply about the two parts of Europe, East and West, indeed about the two parts of the world, North and South, as he did about the two parts of Germany and Berlin. When Helmut Schmidt says that the idea of a European peace order had seemed to him, down the years, the most important thing, we have no good reason to doubt that to him it thus seemed. (One merely has to ask what he meant by it.) For Hans-Dietrich Genscher, pursuing the best possible relations with the largest possible number of states while maintaining the highest possible domestic profile may indeed at times have become almost an end in itself, rather than a means to an end which seemed so remote. And so on down the ranks, with many people at all levels sincerely committed to some vision of a larger European project.

Moreover, when German and European interests were so habitually conflated it would be wrong to assume that a clear private distinction was made between them. Between the national-instrumental usage at the one end and the selfless-visionary usage at the other there was a large area of quite genuine and quite characteristic higher confusion. The point about much German speaking and thinking about Europe was precisely that it was not clear. When, for example, in the early 1980s German interests clashed with Polish interests, many German policymakers and commentators honestly found it difficult to see (let alone to admit) that it was actually national interests that were conflicting. Beside the real difficulty in defining the national interests of an unfree country, such as Poland then was, there was a real confusion between German, European and indeed all-human interests, a confusion much assisted by the elastic and multi-layered concept of 'stability'.

However, in the decades of Ostpolitik the profound unclarities and latent tensions within and between the very diverse forms of German Europeanism produced no major controversy in Germany for three main reasons. Firstly, there undoubtedly was in most of the wartime and immediate post-war generations in German politics a deeply felt revulsion against the preceding perversion of German nationalism, and a correspondingly strong commitment to expand supra-national co-operation and integration in Western Europe; although this went hand-in-hand, or back-to-back, with an equally strong desire to restore Germany's freedom of action as an (at least) half-nation-state.

Secondly, in these decades West European integration did not reach the stage at which it threatened the real core essentials of state power and national sovereignty — such as, for example, the DM. Thirdly, and most importantly, even those who had little genuine commitment to a supranational European project, however defined, could see that, in the circumstances of Yalta Europe, Germany could only achieve her national goals by being demonstratively, emphatically European. As Genscher said: the more European, the more national.

These conditions are interesting not only for historical reasons but also because in the second half of the 1990s all three might no longer apply.

Ostpolitik and the end

What caused what? A simple question which, as we have repeatedly observed, is extraordinarily difficult to answer when looking at East-West relations in the era of hot peace. It is even more difficult to answer when looking at the end (to say 'outcome' is already to prejudge the issue) because German unification came not, as German politicians had hoped, in the course of a gradual transformation of the European scene, but in a revolutionary transformation of the world scene. For the events of 1989 to 1991, from the first snip at the barbed wire along the Austro-Hungarian frontier to the collapse of the Soviet Union, clearly do mark a caesura not just in European but in world history.

The specific causal effect that may tentatively be attributed to German policy is hard to discern between the internal Eastern causes and the effects of the policies of other major Western states. And all of this is bound up in the mystery of truly great events. While compelling reasons may be adduced for the collapse of communism, the reasons why it collapsed then — and not a decade earlier, or later — are much more difficult to pin down. Reference to the old Tocquevillian saw that the most dangerous moment for an autocracy is when it starts to try to reform itself is no doubt helpful. But this is a set of historical events so rich that, like the French Revolution, it offers ample stuff for almost every kind of historical explanation; even Marxist ones.

Some may point to changes in supposedly objective balances of military, economic and political power, what Soviet analysts used to call the 'correlation of forces'. Here the objective, infrastructural shift in the balance of (above all) economic power between the West and the East in general, West Germany and the Soviet Union in particular, was, they might argue, now working through into the formal realities of political superstructure. This is, however, an interpretation that would have been disputed by that well-known Marxist analyst of international relations, Leonid Brezhnev. In one of his confidential letters to Helmut Schmidt,

Brezhnev wrote that 'for all the importance of economics . . . the primacy in international affairs remains, as is well known, with politics'.

Others, mindful of Brezhnev's insight, would point to the significance of individual personalities — and the importance of the particularly good understanding between Kohl, Gorbachev and Bush, Shevardnadze, Baker and Genscher, cannot be ignored. Others again would invoke the *Weltgeist*, God, Time, Life, or, as the veteran Soviet pro-consul in Germany, Vladimir Semyonov, put it in conversation with the author, 'His Majesty History'. Yet others, less philosophically inclined, would point to the role played by Lady Luck — and that often neglected historical agent must certainly be credited with a part in the proceedings. For example, Germany was simply lucky that in the summer of 1990 Gorbachev had reached just the right combination of strength (inside the Soviet party-state) and weakness (all around it). He was weak enough to feel he had to concede German unification within the Western Alliance but still strong enough to push this through at home. Had he been a little stronger, he might not have conceded the deal of the century. Had be been a little weaker, he might no longer have been there to make any deal.

Gorbachev himself, on signing the German-Soviet friendship treaty in Bonn, paid fulsome tribute to the personal contribution of Helmut Kohl, but also to that of the 'Ostpolitik' (German in the original) which he associated with the names of Willy Brandt and Hans-Dietrich Genscher. However, elsewhere he paid equally fulsome tribute to 'my friend Ronald Reagan' and to Pope John Paul II, thus producing, in sum, a truly catholic endorsement of almost every major strain of Western policy.

Naturally enough, German politicians placed slightly different emphases among themselves: Christian Democrats drew a straight line from Konrad Adenauer via Helmut Kohl to unification, Social Democrats drew a great arch from the Willy Brandt of 1970 to the Willy Brandt of 1990, Free Democrats celebrated the triumph of Genscherism — and all ignored the many twists and turns on the way. In outward discourse, they joined in paying tribute to Gorbachev, first and foremost, to the Hungarians, to the Americans and the Western Alliance, to the EC, to the French, to the British, to the Poles, to Uncle Tom Cobley and all.

The most frequent and consensual explanation was, however, 'Helsinki'. President von Weizsäcker referred often to the success of what he called simply *Helsinkipolitik*. The Helsinki process, he averred, had become in Eastern Europe a 'human rights motor'. CSCE, said Genscher, '— that had to lead to German unification'. Thus, characteristically, both chose the most general, multilateral and harmonising form of explanation. In fact, these formulations are less a contribution to the historical explanation of Ostpolitik than a continuation of Ostpolitik in the shape of historical explanation.

As we have seen, Helsinki actually covered a multitude of approaches.

It was a very useful, original and flexible diplomatic form, which could be filled with very different contents. Weizsäcker's version is misleading in at least two respects. Firstly, while human rights activists in Eastern Europe paid generous tribute to 'the favourable atmosphere created by Helsinki' (in the words of a Charter 77 message to the Vienna review conference), his description of Helsinki as a 'human rights *motor*' is an historically indefensible overstatement. Men and women had fought for human rights in Eastern Europe long before Helsinki, and would have done so if Helsinki had never happened. To suggest that Helsinki was the 'motor' that drove Jan Patočka or Andrei Sakharov is like suggesting that the Atlantic Charter was the 'motor' that drove Dietrich Bonhoeffer. Secondly, insofar as a specific linkage was made in Western policy between the Helsinki process and the position of those fighting most actively for respect for human rights in Eastern Europe, it was American rather than German policy that made that linkage. As for Genscher's claim, this is the fallacy of historical inevitability; retrospective determinism in a particularly crass form.

Difficult though it is to establish clear connections between cause and effect, a little more clarity and precision is possible.

German Ostpolitik was a systematic combination of policy towards the Soviet Union, East Germany and the rest of Eastern Europe. While developments in all three areas remained important throughout the events of 1989 to 1991, those in Eastern Europe were most important in the spring, summer and early autumn of 1989, those in East Germany were critical from October 1989 to early 1990, while thereafter it was above all a matter of relations with the Soviet Union.

Broadly speaking, German Ostpolitik made the most direct and substantial contribution to the ultimate success in the area of relations with the Soviet Union, and the overall system of East-West relations. It made a still more direct but much more ambivalent, indeed deeply paradoxical contribution in relations with East Germany. The least substantial and direct contribution was in the area which was always its lowest priority, the rest of Eastern Europe.

The Federal Republic succeeded in what Weizsäcker called 'our most important task': to establish a good relationship with the 'Eastern leading power' while at the same time retaining the protection and support of the leading Western power. The achievement of all that wooing, reassurance, trade and 'honest interpreting', all those treaties, earnest speeches, nocturnal exchanges of war memories, joint economic projects and credits, is clearly reflected in an internal memorandum drafted by the Bogomolov institute in Moscow for one of Gorbachev's key foreign-policy advisers, Georgi Shakhnazarov, in January 1990. 'In principle,' said this memorandum, 'the reunification of Germany does not contradict the interests of the

Soviet Union. A military threat from that side is not very likely, if one considers the radical fracture in the consciousness of the German nation that occurred with the national catastrophe of the past war. In the economic sphere, the Soviet Union can obtain tremendous gains from co-operation and interaction with Germany.'

Here are the two crucial points. Forty-five years after the end of the war, Germany (West) had convinced key Soviet policymakers that it was no longer a threat, and that it was the Soviet Union's most promising and important economic partner in the West. Of course other causes were at work here. In considering the perception of threat we really do have to look at the factor 'time itself'. Gorbachev and Kohl were the first Soviet and German leaders since 1945 not to have experienced the war as adults. On the economic side, the underlying cause was of course the divergent performance of the two systems, Western and Eastern, mixed market and planned. But the contribution of conscious German policy is nonetheless very significant.

There has been some debate about the economic components of power. At least since Ranke, and in the latest version from Paul Kennedy, a great power has been identified by its military might. The economic power of a Germany or Japan is, it has been suggested, qualified and constrained by the multiple dependencies of a trading state. And Leonid Brezhnev's contribution to this scholarly debate should certainly be a caution against any simplistic economic determinism. Nonetheless, West Germany's economic power — that is, at the cutting edge, its *financial* power — demonstrably contributed to the achievement of its goals in German-Soviet relations.

From 1969/70 to 1989/90 the bankers and industrialists preceded or accompanied the diplomats and politicians on the way to Moscow, underpinning and facilitating their work. West Germany, as a prime mover of West European economic integration and a key player in the economy of the developed world, was able to wave the key not just to future economic co-operation with itself, but also to that with the EC and to some extent even with the G7 — as it 'honestly interpreted' Gorbachev's good intentions in the spirit of Genscher's Davos speech. Food supplies and hard currency played a very direct part in the actual diplomacy of German unification.

In the specific circumstances of Europe in the 1980s, where the 'Yalta' dividing line was also one between hard and soft currencies, and many of the soft-currency states had got themselves in debt to hard-currency states, a little hard currency went a long way. This applied even more, in different ways, to relations with Poland, Hungary and the GDR. The power transmission between the economic and the political was quite direct, and the gearing very high. There are circumstances in which a country's riches may not easily be usable for its political ends. But here they definitely were. The DM was indeed the currency of German power.

What of the other, even harder currency of power, arms? Was the success achieved in spite or because of the Federal Republic's continued commitment to the defence as well as the détente track of Nato's Harmel strategy? There are two issues here. The first is the general one of the relative contribution of defence and détente, of a policy of strength and proposals for co-operative security — at the extreme, of SDI or SI — to the revision of Soviet policy in the second half of the 1980s. We have found that evidence can be adduced for both sides, and suggested that the most likely answer is, maddeningly, 'at once neither and both'.

The second issue, however, is the Federal Republic's need to keep the trust of the West. For this, its continued commitment to Nato as a military alliance, including the deployments of the 1980s, was crucial. As Willy Brandt suggested, the term Ostpolitik was to some extent a misnomer, inasmuch as the continuation of Westpolitik was a fundamental premiss and *sine qua non* of this policy. German foreign policy was unavoidably a balancing act between preserving the desirable and changing the undesirable aspects of the status quo, between winning the trust of the East and retaining that of the West, a matter therefore of squaring several circles, reconciling the irreconcilable, of many-sidedness verging on the chameleon-like, of *sowohl-als-auch*.

Some of those most directly involved in the conception and development of Ostpolitik, such as Egon Bahr, pushed for more rapid and generous Western disarmament than Washington (or London) could happily bear. They hoped to yield to Soviet wishes only — judo again! — the better to realise their own. This eastward tilt or gamble was averted twice. First it was averted by Helmut Schmidt becoming Chancellor, thus preventing Bahr from trying out the second part of his 'concept'. Then it was averted by Schmidt ceasing to be Chancellor, thus preventing the Social Democrats from taking another such chance, sustained by an emotional, theological and national tide of protest for 'peace'.

Whether these experiments would have facilitated or delayed the revision of Soviet foreign policy is a hypothetical question, but in the author's judgement Andrei Gromyko might well have accounted them a great success for his own line — and therefore a good reason for continuing with it. Almost certainly, however, they would have rapidly depleted West Germany's 'capital of trust' in the West. While one can never finally know 'what would have happened if', this was a gamble well avoided. As the story of 1989/90 again clearly showed, Bonn needed the trust of both Washington and Moscow to achieve its goals.

In all this, Bonn was successful in the most straightforward and satisfying way. Not only did it achieve all (and even more than) it set out to achieve. It did so more or less in the ways it set out to. What of the other two sides of the Bonn-Moscow-Berlin triangle? The original idea of Brandt and Bahr's Ostpolitik was, after all, to work through Moscow to get back to Berlin, so that Germans could get closer to Germans again. It is hard to overstate the degree to which German-German relations, including those in and around Berlin, were and remained the epicentre, the alpha and omega, of German Ostpolitik.

Now here, too, the end of the story could be considered a remarkable success, going beyond even the highest original expectations. Yet the German-German path to this end was in many respects radically different from that intended or expected. It was hedged with ironies and paved with unconscious as well as conscious paradoxes. We have already presented our interim conclusions to this central chapter, of Ostpolitik and of this book (see p. 203f). A few of the main points should briefly be recapitulated here. By going through Moscow, Bonn got to Berlin. In this sense, the original paradox of only being able to change the status quo by first recognising the status quo proved right. However, the second paradox in the stategy of *Wandel durch Annäherung*, that of liberalisation through stabilisation, proved wrong, while the supplementary, that one could best help dissidents in the GDR by not helping them, was definitely a paradox too far.

The idea of liberalisation through stabilisation, with its behaviourist core of relaxation through reassurance, was always flawed. The West could never provide enough reassurance to make communist rulers relax, because the internal tensions came from the very nature of their regimes and not merely from the external tensions of the Cold War. Somewhere in this theory there was still the idea that a socialist third way, evolving out of reformed communism, could be as attractive as the already reformed capitalism of Western Europe. The theoretical possibility can never finally be disproved. But it has certainly not happened anywhere. And as the reformed capitalism of West Germany became ever more attractive (particularly when seen on television or a short visit) while the unreformed communism of East Germany became ever less attractive, so GDR policy in the original Social Democratic version drove ever deeper into an irresoluble contradiction.

Even if the Federal Republic had, for example, denied its own citizenship to East Germans and recognised the full sovereignty of the East German state in every conceivable way, this would still not have made that state acceptable to its own people. To achieve this end, the only thing would have been to make West Germany poorer, greyer, and altogether less attractive than East Germany. A glimmering of this absurd notion comes through the suggestion made in 1988 by the then Bishop of East Berlin that West Germany might 'try to reduce the temptation a bit'.

At the same time, the lesson of experience in other socialist states, indeed in dictatorships throughout history, was that a degree of tension, opposition, conflict, social pressure from below, was a necessary (though not, of course, a sufficient) condition for desirable change. This was the lesson that some of the best political thinkers in East Central Europe,

Kołakowski and Mischnik, Havel and Kis, had already drawn from the crushing of the Prague Spring. 'Revisionism', change by reforms from above, led by an enlightened Party, would never be enough. In this sense, the Social Democrats were a decade behind the times. They built the hope of revisionism into the heart of their strategy just at the time when the revisionists in Eastern Europe were abandoning it.

Instead of liberalisation through stabilisation, what happened in the GDR was stabilisation without liberalisation. The Federal Republic contributed to this with DM and recognition. Of course the interim benefits for West Berlin, visiting West Germans, and many thousands of individual East Germans — the famous *Menschen* — should by no means be underrated. The 'improvements for people' were great. Perhaps this also contributed to the 'keeping together of the people', although that is more debatable. However, one has to set against these specific alleviations for individual people the disadvantages that flowed from the stabilisation of an unreformed communist state for everyone who lived in it.

Many of the monies paid by West Germany were, in effect, ransom. The main objection to paying ransom was best expressed by Rudyard Kipling:

> That if once you have paid him the Danegeld
> You never get rid of the Dane.

In this case, however, they did ultimately get rid of the Dane. Bonn contributed to his departure in one partly intended and two unintended ways. The partly intended way was to increase contacts between the people in the two states, so the East Germans could see which was better and want to get still closer to it. To some extent this did happen, particularly with the growth of travel from East to West in the late 1980s. But arguably, given the chance, East Germans would always have wanted that anyway.

Curiously enough, one of the two unintended ways was actually the Danegeld itself. Far from helping to encourage a reform of the East German economy, this enabled the GDR to continue without significant reform, economic or political. Precisely that lack of reform, however, made the collapse, when it came, more precipitate and total. The growing direct financial dependency on West Germany was probably not a primary concern for Honecker, but it was for important decision-makers close to him, and contributed very directly to the rapid resignation of those who came after him.

The other main currency of German-German relations, recognition, also worked in an unintended way. Flattered and reassured, Honecker did not, as intended, relax his grip on his subjects in the GDR. In fact, he tightened it. But he did relax his grip on reality. West German illusions about East Germany reinforced his own, thus contributing to hubris, followed by nemesis. Hence our ultimate paradox of West German policy towards the GDR: they got it right because they got it wrong!

However, the successful leap from stabilisation without liberalisation to liberation through destabilisation was only possible because of external circumstances. West Germany had contributed to these directly, consciously and successfully in the development of German-Soviet relations within the overall system of East-West relations. Perhaps those Social Democrats and others who had illusions about the stability and reformability of the GDR also contributed a little to Gorbachev's illusions about the reformability of socialism in Eastern Europe: the illusions of '68 that were so unintentionally helpful in '89. But the other great unexpected cause was the radical yet peaceful push for change from the rest of Eastern Europe, starting in Poland and Hungary.

What was the role of Ostpolitik here? Two major intended effects were to remove the German bogey and to replace it with the attractive image of *Modell Deutschland*, the economic and social Model Germany. In removing, or at least radically diminishing, the fear of a revanchist Germany, the Bonn republic also removed one of the very few effective arguments that East European communist rulers had for securing the support of their own peoples. The policy of reconciliation, however contorted, did achieve this. Willy Brandt in Warsaw will forever remain its great symbol.

As for the attraction: already in the 1950s, first Schumacher and then Adenauer had developed what came to be called the magnet theory. A free, prosperous West Germany — and Adenauer added, in a free, prosperous, uniting Western Europe — would exert an irresistible magnetic pull on the peoples of Eastern Europe. However, what Adenauer thought would happen in years actually took decades — decades in which many other things happened as well.

Not only was the Soviet Union brought to the point where it could be persuaded to let Eastern Europe go — a necessary condition that Adenauer of course also acknowledged. The relative magnetism of Western Europe vis-à-vis Eastern Europe also increased steadily. And the iron curtain was made more permeable, thus allowing the magnet to exert its attractive force. This last was the specific contribution of détente in general, and Ostpolitik in particular. With its strategy of 'weaving', its Helsinki of human contacts, its open door policy for visitors from the East, West Germany did more than any other Western state to bring the full attractions of the West home to 'the people on the quiet streets', to recall John F Kennedy's phrase.

To many East Europeans in 1989, the Federal Republic was the model of a 'normal' Western Europe to which they hoped to 'return'. Such a perception of West Germany had been quite unthinkable in 1950, and still very hard to imagine in 1970. This great change was the combined legacy of Adenauer and Brandt, of West Germany's domestic and foreign, western and eastern policies. Hannah Arendt famously espied in Eichmann the 'banality of evil'. To say that what East Europeans saw in the new West Germany was the banality of good would no doubt be an exaggeration. Yet the West German example of slightly boring, prosperous, civilised, bourgeois — even petit bourgeois — democracy certainly had elements of both banality and good.

In this sense, West Germany made a major indirect contribution to the social and, as it were, psychological preconditions of the revolution of 1989. However, the direct contribution of German Ostpolitik was much smaller, and more ambiguous. As we have seen, relations with East European states had an essentially supporting role in the overall system of Ostpolitik. Following the imperative of synchronisation, they were meant to facilitate, or at least not to disrupt, Bonn's key relationships with Moscow and East Berlin. A little exemplary reform, as seen in Budapest, was a good thing, to encourage the others. But too many demands for freedom, as in the Prague Spring or the Polish August, would upset the whole diplomatic system of Ostpolitik. Soviet-style 'normalisation' in Czechoslovakia was actually a toll-gate on the road to East-West 'normalisation' à la Bahr and Brandt — however much they might personally dislike it.

In his 1989 memoirs, written before the great events of that year, Brandt wrote: 'Whether Warsaw or Prague or whatever other centre in Central and Eastern Europe: Federal German policy could hardly remove much of the burden from those responsible there, but it has not added anything to those burdens.' In one sense this is wrong, because by simply unfolding the magnetic power of its own attractions the Federal Republic did add greatly to East European rulers' problems. But so far as Bonn's intentions were concerned it is clearly right. The question is, however, whether this was something to be proud of. It is an interesting experiment to insert into Brandt's sentence, say, Santiago (under Pinochet) in place of Warsaw (under Jaruzelski), San Salvador instead of Prague, Central and South America instead of Central and Eastern Europe — and then see how it reads.

As we have seen, Bonn's policy was almost exclusively focussed on the powerholders, and ever solicitous not to 'destabilise' their states. The cases of Poland and Hungary do, however, contrast. Bonn's good relations with the reform communist powerholders in Budapest, strengthened by economic leverage through trade and the hard currency debt, contributed directly to the historical breakthrough in 1989. The then Hungarian Foreign Minister, Gyula Horn, records how, after a sleepless night in August 1989 worrying about the number of East German refugees building up in Hungary, he talked to his Prime Minister, Miklós Németh, tired after a sleepless night worrying about the country's economic problems, and especially its hard-currency debt. They decided to fly secretly to Bonn to discuss both problems: the money and the Germans.

According to Németh's recollection of the dramatic meeting in Schloss Gymnich, when the Foreign Minister had indicated to Kohl and Genscher that Hungary would probably open the frontier for the East Germans, Kohl's first response was: what can we give you in return? By Németh's account, it was actually the Hungarians who suggested that a decent interval should elapse before they got — as they did in October — DM 1 billion in new state-guaranteed credits. 'Do you realise,' Horn records the Hungarian Interior Minister commenting on the decision to open the frontier, 'that of the two German states we are choosing the West German one?' No, Horn replied, 'we are choosing *Europe*'!

The Polish case is quite different. Essentially, the Bonn government saw in the Polish revolution of 1980–81 a threat, not an opportunity. German policymakers knew it endangered the whole overall system of German Ostpolitik, and they thought it was the wrong way to go about overcoming Yalta anyway. The reaction to the imposition of martial law was therefore deeply ambivalent. As after the Soviet invasion of Czechoslovakia, a Soviet-style 'normalisation' in another East European country seemed to be necessary for the continued 'normalisation' of West Germany's relations with Moscow and East Berlin. To recall Havel's 1989 Frankfurt speech, for a long painful moment the word 'Ostpolitik' seemed again to signify 'renunciation of freedom' — other people's freedom. In a combination of higher confusion, hypocrisy and self-deception, German policymakers declared the need for 'stability' in the name of 'Europe' and 'world peace'.

In the event, this proved not just morally dubious but also politically short-sighted. For Solidarity made a major contribution to the end of Communism in Eastern Europe, and hence also to German unification. Napoleon said that all empires die of indigestion, and the Poles gave the Soviet empire its biggest stomach-ache. (By comparison, East Germany was positively eupeptic.) In 1989, the Polish Round Table and the subsequent elections led Eastern Europe down the road from refolution to revolution. German policy was focussed on the possibilities of change from the centre of the empire and from above. Poland showed the possibilities of change from the periphery and from below. Neither alone was sufficient. It needed both to achieve the desired result.

'The Germans,' write Jacques Rupnik and Dominique Moïsi, 'did not realise that Solidarity was the first hole in the Berlin Wall.' Really one should say that Solidarity was the second hole. The first was Ostpolitik.

German model

In the 1980s, Ostpolitik was sometimes presented as a model for East-West relations as a whole. This or that aspect of German-Soviet or German-

Hungarian relations, or German Helsinki policy, might, senior politicians would remark with quiet pride, have an 'exemplary' or 'model' character. For a time, German-German relations were also presented as exemplary. In 1984, in a short leading article in *Die Zeit* entitled 'German model', Marion Gräfin Dönhoff quoted two remarks about the necessity for calm negotiations, one from Genscher, the other from Erich Honecker. 'If only,' she concluded, 'the superpowers would show so much insight!' As one analyst has noted, the Federal Republic inclined sometimes to speak like a moralising schoolteacher to a recalcitrant world. So beside Model Germany in domestic policy there was now the German model in foreign policy.

We have found that there was indeed a German model, but its wider applicability is much more questionable. An old Soviet bloc quip defined socialism as the profound and scientific answer to problems that did not even exist in capitalism. A great deal of German Ostpolitik was the answer to problems that did not even exist for other Western states. While it presented itself as the very model of a modern foreign policy, it was actually a mixture of old and new elements: some very new, such as the emphasis on information technology in 'system-opening co-operation' or the desirability of interdependence; some very old, such as the hard *Realpolitik* of German-Soviet deals and the support for minorities defined according to what was ultimately a *völkisch* definition of German nationality. The mixture of old and new elements characterised the whole international environment in which the Federal Republic operated, but, as so often, Germany had both extremes.

Many aspects of this policy contributed, directly or indirectly, to the final achievement of Germany's main foreign-policy goals. However, others also contributed much to this success. Gorbachev did so, by doing something quite different from what he set out to do. He was the greatest 'hero of retreat', to use Hans Magnus Enzensberger's fine phrase. Hungary helped, as an adroit small country changing sides at just the right moment. But neither could count as 'models'. More interesting are two models which West German policy makers often criticised at the time, but which actually helped Germany to succeed. These are the Polish model of dealing with communism from the inside and the American model of dealing with communism from the outside.

In the early 1980s, German policymakers suggested that the Polish model was not good even for Poland. 1989 showed that the Polish model could be good not just for Poland but also for Germany. German politicians thought attempted revolution would never work: look at 1953, 1956, 1968 . . . Anyway, it risked bloodshed and war, than which nothing could be worse. Polish antipoliticians said: even defeats can turn out in the end to be victories, 'for freedom's battle once begun . . .' Different lessons were drawn from the experience of the Second World War. Günter Gaus expressed horror at the very thought of *sterben für Danzig*. Bronisław Geremek wrote: '*on peut mourir pour Dantzig*'.

The 'German realism' of which Brandt spoke in 1973 was, in many ways, realistic. But it underestimated the value of sacrifice, the deeper realism of idealists, even of dreamers such as Dienstbier and Havel. Realistic about the power of the powerholders, it overlooked the power of the powerless. 1989 was not dreamt of in its philosophy.

The history of Ostpolitik raised fundamental issues of values and priorities. In 1954, the Christian Democrat Eugen Gerstenmaier established a famous order of priorities for West Germany: first, freedom; second, peace; third, unity. The Federal Republic stuck to and enhanced freedom in its domestic affairs. No state was more emphatic in its advocacy of peace. Both the adherence to freedom at home and the advocacy of peace abroad helped Germany to achieve unity.

Brandt could say with justified pride that his greatest satisfaction was to see the words 'Germany' and 'peace' taken together. If German leaders had been warmongers in the 1930s, they were veritable peacemongers in the 1970s and 1980s. So much so, in fact, that some detected the old German inclination to swing from one extreme to another. The Marquise von O. And this 'peace' they advocated was a many-layered thing. In the closely related concept of 'stability', and in the very phrase 'European peace order', it also contained the notion of order. Now order, too, is an important value in international relations. But there were moments when West Germany's neighbours would still be tempted to exclaim, like Clawdia Chauchat to poor Hans Castorp in *The Magic Mountain*: '*Vous aimez l'ordre mieux que la liberté, tout l'Europe le sait*'.

In foreign, as opposed to domestic policy, the identification of 'Germany' with the word 'freedom' was much less complete than that with 'peace'. It is, however, very important to stress that this was not just a matter of values and aspirations. West Germany was constrained from being an outspoken advocate of freedom and respect for human rights in Eastern Europe by its geopolitical position at the divided centre, and especially by Berlin's position as the divided centre of the divided centre. Shortly after unification, Horst Teltschik observed that Germany was no longer 'vulnerable to blackmail'. He thus pithily expressed a basic truth about German Ostpolitik.

This was the policy of a state vulnerable to blackmail, by Moscow and East Berlin. Getting on with the powers-that-were in Moscow and East Berlin required caution, restraint, soft speaking, stealth. We have argued that a somewhat more outspoken policy would have been possible, even within these constraints. Particularly in German-German relations, and especially among Social Democrats, there was too much self-censorship, underpinned by a far-reaching relativism and much muddled and wishful thinking. Certainly there was no model for other Western states in the regular payment of ransom for hostages, or in the cross-frontier party politics. Nonetheless, the constraints were real, and a realistic policy had to reckon with them.

All the more reason, however, to be grateful to those in the East who would stand up for human rights — even at the risk of their own lives —, and for those in the West who would support them, and could afford to, because they were not vulnerable to blackmail. This brings us to the American model. Obviously, we are dealing in sweeping generalisations here, for the differences between (and even within) American administrations were much greater than those between (and within) German ones. Yet certain features remained fairly constant.

We have argued that the German debt to the United States does not merely lie on the defence side of the Harmel double-track. It was not just a matter of protection, of successful containment of Soviet power, and even, perhaps, of a policy of military strength. It also lies on the détente side, in the policies of peaceful engagement developed in dialogue between North America and Western Europe. With its policies of 'differentiation' in Eastern Europe, its readiness to use sanctions as well as economic incentives, its offensive public advocacy (since Carter) of human rights, and public and private support of those in the East fighting for them, Washington differed from Bonn. There were arguments, conflicts.

Now our conclusion here is by no means simply that on these points Washington was right and Bonn wrong. The truth is much more complicated. What was right for Washington was not necessarily right for Bonn, and vice versa. Left to itself, Washington might have placed too much emphasis on the sticks, Bonn would have relied too exclusively on the carrots. It was the combination of these approaches, partly intentional and co-ordinated but also partly unintended and conflictual, which produced the necessary mixture of incentive and deterrent, punishment and reward.

Beside the carrots and sticks there were the words. Ostpolitik had a major impact on the language of German politics. Sometimes, in the Bonn republic's little closed circuit of party politics and media, words were mistaken for deeds. Politics was sometimes reduced to phrase-making, or, since this was Germany, concept-coining. Many was the young aspiring politician who cheerfully followed the advice of Mephistopheles (dressed as Faust):

> *Im ganzen: haltet Euch an Worte!*
> *Dann geht Ihr durch die sichre Pforte*
> *Zum Tempel der Gewissheit ein.*

[In general: hold on tight to words!/ Then through the sheltered gate you'll enter/ The temple known as certainty. (Author's translation)]

If one looks more closely at the usage of such concepts as 'security partnership', 'system-opening co-operation', or the many variations played on Bahr's original *Wandel durch Annäherung*, one often finds that the politicians really did not know what they were talking about. They were just making phrases, to gain profile. Yet words, public and private, were also deeds, especially in a period and an area where the guns did not speak. As Havel noted, this was particularly true in relations with regimes that remained at least partly logocratic. Solzhenitsyn's 'one word of truth', and the Pope's, were worth many divisions in the battle against newspeak.

Plain speaking was not Bonn's forte. Waffle was. In vintage Brandt, the inspirational vagueness contained more than a little real wisdom. For no one knew better how much we do not know, how full history is of surprises, good and bad. But the archetypal Bonn waffler was Genscher. There is a fine study to be written of the language of Genscher's speeches, those endless coats of many shades of grey, those layered wedding-cakes of blancmange, those monuments of *sowohl-als-auch*. Yet this vague, harmonising use of language actually did serve Germany's purposes well in this period. For, as we have seen, the Federal Republic had to square many circles, bridge many gaps, above all those between its Eastern and Western ties, and the Genscher compound helped to do just that. It was this getting on with all sides, not the specific advocacy of taking Gorbachev at his word, that was the real essence of Genscherism.

Ostpolitik had the defects of its qualities. Konrad Adenauer's parting admonition to his party in 1966 was to remember that patience was the strongest weapon of a defeated people. West German policy was very patient, consistent, predictable, quietly chiselling away and waiting for the big chance. But at times the consistency hardened into rigidity, the patience became loss of imagination.

Waldemar Besson once wrote that the story of the evolution of a foreign policy is that of experiences becoming maxims. But in the history of Ostpolitik we also see how hypotheses can become burdens. The hypothesis of relaxation through reassurance is the best example. It was original to advance this hypothesis in the 1960s. It was reasonable to try it out in the 1970s, even though some in East Central Europe had already identified its fundamental flaws. But it was foolish to cling to it in the 1980s, ignoring the different course that history was actually taking. As Bahr later acknowledged, in putting disarmament before democratisation, the SPD's second Ostpolitik got things back to front.

The so-called policy intellectuals and the political scientists had a particular responsibility here. For many of them, having become so involved in supporting the policy of their state, trimmed reality to fit theory rather than adjusting theory to fit — and producing hypotheses for — the new reality. More critical independence would better have served the making of policy. Politicians have to work with half-truths and terrible simplifications; intellectuals have a duty not to. A wider penumbra of published opinion also contributed to German misjudgements, above all of the other Germany. Understandably enough, the strain of partition produced its own particular neuroses and hysteria.

Taken all in all, the record of Ostpolitik was thus a mixed one. How could it be otherwise? Some aspects were indeed exemplary and worthy of imitation — the open door policy, for example, the 'weaving' and the Helsinki of human contacts. Others were not. Some strands led directly, in the intended fashion, to the desired result; others led to the intended goal, but by quite unintended and curious paths; yet others led nowhere; a few led into dark alleys, down which it would have been better not to have gone.

Brandt, with his love of northern understatement, might have said this was 'not the worst' chapter in the history of German foreign policy. Given the rather low standards set through much of that history, this seems too little. One can go further: this was one of the better chapters in the history of German foreign policy. It was not by any means simply a policy conducted by Europeans for Europe. But nor was it just the policy of Germans for Germany. At its best, it was the work — Brandt again finds the right words — 'of German patriots in European responsibility'. That description could be applied to most of the leading actors, to Schröder, Kiesinger, Scheel, Bahr, Schmidt, Genscher, Weizsäcker, Kohl, each in their very different way. Close up, you see the smallness and the faults; in Brandt too. Yet in Willy Brandt, as in Konrad Adenauer, Germany has a historical figure at least touched with greatness. This matters. It is important for a country to have such figures.

Was it good for Germany, good for Europe? Here we come to the limits of writing contemporary history. For, alas, it really is too soon to say. As the judgement of Bismarck's achievement changed in the light of what happened in Germany and Europe after 1890, so would that of the Federal Republic's achievement change — for better or for worse — in the light of what happened in Germany and Europe after 1990.

Whether it had been in the German interest, would be for the Germans to decide. What of the European interest? The Germans had made a major contribution to getting the Red Army out of the centre of Europe. Hundreds of millions of Europeans were now free in ways they had not been for half a century or more. This was an incalculable gain. To recall George Bush's invocation of 'Europe whole and free', most of Europe was now more or less free. However, it was very far from whole. To talk of the 'reunification of Europe' was always misleading, because Europe had never properly been united before. Germany had been united, and was now again. Europe had not been, and still had yet to be. The one central Yalta divide was finished. But many smaller divides remained and others re-emerged, with a vengeance. Looking at the former Yugoslavia or the former Soviet Union, the phrase 'European peace order' did not exactly seem to sum up Europe at the end of Ostpolitik.

Beyond this, 'the European interest' had of course to be disaggregated. Russia had lost an empire — but was that loss or gain? Would the Soviet Westernizers' gamble pay off, and Russia now reap the full benefits of full co-operation with a West to which Germany was to be the door? Would the United States find in united Germany its looked-for 'partner in leadership', ready to share the burdens, not just in Europe and not only with the cheque-book?

Of course in many ways all West European countries gained from the end of the Cold War, and all welcomed it. But in some respects Britain and France, at least, lost as well as gained. When Douglas Hurd said in 1989 that the Yalta system was one 'under which we've lived quite happily for forty years', he was speaking more truth than perhaps he knew. The Cold War had preserved Britain in a great-power prominence which its underlying economic strength would no longer sustain. France was some-what better placed, because of the special relationship it had built up with Germany. But in terms of power, France also lost, as its nuclear *force de frappe* no longer counter-balanced the German monetary one, and the European Community's centre of gravity began to move eastwards.

As for the countries of the former Eastern Europe, they won the greatest new chances, and faced the greatest new risks. They were free, but weak; liberated, but unsafe; newly independent, but also in a new dependency.

For everyone involved, the judgement of the past would depend upon the development of the future. That in turn depended on many things, but not least on the behaviour of Germany.

Epilogue

European Answers?

Consequences

In 1965, Konrad Adenauer chose to introduce his memoirs with a wry account of a conversation with an historian. This unnamed 'Professor of Modern History at a German University' was asked by Adenauer how he imagined things would develop. He replied that this was not his task. Historians were not prophets. Adenauer said he had a different view of the historian's task. Historians should at least attempt to recognise in what direction history might be heading. They should point to probable developments, 'and perhaps warn'.

In the more than quarter-century since Adenauer wrote those lines, a few historians but far more political scientists, policy intellectuals and specialists in International Relations, Sovietology and Security Studies have taken up the challenge. On the whole, and with a few notable exceptions, their forecasts, predictions or models have not fared well in the light of what happened in Europe in the years 1989 to 1991. By 1993, German intellectual life had experienced a *Historikerstreit*, about the treatment of the Nazi past, and a *Literaturstreit*, about writers and East Germany, but perhaps it still awaited its *Politologenstreit*. For the end of Soviet communism and of the Cold War posed the largest questions to those disciplines, or branches of disciplines, that made some claim to quasi-scientific prediction.

Most historians make no such methodological claims. Some would agree with E.H.Carr that they should at least have in their bones the question 'whither?' as well as the question 'why?' Others would dispute even that. Yet in his wry way, Adenauer identified a real problem. It surely is reasonable and right for politicians to ask historians to make informed personal guesses — so long as everyone clearly recognises that they are just that: personal guesses. These guesses are related to the history they write, but separable from it. The history may be good but the guesses bad — or even vice versa. At the very least, we can try to identify the new questions to which politicians then have to offer answers. However, what follows is quite deliberately written in the past tense, because these are the guesses and questions of early 1993, when this book went to press. They can be overtaken by events in a way that the historical analysis cannot be. For the one thing historians can confidently predict is surprises.

There is also the question of the relevant past. For the most recent is by no means always the most relevant past. Indeed, the history of Europe before 1939, before 1914, even before 1890, may well provide more analogies or clues for understanding the state of Europe after 1990 than does that of the immediately preceding period. After 1989 it was not just the Europe of Yalta but the Europe of Versailles that began to collapse. To understand the condition of, say, Bosnia-Herzegovina in 1993, Bismarck's Congress of Berlin in 1878 was as relevant as Genscher's (CSCE) Congress of Berlin in 1991. Old books had to be brought out of the stacks, as the new ones were put down there.

Not just Ostpolitik but the whole history of East-West relations in the Cold War belonged to this abruptly closed period. Perhaps the only direct lessons pertained to relations with the last surviving communist states, and above all with China. Here, for all the differences in culture and history, one met again many familiar issues: the degree of necessary recognition, the proper balance between human contacts and human rights, between economic and military carrots and sticks. Here again one found self-styled realists who argued that real change could only come from above, from the centre, from the present powerholders, and that what happened in Tiananmen Square in June 1989, at the very moment of East Central European refolution, showed the folly of insurrection. But here again we could reply that change can also come from below and from the periphery, that people have something to do with their own destiny, and that, in the memorably simple words of the poet James Fenton,

> They'll come again
> To Tiananmen.

Curiously enough, the Western state for which these direct lessons of Ostpolitik might therefore be most immediately relevant in the 1990s was not Germany but Britain. For Britain was directly responsible for the hostage city of Hong Kong. Many of the tensions and dilemmas which West Germany had faced with the hostage city, West Berlin, were now faced by Britain. In one respect, Britain's position was decisively worse than that of the Federal Republic had been. Whereas international law (and British, French and American troops) had upheld the West German position on West Berlin, respect for international law (and a desire to be decently rid of the problem) would have Britain withdraw in 1997. In another respect, however, it was better, because Communism's Wheel of History had now been reversed throughout Europe, and economically in China too.

Germany had no such direct dependencies in the Far East. Yet when its new Foreign Minister, Klaus Kinkel, visited China in the autumn of 1992, he raised human rights issues only discreetly, in his private talks; proclaimed his goal as the 'long overdue normalisation' of relations; described the Chinese Prime Minister partly responsible for the Tiananmen massacre, Li Peng, as 'completely normal and open'; and declared in Peking that 'relations are now normal'. This could have been Moscow or Warsaw twenty years before. Like the Bourbons, the German Foreign Ministry seemed to have forgotten nothing and learned nothing.

What, though, of the new Germany in the new Europe? Despite the vast changes, the history of Ostpolitik was relevant here in at least two respects. Firstly, the combination of West- and Ostpolitik constituted a foreign-policy tradition, although still a short one. The immediate successor generation in German politics, represented in early 1993 by Klaus Kinkel at the Foreign Ministry and Volker Rühe at the Defence Ministry, emphasised continuity. Secondly, the next generation after them had actually grown up in the years of Ostpolitik, and for many it had been formative. The time-lag in politics is often long — Adenauer's political world-view was formed before 1914, or at the latest in the 1920s, Kohl's in the 1940s and 1950s. So in the 2010s and 2020s Germany might have leaders whose truly formative experiences were in the 1970s and 1980s. Even if their delayed response consisted in a rejection of the way things were then said and done, it would still be important to know what they were rejecting.

Yet the situation in which Germany found itself had obviously changed drastically, and the European question was posed anew. After the end of Yalta, every state in Europe had to ask itself again: What sort of power are we? What do we want to be? What are our national interests? What are our priorities? But nowhere were the questions more difficult than for Germany.

What sort of power was united Germany? While neighbours and partners played with ill-defined terms like 'supremacy', 'hegemony', 'domination' or just 'leadership', the range of German self-definitions was immense. At one extreme, Chancellery Minister Rudolf Seiters spoke in November 1990 of the new Germany being 'equipped not with more power but with more responsibility'. A truly ridiculous statement, since every child in Europe could see that Germany had more power. An elephant does not win trust by pretending to be a dove. It merely invites doubt about its sanity — or its honesty. At the other extreme, a Green member of the Bundestag described Germany as a new superpower. In between, there were a hundred variations. Even before unification, one historian had described the Federal Republic as a 'world power against its will'. After unification, another historian described Germany as a new great power. But a political scientist said the Federal Republic should see itself as not as a *Mittelmacht*, let alone as the *Zentralmacht* of Europe, but as a *mittlere Macht*. Fine distinctions.

If they did not know exactly what sort of power Germany was, surely they at least knew where it was? Well, not exactly. Suddenly Hans-Dietrich Genscher spoke of 'we in West *and Central* Europe' (my emphasis). A television newscaster spoke of 'the new Central European *Ordnungsmacht* Germany'. A leading contemporary historian said Germany was now a Central European country. Another analyst suggested that Germany was still 'the East of the West and the West of the East'. In an interview on Austrian television, Chancellor Kohl summoned up the old self-image of Germany as a bridge between East and West, but added 'a bridge as part of the Western world'. So: a bridge all on one bank? Meanwhile, a publisher of the *Frankfurter Allgemeine Zeitung*, who single-handedly did more than any politician to change Bonn's policy towards the former Yugoslavia, could be read on the front page of that newspaper fulminating against the allegedly pro-Serbian policy of what he called 'the Western powers'. By this he meant France, Britain and the United States. But was not Germany a Western power?

The answers were confused. But so was the reality. Nearly two hundred years after Napoleon commented that becoming rather than being seemed to be Germany's natural condition, Germany was still in the condition of becoming. Its frontiers, and therefore its physical shape and size, were now clear. But it did not even have a capital. In a great symbolic decision, the Bundestag voted in June 1991 for Berlin to be Germany's capital and seat of government. But the move from Bonn to Berlin was likely to take many years. Above all, however, the results of the inner unification had yet to be seen. How would the accession of more than sixteen million people with sixty years' experience of two dictatorships, and now experiencing the traumatic impact of a sudden and uniquely sweeping transition, affect the liberal institutions and open society of the old Federal Republic? What would be the economic result?

Here the predictions of the economists, another group of specialists at hand to answer the politicians' questions (and, incidentally, another good candidate for a little professional *Streit*), differed greatly. Yet this was of course a crucial variable, for two reasons. Firstly, because it can plausibly be argued that while the fate of liberal democracy is everywhere closely tied to a certain level (and distribution) of prosperity, this is particularly true in the case of Germany. Certainly democracy in West Germany was consolidated during and after the so-called economic miracle, and had not yet faced the test of real economic hardship. Now, it just might face such a test.

Secondly, the power of united Germany was still above all economic, and, at the cutting edge, financial. We have seen that in its relations with the East, the Federal Republic had effectively used economic power to realise its political goals, albeit sometimes achieving the desired results in unintended ways. After the end of the Soviet empire, its potential to do this was still larger. But in the West, too, whether it liked it or not, it had extraordinary weight.

This was not just a matter of the sheer size of the economy, with a Gross National Product in 1992 roughly one and a half times that of Britain, a good third larger than that of France or Italy — although only half that of Japan and barely a third that of the United States. It was also a matter of the quality of its products, the trade surplus, the savings rate, and the reputation of the currency built up over forty years. While Chancellery Minister Seiters said that Germany had no more power, a word — no, even a silence — from the Bundesbank on interest or exchange rates would directly affect the conduct of domestic policy in many other countries. Here it was not a matter of Germany pursuing any foreign-policy goals, but simply of Germany pursuing its own domestic economic agenda, and above all, the Bundesbank's legal obligation to preserve the stability of the German currency. Even for Germany's neighbours and partners to the west, interdependence thus contained a good measure of dependence.

Helmut Schmidt's reflections on the connections between economic and foreign policy were now more relevant than ever (as he himself did not fail to remind his compatriots). Clearly the future size and quality of Germany's economic power would depend on developments in the world economy, which it could only partly influence (for example, through its contribution to the EC's stance in the GATT negotiations), and on those in Europe, which it could influence more than any other single state. But in the 1990s it would also depend on how it coped with the huge costs of unification, as well as the inherited burdens of what might almost be described as the overdeveloped social market economy of the old Federal Republic (high labour costs, subsidies, perhaps a certain clannish complacency). Germany's budget deficits were projected to be around DM 100 billion a year until 1995. Its total public debt in 1993 was estimated at DM 1,500 billion. A rich country.

Yet beside the economic dimension, the other dimensions of German power should not be ignored. Even with the 2 + 4 Treaty limit on its numbers, and even with financial cuts that might bring the numbers down even further, Germany would have some of the largest armed forces in Europe. In 1992, only those of Russia and Turkey (and possibly, depending what one counted, Ukraine) were numerically larger, but German forces obviously had better technology and better training. Whether they were better at fighting no one could say until they did some, but certainly German forces had been very good at it in the past.

Now whether and, if so, under what auspices, they should actually fight was still a subject of fierce discussion in German politics in early 1993. Both the Gulf War, to which the Federal Republic contributed more than

$6,500 million in cash and kind (but no troops) and the crisis in the former Yugoslovia had sharpened this emotional debate. However, even if the self-imposed constraints were removed, so that German soldiers could risk their lives (and not just German politicians their words) in other parts of the world, as American, British and French soldiers had never ceased to do since 1945; even then, Germany would not be in the same league as Russia, America, France and Britain. For in 1990 Germany had, under most solemn treaty, reaffirmed its renunciation of atomic, biological and chemical weapons.

Now if Germany were to behave as most powers have done over the centuries, one would expect it sooner or later to gain the military cutting-edge to complement (and defend) the economic one: albeit at first in a larger multilateral context (almost certainly containing the adjective European), and quite likely not as the fulfilment of a deliberate policy but rather as a response to an acute and unexpected challenge. But would it so behave? Or had Germany, Europe, international relations in an interdependent world, said good-bye to all that? Perhaps by the year 2000 there would no longer be a fully sovereign, independent German nation-state to face that decision, but rather a Federal (or at least Confederal) Republic of Europe? The Federal Republic of (United) Germany, 1990–2000, hail and farewell?

Before addressing this central German-European question we should mention one other dimension of German power. This third dimension is even more difficult to define than the economic and the military ones, but scarcely less important. It has to do with the overall attractiveness — the magnetism, to recall Schumacher and Adenauer's simile — of a particular society, culture and way of life. This is a dimension of power which Britain had in the late nineteenth century and early twentieth century, which America had in superabundance in the mid-twentieth century, and which, as we have seen, Model Germany developed strongly in the 1970s and 1980s. This attraction is closely related to a country's relative prosperity, but by no means simply a function of it. Other features — individual opportunity, tolerance, culture, security, space, freedom, tradition, beauty — all contribute to the magnetism.

As the Federal Republic discovered at the beginning of the 1990s, such magnetism can bring great problems — above all, immigration. Yet it remains a tremendous asset. As the example of the United States shows, restrictions on immigration do not in themselves necessarily reduce the attraction. They may even increase it. But how people are treated once they are in the country will, of course, very much affect the quality of the attraction. Under the strain of unification, a minority of Germans at the beginning of the 1990s were doing their best to reduce the attraction — with nationalist slogans, racial abuse and fire-bombs. Whether they succeeded would depend on the reaction of the majority.

Yet whatever the evolution of these three dimensions of German power in the 1990s, the united country would remain an awkward size in an awkward place. Germany now had precisely that 'critical size' to which Chancellor Kiesinger had referred back in 1967: 'too big to play no role in the balance of forces . . . too small to keep the forces around it in balance by itself'. Or, in the even pithier formulation of Henry Kissinger: too big for Europe, too small for the world. As for the place: to say that it had returned to the famous old *Mittellage* in the centre of Europe was an over-simplification, ignoring the genuinely new elements in Germany's geopolitical situation, reflected in shorthand by the acronyms EC, Nato and perhaps also OECD. But certainly the new Federal Republic was much closer to the challenges of the nineteenth-century *Mittellage* than the old Federal Republic had been.

The foreign policy of the old Federal Republic had gradually increased its room for manoeuvre and effective sovereignty, but always from a very tightly constrained situation as the divided centre of a divided continent. Now, united Germany had a formidable room for manoeuvre in the centre (though not necessarily *as* the centre) of a still disunited continent. The answers to the European and German questions, new and old, depended more than they had for at least half a century on what the Germans themselves wanted to do.

European Germany, German Europe

What did Germany want to do, indeed — to be? The answers given by most of its political and intellectual leaders at the beginning of the 1990s could be summarised in two words: normal and European. Both raised as many questions as they answered.

'Germany has again become a normal state', said Horst Teltschik a few days after unification, quoting with approval an observation of the British journalist David Marsh. Yet two years later Klaus Kinkel would speak of the need for the 'normalisation' of German foreign policy, notably in committing its troops abroad, and for 'the normalisation of our situation as a nation'. In the debate about Berlin it was argued that to have a large, historic, metropolitan capital was an essential part of being a normal country. The main comparison here was with Paris, London, Rome or Madrid — that is, with the 'normality' of other large historic European nation-states.

As we have seen, the words 'normal', 'normality' and 'normalisation' had a rich and chequered history in German politics since 1945. 'Normalisation' was a key-word of social-liberal Ostpolitik, where it meant establishing full diplomatic and other relations with communist states, at least one of which was simultaneously undergoing Soviet-type 'normalisation'.

In the 1980s, some West German politicians and intellectuals even argued that relations between the two German states were becoming 'normal'. After unification, 'normalisation' became a key-word of the centre-right, and was criticised as such by intellectuals of the centre-left who had enthusiastically embraced the earlier usage.

To say that Germany had become more normal since unification was common sense. Anyone who thought that it was normal to live with a wall through Berlin was not quite normal. It was more normal to take a bus from the Alexanderplatz to Bahnhof Zoo. Altogether, it was more normal for a nation that had once been united in a single state again to live in one. Hans-Peter Schwarz argued that the partition had been the single most important cause of the collective neuroses of the old Federal Republic, including, of course, the endless debates about German identity. It would be premature to suggest that with unification those debates would softly and suddenly vanish away. Nietzsche's famous dictum that what characterises the Germans is that the question 'what is German?' never dies out among them had yet to be disproved. But one could reasonably hope that the debates would become less tortured and obsessive.

Beyond this, however, the critics of the new usage did have a point. To talk seriously of normality and normalisation, you must first specify your norms. And here the comparison with France or Britain would only get you so far. Should one, for example, regard the British gutter press as part of a desirable normality? Should one, more seriously, consider it as normal to have a party of the nationalist, populist right getting around fifteen per cent of the popular vote, as Le Pen's National Front had in France? Could and should Germany really aspire to the foreign policy 'normality' of two of Europe's oldest and most centralised states, with the traditions and reactions of former great powers?

Here we come to the second German answer: Europe. 'Germany is our fatherland, Europe is our future', said Chancellor Kohl in his government programme for the years 1991–94. The aim was 'the political unification of Europe'. 'The *Staatsräson* of a united Germany', said one of his close advisers, 'is its integration in Europe'. In a symbolic act of profound significance, the same article 23 of the Basic Law under which German unification had been achieved was amended in December 1992 so that the Federal Republic, instead of being open for 'other parts of Germany' to join, was now committed to 'the realisation of a united Europe' through the 'European Union'. The European Union, that is, of the existing European Community of twelve member states, as envisaged in the Maastricht Treaty of December 1991.

Maastricht, said President von Weizsäcker, offered Germany 'the chance of being delivered (*erlöst*) from the *Mittellage*'. The twenty-first century, he averred, could become a 'European century', no less. The Bundeswehr's most senior officer, General Naumann, said he looked forward to the day when German soldiers could swear their oath of loyalty on the European flag.

Willy Brandt told the first sitting of the all-German Bundestag that 'German and European belong together, now and hopefully for ever'. The true fulfilment of his political life would be 'to see the day when Europe will have become one'. The dreams of the oldest Bundestag member were apparently shared — no, exceeded — by the youngest. In December 1990, some of the newest members of the Bundestag were asked by a weekly newspaper 'Nation 2000: what does that mean to you?' They answered: 'hope for a liberal, multicultural and tolerant society in united Europe' (25-year-old Free Democrat); 'peaceful Europe in which the East-West conflict is finally overcome and a European Germany' (31-year-old Christian Democrat); 'the future belongs to Europe and the regions!' (35, Social Democrat); 'united Europe of free fatherlands' (33, CSU); 'Germany reconciled with itself and its neighbours — part of the *Staatenbund* Europe' (26, CDU); 'Europe . . . What matters is the internal market, European Union and our responsibility towards the Third World' (35, CDU); or, in a word, 'Europe' (Social Democrat, aged 24!).

Yet it was not just these 'Bonn freshers' who gave such answers. So did seasoned veterans of Ostpolitik. In summer 1991, Egon Bahr — yes, Egon Bahr! — professed to see 'no single national, German foreign policy goal'. 'The foreign policy interests of this larger Germany,' he said, 'are European . . .' And children attending the Chancellor's traditional summer party were informed by Hans-Dietrich Genscher, through an article in the specially printed *Kanzler-Kinderfest-Zeitung*, that the larger Germany 'does not want more power but has more responsibility. We do not aspire to a German Europe but want to live in a European Germany.' This last formula was borrowed from Thomas Mann, and intoned many times like a blessing or a prayer at the birth of united Germany.

Let it not be thought that this was simply what Germany's leaders were telling the children — and the neighbours. It was, by and large, also what they were telling themselves. This was at once the reassuring and the slightly worrying thing. If they also had a clear foreign policy agenda based on fairly well-defined national interests, as the Federal Republic had had in the 1970s and 1980s, that would be fine. As Henry Kissinger observed, the nice thing about dealing with Egon Bahr in the 1970s was that he *did* have a hidden agenda. A little concealment of enlightened national interest behind European or internationalist rhetoric is — dare one say it? — quite normal. You only have to look at France. For more than thirty years the European Community had been built on compromises between such interests, though facilitated, of course — let us not be facile Realists! — by a real desire to learn from the tragedies of European history, cross-border regional experiences, new trans-national challenges, and so on.

Mann's formula, as redeployed by Genscher, is a good starting-point for identifying some of the problems with this German European vision. What does it mean to say 'a European Germany'? Here we must again confront the difference between the prescriptive and the descriptive use of the noun 'Europe' and the adjective 'European'. When Mann coined the phrase, talking to students in Hamburg in 1953, he was using the term 'European' prescriptively. The new Germany should be European, in contrast to Hitler's Germany, which was not, but had instead aimed for a German Europe. But what if we use the term descriptively?

Contemplating the way in which Central Europe had descended into barbarism in the years before 1945, the Germanist J. P. Stern wrote that the heart of Europe had become the heart of darkness. And then he quoted from the novel of that title by the Polish-British writer Joseph Conrad: 'No, they were not inhuman. Well, you know, that was the worst of it — this suspicion of their not being inhuman.' Of the university-educated mass murderers of the Third Reich one has to say: 'No, they were not un-European. Well, you know, that was the worst of it . . .'

Thomas Mann himself had earlier, in 1945, rejected the simplistic distinction between a 'good' and a 'bad' Germany. 'The evil Germany,' he wrote, 'that is the good gone awry, the good in misfortune, in guilt and fall'. And the history of Germany contains, in the most concentrated form, the highest and the lowest of European history. So if we use the term 'European' descriptively, we have to say that, alas, Nazi Germany was also a European Germany. Moreover, the actual words 'Europe' and 'European' have been relentlessly abused throughout European history. *Nation Europa* was the title of a Nazi periodical.

None of this disqualifies the attempt now to use the term 'European' prescriptively. But it does qualify it. 'There are a number of things,' wrote William Hazlitt, 'the idea of which is a clear gain to the mind. Let people, for instance, rail at friendship, genius, freedom, as long as they will — the very names of these despised qualities are better than anything else that could be sustituted for them, and embalm even the most venomed satire against them. It is no small consideration that the mind is capable even of feigning such things.' Is Europe such an idea? There are many, not least, indeed perhaps above all, in Central Europe, who hold with Milan Kundera that Europe is indeed a value in itself. On the other hand there are those (now more often met in London than in Berlin) who would say with Bismarck: '*qui parle Europe a tort. Notion géographique*'.

There is a tenable position in between. This is to say that Europe is less than a value in itself — it cannot and should not be put on the same plane as freedom, truth or justice — but more than merely a geographical notion. Like 'France', like 'England', yes, like 'Germany', we can choose to make it stand for certain things which are found in its past and present, even though many other things are found there as well. But if we do this, we have then to spell out what those things are, the ones we want and those we do not. Thomas Mann, for example, told an Oxford audience in 1949 that he first found his European Germany in Schopenhauer, Nietzsche and Wagner. Is that what was meant in 1992? Just to say 'a European Germany' is to say everything, and therefore nothing.

And 'not a German Europe'? Recalling Mann's remarks, we understand that the new Germany did not want to try and conquer Europe as Hitler did. Now admittedly, at the time of German unification wild Irish and Spanish references to a future 'Fourth Reich' might seem to have invited such reassurances; but did this really need saying? If, however, we take not a 1945 but a 1992 interpretation of 'German Europe', then it was in some respects actually the declared policy of the Federal Republic to seek a German Europe.

The revised article 23 of the Basic Law committed the Federal Republic to seek a European Union 'which is bound to democratic, legal (*rechtstaatliche*), social and federal principles and that of subsidiarity, and secures a protection of basic rights essentially comparable to that of this Basic Law'. 'At the end of this decade, this century,' said Chancellor Kohl, 'the countries of the European Community will have a common currency — a currency which must be just as strong and stable as the German Mark'. The federalism the Federal Government advocated for Europe was German-style, decentralised federalism rather than the centralising federalism of the 'Euro-super-state' so much feared in Britain.

Now these things might be good in themselves. It might indeed be a very good thing to have basic rights protected by a Basic Law. It might be a very good thing to have a currency as strong and stable as the DM. German-style federalism had much to commend it. Europe might very well want to adopt (and adapt) large parts of the Federal German model. But these were German things, and it would be obfuscation to pretend otherwise. (Of course, the French also wanted, in many respects, a French Europe, the Italians an Italian Europe, and so on.)

Where Bismarck had said 'we must put Germany in the saddle', Theo Sommer of *Die Zeit* declared: 'we must put Europe in the saddle'. But who was 'we' in this sentence? The royal we? The Germans? The elites of the main West European powers? And what if the old girl did not, after all, want to go for the ride? Would Sommer have us — whoever 'we' are — adopt the original method of Zeus, and, turning into a bull, carry her off to bed in Crete (or Brussels)? And who is she anyway? Which Europe are we talking about? And why only Europe?

Why Europe? Which Europe?

All the main choices before German foreign policy in the 1990s could be analysed around these two questions. Firstly: Why Europe? If we regard

Europe as a community of values, or of liberal democracies committed to mutual support and defence, the question immediately arises: why not 'the West'? Aren't the values of the West actually easier to define than those of Europe? How far was it actually Europe — specifically, the European Community — that had brought Western Europe peace, co-operation, security and prosperity for forty years, and how far the West — that is, concretely, the Western Alliance, the OECD, the Bretton Woods institutions and so on? How far could Europe now really manage on its own?

Beyond this, there was of course the even larger question: why not the world? This was not just an existential question, about the very survival of life of the planet, or a moral question, about human misery in the Third World, but also a hard political one, about what the miserable of the earth might do to the enclaves of relative peace and prosperity. However, since that was a question that applied equally to all developed countries, we shall frankly duck it here.

Another answer to the question 'why Europe?' was: economic self-interest. Certainly, Germany had done extremely well out of the EC, with its growing trade surpluses far outweighing the cost of its large direct budgetary contribution. Chancellor Kohl declared that the EC had overcome the old European habits of national *sacro egoismo*. But anyone trying to negotiate with the EC on trade matters soon found that economic *sacro egoismo* was very much alive and kicking. Indeed, in many ways the EC did not transcend but rather aggregated the sacred egoisms of nations, regions and, indeed, specific industries and special interests.

Yet the long-term economic self-interest of the trading state Germany clearly also required keeping open existing markets in the wider world — at the very least, in the OECD world — and opening up new ones, particularly in the east. Furthermore, it was by no means self-evident that the German economic interest would best be served by giving up control of its own currency, since even a Euro-Mark was most unlikely to be as strong and stable as the DM had been.

The most characteristic, but also the most singular answer was the political one given by West German Chancellors from Adenauer to Kohl. The European Community was needed to save Germany from itself. This argument continued to be made after unification. One of Germany's most distinguished former diplomats said in 1992 that the aim of German foreign policy must be to prevent German hegemony. In the immediate post-war period, Europe had seen a Western 'double containment': of the Soviet Union and of Germany. As Lord Ismay famously remarked, Nato was designed to keep the Americans in, the Russians out and the Germans down. Was Europe now to see German self-containment?

Genuine and even admirable though this Adenauerian argument had been, could it really be the main sustaining political rationale for German commitment to European integration fifty years after Hitler? Could

Germany's new leaders really say to people born in 1970: 'you know, we have to do this because we really cannot trust ourselves'? 'Why shouldn't we?' those young people would quite reasonably reply. Moreover, until 1990 this rationale always had two sides. In laying on the golden handcuffs, Germany had also been working to set itself free. Having surrendered sovereignty in order to regain it, had it now regained sovereignty in order to surrender it?

There was, however, a further argument that applied specifically to Germany after the end of Yalta. This was that it simply could not cope on its own with the new challenges from the east. Big though it was, these were far bigger. And they were quite literally at Germany's front door: just sixty kilometres from Berlin. Helmut Kohl saw the project of European Union as putting a European roof over Germany. But a roof that just reaches but does not overlap your east wall would not even keep the drizzle out, let alone hail and snow.

This brings us to the second question: Which Europe? After trying to prevent or at least to slow down the unification of Germany at the end of 1989, François Mitterrand was reassured by Helmut Kohl's emphatic commitment to push ahead with the further political and economic integration of the existing EC of twelve member states. This Franco-German understanding was the single most important driving force behind the inter-governmental conferences on what was loosely called European political and monetary union, and hence of the Maastricht treaty. At a meeting with Kohl in April 1990, Mitterrand expanded on his vision of three circles — a geometric image familiar to historians from its earlier and quite different usage, scribbled by Churchill for Adenauer on the back of a menu in 1953.

Whereas Churchill's three circles — the United States, Britain and the Commonwealth, United Europe — were polycentric but intersecting, as in a Venn diagram, Mitterrand's circles were concentric. In the innermost circle were France and Germany. In the next circle was the rest of the existing EC. In the third circle was continental Europe. This was what one might call the Little European idea. It came from the (or at least a) main stream of the original European Communities as they developed from the early 1950s, and even more from the time of the Elysée Treaty between France and Germany in 1963. It also built on older foundations, ranging from post-war social Catholic ideology right back to Charlemagne. It was a vision of Europe close to Helmut Kohl's heart. Indeed, Kohl once described Mainz as being in the middle of Europe.

Until 1989, this Little European project was pretty much what was meant in Bonn by the term *Europapolitik*. There was *Europapolitik* to the West and Ostpolitik to the East. The *pars pro toto* use of the term 'Europe' was always questionable, and questioned, but the real-ities called in shorthand 'Yalta' made the political option defensible.

Little Europe, it could be argued, was to be the magnetic core for a larger Europe.

But could this position be maintained after 1990? If one takes Mitterrand's second circle, then the existing EC of twelve Western and Southern European states was now a very peculiar shape, its outline explicable only by reference to the iron curtain. On grounds of history, culture, economic development, political institutions, the rule of law, civil society — in fact, on every possible domestic ground for membership — there was no reason why Austria should not belong if Portugal did, while for Greece to be in and Sweden out was clearly nonsense.

Yet if one argued from pre-Yalta history, culture, tradition, and the aspiration to West European liberal and democratic norms, then one had to go further. Almost every argument that was made in the 1970s for admitting the fledgling democracies Spain, Portugal and Greece into the EC could be made in the 1990s for, at the very least, Poland, Hungary and the Czech Republic. If the arbitrariness and 'abnormality' of the Yalta divide had been seen most vividly in the divided city of Berlin, then the arbitrariness of this new dividing line could be seen in the divided towns along the River Oder. Was Görlitz in Europe but Zgorzelec (part of the same town until 1945) not in Europe? Had the Oder suddenly become the Bosporus?

However, we cannot stop there. For if one looked at the eastern and south-eastern frontiers of these East Central European states, then very similar arguments could be made, on grounds of history, culture, traditions and aspirations. If the Czech lands, why not Slovakia? If Hungary, why not Romania? If Poland, why not Lithuania? And what of Ukraine? And then the largest question of all: Russia. Certainly there were deep historical fault-lines here, not least between the lands of western and eastern Christianity. Yet the fact is that Europe does not have a single clear eastern end. It merely fades away. (Fortunate are the continents defined by seas.) To be sure, the practical steps to be taken before, say, Romania or Ukraine could seriously be considered for membership of the EC were so numerous and daunting as to make these, politically speaking, questions for the next century.

Mitterrand's definition of the third circle, 'continental Europe', contained a further, still larger problem. Even if one assumed that with the Channel tunnel Britain had physically rejoined the continent, after a short absence of some 5,000 years, there remained the issue of America. In the Helsinki process, North America — that is, the United States and Canada — was explicitly included. When Mitterrand launched his ill-conceived and ill-fated scheme of a 'European Confederation' — a consolation prize for the countries in his third circle —, the participants at what was billed as the founding meeting sat beneath a large map which showed Europe stretching almost to the Kurile islands in the east, but stopping abruptly just to the west of Spain. De Gaulle would have nodded in approval.

Yet for the Federal Republic, the relationship with the United States, though much resented by significant sections of German intellectual and political opinion, had all along been of vital importance. Adenauer, for all his great reconciliation with de Gaulle, had seen this with crystal clarity. And this was not just true of West Germany's position in the West. We have seen in this book how not merely American defence and support in the West, but also active American policies in the East, contributed to the realisation of the goals of German Ostpolitik. Had all that changed now? The American had done his work, the American could go?

Of course, German politicians and diplomats saw all these questions. But, understandably enough, their first inclination was to respond with the old Genscherist *sowohl-als-auch* prose which really had served the Federal Republic rather well for the last quarter-century. France was the most important partner, but so was America. Deepening the EC was the top priority, but so was widening it. Russia was item number one in the East, but so was Poland. And so on. Josef Joffe summed it up in the words of Yogi Berra: if you see a fork in the road, take it. Now up to a point this is what large, powerful countries with a lot of neighbours, partners and petitioners always have to do. But if they are to achieve anything they also have to set priorities. And to set priorities you have first to decide what is most important to you, in other words, what is your national interest. Germany was now too independent, too sovereign, too powerful, to enjoy the luxury of not making choices.

Kohl identified two great tasks on the path to 'the Europe of the future': to deepen the (existing) EC into a European Union, and, secondly, 'the final overcoming of the division of the continent between East and West'. It was far from clear that these two things were compatible. Even if they were, there was a priority choice between them. Looking both west and east there were further big priority choices. Policymakers and policy intellectuals would often discuss these in terms of the relationship between the plethora of multilateral institutions, piling up the acronyms like children's spelling bricks and calling the result a new European architecture. Another way of looking at it would be to chart the real allocation of resources. But one can put it most simply in terms of choices between countries.

Germany could put France first. If France and Germany then did something that could loosely be called uniting, this would be new. If Belgium, the Netherlands and Luxemburg joined in, the result might perhaps be called, with a little poetic licence, a Federal or Confederal Republic of North-Western Europe. But it would not be Europe. Nor was it clear that such a (very) Little Europe would any longer necessarily be the magnetic core of further European integration that many of its German advocates envisaged: *Kleineuropa* as *Kerneuropa*. A process that had seemed to work almost like a successful physics experiment, in the very special, insulated, low-temperature laboratory conditions of divided 'Yalta' Europe, might not work at all in the harsh open air of the new Europe. Or it might work quite differently there. Far from finally overcoming the bad old European habits of forming competing alliances and coalitions, it might actually contribute to their re-emergence.

Thus the pursuit of the Little European strategy might well be at the cost of Germany's relationships with Britain, with other countries in the existing EC, and with those still outside it. America seemed to support moves towards a larger (West) European partner. But that support was by no means guaranteed, particularly if the Gaullist inheritance and an aggregation of French, German and Benelux protectionist reflexes fed into the international economic and security policies of such a *soi-disant* European Union. There might very well, therefore, be an even harder priority choice for Germany — between France and America.

As for the lands to Germany's east, the list of choices was almost endless. But if the most important potential priority conflict to the west was between France and America, the most important one to the east was between Poland and Russia. Traditionally, Germany had given priority to Russia. This old priority was, as we have seen, revived in Ostpolitik — Moscow first! — but for compelling reasons of national interest. Now, however, there was a real choice. Russia was no longer the superpower reaching into the centre of Europe, although it still had the weapons of one. It was not even the neighbour's neighbour. Namier's rule of odd and even numbers (see page 217) might actually now dictate 'friendship' with Ukraine rather than Russia. However, if it wanted to, Germany could even break with tradition and put its neighbour Poland first.

There were arguments for and against each of these priorities. But the one thing Germany could not do was everything. If it tried to do everything it would achieve nothing.

Beyond Ostpolitik

Now obviously Germany did not do nothing. The country was absorbed and obsessed by the costs and strains of its own internal unification, itself a unique version of the 'great transition test' facing all former communist countries. Yet it still had an active policy towards what were loosely described as its neighbours (actually, there were only two) in what was now carefully called 'Central, Eastern, and South-Eastern Europe'. Was this an 'Ostpolitik mark-two', as the *Economist* jauntily remarked? *Should* Germany have a new 'new Ostpolitik'? A second, or, in the case of the Social Democrats, a third Ostpolitik? Or perhaps: a new

'European Ostpolitik', meaning a common Ostpolitik of the European Community?

Our answer may perhaps initially surprise some readers. It is: no! Not an *Ost*politik, that is. The *Ost* in Ostpolitik was a bloc of communist states dominated by the Soviet Union. That bloc no longer existed. Where previously Western states, and especially West Germany, had to deal with the bloc as a bloc whether they wanted to or not — although even then, some 'differentiation' was possible — now they could not deal with the East as a bloc even if they wanted to. Moreover, many of those formerly East European states and peoples were now doing their level best to join — or, as they put it, with varying degrees of historical plausibility, to return to — Europe. And not just to Europe, but to something they called the West, or indeed to what many Russians called simply the world. In most respects, they had a very long way to go. But not in all. Some things — values and ideals, for example — cannot be eradicated by a mere system or partition. If you were to take a teacher from the class of '68 in Frankfurt and a teacher from the class of '68 in Kraków, and soberly compare their values and ideals, you might well conclude that the person to the east was actually closer to the West.

The very word Ostpolitik therefore implies the continued existence of an East. So does the old self-image of Germany as bridge, for it makes no sense to have a bridge between West and West. Yet the passionate aspiration of at least the larger part of the political and intellectual élites of Germany's immediate eastern neighbours was precisely to be — they would say 'again' — part of the West, part of a truly Western Europe. And was not here the real key to that security, that European normality, which Germany's leaders themselves so evidently sought? If Germany wanted to be a normal, European and Western country, like France or Britain, then it had, like France or Britain, to have normal, European and Western neighbours to its east. To say this is, of course, already to suggest a certain priority.

Now in the case of those immediate eastern neighbours, the prospects of achieving this Western, European 'normality' were simply inseparable from the conduct and development, not just external but also internal, of the (currently West and South) European Community. Perhaps the greatest single flaw of the Maastricht treaty was that it had nothing to say about the rest of Europe knocking at Europe's doors. Ostpolitik and Europapolitik, to recall the Bonn terms, could no longer be thought apart. Europe was still very far from being one, but there could now at least be one Europapolitik.

What did Germany actually do to its east, in the first two years after its own 'day of unity'? To tell the story in any detail would distort the proportions of this book. In any case, unlike the history of Ostpolitik told above, this is a story without an end. There are areas and periods in which the only safe form of commentary is the hourly radio broadcast. But a few points may nonetheless be singled out.

Until the Soviet ambassador to Bonn handed over the Soviet ratification document on the 2 + 4 Treaty in March 1991, the Bonn government's overwhelming concern was to keep the Soviet Union together and co-operative. Even after ratification, the Soviet troops still had to be got out of what was now eastern (rather than East) Germany. The Baltic republics continued to be told to go slow. This changed with the failed Soviet coup in August 1991. Immediately thereafter, Germany recognised — or, strictly speaking, restored diplomatic relations with — what were now again described as the Baltic states. Kohl called this 'a moving moment'. At the same time, he looked forward, publicly at least, to a 'renewed Soviet Union', which should take its place next to what the Bonn government insisted on calling the 'reform states' of the former Eastern Europe. Instead, the Soviet Union broke up.

The Federal Republic rightly claimed that it contributed the largest share of Western financial transfers to the former Soviet Union, although if one looked closely at the dramatic headline figures produced by the German government one found that these included all the very large payments for German unification, exports from the former GDR paid for in transferable roubles, export credit guarantees and even private donations. In terms of direct grants and aid, the American contribution was at least comparable.

In December 1992, Kohl agreed with Yeltsin that Soviet troops would withdraw by the end of August 1994, four months before the deadline in the 1990 treaty. Former Foreign Minister Hans-Dietrich Genscher called for a new comprehensive *Russlandpolitik* of the West, and specifically of the EC. What this would be was still wholly unclear, not least because nobody knew what Russia would be. Even less clear was whether Germany, the EC, or anybody in the West had what, in time, might be almost as important: a *Ukrainepolitik*.

What of the other large multi-national communist state, Yugoslavia? In the immediate aftermath of German unification, the general Western hope of keeping together the so-called federal republic of Yugoslavia accorded both with Bonn's general wish for stability (order/peace) and with its specific concern not to countenance any bad example of republican self-determination which might 'destabilise' the Soviet Union. But this also changed in the summer of 1991. After Slovenia and Croatia declared their independence, in the face of Serbian aggression, Hans-Dietrich Genscher, then still Foreign Minister, found himself confronted with a growing barrage of moral outrage and criticism from the media and politicians of all parties in Bonn. He then ran out ahead of his critics, and declared that Slovenia and Croatia should be recognised as sovereign states. It must be done; he insisted on it; how could he — for whom

396 · *In Europe's Name*

human rights and self-determination were sacred — ever be thought to have thought anything else?

German diplomacy then devoted its considerable skills, and new muscle, to securing a 'European' (that is, EC) initiative for recognition. The task was intricate. To give just one small example: according to a credible source, Genscher at one point put heavy pressure on Bulgaria not (yet) to recognise Macedonia, although this was actually a very bold and construct-ive move by Bulgaria — in fact, almost the Bulgarian equivalent of Germany's recognition of the Oder-Neisse line. Why did Genscher do this? Could it possibly be something to do with Greece, so often the joker in the EC pack, and now, in a fashion more often loosely identified with 'Eastern Europe', furiously opposing the recognition of Macedonia? Could it, just possibly, be a deal: Germany would not (yet) support the recognition of Macedonia if Greece did not oppose the recognition of Slovenia and Croatia? Oh, brave new world!

For all this diplomatic finesse, Germany was still unable to persuade its main West European partners of the wisdom of the step. It therefore bounced them into it, by declaring that it would go ahead with the recognition itself anyway, and before Christmas. Having then secured a reluctant resolution of all the EC member states to extend recognition on 15 January 1992, provided certain conditions were met, it proceeded to do so itself, before Christmas, declaring that the conditions had already been satisfied.

There are at least four different issues here. The first is how this was done, which was extremely European in the descriptive, historical sense, but not inordinately European in the prescriptive, futuristic sense. The second is why it was done. One can safely say that most of the Germans who supported this step did so with the very best of intentions, which had nothing in common with Hitler's wartime alliance with Croatia. On the contrary. Milošević's Serbia had been presented to them as the new Nazi Germany and this time they wanted to be on the right side. (One result was that the Federal Republic was presented by Milošević to the Serbs as the new Nazi Germany.) What one could not say, however, is that this sudden turn in German policy was the result of any sober calculation of national interest. It was a hasty over-reaction, following public and especially published opinion rather than leading it. Of course, it was by no means only in Bonn that this was liable to happen. It was one of the structural problems of making foreign policy in a television democracy.

The third issue is the consequences of the decision in the former Yugoslavia. Did it ameliorate the situation, by sending a clear warning to the military-political leadership in Belgrade, or did it exacerbate it, as many American, British and French policymakers feared it would? The real problem with recognition was not Croatia and Slovenia in themselves, but the remaining republic of Bosnia-Herzegovina. Here a nightmare developed to which the principle of self-determination could provide no easy cure — and may even have been part of the disease. The fourth issue is: who faced the consequences? Above all, of course, the bereaved, maimed, brutalised and dispossessed men, women and children of the former Yugoslavia. Yet Germany faced the consequences indirectly, by taking in some 250,000 refugees from the former Yugoslavia in 1992, compared with just 4,000 taken by Britain and just over 1,000 taken by France. The usually humane and generous reception given to these people was something of which Germany could be proud.

But what of tackling causes rather than results? In 1990–91, German diplomacy had hoped that new conflicts in the rest of Europe could be restrained by a strengthened CSCE. The Helsinki process was seen as a golden bridge between the European Community and the long-sought European peace order. Unfortunately, the CSCE 'crisis mechanism' inaugurated at Genscher's Congress of Berlin proved even more powerless to prevent mayhem in Bosnia than the solution found at Bismarck's Congress of Berlin. Instead, the West had to resort to methods which would have been more familiar to Bismarck. Multilateral diplomacy, the cheque-book and the telephone were not enough.

Under joint United Nations and EC auspices, soldiers from France, Britain and many smaller European nations tried to help 'make peace'. The United States initially said this was Europe's business, and a test of the EC's much-vaunted new common foreign and security policy. Yet, willy-nilly, America once again found itself playing a major role. In early 1993, German soldiers were still notable by their absence, although the political parties in Bonn were edging towards the removal of the constitutional impediments to their deployment under UN auspices. Meanwhile, Britain and France sent the soldiers, Germany took the refugees. To describe this as a European division of labour would no doubt be too harmonious an interpretation.

To raise these issues in this cursory way is not to offer any comprehensive or final judgements. It is merely to help concentrate minds on questions. In the former Eastern Europe, by contrast with the former Yugoslavia and the former Soviet Union, the picture was more encouraging. To be sure, there were no simple lines between black and white. To call Romania in 1992 a democracy would be a romanesque — not to say, a baroque — use of the word. In Czechoslovakia, which had generally been regarded as the most Western of the former East European countries, there erupted a quite bitter nationality conflict which resulted in a peaceful separation into two different states: the Czech Republic and Slovakia. In the domestic politics of Poland and Hungary there were, in high and even in the highest places, strong elements not just of the European (prescriptive) but also of the European (descriptive) — the latter being described by the former as nationalist, populist, chauvinist, xenophobic and so on.

Nonetheless, there was some real progress here, and Germany played a notably constructive part. Together with the United States, Germany was instrumental in bringing the East Central European states into a new Nato Co-operation Council, although the fact that all the other post-Soviet states were brought in at the same time rather diminished the attraction. Quiet bilateral co-operation in the security field went further and was more promising. As (West) Germany had itself been welcomed into the Council of Europe, just a few years after being liberated from a dictatorship, so now Germany was able to join other established Western democracies in welcoming the new democracies into that often neglected institution of democratic Europe.

Meanwhile, Germany played a leading role in the negotiation of the so-called 'Europe Agreements' signed between the European Community and the 'Visegrád three' — Hungary, Poland and (then still) Czechoslovakia. In most of the crucial economic sectors where these countries could immediately hope to export more goods to the EC (agriculture, coal, steel, textiles), these agreements were in fact still protectionist, perfectly illustrating the way in which the EC could, at its worst, function as the aggregation of national, regional and sectoral *sacro egoismo*. But here the responsibility lay much more with France and the weaker economies of the south than it did with Germany.

Nonetheless, the treaties set the goal of creating a free-trade relationship in ten years, and this was interpreted in Germany as suggesting a possible time-scale for the opening of negotiations for full membership of the European Community. Moreover, in the bilateral treaties which Germany negotiated with Poland, Hungary and Czechoslovakia, the Federal Republic also committed itself to supporting those countries' progress towards eventual membership of the EC. Similar treaties with Bulgaria and Romania mentioned progress towards the EC, but not membership. Altogether, these bilateral treaties signalled the Federal Republic's desire to place its relations with its eastern neighbours on a new footing; building, of course, on the achievements of Ostpolitik.

Not just on paper but in practice, not just in trade but in assistance for building new democratic, legal and educational institutions, Germany was in the front line — whether through direct action by the Federal Government, by the federal states, by individual towns, by the wealthy party foundations, by other 'quangos' (quasi non-governmental organisations), by the churches, by private foundations or simply by individual initiative. Moreover, insofar as any Western model was applicable to post-communist Europe it would be Model Germany: not just because it was the closest but also because it was a social market economy, a legal system and a liberal democracy built on the ruins of a totalitarian system and designed specifically to prevent the return of totalitarianism. Who would have thought forty or even twenty years before that it would be to Germany that Hungarians, Czechs and Poles would turn first when it came to drafting the constitutions of liberty? This was an extraordinary and heartening novelty.

Recalling a leitmotif of Ostpolitik, one could almost imagine a huge sign hovering over Central and Eastern Europe with the inscription: 'Weaving in progress'. German language-teaching was one of the region's great growth industries. In line with a central tenet of weaving, the Federal Republic also led the way in abolishing visa requirements for Poles as well as Hungarians, Czechs and Slovaks. The millions of visitors, and travellers in transit, provoked not a little hostility, above all in the former East Germany. Yet on balance this bold step was remarkably successful. In early 1992, a Polish quality newspaper could write that never in the twentieth century had Polish-German relations been as good.

Nonetheless, there were still (or again) problems. While the Polish frontier issue was closed by treaty, that of reparations for Poles deported to work in the Third Reich continued to rumble on. The negotiation of the bilateral treaty with Czechoslovakia proved unexpectedly tense, because of continued differences over the date from which the Munich Agreement of 1938 should be deemed invalid (*ex tunc* or *ex nunc*?) and because of demands raised by the organisation of the Sudeten German expellees.

While President Havel had handsomely apologised for the post-war expulsions, and demonstratively made his first visit as President to Germany (even before visiting Slovakia), the Sudeten German leaders stubbornly insisted on the right to resettle in the Sudetenland as German citizens and on compensation for the German property expropriated after the war. At one point they even demanded a halt to the programme of privatisation of state property in Czechoslovakia until this issue had been resolved. Through their influence in the CSU they plagued the progress of the treaty right up to its final ratification in the Bundesrat, where the state of Bavaria still opposed it. And then, with the separation of the Czech lands and Slovakia, they tried to reopen the whole issue yet again.

Elsewhere, there was still the problem of the remaining German minorities. In Romania, the centuries-old German communities had been almost extinguished by emigration to Germany. But there remained up to a million Germans 'in the sense of the Basic Law' (see page 234f) in Poland, and over two million in the former Soviet Union. The German government, working mainly through the department of the Interior Ministry responsible for 'out-settlers', now concentrated on trying to ensure that, as Chancellor Kohl put it, they would 'see a future in the ancestral *Heimat*'.

The numbers of out-settlers from Poland actually fell dramatically, from more than 133,000 in 1990 to less than 18,000 in 1992. Partly this was because the rules for the admission of out-settlers had been tightened in summer 1990. Partly, it was because the general prospects for anyone remaining in Poland had improved. (Polish emigration from Poland had also been high in the 1980s.) But it was also because the democratic Polish government had recognised the cultural rights of the German minority, and the German government was pumping money into their towns and villages. To have a German passport but stay in Silesia could now be an attractive option.

However, the number of out-settlers from the former Soviet Union rose rather than fell, in spite of German-Russian, German-Ukrainian and even German-Kazakh agreements to provide better facilities for Germans in old and new areas of settlement. As a result, the Federal Republic still took a total of just over 230,000 out-settlers in 1992. From the point of view of the ordinary German voter, this was only part of a much larger overall challenge. Immigration had replaced the Red Army as the new threat from the east, and become a (sometimes all too literally) burning issue in German domestic politics. The reaction of the sheltered consumer society of the old Federal Republic to immigration, and even more that of the traumatised society of the former GDR, ranged from the nervous to the hysterical. 'The boat is full', headlines proclaimed, although as Hans Magnus Enzensberger pointed out, the people who were actually at sea in a leaking lifeboat were the refugees.

Nonetheless, the total numbers were very large. In addition to the 230,000 ethnic German out-settlers, there were in 1992 more than 250,000 refugees, nearly 440,000 people using and abusing Germany's exceptionally liberal right of asylum to stay in the country as 'asylum-seekers', and, according to the Interior Minister, some 310,000 people who had 'illegally entered' the country. There was a considerable overlap between these figures, especially since Sunday's illegal immigrant or refugee often became Monday's asylum-seeker. But the total was equivalent to more than one per cent of Germany's existing population, in one year. As usual, Germany looked for a 'European solution' of its problem. But when that was not forthcoming it produced its own attempt, presented as paving the way for a European solution.

After tortuous negotiations between the main parties, agreement was reached to limit the right of asylum so it did not apply to people from countries where there was no longer political persecution. Bogus asylum-seekers who came to Germany through 'secure third countries' would be returned to them. Poland and the Czech Republic were now classified as 'secure third countries'. The burden was therefore to be passed back to Germany's immediate eastern neighbours, although Bonn was ready to pay something for the service — and to help them improve the walls and fences on their own eastern frontiers. To describe this as European burden-sharing would again be a too harmonious interpretation.

This whole complex of issues — minorities, out-settlers, asylum-seekers, immigration and the treatment of foreigners — raised further questions. One of them could hardly be more fundamental. It was: Who is a German? The answer given by the old Federal Republic had not been solely *völkisch*. But in the interpretation of article 116 of the Basic Law there had undoubtedly still been what Johannes Gross has called 'the *völkisch* worm'. The problems this caused were compounded by an exceptionally liberal asylum law but also by a quite illiberal law on the acquisition of citizenship for foreigners living in Germany. The result was a mess.

Foreigners could secure long-term residence in Germany by pretending to be persecuted at home, when they clearly were not. Meanwhile, a young Turkish man who had been born and lived his whole life in Germany, attended German schools and spoke fluent German, could not become a German citizen unless he renounced Turkish citizenship. Yet at the same time, Germany was handing out German citizenship to thousands of Polish citizens, according to criteria such as descent, 'inclination to Germanity', and ancestors in the *Wehrmacht* (see page 236).

The matter should not be made simpler than it was. Many people really had suffered, in Poland and even more in the Soviet Union, just for being Germans. France had felt a responsibility to its *pieds noirs*, Britain to its Falklanders. Simply to abandon the Germans in the East would not necessarily be a noble thing. But the question 'who is a German?' was too important to be left for ever as a hostage of history. Would the Germans leave the primary emphasis on the *Volk*, the tribe, the *ethnos*, or would they shift the emphasis to a more modern, liberal version of citizenship, as they had in most other fields? 'That only those of German origin can be true Germans,' wrote Johannes Gross, 'is a barbaric superstition.' And the East Berlin theologian, Richard Schröder, sharpened the debate by defining a desirable normality as one in which there would be full acceptance of *black Germans*. To put it another way: Did Germany want to stop at being a 'normal European nation-state', or would it try to become a, historically speaking, somewhat less normal state-nation?

Now this was, of course, a question for all European countries. But it was a question particularly for Germany, and Germany would have first to answer for itself. Europe would not do the job for it, even if, in the longer term, the EC were to develop a real European citizenship. And this was not just a matter of self-definition, in Germany's condition of stillbecoming. It also concerned the example that Germany would give to the countries to its east. The provisions for the German minorities sought by the German government, and written in to the bilateral treaties, were presented as being in line with multilateral agreements, with CSCE and European norms. This was no doubt true. But it was also true that one powerful nation-state was making bilateral arrangements to support, culturally, economically and legally, a minority of its own nationals (by its own definition) inside other states. The degree of support and protection accorded them depended on the will and power of the protector-state. It was mainly done through a department of the German *Interior* Ministry.

Hans-Dietrich Genscher said the foreign policy of united Germany should be a 'policy of the good example'. But was this really such a good example? If Germany acted like this, then why should not Hungary, in relation to the large Hungarian minorities in Slovakia, Transylvania and the former Yugoslavia? And Poland in relation to the Polish minority in Lithuania? And Russia for the huge new Russian minorities in other states of the former Soviet Union? And then, what of Croatia? What, even, of Serbia? The German minorities had suffered in the past. But so had most other minorities. To be sure, unlike Serbia (and, in smaller measure, Croatia and Russia), Germany was not using force, the threat of force, or even the hint of a threat of force. But was this model of the protector-state the cure or part of the disease?

In Poland, German officials, and the more enlightened representatives of the expellee organisations through which some of the public funds were channelled, exerted themselves to see that the subsidies benefited Poles as well as Germans and to respect local sensibilities. But some of the local Germans were not so restrained. Here as elsewhere, old-fashioned nationalism had been stoked rather than dampened by oppression. And in this the locals were sometimes encouraged by unrepentant expellees and marginal nationalists from Germany itself. Genuine irredentism was still very unlikely, not least because the German minority (unlike, say, the Hungarian minority in Slovakia) was not contiguous to the fatherland, but concentrated in the area around Opole (Oppeln). Local friction was likely.

Hartmut Koschyk, a Christian Democrat member of the Bundestag working for a genuinely constructive peaceful engagement of the expellees in the area, wrote that 'European normality must be seen as the ultimate goal.' A familiar invocation! But he went on: 'a normality that was practised as a matter of course in Central Europe — which is more than just an idea — for centuries'. If one considers soberly, without nostalgia or wishful thinking, what the normality of Central Europe had really been over at least the previous century and a half, this was not a very encouraging perspective.

All this was of course bound up with the further question of the German economic presence in the region. Despite much loose talk of 'hegemony', 'supremacy' or 'domination', this presence was still difficult to quantify at the end of 1992, both because trade patterns had not fully settled down after the end of East Germany, Comecon and the Soviet Union, and because investment patterns had not yet built up. For what they are worth, the trade patterns for three countries in 1991 and 1992 are given in Table IV. At the end of 1992, German investment was said to account for more than eighty per cent of total foreign investment in the Czech Republic. Rather surprisingly, there was significantly more American than

German investment in Hungary, while in Poland the German share was estimated at about one third. But the total figures for investment were still so small that these proportions could quickly change.

That in the Czech Republic, for example, was substantially affected by one big investment, of Volkswagen in the Skoda car factory. The fact that Skoda went to Volkswagen rather than to Renault was, however, widely interpreted as a sign of things to come. Even with the huge drain of public monies and private capital to eastern Germany, Germany was still a far larger and more active presence than any other West European country. It seemed to be a reasonable guess that German investment would sooner or later pull further ahead, when the former GDR began to be less of a drain on German resources.

This naturally produced fears as well as hopes. The Polish writer Andrzej Szczypiorski commented that whereas previously the Poles had been afraid of the Germans coming with guns now they were afraid of them coming with cheque-books. Yet one has to say that the one thing worse than the Germans coming with their cheque-books would be for the Germans not to come with their cheque-books. These post-communist countries wanted some version of a market economy; that is, of capitalism. Capitalism requires capital. Capital is what they did not have. Therefore, as so often before in the history of the region, the capital had to come from outside. Germany was next door and had a lot of capital.

Under the strain of unification, Germany was actually a net importer of capital in 1992, but within a few years this would almost certainly change for the better. Yet why should this capital then flow to the former Eastern Europe rather than to other European areas with low wages but better communications and guaranteed market access, such as Spain or Portugal? And if it were to go east, why not to the Far East? Beside physical proximity, the main competitive advantage that the former Eastern Europe had to offer would be very cheap skilled and unskilled labour. An unkind word for seizing this advantage would be 'exploitation'. Yet it was not realistic to expect capital to behave philanthropically in a highly competitive world where even Western Europe would have its work cut out to keep up with the Far East. So if there was no way to avoid this dilemma, it would be necessary to confront it.

'Nothing might do greater harm to German-Slav relationships,' wrote Elizabeth Wiskemann in 1956, 'than for Poles and Czechs to feel that, no sooner are they free of the communist yoke than they must go into German economic harness.' A prophecy come true? Wiskemann continued: 'It would call for exquisite tact for this impression to be avoided: the very same German who worked very well with the French or Italian or Benelux representatives in the West might find it traditionally too difficult to keep his manners as good in the East.' Wiskemann, writing just a decade after Hitler, was being ironical, even sarcastic. But might we not now repeat her sentence quite calmly and seriously? Was it not, precisely, exquisite tact that was called for of the Germans in this region in the 1990s?

Here we must dwell for a moment on Wiskemann's word 'traditionally'. In the new bilateral treaties there was talk in the preambles of continuing the 'good traditions ... in the centuries-old history of Germany and Poland', of 'fruitful traditions' with Bulgaria, 'the tradition of fruitful relations' with Romania, 'centuries-old fruitful traditions' with Czechoslovakia and even 'traditional friendship developed over centuries' with Hungary. But did most Germans have any inkling of Germany's history and traditions in the east? In the Third Reich, German studies of the lands to Germany's east were poisoned by Nazism. The poisoned chalice was carried forward by some of the same scholars after 1945. Then there was a sharp break, and 'the East' — now in the ahistorical 'Yalta' definition — became the territory of political science, security studies, policy intellectuals, journalists and professional policymakers. With some notable scholarly exceptions, the history and traditions of the German presence east of the Oder and Neisse rivers, and south-east of the Erz mountains, were left for expellees to brood on. As has often been observed, for most younger West Germans Majorca was closer than Leipzig and California more familiar than Silesia. They lived with their backs to the Wall — and more protected by it than was quite comfortable to admit.

Now all this had changed. Unification opened the window to the east. But what would people see? How would it be presented to them? What were those 'good traditions' to be carried forward? Were there any? One of Germany's most influential and enterprising publishers, Wolf Jobst Siedler, announced a lavish scholarly ten-volume series entitled 'German History in the East of Europe'. It should, he said, describe the world of 'the German-settled or German-permeated East Central and Eastern Europe' — a world 'sunk in the cataracts of history and finally, guiltily gambled away'. A timely undertaking.

Yet this same distinguished publisher could be found, in a book he published in 1991 entitled *Germany, what now?* (as in Fallada's *Little man, what now?*), talking expansively of Germany as 'again the hegemonial power of the whole of Central-Eastern Europe'. Germany, he said, would be for Czechoslovakia, Hungary and partly for Poland 'the leading power' (*Führungsmacht*). Germany might possibly, he suggested, 'be regaining her traditional role in Eastern Europe'. 'Bohemia and Moravia,' he observed, 'are a part of Europe, of the German world, I would almost have said.' Germany could not avoid a 'supremacy'. It would have to take over a 'key role' for Hungary, Czechoslovakia and above all for Poland. 'Of course we don't want to drive out the Poles, but I do indeed believe that one day Pomerania and Silesia and Bohemia-Moravia will orient themselves again towards Germany.'

The historian Arnulf Baring, under whose name the book appeared, was more sceptical. He thought the Germans were more likely to duck the challenge, and erect new walls to protect their modest, bourgeois idyll. If they did take up the challenge, however, he doubted their capacity to do it 'cautiously and yet energetically, tactfully and yet purposefully'. Yet even he, in trying to find the terms in which to present this task to his compatriots, found himself talking about 'a colonisation task, a new *Ostkolonisation*', and about the formerly German territories immediately to the east (i.e. Pomerania and Silesia) as 'these, if you like, common territories'. Now one understands and applauds the intention: to provoke realistic discussion of issues that were urgently in need of it. But such formulations themselves illustrate the difficulty of finding the 'good traditions'. Exquisite tact this was not. Imagine a British historian talking of a British 'colonisation task' in Ireland!

At this point one has to say something slightly shocking. In 1991, many people, in Germany and elsewhere, hoped and believed that at least the territorial questions for the Germans were resolved for good and all. But even of that one could not be certain. All over the former Eastern Europe, the former Soviet Union, the former Yugoslavia, territorial questions were coming open again. It has been said that half the frontiers in Europe are newer than those of Africa, and some already proved to be less durable. For Germany, one territorial question already on the agenda was that of the Kaliningrad region, now a highly militarised Russian exclave between Lithuania and Poland, but formerly Kant's city of Königsberg and a part of East Prussia.

As early as 1988, the banker Friedrich Wilhelm Christians had suggested turning this area into a special economic zone: a 'Baltic region K'. As the perestroika of the Soviet Union turned to the collapse of the Soviet Union, the proposal was seriously discussed in the Russian press. It was by no means impossible that Russia would at some stage in the 1990s be prepared to, in effect, sell the area for hard currency and the promise of more Western 'co-operation'.

How would the Germans react to such an offer? At a conference in mid-1992, an Israeli journalist posed this question, and answered himself: They would say 'yes, but in a European framework'. Some three months later the historian Michael Stürmer, who had been present at this conference, contributed a leading article to the *Frankfurter Allgemeine Zeitung*. It was entitled 'A Task called Königsberg'. After describing the miserable and threatening condition of the Russian military region, he endorsed the idea of a free-trade zone, although not the suggestion (which had been supported by Christians) that the ethnic Germans from the former Soviet Union should be resettled there.

'The German interest,' wrote Stürmer, 'does not only come from the past and history. It must above all be directed to making the Baltic coasts a zone of stability and prosperity.' However, Germany could not alone make such proposals: 'The European Community must be given precedence, in thought and action'. An overall concept of the EC 'should within the foreseeable future bring Königsberg into the EC's internal market. Russia would thus get partial membership and so also an advantageous special status vis-à-vis the European Community.' Whatever was to be done, he wrote, 'it can only be done with Russia'. Although there was mention of the interests of all the Baltic basin states, the words 'Lithuania' and 'Poland' did not appear.

Now this delightful combination of Euro-planning and neo-Bismarckian *Russlandpolitik* should not, of course, be taken as representing official German policy, although Professor Stürmer was the head of the country's leading government-funded foreign policy think-tank. But the question of Königsberg would not go away. In fact, the better things went in Russia the more likely it was to be posed. If things went badly, the Russian military would simply hold on to their desirable base. A more western-oriented, civilian government would be more likely to open talks about it.

It is important to stress that the demilitarisation of the Kaliningrad area might also be in the interests of Poland and Lithuania. However a free-trade zone, as part of a re-emerging Hanseatic league, would be for them a mixed blessing, since it would almost certainly attract investment — above all, German investment — which might otherwise go to Gdańsk or Klaipeda. The precise legal status of the area would obviously be the subject of delicate negotiations. Writing in *Die Zeit*, Marion Gräfin Dönhoff suggested a four-power condominium, the powers being Russia, Poland, Lithuania and — since some might still object to Germany — Sweden! After the four-power city of Berlin, the four-power city of Königsberg? But even if formal sovereignty remained with Russia, a heavy economic commitment would involve Germany very directly at an extraordinarily sensitive point.

What of the territories immediately to Germany's east? Reflecting in his memoirs on the arrogation to Poland, at Stalin's insistence, of the large part of Silesia between the eastern and western Neisse rivers, Churchill wrote: 'One day the Germans would want their territory back, and the Poles would not be able to stop them'. This was a brutally harsh statement which nonetheless accurately reflected what had generally happened in Central and Eastern Europe over the centuries. If strong states were next to weak states which had territory they coveted, and to which they could construct some historical claim, they sooner or later took it. That was, after all, how Prussia had got Silesia in the first place. Of course, there was now a quite different Germany in a quite different Europe. But the co-operation between strong and weak states, in historically disputed territories, with remaining national minorities, would still be a very delicate affair. And Poland was not just economically but also politically a weak state.

One did not need to share Günter Grass's nightmare vision of a Germany economically subordinating 'a good chunk of Silesia, a little slice of Pomerania', in order to foresee tensions here. The German border town of Görlitz advertised itself in the *Financial Times* as the 'Centre of Lower Silesia'. Exquisite tact? German policymakers were particularly keen on co-operation in what were described as 'Euroregions', spanning the borders between Germany, the Czech Republic and Poland, or, in regional terms, between Bavaria, Saxony and Bohemia, Saxony, Brandenburg and Lower Silesia, Mecklenburg-Vorpommern and Pomerania. Here, to Germany's east, as previously to Germany's west, frontiers should be opened and gradually deprived of their importance. They should unite people rather than dividing them. But, as Siedler's remarks suggest, regionalism could mean something rather different in East Central Europe than it did between old-established states of roughly comparable strength in Western Europe.

As we have noticed throughout this book, the history of Ostpolitik abounded in paradoxes, both deliberate and unintentional. In crafting a new Europapolitik, German policymakers might need to consider a further paradox. In the former Eastern Europe, the path to going beyond the state-nation might lead through first consolidating the state-nation. It would be nice to think otherwise, but no better guarantor of human and civil rights had yet been found in Europe than the established, constitutional, liberal and democratic state-nation. That the EC, or the CSCE, or the UN, could substitute for the state in that regard remained still a hope, but not a reality.

Let it again be stressed that none of this is for a moment to doubt German policymakers' good intentions. Indeed, if there was a problem with the formulation of German foreign policy in the first years after unification it was not that there were any bad intentions but that there were too many good ones. What we have tried to do here is simply — following Adenauer's exhortation — to identify a few questions that might soon arise, 'and perhaps [to] warn'. It is hard to overstate the difficulty and sensitivity of the challenges that Germany still faced to its east. The great work of reconciliation would take at least another generation. It would require an honest and unsentimental reading of history, respect for the different achievements even of poor neighbours, and great sensitivity.

Sitting on a bench in front of the Strahov monastery in Prague, a German editor asked an elderly Czech whether the Germans should come back again. 'To be sure,' he replied, 'but you would have to bring the Jews with you.' Central Europe would never again be what it once was. But it could in some ways actually be better: hardly in high culture, but politically, economically and socially. This would require extraordinary commitment from Germany, but also exceptional self-restraint. After forty-five years of steadily working to widen the bounds of German power, the Germans would now have to aquire the new habit of not fully exerting the power they had. More dramatically still: they had the particular task of helping the consolidation of other democratic state-nations in territories where Germans had until quite recently lived and ruled.

Possibilities

Shortly before his death in the autumn of 1992, Willy Brandt wrote a valedictory message in almost Old Testament style. 'Our time,' he wrote, 'like hardly any before, is full of possibilities — for good and ill. Nothing comes of itself. And little lasts. So — reflect on your strength, and on the fact that every period demands its own answers . . .' As the grand old man of Ostpolitik penned his delphic parting words, the range of possibilities in Europe was indeed vast.

It was possible that, in the early twenty-first century, at least part of the former Eastern Europe would be an area of secure, liberal, democratic states, co-operating with neighbours and partners in a larger European Community and Western Alliance. It was possible that Polish, Hungarian and Czech citizens would have rights, freedoms and life-chances comparable to those enjoyed by Spanish, Portuguese and Greek citizens in the 1980s. It was possible that tolerance, pluralism, democracy and the virtues of ever closer co-operation would spread from west to east, so that Germany would at last find itself between West and West — and therefore indeed, to recall Weizsäcker's phrase, 'delivered from the *Mittellage*'. This would not be the final 'unification' or 'healing' of Europe, of which people had dreamed in the early 1980s, in Prague, in Berlin, even in Oxford. But it would be a great step closer to it.

It was also possible that intolerance, tribalism and the forces of disintegration would spread from east to west, threatening even the substance of what had already been achieved in the European Community. In Brecht's words, 'the womb is fertile still, from which that crawled': and the womb was of course not capitalism, as Brecht had claimed to think, but Europe — and human nature. The examples of the former Yugoslavia and parts of the former Soviet Union showed what could happen. And they were not far away. 'Easter holidaymakers in civil war' proclaimed a horrified headline in an Austrian tabloid newspaper. Germany was already shaken.

Altogether, Central Europe was the area in which this new European question was posed most sharply. The peoples of East Central Europe had the first and best chance of gaining from the former, optimistic variant. Those of West Central Europe, the Germans and the Austrians, stood in most immediate danger of suffering from the latter. Perhaps one should again call this not the European question but the Central European question. But once again, the Central European question bid fair to be the central European one.

Germany, specifically, had what the historian Fritz Stern has called its 'second chance'. At the end of the nineteenth century, Germany was the emergent major power in the centre of Europe, a powerhouse of economic and scientific modernity. It had a chance to use this power peacefully and constructively. It spectacularly failed so to do. Now, at the end of the twentieth century, it was again a major power in the centre of Europe. For all the new quality of institutionalised co-operation and permanent communication between allies and partners in the European Community, the Western Alliance, and altogether in the Western world, it was Germany that had this second chance and Germany that faced these particular challenges. Burden-sharing would only go so far, because other Western states had other vital interests, other special problems, other priorities. Britain and America had to look to their own battered economies and tattered social fabric. France, Italy and Spain had also to look south, across the Mediterranean to North Africa. To say that Germany's problems were also Europe's did not mean that Europe would solve them.

Could Germany do it? Could it not only preserve but also help to spread the achievements that had made it a magnet and a model? In another twenty years could another Willy Brandt have the satisfaction of seeing the word Germany become a synonym not just for peace but also for freedom? Some said that Germany lacked the 'internationalist élite' for the task. Yet it did not want for highly educated, well-travelled, idealistic men and women. True, what they had experienced before was little preparation for what they faced now. They were somewhat like the pilot of a barge on the Rhine who suddenly finds himself in charge of an oil-tanker on a high sea. But to some extent that had also been true of America's élites in 1945. And the American half-century had not been Europe's worst (for those in the West, that is).

There were perhaps a few very general lessons they could take with them from that half-century, and more particularly from the quarter-century of Ostpolitik. Firstly, they would need to define anew their own national interest. It would be useful if they did not try to define other people's. Making unilateral, national definitions of the European interest was a habit as old as the nation-states in Europe. But it was a bad habit. Unless and until there was a directly-elected all-European parliament and government, a fair definition of European interest could only be reached as a series of compromises between national interests. Moreover, if they did not define their own national interest consciously and clearly, it would be made up as they went along, in reaction to external challenges and to the pressures of public and published opinion in a television democracy.

They would need to watch out for those abstract nouns ('stability', 'normalisation'), and to remember not to take Mephistopheles' advice.

Hypotheses would, however, be useful. But the history of Ostpolitik also shows how hypotheses can become burdens. So they would need to keep revising the hypotheses against reality. In trying to build a new Europe, they would need always to remember the West — in trade, in defence, above all, in values. Those values could not always be borne aloft at full mast. It would sometimes be necessary to be a 'cunning idealist', to borrow Golo Mann's description of Adenauer. But if they were again to play down, conceal or relativise those values, they would have to be quite sure they knew to what purpose and with what effect. The history of Ostpolitik shows just how little one can ever be certain of the effects. When in doubt, they might therefore remember Mark Twain's advice: If you don't know what to do, do the right thing.

They would still have to beware the tendency to emotional overreaction. If Kleist and Thomas Mann were not sufficient authorities on this point, they might take it from Boris Becker. 'I have the impression,' said the young tennis star, 'that with success — and this nation has great success — many Germans have a certain tendency to flip their top.' They would do well not to overestimate what Germany could achieve, with the best will in the world. One of Germany's most gifted young political scientists declared in an inaugural lecture in 1991 that the 'European tasks' of 'the Germans in their second nation-state' would include above all 'the task of keeping the national and European consciousness of all countries of the continent in harmony'. When Britain was the most powerful country in the world it could barely maintain the balance of power on the continent of Europe, yet now Germany, troubled, burdened, medium-heavyweight Germany, was to hold the balance of consciousness?

Finally, they could not expect to be thanked for what they were doing. If they thought neighbours and partners were being ungrateful (which they would be), they could do worse than to remember what many Germans had said about America over the previous half-century.

This was not much to be getting on with. But who said history teaches any plain lessons? These younger Germans could still count on help from their friends. However, like it or not, it was they who would face the main challenge, and the main chance.

'And,' the ghost of Adenauer might still insist, 'your best guess?' The earlier history of German foreign policy did not give grounds for excessive optimism. Even the largely constructive period of that history described and analysed in this book had some worrying features. Taking all in all, the favourable variant that we have imagined for Germany and Europe at the beginning of the twenty-first century did not seem probable. But it was still possible. There are worse combinations than that of scepticism and hope.

Abbreviations

Wherever possible, we have tried to avoid the use of abbreviations in the main text. The exceptions — such as EC, Nato and GDR — have virtually become words in their own right. The following abbreviations have been used when it seemed unavoidable, especially in direct quotations from documents, and throughout the Notes.

ACDP   *Archiv für Christlich-Demokratische Politik*

AdDL   *Archiv des Deutschen Liberalismus*

AdsD   *Archiv der sozialen Demokratie*

APZ   *Aus Politik und Zeitgeschichte*. A supplement to the weekly *Das Parlament*.

BBC   British Broadcasting Corporation

BPA   *Bundespresseamt*, formally the *Presse- und Informationsamt der Bundesregierung*. This abbreviation refers mainly to transcripts prepared by the federal press office.

CC   Central Committee. As used in Soviet, East German and other Soviet bloc documents.

CDU   *Christlich-Demokratische Union*. Christian Democratic Union. A party of the Federal Republic of Germany. Usually referred to in the main text, together with the Bavarian CSU, as 'Christian Democrats'.

CMEA   Council for Mutual Economic Assistance. Usually referred to in the main text as 'Comecon'.

CoCom   Co-ordinating Committee for Multilateral Export Controls

Comecon	Council for Mutual Economic Assistance. The CMEA.
CPSU	Communist Party of the Soviet Union
CSCE	Conference on Security and Co-operation in Europe. Often referred to in the main text as 'Helsinki'.
CSU	*Christlich-Soziale Union*. Christian Social Union. A party of Bavaria and the Federal Republic of Germany. Usually referred to in the main text, together with the CDU, as 'Christian Democrats'.
DA	*Deutschland Archiv*
DM	*Deutsche Mark*. German Mark. The D-Mark.
EA	*Europa-Archiv*
EC	European Community. Originally, and still in some formal usage, the European Communities.
EDC	European Defence Community
EEC	European Economic Community
EKD	*Evangelische Kirche in Deutschland*. The Protestant Church in Germany. In 1969–90 there was a separate church organisation in East Germany, the Federation of Protestant Churches in the GDR. In this period, the EKD was therefore, in effect, the Protestant Church in West Germany.
EPC	European Political Co-operation
FAZ	*Frankfurter Allgemeine Zeitung*
FDJ	*Freie Deutsche Jugend*. Free German Youth. The mass youth organisation of the GDR.
FDP	*Freie Demokratische Partei*. Free Democratic Party. A party of the Federal Republic of Germany. Usually referred to in the main text as 'Free Democrats'.
FRG	Federal Republic of Germany. The abbreviation was used systematically by the East German and Soviet authorities, to

put the FRG on the same level as the GDR. It was as carefully avoided by the West German authorities.

G7   The Group of Seven

GATT   General Agreement on Tariffs and Trade

GDR   German Democratic Republic

HVA   *Hauptverwaltung Aufklärung*. The espionage section of the MfS.

HZ   *Historische Zeitschrift*

IMF   International Monetary Fund

INF   Intermediate-range Nuclear Forces

KoKo   *Bereich Kommerzielle Koordinierung*. The GDR's 'Commercial Co-ordination' agency, for dealings in hard currency.

KOR   *Komitet Obrony Robotników*. Workers' Defence Committee.

LDPD   *Liberaldemokratische Partei Deutschlands*. The so-called Liberal Democratic Party of Germany was one of the 'bloc' parties in the GDR.

MBFR   Mutual and Balanced Force Reduction talks

MFN   Most Favored Nation. A status granted by the United States of America.

MfS   *Ministerium für Staatssicherheit*. The Ministry for State Security of the GDR. The 'Stasi'.

Nato   North Atlantic Treaty Organisation

ND   *Neues Deutschland*

NG   *Neue Gesellschaft*. Since 1985: *Neue Gesellschaft/ Frankfurter Hefte*.

OECD   Organisation for Economic Co-operation and Development

RFE   Radio Free Europe

SALT	Strategic Arms Limitation Talks, and subsequently treaties.
SDI	Strategic Defense Initiative. Also known as 'star wars'.
SED	*Sozialistische Einheitspartei Deutschlands.* Socialist Unity Party of Germany. The ruling communist party of the GDR, founded by a forced merger of KPD and SPD in the Soviet zone of occupation.
SI	Socialist International
SPD	*Sozialdemokratische Partei Deutschlands.* Social Democratic Party of Germany. A party which predates the Federal Republic of Germany, but references to 'Social Democrats' in the main text are usually to the SPD in the Federal Republic.
START	Strategic Arms Reduction Talks, and subsequently treaty.
SZ	*Süddeutsche Zeitung*
TAZ	*Die Tageszeitung*
USSR	Union of Soviet Socialist Republics
VfZ	*Vierteljahrshefte für Zeitgeschichte*
WEU	Western European Union
ZAIG	*Zentrale Auswertungs- und Informationsgruppe.* The Central Evaluation and Information Group of the MfS.
ZPA	*Zentrales Parteiarchiv.* The Central Party Archive of the SED.

Unpublished Sources

Some of the most interesting, though least reliable, unpublished sources are people's memories, unpacked in conversation. Conversations with the author in connection with this book are cited in the Notes by name, place and date, thus: Helmut Kohl, Bonn, 1 October 1991; Erich Honecker, Berlin-Moabit, 27 November 1992, and so forth.

Obviously these memories, and those in published memoirs, often do not tally with papers produced at the time. Many of these are still unavailable. However, some important documents have already been published, while the following archival collections have been both accessible and useful. Only the main holdings consulted are listed. Abbreviations used in the Notes are given in brackets. Note that reference numbers are those in 1992. Particularly in the case of the East German records, they are quite likely to change.

Archiv für Christlich-Demokratische Politik (ACDP)
    Werner Marx papers (I–356)
    Alois Mertes papers (I–403)

Archiv des Deutschen Liberalismus (AdDL)
    Akten des Bundesvorsitzenden Walter Scheel
    Akten des Bundesvorsitzenden Hans-Dietrich Genscher (Bundesvorsitzender Genscher)
    Wolfgang Schollwer, *Tagebücher*, 1966–1970 (Schollwer *Tagebuch*)

Archiv der sozialen Demokratie (AdsD)
    Egon Bahr papers (Dep EB)
    – Individual documents
    Depositum Willy Brandt (Dep WB)
        – *Beruflicher Werdegang und politisches Wirken in Berlin, 1947–1966* (Rbm)
        – *Bundesminister des Auswärtigen, 1966–1969* (BA)
        – *Bundeskanzler und Bundesregierung, 1969–1974* (BK)
        – *Publisistische Tätigkeit* (Publ)

Helmut Schmidt papers (HS)
- *Person und Werk*
- *Gespräche*
- *Reisen*
- *Schriftwechsel*
- *Reden als Bundeskanzler*
- *Sacharchiv*

(Files are continuously numbered through the whole collection)

Der Bundesbeauftragte für die Unterlagen des Staatssicherheitsdienstes der ehemaligen Deutschen Demokratischen Republik (The *Gauck-Behörde*)

Reports of the *Zentrale Auswertungs- und Informationsgruppe* (ZAIG)

Individual documents

Documents from the *Gauck-Behörde* are cited as MfS-and then the reference number, which is sometimes new and sometimes still the original.

Zentrales Parteiarchiv (ZPA)

Politburo internal archive, minutes and working papers (JIV 2/2, JIV 2/2A etc)

Central Committee records (IV 2/1)

Büro Axen (IV 2/2.035)

Büro Hager (IV B 2/2.024)

Büro Herrmann (IV 2/2.037)

Documents collected in the preparation of Baring, *Machtwechsel* (Baring Papers)

Short Titles

The following published works are cited in the Notes in a short title form. For ease of reference, documentary series and collections, memoirs, monographs and tracts are listed here in a single alphabetical sequence of short titles, together with full publication details. This is not a full bibliography. Guidance to further reading on individual subjects can be found in the Notes.

Apel, *Abstieg*: Hans Apel, *Der Abstieg. Politisches Tagebuch, 1978–1988* (Stuttgart: Deutsche Verlags-Anstalt, 1991)

Arndt, *Verträge*: Claus Arndt, *Die Verträge von Moskau und Warschau. Politische, verfassungsrechtliche und völkerrechtliche Aspekte* (2nd edition, Bonn: Verlag Neue Gesellschaft, 1982)

Aussiedler 1: Wilhelm Arnold, ed., *Die Aussiedler in der Bundesrepublik Deutschland. Forschungen der AWR Deutsche Sektion 1. Ergebnisbericht. Herkunft, Ausreise, Aufnahme* (Vienna: Wilhelm Braumüller, 1980 = Association for the Study of the World Refugee Problem, Treatises on Refugee Problems, Vol. XII/1)

Aussiedler 2: Hans Harmsen, ed., *Die Aussiedler in der Bundesrepublik Deutschland. Forschungen der AWR Deutsche Sektion. 2. Ergebnisbericht. Anpassung, Umstellung, Eingliederung* (Vienna: Wilhelm Braumüller, 1983 = Association for the Study of the World Refugee Problem, Treatises on Refugee Problems, Vol. XII/2).

Bahr, *Sicherheit*: Egon Bahr, *Sicherheit für und vor Deutschland. Vom Wandel durch Annäherung zur Europäischen Sicherheitsgemeinschaft* (Munich: Hanser, 1991)

Bahr, *Zum europäischen Frieden*: Egon Bahr, *Zum europäischen Frieden. Eine Antwort auf Gorbatschow* (Berlin: Corso bei Siedler, 1988)

Baring, *Anfang*: Arnulf Baring, *Im Anfang war Adenauer. Die Entstehung der Kanzlerdemokratie* (Munich: Deutscher Taschenbuch Verlag, 1971)

Baring, *Deutschland*: Arnulf Baring, *Deutschland, was nun? Ein Gespräch mit Dirk Rumberg und Wolf Jobst Siedler* (Berlin: Siedler, 1991)

Baring, *Grössenwahn*: Arnulf Baring, *Unser neuer Grössenwahn. Deutschland zwischen Ost und West* (Stuttgart: Deutsche Verlags-Anstalt, 1988)

Baring, *Machtwechsel*: Arnulf Baring, in Zusammenarbeit mit Manfred Görtemaker, *Machtwechsel. Die Ära Brandt-Scheel* (Stuttgart: Deutsche Verlags-Anstalt, 1982)

Bark & Gress, *Democracy and its Discontents*: Dennis L Bark & David R Gress, *Democracy and its Discontents, 1963–1988* (Oxford: Blackwell, 1989 = A History of West Germany Vol. 2)

Bender, *Neue Ostpolitik*: Peter Bender, *Neue Ostpolitik. Vom Mauerbau zum Moskauer Vertrag* (Munich: Deutscher Taschenbuch Verlag, 1986)

Benz & Graml, *Aspekte*: Benz, Wolfgang & Graml, Hermann, eds, *Aspekte der deutschen Aussenpolitik im 20. Jahrhundert. Aufsätze Hans Rothfels zum Gedächtnis* (Stuttgart: Deutsche Verlags-Anstalt, 1976)

Benz, *Vertreibung*: Wolfgang Benz, ed., *Die Vertreibung der Deutschen aus dem Osten. Ursachen, Ereignisse, Folgen* (Frankfurt: Fischer, 1985)

Bergedorfer Gesprächskreis: The privately circulated stenographic records of the series of high-level conferences organised by the Körber-Stiftung (Hamburg-Bergedorf), are cited here by the number and date of the conference. Thus *Bergerdorfer Gesprächskreis 97* (15–16 October 1992), is the record of the 97th conference, which took place on those days.

Bergsdorf, *Sprache*: Wolfgang Bergsdorf, *Herrschaft und Sprache. Studie zur politischen Terminologie der Bundesrepublik Deutschland* (Pfullingen: Neske, 1983)

Beschloss & Talbott, *Highest Levels*: Michael R Beschloss & Strobe Talbott, *At The Highest Levels. The Inside Story of the End of the Cold War* (New York: Little, Brown, 1993)

Besson, *Aussenpolitik*: Waldemar Besson, *Die Aussenpolitik der Bundesrepublik Deutschland. Erfahrungen und Massstäbe* (Munich: Piper, 1970)

Besuch: Der Besuch von Generalsekretär Honecker in der Bundesrepublik Deutschland. Dokumentation zum Arbeitsbesuch des Generalsekretärs der SED und Staatsratsvorsitzenden der DDR, Erich Honecker, in der Bundesrepublik Deutschland im September 1987 (Bonn: Bundesministerium für innerdeutsche Beziehungen, 1988)

Bingen, *Bonn-Warschau*: Dieter Bingen, *Bonn-Warschau 1949–1988. Von der kontroversen Grenzfrage zur gemeinsamen europäischen Perspektive?* (Köln: Berichte des Bundesinstituts für ostwissenschaftliche und internationale Studien, 13–1988)

Birrenbach, *Sondermissionen*: Kurt Birrenbach, *Meine Sondermissionen. Rückblick auf zwei Jahrzehnte bundesdeutscher Aussenpolitik* (Düsseldorf: Econ, 1984)

Bismarck, *Reden*: Lothar Gall, ed., *Bismarck. Die grossen Reden* (Berlin: Severin & Siedler, 1981)

Böll, *Verantwortlich*: Heinrich Böll, Freimut Duve, Klaus Stäck, eds., *Verantwortlich für Polen?* (Reinbek: Rowohlt, 1982)

Bölling, *Die fernen Nachbarn*: Klaus Bölling, *Die fernen Nachbarn. Erfahrungen in der DDR* (Hamburg: Stern-Buch, 1983)

Brandt, *Erinnerungen*: Willy Brandt, *Erinnerungen* (Frankfurt: Propyläen, 1989)

Brandt, *People and Politics*: Willy Brandt, *People and Politics. The Years 1960–1975* (Boston: Little, Brown, 1978). A slightly abridged and edited version of the German original, *Begegnungen und Einsichten. Die Jahre 1960–1975* (Hamburg: Hoffmann & Campe, 1976).

Brandt, *Zusammen*: Willy Brandt, *". . . was zusammengehört" Reden zu Deutschland* (Bonn: Dietz, 1990)

Broszat, *Polenpolitik*: Martin Broszat, *Zweihundert Jahre deutsche Polenpolitik* (Frankfurt: Suhrkamp, 1972)

Bruns, *DDR-Politik*: Wilhelm Bruns, *Von der Deutschlandpolitik zur DDR-Politik? Prämissen. Probleme. Perspektive* (Opladen: Leske & Budrich, 1989)

Bulletin: The *Bulletin* of the Federal Government's Press and Information Office (*Presse- und Informationsamt der Bundesregierung*), which reproduces a wide range of official speeches, lectures and statements, is here cited simply as *Bulletin*, with date and page reference.

Bundestag Drucksachen/Bundestag Plenarprotokolle: The reports of the West German parliamant (*Verhandlungen des Deutschen Bundestages*) are published in two series: the Plenary Protocols (*Plenarprotokolle*), which give a Hansard-like, stenographic record of the main parliamentary proceedings, and the Printed Matter (*Drucksachen*), which contains committee records, draft motions, reports and so forth. A reference to *Bundestag Plenarprotokolle* is a reference to the former, main series. These stenographic records are identified by electoral period (*Wahlperiode*), sitting (*Sitzung*), and date. We have slightly simplified the reference system, so that, for example, *Verhandlungen des Deutschen Bundestages. Plenarprotokolle.* — 6. Wahlperiode. — 59. Sitzung. Bonn, Mittwoch, den 17. Juni 1970, S.3269, becomes *Bundestag Plenarprotokolle*, 6/59, p.3269 (17 June 1970). *Drucksachen* are identified by electoral period and number: e.g. 10/914 means 10th electoral period/914th printed item.

Burleigh, *Ostforschung*: Michael Burleigh, *Germany Turns Eastwards. A Study of Ostforschung in the Third Reich* (Cambridge: Cambridge University Press, 1988)

Christians, *Wege*: F. Wilhelm Christians, *Wege nach Russland. Bankier im Spannungsfeld zwischen Ost und West* (Hamburg: Hoffmann & Campe, 1989)

Clemens, *Reluctant Realists*: Clay Clemens, *Reluctant Realists. The Christian Democrats and West German Ostpolitik* (Durham, NC: Duke University Press, 1989)

Cramer, *Bahr*: Dettmar Cramer, *Gefragt. Egon Bahr* (Bornheim: Dangmar Zirngibl-Verlag, 1975)

Davy, *Détente*: Richard Davy, ed., *European Détente. A Reappraisal* (London: Sage for the Royal Institute of International Affairs, 1992)

DDR-Reisebarometer: DDR-Reisebarometer '88 (Munich: Infratest Kommunikationsforschung, 1989)

DDR Handbuch: Hartmut Zimmermann, ed., *DDR Handbuch* (3rd revised edition, Köln: Verlag Wissenschaft und Politik, 1985)

Deutschland 1989: The extraordinary twenty-five volumes of photocopies of media coverage of the events in Germany in 1989, produced in 1992 by the indefatigable archivists of the *Zentrales Dokumentationssystem* of the *Presse- und Informationsamt der Bundesregierung*, are cited here by short title and volume number.

Dokumente: *Dokumente zur Deutschlandpolitik*. Volumes of this magisterial documentation, published under the auspices of the *Bundesministerium für innerdeutsche Beziehungen* are cited by Series and Volume number. Thus *Dokumente*, IV/7, is Series IV, Volume 7. Series IV covers the period from 10 November 1958 to 30 November 1966, Series V from 1 December 1966 onward.

Dralle, *Deutsche*: Lothar Dralle, *Die Deutschen in Ostmittel-und Osteuropa. Ein Jahrtausend europäischer Geschichte* (Darmstadt: Wissenschaftliche Buchgesellschaft, 1991)

Ehmke, *Zwanzig Jahre*: Horst Ehmke, Karlheinz Koppe, Herbert Wehner, eds., *Zwanzig Jahre Ostpolitik. Bilanz und Perspektiven* (Bonn: Verlag Neue Gesellschaft, 1986)

Freedman, *Europe Transformed*: Lawrence Freedman, ed., *Europe Transformed. Documents on the End of the Cold War* (New York: St Martin's Press, 1990)

Fricke, *Opposition*: Karl Wilhelm Fricke, *Opposition und Widerstand in der DDR. Ein politischer Report* (Köln: Verlag Wissenschaft und Politik, 1984)

Fritsch-Bournazel, *Europa*: Renata Fritsch-Bournazel, *Europa und die deutsche Einheit* (Stuttgart: Bonn Aktuell, 1990)

Funke, *Demokratie und Diktatur*: Manfred Funke *et al.*, eds, *Demokratie und Diktatur. Geist und Gestalt politischer Herrschaft in Deutschland und Europa* (Bonn: Bundeszentrale für politische Bildung, 1987 = *Schriftenreihe der Bundeszentrale für politische Bildung*, Vol. 250

Garthoff, *Détente*: Raymond L Garthoff, *Détente and Confrontation* (Washington DC: Brookings Institution, 1985)

Garton Ash, *DDR*: Timothy Garton Ash, *'Und willst Du nicht mein Bruder sein . . .' Die DDR heute* (Reinbek: Rowohlt, 1981)

Garton Ash, *Solidarity*: Timothy Garton Ash, *The Polish Revolution. Solidarity* (2nd, revised edition, London: Granta Books, 1991)

Garton Ash, *Uses*: Timothy Garton Ash, *The Uses of Adversity. Essays on the Fate of Central Europe* (2nd, revised edition, London: Granta Books, 1991)

Garton Ash, *We*: Timothy Garton Ash, *We the People. The Revolution of '89 Witnessed in Warsaw, Budapest, Berlin & Prague* (London: Granta Books, 1991)

Gaus, *Deutschland*: Günter Gaus, *Wo Deutschland liegt. Eine Ortsbestimmung* (Hamburg: Hoffmann & Campe, 1983)

Geissel, *Unterhändler*: Ludwig Geissel, *Unterhändler der Menschlichkeit. Erinnerungen. Mit einem Begleitwort von Manfred Stolpe* (Stuttgart: Quell, 1991)

Genscher, *Unterwegs*: Hans-Dietrich Genscher, *Unterwegs zur Einheit. Reden und Dokumente aus bewegter Zeit* (Berlin: Siedler, 1991)

Gipfelgespräche: Michail Gorbatschow, *Gipfelgespräche. Geheime Protokolle aus meiner Amtszeit* (Berlin: Rowohlt, 1993)

Gorbachev, *Haus Europa*: Michail Gorbatschow, *Das gemeinsame Haus Europa und die Zukunft der Deutschen. Mit Beiträgen sowjetischer Wissenschaftler und Politiker* (Revised edition, Düsseldorf: Econ, 1990)

Gordon, *Eroding Empire*: Lincoln Gordon, ed., *Eroding Empire* (Washington DC: Brookings, 1987)

Grenville, *Treaties*: JAS Grenville and Bernard Wasserstein, *The Major International Treaties Since 1945. A History and Guide with Texts* (London: Methuen, 1987)

Grewe, *Rückblenden*: Wilhelm G Grewe, *Rückblenden. 1976–1951* (Frankfurt: Propyläen, 1979)

Griffith, *Ostpolitik*: William E Griffith, *The Ostpolitik of the Federal Republic of Germany* (Cambridge, Mass.: MIT Press, 1978)

Gromyko, *Memories*: Andrei Gromyko, *Memories* (London: Hutchinson, 1989). Translated and edited by Harold Shukman

Grosser, *Unification*: Dieter Grosser, ed., *German Unification. The Unexpected Challenge* (Oxford: Berg, 1992 = German Historical Perspectives, Vol. VII)

Haberl & Hecker, *Unfertige Nachbarschaften*: Othmar Nikola Haberl & Hans Hecker, eds, *Unfertige Nachbarschaften. Die Staaten Osteuropas und die Bundesrepublik Deutschland* (Essen: Reimar Hobbing, 1989)

Hacke, *Wege und Irrwege*: Christian Hacke, *Die Ost- und Deutschlandpolitik der CDU/CSU. Wege und Irrwege der Opposition seit 1969* (Köln: Verlag Wissenschaft und Politik, 1975)

Haftendorn, *Aussenpolitik*: Helga Haftendorn, Lothar Wilker, Claudia Wörmann, *Die Aussenpolitik der Bundesrepublik Deutschland* (Berlin: Wissenschaftlicher Autoren-Verlag, 1982)

Haftendorn, *Sicherheit*: Helga Haftendorn, *Sicherheit und Stabilität. Aussenbeziehungen der Bundesrepublik zwischen Ölkrise und Nato-Doppelbeschluss* (Munich: Deutscher Taschenbuch Verlag, 1986)

Haftendorn, *Verwaltete Aussenpolitik*: Helga Haftendorn & ors, eds, *Verwaltete Aussenpolitik. Sicherheits- und Entspannungspolitische Entscheidungsprozesse in Bonn* (Köln: Verlag Wissenschaft und Politik, 1978)

Hanrieder, *Germany, America, Europe*: Wolfram F Hanrieder, *Germany, America, Europe. Forty Years of German Foreign Policy* (New Haven: Yale University Press, 1989)

Hanson, *Western Economic Statecraft*: Philip Hanson, *Western Economic Statecraft in East-West Relations* (London: Routledge & Kegan Paul, 1988)

Heep, *Schmidt und Amerika*: Barbara D Heep, *Helmut Schmidt und Amerika. Eine schwierige Partnerschaft* (Bonn: Bouvier, 1990)

Hildebrand, *Von Erhard zur Grossen Koalition*: Klaus Hildebrand, *Von Erhard zur Grossen Koalition 1963–1969* (Stuttgart: Deutsche Verlags-Anstalt, 1984 = *Geschichte der Bundesrepublik Deutschland*, Vol 4)

Holzer, *Solidarität*: Jerzy Holzer, *"Solidarität" Die Geschichte einer freien Gewerkschaft in Polen* (Munich: Beck, 1985). Edited by Hans Henning Hahn.

Horn, *Erinnerungen*: Gyula Horn, *Freiheit, die ich meine. Erinnerungen des ungarischen Aussenministers, der den eisernen Vorhang öffnete* (Hamburg: Hoffmann & Campe, 1991)

Innerdeutsche Beziehungen: *Innerdeutsche Beziehungen. Die Entwicklung der Beziehungen zwischen der Bundesrepublik Deutschland und der Deutschen Demokratischen Republik 1980–1986. Eine Dokumentation* (Bonn: Bundesministerium für innerdeutsche Beziehungen, 1986)

Jacobsen, *Bonn-Warschau*: Hans-Adolf Jacobsen & Mieczysław Tomala, eds, *Bonn-Warschau, 1945–1991. Die deutsch-polnischen Beziehungen* (Köln: Verlag Wissenschaft und Politik, 1992)

Jacobsen, *Bundesrepublik-Volksrepublik*: Hans-Adolf Jacobsen, *Bundesrepublik Deutschland. Volksrepublik Polen. Bilanz der Beziehungen. Probleme und Perspektiven ihrer Normalisierung* (Frankfurt: Alfred Metzner, 1979)

Jacobsen, *Nachbarn*: Hans-Adolf Jacobsen, ed., *Misstrauische Nachbarn. Deutsche Ostpolitik 1919/1970. Dokumentation und Analyse* (Düsseldorf: Droste, 1970)

Jentleson, *Pipeline Politics*: Bruce W. Jentleson, *Pipeline Politics. The Complex Political Economy of East-West Trade* (Ithaca, NY: Cornell University Press, 1986)

Jesse & Mitter, *Einheit*: Eckhard Jesse & Armin Mitter, *Die Gestaltung der deutschen Einheit. Geschichte — Politik — Gesellschaft* (Bonn: Bundeszentrale für politische Bildung, 1992)

Kaiser, *Vereinigung*: Karl Kaiser, *Deutschlands Vereinigung. Die internationalen Aspekte. Mit den wichtigen Dokumenten* (Bergisch-Gladbach: Bastei-Lübbe, 1991)

Kissinger, *White House Years*: Henry Kissinger, *The White House Years* (London: Weidenfeld & Nicolson, 1979)

Kissinger, *Years of Upheaval*: Henry Kissinger, *Years of Upheaval* (London: Weidenfeld & Nicolson, 1982)

Koch, *Brandt*: Peter Koch, *Willy Brandt. Eine politische Biographie* (Bergisch Gladbach: Bastei Lübbe, 1989)

Kovrig, *Walls and Bridges*: Bennett Kovrig, *Of Walls and Bridges. The United States and Eastern Europe* (New York: New York University Press, 1991)

Kreile, *Osthandel*: Michael Kreile, *Osthandel und Ostpolitik* (Baden-Baden: Nomos, 1978)

KSZE Dokumentation: *Sicherheit und Zusammenarbeit in Europa. Dokumente zum KSZE-Prozess, einschliesslich der KVAE* (7th revised edition, Bonn: Auswärtiges Amt, 1990)

KSZE Dokumentation 1990/91: *Sicherheit und Zusammenarbeit in Europa. Dokumentation zum KSZE-Prozess 1990/91* (Bonn: Auswärtiges Amt, 1991)

Kuwaczka, *Entspannung von Unten*: Waldemar Kuwaczka, *Entspannung von Unten. Möglichkeiten und Grenzen des Deutsch-Polnischen Dialogs* (Stuttgart: Burg Verlag, 1988)

Lehmann, *Oder-Neisse*: Hans Georg Lehmann, *Der Oder-Neisse-Konflikt* (Munich: Beck, 1979)

Lehmann, *Öffnung*: Hans Georg Lehmann, *Öffnung nach Osten. Die Ostreisen Helmut Schmidts und die Entstehung der Ost- und Entspannungspolitik* (Bonn: Neue Gesellschaft, 1984)

Liesner, *Aussiedler*: Ernst Liesner, *Aussiedler. Die Voraussetzungen für die Anerkennung als Vertriebener. Arbeitshandbuch für Behörden, Gerichte und Verbände* (Herford: Maximilian-Verlag, 1988)

Link, *Ära Brandt*: Karl Dietrich Bracher, Wolfgang Jäger, Werner Link, *Republik im Wandel 1969–1974. Die Ära Brandt* (Stuttgart: Deutsche Verlags-Anstalt, 1986 = *Geschichte der Bundesrepublik Deutschland*, Vol. 5/I). Chapters on foreign policy by Werner Link.

Link, *Ära Schmidt*: Wolfgang Jäger, Werner Link, *Republik im Wandel 1974–1982. Die Ära Schmidt* (Stuttgart: Deutsche Verlags-Anstalt, 1987 = *Geschichte der Bundesrepublik Deutschland*, Vol. 5/II). Chapters on foreign policy by Werner Link.

Löwenthal, *Vom kalten Krieg*: Richard Löwenthal, *Vom kalten Krieg zur Ostpolitik* (Stuttgart: Seewald, 1974). Originally published as a chapter in Richard Löwenthal and Hans-Peter Schwarz, eds, *Die zweite Republik* (Stuttgart: Seewald, 1974)

Lutz, *Bahr*: Dieter S. Lutz, ed., *Das Undenkbare denken. Festschrift für Egon Bahr zum siebzigsten Geburtstag* (Baden-Baden: Nomos, 1992)

Maresca, *Helsinki*: John J. Maresca, *To Helsinki. The Conference on Security and Cooperation in Europe, 1973–1975* (New edition, Durham: Duke University Press, 1987)

Mastny, *Helsinki I*: Vojtech Mastny, *Helsinki, Human Rights and European Security. Analysis and Documentation* (Durham NC: Duke University Press, 1986)

Mastny, *Helsinki II*: Vojtech Mastny, *The Helsinki Process and the Reintegration of Europe, 1986–1991. Analysis and Documentation* (London: Pinter, 1992)

Mastny & Zielonka: Vojtech Mastny & Jan Zielonka, eds, *Human Rights and Security. Europe on the Eve of a New Era* (Boulder: Westview Press, 1991)

Materialien: *Materialien zum Bericht zur Lage der Nation im geteilten Deutschland 1987* (Bonn: Bundesministerium für innerdeutsche Beziehungen, 1987)

Meissner, *Deutsche Ostpolitik*: Boris Meissner, ed., *Die deutsche Ostpolitik 1961–1970. Kontinuität und Wandel. Eine Dokumentation* (Köln: Verlag Wissenschaft und Politik, 1970)

Meissner, *Moskau-Bonn*: Boris Meissner, ed., *Moskau-Bonn. Die Beziehungen zwischen der Sowjetunion und der Bundesrepublik Deutschland 1955–1973. Dokumentation* (Köln: Verlag Wissenschaft und Politik, 1975 = *Dokumente zur Aussenpolitik*, Vol. III/1 & 2)

Meuschel, *Legitimation*: Sigrid Meuschel, *Legitimation und Parteiherrschaft. Zum Paradox von Stabilität und Revolution in der DDR, 1945–1989* (Frankfurt: Suhrkamp, 1992)

Mittag, *Preis*: Günter Mittag, *Um jeden Preis. Im Spannungsfeld zweier Systeme* (Berlin: Aufbau, 1991)

Mitter & Wolle, *Lageberichte*: Armin Mitter & Stefan Wolle, eds, *'Ich liebe Euch doch alle!' Befehle und Lageberichte des MfS. January–November 1989* (Berlin: BasisDruck Verlagsgesellschaft, 1990)

Moreton, *Germany*: Edwina Moreton, ed., *Germany between East and West* (Cambridge: Cambridge University Press, 1987)

Morsey & Repgen, *Adenauer Studien III*: Rudolf Morsey & Konrad Repgen, eds, *Adenauer Studien. Bd. III. Untersuchungen und Dokumente zur Ostpolitik und Biographie* (Mainz: Matthias-Grünewald-Verlag, 1974)

Moseleit, *Zweite Phase*: Klaus Moseleit, *Die "Zweite" Phase der Entspannungspolitik der SPD, 1983–1989. Eine Analyse ihrer Entstehungsgeschichte, Entwicklung und der konzeptionellen Ansätze. Mit einem Vorwort von Willy Brandt* (Frankfurt: Peter Lang, 1991 = European University Studies, Series XXXI, Vol. 180)

Oberdorfer, *Turn*: Don Oberdorfer, *The Turn. How the Cold War came to an end. The United States and the Soviet Union, 1983–1990* (London: Jonathan Cape, 1992)

Pravda, *End*: Alex Pravda, ed., *The End of the Outer Empire. Soviet-East European Relations in Transition, 1985–90* (London: Sage for the Royal Institute of International Affairs, 1992)

Przybylski, *Tatort 1*: Peter Przybylski, *Tatort Politbüro. Die Akte Honecker* (Berlin: Rowohlt, 1991)

Przybylski, *Tatort 2*: Peter Przybylski, *Tatort Politbüro. Band 2. Honecker, Mittag und Schalck-Golodkowski* (Berlin: Rowohlt, 1992)

Rehlinger, *Freikauf*: Ludwig A Rehlinger, *Freikauf. Die Geschäfte der DDR mit politisch Verfolgten 1963–1989* (Berlin: Ullstein, 1991)

Reissmüller, *Vergessene Hälfte*: Johann-Georg Reissmüller, *Die vergessene Hälfte. Osteuropa und wir* (Munich: Langen Müller, 1986)

Schevardnadse, *Zukunft*: Eduard Schevardnadse, *Die Zukunft gehört der Freiheit* (Berlin: Rowohlt, 1991)

Schmid, *Entscheidung*: Günther Schmid, *Entscheidung in Bonn. Die Entstehung der Ost- und Deutschlandpolitik 1969/70* (Köln: Verlag Wissenschaft und Politik, 1979)

Schmid, *Politik*: Günther Schmid, *Politik des Ausverkaufs? Die Deutschlandpolitik der Regierung Brandt/Scheel (*Munich: tuduv, *1975)*

Schmidt, *Menschen und Mächte*: Helmut Schmidt, *Menschen und Mächte* (Berlin: Siedler, 1987)

Schmidt, *Nachbarn*: Helmut Schmidt, *Die Deutschen und ihre Nachbarn. Menschen und Mächte II* (Berlin: Siedler, 1990)

Schröder, *Bahr*: Karsten Schröder, *Egon Bahr* (Rastatt: Verlag Arthur Moewig, 1988)

Schulz-Vobach, *Die Deutschen im Osten*: Klaus-Dieter Schulz-Vobach, *Die Deutschen im Osten. Vom Balkan bis Sibirien* (Hamburg: Hoffmann & Campe, 1989)

Schwarz, *Adenauer I*: Hans-Peter Schwarz, *Adenauer. Der Aufstieg: 1876–1952* (Stuttgart: Deutsche Verlags-Anstalt, 1986)

Schwarz, *Adenauer II*: Hans-Peter Schwarz, *Adenauer. Der Staatsmann: 1952–1967* (Stuttgart: Deutsche Verlags-Anstalt, 1991)

Schwarz, *Gezähmten Deutschen*: Hans-Peter Schwarz, *Die gezähmten Deutschen. Von der Machtbesessenheit zur Machtvergessenheit* (Stuttgart: Deutsche Verlags-Anstalt, 1985)

Schweigler, *Grundlagen*: Gebhard Schweigler, *Grundlagen der aussenpolitischen Orientierung der Bundesrepublik Deutschland. Rahmenbedingungen, Motive, Einstellungen* (Baden-Baden: Nomos, 1985)

Siebenmorgen, *Gezeitenwechsel*: Peter Siebenmorgen, *Gezeitenwechsel. Aufbruch zur Entspannungspolitik* (Bonn: Bouvier, 1990)

Spangenberg, *Mitteleuropa*: Dietrich Spangenberg, ed., *Die blockierte Vergangenheit. Nachdenken über Mitteleuropa* (Berlin: Argon, 1987)

Stares, *New Germany*: Paul B Stares, ed., *The New Germany and the New Europe* (Washington DC: Brookings, 1992)

Stent, *Embargo to Ostpolitik*: Angela Stent, *From Embargo to Ostpolitik. The Political Economy of West German-Soviet Relations 1955–1980* (Cambridge: Cambridge University Press, 1981)

Stern, *Brandt*: Carola Stern, *Willy Brandt* (Hamburg: Rowohlt, 1988)

Stökl, *Osteuropa*: Günther Stökl, *Osteuropa und die Deutschen* (3rd revised edition, Stuttgart: S. Hirzel Verlag, 1982)

Strauss, *Erinnerungen*: Franz Josef Strauss, *Die Erinnerungen* (Berlin: Siedler, 1989)

Szabo, *Diplomacy*: Stephen F Szabo, *The Diplomacy of German Unification* (New York: St Martin's Press, 1992)

Teltschik, *329 Tage*: Horst Teltschik, *329 Tage. Innenansichten der Einigung* (Berlin: Siedler, 1991)

Texte: *Texte zur Deutschlandpolitik.* Published, like the *Dokumente zur Deutschlandpolitik*, under the auspices of the *Bundesministerium für innerdeutsche Beziehungen*, the *Texte* are also cited by series and volume number. Series I covers the period 13 December 1966–20 June 1973; Series II, 22 June 1973–1 October 1982; Series III, 13 October 1982–31 December 1990.

Umbruch: *Umbruch in Europa. Die Ereignisse im 2. Halbjahr 1989. Eine Dokumentation* (Bonn: Auswärtiges Amt, 1990)

Uschner, *Ostpolitik*: Manfred Uschner, *Die Ostpolitik der SPD. Sieg und Niederlage einer Strategie* (Berlin: Dietz, 1991)

Van Oudenaren, *Détente*: John Van Oudenaren, *Détente in Europe. The Soviet Union and the West since 1953* (Durham NC: Duke University Press, 1991)

Verträge: *Dokumentation zur Ostpolitik der Bundesregierung. Verträge und Vereinbarungen* (11th edition, Bonn: Presse- und Informationsamt der Bundesregierung, 1986)

Vierzig Jahre: Auswärtiges Amt, *40 Jahre Aussenpolitik der Bundesrepublik Deutschland. Eine Dokumentation* (Stuttgart: Bonn Aktuell, 1989)

Volle & Wagner, *KSZE*: Hermann Volle & Wolfgang Wagner, eds, *KSZE. Konferenz über Sicherheit und Zusammenarbeit in Europa in Beiträgen und Dokumenten aus dem Europa-Archiv* (Bonn: Verlag für Internationale Politik, 1976)

Weber, *DDR* (1988): Hermann Weber, *Die DDR 1945–1986* (Munich: Oldenbourg, 1988 = *Oldenbourg-Grundriss der Geschichte* Vol. 20)

Weber, *DDR* (1991): Hermann Weber, *DDR. Grundriss der Geschichte. 1945–1990* (new edition, Hannover: Fackelträger, 1976)

Weber, *Links*: Hermann Weber, *Das Prinzip Links. Beiträge zur Diskussion des demokratischen Sozialismus in Deutschland, 1848–1990. Eine Dokumentation* (Berlin: Ch. Links, 1991)

Weizsäcker, *Deutsche Geschichte*: Richard von Weizsäcker, *Die deutsche Geschichte geht weiter* (Berlin: Siedler, 1983)

Wiskemann, *Eastern Neighbours*: Elizabeth Wiskemann, *Germany's Eastern Neighbours. Problems Relating to the Oder-Neisse Line and the Czech Frontier Regions* (London: Oxford University Press for the Royal Institute of International Affairs, 1956)

Witte, *Kulturpolitik*: Barthold C Witte, *Dialog über Grenzen. Beiträge zur auswärtigen Kulturpolitik* (Pfullingen: Neske, 1988)

Wörmann, *Osthandel*: Claudia Wörmann, *Der Osthandel der Bundesrepublik*

Deutschland. Politische Rahmenbedingungen und ökonomische Bedeutung (Frankfurt: Campus, 1982)

Wörmann, *Problem*: Claudia Wörmann, *Osthandel als Problem der Atlantischen Allianz. Erfahrungen aus dem Erdgas-Röhren-Geschäft mit der UdSSR* (Bonn: Forschungsinstitut der Deutschen Gesellschaft für Auswärtige Politik, 1986 = *Arbeitspapiere zur internationalen Politik*, 38)

Zahlenspiegel: Zahlenspiegel. Bundesrepublik Deutschland/Deutsche Demokratische Republik: Ein Vergleich (3rd revised edition, Bonn: Bundesministerium für innerdeutsche Beziehungen, 1988)

Zehn Jahre: Zehn Jahre Deutschlandpolitik. Die Entwicklungen der Beziehungen zwischen der Bundesrepublik Deutschland und der Deutschen Demokratischen Republik 1969–1979. Bericht und Dokumentation (Bonn: Bundesministerium für innerdeutsche Beziehungen, 1980)

Zernack, *Osteuropa*: Klaus Zernack, *Osteuropa. Eine Einführung in seine Geschichte* (Munich: Beck, 1977)

Zündorf, *Ostverträge*: Benno Zündorf, *Die Ostverträge. Die Verträge von Moskau, Warschau, Prag, das Berlin-Abkommen und die Verträge mit der DDR* (Munich: Beck, 1979). Benno Zündorf is a pseudonym for Antonius Eitel.

Notes

Prologue: European Question

... **West Central Europe** ... The distinction between East Central and West Central Europe was made by, among others, Oskar Halecki in Chapter VII of his *The Limits and Divisions of European History* (London: Sheed & Ward, 1950). East Central Europe was, he argued, 'inhabited by a great variety of ethnic and linguistic groups in contradistinction to the homogeneously German West-Central Europe', ibid., p. 127. But see also critical remarks by Philip Longworth in *The Slavonic and East European Review*, Vol. 65, No. 3, July 1987, pp. 422–29, the excellent discussion in Zernack, *Osteuropa*, Werner Conze, *Ostmitteleuropa. Von der Spätantike bis zum 18. Jahrhundert* (Munich: Beck, 1992), edited by Klaus Zernack and Winfried Eberhard & ors, eds, *Westmitteleuropa-Ostmitteleuropa. Festschrift für Ferdinand Seibt* (Munich: Oldenbourg, 1992).

In the context of 'Yalta' Europe, we have used the term West Central Europe to refer mainly to West Germany and Austria; East Central Europe refers mainly to Poland, Hungary and Czechoslovakia. East Germany was obviously a special case.

The terms Eastern and Western Europe, East European and West European, are used in the sense of the 'Yalta' political shorthand, as discussed in this Prologue. The Epilogue considers the cacophony of usages after 1989.

... **arguing that it had brought peace and stability** ... An attitude that provoked the following observation from the distinguished British historian of Central and Eastern Europe, Hugh Seton-Watson, in one of the last texts he wrote. Having asserted that the peoples of 'the eastern half of Europe' would not reconcile themselves to the division of Europe, he continued: 'My last sentence probably suffices to damn me in many minds as a "cold warrior". But all that I have done is to state in simple words the basic fact of which forty years of study have convinced me. Yet such has been the impact of propaganda, counter-propaganda, and disinformation that in the minds of hundreds of thousands of enlightened Western men and women, firmly devoted to freedom in their own countries, the present division of Europe has acquired a sanctity which they will fanatically justify; and to say that this division is permanently unacceptable for more than a hundred million Europeans, and will not last, is seen by them as tantamount to preaching nuclear war.' The eleventh Martin Wight lecture, Royal Institute of International Affairs, reprinted as 'What is Europe, Where is Europe?'

in *Encounter*, July/August 1985, this quotation on p. 14, and in George Schöplin & Nancy Wood, eds, *In Search of Central Europe* (Oxford: Polity Press, 1989), pp. 30–46, quotation on p. 41.

'The peace of Europe ...' This was Günter Gaus, a leading political commentator close to the Social Democrats, and appointed by the Brandt government to be West Germany's first Permanent Representative in the GDR. See Gaus, *Deutschland* p. 283. At a seminar at the Free University in Berlin on 4 February 1987, Gaus said simply: 'the Yalta system is the guarantee of peace in Europe' (author's notes).

More diplomatic versions ... a lucid analytical presentation of the argument was A Wde Porte's *Europe between the Superpowers. The Enduring Balance* (2nd edition, New Haven: Yale University Press, 1986). The first edition was completed in 1978. The jacket of the second edition observes that the author contributed a new Preface 'noting how recent developments have confirmed the book's thesis that the Atlantic alliance system and the division of Europe between East and West are likely to survive indefinitely'.

'under which we've lived quite happily ...' The *Independent*, 22 December 1989 (interview with the author).

'We deplore the division ...' quoted in *The Times*, 4 May 1985, p. 5.

... a 'Prague Appeal' ... Charter 77 document 5/1985, reprinted in the journal *East European Reporter* (London), Vol. 1, No. 1, Spring 1985, pp. 27–28.

'the goal of Europeans ...' quoted in *KOS* (Warsaw), No. 14 (144), 18 September 1988.

Even before he became Party leader ... Gorbachev seems first to have used the image in his remarks to a group of parliamentarians during his visit to Britain in December 1984, three months before he became Party leader. See the text in *Pravda*, 19 December 1984, English in *Current Digest of the Soviet Press*, Vol. XXXVI, No. 51, esp. p. 4. I owe this reference to a typescript by Ernst Kux on Gorbachev and the Common European Home.

... used by Brezhnev ... 'Whatever divides us, Europe remains our common home,' *Bulletin*, 26 November 1981, p. 966. Writing in *Osteuropa*, 8/1991, p. 352, Fred Oldenburg attributes the coinage to Andrei Alexandrov-Agentov, a leading foreign policy aide to Brezhnev and to Gorbachev in his first years in office.
  'This metaphor,' Gorbachev writes in his book *Perestroika*, 'came to my mind in one of my discussions. Although seemingly I voiced it in passing, in my mind I had been looking for such a formula for a long time.' *Perestroika. New Thinking for Our Country and the World* (London: Collins, 1987) p. 194. Clearly great minds think alike.

This Declaration stated ... see *Bulletin*, 15 June 1989, p. 542.

... the Russian text ... see *Pravda*, 14 June 1989.

Soviet commentators ... see for example the interesting commentary by V. Zhurkin in *Pravda*, 17 May 1989, which offered the following definition of the common European home: 'It is a new system of security and co-operation growing out of the all-European process and extending it, a system based on gradually eliminating the military-political and economic division of Europe and replacing it with effective and mutually beneficial forms of co-existence among states with different social systems . . .' Quoted from *Current Digest of the Soviet Press*, vol. XLI, No. 22, 1989, p. 15. Zhurkin was the head of a newly formed Institute of Europe, which itself symbolised this new approach. Vitaly Zhurkin, Moscow, 7 February 1992.

. . . **'a relic of the Cold War'** . . . this comment came from Vyacheslav Dashitchev, a maverick but, as it proved, vanguard Soviet specialist on Germany, as early as June 1988. See the report in *FAZ*, 8 June 1988, p. 1, and summary of the ensuing controversy in the *Monatsbericht* of the Bundesanstalt für gesamtdeutsche Fragen for June 1988.

. . . **different 'social systems'** . . . even Dashitchev could aver in an interview in *Der Spiegel*, 27/1988, that socialism had established deep roots in Eastern Europe. See also the commentary by Zhurkin quoted above.

. . . **'I know that many in the West . . .'** Russian text in *Pravda*, 7 July 1989, pp. 1–2. English in *Current Digest of the Soviet Press*, Vol. XLI, No. 27, 1989, p. 6.

. . . **'Let Europe be whole and free.'** . . . this and following quotations are from the text reprinted in Freedman, *Europe Transformed*, pp. 289–94.

. . . **he went on to underline this message** . . . see the authoritative account by the former Deputy Assistant Secretary of State responsible for relations with the Soviet Union and Eastern Europe, Thomas W Simons, *The End of the Cold War?* (New York: St Martin's Press, 1990), p. 155 f. Simons suggests that there was basic agreement between the two Presidents on the need to end the division of Europe. See also Oberdorfer, *Turn*.

In events which, taken together . . . see the account in Garton Ash, *We*, p. 20 and *passim*, and Ralf Dahrendorf, *Reflections on the Revolution in Europe* (London: Chatto & Windus, 1990), esp. p. 5 ff. François Furet, the distinguished historian of the French Revolution, has argued that the events of 1989 cannot be described as a 'revolution' in the same sense as the French Revolution of 1789 or the Russian Revolution of 1917, both because of the decisive importance of the external factor — Gorbachev and Soviet policy — and because no new ideas were brought to power by these revolutions. In this sense, intellectually, they could even be described as 'counter-revolution', since they aimed to sweep away all traces of the heritage of the Russian October revolution, and restore or imitate the existing liberal capitalist order. See his article in *Politische Studien*, No. 318/1991. Yet this was an extraordinarily swift and sweeping removal of an *ancien régime* in six countries, which changed the political map of Europe out of recognition, and paved the way for the end of Communism in the Soviet Union itself.

. . . **faster and farther** . . . It is extremely difficult to say what exactly Gorbachev and his closest associates hoped for or expected, particularly since they may not themselves have had a very clear idea at the time, and certainly see things slightly differently with hindsight. For more discussion on this very important point see p. 123 f.

... refused all siren calls ... see Schewardnadse, *Zukunft*, pp. 215–17. In English, Eduard Shevardnadze, *The Future belongs to Freedom.* (London: Sinclair-Stevenson, 1991)

'We now have the Frank Sinatra Doctrine ...' quoted by Michael Simmons in the *Guardian*, 26 October 1989, p. 8.

'No more let us falter!' ... see *Foreign Relations of the United States. The Conferences at Malta and Yalta* (Westport: Greenwood Press, 1976, reprint of 1st edition of 1955), p. 26.

'The post-war split ...' quoted from BBC, Summary of World Broadcasts, SU/0652, B/I, 3 January 1990.

... 'the iron curtain' ... Churchill's classic description of the 'iron curtain' in his 1946 Fulton speech had it running 'from Stettin in the Baltic to Trieste in the Adriatic ...', quoted in Martin Gilbert, *Never Despair* (London: Heinemann, 1988), p. 200. In practice, after the creation of East Germany, the Soviet split with Yugoslavia, and the Austrian State Treaty, the line ran from Pötenitz on the Baltic to Rezovo on the Black Sea.

... the European question ... two earlier usages of the term may be of interest here. AJP Taylor concluded the Introduction to his *The Struggle for Mastery in Europe. 1848–1914* (Oxford: Clarendon Press, 1954) with the observation (p. xxxvi) that following the First World War the traditional Balance of Power was not restored and 'Henceforward, what had been the centre of the world became merely "the European question".' In his *Pan-Europa*, Richard Coudenhove-Kalergi wrote: 'The European question is: "Can Europe, in its political and economic fragmentation, preserve its peace and autonomy against the growing extra-European world powers — or is it compelled to organise itself into a state-federation (*Staatenbund*) to save its existence?"', Richard N. Coudenhove-Kalergi, *Pan-Europa* (Vienna: Pan-Europa-Verlag, 1923), p. IX.

Mitterrand ... 'sortir de Yalta' ... see *Le Monde*, 2 January 1982. See also his elegantly non-committal comments in François Mitterrand, *Réflexions sur la Politique Extérieure de la France* (Paris: Fayard, 1986), pp. 68–70.

When Zbigniew Brzezinski ... Zbigniew Brzezinski, 'The Future of Yalta', *Foreign Affairs*, Vol. 63, No. 2, Winter 1984/85, pp. 279–302.

... usually in the forms 'post-Yalta' or 'anti-Yalta' ... See, for example, the first chapter of György Konrád's *Antipolitics* (London: Quartet, 1984), entitled 'Peace: Anti-Yalta'; Ferenc Fehér, 'Eastern Europe's Long Revolution Against Yalta', *East European Politics and Societies* (EEPS), Vol. 2, No. 1, Winter 1988, pp. 1–34; Barbara Toruńczyk, 'Kings and Spirits in the East European Tales' in *Cross Currents*, No. 7, esp. pp. 185, 187, 205; and the East European contributions in Initiative Ost-West-Dialog, ed., *Frieden im geteilten Europa 40 Jahre nach Jalta* (Dokumentation eines Diskussions-Forums in Berlin, Februar 1985). Many more examples can be found in Polish, Hungarian and Czech independent publications.

... **earlier political-military decisions** ... on this, see the author's review articles in the *New York Review of Books*, 7 May and 11 June 1987. A good starting point for this whole subject is now Robin Edmonds, *The Big Three. Churchill, Roosevelt and Stalin in Peace and War* (London: Hamish Hamilton, 1991). On the importance of Tehran see Keith Sainsbury, *The Turning Point* (Oxford: Oxford University Press, 1986).

... **Hajo Holborn** ... Hajo Holborn, *The Political Collapse of Europe* (New York: Knopf, 1951).

... **assertions about Western failures over Yalta** ... see the discussion in Theodore Draper, 'Neoconservative History', *New York Review of Books*, 16 January 1986, and the ensuing controversy.

... **Rolf Steininger's influential book** ... Rolf Steininger, *Eine vertane Chance. Die Stalin-Note vom 10. Marz und die Wiedervereinigung* (Bonn: Dietz, 1985), which is actually a paperback edition of the introduction to a larger documentation. This smaller volume went through three editions in five years. An English translation, with a selection of the most important documents, has been published as *The German Question. The Stalin Note of 1952 and the Problem of Reunification* (New York: Columbia University Press, 1990). For further reading on this controversy see Notes to p. 48.

... **'a Germany ... such as Stalin offered in 1952'** ... ibid., p. 128.

John Lewis Gaddis observed ... John Lewis Gaddis, *Strategies of Containment. A Critical Appraisal of Postwar American National Security Policy* (Oxford: Oxford University Press, 1982), p. 354.

... **Bernhard Friedmann** ... Friedmann's proposal was originally proffered as the basis for a discussion in the CDU/CSU parliamentary party about Deutschlandpolitik and security policy, see his *Thesenpapier. Die Wiedervereinigung der Deutschen als Sicherheitskonzept* (Typescript, dated 16 May 1987) and the attached covering letter to the parliamentary leader of the CDU/CSU, Alfred Dregger, of the same date, where he suggests that the paper was written at Dregger's request. Friedmann subsequently developed his ideas into a book, pregnantly entitled 'Unity instead of Missiles': *Einheit statt Raketen* (Herford: BusseSeewald, 1987), which also reprints the original memorandum on pp. 145–52. In his Introduction he makes it clear that the catalyst for his proposal was the Reagan-Gorbachev summit meeting in Reykjavik in October 1986, with its dramatic suggestion of total nuclear disarmament. What he makes less clear is the significance of the proposal in the internal debate about Deutschlandpolitik and security policy inside the CDU and CSU, with himself belonging to a conservative nationalist minority tendency led by the original addressee, Alfred Dregger, and irreverently described — by its opponents — as the 'Stahlhelm fraction'.

... **Wilhelm Grewe** ... reader's letter entitled 'Alte Hüte in wölkiger Drapierung', *FAZ*, 5 June 1987.

... **the way in which the division was completed, sealed and acknowledged** ... a useful, if not wholly persuasive account is given by Wilfried Loth, *The Division of the World* (London: Routledge, 1988).

'The United States and its allies . . .' quoted in a report by John M. Goshko in the *International Herald Tribune*, 9 September 1985. In a speech about US policy to Central and Eastern Europe delivered to the Austrian Association for Foreign Policy and International Relations in Vienna on 21 September 1983 the then Vice-President George Bush went so far as to call it 'this fictitious division'.

. . . the Treaty of Trianon . . . It will be recalled that the 1920 Treaty of Trianon, part of the post-war peace settlement whose main architects were Woodrow Wilson, Clemenceau and Lloyd George, stripped Hungary of more than two-thirds of its pre-1914 territory, including the Slovakia in what then became Czechoslovakia; Transylvania, which went to Romania; and Croatia, to what then became Yugoslavia.

. . . many attempts have been made . . . on this see Zernack, *Osteuropa*.

. . . those of Charlemagne's empire . . . see the map in William Wallace, *The Transformation of Western Europe* (London: Royal Institute of International Affairs, 1990), p. 16.

. . . economic historians have argued . . . see, for example, the important essay by Jenő Szűcs, 'Three Historical Regions of Europe', reprinted in John Keane, ed., *Civil Society and the State. New European Perspectives* (London: Verso, 1988), pp. 291–332. But see also Péter Hanák, 'Central Europe: A Historical Region in Modern Times' in George Schöpflin and Nancy Wood, eds, *In Search of Central Europe* (Oxford: Polity Press, 1989), pp. 57–70, and the detailed discussion in Daniel Chirot, ed., *The Origins of Backwardness in Eastern Europe. Economics and Politics from the Middle Ages until the early Twentieth Century* (Berkeley: University of California Press, 1989). Piotr Wandycz, *The Price of Freedom. A History of East Central Europe from the Middle Ages to the Present* (London: Routledge, 1992), argues persuasively that it makes most sense to think in terms of 'centre' and 'periphery' rather than developed West and backward East.

. . . running far to the east of the Yalta line . . . see the map in William Wallace, *The Transformation of Western Europe* (London: Royal Institute of International Affairs, 1990), p. 18.

. . . lines . . . finally agreed . . . See Tony Sharp, *The Wartime Alliance and the Zonal Division of Germany* (Oxford: Clarendon Press, 1975), p. 203. For a description of the lines dividing Berlin and Germany, as they appeared in the 1980s, see Garton Ash, *DDR*, Chapter 2; Anthony Bailey, *Along the Edge of the Forest. An Iron Curtain Journey* (New York: Random House, 1983); *Die innerdeutsche Grenze* (Bonn: Bundesministerium für innerdeutsche Beziehungen, 1987).

According to Western specialists . . . quoted in Adam Bromke, *Eastern Europe in the Aftermath of Solidarity* (New York: Columbia University Press, 1985), p. 22.

When Czech, Hungarian and Polish intellectuals . . . see Garton Ash, *Uses*, especially the essay entitled 'Does Central Europe Exist?'; George Schöpflin & Nancy Wood, eds, *In Search of Central Europe* (Oxford: Polity Press, 1989); and the special issue of *Daedalus*, Winter 1990, entitled 'Eastern Europe . . . Central

Europe... Europe', republished as Stephen Graubard, ed., *Eastern Europe...
Central Europe ... Europe* (Boulder: Westview Press, 1991).

... the Trabant and *soljanka*... for future generations one should perhaps
record that the Trabant was a tiny motor-car produced in the GDR, with a
noxious two-stroke engine, while *soljanka* was an East German version of a
Ukrainian peasant soup.

... a matter of the hottest dispute... The development of the dispute was
also the development of a dialogue between parts of the West European peace
movement and parts of the democratic opposition in Eastern Europe. This could
be followed in the journals, occasional papers and pamphlets of such groups as
European Nuclear Disarmament (END), the Dutch Inter-Church Peace Council
(IKV), and the West Berlin-based Network for East-West Dialogue. The East
European side of the debate is well-documented in such journals as *L'Alternative*
(Paris, 1979–85) — subsequently relaunched as *La Nouvelle Alternative* — and the
East European Reporter (London, 1985–   ).

... more need for change in Eastern than in Western Europe... A fairly
characteristic and grudging admission of this asymmetry, from one of the most
eloquent exponents of the 'symmetry' thesis, came in EP Thompson's 1984 essay
on 'The Two Sides of Yalta'. 'The Soviet and American presences in Europe have
of course been of a different order,' he wrote. 'If we leave aside the case of Greece
(1945–50) the United States' presence has not imposed regimes of its choice by
military force. But while operating in a different mode and under different
constraints, it has been an immensely powerful and distorting presence nonetheless.' Quoted from EP Thompson, *The Heavy Dancers* (London: Merlin Press,
1985), p. 175.

Needless to say, the overwhelming emphasis in his own extensive and rich
pamphleteering work, and in the statements of the European Nuclear Disarmament (END) movement, was on the symmetry rather than the asymmetry. Thus
END's response to the imposition of martial law in Poland in December 1981 was
a statement of protest reprinted in the movement's journal with an interpretative
gloss saying that 'along with Italy (1948), Hungary (1956), Greece (1967),
Czechoslovakia (1968), Turkey (1980), it [i.e. the coup in Poland] demonstrates
the limits of independent political development for European countries within the
framework of military blocs'. See *END Bulletin*, No. 8, Spring 1982, p. 8.
Thompson himself described the effects of the original Cold War as follows:
'Those who worked for freedom in the East were suspected or exposed as agents
of Western imperialism. Those who worked for peace in the West were suspected
or exposed as pro-Soviet "fellow-travellers" or dupes of the Kremlin. In this way
the rival ideologies of the Cold War disarmed those, on both sides, who might
have put Europe back together', quoted from his lecture 'Beyond the Cold War',
reprinted in *Zero Option* (London: Merlin Press, 1982), p. 160.

The original END appeal of April 1980 declared that 'The powers of the
military and of internal security forces are enlarged, limitations are placed upon
free exchanges of ideas and between persons, and civil rights of independent-
minded individuals are threatened, in the West as well as the East. We do not
wish to apportion guilt between the political and military leaders of East and

West. Guilt lies squarely upon both parties', quoted from E. P. Thompson & Dan Smith eds, *Protest and Survive* (London: Penguin, 1980), p. 224

Petra Kelly, one of the best known figures among the West German Greens, applied the argument specifically to Germany: 'To people who advise us to "Go East, if you don't like it here," we say East German principles apply in our country too. There is minimal provision for the poor and less and less of an opportunity to speak out. The system is the same; the differences are only of degree', quoted from Petra Kelly, *Fighting for Hope* (Boston, Mass.: South End Press, 1984), p. 14.

. . . the position of West European states vis-à-vis the United States . . . Again, the clearest and most eloquent statements in English came from E P Thompson, see the three books mentioned above, and the collection of essays by Thompson and others entitled *Exterminism and Cold War* (London: Verso, 1982). One might also mentioned the extraordinary remark of the playwright Harold Pinter, speaking in 1988: 'It seems to me that we [i.e. Britain] are as much a satellite of the USA as Czechoslovakia was (sic) of Russia.' Quoted in the *Independent*, 18 October 1988.

. . . the more independent East European states became from the Soviet Union . . . An emphatic statement of this view could be found in Peter Bender's stimulating and influential book, *Das Ende des ideologischen Zeitalters. Die Europäisierung Europas* (Berlin: Severin & Siedler, 1981). Bender wrote: Eastern Europe cannot emancipate itself from the Soviet Union unless Western Europe emancipates itself from the USA—like the forces so also the losses must remain in balance' (p. 260). Of course the basic idea can be traced back to the disengagement proposals of the 1950s, and even more directly to de Gaulle's proposals of the mid-1960s, see the concise summary by Pierre Hassner in Gordon, *Eroding Empire*, p. 196.

. . . 'in the second half of the 1980s . . .' 'Europa muss sich selbst behaupten,' in *Die Zeit*, 28 November 1986.

Independent intellectuals and opposition activists in Eastern Europe, by contrast, . . . The most eloquent and thoughtful exposition of the position summarised in these two paragraphs is that of Václav Havel in his 1985 essay 'The Anatomy of a Reticence', published as a pamphlet by the Charta 77 Foundation, Stockholm, as the first in their series 'Voices from Czechoslovakia', and reprinted in Jan Vladislav, ed., *Václav Havel or Living in Truth* (London: Faber, 1987), pp. 164–95. Among many other contributions to this debate see, for example, the response of the Hungarian philosopher and leading opposition activist János Kis to Charter 77's 'Prague Appeal' [see note below], reprinted in the *East European Reporter*, Vol. 1, No. 4, Winter 1986, pp. 52–56; the Polish contributions to Initiative Ost-West Dialog, ed., *Frieden im geteilten Europa 40 Jahre nach Jalta* (Dokumentation eines Diskussions-Forums in Berlin, Februar 1985); the Czechoslovak essays collected in Jan Kavan and Zdena Tomin, eds, *Voices from Prague. Czechoslovakia, Human Rights and the Peace Movement* (London: END & Palach Press, 1983); and the article by the Yugoslav philosopher Mihailo Marković 'On peace and human rights' in *END Journal* No. 12, Oct-Nov 1984.

... **these East Europeans said: Europe has not been at peace since 1945** ...
The classic statement is the 'Prague Appeal' of Charter 77, launched in March
1985. Charter 77 Document No. 5/85, reprinted in the *East European Reporter*,
Vol. 1, No. 1, Spring 1985, pp. 27–28. There also the formulation 'a state of
non-war'.

'Without internal peace ...' Jan Vladislav, ed., *Václav Havel or Living in Truth*
(London: Faber, 1987), p. 187.

... **the contrasting positions** ... A serious attempt to map out common
ground, under the general motto of 'détente from below', was the memorandum
'Giving real life to the Helsinki Accords', co-ordinated and published by the
European Network for East-West Dialogue in November 1986, and reprinted in
the *East European Reporter*, Vol. 2, No. 2, pp. 52–60.

Chapter I: *German Answers*

... **a long line of German historians** ... a few are mentioned by Harold James
in his *A German Identity 1770–1990* (London: Weidenfeld & Nicolson, 1989),
p. 211. See also Renata Fritsch-Bournazel, *Confronting the German Question.*
Germans on the East-West Divide (Oxford: Berg, 1988), esp. p. 76 f. The book was
originally published in German under the title *Das Land in der Mitte. Die*
Deutschen im europäischen Kräftefeld. (Munich: iudicium Verlag, 1986). A repres-
entative and influential contemporary statement of the argument can be found in
the work of the conservative historian Michael Stürmer, see for example his
Dissonanzen des Fortschritts. Essays über Geschichte und Politik in Deutschland
(Munich: Piper, 1986). Andreas Hillgruber, in his *Zweierlei Untergang. Die*
Zerschlagung des Deutschen Reiches und das Ende des europäischen Judentums (Berlin:
Siedler, 1986), a book which played some part in the German 'historians' debate'
(*Historikerstreit*) of the late 1980s, refers at one point (p. 25) to 'the events [i.e.
the Second World War], that would bring the German Reich *and thus the European*
centre to an end ...' (my italics). An academically partisan but stimulating
discussion of the 'centre' as a historical category is given by Immanuel Geiss in
Zeitschrift für Geschichtswissenschaft, 10/1991, pp. 979–94.

... **Polish historians** ... see Norman Davies, *God's Playground. A History of*
Poland, Volume 1 (Oxford: Clarendon Press, 1981), p. 23 ff and references.

... **'the heart of Europe'** ... Renata Fritsch-Bournazel traces the use of this
metaphor for Germany back to Madame de Staël's famous book of 1810, see
Fritsch-Bournazel, *Europa*, p. 171. As we shall see (below, p. 75), in his negotia-
tions with Gromyko, Egon Bahr referred to Berlin as the heart of Europe. Norman
Davies traces the use of this metaphor for Warsaw back to the poet Juliusz
Słowacki, as well as using it himself for Poland, see his *Heart of Europe. A Short*
History of Poland (Oxford: Clarendon Press, 1984). For a spontaneous popular
identification of Prague as the heart of Europe see Garton Ash, *We*, p. 123.

... **no other country** ... except, of course, Austria until the State Treaty of
1955.

... **Germany was the divided centre** ... a point succinctly recalled in Weizsäcker, *Deutsche Geschichte*, p. 12.

... **'found in the West only ...'** Jiří Dienstbier, *Träumen von Europa* (Berlin: Rowohlt, 1991), p. 13.

... **the Soviet Union's diplomatic note** ... see Meissner, *Moskau-Bonn*, pp. 71–73.

... **Adenauer took up the word** ... ibid., pp. 85–88, the quotation on p. 87.

An important Bundestag resolution ... *Bundestag Drucksachen* 3/2740, also quoted in Meissner, *Deutsche Ostpolitik*, p. 17.

... **'nothing but the attempt ...'** *Bundestag Plenarprotokolle*, 6/53, p. 2685 (27 May 1970), also reprinted in *Texte* I/5, p.171 ff. For a powerful critique of this usage, see the contribution by Karl Theodor Freiherr von und zu Guttenberg, also reprinted in *Texte* I/5, esp. p. 197.

The term was then used ... Thus Article I of the August 1970 treaty with the Soviet Union proclaims the parties' common desire to advance the 'normalisation of the situation in Europe' (*Verträge*, p. 13). The December 1970 treaty with the People's Republic of Poland is formally entitled a 'Treaty ... on the bases of a normalisation of mutual relations' and Article III (1) reads: 'The Federal Republic of Germany and the People's Republic of Poland will undertake further steps towards the full normalisation and comprehensive development of their mutual relations, whose firm basis is this Treaty' (*Verträge*, pp. 21–22. My italics.) The December 1972 Basic Treaty with the GDR speaks in Article 1 of developing 'normal good-neighbourly relations' and in Article 7 of 'the normalisation of ... relations' (*Zehn Jahre*, p. 206). The treaty of December 1973 with Czechoslovakia speaks only of 'good-neighbourly relations' (*Verträge*, p. 50). English texts in Grenville, *Treaties*, pp. 192–200.

... **they wanted to change, not the frontiers in Europe** ... The point being, of course, that official East European propaganda had as tirelessly claimed that the Federal Republic — or certain 'revanchist' circles within the Federal Republic — *did* want to restore the 1937 frontiers of the German Reich.

... **in Helmut Schmidt's 1978 state of the nation address** ... what we have referred to throughout as the 'state of the nation' address was proposed by an all-Party resolution of 1967 (see *Texte* I/4, p. 149) and formally instituted by Chancellor Kiesinger in 1968 under the title 'Report on the state of the nation in divided Germany' — 'Bericht über die Lage der Nation im geteilten Deutschland', see *Bundestag Plenarprotokolle*, 5/158, p. 8168 (11 March 1968). In the last years of Schmidt's Chancellorship, the annual address was simply entitled 'Report on the state of the nation' — 'Bericht zur Lage der Nation', see, for example, *Bundestag Plenarprotokolle*, 8/208, p. 16615 (20 March 1980), 9/31, p. 1541 (9 April 1981), 9/111, p. 6745 (9 September 1982). When he came to power, Chancellor Kohl made a great point of this dropping of the explicit reference to 'divided Germany', suggesting that the emphasis of the addresses under Schmidt had shifted to a discussion of the political situation inside the Federal Republic.

'We Germans will not reconcile ourselves to the division of our fatherland,' he roundly declared, *Bundestag Plenarprotokolle*, 10/16, p. 987 (23 June 1983). But a look back through Chancellor Schmidt's 'state of the nation' addresses hardly bears out the contention that he was, in substance, neglecting the issue of the German and European divisions.

'**gradually a situation of matter-of-course normality . . .**' *Bundestag Plenarprotokolle*, 8/78, p. 6115 (9 March 1978). Emphasis in the original. Wolfgang Schäuble, a key political appointee responsible for Deutschlandpolitik under Chancellor Kohl from 1984 to 1989, himself pointed to the difficulty of determining what 'normality' between the two German states would be, in a lecture in 1986: see 'Deutsche Einheit und menschliche Erleichterungen', in *Bulletin*, 29 April 1986, pp. 379–87, also reprinted in *Innerdeutsche Beziehungen*, pp. 246–53.

It seems to have appeared for the first time . . . this is according to Meissner, *Moskau-Bonn*, p. 27, footnote 50, and text of the declaration on pp. 283–85.

. . . used fitfully, but with growing frequency . . . see, for example, the conclusion of a speech by the Christian Democrat Kopf, welcoming the Jaksch report and resolution in June 1961: 'As a goal we see the creation of a European peace order which includes all the countries of Europe and in which the free united Germany also cheerfully and responsibly takes its place'. *Bundestag Plenarprotokolle*, 3/162, p. 9367 (14 June 1961). In June 1962 Foreign Minister Schröder declared that 'our goal is a just new European order, based on peaceful agreements . . .', quoted in Jacobsen, *Nachbarn*, p. 348. The Federal Government's so-called 'peace note' of March 1966 used an almost identical formulation: 'a just European order, based on peaceful agreements', ibid., p. 385.

. . . in the first government declaration of the 'Grand Coalition' . . . see *Bundestag Plenarprotokolle*, 5/8, p. 3663 (13 December 1966).

. . . used repeatedly . . . see the entries under 'Europäische Friedensordnung' in the index volume to *Texte I*. One version of Brandt's vision of a 'European peace order, that is, an order which really overcomes the Cold War and the political tensions', is given in an interview of July 1967, reprinted in Haftendorn, *Aussenpolitik*, pp. 326–28. But the formulations were vague and varied.

. . . in Nato's 1967 Harmel report . . . this talks variously of a 'peaceful order in Europe', a 'final and stable settlement in Europe' (both in paragraph 8, concentrating on the division of Germany and Europe) and, in paragraph 12, of 'policies designed to achieve a just and stable order in Europe, to overcome the division of Germany and to foster European security', see *Texts of Final Communiqués issued by Ministerial Sessions of the North Atlantic Council, the Defence Planning Committee, and the Nuclear Planning Group* (Brussels: Nato Information Service, 1975), pp. 198–202. German text in EA, 23/1968, pp. D75–77. An important article on the background to the Harmel report is that by Helga Haftendorn in *VfZ*, 40/2, 1992, pp. 169–221.

Helmut Schmidt expresses . . . Schmidt, *Menschen und Mächte*, p. 11

. . . a high level of conceptual imprecision . . . Siebenmorgen, *Gezeitenwechsel*,

p. 327, suggests that Willy Brandt's conceptual imprecision was deliberate and tactical, enabling him not be pinned down by critics or opponents to any precise definition, such as the earlier usage of a 'European security system' had seemed to demand. Bender, *Neue Ostpolitik*, p. 163, suggests that Brandt's conceptual imprecision was deliberate but philosophical, reflecting a genuine humility before the openness of history. Could it not be both?

The objective of the new Ostpolitik, said Scheel in 1970 . . . both quotations are from *Bundestag Plenarprotokolle*, 6/59, pp. 3269–70 (17 June 1970). He restated this goal, retrospectively, in the journal *Liberal*, 30. Jg., Heft 1, February 1988, p. 39.

'The development is inexorably . . .' Rede des Bundesministers des Auswärtigen Hans-Dietrich Genscher aus Anlass der Verleihung des 'Thomas-Dehler-Medaille' am Sonnabend, dem 03. Januar 1987. Der Bundesminister des Auswärtigen, Mitteilung für die Presse Nr. 1005/87, p. 63. An almost identical formulation is to be found in his 11 June 1988 speech to a conference of the Institute for East-West Security Studies at Potsdam. Der Bundesminister des Auswärtigen, Mitteilung für die Presse Nr. 1140/88, p. 15. This speech is reprinted in Genscher, *Unterwegs*, pp. 151–69.

. . . **'last week influential politicians . . .'** Marion Gräfin Dönhoff, 'Ein Dach für ganz Europa,' in *Die Zeit*, 1 April 1988.

. . . **'the necessary structure of international law'** . . . Egon Bahr, *Zum europäischen Frieden*, p. 90.

. . . **could be achieved by the end of the century** . . . ibid., p. 84.

. . . **'would be equivalent to European peace'** . . . ibid., p. 92.

. . . **'the western principles of the Helsinki Final Act . . .'** ibid., p. 92. What 'binding' quality these principles would acquire, and how or why, is not explained.

. . . **'to be historically resolved'** . . . ibid., p. 31.

. . . **'could be very exciting'** . . . ibid., p. 34.

. . . **'guaranteed peaceful competition . . .'** ibid., p. 83.

. . . **'culture of dispute'** . . . ibid., p. 99.

. . . **'growing co-operation in unchanged political structures'** . . . ibid., p. 42. One should note that the nationally-minded CDU parliamentarian, Bernhard Friedmann, came up with a not altogether dissimilar vision: that of the two German states increasingly co-operating on 'questions of ecology, energy, technology and so forth' while retaining 'wholly different social systems'. Friedmann was less circumspect than Bahr, and talked of a 'Confederation' in which, amongst other things, the Federal Republic and the GDR would conduct a 'more or less common foreign policy'. See Bernhard Friedmann, *Einheit statt Raketen* (Herford: BusseSeewald, 1987), p. 137.

. . . **'everything that one says must be true . . .'** Interview in Bayerischer Rundfunk, 19 May 1973.

Social Democrats in government had firmly and consistently maintained . . . A classic forum for such statements was the American journal *Foreign Affairs*. See, for example, Willy Brandt, 'German policy toward the East,' in *Foreign Affairs*, Spring 1968, pp. 476–86, and Helmut Schmidt, 'A policy of reliable partnership,' in *Foreign Affairs*, Spring 1981, pp. 743–55.

. . . **'And therein lies the real problem . . .'** *Bundestag Plenarprotokolle*, 10/59, p. 4164 (15 March 1984).

. . . **'the basic freedoms are realised . . .'** *Bundestag Plenarprotokolle*, 11/33, p. 2160 (15 October 1987).

. . . **'The clear articulation of our own goals . . .'** Wolfgang Schäuble, 'Die deutsche Frage im europäischen und weltpolitischen Rahmen,' EA, 12/1986, p. 342 (based on the text of a lecture to the Swedish Institute for International Relations on 15 May 1986). Schäuble was Chancellery Minister from 1984 to 1989, when he became Interior Minister.

. . . **'To be sure, it verbally subordinates . . .'** ibid., p. 342.

. . . **'Peace begins with respect . . .'** Kohl used this formula in his televised keynote speech during Erich Honecker's visit to Bonn in September 1987: see the *Bulletin*, 10 September 1987, p. 706. He repeated an almost identical formula in his state of the nation address the same year: see *Bundestag Plenarprotokolle*, 11/33, p. 2163 (15 October 1987).

Chancellor Kohl echoed Chancellor Schmidt . . . For Kohl see his 1983 state of the nation address in *Bundestag Plenarprotokolle*, 10/16, p. 988 (23 June 1983). For Schmidt see his 1980 state of the nation address in *Bundestag Plenarprotokolle*, 8/208, p. 16623 (20 March 1980).

. . . **Genscher said simply: 'the division of Germany is the division of our European continent'.** Rede des Bundesministers des Auswärtigen Hans-Dietrich Genscher aus Anlass der Verleihung des 'Thomas-Dehler-Medaille' am Sonnabend, dem 03. Januar 1987. Der Bundesminister des Auswärtigen, Mitteilung für die Presse Nr. 1005/87, p. 10.

. . . **'above all a matter for the Germans'** . . . quoted from his 1985 speech on 'The Germans and their Identity', reprinted in Richard von Weizsäcker, *Von Deutschland aus. Reden des Bundespräsidenten* (Munich: Deutscher Taschenbuch Verlag, 1987), p. 56. An English edition is *A Voice from Germany. Speeches by Richard von Weizsäcker*, translated by Karin von Abrams (London: Weidenfeld & Nicolson, 1986), this passage on p. 78.

'To overcome the division of Germany is simultaneously . . .' Wolfgang Schäuble, 'Die deutsche Frage im europäischen und weltpolitischen Rahmen', EA, 12/1986, p. 344.

. . . **always and simultaneously 'European peace policy'** . . . This particular formula seems to have been coined, and was most often repeated by Hans-Dietrich Genscher. As early as January 1971, while still Interior Minister, he declared in a speech in New York: 'The Ostpolitik of the Federal Government is thus in its substance and its goals at once Deutschlandpolitik and European peace policy', *Bulletin*, 15 January 1971, p. 27. For typical later usages see, for example, his remarks in *Bundestag Plenarprotokolle*, 11/33, p. 2193 (15 October 1987), and his 11 June 1988 speech to a conference of the Institute for East-West Security Studies at Potsdam, Der Bundesminister des Auswärtigen, Mitteilung für die Presse Nr. 1140/88, p. 3. This speech is also reprinted in Genscher, *Unterwegs*, pp. 151–69.

. . . **no contradiction between West European integration and Ostpolitik** . . . An argument made forcefully by Walter Scheel in the original debates about the Eastern treaties and restated most emphatically by Helmut Kohl in the late 1980s. 'We should,' he told his party's foreign policy congress in April 1988, 'avoid a phoney debate about the question of whether and to what extent our Germany-political (*deutschlandpolitische*) goals can be brought into harmony with the policy of European integration.' See the typescript of the speech, pp. 7 ff. In his 1984 state of the nation address Kohl declared that 'for us, Europapolitik [i.e. the policies related to West European integration] and Deutschlandpolitik are like two sides of the same coin'. *Bundestag Plenarprotokolle*, 10/59, p. 4163 (15 March 1984).

'. . . **the identity of our interests with the interests of Europe.**' *Bundestag Plenarprotokolle*, 6/23, p. 915 (15 January 1970).

'**I have always found** . . .' dictated by Bismarck on 9 November 1876, see Johannes Lepsius & ors, eds, *Die Grosse Politik der Europäischen Kabinette 1871–1914* (Vol. 2, Berlin: Deutsche Verlagsgesellschaft für Politik und Geschichte, 1922), No. 256, p. 88.

. . . **how often and how eloquently Hitler spoke of Europe** . . . with consummate mendacity, of course, and only in the pre-war years. Thus in the subject index to Max Domarus, *Hitler: Reden und Proklamationen* (Wiesbaden: R Löwit, 4 Vols, 1973) there are twenty-two references to 'Europe' for the period 1932–38, but only one reference for the period 1939–45. Europe had done its work. Europe could go. For peace, respect and equal rights for neighbours, see, for example, Domarus, *op. cit.*, pp. 193, 273. Perhaps the high-point of Hitler's 'European' humbug is his speech to the Reichstag on 7 March 1936, with its eloquent references to German-French reconciliation, 'European co-operation', and the need for a peaceful solution of Europe's problems — all in fact justifying the remilitarisation of the Rhineland. See Domarus, *op. cit.*, pp. 583–97. For his private, wartime talk of 'Europe' in quite a different vein — although still repeating some of the same leitmotifs — see Henry Picker, *Hitlers Tischgespräche im Führerhauptquartier* (Seewald, Stuttgart, 1976), and in English, *Hitler's Table Talk* (London: Weidenfeld & Nicolson, 1953).

. . . **wrote his biographer Alan Bullock** . . . *Hitler. A Study in Tyranny* (London: Penguin, 1962), p. 335.

. . . **Willy Brandt, Helmut Kohl and Hans-Dietrich Genscher** . . . For Brandt, see his very interesting 10 May 1968 speech at the Stresemann-Gedenkfeier in Mainz, reprinted as the introduction to Arnold Harttung, ed., *Gustav Stresemann. Schriften* (Berlin: Berlin-Verlag, 1976), esp. pp. XI, XIII–XV, where he explicitly compares his own proposed new policy with that of Stresemann. He also made the comparison in his December 1971 Nobel Peace Prize lecture, see *Texte* I/9, pp. 309–10. For Kohl, see, for example, his 2 May 1984 Adenauer Memorial Lecture in Oxford, where he presents Locarno as the first great attempt at — and missed opportunity for — that Western integration of Germany which Adenauer finally achieved. German text in *Bulletin*, 9 May 1984, p. 433; English text published as *German Foreign Policy Today* (London: St Antony's College/Konrad Adenauer Foundation, 1984). For Genscher, see Helmut R. Schulze & Richard Kiessler, *Hans-Dietrich Genscher. Ein deutscher Aussenminister* (Munich: Bertelsmann, 1990), p. 29.

... a means to the achievement of national ends ... For contrasting judgements on the vexed, and perhaps falsely posed question of whether or in what sense Stresemann was 'a good European' see Gordon A. Craig, *Germany 1866–1945* (Oxford: Clarendon Press, 1978), pp. 511–24 (with further references); Griffith, *Ostpolitik*, pp. 6–15 (and further references on pp. 239–41); A. J. Nicholls, *Weimar and the Rise of Hitler* (London: Macmillan, 1968), pp. 120–22; Golo Mann, *The History of Germany Since 1789* (London: Peregrine Books, 1987), pp. 636–37; Sebastian Haffner, *Von Bismarck zu Hitler* (Munich: Kindler, 1987), pp. 193–95. Two hostile but vivid assessments by contemporary observers may be found in F. W. Foerster, *Europe and the German Question* (London: Allen & Unwin, 1941), pp. 305–06, and Claud Cockburn, *Cockburn Sums Up* (London: Quartet Books, 1981) p. 36. Now see also the biography by Kurt Koszyk, *Gustav Stresemann. Der Kaisertreue Demokrat* (Köln: Kiepenheuer & Witsch, 1989). Jonathan Wright of Christ Church, Oxford, is preparing a major biography of Stresemann which will also address this question.

... Konrad Adenauer ... on all that follows see the superb two-volume biography by Hans-Peter Schwarz, cited below as Schwarz, *Adenauer I* and *Adenauer II*.

'The only opportunity left to Germany ...' Michael Stürmer, 'The evolution of the contemporary German question,' in Moreton, *Germany*, pp. 23–4. See also the discussion on p. 48 f and notes.

... two sides ... see, for example, Schwarz, *Adenauer I*, p. 850 ff, *Adenauer II*, pp. 146–48, 285–6, 367, 384, 893. Schwarz emphasises that Adenauer was extremely flexible in his thinking about how 'Europe' might be built, and that, by contrast with Walter Hallstein, he inclined to the inter-governmental rather than the supranational model of EC development. Altogether, the second aspect, that of regaining sovereignty, powers and freedom of manoeuvre for the Federal Republic, seen as the core of the nation-state Germany, comes through most strongly from the portrait Schwarz paints. Adenauer once observed that there were Hyper-Europeans, Europeans and Anti-Europeans. He himself, he said, was a European. Quoted in Schwarz, *Adenauer II*, p. 753.

... he sometimes doubted ... see Baring, *Anfang*, pp. 101–03, Schwarz, *Adenauer II*, p. 152. See also the note by the then Permanent Under-Secretary of the Foreign Office, Sir Ivone Kirkpatrick, of a conversation with the German ambassador to London on 16 December 1955. Noting Adenauer's fear of the

Western allies making a deal with the Soviet Union, perhaps involving a united but demilitarised Germany, he goes on, recording the German ambassador's account of the Chancellor's remarks: 'The bald reason was that Dr Adenauer had no confidence in the German people.' The document is reprinted in Josef Foschepoth, *Adenauer und die deutsche Frage* (Göttingen: Vandenhoeck & Ruprecht, 1988), pp. 000.

. . . the first step . . . Adenauer celebrated this at the time as the 'foundation-stone for the building of a European *Bund*', Schwarz, *Adenauer I*, p. 850. But it is clear that he attached at least as much importance to the security dimension, and the plans for a European Defence Community.

. . . the plan for a European Defence Community . . . see Baring, *Anfang*, *passim*, Schwarz, *Adenauer II*, pp. 121–40, and Edward Fursdon, *The European Defence Community. A History* (London: Macmillan, 1980).

. . . a special, unique commitment . . . on this see Olaf Mager, *Die Stationie-rung der britischen Rheinarmee. Grossbritanniens EVG-Alternative* (Baden-Baden: Nomos, 1980).

. . . the ties with the United States . . . see Schwarz, *Adenauer II*, p. 728 and *passim*. For a vigorous, polemical re-statement of this view see Baring, *Grössen-wahn*.

. . . the striving to become subject rather than object . . . Two interesting German usages of the subject/object terminology: '. . . the Cold War offered the Germans, more particularly those in the West, the opportunity to change their role from object to subject'. Michael Stürmer in Moreton, *Germany*, p. 23. And in the lecture already quoted Wolfgang Schäuble observes 'Without Germany there is no Europe, and without Europe the Germans would only be an object of world policy (*Objekt der Weltpolitik*)', *Bulletin*, 29 April 1986, p. 383.

. . . 'a more self-reliant German policy' . . . the word both Brandt and Scheel used is *selbstständig* which means literally 'self-standing', but with the clear implication, in this context, of greater autonomy. In his seminal 'Government declaration' of 28 October 1969, Brandt spoke of the common interests of the Federal Republic and the United States of America being 'strong enough to sustain a more self-reliant (*selbständigere*) German policy in a more active partnership', *Bundestag Plenarprotokolle*, 6/5, p. 31 (28 October 1969). In a debate early in 1970 Scheel referred to 'the desire for a greater self-reliance (*Selbstständig-digkeit*) of German policy', *Bundestag Plenarprotokolle*, 6/53, p. 2685 (27 May 1970).

. . . West Germany had more ties than any . . . a point well emphasised by Helga Haftendorn in her contribution to Ekkehart Krippendorff & Volker Rittberger, eds, *The Foreign Policy of West Germany. Formation and Contents* (London: Sage, 1980).

. . . with the 'understanding', 'agreement' or 'support' . . . for a political-theological debate about the precise wording see the note on p. 446. For what actually happened, see Chapter VII.

... 'without the assent of the East European peoples'. *Bundestag Plenarprotokolle*, 8/154, p. 12257 (17 May 1979).

'... there was hardly a government in Europe ...' Schmidt, *Menschen und Mächte*, p. 41. At a seminar organised by the author at St Antony's College, Oxford, on 3 May 1988, the veteran British diplomat Sir Frank Roberts put it quite charmingly. By the mid-1960s, he observed, Germany's Western allies felt the commitment to reunification had become 'a bit of a nuisance'.

... perfect understanding of the fears ... see, for example, *Bundestag Plenarprotokolle*, 8/154, p. 12264 (17 May 1979).

... policymakers in Washington ... on this, see now the work of Hermann-Josef Rupieper, *Der besetzte Verbündete. Die amerikanische Deutschlandpolitik 1949–1955* (Opladen: Westdeutscher Verlag, 1991).

... in American State Department discussions ... see, for example, the note of a discussion on 1 April 1952, in *Foreign Relations of the United States. 1952–1954* Volume VII (Washington: US Government Printing Office, 1986), pp. 194–99.

... France, although sporadically interested in overcoming the division of Europe ... see the masterly short survey by Pierre Hassner in Gordon, *Eroding Empire*, pp. 188–231.

... 'The trench that divides my country ...' Notes for a conversation with de Gaulle in Paris, 15 December 1966, in AdsD: Dep WB, BA 17. Brandt gives an account of the conversation in *People and Politics*, pp. 130–35 and *Erinnerungen*, pp. 251–53.

'Our chance lies in the fact ...' Wolfgang Schäuble, 'Die deutsche Frage im europäischen und weltpolitischen Rahmen', in EA, 12/1986, p. 345.

... the phrase 'unifying Europe' ... see, for example, remarks by Helmut Kohl in *Bundestag Plenarprotokolle* 11/125, p. 9130 (16 February 1989).

... what Strauss then described as the chimera of a Greater Europe ... *Bundestag Plenarprotokolle*, 6/53, p. 2713 (27 May 1970).

'The unity of the Germans ...' *Bundestag Plenarprotokolle*, 6/22, p. 843 (14 January 1970).

... a formula from the late 1960s ... Renata Fritsch-Bournazel traces this formula to a 1968 lecture by Klaus Bloemer, then adviser to Franz Josef Strauss on foreign affairs. See Renata Fritsch-Bournazel, *Confronting the German Question* (Oxford: Berg, 1988), p. 131 [German original: *Das Land in der Mitte. Die Deutschen im europäischen Kräftefeld*, Munich: iudicium Verlag, 1986]. The whole theme of the relationship between the German and the European questions is explored with characteristic brilliance by Pierre Hassner in his contribution to Werner Weidenfeld, ed., *Die Identität der Deutschen* (Munich: Hanser, 1983), pp. 294–323, with this formulation on p. 299.

'Do not do unto others. ...' George Bernard Shaw, *Maxims for Revolutionists*.

Chapter II: Ostpolitik

... **true of Willy Brandt** ... see above, p. 62.

... **eminently true of Hans-Dietrich Genscher** ... a serious political biography of Genscher remains to be written. Two journalistic portraits are Werner Filmer & Heribert Schwan, *Hans-Dietrich Genscher* (Düsseldorf: Econ, 1988) and Helmut R Schulze & Richard Kiessler, *Hans-Dietrich Genscher. Ein deutscher Aussenminister* (Munich: Bertelsmann, 1990). Two collections of his speeches are *Deutsche Aussenpolitik. Ausgewählte Reden und Aufsätze 1974–1985* (Stuttgart: Bonn Aktuell, 1985), and *Unterwegs*. These small selections do not, however, begin to give an idea of the sheer volume and diversity of the minister's publicly spoken words.

... **to delay the opening of the Brandenburg Gate** ... see Peter Siebenmorgen, 'Des Kanzlers Jubelplan' in *Die Zeit*, 19 April 1991. Siebenmorgen bases this report on the notes and recollections of the East German emissary Alexander Schalck-Golodkowski, but confirmed it also with West German sources.

... **nearly one fifth of the new state's population** ... Benz, *Vertreibung*, p. 8, quotes a figure of 16.5 per cent of the total population from the September 1950 census. This does not include those who fled from the Soviet Occupied Zone/GDR. *Aussiedler* 2, p. 3, quotes a *Statistisches Bundesamt* calculation according to which there were some 11.9 million refugees and expellees, of whom, in September 1950, 7.6 million were in West Germany (including West Berlin), 3.7 million in East Germany. Of course some who initially fled to East Germany subsequently fled again from East Germany.

... **claimed three million members** ... this in notes in preparation for a meeting of Willy Brandt with leaders of the Federation of Expellees on 17 February 1961, in AdsD: Dep WB, Rbm 63.

... **some two million members** ... the figure of 2.2 million members was claimed in the Federation of Expellees 1991 annual report, which also reported an increase in membership, due to the number of recent German migrants from Eastern Europe. See the report in FAZ, 1 July 1991.

... **Bavaria's 'fourth tribe'** ... Strauss, *Erinnerungen*, p. 66.

... **to pay close attention** ... see, for example, the accounts of Brandt's meetings with expellee leaders in AdsD: Dep WB, Rbm 63

... **the defection** ... **Herbert Hupka** ... see Baring, *Machtwechsel*, pp. 398–400.

... **a February 1984 joint resolution** ... The resolution was a compromise worked out in the Bundestag's Committee for Intra-German Relations between two proposals, one from the Christian and Free Democrats, one from the Social Democrats. The separate proposals were tabled on 22 June 1983, see *Bundestag Drucksachen* 10/187 and 10/192, the joint resolution presented on 24 January 1984, see *Bundestag Drucksachen* 10/914. For the debate on the joint resolution, see *Bundestag Plenarprotokolle* 10/53, pp. 3842–51 (9 February 1984).

... a security *Teilhaberschaft* ... Speech to the Aspen Institute's Berlin conference on 'Perspectives for the 21st Century', 25 October 1987, reprinted in Theo Sommer, ed., *Perspektiven. Europa im 21. Jahrhundert* (Berlin: Argon, 1989), pp. 107–18, this on p. 115.

... the precise terms ... see, for example, the distinction drawn between the Federal Republic's *Westbindungen* and *OstVERbindungen* by Werner Link, 'Die aussenpolitische Staatsräson der Bundesrepublik Deutschland' in Funke, *Demokratie und Diktatur*, pp. 400–16.

... many (though not all) of them had attacked ... An exception, notable also on account of his subsequent elevation, was Richard von Weizsäcker, see Baring, *Machtwechsel*, pp. 437 & 441.

... a government-guaranteed one billion DM loan ... see above, p. 155 and notes.

... few Western visitors were more fulsome ... 'I must say ... that I left with the most agreeable feelings,' 'one can only wish Gorbachev all the best,' East and West might stand 'on the eve of a new age', 'Mars must leave and Mercury take the stage.' see *Der Spiegel*, 1/1988.

'Divided Germany ...' see Herbert Wehner, *Wandel und Bewährung. Ausgewählte Reden und Schriften 1930–1980* (Frankfurt: Ullstein, 1986), pp. 232–48, this quotation on p. 248. The turn was subsequently confirmed by a major resolution on foreign policy at the November 1960 Hannover party congress. 'In the argument between East and West,' declared this resolution, 'the place of the Federal Republic is firmly on the side of the West, the Federal Republic is a reliable ally.' Quoted in Siebenmorgen, *Gezeitenwechsel*, p. 325.

... a long, complex, not to say confused process ... See Clemens, *Reluctant Realists*, Hacke, *Wege und Irrwege*, and the lecture by Alois Mertes, 'Kontinuität und Wandel in der deutschen Aussenpolitik', in *Bulletin*, 14 May 1983, pp. 437–44.

... the May 1972 'Joint Resolution' ... See Baring, *Machtwechsel*, pp. 427–47, with the text of the resolution on pp. 438–40; also in *Verträge*, pp. 66–67.

... an encyclopaedic resolution ... Even after five years of relatively successful government practice of Ostpolitik, and even with the right flank secured by the 'conversion' of Franz Josef Strauss, this theoretical codification produced some ructions inside the Christian Democratic Union.

The original 'discussion paper' produced by a party commission in February 1988, placed a fulsome description of the Federal Republic's commitments to, and hopes for, the Western Alliance and the European Community, before a discussion of Deutschlandpolitik. In the latter section, it declared that the 'core' of Deutschlandpolitik was 'the maintenance of national unity', but without explicitly mentioning the goal of reunification in one state. 'The goal of unity is only to be achieved by the Germans with the agreement (*Einverständnis*) of their neighbours to East and West,' it said. Some party members objected vehemently to the omission of any explicit reference to the goal of reunification, and to the implication that Germany's neighbours might have a veto over Germany's future.

The final resolution passed at the Wiesbaden party conference in June 1988 put the discussion of Deutschlandpolitik before that of the Western Alliance and Western Europe, declared that 'the core of the CDU's Deutschlandpolitik remains "to maintain national *and state* unity" (Preamble of the Basic Law)' [my italics], and observed that 'we need the understanding (*Verständnis*) and support (*Unterstützung*) of our neighbours for the realisation of our nation's right of self-determination'. The overwhelming majority of the long text remained a theoretical affirmation and elaboration of what the Kohl government had, in practice, already been doing for the previous five years.

. . . 'realistic' and 'illusion-free' détente . . . See, for example, the 1978 paper on CDU/CSU policy towards the Soviet Union, prepared by a commission under the chairmanship of Alois Mertes, and published in FAZ, 24 February 1978.

'*Pacta sunt servanda*' . . . Strauss used the phrase in an article in the *Bayernkurier* of 26 May 1972, just nine days after the Joint Resolution. 'The treaties with Moscow and Warsaw are unquestionably valid in international law,' he declared in the Bundestag on 24 January 1973. 'There is now no alternative to them: *pacta sunt servanda.*' *Bundestag Plenarprotokolle*, 7/8, p. 170.

. . . a significant change of rhetoric . . . an important commentary on this will be the planned new edition of Wolfgang Bergsdorf's illuminating *Herrschaft und Sprache. Studien zur politischen Terminologie der Bundesrepublik Deutschland* (Pfullingen: Neske, 1983), hereafter cited as Bergsdorf, *Sprache*. Having dissected the political terminology of federal governments from Konrad Adenauer to Helmut Schmidt, Bergsdorf went on to help mould the political terminology of the Federal Government under Helmut Kohl, as a senior political appointee at the Federal Press and Information Office and adviser to the Chancellor.

'there is no break in the continuity . . .' *Die Zeit*, 28 October 1988.

'Despite all the party-political disputes . . .' see *Bulletin*, 2 February 1988, this quotation on p. 130, from a lecture delivered at the Evangelical Academy in Tutzing on 20 January 1988, entitled 'Im Dienste der Menschen. Unsere Politik gegenüber unseren östlichen und südöstlichen Nachbarn'. It was, of course, at the Tutzing academy that Egon Bahr delivered his seminal lecture in 1963, see p. 65 f.

'there are no more differences between him and me' . . . *Die Zeit*, 7 October 1988. Strauss actually died between the delivery and the publication of this text, which therefore acquired the character almost of a political testament.

President von Weizsäcker declared . . . See *Bulletin*, 24 January 1989, p. 38.

All the major parties . . . agreed . . . this is not to count the Greens as a 'major party'.

. . . to describe it as *German* Ostpolitik . . . a 1971 study by Lawrence L Whetten is even called, simply, *Germany's Ostpolitik*, although the sub-title is 'Relations between the Federal Republic and the Warsaw Pact Countries' (Oxford: Oxford University Press, 1971).

. . . much though the other German state might object . . . whereas the West

German state had an *Ostpolitik* but a *Westbindung*, the East German state had a *Westpolitik* but an *Ostbindung*. The GDR was 'for ever and irrevocably allied to the Union of Soviet Socialist Republics', said Article 6.2 of the 1974 constitution. As the bonds of the Soviet bloc loosened in the 1980s, however, the GDR did increasingly differentiate between its East European partners: for example, welcoming Hungary as an ally in defence of détente in 1984–5 (see pp. 168), but deploring her domestic reforms in 1989 (see remarks by Joachim Herrmann at a Central Committee meeting, ND, 23 June 1989), embracing Ceauşescu's Romania both on account of its relative independence in foreign policy *and* because of its internal political Stalinism. The GDR's East European policy under Honecker was thus almost an ironical perversion of the US policy of 'differentiation' (see p. 178 f). Whereas the US 'rewarded' East European states for relative foreign policy autonomy and/or relative domestic liberalism, the GDR 'rewarded' its fraternal allies for relative foreign policy autonomy and/or domestic *illiberalism*! Although relations between East European states increasingly came to resemble 'normal', or even pre-war relations between European states—witness the cold war between Hungary and Romania, or the frontier dispute about territorial waters between Poland and the GDR—it was still never plausible to talk of the GDR having a distinctive Ostpolitik.

... 'German foreign policy' ... thus the title of Hans-Dietrich Genscher's collected speeches: *Deutsche Aussenpolitik. Ausgewählte Reden und Aufsätze 1974–1985* (Stuttgart: Bonn Aktuell, 1985).

... 'the German Ostpolitik' ... thus also the title of Boris Meissner's documentation of 1970: *Die deutsche Ostpolitik* ...

... sanctified by *Duden* ... *Duden. Das grosse Wörterbuch der deutschen Sprache*, Vol. 5, 1980.

... the concept of 'national interest' ... see the lucid short book by Joseph Frankel, *National Interest* (London: Macmillan, 1970).

... meaning Bavaria, Baden-Württemberg ... thus, welcoming Erich Honecker to Munich in 1987, Franz Josef Strauss said 'Between the Federal Republic of German and the Free State of Bavaria on the one hand, and the German Democratic Republic on the other, a sober co-operation has developed since 1983 ..', quoted in EA, 19/1987, p. D 549. Similar tones could be heard during Strauss's visit to Moscow in December 1987, but also, for example, in Lothar Späth's reception of Gorbachev in Baden-Württemberg in June 1989. Several of the states had their own missions in Brussels, and in Moscow.

... traditionally called *Staatsräson* ... Perhaps the most famous work on this subject was Friedrich Meinecke's *Die Idee der Staatsräson in der neueren Geschichte*.

... Virtually all ... it must be emphasised that the 'all' here refers to the Federal Republic's political and intellectual *élites*, not to a wider public. A public opinion poll in January 1984 asked 'When people talk about Germany, what does that mean to you?' 57 per cent of respondents said 'the Federal Republic' while only 27 per cent said 'Federal Republic and GDR'. Another poll, in July 1986, had 37 per cent of those asked averring that the 'German nation today' means the

Federal Republic, while 35 per cent said Federal Republic and GDR together. But interestingly the figure for those who said 'German nation' meant both Federal Republic and GDR had *risen* three per cent since November 1981, while the proportion of those who said only Federal Republic had *fallen* by six per cent in the same period. For these figures, and an authoritative discussion of them, see Gebhard Schweigler, 'Normalcy in Germany', paper for the Woodrow Wilson Center European Alumni Association conference in Dubrovnik, 1988, published in a revised German version as 'Normalität in Deutschland' in EA, 6/1989, pp. 173–82.

. . . *Josef Joffe called it* . . . in his perceptive discussion of West German policy Joffe distinguishes between 'raison d'état' and 'raison de nation', see Josef Joffe, *The Limited Partnership. Europe, the United States and the Burdens of Alliance* (Cambridge, Mass.: Ballinger, 1987), pp. 22, 33.

. . . *Duden* . . . Duden: *Das grosse Wörterbuch der deutschen Sprache*, Vol. 5, 1980.

. . . *Brockhaus-Wahrig* . . . Brockhaus-Wahrig: *Deutsches Wörterbuch*, Vol. 4, 1982.

Langenscheidt's concise German-English dictionary . . . *Handwörterbuch Englisch*, 1977.

. . . *Oxford English Dictionary* . . . the second edition appeared in 1989, but the entry for Ostpolitik is that from the *Supplement* volume of 1982.

. . . 'will scarcely overlook . . .' the quotation comes from Terence Prittie, *Germany Divided* (London: Hutchinson, 1961), p. 155.

. . . 'Today's German Ostpolitik . . .' quoted from Henry Picker, *Hitlers Tischgespräche im Führerhauptquartier* (Stuttgart: Seewald, 1976), p. 165. See also the slightly different version in *Hitler's Table Talk* (London: Weidenfeld & Nicolson, 1953), p. 379. Of course in pre-1945 usage the term Ostpolitik was only one among a whole family of *Ost*-compounds: *Ostpreussen, Ostmark, Ostmarkenpolitik, Ostsiedlung, Ostkolonisation, Osthilfe, Ostfront, Ostwall, Ostraum* etc.

. . . in his 1971 Nobel Peace Prize speech . . . see *Texte I/9*, pp. 312–13.

'Twenty five years ago yesterday . . .' *Deutschland-Union-Dienst* (Pressedienst der CDU und CSU), No. 170, 10 September 1980, p. 1.

. . . also a party-political statement . . . yet an independent scholar agrees: 'The beginning of an Ostpolitik of the Federal Republic,' writes Lothar Wilker, 'can be dated precisely: to the opening of diplomatic relations with the Soviet Union, agreed in September 1955 . . .' Haftendorn, *Aussenpolitik*, p. 316 (this section by Lothar Wilker).

. . . as Social and Free Democrats generally implied . . . for a fine example of partisan aetiology, see Ehmke, *Zwanzig Jahre*, p. 11.

. . . the milestone at the 13 August 1961 . . . thus Bender, *Neue Ostpolitik*. See below, 'The Road from Berlin', p. 58 f.

. . . with the formation of the Grand Coalition . . . thus Ehmke, *Zwanzig Jahre*.

... **the whole complex of the Eastern treaties** ... see below, p. 67 f.

... **the hope-filled crowds at Erfurt shouting 'Willy! Willy!'** ... this on Brandt's first visit as Chancellor to the GDR, on 19 March 1970. See Brandt, *People and Politics*, pp. 370–72.

... **Willy Brandt falling to his knees** ... this on 7 December 1970, see ibid., p. 399, and Bender, *Neue Ostpolitik*, pp. 178–79.

... **Ostpolitik may therefore also be described as détente policy** ... this is implicit in the title of Richard Löwenthal's masterly study with its opposition of 'Ostpolitik' to 'Cold War': *Vom kalten Krieg zur Ostpolitik*. See also Siebenmorgen, *Gezeitenwechsel*, p. 6.

... **so closely associated** ... **with the years 1969–1972** ... thus the Index to the *Bulletin* has references to 'Ostpolitik' only for these years. After 1972, references are by individual countries, or, from 1976 to 1980, under *Entspannungspolitik*.

... **used already by Konrad Adenauer** ... see Siebenmorgen, *Gezeitenwechsel*, p. 13 ff, Schwarz, *Adenauer II*, p. 19.

... **Americans had made the French word into an English one** ... but Leon Wieseltier has wittily suggested that détente is 'the French word for German goodwill towards Russia', *The New Republic*, 10 February 1982, quoted in Schweigler, *Grundlagen*, p. 141. This was not how it looked from Bonn in the mid-1960s, however, when détente seemed to be rather a French word for American (and French and British) goodwill towards Russia.

... **the adjective 'realistic'** ... see his Bundestag speech about the Helsinki conference on 25 July 1975, reprinted in Hans-Dietrich Genscher, *Deutsche Aussenpolitik. Ausgewählte Reden und Aufsätze 1974–1985* (Bonn: Bonn Aktuell, 1985), p. 77 ff.

... **'the failure of *Entspannungspolitik*'** ... see, for example, Haftendorn, *Sicherheit*, p. 133 ff. The 'End of *Entspannung*' was discussed as early as 1976, when President Ford said he would no longer use the word 'détente'. In response, Helmut Schmidt resorted to the marvellously sophistical argument that 'the renunciation of the foreign word 'détente', which we have never used in German', would not affect the continuity of the American policy of *Entspannung* towards the Soviet Union! See *Bulletin*, 20 April 1976, pp. 429–36, this comment on p. 430.

... **in a Joint Declaration at the end of Brezhnev's visit** ... *Bulletin*, 9 May 1978, pp. 429–30.

... **the Kohl-Genscher government's** ... **'Programme of Renewal'** ... according to Gebhard Schweigler, when the SPD criticised this omission, 'government representatives declared this was just an accident ...', see Schweigler, *Grundlagen*, p. 151 note. For Brandt's criticism, see *Bundestag Plenarprotokolle*, 10/6, p. 274 (6 May 1983).

... **in an official government documentation** ... *Verträge*, p. 7.

In official Bonn usage ... see, for example, the *Bonner Almanach 1987/88*

(Bonn: Presse- und Informationsamt der Bundesregierung, 1987), which has fifteen pages on Deutschlandpolitik and one page on Ostpolitik.

. . . Deutschlandpolitik meant . . . in the 1940s and 1950s, Deutschlandpolitik actually meant the policy of other countries (mainly the victor powers) *towards* Germany. In fact as late as 1976, *Duden* gave this as the only meaning of the term ('the policy of foreign states concerning Germany', *Das Grosse Wörterbuch der deutschen Sprache*, Vol. 2, 1976). *Brockhaus-Wahrig* is once again more canny: 'Policy which concerns the problems arising from the division of Germany', it says, without specifying whose policy (*Deutsches Wörterbuch*, Vol. 2, 1981). Deutschlandpolitik as a term for the policy of the Federal Government towards these problems — and primarily towards the GDR — seems to have become firmly accepted only with Chancellor Kiesinger's programmatic statements at the outset of the Grand Coalition in December 1966 and January 1967. The term Deutschlandpolitik, unlike the terms Ostpolitik or *Entspannungspolitik*, figures continuously in the index of the *Bulletin* since the end of 1966.

The great series of *Dokumente zur Deutschlandpolitik* documents Deutschlandpolitik in both senses: that of the wartime allies and subsequently victor powers, and that of the Federal Republic.

. . . simply as *DDR-Politik* . . . see Bruns, *DDR-Politik*, especially pp. 11 & 123–4, where the coinage is attributed to Günter Gaus, and below, Chapter Four, *passim*.

. . . a quarter of what was once Germany . . . in the December 1937 frontiers of the German Reich, the territories to the east of the Oder-Neisse line comprised roughly twenty-five per cent of the total land-area, but contained only some fifteen per cent of the population, see *Zahlenspiegel*, p. 4.

. . . the policymaking process . . . on this see Haftendorn, *Aussenpolitik*, pp. 9–12; Joffe in Gordon, *Eroding Empire*, pp. 169–78; and more extensively, Haftendorn, *Verwaltete Aussenpolitik*.

. . . the direct control of the Chancellery . . . on this, see below p. 130.

. . . the Foreign Ministry . . . strictly speaking, of course, it is the Foreign Office: *Auswärtiges Amt*. But since British readers assume there is only one Foreign Office, we have used the term Foreign Ministry to avoid confusion.

. . . informal East German emissaries . . . most notable among the East German emissaries were the lawyer Wolfgang Vogel and the financial operator Alexander Schalck-Golodkowski. On all this, see p. 130.

. . . the direct responsibility of the Foreign Ministry . . . although the Economics Ministry was also responsible for East-West (including Intra-German) trade, and the Finance Ministry was, of course, closely involved in all issues that concerned public funds: e.g. credits and loan guarantees.

. . . the role of the Chancellor and his advisers . . . the supremacy of the Chancellery in the crucial first phase of Ostpolitik is emphasised in Schmid, *Entscheidung*, esp. p. 181 ff, although this was a period in which the Foreign Minister was unusually weak, see Baring, *Machtwechsel*, esp. p. 269 ff.

... **unofficial intermediaries and 'back channels'** ... Thus Hans-Peter Schwarz records an extraordinary series of meetings in East Berlin between Adenauer's Finance Minister, Fritz Schäffer, and his former schoolmate, Vinzenz Müller, now chief of staff of the East German 'Garrisoned People's Police', as well as a message from the Polish leadership brought by the industrialist Berthold Beitz. To some extent, Adenauer's unconventional and wilful Ambassador in Moscow, Hans Kroll, could also be regarded as such a channel to Khrushchev. See Schwarz, *Adenauer II*, pp. 190–93, 686, and 699 ff. Günter Buchstab describes Kiesinger's personal soundings in his article in Karl Dietrich Bracher & ors, eds, *Staat und Parteien. Festschrift für Rudolf Morsey zum 65. Geburtstag* (Berlin: Duncker & Humboldt, 1992). Egon Bahr performed this function over many years for Willy Brandt, and set up his own direct lines both to Washington and to Moscow. His special Soviet channel was the journalist Valery Lednyev. Bahr also made his own top-level 'channels', for example to the Central Committee of the Soviet Communist Party, available to Chancellor Kohl's foreign policy adviser, Horst Teltschik. (Horst Teltschik, Bonn, 12 July 1991). Eugen Selbmann, foreign policy adviser to the Social Democrats' parliamentary fraction, played a role much more important than his formal position would suggest, in maintaining top-level, informal contacts with Party leaders in Warsaw, Budapest, Prague and Moscow, both for Willy Brandt and even more for Helmut Schmidt. His real importance was recognised by the presentation to him of a Festschrift with contributions from most of the leading figures in Social Democratic Ostpolitik, see Ehmke, *Zwanzig Jahre*, especially the tributes on pp. 385–90. Selbmann himself is, at the time of writing, working on a volume of analytical memoirs. (Eugen Selbmann, Bonn, 8 July 1991). Senior figures from the world of business also on occasion passed on messages or top-level background information directly to the Chancellor.

... **[Foreign ministry] department** ... formally the department for 'foreign policy questions which concern Berlin and Germany as a whole'. Günther van Well, head of this department from 1967 to 1971, and subsequently the top official in the foreign service, Ambassador to the UN and to Washington, recalls that it included such high-fliers as Gerold von Braunmühl, Otto von der Gablentz and Hans Otto Bräutigam, subsequently the Federal Republic's Permanent Representative in the GDR. Günther van Well, Bonn, 8 July 1991.

... **'so now we are setting you down ...'** quoted in Schröder, *Bahr*, p. 148. There was a double irony in Duckwitz saying this, since he was himself personally close to the Chancellor (they were neighbours on the Venusberg in Bonn), took part in the daily 'situation meeting' at the Chancellery, and caused a minor row between the Chancellor and the Foreign Minister when, during the German-Polish negotiations in 1970, he took a personal letter from Brandt to Gomułka, of which Scheel had not been informed. After this affair, Scheel demanded that Duckwitz no longer be included in the daily 'situation meeting' in the Chancellery, and Duckwitz was retired in June 1970. See Baring, *Machtwechsel*, p. 285 f & 305 f, and Schmid, *Entscheidung*, pp. 112–14, & 187. That Duckwitz was not entirely happy with his departure in the middle of the German-Polish negotiations can be seen from his letters to Willy Brandt, including copies of distinctly aggrieved letters to his successor as State Secretary of the Foreign Ministry, in AdsD: Dep WB, BK4.

... **a high degree of consistency and continuity** ... this extended not only to the civil service and the politicians but even to the media commentators. On the relative inconsistency of the American and French political and policy-making processes, see the relevant chapters in Gordon, *Eroding Empire*. The British political and policymaking process secured a relatively high degree of consistency, but so far as Eastern Europe is concerned this was, until the early 1980s, rather the consistency of disinterest.

... **increasingly a matter of working through multilateral institutions** ... this is well described in Haftendorn, *Verwaltete Aussenpolitik*

... **European Political Co-operation** ... see the valuable book by Simon J Nutall, *European Political Co-operation* (Oxford: Clarendon Press, 1992)

... **pursue different goals or interests through separate instruments** ... but where in this matrix should one fit the competition between Western countries for Eastern trade? And where the attempts not just of West German but of British and French leaders to act as 'intermediaries' between Moscow and Washington? Were Mrs Thatcher 'going between' Reagan and Gorbachev in 1985, or Giscard d'Estaing seeking to mediate between Carter and Brezhnev in 1980, pursuing common or special interests? Both, to be sure.

... **'trading states'** ... on this, see especially Richard N Rosecrance, *The Rise of the Trading State* (New York: Basic Books, 1986)

... **'an insatiable striving ...'** Schwarz, *Gezähmten Deutschen*, pp. 28–35, this on p. 35

... **which Ralf Dahrendorf has argued** ... see Ralf Dahrendorf, *Society and Democracy in Germany* (New York: Norton, 1979), esp. p. 142 ff & 202–03.

Having by 1945 become enemies ... Hans-Peter Schwarz, remarks at a conference of the Woodrow Wilson Center European Alumni Association, Dubrovnik, 1988, and Schwarz, *Gezähmten Deutschen*, *passim*.

... **'an unmanly dream'** ... see the entry for 'Friede' in Wilhelm Janssen & ors, *Geschichtliche Grundbegriffe* Vol. 2, (Stuttgart: Klett, 1975), pp. 543–91, this on pp. 579–80.

It has also been suggested ... for example by Johannes Gross, *Phönix in Asche* (Stuttgart: Deutsche Verlags-Anstalt, 1989), p. 21 ff. See also Ralf Dahrendorf, *Society and Democracy in Germany* (New York: Norton, 1979), p. 9.

... **as the Christian Democrat Jakob Kaiser put it** ... quoted in Besson, *Aussenpolitik*, p. 35.

... **placed the division of Germany at the centre** ... '... the central political issues in Europe, first and foremost the German question ...' (Par. 5), '... no final and stable settlement in Europe is possible without a solution of the German question which lies at the heart of present tensions in Europe' (Par. 8), Harmel report, quoted from *Texts of Final communiqués issued by Ministerial Sessions of the North Atlantic Council, the Defence Planning Committee, and the Nuclear Planning Group* (Brussels: Nato Information Service, 1975), pp. 198–202.

454 · *Notes to Pages 42–47*

... between the interests of the (undemocratic) states and those of their societies ... British and American policy makers sometimes spoke in this connection of relations with 'peoples' and with 'governments' in Eastern Europe. But the term 'societies' (with no ethnic overtones) was more widely used by the democratic oppositions in Eastern Europe, while the governments were, at least until the very end of the decade, merely one arm of a party-state.

'The main characteristic of the "hot peace" ...' Pierre Hassner, *Europe in the Age of Negotiation* = The Washington Papers, Vol. 1, No. 8 (Beverly Hills: Sage, 1973), pp. 69–70. In an article in *Europa-Archiv* in the same year, Josef Joffe described this 'dialectic of social interaction' as one of two key problems for future Ostpolitik, see EA, 4/1973, pp. 111–24, reprinted in Haftendorn, *Aussenpolitik*, pp. 378–93. Hassner recalls having begun to use this formula in late 1969 or early 1970.

... substantial impact of a different policy ... France was a partial exception, see p. 136, but it is very doubtful if this had a substantial impact.

... as Reinhart Koselleck has pointed out ... 'Sprachwandel und Ereignisgeschichte', *Merkur*, August 1989, pp. 657–72.

... in personal encounters at summit meetings ... Thus Helmut Schmidt points out that often no proper record was kept of his summit encounters, for example, when he spoke English with Giscard d'Estaing. Helmut Schmidt, London, 3 June 1991.

... on the telephone ... Jochen Thies records the following from his time working in the Chancellery. With a change of superior, an official exclaimed: 'Thank heavens we won't need to write any more memos. Now it'll only be telephoning.' Jochen Thies, *Helmut Schmidts Rückzug von der Macht. Das Ende der Ära Schmidt aus nächster Nähe* (Stuttgart: Bonn Aktuell, 1988), p. 38.

... or on television ... given the supreme importance of this one medium in contemporary politics, future historians will surely need to spend as much time in front of video screens as in press archives. The Konrad Adenauer Foundation's archive (ACDP) has presciently laid down a collection of television news and current affairs programmes, starting in 1982.

... what Bergson called ... quoted in Dominique Moïsi & Jacques Rupnik, *Le Nouveau Continent. Plaidoyer pour une Europe renaissante* (Paris: Calmann-Lévy, 1991), p. 78.

... legal provisions ... the key provisions are, for the party archives, in the law of 13 March 1992 amending the existing *Bundesarchivgesetz* (see *Bundesgesetzblatt*, 1992, Teil 1, p. 506), and, for the Stasi files, in article 32 of the so-called *Stasi-Unterlagen-Gesetz* (see *Bundesgesetzblatt*, 1991, Teil 1, pp. 2272–87).

... the 'essential triangle' ... Pierre Hassner in Gordon, *Eroding Empire*, p. 194.

Chapter III: Bonn–Moscow–Berlin

'not just the East of the West . . .' Weizsäcker, *Deutsche Geschichte*, p. 12.

The history of these plans and attempts . . . See Hermann Graml, *Die Alliierten und die Teilung Deutschlands. Konflikte und Entscheidungen 1941–1948* (Frankfurt: Fischer, 1985); Hans-Peter Schwarz, *Vom Reich zur Bundesrepublik. Deutschland im Widerstreit der aussenpolitischen Konzeptionen in den Jahren der Besatzungsherrschaft 1945–1949* (2nd edition., Stuttgart: Klett-Cotta, 1980); Theodor Eschenburg, *Jahre der Besatzung. 1945–1949* (Stuttgart: Deutsche Verlags-Anstalt, 1983 = *Geschichte der Bundesrepublik Deutschland* Bd. 1); Hans-Peter Schwarz, *Die Ära Adenauer. Gründer jahre der Republik 1949–1957* (Stuttgart: Deutsche Verlags-Anstalt, 1981 = *Geschichte der Bundesrepublik Deutschland* Bd. 2); Hans-Peter Schwarz, *Die Ära Adenauer 1957–1963. Epochenwechsel* (Stuttgart: Deutsche Verlags-Anstalt, 1983 = *Geschichte der Bundesrepublik Deutschland* Bd. 3); Josef Foschepoth, ed., *Kalter Krieg und deutsche Frage. Deutschland im Widerstreit der Mächte 1945–52* (Göttingen: Vandenhoeck & Ruprecht, 1985). See also, more recently, Hermann-Josef Rupieper, *Der besetzte Verbündete. Die amerikanische Deutschlandpolitik von 1949 bis 1955* (Opladen: Westdeutscher Verlag, 1991).

. . . the possible alternative . . . the best and most balanced short account of Adenauer's reaction is in Schwarz, *Adenauer I*, pp. 906–24. For an account of Adenauer's response by a close associate see Wilhelm G Grewe, *Rückblenden 1976–1951* (Frankfurt: Propyläen, 1979), and the same author's short article, 'Ein zählebiger Mythos. Stalins Note vom März 1952' in FAZ, 10 March 1982. Specifically on the Soviet proposals of 1952–53, see also the well-documented but tendentious book by Rolf Steininger, *Eine vertane Chance. Die Stalin-Note vom 10. März 1952 und die Wiedervereinigung* (Bonn: Dietz, 1985), originally published as the introduction to a collection of documents, and now translated into English as *The German Question. The Stalin Note of 1952 and the Problem of Reunification* (New York: Columbia University Press, 1990); Hans-Peter Schwarz, ed., *Die Legende von der verpassten Gelegenheit. Die Stalin-Note vom 10. März 1952* (Stuttgart: Belser, 1982 = Vol. 5 of *Rhöndorfer Gespräche*); Hermann Graml, 'Die Legende von der verpassten Gelegenheit. Zur sowjetischen Notenkampagne des Jahres 1952', VfZ, 3/1981, pp. 307–41; Hermann-Josef Rupieper, 'Zu den sowjetischen Deutschlandnoten 1952. Das Gespräch Stalin-Nenni', VfZ, 3/1985, pp. 547–57; Gerhard Wettig, 'Die sowjetische Deutschland-Note vom 10. März 1952', DA, 2/1982, pp. 130–48 and most recently his articles in DA, 2/1992, pp. 157–67 and DA, 9/1992, pp. 943–58. See also the still cogent discussion in Löwenthal, *Vom Kalten Krieg*, pp. 14–22.

'it's called Potsdam' . . . quoted in Schwarz, *Adenauer I*, p. 833.

. . . Churchill did in fact . . . see Anthony Glees, 'Churchill's Last Gambit' in *Encounter*, April 1985, pp. 27–35; Martin Gilbert, *Winston S. Churchill. Volume VIII: 'Never Despair' 1945–1965* (London: Heinemann, 1988), pp. 818 ff; Schwarz, *Adenauer II*, p. 73 f.

... **still significantly limited**... for an interesting discussion of these limits see Ludolf Herbst, 'Wie souverän ist die Bundesrepublik?', in Wolfgang Benz, ed., *Sieben Fragen an die Bundesrepublik* (Munich: dtv, 1989), pp. 72–90.

... **'We are a free and independent state**...' see Konrad Adenauer, *Erinnerungen 1953–1955* (Stuttgart: Deutsche Verlags-Anstalt, 1966), pp. 430–34. Text of the declaration also in *Vierzig Jahre*, p. 83.

... **the 'day of sovereignty'**... see, for example, Chancellor Kohl in *Bundestag Plenarprotokolle* 11/33, p. 2160 (15 October 1987).

... **'the interests of peace and European security**...' reprinted in Meissner, *Moskau-Bonn*, pp. 71–3. Hans-Peter Schwarz notes that Adenauer had received an informal signal that the Russians wanted to talk directly but responded that one should first wait until the Paris treaties came into force, see Schwarz, *Adenauer II*, p. 192.

... **tough and dramatic negotiations**... a vivid account is given in Schwarz, *Adenauer II*, pp. 207–22, but see also Meissner, *Moskau-Bonn*, pp. 15 ff, Rainer Salzmann, 'Adenauers Moskaureise in sowjetischer Sicht', in Dieter Blumenwitz & ors., eds, *Konrad Adenauer und seine Zeit* (Stuttgart: Deutsche Verlags-Anstalt, 1976), Vol. 2, pp. 131–59, and, of course, Adenauer's own memoirs.

Adenauer certainly did not belong... for Adenauer's attitudes and policies towards the East see, first and foremost, the two volumes of Schwarz, *Adenauer*. Still valuable is the pioneering study by Klaus Gotto, 'Adenauers Deutschland- und Ostpolitik 1954–1963' (hereafter: Gotto, 'Adenauer') in Morsey & Repgen, *Adenauer Studien III*. See also Dieter Blumenwitz & ors., eds, *Konrad Adenauer und seine Zeit* (2 Vols, Stuttgart: Deutsche Verlags-Anstalt, 1976) and the revisionist treatments in Josef Foschepoth, ed., *Adenauer und die deutsche Frage* (Göttingen: Vandenhoeck & Ruprecht, 1988). In English see Hans-Peter Schwarz, 'Adenauer and Russia' in *Adenauer at Oxford. The Konrad Adenauer Memorial Lectures 1978–82* (Oxford: St Antony's College & Konrad-Adenauer-Stiftung, 1983).

'Asia stands on the Elbe' quoted in Schwarz, *Adenauer I*, p. 466.

... ***The Russian Perpetuum Mobile***... Wilhelm G Grewe, *Rückblenden 1976–1951* (Frankfurt: Propyläen, 1979), p. 635. The book mentioned was by one Dieter Friede. Grewe points out that Adenauer could be unduly if briefly influenced by the last book he had read. But since Adenauer subsequently also presented Friede's book to de Gaulle (see Schwarz, *Adenauer II*, p. 923) it must clearly have made a more lasting impression.

... **got on quite well with the representatives**... Wilhelm G Grewe, Bonn, 6 July 1991. As Hans-Peter Schwarz notes, Adenauer concludes the account in his memoirs with the comment that, with all due scepticism, he had the feeling that one day they might be able to solve Germany's problems with the men in the Kremlin... see Schwarz, *Adenauer II*, p. 961.

... **'this terrible power'**... this in a conversation with Alois Mertes in 1964, recalled by Mertes in Dieter Blumenwitz & ors., eds, *Konrad Adenauer und seine*

Zeit (2 Vols, Stuttgart: Deutsche Verlags-Anstalt, 1976), pp. 673–79. Adenauer also commended to Mertes, as he had to Kennedy and de Gaulle, Dieter Friede's book *The Russian Perpetuum Mobile*.

. . . **holding hands with Bulganin** . . . It is interesting to find Adenauer using, to describe his gesture at the Bolshoi, the same literary device that Brandt uses to describe his gesture of kneeling before the ghetto rising memorial in Warsaw: that is, describing it through the words of an outside observer. See Konrad Adenauer, *Erinnerungen 1953–1955* (Stuttgart: Deutsche Verlags-Anstalt, 1966), pp. 529–30, and compare Brandt, *People and Politics*, p. 399.

. . . **'until now we were like the growing young man** . . .' quoted in Siebenmorgen, *Gezeitenwechsel*, p. 141.

. . . **two main tendencies discernible** . . . Meissner, *Moskau-Bonn*, pp. 47–8.

. . . **Moscow First** . . . a point made particularly clearly in Schwarz, *Adenauer II*, p. 420 and 456–7.

The basic vision from which he started . . . neatly summarised in Klaus Gotto, 'Der Realist als Visionär', in *Die Politische Meinung*, 249/1990, pp. 6–13. One should note, however, that the image of the magnet seems first to have been used by his Social Democratic arch-critic Kurt Schumacher. See Willy Albrecht, *Kurt Schumacher. Ein Leben für den demokratischen Sozialismus* (Bonn: Verlag Neue Gesellschaft, 1985), pp. 54, 126.

'The hour of great disillusionment . . .' Heinrich Krone, 'Aufzeichnungen zur Deutschland- und Ostpolitik 1954–1969' (hereafter: Krone, 'Aufzeichnungen'), in Morsey & Repgen, *Adenauer Studien III*, pp. 134–201, this on p. 162 (entry for 18 August 1961). According to Schwarz, *Adenauer II*, p. 363, between 1957 and 1961 Krone was the second most powerful man in the Federal Republic.

. . . **expected a stronger reaction from Konrad Adenauer** . . . Even the Christian Democrat Eugen Gerstenmaier was dismayed that Adenauer did not fly immediately to Berlin. See Eugen Gerstenmaier, *Streit und Friede hat seine Zeit. Ein Lebensbericht* (Frankfurt: Propyläen, 1981), pp. 451–52. By his own account, Adenauer felt that the Soviet action could have been much worse — for example, a direct challenge to the West's connections with West Berlin; that worse challenges might still be to come; and that the crucial thing was to keep 'strong nerves', calm, and, above all, the support of the Americans, for, as he told a group of trusted journalists in one of his regular 'teatime conversations' on 17 August 1961, 'Without the United States we simply can't stay alive, that's as clear as day.' For all that can be said rationally for this position, the coolness with which he — and his Foreign Minister — reacted to the building of the Berlin Wall was eloquent of the distance between Bonn and Berlin. See Konrad Adenauer, *Teegespräche 1959–61 Bearbeitet von Hanns-Jürgen Küsters* (Berlin: Siedler, 1984), pp. 538–54 (quotation about the Americans on p. 550), Schwarz, *Adenauer II*, pp. 659–66, and also the interesting discussion in Arnulf Baring, *Sehr Verehrter Herr Bundeskanzler! Heinrich von Brentano im Briefwechsel mit Konrad Adenauer 1949–64* (Hamburg: Hoffmann & Campe, 1974), pp. 330–37. See also, most recently, the article by Hanns-Jürgen Küsters, 'Konrad Adenauer und Willy

Brandt in der Berlin-Krise 1958–1963' in VfZ, 40/2, 1992, pp. 483–542, esp. p. 527 ff, and Peter Siebenmorgen, 'Konrad Adenauer und die Berliner Mauer' in Boris Meissner, ed., *Die Deutschlandfrage von der Berliner Mauer bis zum Rücktritt Adenauers* (forthcoming).

'Adenauer probably did not abandon . . .' Andrei Gromyko, *Memories*, translated by Harold Shukman (London: Hutchinson, 1989), pp. 196–97.

. . . more rather than less committed . . . Wilhelm G Grewe, in conversation with the author (Bonn, 6 July 1991), made the simple but illuminating suggestion that it is difficult — while retaining self-respect — to continue publicly to maintain over two decades a position in which you do not privately believe. And since, whatever his private views, Adenauer was plainly convinced that for domestic political reasons he had to maintain a demonstrative commitment to reunification of the Germany 'divided in three', it is not impossible that his private conviction gradually adjusted to his public stance. But plainly this cannot be more than a speculation.

. . . a source of continuing controversy . . . for a useful statement of the 'revisionist' view, see Josef Foschepoth, ed., *Adenauer und die deutsche Frage* (Göttingen: Vandenhoeck & Ruprecht, 1988). Schwarz's biography shows that there is simply no simple answer.

In a 'word to the Soviet Union' . . . *Bundestag Plenarprotokolle*, 4/39 p. 1639 (9 October 1962). He repeated this passage in his government declaration of February 1963, adding 'The Soviet Union has not responded to these words', see *Bundestag Plenarprotokolle*, 4/57, p. 257/6 (6 February 1963). For his informal expressions of the same sentiments earlier in 1962, see Siebenmorgen, *Gezeitenwechsel*, pp. 342–43.

. . . schemes for reaching some *modus vivendi* . . . see the contributions by Klaus Gotto and the so-called 'Globke plans' in Morsey & Repgen, *Adenauer Studien III*, pp. 3–91, 202 ff, and Hans Globke, 'Überlegungen und Planungen in der Ostpolitik Adenauers', in Dieter Blumenwitz & ors., eds, *Konrad Adenauer und seine Zeit* (Stuttgart: Deutsche Verlags-Anstalt, 1976), Vol. 1, pp. 665–72.

. . . an 'Austrian solution' . . . see Siebenmorgen, *Gezeitenwechsel*, pp. 146–51; Gotto, 'Adenauer', in Morsey & Repgen, *Adenauer Studien III*, pp. 34–40; Schwarz, *Adenauer II*, p. 425 ff. Schwarz also records that this was preceded already in 1955–56 by secret discussions between Adenauer's Finance Minister, Fritz Schäffer, and the East German General Vinzenz Müller, in which the idea of a confederation between the two German states was also discussed, see ibid., pp. 190–93, and 416–17.

. . . further tentative advances . . . see Siebenmorgen, *Gezeitenwechsel*, pp. 331–46, Klaus Gotto in Morsey & Repgen, *Adenauer Studien III*, pp. 67 ff.

. . . 'for the rest of his life . . .' Krone, 'Aufzeichnungen', in Morsey & Repgen, *Adenauer Studien III*, p. 164 (entry for 7 December 1961). However Klaus Gotto points out that Adenauer inclined to make such apodictic statements, sometimes saying the opposite a few days later; and that in the same period he at least once indicated another order of priorities. See his comments in Morsey & Repgen, *Adenauer Studien III*, p. 84 (n. 387) and p. 70 (n. 402).

... **The period between**... good introductory accounts in Hildebrand, *Von Erhard zur Grossen Koalition*, Bender, *Neue Ostpolitik*, and Griffith, *Ostpolitik*.

... **an important all-party Bundestag resolution**... reprinted in Meissner, *Deutsche Ostpolitik*, pp. 17–18, Jacobsen, *Nachbarn*, pp. 345–46.

... **based on a report**... *Bundestag Drucksachen*, 3/2740. It is interesting to note that this was paired with another resolution, based on another Jaksch report, on the situation of the German minorities in Eastern Europe, see Chapter Six.

Kennedy's 'strategy of peace'... Kennedy proclaimed his 'strategy of peace' in an eloquent commencement address (drafted by Ted Sorensen) at American University in Washington on 10 June 1963. See *Public Papers of the Presidents: John F. Kennedy* (Washington: US Government Printing Office, 1964), pp. 459–64 & 526–29. Note also the seminal article by Zbigniew Brzezinski and William E Griffith advocating 'Peaceful Engagement in Eastern Europe', *Foreign Affairs*, Summer 1961.

... **Johnson's 'bridge-building'**... Johnson's key-note statement on 'bridge-building' came in a speech at the dedication of the George C Marshall library in Lexington, Virginia, on 23 May 1964, see *Public Papers of the Presidents: Lyndon B Johnson* (Washington: US Government Printing Office, 1965), pp. 708–10.

... **de Gaulle's advocacy of what he called 'détente'**... on this, see Jean Lacouture, *De Gaulle. The Ruler, 1945–1970* (London: Harvill, 1991), Chapter 29.

... **the so-called 'Hallstein Doctrine'**... for an authoritative account of the origins of the so-called 'Hallstein Doctrine', by the man who was perhaps most responsible for it, see Wilhelm G Grewe, *Rückblenden 1951–76* (Frankfurt: Propyläen, 1979), pp. 251–62.

... **since the Federal Republic alone represented Germany**... this was known in German as the *Alleinvertretungsanspruch*, the 'claim to sole representation'.

... **trade missions**... in the light of Grewe's role in formulating the 'Hallstein Doctrine' it is interesting to note that this 'intermediate solution' had already been proposed by the same Wilhelm G Grewe in a memorandum to the Foreign Minister in January 1957, see ibid, pp. 263–65. The opening of trade missions was agreed with Poland, Hungary and Romania in 1963 and with Bulgaria in 1964; with Czechoslovakia only in 1967.

... **demonstratively to ostracise the GDR**... this was the policy advocated by one of the early advocates of 'peaceful engagement', Zbigniew Brzezinski, in his book of 1965, *Alternative to Partition*. 'In these years at least,' writes Hans-Peter Schwarz, 'the concepts of German foreign policy were developed less on the Rhine than on the Hudson and Charles rivers!', Hans-Peter Schwarz & Boris Meissner, eds, *Entspannungspolitik in Ost und West* (Köln: Carl Heymanns Verlag, 1979), p. 177. But challenged on this point by George Urban in 1981, Brzezinski himself said 'My suggestions in the mid-1960s for the isolation of East Germany were tactical. I wanted the Federal Republic to recognise the Oder-Neisse line and the new realities in Eastern Europe so that we could more effectively pursue a policy of "peaceful engagement" with Eastern Europe. I knew that I could not get the West Germans to do that *and* recognise East Germany at the same time. So the best way to induce West Germany to be interested in this approach was to say that Communist East Germany was an embarrassment to the Kremlin and in need of being isolated.' See 'A Long conversation with Dr Zbigniew Brzezinski, *Encounter*, May 1981, p. 25.

. . . **'peace note' of March 1966** . . . reprinted in Meissner, *Deutsche Ostpolitik*, pp. 120–24; Jacobsen, *Nachbarn*, pp. 383–89; *Vierzig Jahre*, pp. 171–75.

'Soviet Russia has entered the ranks . . .' quoted in Morsey & Repgen, *Adenauer Studien III*, p. 189 (n. 27), and see also the analysis by Klaus Gotto in his contribution to that volume. In his memoirs, Wilhelm G Grewe suggests that Adenauer may have been temporarily convinced by de Gaulle, against his own basic judgement. See Wilhelm G Grewe, *Rückblenden 1976–1951* (Frankfurt: Propyläen, 1979), pp. 633–37. A similar view is taken in Schwarz, *Adenauer II*, p. 923 ff.

. . . **his first government declaration** . . . on 13 December 1966, see *Bundestag Plenarprotokolle*, 5/80, pp. 3656–65. According to Schmid, *Politik*, p. 17, Kiesinger drafted this declaration himself.

. . . **enshrined in Nato's Harmel report** . . . see above, p. 17 and note.

. . . **a secret mission** . . . see the article by Günter Buchstab in Karl Dietrich Bracher & ors, eds, *Staat und Parteien. Festschrift für Rudolf Morsey zum 65. Geburtstag* (Berlin: Duncker & Humboldt, 1992).

'We all know . . .' *Bundestag Plenarprotokolle*, 5/115, p. 5667 (14 June 1967).

'Germany, a reunited Germany . . .' see *Bulletin*, 20 June 1967, pp. 541–43, this on p. 542. The speech is also reprinted in Meissner, *Deutsche Ostpolitik*, pp. 205–08.

. . . **'détente through reunification'** . . . see Hildebrand, *Von Erhard zur Grossen Koalition*, pp. 83–98, but note his cautionary remarks about the degree to which Adenauer had already departed from the concept of 'détente through reunification' in his last years as Chancellor. This point is made still more forcefully in Siebenmorgen, *Gezeitenwechsel*, p. 378.

. . . **a list of proposals** . . . see *Bulletin*, 14 April 1967, p. 313, and above p. 127 f.

. . . **'a phenomenon'** . . . *Bundestag Plenarprotokolle*, 5/126, p. 6360, also in *Texte* I/2, pp. 22–32, this on p. 28.

. . . **Herbert Wehner** . . . In the first volume of his memoirs, Helmut Schmidt writes: 'Wehner's ideas about Ostpolitik were already clear before Willy Brandt developed his . . . In the whole period of my Chancellorship I discussed my policy with Herbert Wehner every week, especially my Ostpolitik — and I could always rely on him.' Schmidt, *Menschen und Mächte*, p. 30. The judgement is clearly not a full and fair historical one, but it serves as a useful corrective. In the Brandt papers deposited in the AdsD there are numerous letters from Wehner, concerned primarily with East Germany, but also with Poland and Czechoslovakia. These demonstrate a profound interest in pursuing an Ostpolitik based on dealing with the communist 'powers that be' in Eastern Europe. They do not, however, immediately display an overall *conception* for the pursuit of Ostpolitik, particularly in relation to Moscow. A balanced judgement on this point must, however, await the opening of the Wehner papers, which are already partly deposited in the AdsD.

. . . **by Helmut Schmidt** . . . For an account of Schmidt's part in the early years of Ostpolitik, which, in turn, somewhat exaggerates Schmidt's role, see Lehmann, *Öffnung*.

. . . **Ulrich Sahm** . . . Ulrich Sahm, Bodenwerder, 27 September 1992.

. . . **a somewhat neglected figure** . . . and not just in the history of Ostpolitik. A useful recent book, by two of his former aides, is fittingly entitled 'The Forgotten Government': Reinhard Schmöckel & Bruno Kaiser, *Die vergessene Regierung. Die Grosse Koalition 1966 bis 1969 und ihre langfristigen Wirkungen* (Bonn: Bouvier, 1991).

. . . **'did not do badly . . .'** letter of 9 October 1969 in AdsD: Dep WB, BA 13.

In January 1967 . . . for this and the following two paragraphs see Löwenthal, *Vom kalten Krieg*, pp. 72–74, Meissner, *Moskau-Bonn*, pp. 766–74, and Bender, *Neue Ostpolitik*, pp. 139–41.

. . . **Moscow was prepared to do business** . . . see Griffith, *Ostpolitik*, pp. 158–69, Löwenthal, *Vom kalten Krieg*, pp. 71–79, Meissner, *Moskau-Bonn*, pp. 766–74, Bender, *Neue Ostpolitik*, p. 137 ff.

In a lecture delivered in 1971 . . . Frank's lecture, delivered to the *Deutsche Gesellschaft für Osteuropakunde* on 13 October 1971, is printed in *Bulletin*, 14 October 1971, pp. 1573–79.

'Détente . . . is compelled' . . . quoted by Siebenmorgen, *Gezeitenwechsel*, p. 381, from a marginal comment by Egon Bahr on an article by Richard Löwenthal.

. . . **and specifically for the Prague Spring** . . . see H Gordon Skilling, *Czechoslovakia's Interrupted Revolution* (Princeton: Princeton University Press, 1976), esp. pp. 728 & 732–33.

. . . **one of the main Soviet pretexts** . . . see, for example, the leading article from *Pravda*, 22 August 1968, reprinted in Meissner, *Moskau-Bonn*, p. 1142.

. . . **the reaction of West German leaders** . . . see statements following 21 August 1968 in *Dokumente*, V/2, *Texte*, I/3, Meissner, *Deutsche Ostpolitik* and *Moskau-Bonn*. Specifically for Brandt and Bahr's reaction see Baring, *Machtwechsel*, p. 231 ff, Brandt, *Erinnerungen*, pp. 221–22, *People and Politics*, p. 217 ff.

... the March 1969 Budapest Declaration ... see *Current Digest of the Soviet Press*, Vol. XXI, No. 11, pp. 11–12. While this 'reaffirmed' the proposals of the Warsaw Pact's 1966 Bucharest Declaration, it was much more conciliatory in tone, and did not make the satisfaction of Moscow's demands a precondition for the opening of talks. For the text of the Bucharest Declaration see *Current Digest of the Soviet Press*, Vol. XVIII, No. 27, pp. 3–7.

... after the failure of the 1965 Kosygin economic reforms ... I owe this point to Mark Smith. See also Mikhail Heller and Aleksandr Nekrich, *Utopia in Power. The History of the Soviet Union from 1917 to the Present* (New York: Summit Books, 1986), pp. 629–41.

... unsettled by ... China ... this element is stressed by Griffith, *Ostpolitik*, pp. 162–67, and Arndt, *Verträge*, pp. 20–21. The Chinese 'threat' was dramatised by the Sino-Soviet border clash at Ussuri in March 1969. The Soviet Ambassador in Bonn was instructed to inform Chancellor Kiesinger directly of the Soviet Union's concern, see Meissner, *Moskau-Bonn*, p. 1166.

... no longer made *pre*conditions ... a point subsequently confirmed to Willy Brandt by the Soviet Ambassador, see Löwenthal, *Vom kalten Krieg*, p. 77.

... including Franz Josef Strauss ... see the sharp observations in Bender, *Neue Ostpolitik*, pp. 122–23.

... stuck to, indeed retreated to, ... this is well charted by Schmid, *Politik*, pp. 22–24. The difference, in tone as much as content, can be appreciated by comparing Kiesinger's state of the nation address on 17 June 1969 (see *Bundestag Plenarprotokolle* 5/239, pp. 13246–13254), with Willy Brandt's first government declaration just four months later, on 28 October 1969 (see *Bundestag Plenarprotokolle* 6/5, pp. 19–34). Ulrich Sahm (Bodenwerder, 27 September 1992) recalls that Foreign Ministry drafts of important notes and statements would come back from the Chancellery with all the daring, innovative passages struck out by Karl Theodor Freiherr von und zu Guttenberg or Karl Carstens.

... Kiesinger had sarcastically described ... see *Texte*, I/3, pp. 24–25.

... innovative proposals ... for the discussion initiated by the so-called Schollwer Papers see Baring, *Machtwechsel*, pp. 211–29, and Hildebrand, *Von Erhard zur Grossen Koalition*, pp. 342–47.

... what moved and informed Willy Brandt ... beside Brandt's *People and Politics* and *Erinnerungen*, see also his earlier volume *Mein Weg nach Berlin* (Munich: Kindler, 1960), translated into English as *My Road to Berlin* (London: Peter Davies, 1960), and the collection of writings from his period in exile, *Draussen* (Munich: Kindler, 1966), translated into English as *In Exile* (London: Oswald Wolff, 1971), with a biographical introduction by Terence Prittie. The restrained, simple and moving memoirs of his wife of many years, Rut Brandt, *Freundesland. Erinnerungen* (Hamburg: Hoffmann & Campe, 1992), give extraordinary insights into his character, as well as some interesting incidental detail about his eastern contacts. Among numerous biographies, Stern, *Brandt*, is concise, lucid and sympathetic, Koch, *Brandt* is comprehensive and revealing, although tending to portray Brandt as a selfish and ambitious party politician, whereas Günter Hoffmann, *Willy Brandt. Porträt eines Aufklärers aus Deutschland*, (Reinbek: Rowohlt, 1988) verges on the hagiographical. There are also astute biographical observations in Baring, *Machtwechsel*. The best short biography in English is Barbara Marshall, *Willy Brandt* (London: Cardinal, 1990).

'We consider . . .' in AdsD: Dep WB, Rbm 30. Formally this was a message from the Berlin city government, the *Senat*.

'The barred walls . . .' in AdsD: Dep WB, Rbm 30.

'In my Wedding constituency . . .' Brandt, *Erinnerungen*, p. 11.

'Gentlemen,' Brandt told the Western Allied commanders . . . quoted from Koch, *Brandt*, p. 279, although Koch does not name his source for this version.

Kennedy, he gathered, . . . Brandt, *Erinnerungen*, p. 10. In fact, Kennedy did interrupt his yachting trip, to the extent of staying onshore in his lakeside bungalow! See the blow-by-blow account in Curtis Cate, *The Ides of August. The Berlin Wall Crisis of 1961* (London: Weidenfeld & Nicolson, 1978), pp. 331–33.

In a cool response . . . both letters are reprinted and expertly introduced by Diethelm Prowe, 'Der Brief Kennedys an Brandt vom 18. August 1961', in VfZ, 33/2 (1985), pp. 373–83. See also Prowe's more recent article, drawing on the American documents, in Hans J Reichhardt, ed., *Berlin in Geschichte und Gegenwart. Jahrbuch des Landesarchivs Berlin 1989* (Berlin: Siedler, 1989), pp. 143–67.

'Was it this letter . . .' Brandt, *Erinnerungen*, p. 11. In a conversation with the author (Bonn, 2 October 1991), Willy Brandt recalled his own letter to Kennedy as being above all a gesture to show the dismayed Berliners that he was doing something decisive. He went on to reflect that in the months before the building of the Wall he and his close associates lived in a curious sort of schizophrenia: knowing that this was the American attitude, but also not wanting to know that this was the American attitude. It was thus a moment of truth in the sense of bringing home to them what they already knew.

'I said later . . .' Brandt, *People and Politics*, p. 20.

'I wondered then . . .' Ibid., pp. 290–30. In his 1989 memoirs, Brandt takes a side-swipe at Ronald Reagan for his claim that, had he been President in 1961, he would have had the Wall torn down. 'To be sure,' writes Brandt, 'Reagan publicly called on Gorbachev to get rid of the Wall. But in negotiations with the Russians he set other priorities and certainly did not put in question the division of Germany — *established in 1945 at Yalta*.' *Erinnerungen*, p. 55 (my italics).

. . . the historical Autobahn . . . a seminal treatment remains Diethelm Prowe, 'Die Anfänge der Brandtschen Ostpolitik in Berlin 1961–1963', (hereafter Prowe, 'Anfänge') in Benz & Graml, *Aspekte*, pp. 249–86.

. . . a tight circle of colleagues . . . beside Bahr it included Heinrich Albertz, himself later Governing Mayor of Berlin, Klaus Schütz, who succeeded

Albertz as Governing Mayor, and Dietrich Spangenberg, head of the Senate Chancellery from 1963. See Bender, *Neue Ostpolitik*, pp. 125–26, Siebenmorgen, *Gezeitenwechsel*, pp. 351–71, Prowe 'Anfänge' in Benz & Graml, *Aspekte*, pp. 251, 255, 265.

... the first, strictly unofficial contact ... Bender, *Neue Ostpolitik*, pp. 126–27. The meeting, in December 1961, was between Dietrich Spangenberg and the East German academic Hermann von Berg, who played an important 'middleman' role in German-German relations at this time. Twenty-five years later, in 1986, von Berg emigrated to the Federal Republic, and published a bitterly disillusioned book about the GDR: *Vorbeugende Untwerwerfung. Politik im realen Sozialismus* (Munich: Universitas, 1988). Curiously, he there (pp. 156–58) simply quotes Peter Bender's description of this first contact, without elaborating on it himself. In a conversation with the author (Berlin, 27 June 1991), von Berg explained that he was chosen for this task because, as a leader of the official student organisation in Leipzig in the 1950s, he had made some contacts with Social Democrat student leaders in the West. He recalled that he used to meet Spangenberg by the back entrance of the city hall, 'near the dustbins', so they would not be noticed. He reported to Willi Stoph.

In November 1961 there had been technical contacts on the issue of traffic and telecommunications contacts between the two halves of the divided city, see Prowe, 'Anfänge' in Benz & Graml, *Aspekte*, p. 259.

One of Brandt's Scandinavian connections, Carl Gustav Svingel, was also an important intermediary in these discreet, humanitarian dealings with the GDR. Willy Brandt, Bonn, 2 October 1991. See also the article in *Der Spiegel*, 13/1992, and further detail in Craig Whitney's biography of Wolfgang Vogel, *Spytrader. Germany's legendary spy broker and the darkest secrets of the Cold War* (New York: Times Books, 1993).

... then tried to negotiate ... see *Dokumente*, IV/7, pp. 1166–68.

'Since the total strangulation ...' *Dokumente*, IV/7, p. 1006. The increase in suicides is vividly documented in Dietfried Müller-Hegemann, *Die Berliner Mauerkrankheit. Zur Soziogenese psychischer Störungen* (Herford: Nicolaische Verlags-Buchhandlung, 1973)

... Peter Fechter ... see the official statements in *Dokumente*, IV/8, pp. 948–50, Brandt, *People and Politics*, p. 37, and Bender, *Neue Ostpolitik*, pp. 124–25.

... through unconventional, even conspiratorial channels ... notably through Dr Kurt Leopold of the Trust Office for Inter-Zonal Trade (the West German agency for trade between the two states), through the Protestant churches, and through personal contacts such as those between Spangenberg and von Berg. It seems fair to say that all these contacts had essentially the same basis: the Western side wanted the GDR to grant more elementary freedoms (above all, of movement) to at least a few of their own citizens; the GDR wanted hard currency and/or diplomatic recognition in return. In 1962 there was an attempt to negotiate the first 'Permit Agreement' as a direct *quid pro quo* for a hard currency credit being sought by the GDR: see Prowe, 'Anfänge' in Benz & Graml, *Aspekte*, pp. 262–63 and *Dokumente*, IV/9, p. XI.

... the first so-called 'Permit Agreement' ... For the texts see *Dokumente*, IV/9, pp. 1023–38.

... no less than 790,000 West Berliners ... see Brandt, *Erinnerungen*, p. 81.

... again and again return ... see, for example, the reference in Brandt's 1971 Nobel Peace Prize lecture, *Texte*, I/9, p. 307; in his small book *Menschenrechte misshandelt und missbraucht* (Reinbek: Rowohlt, 1987), pp. 89–90; and, most strikingly, in his speech to the Berliners on the day after the opening of the Berlin Wall, see *Umbruch*, pp. 79–81, this on p. 80.

... this emotional moment ... see, for example, the touching exchange between Dettmar Cramer and Egon Bahr in their conversation of 1975. Bahr recalls the experience of going across to East Berlin at that time, and seeing the many West Berliners:

Cramer: I still remember, the cars six-deep down Unter den Linden
Bahr: Fantastic!
Cramer: ... from the corner of Friedrichstrasse
Bahr: Wonderful!
Cramer: ... up to the [old Prussian] Arsenal
Bahr: Wonderful! That was really splendid. And one saw masses of people and the people's faces were happy.
quoted from Cramer, *Bahr*, pp. 41–42.

'It was then ... that the foundation-stone was laid ...' 'Ein Fortschritt für die Menschen. Passierschein-Regelung war Grundstein für die Ost-Politik,' in *Sozialdemokratischer Pressedienst*, 42. Jg., No. 33, 17 February 1987, p. 5.

... 'an Ostpolitik of their own' ... Krone, 'Aufzeichnungen' in Morsey & Repgen, *Adenauer Studien III*, p. 183 (entry for 31 December 1963).

'What you must do ...' in AdsD: Dep WB, Rbm 39/40.

... the 1969 Bonn coalition was forged on the basis ... see Baring, *Machtwechsel*, p. 199.

'Don't believe ...' quoted from *Der Spiegel*, 13 March 1963, by Prowe, 'Anfänge' in Benz & Graml, *Aspekte*, p. 271, see also ibid. p. 285, and Baring, *Machtwechsel*, pp. 202–03.

'What most people don't know ...' in AdsD: Dep WB, BK 3. However according to a report in *Der Spiegel* 18/1991, papers found since unification suggest that Borm may have worked for — or at least co-operated with — the East German State Security Service.

Two planned personal meetings with Khrushchev ... Stern, *Brandt*, pp. 57–8, Brandt, *People and Politics*, pp. 101–03. Some detail on the preparation for the 1963 meeting is in AdsD: Dep WB, Rbm 73.

'The German side ...' in AdsD: Dep WB, Rbm 72.

'Khrushchev wants a Western signature ...' in AdsD: Dep WB, Rbm 72.

... meetings with ... Abrassimov ... Brandt's notes, and a long memorandum (in Swedish) by the host, the Swedish Consul-General Sven Backlund, are in AdsD: Dep WB, Rbm 74. See also the detailed accounts in Brandt, *People and Politics*, pp. 104–110, and Rut Brandt, *Freundesland. Erinnerungen* (Hamburg: Hoffmann & Campe, 1992), pp. 161–78.

'All this is very stupid.' in AdsD: Dep WB, Rbm 72.

. . . de Gaulle had envisaged . . . see Peter Bender, 'War der Weg zur deutschen Einheit vorhersehbar? Charles de Gaulle — Realist und Prophet' in DA, 3/1991, pp. 258–63.

In a series of meetings . . . see Chapter 5 of Brandt, *People and Politics*, entitled 'Conversations with de Gaulle'.

. . . 'alleviation and encouragement . . .' Note on meeting of 24 April 1963, in AdsD: Dep WB, Rbm 74.

'De Gaulle expressed himself very positively . . .' Note on meeting of 2 June 1965, in AdsD: Dep WB, Rbm 74.

. . . American backing for his practical policy . . . See Prowe, 'Anfänge' in Benz & Graml, *Aspekte*, pp. 272–73, Diethelm Prowe, 'Der Brief Kennedys an Brandt vom 18. August 1961', VfZ, 33/2 (1985), pp. 379–80, and the same author's more recent article in Hans J Reichhardt, ed., *Berlin in Geschichte und Gegenwart. Jahrbuch des Landesarchivs Berlin 1989* (Berlin: Siedler, 1989), pp. 143–67; Brandt, *Erinnerungen*, pp. 65–83; Siebenmorgen, *Gezeitenwechsel*, p. 364.

Encouraged by . . . Klaus Schütz . . . Stern, *Brandt*, p. 64. Egon Bahr, Bonn, 4 July 1991.

. . . a German Kennedy . . . see Prowe, 'Anfänge' in Benz & Graml, *Aspekte*, pp. 272–73, and rather sarcastically, Koch, *Brandt*, pp. 310–11. Following Kennedy's assassination, Brandt penned a short book entitled 'Encounters with Kennedy': *Begegnungen mit Kennedy* (Munich: Kindler, 1964).

. . . 'small steps are better than none' . . . this catchphrase, made memorable in German by a play on words — 'kleine Schritte sind besser als keine — became one of the SPD's slogans during Willy Brandt's second attempt as Chancellor-candidate, in the 1965 federal election. Diethelm Prowe points to the government declaration of the new social-liberal coalition in Berlin, on 18 March 1963, as the first major programmatic declaration of this new approach: see Prowe, 'Anfänge' in Benz & Graml, *Aspekte*, p. 271.

. . . Coexistence: The Need to Dare . . . *Koexistenz — Zwang zum Wagnis* (Stuttgart: Deutsche Verlags-Anstalt, 1963). Extracts in *Dokumente*, IV/8, pp. 1151–55.

'Brandt likes to talk . . .' Krone, 'Aufzeichnungen', pp. 155–56 in Morsey & Repgen, *Adenauer Studien III*. On this, see also Bergsdorf, *Sprache*, p. 210 ff.

. . . in the drafts of his speeches and articles . . . which make a quite formidable holding in the Brandt papers.

. . . still needing to be persuaded . . . this point is made explicitly in a letter of

1 August 1963 from Heinrich Albertz to Willy Brandt, in AdsD: Dep WB, Rbm 38.

. . . **John F Kennedy suddenly proclaimed his 'strategy of peace'** . . . for Kennedy's eloquent 10 June 1963 commencement address (drafted by Ted Sorensen) see *Public Papers of the Presidents: John F Kennedy* (Washington: US Government Printing Office, 1964), pp. 459–64.

. . . **'to redefine the whole . . .'** see Arthur M Schlesinger, *A Thousand Days. John F Kennedy in the White House* (New York: Fawcett Premier, 1965), pp. 821–24. The phrase 'strategy of peace', and some of the ideas, can, however, already be found in a collection of Kennedy's pre-1960 speeches published as *The Strategy of Peace* (London: Hamish Hamilton, 1960).

. . . **'a gift from heaven'** . . . Egon Bahr, Bonn, 4 July 1991.

. . . **at the Free University** . . . on 26 June 1963, see *Public Papers of the Presidents: John F Kennedy* (Washington: US Government Printing Office, 1964), pp. 526–29.

. . . **'Ich bin ein Berliner'** . . . According to Eugen Selbmann (Bonn, 8 July 1991) this famous phrase was actually suggested to Kennedy by the German Social Democrat Max Brauer. Willy Brandt (Bonn, 2 October 1991) had not heard this version of events, but recalled Ted Sorensen mentioning the phrase the night before, and rehearsing it with Kennedy on the morning before the speech. See also the handwritten note in AdsD: Dep WB, Rbm 74 and Willy Brandt, *Begegnungen mit Kennedy* (Munich: Kindler, 1964), pp. 191–215. The phonetic note is reproduced in the article by Diethelm Prowe in Hans J Reichhardt, ed., *Berlin in Geschichte und Gegenwart. Jahrbuch des Landesarchivs Berlin 1989* (Berlin: Siedler, 1989), p. 147.

. . . **the text of his talk** . . . reprinted in *Dokumente*, IV/9, pp. 565–71. On the background to this and Bahr's own talk see Schröder, *Bahr*, p. 111 ff. Drafts in AdsD: Dep WB, Pub 159.

'the application of the strategy of peace . . .' see *Dokumente*, IV/9, pp. 572–75, for this and following quotations. This famous speech is also reprinted in Meissner, *Deutsche Ostpolitik*, pp. 45–48, Jacobsen, *Nachbarn*, pp. 351–56, Haftendorn, *Aussenpolitik*, pp. 255–60, and Bahr, *Sicherheit*, pp. 11–17.

. . . **'a policy of transformation'** . . . see *Dokumente*, IV/9, pp. 567–68.

'The German question . . .' ibid., p. 570.

. . . *Wandel durch Annäherung* . . . In a conversation with Hans Magnus Enzensberger in 1984, Bahr suggested that this formula had made such a career through the 'chance' that his deputy had chosen it as the headline for the circulated copy of his typescript. See *Kursbuch*, Nr. 77, 1984, pp. 97–110, this on p. 98. The same version is given in Schröder, *Bahr*, pp. 111–12, citing a conversation with Bahr. Yet in the passage quoted, Bahr himself offered this formula as the summation of his argument.

. . . **'common thoughts'** . . . Brandt, *Erinnerungen*, p. 73. Brandt says he was slightly unhappy with the formula *Wandel durch Annäherung* — for 'it could nourish the illusion that we sought to come closer to the communist system' — but immediately adds a warm tribute to his 'most conceptually gifted' collaborator. And Bahr comments: 'on the substance, he [Brandt] completely agreed with me', quoted in Schröder, *Bahr*, p. 115.

. . . designed for a specific, transitional phase . . . see Bahr's own comments on the tenth anniversary of his Tutzing speech, published as 'Der Gewaltverzicht und die Allianzen' in *Aussenpolitik* 3/1973, p. 243 ff, and reprinted in Haftendorn, *Aussenpolitik*, pp. 354–67, this on p. 355; similar comments in the discussion on the tenth anniversary of this speech in *Die Zeit*, 15 July 1973, in Cramer, *Bahr*, pp. 43–44, and in Egon Bahr, *Was wird aus den Deutschen?* (Reinbek: Rowohlt, 1982), pp. 219–20.

. . . the courtly, almost exaggerated emphasis . . . the point is made by Brandt himself in the *Erinnerungen*, p. 75. And Peter Bender comments that while Bahr claimed to be applying Kennedy's stategy of peace 'his [Bahr's] thoughts had come earlier', Bender, *Neue Ostpolitik*, p. 126.

Friedrich Naumann said of Bismarck . . . see Baring, *Anfang*, p. 86 ff.

Arnulf Baring has argued . . . ibid.

. . . from Berlin out . . . Diethelm Prowe suggests that the members of Brandt's close circle, mostly not native Berliners, had been drawn to Berlin originally because they believed it was the best place from which to work against the division of Germany. He also makes the interesting comment that Governing Mayors of Berlin received an extraordinary education in foreign affairs, but perhaps at the expense of their grounding in domestic social and economic policy — precisely the strength, and the weakness, that would characterise Brandt's chancellorship. Prowe, 'Anfänge', in Benz & Graml, *Aspekte*, p. 251 and 286. In an article pleading that Berlin should be the capital of united Germany, Brandt himself wrote, in May 1991: 'I stand under suspicion of not having forgotten my time as Governing Mayor — and the preceding years at the side of Ernst Reuter, and the subsequent years with the Ostpolitik, inextricable from Berlin. I am happy to confirm this suspicion.' FAZ, 8 May 1991.

. . . his concept for negotiations . . . see Cramer, *Bahr*, esp. pp. 50–51, 58 ('the whole concept was to hand'), Schröder, *Bahr*, p. 137 ff, Bahr, *Sicherheit*, p. 42, Schmid, *Entscheidung*, esp. pp. 19–20, 225–26.

. . . other senior officials . . . themselves divided . . . Ulrich Sahm, Bodenwerder, 27 September 1992. One should, however, note that the 'Germany department' of the Foreign Ministry worked out its own guidelines and perspectives for negotiations, especially in respect of Berlin. According to the then head of that department, Günther van Well, they did not see the 'concept' worked out in Bahr's planning staff (Günther van Well, Bonn, 8 July 1991). For an example of the careful work of this department see the memorandum (drafted by Hans Otto Bräutigam) quoted in Baring, *Machtwechsel*, pp. 241–42.

. . . every available channel . . . thus the handwritten notes in AdsD: Dep WB,

BA 17–18, record direct encounters with, for example, Piotr Abrassimov, 'my Prague acquaintance W. T.', N. Polyanov of *Izvestia*, the Polish journalist Ryszard Wojna, and a representative of the Czechoslovak trade mission. See also Brandt, *People and Politics*, pp. 171–72, Brandt, *Erinnerungen*, pp. 174–77, and the partial summary of these more or less informal contacts in Schmid, *Entscheidung*, p. 20 f.

... **confidential mediation by Italian communists** ... the mediation here being particularly between SPD and SED, see the account by Heinz Timmermann, 'Im Vorfeld der neuen Ostpolitik', in *Osteuropa*, 6/71, pp. 388–99, Brandt, *People and Politics*, pp. 220–22, Brandt, *Erinnerungen*, p. 182. A key figure in these contacts was Brandt's close associate Leo Bauer, and more details can be found in AdsD: Dep WB, PV, Verbindungen zu Leo Bauer. See also Peter Brandt & ors, *Karrieren eines Aussenseiters. Leo Bauer zwischen Kommunismus und Sozialdemokratie 1912 bis 1972* (Bonn: Dietz, 1983).

... **a discreet lunch in a journalist's flat in Vienna** ... for an interesting account of this encounter between Egon Bahr and a Polish diplomat, in January 1968, and its consequences, see the article by Hansjakob Stehle (in whose flat the meeting took place) in *Die Zeit*, 7 December 1990, pp. 41–2.

... **shared even by Chancellor Kiesinger** ... This can be seen vividly in Brandt's correspondence with Kiesinger in the Brandt papers. On 30 June 1967, for example, Kiesinger wrote to Brandt to complain of an official memorandum of Bahr's conversations in Prague on 12 and 13 June, where it was stated that Bahr 'explained again the readiness of the new Federal Government to live with the GDR in peaceful co-existence'. In January 1969 there then errupted a controversy about Bahr's secret eastern contacts, and in particular about allegations that he had visited the Central Committee of the Socialist Unity Party in East Germany. On 16 January 1969 Brandt wrote to Kiesinger stating plainly that Bahr's contacts were 'on my instructions or with my approval'. On 18 April 1969, Kiesinger wrote with plaintive irritation to say that he gathered from the press that Bahr was going to Washington, and wondered what he would do there! All the above in AdsD: Dep WB, BA 13. In conversation with the conservative journalist Giselher Wirsing, Kiesinger described Egon Bahr as 'a really dangerous man', quoted in Hildebrand, *Von Erhard zur grossen Koalition*, p. 327.

... **'If one wants to maintain ...'** in an interview in December 1968, reproduced in *Dokumente*, V/2, pp. 1610–11.

... **'Reflections on the foreign policy'** ... a copy of this document, datelined New York, 21 September 1969, was kindly made available to the author by Egon Bahr, from his collection now in the AdsD: Dep EB. Brandt was in New York for the annual meeting of the UN general assembly. Bahr confirms that this was the second of the two major working papers of the planning staff, to which he had several times subsequently referred, for example in Bahr, *Sicherheit*, p. 42. He also notes that the paper was prepared on the assumption that the Grand Coalition would probably continue.

That pessimistic assumption ... this was also the optimistic assumption of the East German side. Karl Seidel, Berlin, 30 September 1992.

A shorter version . . . A copy of this was kindly made available to the author by Werner Link. See also Link, *Ära Brandt*, pp. 163–64. A comparison with the longer paper shows this to be essentially an abridgement of it, trimmed for discussion with the Free Democrats.

'Scheel stated in the debate . . .' draft minute by Hans-Jürgen Wischnewski in AdsD: Dep WB, BK 61. The word 'largely' was inserted by Willy Brandt.

. . . **a general treaty with the GDR** . . . see Baring, *Machtwechsel*, pp. 226–29. Bahr recalls: 'Since thinking in the FDP — independently of us — went in a similar direction, we took only, one could almost say, minutes to agree the foreign policy part of the government declaration. So much were the vision and direction of our thinking in harmony.' Egon Bahr, *Was wird aus den Deutschen?* (Reinbek: Rowohlt, 1982), p. 222.

. . . **drawn by Helmut Schmidt and his Social Democratic delegation** . . . see the exhaustive account in Lehmann, *Öffnung*, pp. 71–112.

. . . **the great common ground** . . . 'The regulation of our relationship to the Soviet Union and the East European states including the GDR, was the real, indeed perhaps the only real basis for the social-liberal coalition at the outset', Baring, *Machtwechsel*, p. 199.

. . . **a paper written by Bahr in October 1968** . . . a copy of the paper, headed 'Ostpolitik after the occupation of the CSSR', and dated 1 October 1968, was kindly made available to the author by Egon Bahr from AdsD: Dep EB. Baring, *Machtwechsel*, p. 231 records Bahr as 'remarking spontaneously to his associates' that the end of the Dubček era had not changed the overall conditions for Bonn's policy. In fact it clearly *strengthened* the case for dealing with Moscow first and foremost, see Löwenthal, *Vom kalten Krieg*, p. 78 f. It was not only Bahr and Brandt, however, who concluded that the invasion reinforced the argument for the new Ostpolitik. Asked about the consequences of the invasion in a television interview on 21 August 1968, Chancellor Kiesinger responded that he could only answer for the consequences of 'this event' on the Ostpolitik of the Federal Government: 'Here I can only say: we shall consistently pursue this Ostpolitik', see *Texte*, 1/3, p. 63 ff, this on p. 64. It must again be emphasised, however, that German leaders had special reasons to be restrained in their response — since Soviet propaganda had held them directly responsible for the Prague Spring —, and the same thing was said more strongly by American and French leaders. Thus de Gaulle's prime minister, Michel Debré, famously observed that this was 'a traffic accident on the road to détente', while de Gaulle himself remarked to his ambassador in Moscow: '*la Tchécoslovaquie, je m'en bats l'oeil*', both quoted by Pierre Hassner in Gordon, *Eroding Empire*, pp. 196–97.

. . . **notably Ralf Dahrendorf** . . . see Wolfgang Schollwer, 'Ost-West-Politik eines Europäers' in *Liberal*, 1/88, p. 45, and Schmid, *Entscheidung*, p. 293. Schollwer noted Dahrendorf's insistence on this point in his diary entry for 1 June 1970, AdDL: Schollwer *Tagebuch*.

The secrecy of the negotiations . . . while Gromyko was happy to regard his talks with Bahr as negotiations — which of course in reality they were —, Bahr, in accordance with his brief, insisted that this was only an 'exchange of views'. According to the recollection of Bahr and one of his aides, Antonius Eitel, Gromyko remarked, on once again being reminded of this fine distinction: 'I'll tell you what an "exchange of views" is. An "exchange of views" is when Falin comes to me with his views and goes away with mine.' (Antonius Eitel, Bonn, 1 July 1991. Egon Bahr, Bonn, 4 July 1991).

... **the whole library of works** ... In English, basic narrative and analysis can be found in Griffith, *Ostpolitik*, Chapter 5; Hanrieder, *Germany, America, Europe*, Chapter 7; Bark & Gress, *Democracy and its Discontents*, Part VIII. In German, the best general accounts are to be found in: Link, *Ära Brandt*, pp. 163 ff, and for the Moscow Treaty specifically pp. 179–90; Meissner, *Moskau-Bonn*, pp. 775–808, and the documents contained in the same volume; Löwenthal, *Vom kalten Krieg*, pp. 79–90; Baring, *Machtwechsel*; Bender, *Neue Ostpolitik*. Schmid, *Entscheidung* is a meticulous and perceptive study of the decision-making process in Bonn from Brandt's October 1969 government declaration to the August 1970 signature of the Moscow Treaty. Detailed accounts of the treaties by informed insiders are Zündorf, *Ostverträge* and Arndt, *Verträge*. Among memoirs and biographies one should mention, beside Brandt's two volumes and Baring's *Machtwechsel*, which is itself a kind of collective biography, the two works of Bonn's then ambassador to Moscow, who was at once personally resentful and substantively critical of Bahr's conduct of the negotiations: Helmut Allardt, *Moskauer Tagebuch. Beobachtungen, Notizen, Erlebnisse* (Düsseldorf: Econ Verlag, 1973) and *Politik vor und hinter den Kulissen. Erfahrungen eines Diplomaten zwischen Ost und West* (Düsseldorf: Econ Verlag, 1979). For Bahr's side of the argument see Schröder, *Bahr*, which also gives references to a number of important interviews with Bahr; the selection of his speeches and articles in Bahr, *Sicherheit*; and two revealing interview volumes: Cramer, *Bahr*, and Egon Bahr, *Was wird aus den Deutschen? Fragen und Antworten* (Reinbek: Rowohlt, 1982).

... **three major sweeteners** ... see Meissner, *Moskau-Bonn*, p. 775 ff.

it signed the nuclear non-proliferation treaty ... on 28 November 1969.

... **a European security conference** ... Mastny, *Helsinki I*, p. 3, notes that such a conference was first proposed by Molotov shortly after Stalin's death. It was, of course, also called for in the 1966 Bucharest Declaration and 1969 Budapest Declaration of the Warsaw Pact.

... **the banker F Wilhelm Christians** ... see his own account in his book *Wege nach Russland. Bankier im Spannungsfeld zwischen Ost und West* (Hamburg: Hoffmann & Campe, 1989), pp. 17–44, hereafter Christians, *Wege*.

... **agreements were signed in Essen** ... see Meissner, *Moskau-Bonn*, pp. 1209–10, and the excellent treatment in Wörmann, *Osthandel*, pp. 115–25. DM 494m of the DM 1.2bn credit was guaranteed by the Hermes AG — that is, in effect by the Federal Government. The rate of interest was a closely guarded secret, but contemporary estimates put it at 6.25 per cent.

... **'the existing real situation'** ... the treaty says the two parties '*gehen dabei von der in diesem Raum bestehenden wirklichen Lage aus*', that is, 'proceed from the existing real situation in this region', see *Verträge*, p. 13. On the legal significance — or non-significance — of the formula see Arndt, *Verträge*, pp. 45–50. Zündorf, *Ostverträge*, p. 34, argues that the substitution of the word *wirklich* for the term *real*, used in earlier Warsaw Pact declarations, 'may perhaps mean a greater proximity to the inclusion of legitimate claims. They too can be *wirklich*. The term *real* by contrast was to be interpreted closer to the material.' The difference is hard to see with an untutored eye.

... **'including the Oder-Neisse line'** ... ibid., p. 14.

... **first by Bahr, then in the official negotiations by Walter Scheel** ... the question of Bahr's negotiating ability — or lack of it –, and the significance — or insignificance — of the improvements subsequently achieved by Scheel, is discussed at length in the works listed above.

... **down to 'inviolable'** ... see Griffith, *Ostpolitik*, p. 191 for German and Russian wording.

... **a reference in the preamble of the treaty** ... see Zündorf, *Ostverträge*, pp. 54–55.

... **by Adenauer to Bulganin** ... Meissner, *Moskau-Bonn*, p. 124. The Soviet side merely acknowledged receipt of this letter. Schwarz, *Adenauer II*, p. 219, nonetheless emphasises the importance of this letter for Adenauer's policy, and describes it as the 'letter on German unity', a description more usually applied to that of 1970.

... **'solving the main national problem** ...' for the texts of the letters see Meissner, *Moskau-Bonn*, pp. 122–23. According to the versions there given, while Bulganin's letter talks of the 'national main problem of the whole German people', Adenauer's refers to 'the whole national main problem of the German people'. The formula had been used in the original Soviet note proposing talks about opening diplomatic relations, see above p. 49.

a 'letter on German unity' ... reprinted in *Verträge*, p. 15, Meissner, *Moskau-Bonn*, pp. 1271–72, *Vierzig Jahre*, p. 226.

Twenty years later ... see the letter from Ludwig Mertes in the FAZ, 7 August 1990, and the responses from Dr Claus Arndt and Professor Konrad Repgen (both 3 September), Rainer Barzel and Egon Bahr (both 20 September). In a telegram from Moscow dated 21 May 1970, Bahr reported that he had informally handed to Falin the draft of a letter on the right of self-determination. There follows the text of a somewhat longer and more complicated version of what became the Letter on German Unity. (Copy in possession of the author). Falin claims that he actually contributed to the formulation of the letter, Valentin Falin, Hamburg, 14 May 1992. This does not, however, necessarily contradict the claim made by Christian Democrats that they contributed to this initiative from the German side at an earlier stage.

... **diplomatic notes** ... reprinted in *Verträge*, pp. 16–17, *Vierzig Jahre*, p. 227.

... **the Christian Democratic opposition insisted** ... on the Christian Democratic side see, beside the works listed above, Clemens, *Reluctant Realists* and Hacke, *Wege und Irrwege.* The then Party leader, Rainer Barzel, gives his retrospective account in Rainer Barzel, *Im Streit und umstritten. Anmerkungen zu Konrad Adenauer, Ludwig Erhard und den Ostverträgen* (Frankfurt: Ullstein, 1986). A more concrete and detailed memoir is Birrenbach, *Sondermissionen.* A reasoned retrospective summary of the opposition's position was given by Alois Mertes in *Politik und Kultur*, 2/81, pp. 20–38, and in APZ, 18 December 1982, pp. 3–9. A notable contemporary critique was Karl Theodor Freiherr von und zu Guttenberg, *Die neue Ostpolitik. Wege und Irrwege* (Osnabrück: Verlag A Fromm, 1971), while the same author's posthumous *Fussnoten* (Stuttgart: Seewald, 1973) give some fascinating insights. A wealth of material on this subject can be found in the Marx and Mertes Papers in the ACDP.

... a **Common Resolution of the Bundestag** ... reprinted in *Verträge*, pp. 66–67, and *Vierzig Jahre*, pp. 260–62.

... the **Constitutional Court averred** ... the Constitutional Court delivered two main judgements relating to the Eastern treaties, on 31 July 1973 and 7 July 1975. Although the first of these formally referred to the Basic Treaty with the GDR, whereas the second referred explicitly to the Moscow and Warsaw treaties, it was the first — with its insistence on the continued legal existence of the German Reich — which was both juridically and politically most important. The full verdict can be found in *Zehn Jahre*, pp. 232–43, analytical commentary on all the verdicts (including a further minor one of 2 February 1980) in Arndt, *Verträge*, pp. 224–29.

'Even if two states in Germany exist...' see Link, *Ära Brandt*, pp. 166–67.

... **'the constitutive political statement...'** ibid. quoting from von Weizsäcker's contribution to Diertrich Rollmann, *Die CDU in der Opposition. Eine Selbstdarstellung* (Hamburg: Christian Wegner, 1970), p. 41 f.

.. the **'German signature'** ... see above p. 63.

'When on 12 August 1970...' Bender, *Neue Ostpolitik*, p. 174.

... **resented even by the communist leadership of Poland** ... see Bender, *Neue Ostpolitik*, pp. 176–77, Schmid, *Entscheidung*, p. 115 ff, and 290 ff, and Mieczysław F Rakowski in Lutz, *Bahr*, p. 98. Brandt, in his *Erinnerungen*, pp. 211–12, gives a sensitive account of these Polish sensibilities. He makes the point — also made in many other commentaries — that the Bonn government attempted to take account of them by putting the recognition of the frontier in the first article of the Warsaw Treaty, before the renunciation-of-force clause, whereas in the Moscow Treaty the frontier-recognition was carefully put *after*, and made to follow from, the renunciation-of-force clause. He also reports that when he raised with Gomułka the suggestion that the Warsaw Treaty might be ratified before the Moscow Treaty — thus giving it symbolic priority — Gomułka urged him not to split the two, since any attempt to drive a wedge between Moscow and Warsaw was doomed to fail.

Leaked extracts from the German records ... These were published in the

FAZ and *Die Welt*, both on 18 April 1972. They are reprinted in Meissner, *Moskau-Bonn*, pp. 1473–80, together with the extremely sharp government response, which gives a vivid impression of the atmosphere at that time. The government did not basically deny that the extracts were genuine — indeed they were later to publish one of the fragments themselves (see above p. 74 and note) — but Chancellery Minister Horst Ehmke wrote to the opposition leader, Rainer Barzel, that 'the quotations are torn out of context, changing their sense. In part there are omissions inside individual sentences, in part additions, which are not taken from the records and apparently are meant to be explanatory. In certain cases the text is falsified.' The opposition's suspicions were deepened by the fact that the government did not allow even respected senior Christian Democrats to look through the records of the Moscow and Warsaw negotiations, a bipartisan consensus-building privilege which they claimed Adenauer had given to leading Social Democrats during the negotiation of the Western treaties. Instead, on 6 and 7 May 1972, Egon Bahr read aloud from the records of the Moscow negotiations to a senior Christian Democrat, Kurt Birrenbach, and State Secretary Paul Frank did the same from the records of the Warsaw negotiations. According to Birrenbach, Bahr read him the records for some twenty to twenty-four hours of the total ca. sixty hours of negotiations, with Birrenbach interrupting to ask him to go back or clarify. So far as the authenticity of the leaked extracts is concerned, Birrenbach summarises his impressions thus: 'The fragments published in the press were written by someone who had had direct access to the records. They were, so far as I found them again in the records, reproduced word-for-word. There was only one exception: one quotation was incomplete in an important point. The passages omitted were important, but not crucial for an overall judgement. But to this extent they diminished the value of the publication.' Birrenbach, *Sondermissionen*, pp. 402–04.

In conversation with the author, Egon Bahr said that he did not actually bother to read the records carefully until the opposition started asking for them, and then he was dismayed at what he found. In his judgement, Immo Stabreit, the diplomat at the German Embassy who actually wrote the records, was critical and even 'hostile' to his approach, and this hostility is reflected in the wording and tone of the records. He said, however, that the actual quotations are generally correct. (Egon Bahr, Bonn, 4 July 1991).

Although the leaked fragments must clearly be treated with care, Birrenbach's testimony, the very partial nature of the government denial, and, not least, everything else we know about Bahr's overall approach, all suggest that they give an important insight into the terms and atmosphere of the Bahr-Gromyko talks. A set of the protocols is apparently in AdsD: Dep EB, but Egon Bahr was not yet willing to let the author read them.

In addition to the records, there are the 'delegation reports' sent by telegram to Bonn from the Moscow embassy.

'We had to make sure . . .' This and the following quotations are from Meissner, *Moskau-Bonn*, p. 1476.

At the end of their preliminary talks . . . see Schmid, *Entscheidung*, p. 67.

. . . the 'Bahr paper' . . . this is conveniently printed next to the text of the

Moscow Treaty in Bender, *Neue Ostpolitik*, pp. 233–39. Also in Bahr, *Sicherheit*, pp. 36–39, where Bahr himself comments 'The ten points of the "Bahr paper" were the summation of the single whole of Ost-Politik until the green light for the European conference in Helsinki 1975.'

Its first four points became . . . in the official cover-sheet to the 'Bahr paper' it is clearly stated that '1. Of the attached 10 points, points 1–4 are conceived as the subject of the real treaty negotiations.' Further: '2. A renunciation-of-force treaty to be concluded on the basis of numbers 1–4 will be complemented by a letter averring that the conclusion of the treaty does not signify that the Federal Government gives up its political goal to work towards self-determination for all Germans by peaceful means. During the exchange of views, the Soviet delegation declared that it might, in the right circumstances, accept such a letter without rebuttal.' Baring, *Machtwechsel*, p. 318 and copy of text from Baring Papers.

. . . **joint 'declarations of intent'** . . . see Meissner, *Moskau-Bonn*, pp. 1280–81. There also an interview with Scheel, who says that while these declarations are not binding in international law, they 'form for the future, too, the basis of our behaviour, they have political significance'.

. . . **'Twenty-five years after . . .'** Meissner, *Moskau-Bonn*, pp. 1272–73. An earlier draft has the weaker formulation 'with this treaty nothing is given away, which was not already lost in 1945'. AdsD: Dep WB, Publ 0285.

. . . **'accept[ed] the results of history'** quoted in Bender, *Neue Ostpolitik*, p. 165. The translation given in Brandt, *People and Politics*, p. 407, is 'accepts the consequences of history'.

. . . **'gambled away by a criminal regime . . .'** see the text of his 7 December 1970 television address in *Texte*, I/6, pp. 263–65. Many drafts of this powerful speech are in AdsD: Dep WB, Publ. Responding to a letter of 7 December 1970 from Marion Gräfin Dönhoff, in which she said she had wept the day through, Willy Brandt replied, on 13 December 1970: 'So far as the "weeping" is concerned, it overcame me at my desk, as I was preparing the texts for Warsaw.' AdsD: Dep WB, BK4.

. . . **'If two states agree . . .'** Meissner, *Moskau-Bonn*, p. 1416. Since this passage appeared — word-for-word — in the leaked fragments from the records of the Moscow negotiations (see above p. 72 and note) it rather strengthened the argument for the genuineness of the leaked fragments.

. . . **by German leaders as much** . . . in an interview with *US News and World Report*, 29 December 1969, Brandt said: 'I must confess that I have stopped speaking about reunification'. But stopping speaking and stopping thinking are two slightly different things.

. . . **conceded too much** . . . this impression was strengthened by publication of the so-called 'Gromyko paper', which two leading Christian Democrat opponents of the treaties, Werner Marx and Karl Theodor Freiherr von und zu Guttenberg, claimed had been tabled by Gromyko during his talks with Bahr on 6 March. This bore a remarkable resemblance to the final 'Bahr paper', although with some interesting minor differences. The 'Gromyko paper' spoke, for example, of the 'unalterability' of frontiers. (See Meissner, *Moskau-Bonn*, pp. 1222–23.) In a letter to Brandt ('Lieber W.B.') from Moscow, dated 1 August 1970 — that is, during Scheel's final negotiations — Egon Bahr wrote: 'A small quotation from the negotiations: Gromyko: "The opposition has talked of a Gromyko paper. You sitting round this table will surely not doubt that I am Gromyko, and I don't know this paper." ' AdsD: Dep WB, BK 2. But in the 'delegation report' telegram from Moscow dated 6 March 1970 (copy in the author's possession) there is reference to 'ten theses' handed over by Gromyko, in response to a paper handed over by Bahr the previous day. Insofar as the 'Gromyko paper' existed, it must probably be seen as one of several interim summations, following the more than three weeks of talks that he had already conducted with Bahr.

... **the armchair Metternich** ... while Bahr had direct experience of East Germany, he had little direct experience of the Soviet Union and Eastern Europe, having only negotiated one agreement with Czechoslovakia, and briefly visited Romania. See Lehmann, *Öffnung*, p. 171, who contrasts him in this respect unfavourably with Schmidt, and reports the professional diplomats' sarcastic quip that 'Bahr speculates for Germany'.

... **'a notable success ...'** Meissner, *Moskau-Bonn*, p. 789.

... **'painful' concessions** ... Meissner, *Moskau-Bonn*, p. 1416.

... **'Consistently in favour ...'** Andrei Gromyko, *Memories*, translated by Harold Shukman (London: Hutchinson, 1989), p. 198.

As in a judo throw ... see Bahr's own lapidary summary in Bahr, *Sicherheit*, p. 36.

Brandt's handwritten notes ... in AdsD: Dep WB, BK 91. Brandt's reminiscences of these meetings are in *People and Politics*, Chapter 13, and *Erinnerungen*, pp. 195–210.

... **he would later note** ... Brandt, *Erinnerungen*, p. 205. In conversation with the author (Bonn, 2 October 1991), Brandt observed that this wish to settle the reparations issue once and for all reflected his concern about public opinion in West Germany, for, he observed, support for the Ostpolitik was not really as broad and deep as it seemed in the 1972 election.

... **the 'heart of Europe'** ... recollection of Antonius Eitel, Bonn, 1 July 1991.

... **an explicit linkage** ... for the origins of this linkage see Schmid, *Entscheidung*, p. 62 ff and p. 92. On the 'cover sheet' to the 'Bahr paper' it was plainly noted: '3. It must be stated to the Soviet Union, in addition to the treaty to be concluded, that the Federal Government sees a satisfactory regulation of the situation in and around Berlin as an indispensable part of its détente policy, and will not put the treaty into force until such a satisfactory regulation has been achieved.' Copy from Baring Papers.

... **notes scribbled for his response** ... in AdsD: Dep WB, BK 91. The reading of '*Ml-Eur*' as '*Mitteleuropa*' was given by Brandt himself in conversation with the author (Bonn, 2 October 1991).

This so-called *Berlin-Junktim* . . . One of the Christian Democratic opposition's criticisms was that the Brandt government had signed the Moscow Treaty before getting a satisfactory agreement on Berlin — see, for example, the statements by former Foreign Minister Gerhard Schröder in *Texte* I/6, pp. 308–9 & 378–81. Once again, there is a large literature on just this one point. For two balanced and differentiated accounts, one moderately critical of the Government's conduct, the other moderately supportive, see Meissner, *Moskau-Bonn*, p. 787 ff, and Löwenthal, *Vom kalten Krieg*, p. 82 ff. Brandt and Bahr were certainly the last people to neglect the special interests of Berlin.

Immensely intricate and delicate negotiations . . . a brilliant and vivid account is given in Kissinger, *White House Years*, pp. 801 f, 805 f, and 823–33. See also Brandt, *Erinnerungen*, pp. 229–31, Brandt, *People and Politics*, pp. 387–93, Bark & Gress, *Democracy and its Discontents*, pp. 190–99, Griffith, *Ostpolitik*, p. 196 ff, Bender, *Neue Ostpolitik*, pp. 186–90.

. . . the two Metternichs of détente . . . Bahr and Kissinger had a healthy mutual suspicion and grudging mutual respect. Thus Kissinger, in his memoirs, describes Bahr as 'a German nationalist who wanted to exploit Germany's central position to bargain with both sides' but adds: 'as for his alleged deviousness, I tended to share Metternich's view that in a negotiation the perfectly straightforward person was the most difficult to deal with. I at any rate did not lack the self-confidence to confront Bahr's tactics.' Kissinger, *White House Years*, pp. 410–11. For his part, Bahr paid tribute to Kissinger's deviousness in an interview with Hans Magnus Enzensberger in *Kursbuch*, 77, September 1984, p. 99.

In conversation with the author, Egon Bahr averred that Kissinger's initial mistrust seemed to him to have been largely overcome by the time of the Moscow Treaty, and that they worked together closely and effectively thereafter, especially in the negotiation of the Quadripartite Agreement on Berlin. (Egon Bahr, Potsdam-Berlin, 29 June 1991). A conversation with Henry Kissinger on the same day suggested that perhaps some of the mistrust after all remained. But while describing Bahr as a left-nationalist, and arguing that he was perhaps excessively preoccupied with the Bonn-Moscow-Berlin triangle, Kissinger nonetheless acknowledged Bahr's analytical brilliance and strategic clarity. (Henry Kissinger, Berlin, 29 June 1991).

. . . the resulting Quadripartite Agreement . . . English text in Grenville, *Treaties*, pp. 196–98, German text, with the important annexes, in *Verträge*, pp. 70–87.

. . . 'it is still difficult for me . . .' quoted in Kissinger, *White House Years*, p. 830.

. . . 'three Zs' . . . see Bender, *Neue Ostpolitik*, p. 187 f. For judgements on the agreement overall, compare Bark & Gress, *Democracy and its Discontents*, pp. 196–97, Meissner, *Moskau-Bonn*, pp. 794–95, Griffith, *Ostpolitik*, pp. 196–200, Kissinger, *White House Years*, pp. 830–31.

. . . 'ties' . . . in one of those absurd diplomatic fandangles in which the post-war history of Berlin was replete, the French declined to have the German text of this agreement about Germany recognised as 'official'. As a result, there were two German texts, West and East. The West Germans, for example, translated 'ties' as *Bindungen* while the East Germans used the weaker *Verbindungen*, thus providing stuff for further endless legal-symbolic-theological disputation. See Brandt, *Erinnerungen*, pp. 230–31, and Kissinger, *White House Years*, p. 832.

'Tomorrow [i.e. 13 August 1970] . . .' Meissner, *Moskau-Bonn*, p. 1273.

. . . top of his personal agenda . . . see the handwritten notes in AdsD: Dep WB, BK 92, where the item 'DDR' comes second only to the complex 'ratification/Berlin'.

. . . 'regards the creation of *a modus vivendi* . . .' AdsD: Dep WB, BK 58. In the German he does not use any article, definite or indefinite, before 'central task', thus leaving it open to the reader to guess whether it is *a* or *the* central task of his policy! This omission of the article is a characteristic trick of Brandt's style, one of the small keys to its elevated vagueness.

. . . a message sent with Egon Bahr . . . in AdsD: Dep WB, BK 74.

. . . Bahr spent four hours . . . Schröder, *Bahr*, pp. 204–05.

. . . what direct effect . . . in his 1976 memoirs, Brandt notes that Brezhnev visited East Berlin in November 1971 'after I had been his guest in the Crimea. . . It is likely that he prompted the GDR leaders to take a few initiatives in the matter of intra-German agreements — at any rate, that had been my suggestion to him.' Brandt, *People and Politics*, p. 393.

A few of these documents . . . already accessible . . . notably in the Central Party Archive (ZPA) in East Berlin. At the time of writing, publication of such documents has mostly occurred in the form of more or less sensational 'revelations', generally of documents sold or leaked by people in high places, or with access to high places, in the former ruling apparatus of the GDR. This is the case, for example, with the bestselling Peter Przbylski, *Tatort Politbüro. Die Akte Honecker* (Berlin: Rowohlt, 1991), henceforth cited as Przybylski, *Tatort 1*. This is a selection of documents from the file of the state prosecutor's judicial investigation against Erich Honecker, after his downfall, documents copied, selected, and tendentiously introduced by the former press spokesman of the state prosecutor's office of the GDR. The dubious form of the publication does not seriously put in question the authenticity of the actual documents, although it does increase the risk of taking them out of their proper context. One must hope that a more disinterested, systematic and scholarly publication will follow.

. . . Honecker's own notes . . . typewritten notes dated 2.12.1969 and 15.5.1970. These come from a remarkable source, a synthetic-leather-bound volume of photocopied documents with, embossed in gilt on the front cover, the single word '*Dokumente*'. Almost all the documents in the volume concern relations between the East German and Soviet Party leaderships at critical junctures, in 1953, and then in 1969–71. The collection was apparently put together at the behest of Erich Honecker, and circulated to all members of the Politburo in February 1989, but the copies were then collected in. Kurt Hager recalled this curious sally in conversation with the author (Berlin, 8 May 1992) and interpreted it as part of Honecker's defence against any attempt to replace him. These documents should demonstrate that he had always had the closest ties with Moscow. Similarly Egon Krenz (Berlin, 29 September 1992). Copy 29 of the 'Dokumente' can be found in ZPA: JIV 2/2A/3196.

It should however be noted that these documents were prepared in this form for this particular purpose under Honecker's supervision. A collection of the manuscript originals on which the *'Dokumente'* are based is apparently in the Central Party Archive, but was not available to the author for examination. It is possible that amendments may therefore have been made, or simple errors of transcription.

Many of the documents in Pryzybylski, *Tatort 1*, are actually taken from this source, as he himself notes on pp. 101–14.

... Brezhnev and Honecker on 28 July 1970 ... this also comes from the 'Dokumente' (see note immediately above). For the convenience of readers, page references are given to the version printed in Przybylski, *Tatort 1*, pp. 280–88, but quotations have been checked against the copy in ZPA: JIV 2/2A/3196. However note again the possibility that some changes may have been made in preparing the documents for circulation to the Politburo in 1989.

'*I tell you quite openly* . . .' Przybylski, *Tatort 1*, p. 281.

'This will not solve . . .' ibid, p. 283.

'Brandt is under double pressure . . .' ibid, p. 287.

'It . . . must not come' ibid, p. 283.

. . . 'concentrate everything . . .' ibid, p. 284.

. . . 'objectively one must pay him . . .' this and the following quotation are from the record (*Niederschrift*) of the conversation between Honecker and Brezhnev in the Kremlin on 18 June 1974, now in ZPA: IV 2/2.035/55.

. . . recognise the status quo in order to overcome it . . . Bahr had already come close to this dialectical formula in his Tutzing speech, see above p. 65. In a television discussion in September 1967, he observed that the Bonn government had accepted the status quo: 'When the Federal Government says renunciation-of-force. What else does that mean?' But he went on to say that the Government 'wants to start from the status quo, in order to overcome it'. See *Dokumente* V/1, pp. 1575–87, this on pp. 1579–80. In his Nobel Peace Prize lecture, Brandt returned to the achievement of the first permit agreement in Berlin and said: 'this was in a nutshell the application of the insight that there can be a new, only apparent paradox, which will have benign effects: to improve the situation through recognition of the situation as it is', see *Texte* I/6, p. 307.

. . . 'Alliances, us: Rome, loyal' . . . in AdsD: Dep WB, BK 91.

. . . 'Basic principle: in loyalty to allies . . .' in AdsD: Dep WB, BK 91.

In his Nobel Peace Prize lecture . . . reprinted in *Texte* I/9, pp. 302–19, this on p. 313. He repeats the same point in his *Erinnerungen*, p. 187.

... **to West Germany's Western partners** ... for a wealth of detail on this, see Kurt Birrenbach's account of his trips to Western capitals to sound out reactions to the new Ostpolitik, in Birrenbach, *Sondermissionen.*

... **two working papers** ... this was attested several times by Bahr, for example in Bahr, *Sicherheit*, p. 42, and Egon Bahr, *Was wird aus den Deutschen?* (Reinbek: Rowohlt, 1982), pp. 221–22. In his interview with Hans Magnus Enzensberger in *Kursbuch*, 77, September 1984, p. 99, he notes that 'the paper' (presumably that on security) was also shown to Walter Scheel.

... **to 'analyse German interests** ...' this paper was first published, as a leak, in the weekly *Quick*, 27 September 1973, under the provocative title 'How Egon Bahr wants to neutralise Germany'. Bahr himself reprints it in Bahr, *Sicherheit*, pp. 42–52, commenting that 'the overcoming of the two blocs through a European security system, in order to achieve unity, remains a task, after unity has been achieved'. Egon Bahr kindly made available to the author a copy of the original paper, which is datelined Bonn, 27 June 1968.

... **from Conception A to Conception C** ... Conception B was an intermediate stage in which Nato and Warsaw Pact would be 'tied together' by common organs, eventually becoming an 'institutional roof (permanent European security conference) over the pacts ...' ibid.

... **Walter Hahn** ... see Walter F Hahn, 'West Germany's Ostpolitik. The Grand Design of Egon Bahr', in *Orbis*, Winter 1973, pp. 859–80. This is not only a vivid report but also a fine analysis. In a note to Willy Brandt dated 19 August 1968, Bahr reported on an evening discussion of the security paper *'bei Ducki'* (that is, Duckwitz). The consensus was, he wrote, that C was the really interesting part, on which more preparatory work needed to be done. This from AdsD: Dep EB.

... **what the Federal Republic's Western allies feared** ... for a measured account of such fears see Kissinger, *White House Years.* Kissinger's mistrust of the new German Ostpolitik is more sharply and critically recalled in Seymour M Hersh, *Kissinger: The Price of Power* (London: Faber, 1983), pp. 415–22.

... **'in foreign policy** ...' in AdsD: Dep WB, BK 68.

... **pressed hard but unsuccessfully** ... note that Article 5 of the Basic Treaty with the GDR made an emphatic commitment of both states to supporting both conventional and nuclear arms reductions in Europe. For the exact wording see *Zehn Jahre*, p. 206.

'We deflected the German initiative ...' Kissinger, *White House Years*, p. 534.

... **simply exhausted** ... Egon Bahr, Bonn, 4 July 1991.

... **motives and attitudes** ... this point is made by, among others, Schmid, *Politik*, p. 92 f and Schmid, *Entscheidung, passim*; Meissner, *Moskau-Bonn*, p. 777 ff; Wolfgang Schollwer in *Liberal*, 1/88, p. 46.

... **the support of Germany's Western partners** ... probably not untypical of British attitudes was Peter Carrington's comment to Kurt Birrenbach that he had 'put aside' his initial fears after seeing the commitment with which Helmut Schmidt, as Defence Minister, supported the development of Nato and the maintenance of close ties with the United States, see Birrenbach, *Sondermissionen*, pp. 377–78.

The existential argument . . . this argument is made most clearly and forcefully in Baring, *Grössenwahn*.

. . . **urged most forcefully by Helmut Schmidt** . . . see his book *Strategie des Gleichgewichts. Deutsche Friedenspolitik und die Weltmächte* (Stuttgart: Seewald, 1969), translated into English as *The Balance of Power. Germany's Peace Policy and the Superpowers* (London: Kimber, 1971).

. . . **a leitmotif of the new policy** . . . see above p. 22 f. Brandt, *Erinnerungen*, pp. 185–95. Link, *Ära Brandt*, p. 224, notes that when Brandt arranged to meet Brezhnev at Oreanda in the Crimea in September 1971, 'the Western allies were merely informed, not consulted'.

'I think it is no exaggeration . . .' in AdsD: Dep WB, BK 42

. . . **tactical for some** . . . Thus Bahr's working paper of 21 September 1969 concludes by considering two possible German tactics inside the EEC, and comes down in favour of the more conciliatory one partly because the Federal Republic would need the 'good will' (in English in the original) of its closest European allies for its alliance policy and Ostpolitik. Copy from AdsD: Dep EB, in the author's possession.

. . . **its multilateral development** . . . see, for example, an interview Brandt gave to the London *Times*, reprinted in *Bulletin*, 1 March 1973, pp. 225–30, esp. p. 229.

'After public opinion in our country . . .' letter of 30 May 1973, in AdsD: Dep WB, BK 58.

. . . **Falin, said** . . . note of 1 June 1973 by Carl-Werner Sanne, in AdsD: Dep WB, BK 58

'The Soviet side may not realise . . .' letter of 30 December 1973, in AdsD: Dep WB, BK 58.

. . . **the two sets of talks as intimately linked** . . . in a letter to Brezhnev dated 4 May 1973 he reported his full agreement with Nixon on the 'inner connection' between 'the subjects treated in Helsinki and in Vienna'. AdsD: Dep WB, BK 58. For a clear public statement see *Bulletin*, 14 July 1972, p. 1361.

. . . **a time-scale of five years** . . . see his notes for his meeting with Brezhnev in Bonn, dated 18 May 1973, and those dated 20 May 1973, in AdsD: Dep WB, BK 94.

. . . **Waldemar Besson** . . . Waldemar Besson, 'The Conflict of Traditions. The Historical Basis of German Foreign Policy', in Karl Kaiser & Roger Morgan, eds., *Britain and West Germany. Changing Societies and the Future of Foreign Policy* (Oxford: Oxford University Press, 1971), pp. 61–80.

Henry Kissinger ... Kissinger, *Years of Upheaval*, p. 147, see also Kissinger, *White House Years*, pp. 410–12.

'I have been fascinated ...' Cramer, *Bahr*, p. 65.

... **'the real mastery ...'** ibid., p. 66.

'one of the great statesmen ...' reprinted in *Texte* I/6, pp. 351–2. For other indications of Brandt's ambivalent and qualified respect for Bismarck see Prowe, 'Anfänge' in Benz & Graml, *Aspekte*, p. 251, and the references in Brandt, *People and Politics*.

... **the system demanded** ... the next three paragraphs owe a significant debt to the very stimulating chapter by Josef Joffe in Gordon, *Eroding Empire*. He uses there the term 'synchronisation'; the distinction between 'horizontal' and 'vertical' synchronisation is, I believe, mine.

... **a principle of synchronisation** ... this was implicit already in the crucial statement in the 'Bahr paper' that the treaties with the Soviet Union, the GDR, Poland and Czechoslovakia formed 'a single whole' (see above, p. 73). Bahr spells out the imperative of horizontal synchronisation clearly in Cramer, *Bahr*, p. 70. For a clear public statement by Schmidt see *Bundestag Plenarprotokolle*, 7/218, p. 15085 (29 January 1976). The contrast with American 'differentiation' is made by Joffe in Gordon, *Eroding Empire*, pp. 162–64.

Similarly, but *a fortiori*, ... this was clearly spelled out by Schmidt in his 1975 state of the nation address, to a chorus of 'very true!' from Herbert Wehner, see *Bundestag Plenarprotokolle*, 7/146, p. 10038 (30 January 1975).

... **the first external preoccupation** ... two excellent general treatments of German foreign policy in the Schmidt period are Haftendorn, *Sicherheit* and Link, *Ära Schmidt*.

'Never since ...' This and following quotations are from the 10 April 1977 typescript version of the paper, which was originally written over the New Year holiday. Now in AdsD: HS 002.

... **Hans Georg Lehmann** ... see Lehmann, *Öffnung*, p. 201 and passim.

... **a representative of this** *Frontgeneration* ... this element emerges very clearly from Schmidt's own memoirs and statements. Franz Josef Strauss himself observed in his review of the first volume of the memoirs that this was a formative experience which he and Schmidt had in common, and which had a decisive influence on both their subsequent approaches to the Soviet Union, see *Die Zeit*, 7 October 1988. A brief account of Schmidt's war years can be found in Harald Steffahn, *Helmut Schmidt* (Reinbek: Rowohlt, 1990).

... **methods and manners** ... this is quite vividly apparent in the contrast between the organisation of the official papers of the Chancellery under Brandt and under Schmidt. The point was also made by Holger Börner in conversation with the author, Bonn, 11 July 1991. It is interesting to note that Schmidt enrolled in the Bundeswehr Reserve forces, in his old rank of first lieutenant, and in 1958 was promoted to Captain, see the brief account (with picture) in Harald Steffahn,

Helmut Schmidt (Reinbek: Rowohlt, 1990), pp. 69–70. Gromyko wrote sourly that 'although capable and strong-willed, he had not fully freed himself from the outlook of an officer in the German Wehrmacht', Andrei Gromyko, *Memories* (London: Hutchinson, 1989), p. 202.

'We seek . . .' Helmut Schmidt, *The Balance of Power. German Peace Policy and the Superpowers* (London: Kimber, 1971), p. 24. German edition: *Strategie des Gleichgewichts. Deutsche Friedenspolitik und die Weltmächte* (Stuttgart: Seewald, 1969).

. . . in his bilateral discussions with the United States . . . a thorough treatment of this aspect of his Chancellorship is Heep, *Schmidt und Amerika*.

. . . 'in the eyes of the world . . .' this and following quotations from the 10 April 1977 typescript version in AdsD: HS 002.

. . . summit meetings . . . on this see Schmidt's own comments in his essay, 'Glanz und Elend der Gipfeldiplomatie—und ihre Notwendigkeit' in Helmut Schmidt and Walter Hesselbach, eds., *Kämpfer ohne Pathos. Festschrift für Hans Matthöfer zum 60. Geburtstag am 25. September 1985* (Bonn: Verlag Neue Gesellschaft, 1985), pp. 235–39. See also Dieter Rebentisch, 'Gipfeldemokratie und Weltökonomie', in *Archiv für Sozialgeschichte*, Vol. XXVIII, 1988, pp. 307–32.

. . . described as *Staatslenker* . . . see, for example, Schmidt, *Menschen und Mächte*, pp. 141, 459.

. . . 'the role of the Federal Republic . . .' this and following quotation from the protocol by the Foreign Ministry interpreter E Hartmann of the conversation between Schmidt and Brezhnev on 4 May 1978, with manuscript corrections in Schmidt's hand. Now in AdsD: HS 174.

. . . a good and even sentimental relationship . . . In a conversation with Mrs Thatcher on 18 November 1981, Schmidt said that Brezhnev 'reminded him of the Russian characters that we know from the great Russian novels . . . After six meetings, he [i.e. Schmidt] had developed a personal sympathy for him. His wish for peace is genuine. He is deeply afraid of a new war. He comes back again and again to his own wartime experiences.' This from a minute of the conversation by the then head of the foreign policy department in the Chancellery, Otto von der Gablentz, now in AdsD: HS 199. In his memoirs, Schmidt also characterises Brezhnev as a man such as Maxim Gorky and other Russian writers might have described, see Schmidt, *Menschen und Mächte*, p. 71.

. . . Schmidt responded . . . Schmidt's account is in *Menschen und Mächte*, pp. 19–20. See also Brandt's account in *People and Politics*, p. 364, where he writes that 'Brezhnev was deeply moved by the reminiscences of the then Finance and former Defence Minister'. Also in Brandt, *Erinnerungen*, pp. 201–2.

. . . 'when war reminiscences are exchanged . . .' Brandt, *Erinnerungen*, p. 201. The comment is related directly to his account of Schmidt's response to Brezhnev.

. . . genuine sorrow . . . Schmidt, *Menschen und Mächte*, p. 131.

484 · *Notes to Pages 88–90*

. . . **better understood** . . . ibid., p. 228. Schmidt repeated this in conversation with the author, London, 3 June 1991. The point is also picked up by Brandt, *Erinnerungen*, p. 359.

. . . **a conversation with** . . . **Falin** . . . minute of the conversation on 25 September 1974 by the then head of the foreign policy department in the Chancellery, Carl-Werner Sanne, now in AdsD: HS 130.

. . . **the GDR announced** . . . see Link, *Ära Schmidt*, p. 293.

. . . **Berlin, which occupied a great deal of time** . . . on this, see the useful summary in Avril Pittman, *From Ostpolitik to Reunification. West German-Soviet Political Relations since 1974* (Cambridge: Cambridge University Press, 1992), Chapter 3.

. . . **Gromyko spoke dismissively** . . . following quotations are from the minute of a conversation between Schmidt and Gromyko on 16 September 1974, in preparation for the Chancellor's visit to Moscow. The note seems to have been written by the then head of the foreign policy department of the Chancellery, Carl-Werner Sanne, and is now in AdsD: HS 129.

. . . . **'strict observance and full application'** . . . Brandt, *People and Politics*, p. 365.

. . **a personal letter** . . . datelined Hamburg [not Bonn!], 5 April 1975. A copy of this letter was made available to me from AdsD: Dep EB, 409, by kind permission of Helmut Schmidt and Egon Bahr. The first copies of the whole correspondence with Brezhnev are presumably in Schmidt's private archive in Hamburg.

. . . **somewhat at odds with the Foreign Ministry** . . . the tougher and more status-oriented line of the Foreign Ministry was authoritatively expressed by Günther van Well in an article entitled 'The participation of Berlin in international affairs. An urgent point on the East-West agenda', in EA, 20/1976, pp. 647–56.

. . . **the presence of Federal Government institutions.** . . the siting of the Federal Office for Environmental Protection in West Berlin in 1974 had provoked strong Soviet protests.

. . . **openly and contemptuously dismissive** . . . even in his memoirs he described the Carter human rights campaign as as 'mistake' and a 'threat to the détente process', Schmidt, *Menschen und Mächte*, pp. 222–23.

. . . **in a lecture in 1991** . . . this was a lecture to members of the German Society for Foreign Policy (DGAP) in Bonn in September 1991, printed as 'Germany's role in the new Europe' in EA 21/1991, pp. 611–24, this on p. 624.

His book published in 1969 . . . Published under this title in English in 1971. The original German title was *Strategie des Gleichgewichts. Deutsche Friedenspolitik und die Weltmächte* (Stuttgart: Seewald, 1969).

The foreign policy of a state . . . attributed to Georges Pompidou by Michael

Stürmer in Peter R Weilemann, ed., *Aspects of the German Question* (Sankt Augustin: Konrad-Adenauer-Stiftung, 1985), p. 9.

... **a key element in that Westpolitik of Brezhnev** ... this is clearly brought out in the excellent discussion in Stent, *Embargo to Ostpolitik*. (See also the further discussion in Chapter Four, below.)

... **jumped into a gleaming new Mercedes** ... ibid., p. 192.

... **in glowing terms** ... ibid., p. 193. Brandt, *People and Politics*, p. 360 ff.

... **'the political motive ...'** minute of a conversation between Schmidt and Gromyko on 16 September 1974, now in AdsD: HS 129.

... **some economic motives** ... see the balanced discussion in Stent, *Embargo to Ostpolitik*, Chapter 9. See also Chapter Five, below, pp. 244 f. In conversation with the Chancellor on 25 February 1974, the Soviet Ambassador, Valentin Falin, noted in passing that the Soviet Union would buy 10,000 lorries from the firm Klöckner-Humboldt-Deutz. This, he observed, was one third of the annual output of that firm! See the minute now in AdsD: HS 130.

... **a clear complementarity** ... this point was made frequently by both sides. Thus, in the aforementioned conversation with Gromyko in September 1974, Schmidt said: 'We proceeded on the assumption that the conditions and products of the two economies were complementary. The Federal Republic could supply investment goods and technology in large quantities to the Soviet Union ... The Soviet Union could supply us with raw materials and processed raw materials'. Note in AdsD: HS 129. In a personal letter from Brezhnev to Schmidt, dated 23 September 1974, the Soviet leader expressed his satisfaction 'that we agree to pay special attention to the economic theme during your stay in Moscow' — German version ('unofficial translation') now in AdsD: HS 130.

... **some 300,000 jobs** ... Stent, *Embargo to Ostpolitik*, p. 217.

... **for advancing German national interests** ... Schmidt, *Menschen und Mächte*, pp. 138–40. In Schmidt, *Nachbarn*, p. 448, he goes so far as to say that to the Bonn government eastern trade and eastern credits were 'of purely political interest'.

... **'the long-term securing ...'** the memorandum, dated 17 October 1977, was signed by the then head of the Chancellery department for economic and financial policy, and is now in AdsD: HS 168.

... **the barter deals frowned upon** ... this was a major subject at the aforementioned brainstorming session, on 18 October 1977, see the minute now in AdsD: HS 168.

... **Kaliningrad ... Kursk** ... see Stent, *Embargo to Ostpolitik*, pp. 223–32.

... **'into the third millennium'** ... this, in direct quotation marks, in the minute of the meeting on 18 October 1977, now in AdsD: HS 168.

... **a very broadly framed agreement** ... text in *Bulletin*, 9 May 1978, pp. 431–2.

... 'political act without parallel ...' quoted in Stent, *Embargo to Ostpolitik*, p. 206.

... 'It is not a historic accord.' ibid., p. 207.

The total volume ... this and further figures in this paragraph are taken from ibid., pp. 209–15.

... nearly thirty per cent ... Stent, *Embargo to Ostpolitik*, pp. 212–13, gives a figure of 28 per cent by 1990, which she says would represent five per cent of total energy supplies. Schmidt set a ceiling of 30 per cent, which he says would be six per cent of the Federal Republic's total energy imports, see Schmidt, *Menschen und Mächte*, p. 79. The actual figures for 1989 were 30 per cent of West Germany's natural gas supplies and 4.99 per cent of the total value of its energy imports. Figures from the Foreign Ministry.

... confidential personal letters ... the author has at the time of writing only been able to see a few letters from this remarkable correspondence, in copies from AdsD: Dep EB. Nonetheless, even from these the warming of tone is apparent.

... the already seriously ill Soviet leader ... Schmidt notes that he was dismayed by the obvious deterioration in Brezhnev's health, *Menschen und Mächte*, p. 98. Valentin Falin says that Brezhnev was 'mortally sick' from as early as 1975. Valentin Falin, Hamburg, 14 May 1992.

... a Joint Declaration ... *Bulletin*, 9 May 1978, pp. 429–31. As already noted, the word 'détente' here occurs seven times in two pages.

... a sharp polarisation ... this argument produced an immense and largely ephemeral literature. For those who wish to get a taste of the argument at a fairly high level one might recommend the sharply contrasting books of Robert Conquest, *Present Danger. Towards a Foreign Policy* (Oxford: Blackwell, 1979) and Fred Halliday, *The Making of the Second Cold War* (London: Verso, 1983).

... withering criticism ... see, for example, Schewardnadse, *Zukunft*, p. 109 f and the devastating passage on p. 116. For an early public expression, see the article by the Soviet policy intellectual and Foreign Ministry adviser, Vyacheslav Dashitschev, in *Literaturnaya Gazeta*, 18 May 1988. It is reprinted in Wolfgang Seiffert, *Die Deutschen und Gorbatschow. Chancen für einen Interessenausgleich* (Erlangen: Straube, 1989), pp. 211–25.

... influence in the Third World ... this is, of course, a highly complex and controversial subject. For a very measured discussion of this and the impact on Soviet-American relations, see Garthoff, *Détente*, esp. Chapter 19. For a more critical view, which was to become highly influential under the Reagan Administration, see the 11 November 1976 policy statement of the Committee on the Present Danger, reprinted in Charles Tyroler, ed., *Alerting America. The Papers of the Committee on the Present Danger* (Washington: Pergamon Brassey's, 1984), pp. 3–5. For accounts more sympathetic to the Soviet position see Fred Halliday, *The Making of the Second Cold War* (London: Verso, 1983), especially Chapter 4, and Jonathan Steele, *World Power. Soviet Foreign Policy under Brezhnev and Andropov* (London: Michael Joseph, 1983).

... 'in my view'... Letter of 13 February 1976. Copy in AdsD: Dep EB, 409.

'Altogether...' this in a luncheon speech on 5 May 1978, see *Bulletin*, 9 May 1978, p. 428.

... 'he liked to think...' minute of their conversation on 16 September 1974, now in AdsD: HS 129.

Defence or Retaliation... *Verteidigung oder Vergeltung. Ein deutscher Beitrag zum strategischen Problem der Nato* (Stuttgart: Seewald, 1961). English edition: *Defence or Retaliation. A German Contribution to the Consideration of Nato's Strategic Problem* (Edinburgh: Oliver and Boyd, 1962).

... a memorable speech to the Bundestag... see *Bundestag Plenarprotokolle*, 3/87, pp. 4758–4767 (5 November 1959).

... 'Why?'... Lehmann, *Öffnung*, p. 172

... the West German leader had serious concerns... by some accounts, Schmidt was significantly influenced in this concern about the gap in the chain of deterrence by a group of American and European defence intellectuals headed by Albert Wohlstetter, see Garthoff, *Détente*, p. 855, and the article referred to there by Fred Kaplan in the *New York Times Magazine*, 9 December 1979. It is interesting to find that this claim was taken up by one of the leading Soviet specialists on the United States, Georgi Arbatov, see Georgi A. Arbatov, *Cold War or Détente? The Soviet Viewpoint* (London: Zed Books, 1983), p. 126. Schmidt himself makes favourable mention of Wohlstetter in *Menschen und Mächte*, p. 274 but in a letter to the author (13 November 1992) Schmidt denied that there was a specific influence with regard to the SS-20 build-up.

By his own account... Schmidt, *Menschen und Mächte*, p. 64

In what was to become a famous speech... the best account of this whole episode is in Haftendorn, *Sicherheit*, pp. 1–31, with the most important parts of the speech reprinted on pp. 195–212. English text in *Survival*, Vol. 20, No. 1, Jan-Feb 1978, pp. 2–10. It is remarkable how little of the speech was actually devoted to this subject. Schmidt's own brief account is in *Menschen und Mächte*, pp. 230–31. In a letter to the author (13 November 1992) he himself stressed that the speech itself was rather diplomatic and what he called 'the real burst-out' happened over dinner.

... Michael Howard, would describe... conversation with the author.

... a transatlantic comedy of errors... this is, of course, a slightly frivolous summary of an immensely complicated story, with intricate military and political arguments on both sides of the Atlantic. Good summary accounts are given by Garthoff, *Détente*, Chapter 25, Haftendorn, *Sicherheit*, Chapter 3, Link, *Ära Schmidt*, pp. 315–21, and Heep, *Schmidt und Amerika*, pp. 113–51. Writing in 1982, Zbigniew Brzezinski observed: 'I was personally never persuaded that we needed [the new weapons] for military reasons. I was persuaded reluctantly that we needed [them] to obtain European support for SALT. This was largely because Chancellor Schmidt made such a big deal out of the so-called Eurostrategic imbalance that was being generated by the Soviet deployment of the SS-20. To keep him in line we felt that some response in Europe on the intermediate level would be necessary.' Quoted in Strobe Talbott, *Deadly Gambits. The Reagan Administration and the Stalemate in Nuclear Arms Control* (London: Picador, 1985), p. 33

. . . **Guadeloupe** . . . see Schmidt's account in *Menschen und Mächte*, pp. 231–32. However both Link, *Ära Schmidt*, p. 318 and Heep, *Schmidt und Amerika*, pp. 130–32, point out that, according to reports at the time and the memoirs of Carter and Brzezinski, Schmidt was more or less explicitly criticised by the American, French and British leaders for what they saw as his excessive fear of offending the Soviet Union by a new deployment.

. . . **set for 1983** . . . Hans Apel, the then German Defence Minister, notes in his 'political diary' that one reason for this deadline was that the Pershing II and Cruise missiles would simply not be ready before 1983. See Apel, *Abstieg*, p.72.

. . . **'détente could not survive** . . .' text in Haftendorn, *Sicherheit*, pp. 232–3. For good summary accounts of American and German reactions see Garthoff, *Détente*, Chapters 26 and 27, and Heep, *Schmidt und Amerika*, pp. 153–92.

. . . **to visit Moscow** . . . see Schmidt, *Menschen und Mächte*, pp. 108–25, Link, *Ära Schmidt*, p. 335 ff, Heep, *Schmidt und Amerika*, pp. 186–89.

. . . **a high-risk visit** . . . but Link, *Ära Schmidt*, p. 335, points out that on 19 June 1980 Schmidt had been given an indication, by someone identified by Link only as a high-placed 'American personality not in the government', following a conversation with Ambassador Dobrynin in Washington, that the Chancellor could expect some 'success' on this trip.

. . . **to negotiate** . . . thus letting fall the 'conditions' of prior ratification of SALT II, and a withdrawal of the Nato two-track decision. See report and quotations from leaked protocols of the meeting in *Die Welt*, 7 July 1980. The Soviet party leadership's report of this meeting sent to the East German party leadership can be found in ZPA: IV 2/2.035/65.

'The dialogue . . .' Klaus Bölling, *Die letzten 30 Tage des Kanzlers Helmut Schmidt. Ein Tagebuch* (Reinbek: Rowohlt, 1982), p. 116. In this quotation Bölling appears to be summarising, in indirect speech, the gist of what Schmidt himself said.

The Polish revolution . . . on this see Garton Ash, *Solidarity*, and Jerzy Holzer, 'Solidarność 1980–81. Geneza i Historia (Warsaw: Kraag, 1983), translated into German as 'Solidarität'. Die Geschichte einer freien Gewerkschaft in Polen (Munich: Beck, 1985), edited by Hans Henning Hahn.

'If the Russians invade . . .' quoted by Josef Joffe in Gordon, *Eroding Empire*, p. 161. See *Der Spiegel*, 1/1982.

. . . **the Bonn government was not entirely clear** . . . this is discussed in more detail in Chapter Five, pp. 288 ff.

... 'only a postman' ... quoted from leaked protocols of the meeting in *Die Welt* of 7 July 1980.

... 'the one was talking Eskimo ...' Helmut Schmidt to the author, London, 3 June 1991.

... 'honest broker' ... this famous comment came in a speech to the Reichstag on 19 February 1878. It is interesting to note that the context was Bismarck insisting that Germany could *not* play the role of a mediator, let alone that of a 'referee', just the modest part of an honest broker ... See Bismarck, *Reden*, pp. 140–67, this on p. 152.

... 'honest interpreters ...' in a speech to the Federal Association of German Publishers on 10 November 1981, reprinted in *Bulletin*, 19 November 1981, pp. 921–28, this on p. 925. Asked about this image in a television discussion on the occasion of Brezhnev's visit to Bonn, Schmidt said that 'we are probably at the moment the best interpreters in both directions', see the transcript, BPA — DFS/26.11.81/20.15, p. 4. For further discussion of the interpreter image see Haftendorn, *Sicherheit*, p. 150, Joffe in Gordon, *Eroding Empire*, p. 184 f, and Avril Pittman, *From Ostpolitik to Reunification. West German-Soviet Political Relations since 1974* (Cambridge: Cambridge University Press, 1992), pp. 101–08.

... revived by Chancellor Kiesinger ... in his initial government declaration, Kiesinger said: 'Germany was for centuries a bridge between Western and Eastern Europe. We would be happy to perform these tasks in our age too.' *Bundestag Plenarprotokolle*, 5/80, p. 3662 (13 December 1966).

... used by Schmidt himself ... 'Our task is to perform the function of a bridge' he declared in a speech to the extraordinary party conference of the SPD in Cologne on 10 December 1978, quoted in Link, *Ära Schmidt*, p. 309.

... the proposed deployment ... provoked ... a recent book on this is Jeffrey Herf, *War by Other Means. Soviet Power, West German Resistance and the Battle of the Euromissiles.* (New York: Free Press, 1991).

... deep into Schmidt's own party ... a vivid account, by someone very hostile to this development, is given in Apel, *Abstieg*.

... both overtly and covertly ... Schmidt refers in passing to the covert actions, disinformation etc in *Menschen und Mächte*, p. 108. After the end of the GDR, more evidence emerged of how active the East German State Security Service had been in this connection. While it is important to establish the facts about this support, which was more important and substantial than many in the peace movement would have like to believe, it does not amount to an 'explanation' of it, any more than the overt and covert support given to Solidarity in Poland by the United States amounts to an 'explanation' of that movement.

... 'with God's and your help' ... quoted from the report by Herbert Häber, head of the SED's Western Department, on his trip to West Germany, 16–22 February 1981, now in ZPA: JIV 2/10.02/12.

... encouraged the key foreign-policy decision-makers ... Valentin Falin argues, retrospectively, that from as early as 1975, when Brezhnev became seriously ill, Soviet foreign policy was really made by what he calls a 'gang of four' consisting of Gromyko, Ustinov, Andropov and Suslov. Valentin Falin, Hamburg, 14 May 1992.

... the Social Democrats' party conference ... see *Parteitag der Sozialdemokratischen Partei Deutschlands. 19. bis 23. April 1982. München, Olympiahalle. Vol 1: Protokoll der Verhandlungen* (Bonn: Vorstand der SPD, 1982), especially the discussion on the report by Egon Bahr on 'peace and security policy', pp. 305–83. For more on this, see Chapter Six.

... this decision was put off ... according to Apel, *Abstieg*, p. 198, the decision to postpone was made already at the beginning of the year, due to the atmosphere in the regional party organisations.

... planning staff paper ... published in *Der Spiegel*, 20/1982, pp. 22–3. There also all the following quotations. According to *Der Spiegel*, the government spokesman, Klaus Bölling, confirmed the authenticity of the paper. The head of the planning staff and main author of the paper, Albrecht Müller, recalls that he had prepared similar planning papers for Schmidt in 1980 and 1981. The particular concern, he says, was the fraught relationship with the Free Democrats. The public opinion polls referred to included some specially commissioned by the government itself. Albrecht Müller, Bonn, 20 March 1992.

... Kant but also Cruise ... Schmidt paid considerable attention to the philosophical and ethical underpinnings of his political work, to what he called at the end of his valedictory speech to the Bundestag in 1986, 'the sober passion for practical reason'. See *Bundestag Plenarprotokolle* 10/228, p. 17685 (10 September 1986). This favourite phrase of his was then taken up as the title of a Festschrift in his honour, Manfred Lahnstein, ed., *Leidenschaft zur praktischen Vernunft* (Berlin: Siedler, 1989). Both Kant and Popper earn several mentions in his memoirs. There is some evidence that he suffered under his image of the *Macher*, the businessman-manager in politics. Thus in a rather touching note to the head of the Chancellery dated 7 January 1975, Schmidt suggests that he should deliver a speech to mark a noteworthy cultural or historical date, such as the 100th birthday of Albert Schweitzer or Thomas Mann. 'I could imagine,' he writes, 'that in this way the strongly economically coloured *Macher*-image could be complemented by a part of the components [i.e. of Helmut Schmidt] which are really present but lacking in the public awareness.' Now in AdsD: HS 1. Yet clearly his philosophical and ethical concerns went far deeper than just concern about the image. They were strongly held and vividly and personally expressed. See, for example, his response to the author in the protocol of the *Bergedorfer Gesprächskreis* 88 (6–7 September 1989), pp. 66–7.

... 'if an agreement cannot be reached...' dinner speech on 23 November 1981, reprinted in *Bulletin*, 26 November 1981, pp. 963–66, this on p. 965.

... other, more direct causes ... for a partisan but vivid account of the break-up of the social-liberal coalition, see Klaus Bölling, *Die letzten 30 Tage des Kanzlers Helmut Schmidt. Ein Tagebuch* (Reinbek: Rowohlt, 1982). A more scholarly and critical account is given by Wolfgang Jäger in Wolfgang Jäger and Werner Link, *Republik im Wandel. 1974–1982. Die Ära Schmidt* [= Geschichte der *Bundesrepublik Deutschland* Vol 5/II] (Stuttgart: Deutsche Verlags-Anstalt, 1987), pp. 188–263.

. . . **truly unprecedented movement in American-Soviet relations** . . . Oberdorfer, *Turn*, and Beschloss & Talbott, *Highest Levels*, are both excellent and accessible chronicles, displaying the best of American quality journalism. But see also Seweryn Bialer and Michael Mandelbaum, eds, *Gorbachev's Russia and American Foreign Policy* (Boulder: Westview Press, 1988), and the account of a policy maker closely involved, Thomas W Simons, *The End of the Cold War?* (New York: St Martin's Press, 1990).

'The Alliance,' said Kohl . . . see *Bundestag Plenarprotokolle* 9/121, pp. 7213–7229 (13 October 1982), this on p. 7220. (See also Genscher's speech on pp. 7254–64.) The Government rather pointedly included the Social Democrats' heckling reaction in the version printed in *Bulletin*, 14 October 1982, this on p. 860.

. . . **'not only to keep** . . .' this from point (19) of the CDU-CSU coalition agreement on foreign, security, EC, Ostpolitik and Deutschlandpolitik issues, as circulated to CSU parliamentarians by the General Secretary of the CSU on 13 May 1983. Copy in the papers of Werner Marx, ACDP: I–356, 005/3.

Helmut Kohl, the Catholic from the Rhineland-Palatinate . . . in the not very impressive literature on Helmut Kohl see the rather partisan biography by Werner Maser, *Helmut Kohl. Der Deutsche Kanzler* (Frankfurt: Ullstein, 1990); an interesting collection of critical articles, Reinhard Appel, ed., *Helmut Kohl im Spiegel seiner Macht* (Bonn: Bouvier, 1990); and the rather good essay by Peter Scholl-Latour in a volume of photographs by Konrad R Müller, *Helmut Kohl* (Bergisch Gladbach: Gustav Lübber Verlag, 1990). A good summary of Kohl's own views on German foreign policy is given in his 1984 Konrad Adenauer Memorial lecture (Oxford: St Antony's College, 1984).

The record of his meeting with Alexei Kosygin . . . a copy of the twenty-one page record of the conversation on 30 September 1975 is in the Werner Marx papers, ACDP: I–356, 022/4. All following quotations are from that copy. Unfortunately this record does not cover the concluding forty-five minute one-to-one conversation.

. . . **'We wouldn't dream** . . .' this from the copy of Weizsäcker's five-page 'Note for the Moscow Visit', dated 18 September 1975, also in ACDP: I–356, 022/4.

. . . **all the stages** . . . for a first attempt see Clemens, *Reluctant Realists*, and the same author's 1992 Alois Mertes Memorial Lecture on *CDU Deutschlandpolitik and Reunification, 1985–1989* (Washington: German Historical Institute, 1992).

. . . **'the object in East-West relations** . . .' quoted from the Free Democrats' protocol of the coalition talks on the evening of 22 March 1983, now in AdDL: Bundesvorsitzender Genscher, 13544.

... **the most solicitous attention** ... Note, for example, the despatch of no less a figure than the Economics Minister, Otto Graf Lambsdorff, to chair the meeting of the German-Soviet economic commission in Moscow in November 1983, just a week before the Bundestag vote on the deployment.

The confidential note on these talks ... The note is dated 14 July 1983. Following quotations are from the copy in the office papers of Hermann Axen, ZPA: IV 2/2.035/65.

... **the Bundestag's vote** ... The actual vote was on 22 November 1983. For the debate see *Bundestag Plenarprotokolle*, 10/35 & 36 (21 & 22 November 1983).

... **'limit the damage'** ... see the text in ND, 26/27 November 1983, also reprinted in *Texte* III/1, pp. 267–71.

... **'a coalition of reason'** ... see Ronald D Asmus, 'The Dialectics of Détente, and Discord. The Moscow-East Berlin-Bonn Triangle,' in *Orbis*, Winter 1985, pp. 743–74, and A James McAdams, 'The New Logic in Soviet-GDR Relations', in *Problems of Communism*, September-October 1988, pp. 47–60.

While Soviet negotiators walked out ... for a good contemporary documentation see Ronald D Asmus, *East Berlin and Moscow. The Documentation of a Dispute* (Munich: Radio Free Europe, 1985 = RFE Occasional Papers No. 1). It will, however, now be possible to write an account based on the East German and perhaps also on the Soviet archives.

... **joined in this by Hungary** ... ibid., especially pp. 9–10, 21 ff, 27 ff.

As Honecker himself recalled ... Erich Honecker, Berlin-Moabit, 27 November 1992.

... **a stormy meeting with the Soviet leadership** ... see p. 169. The East German record is in ZPA: JIV 2/2A/2678.

... **a public lesson, in the Bundestag** ... *Bundestag Plenarprotokolle* 10/81, pp. 5896–5902 (12 September 1984).

'The Soviet Union ...' ibid., p. 5903.

... **Moscow First** ... see his article in APZ, 16 February 1985, pp. 3–13, especially p. 11.

... **the obdurate Gromykos and Ustinovs** ... in conversation with the author, Valentin Falin argued that a 'gang of four' consisting of Gromyko, Ustinov, Andropov and Suslov, had been effectively making — and blocking — Soviet foreign policy since Brezhnev became seriously ill in the mid-1970s. Valentin Falin, Hamburg, 14 May 1992. In the meeting with Honecker and the East German leadership on 17 August 1984, Ustinov was particularly outspoken in his criticism.

... **Europe remained a subsidiary theatre** ... on Gorbachev's policy towards Europe see Neil Malcolm *Soviet Policy Perspectives on Western Europe* (London: Routledge, 1989). Anatoly Chernyaev specifically confirmed this in a lecture in

1992, printed in Gabriel Gorodetsky, ed., *Soviet Foreign Policy, 1917–1922. A Retrospective* (London: Frank Cass, forthcoming).

. . . **in the frontiers of 1937** . . . the bald statement 'The German Reich continues to exist in the frontiers of 1937' actually appears in point 20 of the spring 1983 coalition agreement of CDU and CSU. Quoted from the copy in the papers of Werner Marx, ACDP: I–356, 005/3.

. . . **not reflect the real convictions** . . . this was certainly Brandt's impression of Gorbachev from their first meeting, see his account in Brandt, *Erinnerungen*, p. 405 ff, esp. p. 407.

. . . **F Wilhelm Christians** . . . See his own account in Christians, *Wege*, pp. 136–47.

. . . **only after the Kohl-Genscher government** . . . In 1989, Horst Teltschik wrote that 'it [Soviet policy towards Germany] changed after Chancellor Helmut Kohl's re-election in January 1987', see his article in *Aussenpolitik* (English-language edition), 3/1989, pp. 201–14, this on p. 208.

. . . **letter to Gorbachev dated 30 January 1986** . . . a copy of this letter was passed by the Soviet to the East German Party leadership and is now in ZPA: IV 2/2.035/65.

. . . **the quantitative reduction** . . . the reference was of course to the very sharp downturn in the number of ethnic Germans allowed to emigrate, down from a high point of more than 9,000 in 1977 to just 460 in 1985.

Genscher recalls . . . Hans-Dietrich Genscher, Bonn, 23 June 1992.

. . . **a new page** . . . Genscher's speech in Moscow is reprinted in *Bulletin*, 24 July 1986, pp. 745–48. A very useful account of the development of German-Soviet relations from 1986 to mid-1989 is Fred Oldenburg, *Sowjetische Deutschland-Politik nach den Treffen von Moskau und Bonn 1988/89* (Köln: Bundesinstitut für ostwissenschaftliche und internationale Studien, 1989 = *Bericht des BIOst* 63/1989), hereafter Oldenburg, *Sowjetische Deutschland-Politik*.

. . . **'He [Gorbachev] is a modern communist leader** . . .' *Newsweek*, 27 October 1986. See also *Der Spiegel* 44/1986

. . . **the Politburo actually decided to freeze** . . . this emerges clearly from the record of a meeting between Hermann Axen and the Soviet Central Committee Secretaries Anatoly Dobrynin and Vadim Medvedev in Moscow on 27 July 1987, now in ZPA: IV 2/2.035/59, pp. 108–25. 'After Kohl's attacks,' Dobrynin is there recorded as reporting, 'the Politburo of the CPSU had passed a resolution to freeze all political contacts with the FRG for the time being'.

. . . **a widely reported speech** . . . this now famous Davos speech, drafted by Konrad Seitz, is reprinted in Genscher, *Unterwegs*, pp. 137–50.

. . . **'worst case analysis'** . . . ibid., p. 146

. . . **'take Gorbachev seriously, take him at his word!'** . . . ibid., p. 150. In the ensuing discussion, some Foreign Ministry officials insisted that the correct translation of the German would be 'hold him to his word'. The German phrase says literally 'take him by his word' but the correct English translation is certainly 'take him at his word'!

... 'pacemaker' ... See, for example, an interview with Genscher in Deutschlandfunk, 12 September 1988 (BPA transcript).

... as much a rival ... the notes of the head of the Western Department of the SED, Herbert Häber, on a conversation with Weizsäcker on 4 March 1980, record the following: 'so far as Helmut Kohl is concerned, it had proved to be a mistake that he had come from Mainz to Bonn. He would never become Chancellor and did not possess the abilities for it. In the two main areas which really matter — economic and foreign policy — he had learned nothing.' ZPA: J IV 2/10.02/10.

'However,' as one of his hosts recorded him saying ... Note of 28 May 1984 by Herbert Häber on the meeting of Richard von Weizsäcker with Horst Sindermann and Herbert Häber in the Hubertusstock, now in ZPA: J IV 2/10.04/14.

... giving Gorbachev a marvellous pretext ... Oberdorfer, *Turn*, p. 230 records a senior Soviet official joking that for this reason Rust should be awarded the Order of Lenin. In a sense, this obviously disturbed young man also deserved the West German *Bundesverdienstkreuz*, for the political results of his madcap venture were clearly to West Germany's long-term advantage.

... 'for the time being, however ...' This is the official Soviet version of the talks, given in *Pravda*, 8 July 1987 and reprinted in Gorbachev, *Haus Europa*, pp. 103–06.

... history would decide ... ibid., p. 106. Note that this is the official published version. What Gorbachev actually said may therefore be slightly different, but neither the Soviet nor the German protocols of the conversation were accessible to the author at this writing. Gorbachev repeated this formula in his book *Perestroika*, see Mikhail Gorbachev, *Perestroika. New Thinking for Our Country and the World* (London: Collins Harvill, 1987), p. 200, and, for comparison of the Russian and German texts, Oldenburg, *Sowjetische Deutschland-Politik*, p. 45.

Weizsäcker recalls ... Richard von Weizsäcker, Bonn, 30 September 1991.

'Already in 1986' ... Schewardnadse, *Zukunft*, p. 233.

Asked about this by the author ... Eduard Shevardnadze, Moscow, 7 February 1992. I am grateful to Gabriel Gorodetsky for giving me the opportunity of this discussion in a small group.

Anatoly Chernyaev ... see his lecture printed in Gabriel Gorodetsky, ed., *Soviet Foreign Policy, 1917–1992. A Retrospective* (London: Frank Cass, forthcoming).

In a separate conversation ... Alexander Yakovlev, Oxford, 29 January 1992. I am grateful to my colleague Archie Brown for enabling me to join in this discussion in a small group at St Antony's College.

... **Vyacheslav Dashitschev** ... Vyacheslav Dashitschev, Berlin, 26 June 1991. See also his interview in *Der Spiegel* 4/1991, where he also mentions a subsequent presentation in the International Department of the Central Committee. This interview provoked a furious response from Valentin Falin (reader's letter, *Der Spiegel*, 20/1991) who claimed there, and repeated in conversation with the author (Hamburg, 14 May 1992), that he had no recollection of such a presentation, and that Dashitschev was not an adviser to Gorbachev. Dashitschev, head of the foreign policy department in the then Institute for the Economics of the World Socialist System (the 'Bogomolov Institute'), says that he was an adviser in the sense that some of his papers came back with marginal annotations by Gorbachev (letter to *Der Spiegel*, 34/1991, and in conversation with the author). Certainly by 1988 Dashitschev was going public, both inside the Soviet Union and in Germany, with extremely outspoken criticism of Soviet foreign policy in the Soviet years. See, for example, his well-known article in *Literaturnaya Gazeta*, 18 May 1988, reports of his remarks in FAZ, 8 June 1988, interview in *Der Spiegel*, 27/1988. In *International Affairs* (Moscow), 10/1992, p. 132 ff, Oleg Bogomolov retrospectively described this as the general line of his Institute since about 1986. See also remarks by Bogomolov himself in June 1988, quoted in Garton Ash, *Uses*, p. 221.

... **Honecker remembered** ... in Reinhold Andert & Wolfgang Herberg, *Der Sturz. Erich Honecker im Kreuzverhör* (Berlin: Aufbau, 1990), p. 21.

In a television interview ... on ARD, 10 October 1991.

Dashitschev himself says ... Vyacheslav Dashitschev, Berlin, 26 June 1991, and in *Der Spiegel* 4/1991, 34/1991

... **wrangling over** ... **German-Soviet agreements** ... Dieter Kastrup, Bonn, 18 March 1992. For detail on Berlin and the so-called 'PO Box solution' of 1986 — whereby Berlin participants in German-Soviet agreements were listed only with a PO Box address — see Oldenburg, *Sowjetische Deutschland-Politik*, pp. 29–35.

The East German record ... This extremely revealing document is in ZPA: IV 2/2. 035/59, pp. 108–25, from which the following quotations are drawn. The consultation was in preparation for Honecker's visit to Bonn. Its formal basis was an 'Analysis of the situation in the FRG — conclusions for a common policy' (now in ZPA: IV 2/2. 035/14) which had been prepared on the instructions of the East German Politburo, and sent to the Soviet leadership, with a covering letter from Honecker to Gorbachev, on 23 June 1987. Axen opined in a memorandum to Honecker on 29 July 1987 (now in ZPA: IV 2/2.035/59, pp. 153–55), enclosing the formal report on the visit and draft resolution for the Politburo (pp. 146–52), that the fact that the Soviet side had accepted the East German analysis and conclusions for a common policy of the 'socialist community' towards West Germany was 'undoubtedly a success for the policy of the SED'. He also noted a difference of emphasis between Dobrynin and Medvedev, with the latter having 'passages which contained the old, false reservations and misjudgements of the correlation of forces between the GDR and the FRG and the situation in the GDR and the FRG'. For further detail, see p. 170 f.

... **with the most agreeable feelings** ...' report and quotations in *Der Spiegel*, 1/1988.

... **Shevardnadze visited Bonn** ... see *Bulletin*, 21 January 1988, pp. 53–57, Oldenburg, *Sowjetische Deutschland-Politik*, pp. 9–10.

... **sacrificing** ... **Pershing 1A missiles** ... this story is well told in Michael Inacker's useful account of the security policy of the Kohl government in Reinhard Appel, ed., *Helmut Kohl im Spiegel seiner Macht* (Bonn: Bouvier, 1990), pp. 73–112, on this esp. pp. 89–98.

The Soviet information note ... one of the German texts of the note, dated 19 February 1988, is in ZPA: IV 2/2.035/65, pp. 209–16. Following quotations are all from this text.

'The CDU,' he said ... in a long interview in *Blätter für deutsche und internationale Politik* 11/1987, pp. 1392–1404, this on p. 1396.

... **that Kohl at last visited Moscow** ... for details of this visit see *Bulletin*, 1 November 1988, pp. 1265–76, Oldenburg, *Sowjetische Deutschland-Politik*, and extensive press reports in the second half of October.

'Now,' said Gorbachev ... *Bulletin*, 1 November 1988, p. 1265.

... **the beginnings** ... **rapport** ... Anatoly Chernyaev in Gabriel Gorodetsky, ed., *Soviet Foreign Policy, 1917–1992. A Retrospective* (London: Frank Cass, forthcoming).

... **'new chapter'** ... *Bulletin*, 1 November 1988, p. 1271.

... **the reception given to Gorbachev** ... the following paragraph is based on my observations in Bonn at the time. For the main official documents and speeches of this visit see *Bulletin*, 15 June 1989, pp. 537–48; EA, 13/1989, pp. D371 ff; and, with more of Gorbachev's speeches, *Gorbatschow in Bonn. Die Zukunft der deutsch-sowjetischen Beziehungen. Reden und Dokumente vom Staatsbesuch* (Köln: Pahl-Rugenstein, 1989).

... **'Gorbasm'** ... that is, in German, *Gorbasmus*. The coinage was attributed to Günter Diehl, see *Der Spiegel* 24/1989.

... **'A kiss for Annette** ...' *Bild*, 13 June 1989.

... **'the object of desire'** ... TAZ 13 June 1989.

'After a good sowing ...' from Kohl's speech on 12 June, *Bulletin*, 15 June 1989, p. 537.

... **eleven agreements** ... details from an information sheet of the *Presse- und Informationsamt der Bundesregierung*, 12 June 1989.

... **similar connections** ... reported in FAZ, 11 February 1989 (from which it appears that the 'hot line' was actually installed in the run-up to the visit).

'We are drawing the line ...' from Gorbachev's speech on 12 June, *Bulletin*, 15 June 1989, p. 541.

'This must be . . .' ibid.

This remarkable document . . . all following quotations from the text in *Bulletin*, 15 June 1989, pp. 542–544. Also in *Vierzig Jahre*, pp. 591–594.

. . . 'a catalyst for new relations . . .' in a speech on 13 June, *Bulletin*, 15 June 1989, p. 547.

. . . 'the growing young man' . . . see above p. 51 and notes.

. . . 'partners in leadership' . . . English text in Freedman, *Europe Transformed*, pp. 289–94, this on p. 289.

Connoisseurs pointed out . . . see Hannes Adomeit, 'Gorbachev and German Unification' in *Problems of Communism*, July-August 1990, pp. 1–23, this on p. 5. (This important article is hereafter cited as Adomeit, 'Gorbachev and German Unification'.) Oldenburg, *Sowjetische Deutschland-Politik*, p. 44, notes that the changed usage was subsequently adopted in the Soviet press.

. . . the only comparable bilateral document . . . the Soviet Foreign Ministry spokesman, Genady Gerassimov, compared it to the Delhi Declaration between the Soviet Union and India (author's notes). But India's position could hardly be compared with that of the most important West European state, on the front line of the East-West conflict.

'I must admit . . .' quoted in SZ, 14 June 1989.

'Differences in ideology . . .' See the full text in Grenville, *Treaties*, pp. 456–58. It is interesting to note that Egon Bahr, in praising the Bonn Declaration, also compared it to this one. See his speech in *Bundestag Plenarprotokolle*, 11/150, pp. 11202–204 (16 June 1989).

. . . already well on the way . . . on this, see Garton Ash, *We*.

. . . 'to promote free elections . . .' see the text of his Mainz speech reprinted in Freedman, *Europe Transformed*, pp. 289–94, this on p. 291, and extracts from his speech to the Polish parliament on pp. 333–35.

. . . 'an open wound' . . . this and following quotations from his speech on 12 June, *Bulletin*, 15 June 1989, p. 537–39.

. . . a major controversy with Washington . . . a clear and detailed account is given by Michael J Inacker in Reinhard Appel, ed., *Helmut Kohl im Spiegel seiner Macht* (Bonn: Bouvier, 1990), p. 92 ff.

'The shorter the range . . .' quoted in ibid., p. 93.

. . . 'the continental Europeans' . . . ibid., p. 103, and see also the commentary by Thomas Kielinger in *Rheinischer Merkur*, 28 April 1989.

. . . 'the opening of Eastern societies . . .' see the text reprinted in Freedman, *Europe Transformed*, pp. 295–303, this on p. 300.

He recalls, in particular . . . Helmut Kohl, Bonn, 1 October 1991. See also his account in *Die Welt am Sonntag*, 27 September 1992. Kohl referred back to this particular conversation in a crucial meeting with Gorbachev in Moscow on 15 July 1990, see Teltschik, *329 Tage*, p. 320, and publicly in an extraordinary televised telephone chat with Mikhail Gorbachev on the first anniversary of the unification of Germany, ARD 3 October 1991.

. . . **'the decisive moment'** . . . Helmut Kohl, Bonn, 1 October 1991.

. . . **'Du'** . . . **'Sie'** . . . see the telegrams to Bush and Gorbachev reproduced in *Bulletin*, 5 November 1991, p. 969.

. . . **a long track-record** . . . see above p. 101 and the handwritten letter of thanks from Alois Mertes following Kohl's trip to Moscow in July 1983, ACDP: I–403, A–000.

Willy Brandt . . . **poured gentle scorn** . . . Brandt, *Erinnerungen*, pp. 354, 405.

. . . **highlighted the influence** . . . ibid., pp. 404, 407, and 426–36. See also, Mikhail Gorbachev, *Perestroika. New Thinking for Our country and the World* (London: Collins Harvill, 1987), p. 207.

. . . **compelled the decisive turn** . . . a very lucid and valuable treatment of this subject is Jonathan Haslam, *The Soviet Union and the Politics of Nuclear Weapons in Europe, 1969–1987* (London: Macmillan, 1989).

. . . **via Georgi Arbatov to Gorbachev** . . . Egon Bahr, Potsdam, 29 June 1991, Willy Brandt, Bonn, 2 October 1991.

. . . **'without Ostpolitik, no Gorbachev'** . . . Willy Brandt, Bonn, 2 October 1991. Egon Bahr in SZ *Magazin*, 27 September 1991, p. 18.

. . . **in an interview with** *Die Zeit* . . . *Die Zeit*, 13 March 1992.

Schmidt, Kohl and Genscher all stressed . . . Helmut Schmidt, London, 3 June 1991; Helmut Kohl, Bonn, 1 October 1991; Hans-Dietrich Genscher, Bonn, 23 June 1992. For an interesting though slightly confused discussion of the relationship between INF and the revision of Soviet foreign policy, see the article by Thomas Risse-Kappen in *International Security*, 16/1, Summer 1991, pp. 162–88.

Yes, said ex-Chancellor Brandt . . . Willy Brandt, Bonn, 2 October 1991.

. . . **perhaps Palme and SI pointed to a possible way out** . . . Vitaly Zhurkin, Director of the Institute of Europe created in Moscow in 1988 and an active participant in the revision of Soviet foreign policy thinking, believes this was true particularly of the earlier years, ca. 1985–87, when the focus of discussion was on security issues. Vitaly Zhurkin, Moscow, 7 February 1992.

. . . **alarmed and goaded the Gorbachev leadership** . . . for Gorbachev's concern about the economic development of the EC, and a security dimension of the Franco-German relationship, see Neil Malcolm, *Soviet Policy Perspectives on Western Europe* (London: Routledge, 1989).

'our firm anchoring in the West . . .' *Bulletin*, 1 November 1988, p. 1269.

... 'no destabilisation' ... author's notes of remarks by Hans Klein. See also reports in SZ and FAZ, 14 June 1989.

... 'a commensurate change on the Soviet side ...' Meissner, *Moskau-Bonn*, p. 824.

... ten ... i.e. since Brezhnev's growing incapacity ushered in a decade of growing inflexibility and 'stagnation' in Soviet foreign and domestic policy.

... some even as twenty ... i.e., since the fall of Khrushchev.

... by no means be underrated. ... Hannes Adomeit nonetheless surely goes too far in the other direction when he writes that 'the conceptual basis for the collapse of the GDR was supplemented by a practical precondition: the removal of the Berlin Wall'. Some supplement! See Adomeit, 'Gorbachev and Unification', p. 5.

... the main components of 'new thinking'. ... Among the many good treatments of this subject one might mention, Archie Brown, ed., *New Thinking in Soviet Politics* (London: Macmillan, 1992), Gerhard Wettig, *Changes in Soviet Policy Towards the West* (London: Pinter, 1991), Adomeit's excellent article, quoted here as 'Germany and Unification', and a characteristically precise and lucid article by Boris Meissner in *Aussenpolitik* (English-language edition), 2/1989, pp. 101–18.

... especially when it came to Germany ... see the revealing remark by Georgy Shakhnazarov, quoted in Beschloss & Talbott, *Highest Levels*, p. 82.

... what Seweryn Bialer has called ... see his *The Soviet Paradox. External Expansion, Internal Decline* (New York: Knopf, 1986), p. 191.

... not least ... Uzbekistan ... the point is made by Oldenburg, *Sowjetische Deutschland-Politik*, p. 11.

... Soviet policy towards Eastern Europe ... an excellent introduction to this topic is Pravda, *End*, especially the editor's own introductory chapter.

... a short memorandum to the Politburo ... and communicated in general terms ... this was mentioned by Alexander Kaptov in his speech to the 19th Party Conference in June 1988, reprinted in *International Affairs* (Moscow), November 1988, pp. 28–32, this on p. 29. Its significance was confirmed to the author by Oleg Bogomolov, Moscow, 7 February 1992, and Nikolai Kolikov, Moscow, 10 February 1992. Kolikov, a consultant to the Central Committee department for relations with socialist countries, recalls that an earlier draft of this memorandum contained the key formulation 'more socialism, more democracy'. Subsequently it was changed to the more cautious 'more socialism — more democracy', thus implying that more socialism would lead to more democracy. From the East European side, Erich Honecker (Berlin-Moabit, 27 November 1992) and Egon Krenz (Berlin, 20 February 1990) both confirmed in conversation with the author that autumn 1986 was the moment at which the East German leadership understood that they had, as Krenz put it, a 'green light' to change — or not to change. Honecker recalled what he described as the 'meeting of General

Secretaries' in Moscow when Gorbachev explained that the Soviet Union did not have a monopoly of the truth — 'we'd known that for some time', Honecker commented tartly — and proposed a new relationship of 'partnership'. He recalled Zhivkov asking what exactly this meant, and receiving only a vague reply. It would clearly be very interesting to see a record of this meeting.

... **practice lagged a long way behind** ... a point made very forcibly to the author by Oleg Bogomolov (Moscow, 7 February 1992) and confirmed by numerous East European sources. Erich Honecker (Berlin-Moabit, 27 November 1992) said emphatically that at no point did the Soviet Union refrain from 'interfering' (*sich einmischen*) in the GDR. He described the consular officials of the Soviet Embassy in the provinces of the GDR as *Provinzgouverneure*.

... **Gorbachev** ... **extremely cautious** ... witness, for example, his non-response to a question on this subject from a Polish intellectual, Marcin Krol, during Gorbachev's visit to Warsaw in July 1988, see Garton Ash, *Uses*, p. 222.

... **Gorbachev gave his assent** ... see Pravda, *End*, pp. 24–25. Miklás Németh, Oxford, 22 January 1991.

... **'beyond containment'** ... see Oberdorfer, *Turn*, p. 345 ff, Beschloss & Talbott, *Highest Levels*, p. 69 ff, and Thomas W Simons, *The End of the Cold War?* (New York: St Martin's Press, 1990), p. 154 ff.

'This isn't meant ...' quoted in Oberdorfer, *Turn*, p. 342.

... **he also warned** ... ibid., p. 360.

'Yes, we had in principle ...' quoted in Adomeit, 'Gorbachev and Unification', p. 22, citing *Pravda*, 5 July 1990. See also the translation in *Current Digest of the Soviet Press* XLII, No. 29, 1990, pp. 12–13.

... **a report from the Soviet ambassador to Bonn** ... Schevardnadse, *Zukunft*, p. 258.

... **other Soviet specialists** ... the best known of these is a memorandum by Dashitschev of April 1989, reprinted in *Der Spiegel* 6/1989. But this was only one of a number of memoranda prepared by, among others, the Bogomolov Institute, the Foreign Ministry and the Central Committee on Moscow's relations with Eastern Europe (copies in the possession of the author). *Die Welt*, 15 September 1989, reported a West German Federal Intelligence Service (BND) report of early August 1989 which in turn contained a report by Valentin Falin on dangerous instability in the GDR.

Sergei Tarasenko ... Moscow, 10 February 1992.

... **'would be the end of perestroika'** ... quoted in Oberdorfer, *Turn*, p. 360.

... **strongly influenced by the Prague Spring** ... on this, see Pravda, *End*, p. 3, and Archie Brown, *The Gorbachev Factor in Soviet Politics* (forthcoming).

... **'nineteen years'** ... quoted in William E Griffith, ed, *Central & Eastern Europe: The Opening Curtain?* (Boulder: Westview Press, 1989), p. 423.

... 'reveal the human face of socialism' ... this in a speech in Kiev in February 1989, quoted by Adomeit, 'Gorbachev and Unification', p. 3, citing *Pravda*, 24 February 1989. See also his note of 2 February 1989 'On Stalin', reprinted in *Gipfelgespräche*, pp. 258–63, this on p. 263.

... 'a particular significance ...' Horst Teltschik, 'Gorbachev's Reform Policy and the Outlook for East-West Relations', in *Aussenpolitik* (English-language edition) 3/1989, pp. 201–214, this on p. 212.

... the time-scale Teltschik imagined ... Horst Teltschik, Bonn, 12 July 1991.

Chapter IV: Germany and Germany

... all Ostpolitik was Deutschlandpolitik ... 'The new Ostpolitik,' writes a leading West German specialist, Werner Link, 'was at the same time and in its innermost intentions, Deutschlandpolitik', in Link, *Ära Brandt*, p. 214.

... the Brandt government re-named ... this was announced in the first Government declaration, see *Bundestag Plenarprotokolle*, 6/5, p. 21 (28 October 1969).

... 'German-German relations' ... a leading article in the FAZ, 13 August 1973, denounced this usage as a further concession to the GDR.

Egon Bahr memorably commented ... Quoted, by Bahr himself, in Schmid, *Politik*, p. 257, and Bender, *Neue Ostpolitik*, p. 195.

The Berlin Agreement of September 1951 ... see *Materialien*, p. 627, the article on 'Innerdeutscher Handel' in *DDR-Handbuch*, and further references given below.

Starting in 1963 ... see p. 142 f for further detail.

Chancellor Kiesinger's April 1967 declaration ... text in *Bundestag Plenar-protokolle*, 5/101, pp. 4686 ff (12 April 1967). There also Barzel's response.

... some heavy use of the Bonn-Moscow-Berlin triangle ... see Baring, *Machtwechsel*, pp. 475 ff, 490–91.

'The day of Erfurt ...' Brandt, *Erinnerungen*, p. 226.

... merely exchanged numbers ... Ulrich Sahm, Bodenwerder, 27 September 1992.

The Politburo briefing book ... attached as an appendix to the minutes of the Politburo meeting on 19 May 1970, now in ZPA: JIV 2/2/1283.

... forgot to remove his hat ... thus Karl Seidel, Berlin, 30 September 1992.

... that same official ... Karl Seidel again. He retells both stories in Lutz, *Bahr*, p. 101.

... drawing on the wealth of documents ... some at least of the East German records of the Kohl-Bahr negotiations are in ZPA: B2/20/433 and 434. Egon Bahr holds a set of the West German records in his papers deposited in the Archiv der sozialen Demokratie in Bonn. For two complimentary assessments see the contributions by Hans-Otto Bräutigam and Karl Seidel in Lutz, *Bahr*, pp. 81–88, 101–02.

... the '20 Points' ... text in *Zehn Jahre*, pp. 138–39.

... already agreed in Erfurt ... Brandt, *Erinnerungen*, p. 227. Ulrich Sahm, who was directly responsible for putting the phrase in as one of the 20 points, suggests that its origins go back much farther, even to the Potsdam agreement or the Atlantic Charter (Bodenwerder, 27 September 1992).

The treaty itself ... a comprehensive and learned insider's commentary is given by Bahr's legal adviser, Antonius Eitel, in Zündorf, *Ostverträge*, pp. 211–310. See also Baring, *Machtwechsel*, pp. 491–98, Bender, *Neue Ostpolitik*, pp. 192–95, Link, *Ära Brandt*, pp. 222–24, Brandt, *People and Politics*, pp. 394–96.

... 'without prejudice to the different views ...' text in *Zehn Jahre*, p. 205–16, together with the important accompanying letters, protocols and declarations, and the Federal Government's memorandum expounding the treaty. The following quotations are taken from those pages. English text of the main treaty in Grenville, *Treaties*, pp. 198–99.

In a statement to mark the initialling of the treaty ... see *Texte*, I/11, pp. 320–21. The same formula was used by Bahr in a statement at the actual initialling of the treaty, ibid., pp. 311–13.

... a letter accompanying the treaty ... see *Zehn Jahre*, p. 208.

... detailed provision for easier travel ... see *Zehn Jahre*, pp. 208–10.

'*Wandel durch Annäherung* ...' the lecture is reprinted in Bahr, *Sicherheit*, pp. 44–59, this on p. 45.

... 'the respective seats of government' ... the formula is in Article 8 of the Basic Treaty, see *Zehn Jahre*, p. 206.

... reported directly to the Chancellor ... the precise lines of reporting and command were laid down in memoranda dated 10 July 1974 from the head of the Chancellery, Manfred Schüler. AdsD: HS, 449.

... policy had to be co-ordinated ... see Gaus, *Deutschland*, p. 255 ff. In conversation with the author, Gaus recalled what he called a 'gang of four' chaired by the Chancellery minister and including the state secretaries from the Chancellery (Gaus himself, in a personal union!), the Foreign Ministry and the Intra-German Ministry. Günter Gaus, Hamburg, 14 May 1992. For a later period, one of the heads of the *Arbeitstab Deutschlandpolitik* in the Chancellery recalls a co-ordinating group of five, with the Chancellery Minister, the state secretaries from the Foreign Ministry, Intra-German Ministry and Economics Ministry, and the federal plenipotentiary for Berlin. Hermann von Richthofen, London, 3 March 1992.

After Brandt's re-election in 1972, there was a serious discussion inside the

Brandt Chancellery about dissolving the Intra-German Ministry altogether, and gathering the operative part of its work in a new 'Germany- and Berlin-political department' in the Chancellery. See the confidential memorandum from Horst Ehmke as head of the Chancellery dated 13 November 1972, memorandum from Egon Bahr dated 14 November 1972, and further memorandum from Ehmke dated 27 November 1972, all in AdsD: Dep WB, BK 68. Günter Gaus restates the argument that this would have been a better way to organise things in Gaus, *Deutschland*, p. 256. According to Gaus's recollection, this did not happen mainly for party-political and coalition reasons: the Intra-German Minister, Egon Franke, was a pillar of the right-wing SPD, Herbert Wehner did not wish to see his old ministry dissolved, and there were concerns about the FDP's response to such a reshuffling of cabinet-level responsibilities. Günter Gaus, Hamburg, 14 May 1992.

. . . **the man who took the key decisions** . . . Honecker confirmed his own direct responsibility for foreign policy, and especially for relations with West Germany, in conversation with Helmut Schmidt during their summit meeting in December 1981, see Schmidt, *Nachbarn*, p. 71. In conversation with the author, the former Politburo member Günter Schabowski said that Honecker kept four key areas to himself: foreign policy, especially relations with the Federal Republic, internal security, the media, and 'cadre questions' (i.e. who should get what post). Günter Schabowski, Berlin, 29 June 1991.

. . . **'Working Group FRG'** . . . this group was supposed to deal mainly with the economic aspects of relations with West Germany, but there were few German-German ties which did not have an economic aspect. (Information from Günter Mittag, Gerhard Schürer, Alexander Schalck-Golodkowski, Karl Seidel.) Its secretary was Alexander Schalck-Golodkowski. See also Mittag, *Preis*, p. 91 ff. Regrettably, the papers of this working group now deposited in the Central Party Archive had not been catalogued at the time of writing.

. . . **the Foreign Ministry's 'FRG Department'** . . . thus the head of that department could say that he was 'his own boss'. Most of the Foreign Ministry, like most other ministries, was directly subordinated to the Central Committee apparatus. Karl Seidel, Berlin, 30 September 1992.

From 1976 . . . **Schalck** . . . Gaus's first negotiating contact with Schalck dates from 1976. Günter Gaus, Hamburg, 14 May 1992. The significance of the date is by now well-established, as Schalck's 'Commercial Co-ordination' agency was given wider responsibilities following the 9th party congress and a Politburo decision of 2 November 1976. See the appendix to the Politburo minutes in ZPA: JIV 2/2/1642. However, in testimony to the Bundestag special committee Schalck mentioned earlier contacts with Carl-Werner Sanne and Karl-Otto Pöhl, both important senior officials in the Bonn government in the early 1970s, see the transcript in *Die Zeit*, 4 October 1991. The central importance of Schalck as a negotiating partner for the Bonn government was confirmed to the author by, among others, Wolfgang Schäuble, Bonn, 17 March 1992, and Hermann von Richthofen, London, 3 March 1992. His standing as a key negotiator for the East German side was confirmed to the author by, among others, Günter Mittag,

Berlin, 28 June 1992, and the head of Honecker's personal office in the Council of State, Frank-Joachim Hermann, Berlin, 8 October 1991. In his testimony to the Bundestag special committee, Schäuble described Schalck as not merely a messenger but a plenipotentiary (*Bevollmächtigter*), see *Deutscher Bundestag. 12. Wahlperiode. I. Untersuchungsausschuss "Kommerzielle Koordinierung"* [hereafter cited as *Schalck-Ausschuss*], Protokoll Nr. 24, p. 28 f.

... a Bundestag special committee struggled ... Author's observation at the hearing with Schalck on 24 June 1992. See now the special committee's first two reports, *Bundestag Drucksachen*, 12/3462 and 12/3920. Günter Mittag insists that he was not empowered to give direct orders to Schalck, see Mittag, *Preis*, p. 92, but the evidence makes it clear that he (but not only he!) was.

... taking orders ... see p. 165 and notes.

... and especially ... Abrassimov ... a taste of Abrassimov's fierce criticism of the 1978 package of German-German agreements, negotiated by Gaus and Schalck on behalf of Schmidt and Honecker, can be had from the East German documents now in ZPA: IV 2/2.035/65.

Wolfgang Mischnick ... recalls ... Bonn, 17 March 1992.

Wolfgang Schäuble suggests ... see his testimony in *Schalck-Ausschuss*, Protokoll Nr. 24, p. 4 ff.

... Günter Gaus, subsequently described ... according to Bruns, *DDR-Politik*, p. 123, Gaus first publicly used this term in an important interview in *Der Spiegel*, 6/1977.

... much criticised in West Germany ... for a taste of the immediate reaction see *Der Spiegel*, 7/1977. Copies of this and the original interview and lead story are in the Schmidt papers, a small indication of the importance attached to it at the time.

... an 'inner' recognition ... Gaus, *Deutschland*, p. 274.

Yet can one thus separate it? ... Bruns, *DDR-Politik*, pleads for the analytical usefulness of the term, but also himself argues in a partisan, Gausian direction.

... somewhat in the tones of the Spanish inquisition ... see Jens Hacker, *Deutsche Irrtümer. Schönfärber und Helfershelfer der SED-Diktatur im Westen* (Berlin: Ullstein, 1992), *passim*.

... that reunification was the *Lebenslüge* ... Brandt appears first to have used this term, in passing, in a lecture delivered in Munich in 1984. See *Nachdenken über Deutschland* (Munich: Bertelsmann, 1988), pp. 177–190, this on p. 183. His more emphatic and deliberate use of it was, however, in a lecture in Berlin on 11 September 1988, reprinted in Wolf Jobst Siedler, ed., *Berliner Lektionen* (Berlin: Siedler, 1989), pp. 72–88. He repeated it shortly thereafter in a lecture to mark the fortieth anniversary of the Basic Law, at the Friedrich Ebert Stiftung in Bonn on 14 September 1988.

... came the somewhat strained reply ... in a letter from Brandt to the CSU

Chairman Theo Waigel, reprinted in *Frankfurter Rundschau*, 2 November 1990. Brandt traced the sense in which he used the word back to Ibsen.

. . . **not see German unity in his lifetime** . . . quoted by Angela Stent in *Foreign Policy* No. 81, Winter 1990/91, pp. 53–70, this on p. 60.

The few who did thus speak or write . . . See, for example, Wolfgang Venohr, *Die deutsche Einheit Kommt bestimmt* (Bergisch Gladbach: Gustav Lübbe Verlag). But in a book published in 1989, Venohr wrote: 'All the indications are that the GDR will still celebrate its fiftieth anniversary in October 1999,' although he did suggest that this would be 'hopefully as member-state of Democratic Confeder- ation of Germany . . .' Wolfgang Venohr, *Die roten Preussen. Vom wundersamen Aufstieg der DDR in Deutschland* (Erlangen: Straube, 1989), p. 323.

. . . **whereas in the 1950s and 1960s** . . . see Schweigler, *Grundlagen*, p. 118, note 72

'The time seems to me to have come . . .' reprinted in *Zehn Jahre*, pp. 122–23. The original is in AdsD: Dep WB, BK 41.

. . . **'I must confess that I have stopped speaking** . . .' interview in *US News and World Report*, 29 December 1969.

. . . **German unity could only be achieved** . . . the thought was expressed to me — retrospectively — in precisely this paradoxical way by one of the key practitioners of policy towards the GDR, Hans Otto Bräutigam, who was deputy head of the Permanent Representation in East Berlin, then leader of the working group on Deutschlandpolitik in the Federal Chancellery under Helmut Schmidt, then the Federal Republic's Permanent Representative in East Berlin. Hans Otto Bräutigam, Potsdam, 25 June 1991.

. . . **hard-fought negotiations and agreements** . . . the basic agreement was made simultaneously with the initialling of the Basic Treaty, on 8 November 1972, see *Zehn Jahre*, pp. 203–05. But the role and possibilities of Western journalists remained a major bone of contention, with such incidents as the expulsion of the ARD correspondent Lothar Loewe and the closure of the *Spiegel* office counting as minor 'crises' in German-German relations.

. . . **France** . . . **a distinctive policy** . . . this was, at least, the clear impression of the East German leadership. See Honecker's remark quoted above, p. 336. Also Erich Honecker, Berlin-Moabit, 27 November 1992; Kurt Hager, Berlin, 8 May 1992; Karl Seidel, Berlin, 30 September 1992.

. . . **essentially supportive of Bonn's** . . . Jonathan Greenwald (US Embassy), East Berlin, 6 July 1989.

'The intra-German treaty policy . . .' *Bundestag Drucksachen* 10/914.

No one talked more movingly . . . yet this emphasis, like so much else in Deutschlandpolitik, owed a great deal to Herbert Wehner as well. See, for example, Baring, *Machtwechsel*, pp. 611–12.

... 'when considerable German payments-in-advance ...' *Bundestag Plenarprotokolle*, 6/22, p. 847 (14 January 1970).

... 'We are aware ...' *Bundestag Plenarprotokolle*, 11/33, p. 2161 (15 October 1987).

... negotiations with the East German authorities ... the most comprehensive and detailed summary accounts are contained in *Zehn Jahre* (for 1969–79) and *Innerdeutsche Beziehungen* (for 1980–86), while the last years (1987–89) are summarised in the annual reports (*Jahresberichte*) and other publications of the Ministry for Intra-German Relations.

... *Verklammerung* ... For the slogan of *Verklammerung* already in the FDP's 'Schollwer paper' in the mid-1960s see Hildebrand, *Von Erhard zur Grossen Koalition*, p. 342.

... fifteen of the seventeen agreements ... Bender, *Neue Ostpolitik*, p. 211.

... an agreement on cultural co-operation ... see *Innerdeutsche Beziehungen*, pp. 15 and 259–62. The main obstacle to the signature of such an agreement was the dispute about former Prussian state museum and library holdings, which, due to wartime evacuations, often ended up in the West when they had originally been in the East, or vice versa. As so often in German-German relations this dispute was not resolved but rather put aside, in this case with a 'common protocol declaration' which read: 'The different standpoints on the question of cultural property moved as a result of war are not affected. The partners to the agreement declare their readiness insofar as possible to seek solutions in the areas of cultural goods moved as a result of war.' This, in several cases, they actually proceeded to do.

... fifty-eight such agreements ... for an exhaustive study of these town-twinnings see Beatrice von Weizsäcker, *Verschwisterung im Bruderland. Städtepartnerschaften in Deutschland* (Bonn: Bouvier, 1990), these statistics on pp. 365–66. For a very interesting top-level East German assessment of the town-twinnings see the appendix to the minutes of the Politburo meeting on 6 September 1988 in ZPA: JIV 2/2/2292.

... 1969 ... just half a million ... *Zahlenspiegel*, p. 130.

... 1988 ... 40 million ... see *Texte*, III/6, p. 543.

... little more than one million visits ... this and following statistics in *Zahlenspiegel*, p. 124, supplemented by *DDR-Reisebarometer*. See Table VII.

... some 60,000 a year ... *Zahlenspiegel*, p. 124.

... the numbers who travelled by land to West Berlin ... *Zahlenspiegel*, p. 126.

... 1988 ... some one and a half million visits ... *DDR-Reisebarometer*, p. 17.

... phone calls ... *Zahlenspiegel*, p. 130.

... among them Hans-Dietrich Genscher ... for Genscher's flight see Werner

Filmer, Heribert Schwan, *Hans-Dietrich Genscher* (Düsseldorf: Econ Verlag, 1988), pp. 102–7.

. . . his heart remained in Halle . . . In a speech in Potsdam in June 1988 Genscher said: 'The GDR is the part of Germany in which, in Halle on the Saale, there stands the house of my birth, in which I grew up, in which I went to school, in which I studied at the Universities of Halle and Leipzig — here my father, my grandparents are buried — here I have my *Heimat.*' Genscher, *Unterwegs*, p. 153. In a 1985 eulogy for Alois Mertes, Genscher also described himself as 'a Protestant from the heart of our fatherland'. Der Bundesminister des Auswärtigen, Mitteilung für die Presse, Nr. 1074/85. In a speech of thanks on receiving the honorary citizenship of Halle, after unification, he remarked that his associates had sometimes got the impression that Halle was larger than Shanghai, FAZ, 10 June 1991.

. . . becoming easier for Poles and Czechs . . . According to figures in the *UN Statistical Yearbook* the number of Hungarians visiting Austria rose from just 9,000 in 1960 to 45,000 in 1970, and 126,000 in 1980. These are almost certainly underestimates, since they are based on registrations at places of overnight stay. To this period, one might note, belongs a minor sub-genre of East Central European literature: the account of the first visit to the West. See, for example, Zbigniew Herbert's marvellous *A Barbarian in the Garden* (Manchester: Carcanet, 1985).

. . . top operative priority . . . 'Our most important goal, Ladies and Gentlemen, remains the achievement of more freedom of movement in Germany,' Chancellor Kohl in his 1987 state of the nation address, *Bundestag Plenarprotokolle* 11/33, p. 2163 (15 October 1987).

It began with the Protestant Church . . . for this and the following see Geissel, *Unterhändler*, pp. 328–334 and *passim*. See also the important article by Armin Volze, 'Kirchliche Transferleistungen in die DDR', in DA, 1/1991, pp. 59–63 (hereafter Volze, 'Kirchliche Transferleistungen'), Rehlinger, *Freikauf*, pp. 14–15, the long investigative article by Thomas Kleine-Brockhoff and Oliver Schröm in *Die Zeit*, 28 August 1992, which draws on material from the Schalck investigations, but also Volze's critical commentary on it in DA, 1/1993 pp. 58–66. These sources, together with the figures in Figure X, supplant the earlier and necessarily speculative work of the French journalist Michel Meyer, *Freikauf. Menschenhandel in Deutschland* (Vienna: Paul Zsolnay, 1978). This is clearly the subject for an important book, although one that will be very difficult to write given the lack of written evidence and the often conflicting testimonies.

. . . an intervention by the publisher Axel Springer . . . Rainer Barzel, Bonn, 2 October 1991. Rehlinger, *Freikauf*, pp. 17–18. Springer was responding to a suggestion from the West Berlin lawyer Jürgen Stange, who in turn had got the hint from Wolfgang Vogel.

. . . Ludwig Rehlinger describes . . . in Rehlinger, *Freikauf*, p. 23 ff.

. . . in a large unmarked envelope . . . ibid., pp. 32–35. Jürgen Stange, Berlin, 9 October 1991.

In August 1964 the first 'regular' transports ... Wolfgang Vogel, Berlin, 9 October 1991.

... the East Berlin lawyer extraordinary ... a first attempt at a biography of this controversial figure was Jens Schmidthammer, *Rechtsanwalt Wolfgang Vogel. Mittler zwischen Ost und West* (Hamburg: Hoffmann & Campe, 1987). A biography by Craig Whitney, *Spy Trader. Germany's Legendary Spy Broker and the Darkest Secrets of the Cold War* (New York: Times Books, 1993), was made available to the author in typescript as this book was going to press. A fine example of American investigative journalism, it contains many new details.

... a certain Heinz Volpert ... see Przybylski, *Tatort 2*, the special report in *Die Zeit*, 28 August 1992, Whitney's *Spy Trader*, and the reports of the Bundestag special committee.

... a price on the head ... in an interview in *Der Spiegel*, 15/1990, Vogel claimed that the criterion was the length of sentence. But see Rehlinger, *Freikauf*, p. 28.

... a detailed record of what it called 'B-Deals' ... see Volze, 'Kirchliche Transferleistungen', pp. 62–64. The East German side also referred to 'C-Deals', which were payments from the Roman Catholic Church. Alexander Schalck, Berlin, 1 July 1992.

... Commercial Co-ordination (*KoKo* ...) An authoritative book on *KoKo*, drawing on the mass of documents collected by the Bundestag special committee, other documents in the Party, state and Stasi archives, and the testimonies of Schalck and other participants, remains to be written. The first two reports of the Bundestag special committee, *Bundestag Drucksachen*, 12/3462 and 12/3920, present much basic information. On three 'instant' Schalck books to appear on the market see the review by Armin Volze in DA, 6/1992, pp. 646–56. For the specific relationship with the Protestant church see Geissel, *Unterhändler*, p. 346 ff and *passim*.

The first delivery ... the following two paragraphs are based on the work of Armin Volze, the special report in *Die Zeit*, 28 August 1992, reports by Wolfgang Stock in the FAZ, and the official records of the Bundestag special committee.

... oil, copper, silver and industrial diamonds ... see the table in Volze, 'Kirchliche Transferleistungen', p. 63.

Jürgen Stange estimates that ... Jürgen Stange, Berlin, 9 October 1991.

... a letter ... August 1972 ... this letter, dated 1 August 1972, is in AdsD: HS, 347, a file of correspondence with the Minister for Intra-German Relations.

... proposed to take this seriously ... Günter Gaus, Hamburg, 14 May 1992.

... broke off the talks ... Rehlinger, *Freikauf*, p. 77.

According to Wolfgang Vogel ... Wolfgang Vogel, Berlin, 9 October 1991.

... **Wehner** ... **travelled to East Berlin** ... for this at the time famous incident see Baring, *Machtwechsel*, pp. 608–14, Rehlinger, *Freikauf*, p. 77, and Wehner and Mischnick's statements reproduced in *Texte*, I/12, pp. 676–81. Wehner's fascinating correspondence with Brandt following this episode is in AdsD: Dep WB, BK 75, while Wehner's own collection of his interviews and speeches on the subject in the second half of 1973 fills a fat file in BK 76. Mischnick joined Wehner and Honecker somewhat later in the day, Wolfgang Mischnick, Bonn, 17 March 1992. Honecker's own account in Reinhold Andert & Wolfgang Herzberg, *Der Sturz. Erich Honecker im Kreuzverhör* (Berlin: Aufbau-Verlag, 1991), pp. 348–49, confirms the details.

'**They will get serious** ...' letter of 24 June 1973 in AdsD: Dep WB, BK 75.

... **a memorandum of a conversation** ... the memorandum, dated 2 December 1973, is in AdsD: Dep WB, BK 75. The memorandum contains both Wehner's summary of this 'verbal report' and his own commentary upon it. It is clear from accompanying notes that Wehner actually sent this to Honecker, as well as to Brandt, who asked Horst Ehmke to discuss it with Egon Bahr and Günter Gaus. More remarkably, Honecker wrote a long reply, dated 2 February 1974, of which more below.

Talking to Leonid Brezhnev ... record (*Niederschrift*) of their conversation in Moscow on 18 June 1974, now in ZPA: IV 2/2.035/55.

... **happy with us** ... for one contrary example see Garton Ash, *DDR*, pp. 21–22.

... **emotional relationship** ... see also p. 321.

... **neither Vogel nor Schalck will aver** ... Wolfgang Vogel, Berlin, 9 October 1991, Alexander Schalck-Golodkowski, Rottach-Egern, 10 October 1991.

... **set at DM 40,000** ... Wolfgang Vogel in *Der Spiegel*, 15/1990. There also the following details and quotation.

... **DM 4,500 a head** ... this figure from Wolfgang Vogel, Berlin, 9 October 1991.

... **in sum** ... the Rehlinger, *Freikauf*, p. 247. They tally with those given by Vogel in *Der Spiegel*, 15/1990. For the payments, the most precise figures are given by Volze, 'Kirchliche Transferleistungen', p. 64, who lists both the Church figure of DM 3,436,900 (cf. Geissel, *Unterhändler*, p. 470) and the federal budget figure of DM 3,464,900. Rehlinger gives a slightly higher figure of 'over 3.5 billion'. The uncontrolled nature of these transfers led to a scandal in the Ministry for Intra-German Relations, where the senior official responsible for these proceedings under the social-liberal coalition was convicted of having misappropriated large sums. For further detail, see the special report in *Die Zeit*, 28 August 1992. The lawyers also took a number of cases in which private individuals paid to 'buy free' people from the GDR.

... '**The government of the German Democratic Republic** ...' *Zehn Jahre*,

p. 188. See also the account of these negotiations in Baring, *Machtwechsel*, pp. 457–62.

. . . the formula 'urgent family matters' . . . it seems first to have been used in the second permit agreement of September 1964, see *Dokumente*, IV/10, pp. 987–90, and Egon Bahr's commentary, pp. 996–97.

. . . a directive according to which . . . *Zehn Jahre*, p. 199. The one word 'Westberlin' reflected the GDR's position that West Berlin was a separate unit, neither half a divided city nor an integral part of the Federal Republic, but a land unto itself . . .

. . . the GDR promising to take further steps . . . *Zehn Jahre*, p. 208.

. . . a set of detailed notes . . . ibid., pp. 208–10.

. . . a further directive of June 1973 . . . ibid., pp. 231–2.

. . . a new travel decree . . . on visits to 'non-socialist states and Berlin (West)' of 15 February 1982, replacing those of October 1972 and June 1973. Text in *Innerdeutsche Beziehungen*, p. 100.

. . . West German statistics . . . see Table VI and notes.

. . . the introduction in January 1989 . . . see reports in FAZ, 15 December 1988, and for the criticism, FAZ 20 February 1989 and 23 March 1989. Text of the decree in *Texte*, III/6, pp. 554–562.

. . . no less than eighty-four per cent . . . *DDR-Reisebarometer*, p. 94.

. . . 'the most important achievement . . .' *Bundestag Plenarprotokolle*, 11/33, p. 2159 (15 October 1987).

. . . a 'meeting about GDR issues' . . . the minute, signed by Carl-Werner Sanne, is in AdsD: HS 127. Part of the follow-up can be seen in the exchange of letters between Schmidt and Honecker in ZPA: JIV 2/2A/1815.

. . . with Schalck, Vogel . . . see, for example, Gaus, *Deutschland*, pp. 257–62, Bölling, *Die fernen Nachbarn*, Chapter V. For a conversation between Schmidt and Vogel, in preparation for the Chancellor's planned summit with Honecker in 1980, see the note of 16 July 1980 in AdsD: HS 322. Some of Gaus's reports on his talks with Schalck are in AdsD: HS 449. Many East German reports of these talks emerged in a fragmentary way through the work of the Bundestag special committee on Schalck, which sifted the holdings of the Central Party Archive in Berlin.

. . . Karl Seidel . . . the papers of Seidel's department would be an indispensable source for any serious treatment of this subject. But at the time of writing they were under lock and key in the archives taken over directly by the West German Foreign Ministry. Even the archivists themselves had only limited access to them.

. . . to be found in the Schmidt papers . . . notably the correspondence with the Permanent Representation in AdsD: HS 449. See also the illuminating discussion in Link, *Ära Schmidt*, p. 353 ff.

... **when, for example, men and women took refuge** ... a moving description of one such case was given by Klaus Bölling in a confidential letter to the Chancellor dated 26 February 1981, in AdsD: HS 449. For a fine account see Rehlinger, *Freikauf*, pp. 121–93.

... **'I.** *Introduction*: **20 years** ...' these notes, the outline for the speechwriters, are in AdsD: HS 2439. Schmidt actually used the terms near the end of the final version of his speech, adding 'Moderation, persistence and predictability are not exactly traditional virtues of the Germans. Instead we must make them German virtues, if we want to survive in our very special historical and very special geographical situation.' *Bundestag Plenarprotokolle* 9/31, pp. 1548–49 (9 April 1981).

... **the 'Church in socialism'** ... see references in note on p. 530.

... **Stolpe** ... On Stolpe, as on Schalck, there is already a vast literature. The case against Stolpe is well summarised in Ralf Georg Reuth, *IM "SEKRETÄR". Die "Gauck-Recherche" und die Dokumente zum "Fall Stolpe"* (2nd, revised edition, Frankfurt: Ullstein, 1992), which reprints many of the most important documents. Stolpe's own successive versions can be followed in Manfred Stolpe, *Den Menschen Hoffnung geben. Reden, Aufsätze und Interviews aus zwölf Jahren* (Berlin: Wichern Verlag, 1991), and Manfred Stolpe, *Schwieriger Aufbruch* (Berlin: Siedler, 1992). Among innumerable articles on the case one might single out that by Richard Schröder in *Die Zeit*, 9 October 1992.

'Stolpe was a détente politician ...' this in an open letter to Bärbel Bohley in FAZ, 13 February 1992.

... **close to Stolpe's methods** ... report on an interview by Peter Jochen Winters in FAZ, 3 February 1992.

When Günter Gaus first made contact ... this story from Günter Gaus, Hamburg, 14 May 1992.

... **heartily relieved** ... Hans Otto Bräutigam, Berlin, 28 June 1992.

... **Strauss** ... **secret communications with Schalck** ... copies of documents originally made available by the CSU were kindly placed at the author's disposal by Wolfgang Stock.

... **Schäuble, tried to regularise** ... see his own account in *Schalck-Ausschuss*, Protokoll Nr. 24., p. 13 ff.

... **pending the necessary masterwork** ... short accounts are given in *Materialien*, pp. 626–35, a section written by specialists from the Deutsches Institut für Wirtschaftsforschung, and Karl C Thalheim, *Die wirtschaftliche Entwicklung der beiden Staaten in Deutschland* (Opladen: Leske & Budrich, 1988), Chapter 10. The best starting-points in English are the chapter by Michael Kaser in Moreton, *Germany*, John Garland, 'FRG-GDR Economic Relations', in *East European Economies. Slow Growth in the 1980s* (Washington: US Government Printing Office, 1986 = Selected Papers submitted to the Joint Economic Committee, Congress of the United States), Vol. 3, pp. 169–206 (hereafter, Garland

'FRG-GDR'), and H-D Jacobsen, *Security Implications of Inner-German Economic Relations* (Washington DC: Wilson Center International Security Studies Program Working Paper No. 77, 1986). (After unification, Jacobsen was reportedly discovered to have been collaborating with the Stasi, which gives a certain piquancy to this last title.)

... 'intra-German trade' ... on this see the article by Siegfried Kupper in *DDR-Handbuch*, Bruns, *DDR-Politik*, pp. 98–107, Siegfried Kupper's earlier book, *Der innerdeutsche Handel* (Köln: Markus, 1972), Doris Cornelsen & ors, *Die Bedeutung des innerdeutschen Handels* (Berlin: Duncker und Humboldt, 1984) and Reinhold Biskup, *Deutschlands offene Handelsgrenze. Die DDR als Nutzniesser des EWG-Protokolls über den innerdeutschen Handel* (Berlin: Ullstein, 1976).

... 'a part of internal German trade' ... see *Treaties establishing the European Communities* (Luxemburg: Office for Official Publications of the European Communities, 1987), Vol. I, pp. 513–14. The precise wording of the first paragraph is: 'Since trade between the German territories subject to the Basic Law for the Federal Republic of Germany and the German territories in which the Basic Law does not apply is a part of German internal trade, the application of this Treaty in Germany requires no change in the treatment currently accorded this trade.' In a discussion to mark the twentieth anniversary of Bahr's Tutzing speech, Alois Mertes recalled Walter Hallstein telling him about the 'hard struggle' he had to get the above-mentioned Protocol on Intra-German Trade accepted by the Federal Republic's new partners in the EEC. See *Die Zeit*, 15 July 1983. The formula 'German territories in which the Basic Law does not apply' reflected the Bonn government's then non-recognition of the sovereignty of both the GDR and the Polish and Soviet states over former German territories to the East. Needless to say, the benefits of Intra-German Trade were only ever extended to the GDR, or what was then known as the Soviet Occupation Zone. The agency which dealt with Intra-German Trade was actually known as the 'Trust Office for Intra-Zonal Trade' until the end of 1981, when it was renamed the 'Trust Office for Industry and Trade.'

... a drizzle of discontent ... see the balanced discussion in Garland, 'FRG-GDR', pp. 204–5.

... more than half its western trade ... According to GDR official statistics, in 1984 only 30 per cent of the GDR's total Western trade was with the Federal Republic, but the statistics of its trading partners produce a figure of about 50 per cent (*Materialien*, p. 630). In his calculations for 1985, Lincoln Gordon concludes that trade with West Germany comprised 59.4 per cent of East Germany's trade with 'industrial countries' (Gordon, *Eroding Empire*, Table A–12). For a fine analysis of the amazingly diverse statistics see Raimund Dietz, 'Der Westhandel der DDR', in DA, 3/1985.

... 'Swing' ... as a card ... see Link, *Ära Schmidt*, pp. 358–59.

... even more cautiously ... in 1980–81 ... see Schmidt, *Nachbarn*, pp. 70–71, Mittag, *Preis*, pp. 94–95.

In 1985, the Kohl government privately... see Schäuble's testimony in *Schalck-Ausschuss*, Protokoll Nr. 24, p. 12.

...public and private transfers... the best summary account is now given in three scrupulous articles by Armin Volze, 'Geld und Politik in den innerdeutschen Beziehungen 1970–1989', in DA, 3/1990 (hereafter Volze, 'Geld und Politik'), the already cited 'Kirchliche Transferleistungen' (DA, 1/1991, pp. 59–66), and 'Die Devisengeschäfte der DDR. Genex und Intershop', DA, 11/1991, pp. 1145–1159 (hereafter Volze, 'Devisengeschäfte'). A critical account is given by Jerzy Lisiecki, 'Financial and Material Transfers between East and West Germany', in *Soviet Studies*, Vol. 42, No. 3, July 1990, pp. 513–34. Some additional detail can be found in the *Materialien*, and in an earlier article by Armin Volze, 'Zu den Besonderheiten der innerdeutschen Wirtschaftsbeziehungen im Ost-West Verhältnis' in *Deutsche Studien*, No. 83, September 1983, pp. 184–99.

...some DM 2 billion... Volze, 'Geld und Politik', p. 386. The 'greeting money' was raised from DM 30 to DM 100 per head in 1987.

...a leading specialist estimates... ibid.

...some DM 2.2 billion... calculated from the table in Volze, 'Kirchliche Transferleistungen', p. 64.

...of the order of $1—$1.5 billion... see Jacek Rostowski's contribution to Stanisław Gomułka and Antony Polonsky, eds, *Polish Paradoxes* (London: Routledge, 1990), p. 219, with further detail from the author's original typescript.

...some DM 5 billion... Volze, 'Geld und Politik', p. 386.

...some DM 3.2 billion... calculated from the table in Volze, 'Kirchliche Transferleistungen', p. 64.

...by Willy Brandt to Piotr Abrassimov... 'In this connection [links with West Berlin] Abrassimov reacted extremely positively to a passing comment of mine that it would be sensible to negotiate a lump-sum payment for the use of the motorway etc.' — Brandt's handwritten notes of a conversation with Abrassimov, 18 June 1968, in AdsD: Dep WB, BA 18.

...a lump-sum payment for the transit and other 'road use' fees... see *Materialien*, Table 7–6, p. 796. Strictly speaking, the DM 575 million was DM 525 million for transit fees plus a further DM 50 million for 'road-use fees'. This did not include sums paid by other travellers in transit, or special 'road use fees' for lorries etc. The overall figure of DM 8.3 billion is given by Volze, 'Geld und Politik', p. 384.

...under an agreement signed in October 1988... see *Texte*, III/6, pp. 343–57. Formally speaking, this was an annual DM 860 million for transit plus DM 55 million for 'road use'. The GDR undertook to open a new frontier crossing and to use some of these DM to improve the transit routes. In the formal agreements, provision was made for a negotiation in 1999, to agree a rate for the first decade of the twenty-first century.

...the papers presented to the Politburo... for the meeting of 30 August

1988. In the draft 'informal verbal declaration', the GDR said it would 'continue the measures taken and alleviations which have led to an increase in the travel — and visit-traffic of citizens of the GDR to non-socialist foreign countries'. Now in ZPA: JIV 2/2/2291. As noted above, new regulations on visits to the West were introduced at the end of 1988.

... **more than DM 2.4 billion** ... Volze, 'Geld und Politik', p. 385 says 'nearly' DM 2.4 billion, but if one adds payments from the Berlin and Bavarian governments for sewage disposal etc., the figure is slightly more.

... **that Bonn got 'value for money'** ... this was emphatically confirmed by one former Permanent Representative, Klaus Bölling, in conversation with the author (Berlin, 26 June 1991).

... **West German investigators found** ... see the report in *Handelsblatt*, 24 October 1990, p. 6. I am grateful to Jurek Lisiecki for drawing my attention to this detail.

... **initially negotiated** ... for Strauss's own account, which includes his drafting the letter for the East German Finance Minister to send to the West German Finance Minister, see Strauss, *Erinnerungen*, pp. 470–74.

... **unusually favourable terms** ... As befitted a Strauss initiative, the consortium of banks was led by the Bayerische Landesbank. Exceptionally, the guarantee covered 100 per cent of the loan and the banks had to pay nothing for the guarantee. The conservative-liberal government thus went further in helping the GDR than the social-liberal government ever had. See Bruns, *DDR-Politik*, pp. 164–67. On the second loan, the banks did have to pay the usual 'provision' for the guarantee. See *Materialien*, p. 634. The 'security' offered by the GDR was an undertaking to renounce the equivalent amount of the lump-sum payment on transit fees, if it failed to repay the loan.

... **that it would pay off in other fields** ... a specific example is a letter from Gaus to Chancellor Schmidt dated 24 October 1978, in which, noting that the financial difference between Bonn and the GDR's proposals for a package of projects is DM 137.5 million, he then writes: 'My recommendation is that in the final version we should meet the GDR's demands in this area, because our prospects of their giving ground on other questions could thereby be decisively improved.' AdsD: HS 449

... **'the principle of a balance of give and take** ...' Bölling, *Die fernen Nachbarn*, p. 93

... **'cash against hope'** ... thus Rainer Barzel in *Bundestag Plenarprotokolle*, 9/118, p. 7169, 1 October 1982.

... **the Social Democrats could hardly resist retorting** ... see the speech by Hans Apel, responding to Chancellor Kohl's 1985 state of the nation address, in *Bundestag Plenarprotokolle*, 10/122, p. 9017 (27 February 1985).

... **they would point** ... these arguments were mustered by Wolfgang Schäuble in a clear defence of the policy, see the report by Karl Feldmeyer in FAZ, 17 August 1991.

. . . **a political signal** . . . this was said in so many words by Chancellor Kohl in his 1984 state of the nation address, see the discussion in *Innerdeutsche Beziehungen*, p. 11.

. . . **Schalck's internal note** . . . copy of report dated Berlin, 12.03.1984, from papers of the *Schalck-Ausschuss*. For Honecker's acceptance of such linkages in connection with the first billion credit, see Strauss, *Erinnerungen*, p. 473.

. . . **the hard currency balance of payments deficit** . . . one of the first to point this up was Schalck himself, see the report in FAZ, 2 January 1990, referring to an interview with Schalck on ARD television. It has subsequently been extensively referred to, not only by Schalck but also, notably, by the head of the State Plan Commission, Gerhard Schürer, who also chaired the operative Balance of Payments Working Group. See also Mittag, *Preis*, pp. 82 ff, 287 ff, and the embittered memoirs of one of his associates, Carl-Heinz Janson, *Totengräber der DDR. Wie Günter Mittag den SED-Staat ruinierte* (Düsseldorf: Econ, 1991), p. 33 ff.

. . . **Schalck and others now testify** . . . Alexander Schalck-Golodkowski, Berlin, 1 July 1992. Gerhard Schürer, Berlin, 7 October 1991.

Günter Mittag goes so far . . . Günter Mittag, Berlin, 28 June 1992, and see Mittag, *Preis*, p. 82 ff.

Gerhard Schürer . . . suggests . . . Berlin, 7 October 1991 and 30 June 1992.

. . . **the key operational Balance of Payments Working Group** . . . one must distinguish between the Politburo Balance of Payments Working Group, set up by the Politburo resolution of 2 November 1976 and chaired by Mittag, and the *operational* Balance of Payments Working Group, chaired by Schürer.

The internal statistics of the GDR in this field . . . The most important series of statistics would appear to be that kept by the hard currency department of the Finance Ministry, under Deputy Minister Herta König, who was also a member of the Balance of Payments Working Group.

. . . **about 2 billion Valutamarks** . . . Carl-Heinz Janson, *Totengräber der DRR. Wie Günter Mittag den SED-Staat ruinierte* (Düsseldorf: Econ, 1991), p. 65, gives a figure of 2.2 billion for 1970 and 25.3 billion for 1985. These figures were confirmed to the author by Gerhard Schürer (letter of 13 November 1992) on the basis of his own papers.

. . . **this 'plinth'** . . . in German, *Sockel*. The term is used frequently by Mittag, *Preis*, and by those responsible in conversation with the author.

. . . **more consumer than producer** . . . Schürer gives a figure of sixty per cent consumer to forty per cent producer goods for the early 1970s. Gerhard Schürer, Berlin, 7 October 1991. This general critique of Honecker's strategy is made in a number of memoirs and recollections. Mittag, *Preis*, blames it all on Honecker. Carl-Heinz Janson, *Totengräber der DDR. Wie Günter Mittag den SED-Staat* *ruinierte* (Düsseldorf: Econ, 1991) blames it all on Mittag. Most others blame it on both Honecker and Mittag. See, for example, the notes by Werner Krolikowski reprinted in Przybylski, *Tatort 1*, p. 321 ff. Schürer gives his account in a memoir entitled *Gewagt und Verloren. Die Planwirtschaft der DDR und ihr Untergang* (typescript, October 1991, copy in the author's possession).

. . . **constantly warning** . . . this was a point made to me by almost all the former members of the East German Politburo, with the signal exception of Erich Honecker, who flatly denied that Brezhnev had given any such warning.

. . . **'did not reach a dangerous level'** . . . report on Brezhnev's meeting with the Czechoslovak politburo in April 1981 in ZPA: IV 2/2.035/54.

. . . **also warned** . . . Günter Schabowski, *Der Absturz* (Berlin: Rowohlt, 1991), p. 121 f, credits Schürer with making a first protest in 1972, a version also given by Schürer himself. Werner Krolikowski also claims to have warned about the consequences at an early stage (see the documents in Przybylski, *Tatort 1*), a claim broadly confirmed by Schürer. See also Przybylski, *Tatort 2*, p. 49 ff. For Schürer's 1988 attempt see below.

Ludwig Geissel recalls . . . Geissel, *Unterhändler*, pp. 264–65.

. . . **an enclave of real-price, market-oriented economic activity** . . . an interpretation given by Schalck himself (Berlin, 1 July 1992), this is nonetheless plausible.

. . . **formally in 1972 and again in 1976** . . . that is, after the 8th and 9th party congresses. A rather vivid account of the irresistible rise of Alexander Schalck is given in Przybylski, *Tatort 2*.

. . . *de facto* **even more thereafter** . . . see, for example, the letter dated 23/24 April 1981 from Mittag to Honecker, reprinted in *Bundestag Drucksachen*, 12/3462, pp. 898–900, and all the evidence cited above about his crucial role as German-German intermediary.

Karl Seidel . . . Berlin, 30 September 1992.

. . . **Gerhard Schürer rightly points out** . . . Berlin, 30 June 1992.

. . . **'secured'** . . . **DM 50 billion** . . . thus Schalck many times, for example in testimony to the *Schalck-Ausschuss*, Bonn, 24 June 1992.

. . . **DM 27 billion** . . . **DM 23 billion** . . . Alexander Schalck-Golodkowski, Berlin, 1 July 1992.

. . . **casually mentioned** . . . ibid.

. . . **corresponds almost exactly** . . . The precise total from the ten years' transit and road-use lump-sum payments would have been DM 9.15 billion. Subtracting this from the round figure of DM 23 billion we get DM 13.85 billion. The total of the state-to-state transfers, as calculated by Armin Volze on the basis of the West German figures, is DM 13.9 billion.

. . . **of the order of 2 billion Valutamarks** . . . Gerhard Schürer, Berlin, 30 June 1992 and letter of 13 November 1992. One should also note that the so-called

Staatsdevisenreserve (state hard currency reserve), which was controlled by the Council of Ministers, was probably also fed directly from the hard currency visa and minimum compulsory exchange income from Western visitors.

. . . **about 5 billion Valutamarks** . . . ibid. Of course these figures should be verified if and when the full, internal statistics are available. But Schürer's round figures give a good sense of the orders of magnitude.

. . . **figures used by Schürer and others** . . . Carl-Heinz Janson, *Totengräber der DDR. Wie Günter Mittag den SED-Staat ruinierte* (Düsseldorf: Econ, 1991), p. 65, gives the figures as 30.0 billion for 1985 and 34.7 billion for 1987.

A memorandum . . . memorandum of 30 October 1989, reprinted in DA, 10/1992, pp. 1112–20, this on p. 1116.

. . . **the Bundesbank** . . . see its *Monatsbericht*, 7/1990. Further detail in this paragraph comes from Gerhard Schürer, and from the leading West German specialist, Armin Volze (letter of 11 January 1993).

. . . **including arms and ammunition** . . . these raids on the strategic reserves had formally to be approved by the Politburo, see, for example, the appendices in ZPA: JIV 2/2A/2582.

. . . **Schürer and Schalck would privately discuss** . . . Gerhard Schürer, Berlin, 7 October 1991. The first serious journalistic treatment of this story came in an article by Peter Siebenmorgen in *Die Zeit*, 3 May 1991. More details can be found in Hans-Hermann Hertle, *Vor dem Bankrott der DDR = Berliner Arbeitshefte und Berichte zur sozialwissenschaftlichen Forschung Nr. 63* (Berlin: Zentralinstitut für sozialwissenschaftliche Forschung, 1991), which contains both a transcript of a long interview with Schürer and copies of the actual documents submitted to Honecker and then to the Politburo.

. . . **Mittag would claim, retrospectively** . . . Günter Mittag, Berlin, 28 June 1992, and Mittag, *Preis*, p. 97 ff. Mittag there credits Gerhard Beil with also thinking in terms of an eventual confederation. Gerhard Beil was unfortunately not prepared to talk to the author.

. . . **slightly less alarming** . . . Günter Schabowski, Berlin, 29 June 1991. Egon Krenz, Berlin, 29 September 1992. Among other things, monies owed to the GDR were credited in full, even where there was effectively no chance of their being repaid.

'When you took over . . .' quoted by Gerhard Schürer in his (at the time of writing, unpublished) memoirs, *Gewagt und Verloren. Die Planwirtschaft der DDR und ihr Untergang* (typescript, October 1991, copy in the author's possession).

Egon Krenz knew the true facts . . . Egon Krenz, Berlin, 29 September 1992.

. . . **Werner Krolikowski colourfully remarked** . . . the memorandum is reprinted in Przybylski, *Tatort 1*, pp. 321–339, this on p. 327.

. . . **the above-mentioned Schürer memorandum** . . . DA, 10/1992, pp. 1112–20, this on p. 1116.

'Where has all the hard currency gone?' . . . Garton Ash, *We*, p. 70.

. . . understood little of economics . . . Gerhard Schürer, Berlin, 7 October 1991; Mittag, *Preis*; and see below, p. 198.

. . . to make quite sure . . . thus, explicitly, Strauss, *Erinnerungen*, p. 476. Also Wolfgang Schäuble, Bonn, 17 March 1992.

. . . Schäuble recalls . . . Wolfgang Schäuble, Bonn, 17 March 1992.

. . . Schalck recalls . . . Alexander Schalck-Golodkowski, Rottach-Egern, 10 October 1991.

. . . some of West Germany's economic experts . . . on the political-academic tensions behind the 1987 *Materialien* see the brief and distinctly partisan account in Jens Hacker, *Deutsche Irrtümer. Schönfärber und Helfershelfer der SED-Diktatur im Westen* (Berlin: Ullstein, 1992), pp. 442–49.

. . . the average East German cow . . . *Materialien*, p. 442.

. . . enough to cover the interest payments . . . ibid., p, 634. In the event, this almost certainly underestimated the debt service burden. The authors' guesstimate was based on the work of Armin Volze. In the light of Hacker's criticisms it should perhaps be noted that this passage comes in the part of the *Materialien* prepared by the Deutsches Institut für Wirtschaftsforschung.

. . . 'choreograph the West German grande bourgeoisie' . . . Günter Schabowski, Berlin, 29 June 1991.

Did not the World Bank say . . . quoted, with apparent relish, by Jonathan Steele, *Socialism with a German Face. The State that Came in From the Cold* (London: Jonathan Cape, 1977), p. 7. The GDR was said to have 'overtaken' Britain in 1974.

. . . James McAdams . . . 'Inter-German Détente. A New Balance', in *Foreign Affairs*, Fall 1986, pp. 136–53. This article developed the argument of his earlier book *East Germany and détente. Building Authority after the Wall* (Cambridge: Cambridge University Press, 1985). See also his delightfully titled article 'The GDR at Forty. The Perils of Success' in *German Politics and Society* (Harvard) Issue 17, Summer 1989. McAdams's notable book on German-German relations, *Germany Divided. From the Wall to Unification* (Princeton: Princeton University Press, 1993) appeared too late to be used in the preparation of this chapter.

. . . the subject of fierce debate . . . see the illuminating discussion in Bergsdorf, *Sprache*, p. 212 f.

. . . a more important distinction . . . this distinction was drawn with characteristic clarity by Ralf Dahrendorf, see *Bundestag Plenarprotokolle*, 6/23, p. 925 (15 January 1970).

. . . Christian Democratic opponents . . . see Clemens, *Reluctant Realists* and Hacke, *Wege und Irrwege* for more detail. In his last state of the nation address, in June 1969, Chancellor Kiesinger himself made this point quite forcefully. The people in East Germany did not support either the regime or the imposed constitution or even the very existence of a second German state, he said. 'A recognition by us or by others could not substitute for this lacking support.' See *Bundestag Plenarprotokolle*, 5/239, p. 13246 (17 June 1969), also in *Texte* I/3, p. 256 ff.

'**We . . . are not prepared**' . . . reprinted in *Texte* I/5, pp. 189–201, this on p. 193.

Social and Free Democrats replied . . . see the speeches by Brandt and others listed under 'Anerkennung' in the index to *Texte* I. See also the brief discussion in Brandt, *Erinnerungen*, p. 234 ff, Bender, *Neue Ostpolitik*, p. 160 ff, and for an eloquent publicistic statement of the case, Peter Bender, *Zehn Gründe für die Anerkennung der DDR* (Frankfurt: Fischer, 1968)

Willy Brandt quoted . . . see *Bundestag Plenarprotokolle*, 6/94, p. 5183 (29 January 1971) and Brandt, *Erinnerungen*, p. 235

. . . Erich Honecker proudly announced . . . personal observation by the author. He was still trumpeting this achievement in his defence speech before the West Berlin court in 1992, see DA, 1/1993, pp. 97–105, this on p. 97.

In a speech at Gera . . . for the demands, and their context, see Bruns, *DDR-Politik*, pp. 139–43, and, in English, A. James McAdams, *East Germany and Détente. Building Authority after the Wall* (Cambridge: Cambridge University Press, 1985), pp. 170–72.

Häber's records of his conversations . . . these are now in ZPA with the signatures (in 1992) JIV 2/10.02/10–14 and JIV 2/10.04/14–17.

. . . the delight expressed . . . this in Häber's reports in ZPA: JIV 2/10.02/13. The tendency to sycophancy is particularly apparent in Häber's reports — perhaps one reason why Honecker lifted him so unexpectedly into the Politburo?

. . . 'a fanatical Polish nationalist' . . . quoted from Häber's report of 27 June 1978 on a trip to West Germany, 19–24 June, now (1992) in ZPA: JIV 2/10.02/10.

. . . 'there was hardly an interlocutor . . .' from Häber's report on his trip of 2–8 March 1980, in ZPA: JIV 2/10.02/10.

. . . 'the difference between Carter and Reagan . . .' from Häber's report of 15 September 1980 on his trip of 5–14 September, in ZPA: JIV 2/10.02/10.

Herbert Wehner, among others, . . . see the correspondence in AdsD: Dep WB, BK 75. Another example in a letter of 19 May 1981 from Egon Franke to Chancellor Schmidt in AdsD: HS 347. See also the testimonial given by Schmidt, *Nachbarn*, p. 40,

. . . Hermann Axen, hurried off . . . Axens's notes on his conversations with Suslov, Ponomaryev and Zagladin on 23 and 24 January 1980 are now in ZPA: IV 2/2.035/57. There all the quotations in this paragraph.

The East German record . . . record (*Niederschrift*) of the meeting in Belgrade on 8 May 1980, in ZPA: IV 2/2.035/86.

... **Bahr's hope** ... see, for example, his statement on the signing of the treaty in *Texte* I/11, pp. 311–13.

... **solemnly exchanged that code-phrase** ... in his state of the nation address in March 1980, Chancellor Schmidt noted 'In December last year the Chairman of the Council of State, Erich Honecker, and I said in Berlin, independently of one another but in full agreement: war may never again go out from German soil.' See *Bundestag Plenarprotokolle*, 8/208, p. 16617 (20 March 1980).

'We have signed ...' quoted in Bölling, *Die fernen Nachbarn*, p. 135

'We don't want to show off ...' ibid., p. 140. Obviously there was a strong element of tactical flattery in this.

... **a dark shadow** ... see Schmidt, *Nachbarn*, p. 73 ff, Bölling, *Die fernen Nachbarn*, p. 152 ff.

... **Walther Leisler Kiep** ... this in a report of 8 February 1982 on a trip to West Germany, 1–6 February 1982, in ZPA: JIV 2/10.02/13.

... **real concerns on the East German side** ... Thus the Minister for State Security, Erich Mielke, gave a dark warning about the dangers of increased subversion, embargoes and sanctions in his speech to a 'central service conference' of the Stasi in Potsdam on 11 October 1982. MfS: GVS o008–12/82. On a memorandum from Herbert Häber reporting a lunch with Hans Otto Bräutigam on 5 October 1982, Honecker scribbled: 'Our position [?] is clear — Kohl's "accents" will be decisive for how relations develop. Elections 6 March. i.e. Kohl is transitional government?' ZPA: JIV 2/10.02/11. But Kohl was confirmed in office, and Honecker clearly did not like the initial 'accents', see the message he sent to Kohl via Häber and Bräutigam in April 1983, in ZPA: JIV 2/10.02/11.

... **'these days it is almost ...'** this in a report of 17 October 1983 on trip to West Germany, 9–16 October 1983, in ZPA: JIV 2/10.02/13.

... **'As genuine advocates of peace ...'** ND, 26/27 November 1983.

... **other signals the Kohl government gave** ... see, for example, the letter sent by Kohl to Honecker on 24 October 1983, in response to Honecker's letter of 5 October, ZPA: 2/2.035/87. Here Kohl has already picked up the phrase 'coalition of reason'. This was in response to a letter from Honecker, published in ND, 10 October 1983. Both letters are reproduced in *Texte*, III/1, pp. 242–44 and 255–59.

'The two states in Germany ...' in ZPA: IV 2/2.035/87. Kohl was responding to a letter from Honecker on 25 November 1983.

Two months later, Honecker replied ... letter of 17 February 1984 in ZPA: IV 2/2.035/87.

... **in a guesthouse in the Lenin Hills** ... both Helmut Kohl (Bonn, 1 October 1991) and Erich Honecker (Berlin-Moabit, 27 November 1992) recalled the importance of this first personal meeting.

... **blamed this** ... **offensive commentaries** ... see Ronald D Asmus, *East Berlin and Moscow. The Documentation of a Dispute* (Munich: Radio Free Europe, 1985), pp. 14, 76–77.

'the future of the Federal Republic ...' *Die Welt*, 21 August 1984.

As late as mid-August ... see the minutes of the Politburo meeting on 14 August 1984, which sanctioned an extensive briefing paper for the Party (*Informationen* 1984/6, Nr. 209) arguing in this direction, ZPA: JIV 2/2/2070. The *Pravda* article, of 2 August 1984, ostensibly attacking the *West* German position, is reprinted in *Texte* III/2, pp. 297–98. Honecker seems to have believed that he had Chernenko's sanction from their earlier conversation on 14 June 1984, see the record in ZPA: JIV 2/2A/2660. At a Politburo meeting on 17 August 1984 (ZPA: JIV 2/2/2071) those who were not accompanying Honecker agreed the text of his plea to be allowed to go, and the text (already in proof form) of his interview in ND, 18 August 1984.

A dramatic encounter ... see the record in ZPA: JIV 2/2A/2678.

... **Honecker recounted proudly** ... Erich Honecker, Berlin-Moabit, 27 November 1992.

Egon Krenz vividly recalls ... Berlin, 29 September 1992. The minutes of the meeting, on 20 August 1984, are in ZPA: JIV 2/2/2072.

... **minutes for 28 August** ... ZPA: JIV 2/2/2073

... **the word 'peace'** ... see the discussion in Bergsdorf, *Sprache*, p. 246 ff.

... **a joint statement** ... the declaration, dated 12 March 1985, is reprinted in *Innerdeutsche Beziehungen*, p. 212.

How can I explain to the Soviet people ... Egon Krenz, Berlin, 29 September 1992. At the time of writing, a documentation of the Honecker-Gorbachev meetings was promised by Daniel Küchenmeister, but not yet available. He gave a very preliminary account of his findings in DA, 1/1993, pp. 30–40.

... **Hermann Axen to Moscow** ... Axen's records of this 'consultation' on 27 July 1987 are in ZPA: IV 2/2.035/59.

... **a long document** ... the original text is in ZPA: IV 2/2.035/14. It was given to the Soviet leadership on 23 June. Another copy, from the papers of the East German trades union head, Harry Tisch, is usefully reproduced in Hans-Hermann Hertle, & ors, *Der Staatsbesuch. Honecker in Bonn: Dokumente zur deutsch-deutschen Konstellation des Jahres 1987* (Berlin: Freie Universität, 1991 = FU Informationen aus Lehre und Forschung, 2/1991).

'That sounded exactly ...' internal memorandum from Axen to Honecker, 29 July 1987, in ZPA: IV 2/2.035/59.

'The visit would be ...' quoted from the record (*Niederschrift*) of the meeting in ZPA: IV 2/2.035/59. Of course the GDR only became a member of the United Nations in 1973.

... **merely informed** ... Kurt Hager, Berlin, 8 May 1992. Egon Krenz, Berlin, 29 September 1992. The author had not, at the time of writing, been able to find the precise documentation of the 'information' to Moscow.

... **Helmut Kohl** ... **very far from enthusiastic** ... Wolfgang Schäuble, Bonn, 17 March 1992. Schäuble recalls Kohl saying 'this is a bad day'.

... **virtually all the honours** ... But not the full number of police outriders due in protocol to a head of state. In Bonn, Honecker got only seven. But, characteristically, Franz Josef Strauss gave him the full head of state's complement — fifteen — for his day in the capital of the Free State of Bavaria. See *Der Spiegel*, 1/1988, p. 22.

... **two German leaders stood to attention side by side** ... see, for example, the photographs on the front-page of the tabloid *Bild*, 8 September 1987, which, however, offered the headline: 'Two Flags, Two Anthems, One Fatherland'.

... **keynote dinner speech** ... most of the speeches and statements of the Honecker visit are usefully collected in a Ministry for Intra-German Relations booklet, *Der Besuch von Generalsekretär Honecker in der Bundesrepublik Deutschland* (Bonn, 1988), hereafter *Besuch*, this on p. 26 ff. The keynote speeches can also be found in *Bulletin*, 10 September 1987. All the following quotations from the speeches can be found there.

... **reported on 9 September** ... in MfS: Z4229.

... **talking to the Free Democrat Otto Graf Lambsdorff** ... record of a conversation on 4 February 1988 in ZPA: IV 2/2.035/83.

Their joint communiqué ... *Besuch*, p. 36 ff. It should be noted that the communiqué emphasised the different positions on arms control as 'Chancellor Kohl presented the concept agreed in the Atlantic Alliance ...' while 'General Secretary Honecker drew attention to the proposals of the member states of the Warsaw Treaty ...'

... **offering hitherto unexposed charms** ... of course there were other motives, including concerns about a weakening American commitment, defence costs, and a rethinking of French military strategy. See, for example, Pierre Lellouche, *L'Avenir de la Guerre* (Paris: Mazarine, 1985). Nonetheless, the concern about a possible German eastward or national-neutralist drift remained a dominant motive. An extreme but highly successful example was Alain Minc, *La Grande Illusion* (Paris: Bernard Grasset, 1989).

... **point 9** ... see the neatly organised agenda issued in a briefing package for the Washington Summit. Reagan's speech in front of the Brandenburg Gate on 12 June 1987 is reprinted in *Texte* III/5, pp. 96–100.

Publicistic reaction ... see Karl Wilhelm Fricke, 'Der Besuch Erich Honeckers in der Bundesrepublik Deutschland', EA, 23/1987, pp. 683–90.

... **presciently formulated by** ... Pierre Hassner ... see his essay 'Zwei deutsche Staaten in Europa: Gibt es gemeinsame Interessen in der internationalen

Politik?' in Werner Weidenfeld, ed., *Die Identität der Deutschen* (Munich: Hanser, 1983), pp. 294–323, this on p. 301.

... **to influence its own alliance**... in a prepared statement to open the first round of talks, Chancellor Kohl referred to the desirability of arms control measures on short-range nuclear forces, conventional arms and chemical weapons, and then said 'We expect that the GDR will make its influence felt in the framework of its alliance so that here too it soon comes to concrete steps.' *Bulletin*, 10 September 1987, p. 709.

... **the Federal Republic's role, influence and room for manoeuvre in Nato**... on this, see Josef Joffe, *The Limited Partnership. Europe, the United States, and the Burdens of Alliance* (Cambridge: Ballinger, 1987) and David P. Calleo, *Beyond American Hegemony. The Future of the Western Alliance* (New York: Basic Books, 1987).

'It's a short step ...' *Frankfurter Rundschau*, 26 June 1982.

'Incidentally... if your neighbour put up some new wallpaper ...' ND, 10 April 1987.

The basic lesson of the Cold War... see Peter Bender, *Offensive Entspannung. Möglichkeit für Deutschland* (Köln: Kiepenheuer & Witsch, 1964), Bender, *Neue Ostpolitik*, p. 163.

'Increasing tension...' for this and following quotations from the Tutzing speech see p. 65 f. and notes.

'This weakness...' Peter Bender, *Offensive Entspannung. Möglichkeit für Deutschland* (Köln: Kiepenheuer & Witsch, 1964), p. 110.

'A material improvement...' see p. 66 above and notes.

Josef Joffe has forcefully argued... See his chapter in Gordon, *Eroding Empire*, pp. 129–87, especially pp. 15–51, 161–62, 178–80.

... **a 'virtuous circle'**... ibid., p. 151.

... **with deliberate oversimplification**... The complexity of the German origins of détente has already been indicated. For the complexity of the American origins of détente see, for example, Kovrig, *Walls and Bridges*, and John Lewis Gaddis, *Strategies of Containment. A Critical Appraisal of Postwar American National Security Policy* (Oxford: Oxford University Press, 1982).

... **the United States' policy of 'differentiation'**... for 'differentiation' see, out of a large literature, Kovrig, *Walls and Bridges*, *passim*; Gordon, *Eroding Empire*, esp. pp. 73–74, and Charles Gati, *Hungary and the Soviet Bloc* (Durham NC: Duke University Press, 1986), Chapter 10.

... **rather childish simplifications**... Hans-Peter Schwarz suggests that the correct distinction is rather between (American or German) *liberal* notions of détente, and (American or German) *conservative* notions of détente. Yet in the end, when it came to actual policy-making, did the conservative Kissinger have more in common with the conservative Strauss or with the liberals Carter and

Brzezinski? Conversely, when it came to actual policy-making, did the conservative Strauss have more in common with the conservative Kissinger or with the 'social-liberal' Schmidt and Genscher? See Hans-Peter Schwarz, 'Supermacht und Juniorpartner. Ansätze amerikanischer und westdeutscher Ostpolitik', in Hans-Peter Schwarz & Boris Meissner, eds., *Entspannungspolitik in Ost und West* (Köln: Heymann, 1979), p. 159 ff.

. . . 'only the *unconditional* recognition of the status quo . . .' Italics mine. Peter Glotz, *Manifest für eine neue Europäische Linke* (Berlin: Siedler, 1985), p. 65. So also Günter Gaus: 'We must firmly hold fast to the fact that peace in Europe — enriched by a relative détente — remains bound for the foreseeable future to the unconditional recognition of the status quo, of the political property relations as they are', from a speech of 1981, reprinted in Günter Gaus, *Deutschland und die Nato. Drei Reden* (Hamburg: Rowohlt, 1984), p. 103.

. . . the distinction between state and system was relatively easy to make . . . Which does not mean, however, that West German policymakers always managed to make it, see p. 280 ff.

. . . 'only thinkable . . .' Prof. Otto Reinhold on Radio DDR II, 19 August 1989, quoted here from the BPA/DDR-Spiegel transcript, 22 August 1989.

'The more firmly entrenched the SED leadership . . .' Wilhelm Bruns quoted in an article by Joachim Nawrocki in *Die Zeit*, 15 June 1979.

'Only a consolidation of the GDR . . .' Michael Kreile, 'Ostpolitik Reconsidered', in Ekkehart Krippendorff & Volker Rittberger, eds, *The Foreign Policy of West Germany* (London: Sage, 1980), p. 140.

Bahr himself modified and qualified . . . see above p. 67 f. and references.

Willy Brandt cautioned . . . ' . . . interests, power relations and social differences are neither dialectically to be resolved, nor should they be obscured', government declaration of 28 October 1969, *Bundestag Plenarprotokolle*, 6/5, p. 32. He quoted this passage again in his 1974 state of the nation address, see *Bundestag Plenarprotokolle*, 7/76, p. 4771 (24 January 1974).

Richard von Weizsäcker described . . . Weizsäcker, *Deutsche Geschichte*, pp. 13–14.

Peter Bender, wrote . . . see *Vorwärts*, 16 July 1988.

. . . 'not aimed at a destabilisation . . .' EA, 12/1986, p. 346. In the same article Schäuble wrote: 'The Federal Government knows that steps forward in the intra-German relationship are only possible in homeopathic doses' (ibid., p. 343). Did he realise that he was using the exact metaphor — homeopathic doses — that Bahr had used in Tutzing in 1963?

'We have no intention of harming . . .' see his article 'The Two States in Germany', *Aussenpolitik* (English edition), 3/1984, p. 241.

. . . as Eberhard Schulz well described it . . . see Ehmke, *Zwanzig Jahre*, p. 219. Schulz uses the term *Stabilitätsgebot* here in the specific context of security, alliance and frontier issues, but it has a wider application. See also the revealing discussion by Peter Hardi, then of the Karl Marx University in Budapest, in EA, 13/1986, pp. 387–90. 'The most important security question for East European governments,' writes Hardi, 'is the preservation of social and political stability. This means a stable socialist society under the leadership of a communist party.'

... 'a serious domestic crisis' ... *Bundestag Plenarprotokolle*, 8/78, p. 6112 (9 March 1978).

... simply did not believe ... this was evident from conversations the author had with German policymakers at the time. Of course it will only be possible to document this more precisely when the West German official papers are opened, in 2011.

... 'unrealism' of the Poles ... see, for example, Bölling, *Die fernen Nachbarn*, p. 120. Although Bölling ascribes these views to thoughtful Germans in the GDR, they could be heard in Bonn almost as much as in East Berlin.

... seemed only to bear out ... See Schmidt's own recollection of his remarks to Mitterand in January 1982: 'Unfortunately Solidarność wanted to advance the process of change too quickly, which led to the recent reverse ...' Schmidt, *Nachbarn*, p. 259 ff, this on p. 264. For analysis of this general judgement see Garton Ash, *Solidarity*, p. 297 ff.

'It is in the liberal and socialist traditions ...' letter dated 20/22 August 1963 in AdsD: Dep WB, Rbm 38.

... Alois Mertes would later make ... in a discussion reprinted in *Politik und Kultur* 2/1981, p. 34.

Brandt at the window ... the photograph on which the gesture can be seen is in Koch, *Brandt*, also in *Die Zeit*, 9 March 1990.

'I was moved, but ...' Brandt, *People and Politics*, p. 372. Similarly, Brandt, *Erinnerungen*, p. 226.

'For freedom's battle ...' these lines from Byron's 'Giaour', well-known in Poland through the translation by Adam Mickiewicz, were scribbled on a piece of paper pinned to the wooden cross erected outside the Lenin Shipyard, during the strike that gave birth to Solidarity. But the unknown striker who made the dedication omitted the word 'bleeding'. See Garton Ash, *Solidarity*, p. 49.

In nineteenth-century Poland ... see the discussion in Norman Davies, *God's Playground. A History of Poland* (Oxford: Clarendon Press, 1981), especially Volume 2, Chapter 1.

In the twentieth century ... thus the title of a book by Adam Bromke, *Poland's Politics. Idealism vs. Realism* (Cambridge, Mass.: Harvard University Press, 1967).

... 'German realism' ... speech to the Bundestag on 11 May 1973, reprinted in *Texte* I/12, pp. 523–31, this on p. 526.

... 'Polish conditions such as ...' Gaus, *Deutschland*, pp. 270–71.

The Minister for Intra-German relations talked . . . see the report in FAZ, 2 January 1989.

Hans Otto Bräutigam . . . spoke . . . lecture at St Antony's College, Oxford, 6 June 1988. An earlier, internal usage, where he talks of the 'stabilisation' of German-German relations, is to be found in his memorandum of 9 January 1979 on 'Germany-and Berlin-policy at the beginning of 1979' in AdsD: HS 01442.

. . . a reliable and forthcoming partner in negotiations . . . in an interview immediately after his retirement as Permanent Representative, Günter Gaus argued explicitly 'that we need the GDR as a strong partner. We don't gain when the GDR is weak.' See his interview in NG 8/1982, pp. 712–21, this on p. 714. Bräutigam expressed a similar view, albeit somewhat more cautiously.

. . . nor the West German government should put too much pressure . . . 'If we now forcefully urge the GDR to change itself, or else this or that won't work any more, that only strengthens the *Abgrenzung* [i.e. the defensive policy of the GDR against West German influence] and can completely halt the little there is of inner movement', Hans Otto Bräutigam in *Die Zeit*, 3/1989.

'I wanted to help to increase . . .' Schmidt, *Nachbarn*, p. 67.

. . . the available East German records . . . in 1991–92, the most important sources available for research on this topic were the minutes and working papers of the Politburo, some other holdings in the internal archive of the Politburo, and the papers of the office of Hermann Axen (Büro Axen). Also available for consultation were the papers of the offices of Kurt Hager and Joachim Herrmann. Those of Honecker's own office were not available for systematic research, while those of Egon Krenz's office were catalogued but then closed by the state prosecutors' office. Still unavailable were most of the papers of the so-called Western Department (subsequently Department for International Politics and Economics) and the curiously named Traffic Department, which actually dealt in the covert 'traffic' (including financial traffic) with organisations and parties in the West.

Perhaps the most important records *not* available, however, were the papers of the 'FRG Department' of the East German Foreign Ministry, which the West German Foreign Ministry took over at unification and then firmly closed. For it was the head of this department, Karl Seidel, who was generally the note-taker at the meetings of prominent West German visitors with the East German leader. A number of these records are to be found in the party archives, but all of them, in a matchless series from 1970 to 1990, were, by Seidel's own account, left neatly in his office cupboard when — the correct functionary to the last — he handed over the keys and departed in early 1990. Karl Seidel, Berlin, 30 September 1992.

Those of Seidel's protocols that we have thus far been able to examine are generally credible, on two grounds. Firstly, on account of the great detail, the generally authentic vocabulary, and the significant variations between the records of individual conversations. Secondly, on account of the personal credibility of Karl Seidel as a note-taker. Seidel took shorthand notes. Returning to his office, he dictated a full record as soon as possible to his secretary. He insists that, while he may have very slightly emphasised the praise and de-emphasised the criticism, both praise and criticism were mentioned if and when they came. (Karl Seidel, Berlin, 30 September 1992). The variations between, for example, the record of Honecker's conversation with Volker Rühe and those of his conversations with Oskar Lafontaine, bear out this contention. Moreover, Seidel is himself personally credible, as a no doubt limited but also calm and conscientious official. His West German partners would certainly confirm this. While all official papers, and especially the papers of a dictatorship, clearly have to be treated with care, these particular records cannot be disqualified with sweeping statements about 'documents that lie'.

... only a few ... the most notable example we have come across so far is the conversation between Volker Rühe and Erich Honecker on 28 April 1988, of which the record is now in ZPA: IV 2/2.035/84. However, Karl Seidel recalls that Rühe was desperately keen to be received by Honecker, and remained polite and respectful in tone. Karl Seidel, Berlin, 30 September 1992. In a conversation in 1992, Erich Honecker could not recall his meeting with Volker Rühe (Erich Honecker, Berlin-Moabit, 27 November 1992).

... summarising his own conversation ... this in an internal memorandum for Honecker dated 28 April 1988, in ZPA: IV 2/2.035/84.

... perhaps the most outspoken ... however, the files on contacts with CDU politicians in the Party archives are relatively thin. For historians to be able to make a fair and balanced judgement, the Bonn government will need to open the files now controlled by its own Foreign Ministry.

Wolfgang Leonhard made a powerful critique ... in NG 10/1982 (responding to the Gaus interview mentioned above), and reprinted in Wolfgang Leonhard, *Das kurze Leben der DDR. Berichte und Kommentare aus vier Jahrzehnten* (Stuttgart: Deutsche Verlags-Anstalt, 1990), pp. 174–78. This volume also contains his earlier analysis of the possible connection between Western economic help and lack of reforms, for example p. 164. A commentary by Ilse Spittmann in DA 8/1981, also deserves mention. It is reprinted in Ilse Spittmann, *Die DDR unter Honecker* (Köln: Verlag Wissenschaft und Politik, 1990), pp. 83–87.

... an even more swingeing critique ... in DA, 7/1988, pp. 738–46.

... Hermann von Berg, Franz Loeser and Wolfgang Seiffert ... see their co-authored *Die DRR auf dem Weg in das Jahr 2000* (Köln: Bund-Verlag, 1987), pp. 179–88. See also Hermann von Berg, *Vorbeugende Unterwerfung. Politik im realen Sozialismus* (Munich: Universitas, 1988), Wolfgang Seiffert, *Das ganze Deutschland. Perspektiven der Wiedervereinigung* (Munich: Piper, 1986), and brief critical articles by Hermann Rudolph, SZ, 16 January 1989, and Ernst-Otto Maetzke in FAZ, 4 February 1988 and 28 November 1988.

At least until 1988 ... in a lecture in spring 1988, Wolfgang Schäuble talked of the need for a 'new stability' in the GDR, see EA, 14/1988, p. 417. In a note under the title 'correct pressure for reform' (*Richtiger Reformdruck*) in the FAZ, 9 August 1988, Ernst-Otto Maetzke noted that the Kohl government seemed inclined to step up the pressure for reform in the GDR. This slight shift was reflected also in the explicit criticism of political conditions inside the GDR with which Chancellor Kohl opened his state of the nation address for 1988, see *Bundestag Plenarprotokolle, Bundestag Plenarprotokolle*, 11/113, p. 8094 f (1 December 1988).

... **Hans Otto Bräutigam** ... Potsdam, 25 June 1991.

... **the politics of the GDR** ... since GDR-studies was a large scholarly field in West Germany, with hundreds of scholars and publications, any small selection is bound to be invidious and unsatisfactory. Probably the most useful single introduction to the subject, indicating most of the major problems and themes, is Weber, *DDR* (1991). The earlier edition, Weber, *DDR* (1988) is still useful, and has a very clear and extensive bibliography. The third edition of the *DDR-Handbuch*, edited by Hartmut Zimmermann, also contains invaluable articles on individual topics and a comprehensive bibliography. No other East European state could boast a Western chronicle to compare with the *Deutschland Archiv* (DA). In the notes for this section I have not attempted to indicate primary and secondary sources for the overall assessment, but only for specific assertions, quotations etc.

... **the strategies by which it endeavoured** ... in the analysis of these strategies and their effects I have found particularly stimulating and useful the Habilitation thesis of Sigrid Meuschel, 'Legitimation und Parteiherrschaft. Zum Wandel der Legitimitätsansprüche der SED 1945–1989' (Free University, Berlin, November 1990) now published as *Legitimation und Parteiherrschaft. Zum Paradox von Stabilität und Revolution in der DDR 1945–1989* (Frankfurt: Suhrkamp, 1992), hereafter cited as Meuschel, *Legitimation*. She gives a useful short summary of some of her main points in Rainer Deppe & ors, eds, *Demokratischer Umbruch in Osteuropa* (Frankfurt: Suhrkamp, 1991), pp. 26–47.

... **a 'hypertrophied function'** ... Markus Wolf at a press conference in Munich, 10 October 1991.

... **in direct consultation** ... see the account in Günter Schabowski, *Der Absturz* (Berlin: Rowohlt, 1991), pp. 115–17.

... **as attractive as by its nature** ... my attention was drawn to this fine piece of ideological casuistry by Honecker's former aide Frank-Joachim Hernmann, Berlin, 8 October 1991.

... **the key-word *Geborgenheit*** ... see Weber, *DDR* (1988), pp. 97–98.

... **an understanding of socialism** ... the point was made by, among others, Hans Modrow, as quoted in Volze 'Devisengeschäfte', p. 1144, citing the FAZ, 18 March 1990. Talking to the author in Moabit prison in late 1992, Honecker dilated at length on this aspect of his achievement. Erich Honecker, Berlin-Moabit, 27 November 1992.

... **a consolidation of traditional, Soviet-type central planning** ... and a further nationalisation of small-scale private enterprise, see Anders Åslund, *Private Enterprise in Eastern Europe. The Non-Agricultural Private Sector in Poland and the GDR, 1945–83* (London: Macmillan, 1985), Chapter 3.

... **one of the main substitutes for reform was — imports** ... this was the central burden of the charge made against Honecker by the former Politburo member, Werner Krolikowski, in a memorandum of 16 January 1990, reprinted in Przybylski, *Tatort 1*, pp. 321–39. Krolikowski claims that as early as 1973 he pointed out to Honecker the dangers of concentrating on consumer goods at the expense of capital investment, and warned against the soaring debts to the West. In the same place, pp. 340–56, are reprinted what are claimed to be notes by Krolikowski from the period 1980–83, showing that not only he but also Erich Mielke and Willi Stoph were afraid of the dangers of Honecker getting too close and too indebted to West Germany. But as Krolikowski himself notes, they did not stop him. The basic point about too many consumer imports was also made to Honecker at the time by Gerhard Schürer (see above, p. 516), and in retrospect by Mittag, Schabowski and many other former members of the Party leadership.

. . . 'peaceful co-existence' . . . see, for example, the entries for 'Entspannungspolitik' and 'Friedliche Koexistenz' in the *Kleines Politisches Wörterbuch* (3rd edition, Berlin: Dietz, 1978).

. . . a series of top-level internal briefings . . . these were delivered to meetings of the so-called *Kollegium* or to the 'central service conferences' of the Ministry.

. . . 'above all struggle'. . . . this in 'Theses' for the *Kollegiumssitzung* on 29 September 1971, now in MFS: 4751. A handwritten annotation indicates that the meeting did not actually take place, but the text is nonetheless a good expression of Mielke's concerns.

. . . Erfurt should never be repeated . . . see his 'Theses' for the *Kollegiumssitzung* on 29 May 1970 (MfS: 4739), which clearly convey his anger at what had happened in Erfurt eight days before.

. . . 'hard and complicated' . . . this and the following quotations from a massive 111-page lecture delivered to the central service conference on 16 November 1972, MfS: 4770.

. . . the 1968 constitution . . . see Bruns, *DDR-Politik*, p. 32.

. . . the words of the GDR's 'national anthem' . . . see the entry for 'Nationalhymne' in *DDR Handbuch*, p. 939. The text was written by the poet Johannes R. Becher in 1949.

. . . the GDR . . . a 'socialist nation' . . . see the entry for 'Nation und nationale Frage' in *DDR Handbuch*, the extensive discussion in Meuschel, *Legitimation*, and Gerhard Naumann & Eckhard Trumpler, *Der Flop mit der DDR-Nation 1971* (Berlin: Dietz, 1991).

. . . 'a socialist German nation' . . . ND, 10 April 1987.

Looking back from 1992 . . . Erich Honecker, Berlin-Moabit, 27 November 1992.

. . . still 'German' . . . quoted in *DDR-Handbuch*, from ND, 13 December 1974.

See also the entries for 'Nation' and 'Nationalität' in *Kleines Politisches Wörterbuch* (3rd edition, Berlin: Dietz, 1978).

. . . to acknowledge its own indubitable Germanness . . . this is one of the main themes of Garton Ash, *DDR*. The rediscovery and reassessment of German history in the GDR was noted by Helmut Schmidt in his state of the nation address for 1981, *Bundestag Plenarprotokolle*, 9/31, p. 1541 (9 April 1981).

'Defence education' . . . see the entry under 'Wehrerziehung' in *DDR-Handbuch*, and the discussion in Klaus Ehring/Martin Dallwitz [a pseudonym for Hubertus Knabe], *Schwerter zu Pflugscharen. Friedensbewegung in der DDR* (Hamburg: Rowohlt, 1982) and Wolgang Büscher & ors, *Friedensbewegung in der DDR. Texte 1978–1982* (Hattingen: Scandica Verlag, 1982 = edition transit, Vol. 2).

. . . 'perhaps my brother . . .' quoted in Garton Ash, *DDR*, p. 144 f.

. . . relations with the Protestant Church . . . strictly speaking one should say Churches, because there were no less than eight different *Landeskirchen* in the GDR, often jealously guarding their particular traditions, although since 1969 joined in a Federation of Protestant Churches in the GDR. To avoid confusion, we have used the more usual English singular. Developments in the Church could best be followed in the excellent bi-monthly journal of the Berlin Arbeitsgemeinschaft für Kirchliche Publizistik, *Kirche im Sozialismus*. The best short introduction was Reinhard Henkys, *Gottes Volk im Sozialismus. Wie Christen in der DDR leben* (Berlin: Wichern-Verlag, 1983); a more extensive survey, Reinhard Henkys, ed., *Die Evangelischen Kirchen in der DDR* (Munich: Kaiser, 1982). A new study in English is Robert F Goeckel, *The Lutheran Church and the East German State. Political conflict and change under Ulbricht and Honecker* (Ithaca: Cornell University Press, 1990). A controversial analysis and detailed documentation of Church relations with the Stasi is Gerhard Besier & Stephan Wolf, eds, *'Pfarrer, Christen und Katholiken'. Das Ministerium für Staatssicherheit der ehemaligen DDR und die Kirchen* (2nd edition, Neukirchen-Vluyn: Neukirchener, 1992). Much of the following analysis is, however, based on the author's own personal enquiries, observations and conversations, in which he owes a very special debt of gratitude to Werner Krätschell.

. . . Manfred Stolpe . . . for references, see above, p. 511.

. . . 'swords into ploughshares'. . . . on the peace groups and initiatives more or less under Church auspices see Wolfgang Büsche, & ors, eds, *Friedensbewegung in der DDR. Texte 1978–82* (Hattingen: Scandica-Verlag, 1982 = edition transit Vol. 2), Klaus Ehring/Martin Dallwitz [pseudonym of Hubertus Knabe], *Schwerter zu Pflugscharen. Friedensbewegung in der DDR* (Hamburg: Rowohlt, 1982), and Chapter 14 in Fricke, *Opposition*. In English, see John Sandford, *The Sword and the Ploughshare. Autonomous Peace Initiatives in East Germany* (London: Merlin Press/END, 1983) and the relevant sections of Roger Woods, *Opposition in the GDR under Honecker, 1971–85* (London: Macmillan, 1986).

. . . the authorities dealt decisively . . . by far the best single survey is Fricke, *Opposition*. In English, see Roger Woods, *Opposition in the GDR under Honecker, 1971–85* (London, Macmillan, 1986).

. . . **as one young Christian put it** . . . Joachim Krätschell, Berlin, 6 July 1989.

. . . **most . . . chose emigration** . . . the authorities resorted to direct deportation in the case of the Jena peace activist, Roland Jahn, see the detailed and vivid report by Helmut Loelhoeffel in SZ, 9 June 1983. In 1988, Bärbel Bohley and others agreed to leave only temporarily, and on condition that they would be allowed to return.

. . . **that the 'Zone' was behind** . . . *Dokumente*, IV/9, p. 573

. . . **'niche society'** . . . see Gaus, *Deutschland*, p. 156 ff.

. . . **nothing that seriously deserved the name of reform** . . . on the definition of reform see Garton Ash, *Uses*, p. 252 ff.

West German historians agreed . . . on this see Weber, *DDR*, and compare such official histories as Zentral Institut für Geschichte der Akademie der Wissenschaften der DDR, ed., *Grundriss der deutschen Geschichte. Von den Anfängen der Geschichte des deutschen Volkes bis zur Gestaltung der entwickelten sozialistischen Gesellschaft in der Deutschen Demokratischen Republik* [!] (Berlin: VEB Deutscher Verlag der Wissenschaften, 1979), and, more concisely, Heinz Heitzer, *DDR. Geschichtlicher Überblick* (Berlin: Dietz, 1979).

'Important, important strong GDR' . . . Ulrich Bürger, *Das sagen wir natürlich so nicht! Donnerstag-Argus bei Herrn Gegel* (Berlin: Dietz, 1990), p. 189 f. This book gives vivid insights into the arguments, and delusions, of the party leadership in the 1980s.

. . . **three former East German intellectuals suggested** . . . Hermann von Berg, Franz Loeser and Wolfgang Seiffert in their co-authored *Die DRR auf dem Weg in das Jahr 2000* (Köln: Bund-Verlag, 1987), p. 186.

. . . **Ludwig Rehlinger has argued** . . . Rehlinger, *Freikauf*, p. 110, and in conversation with the author, Bonn, 6 December 1990.

. . . **a circle of activists.** . . . this group was kindly brought together by one of the leading activists of the Initiative for Peace and Human Rights, Gerd Poppe, in East Berlin.

. . . **'slice-by-slice'** . . . Bärbel Bohley in FAZ, 25 January 1992. It appears that in the early 1988 crisis, following the Luxemburg/Liebknecht demonstration, the Federal Government did pay directly for the release of some dissenters to the West. Wolfgang Vogel, Berlin, 9 October 1991. Leslie Collitt and David Marsh reported in the *Financial Times*, 4 February 1988: '. . . East German supporters of the four released dissidents complained that Bonn was helping the East Berlin authorities to undermine the civil rights movement'. Other activists, including Bärbel Bohley herself, were, however, allowed out for six months, and subsequently returned to play an important part in the revolution of autumn 1989.

. . . **the one to two thousand members of the democratic oppositions** . . . The democratic oppositions in Hungary and Czechoslovakia were probably nearer to one thousand than two until the late 1980s. Obviously it is impossible to give a precise 'membership', and there were many more sympathisers than activists.

Charter 77, for example, had 242 signatories at the outset, 617 by March 1977, 1,065 by June 1980, and 'more than 1,300' by the end of 1986, with the proviso that some of the earlier signatories subsequently emigrated, or ceased to be so active. See *A Decade of Dedication. Charter 77 1977–1987* (New York: Helsinki Watch, 1987), p. 7. For Poland this figure plainly applies only for the period up to August 1980.

. . . between one and three thousand of East Germany's most active citizens . . . see Table VIII.

. . . Gorbachev was indicating to East European rulers . . . see above, p. 123. Erich Honecker specifically recalled the meeting of East European leaders in autumn 1986 when Gorbachev delivered this general message, Erich Honecker, Berlin-Moabit, 27 November 1992. Egon Krenz confirmed in conversation with the author (Berlin, 20 February 1990) that this was certainly the message which Honecker chose to hear from Gorbachev in 1986.

Honecker's last gamble . . . the following section is based on sources in the Party archive, a wide range of conversations with senior officials and Politburo members, including one with Honecker himself, and published sources. There is as yet no good life of the East German Party leader. Before his fall, Honecker gave his own version, courtesy of Robert Maxwell, in *Erich Honecker, From My Life* (Oxford: Pergamon Press, 1981). After his fall, he gave a series of long, self-justificatory, illusion-ridden, but nonetheless sometimes revealing interviews to Reinhold Andert and Wolfgang Herzberg, who published them as *Der Sturz. Erich Honecker im Kreuzverhör* (Berlin: Aufbau-Verlag, 1990). His successor Egon Krenz, wrote a highly critical, but also quite revealing review in *Der Spiegel* 6/1991, as well as giving his own first, hastily (ghost-)written account in Egon Krenz, *Wenn Mauern fallen. Die friedliche Revolution: Vorgeschichte-Ablauf-Auswirkungen* (Vienna: Neff, 1990). Another witness quick to the press was Krenz's fellow 'conspirator' in overthrowing Honecker, Günter Schabowski, see his *Der Absturz* (Berlin: Rowohlt, 1991) and *Das Politbüro. Ende eines Mythos* (Hamburg: Rowohlt, 1990). See also the documents and discussion in Przybylski, *Tatort 1* and *Tatort 2*, and Mittag, *Preis*. All witnesses confirm the supremacy of Honecker in decisions regarding relations with the West.

. . . a church weekly was forbidden to reprint . . . see the commentary by Gisela Helwig in DA, 8/1988, p. 602. The weekly in question, *Die Kirche*, played a modest but important role in the development of Church-protected freedom of expression, comparable in some ways to that of the weekly *Tygodnik Powszechny* in Poland.

. . . the Soviet journal *Sputnik* was banned . . . According to the GDR's Postal Ministry, *Sputnik* had no articles 'which served the strengthening of German-Soviet friendship, but instead distorting historical articles'. see FAZ, 21 November 1988. On the subsequent protests from Party members see *Der Spiegel*, 48/1988.

. . . 'socialism in the colours of the GDR' . . . he used this phrase at the 7th plenum of the Central Committee in December 1988, see ND 2 December 1988. Of course the colours of the GDR were the same as those of the Federal Republic.

... **referred to in Politburo minutes** ... see, for example, the minutes of the meeting on 3 May 1988, now in ZPA: JIV 2/2/2271.

Egon Krenz ... Berlin, 29 September 1992.

... **even a penchant for taking risks** ... thus, for example, Günter Schabowski, Berlin, 29 June 1991, and one of Honecker's personal assistants, Frank-Joachim Herrmann, Berlin, 8 October 1991.

... **Erich Honecker himself** ... Berlin-Moabit, 27 November 1992.

'**The German Democratic Republic** ...' EA, 19/1987, p. D549, quoting ND, 11 September 1987.

Gerhard Schürer recalls ... Gerhard Schürer, Berlin, 25 November 1992.

... **talking to the author in 1992** ... Erich Honecker, Berlin-Moabit, 27 November 1992.

... '**only' about DM 30 billion** ... Honecker added that even this was an overestimate, since it did not show the credits with such countries as Iran, Iraq, Syria etc, that were regularly shown in the figures given to the Politburo.

... '**the last all-German'** ... He went on: 'Those who follow are GDR-Germans', quoted in *Der Spiegel*, 48/1985.

Honecker became 'more German' ... see his article in *Die Zeit*, 31/1987.

Old men remember ... Schmidt, *Nachbarn*, p. 26. This impression was confirmed by others who spoke to him at this time.

... **of whom he would often speak** ... this is confirmed by numerous sources. It is interesting to note that the role of Herbert Wehner was also singled out for special remark by the head of the Agitation department of the Central Committee, in his briefing for senior editors at the time of Honecker's visit to West Germany, see Ulrich Bürger, *Das sagen wir natürlich so nicht! Donnerstag-Argus bei Herrn Gegel* (Berlin: Dietz, 1990), p. 189.

... **a remarkable text** ... in AdsD: Dep WB, BK 75.

... **in or near East Berlin** ... Erich Honecker, Berlin-Moabit, 27 November 1992.

... '**his goal was still** ...' in Reinhold Andert & Wolfgang Herzberg, *Der Sturz. Erich Honecker im Kreuzverhör* (Berlin: Aufbau-Verlag, 1990), p. 348. Honecker also made a special point of mentioning the part played by his regular contact with Herbert Wehner (also through Wolfgang Vogel) in a statement on his attitude to humanitarian questions in early 1990, reproduced in Przybylski, *Tatort 1*, pp. 363–66. He and Wehner, wrote Honecker, 'worked together in a comradely way'.

In 1992 he affirmed ... Erich Honecker, Berlin-Moabit, 27 November 1992.

... '**we are going the German way'** ... quoted by Brigitte Seebacher-Brandt in Jesse & Mitter, *Einheit*, p. 36.

... **the element of simple vanity** ... Honecker's vanity is attested by many who worked with him. This was also stressed by Hans-Otto Bräutigam in a conversation with the author (Potsdam, 25 June 1991).

... *hubris* ... an interpretation also subscribed to by Helmut Schmidt in conversation with the author (London, 3 June 1991). Confirmed from close observation by Frank-Joachim Herrmann, Berlin, 8 October 1991.

... **the growing distance from everyday reality** ... first-hand evidence of his growing distance from reality is given in the books by Krenz and Schabowski.

... **refer to the happy expression** ... Wolfgang Vogel, Berlin, 9 October 1991

... **'that the majority of the population ...'** Note of 6 February 1989 on a conversation in Berlin, 3 February 1989, in ZPA: IV 2/2.035/54. Talking to the author in November 1992, Honecker also stressed that the GDR was, as he put it, 'the only socialist country' where to the end everyone could go into a shop and buy sausage, butter etc. Erich Honecker, Berlin-Moabit, 27 November 1992.

... **'I would wish every one who rules over us ...'** in *Der Spiegel*, 11/1987. Gabriele Eckart had earlier made a collection of long interviews, *So sehe ick die Sache. Protokolle aus der DDR* (Köln: Kiepenheuer & Witsch, 1984), which give a very good insight into the ground-floor reality of life in the GDR.

... **their reactions to some aspects of West German life** ... 'Sodom and Gomorrah!' was the not wholly untypical commentary of one East German friend on the obscene profusion of food and drink displayed in the famous top-floor delicatessen of West Berlin's *Kaufhaus des Westens*.

... **'one of the freest countries ...'** quoted in Weber, *DDR* (1988), p. 103.

... **young East Berliners gathered** ... Their other chant was 'the Wall must go' (*Die Mauer muss weg*). These were the most serious public disorders in East Germany for a decade. See reports in *Washington Post*, 10 June 1987, FAZ, 10 June 1987, and *Der Spiegel*, 25/1987.

... **Honecker** ... **youth** ... for one example, see above p. 336.

Whereas in 1985 ... these results are quoted in Michael Brie/Dieter Klein, eds, *Zwischen den Zeiten. Ein Jahrhundert verabschiedet sich* (Hamburg: VSA-Verlag, 1992), p. 147.

Figures to the Politburo ... Item 3 on the minutes of the Politburo meeting on 19 April 1988, now in ZPA: JIV 2/2/2269. Interestingly, no less than 30,000 of these applications came from Dresden, in the so-called 'valley of the clueless', where people could not receive West German television.

Western estimates in 1988–89 ... *Der Spiegel*, 36/1988, declared, with characteristic omniscience, that 'a quarter of a million GDR citizens have filed applications to leave. Five to six million count as GDR-tired.' The *Frankfurter Rundschau*, 29 July 1988, spoke of an estimate in 'well-informed West Berlin circles' of 300–400,000 applications, but indicated that the *Tagesspiegel* had recently cited 'information from Bonn' to give a figure of 500,000 applications for a total of no less than 1.5 million people. Another organisation put the figure at

1.2 million in November 1988, see FAZ, 28 November 1988. When I asked the Permanent Representative of the Federal Republic to the GDR, Franz Bertele, for his guesstimate in July 1989, he indicated a similar range, but declined to name his own figure (Berlin, 6 July 1989). Rehlinger, *Freikauf*, p. 115, says that estimates of over one million came from 'the various services', by which he presumably means the West German intelligence services.

... **grew in strength and boldness** ... a good short account is given in the introduction to Hubertus Knabe, ed., *Aufbruch in eine andere DDR* (Reinbek: Rowohlt, 1990), p. 12 f.

... **'freedom is always...'** see report and photograph in *Der Spiegel*, 5/1988.

... **more or less compelled to leave** ... here again the traditional 'heaven or hell' method was used. The balladeer Stephan Krawczyk and his wife Freya Klier, for example, said they did not leave the GDR 'voluntarily', but faced with the threat of heavy charges they did actually fill out applications to leave. See *Der Spiegel*, 6/1988. Speaking in an East Berlin church in April 1989, the former Party functionary Rolf Heinrich confirmed that he, too, after writing a book critical of the system, had been urged to file an application to leave. See report in FAZ, 13 April 1989.

... **20 Theses for a reformation of the GDR** ... these were not actually pinned to the church door, like Luther's 95 Theses, but were first presented to a synod in Halle by the Wittenberg theologian Friedrich Schorlemmer, see the report in DA, 8/1988, pp. 801–02.

... **the dissidence acquired — for the first time** ... this is also the judgement of Hubertus Knabe, who closely followed the evolution of this Church-based dissidence throughout the 1980s, see Hubertus Knabe, ed., *Aufbruch in eine andere DDR* (Reinbek: Rowohlt, 1990), p. 14.

... **to monitor local elections of May 1989** ... according to the official figures, there were 142,301 (1.15 per cent) votes against, compared with 14,683 (0.1 per cent) in 1984, and the turn-out was a mere 98.77 per cent, compared with 99.37 per cent in 1984. Opposition monitors reckoned that in, for example, the East Berlin borough of Friedrichshain, there were 6.93 per cent votes against, whereas the official result was 1.89 per cent. Opposition protests took the form of letters and petitions to the Council of State, and even laying charges on the suspicion of electoral fraud — a crime under Article 211 of the GDR's Penal Code! *Monatsbericht* of the *Gesamtdeutsches Institut*, May 1989, p. 1. Report in *Der Spiegel*, 20/1989.

... **a report to Honecker** ... the report, dated 1 June 1989, is printed in Mitter & Wolle, *Lageberichte*, pp. 46–71. It went to all the senior functionaries concerned with internal security.

... **'is it that tomorrow...'** ibid., p. 125.

... **'so far as the power question is concerned...'** ibid., p. 127.

... **'refolutions'** ... on 'refolution' see Garton Ash *We*, p. 14 f.

... **Willy Brandt once again at the window** ... see the report and photographs in *Die Zeit*, 9 March 1990.

... **'the final measure ...'** quoted by Klaus Gotto in *Die Politische Meinung* 249/1990, p. 12.

As Robert Leicht observed ... in *Die Zeit*, 6 October 1989, quoted by Sigrid Meuschel in Rainer Deppe & ors, eds, *Demokratischer Umbruch in Osteuropa* (Frankfurt: Suhrkamp, 1991).

... **in a conversation in June 1991** ... Egon Bahr, Potsdam-Berlin, 29 June 1991. But at the end of this conversation, in a taxi driving from Potsdam to central Berlin, the East German taxi-driver, who had obviously listened closely to my critical questioning, turned to Egon Bahr and demonstratively thanked him 'for everything that you have done for us over the years'. With tributes like that, who needs to worry about the carping of historians?

... **'If our demands add up ...'** *Bergedorfer Gesprächskreis* 88 (6–7 September 1989), this on p. 62. One should note that it is the custom of the organisers to send the typescript of the stenographic record to individual participants to be checked and authorised before publication.

Until very late in the day... this distinction was, however, made by Horst Teltschik in a spontaneous response to the remarks by Egon Bahr quoted above. By putting in question the recognition of the GDR, said Teltschik, Bonn would block reforms there: 'But the population of the GDR can of course themselves put this state in question. If one day they really can exercise the right to self-determination, it is quite possible that the majority of the people in the GDR will decide for an *Anschluss* to the Federal Republic. Then we cannot be against it. Just as we cannot be against it if the majority of the population of the GDR should decide that they wish to remain a second German state. I must add that I am profoundly convinced that if the population of the GDR could freely exercise their right of self-determination today, they would decide for *Anschluss*.' ibid., p. 63. A very sound judgement.

... **might have saved the GDR** ... this is suggested by Sigrid Meuschel in the original (Free University, Berlin, 1990) version of her Habilitation thesis, p. 495, footnote 8. See also various contributions to Hubertus Knabe, ed., *Aufbruch in eine andere DDR* (Reinbek: Rowohlt, 1989). In an interview in October 1989, Egon Bahr spoke of a possible process 'at the end of which we will have another GDR, sustained by the overwhelming will of its own population,' *Der Spiegel*, 42/1989.

... **which 1989 marked the end of** ... see Garton Ash, *We*, p. 151 f.

... **eighty-four per cent** ... see above, p. 148 and note.

When the mayor of Bonn ... see reports in FAZ, 28 January 1988, *Express*, 29 June 1988, and *Neue Zürcher Zeitung*, 30 June 1988. According to an 'Information' now in the files of the Büro Axen, and dated 28 January 1988, the then deputy head of West Germany's Permanent Representation observed that Mayor Daniels had clearly gone too far, confusing Potsdam with the marketplace in Bonn. ZPA: IV 2/2.035/88. However, it is not clear whether this was a private comment, obtained by secret police methods, or the report of an actual conversation with the diplomat. Even if it is the latter, it may be distorted. According to the report to the Politburo on Wolfgang Schäuble's visit to the GDR on 9–10 November 1988, the then Chancellery Minister brought a 'declaration' which enabled the Bonn-Potsdam relationship to be resumed. Although, the SED report says, 'the expectation will be expressed that in future no such disturbances of the relations between the two towns will be permitted'. ZPA: JIV 2/2/2303.

To substantiate this generalisation . . . One crude experiment made by the author was to ask the Central Documentation System of the Federal Government to put into its computerised media database the combination 'dictatorship-GDR' for the years 1987 and 1991. The pile of cuttings produced for 1991 was some five times as high as that for 1987! I am most grateful to Frau Anna Maria Kuppe for this as for numerous other researches.

'As a result . . .' the letter, dated 25 February 1970, is in AdsD: Dep WB, BK 6.

Out of the attempt at 'normalisation' . . . Martin Kriele, a Professor of Law who defended the Basic Treaty in the Constitutional Court for the Brandt government, and then became bitterly disillusioned with what he saw as the rampant relativism and self-censorship on human rights resulting from the social-liberal 'peace policy', offered a more general version of this explanation. Starting from the well-known legal concept of 'the normative force of the given' — i.e. that people accept as normal and right what they have been used to — he argued that there was something one could call 'the normative force of the Red Army'. As Soviet power seemed to be so overwhelming, and, in the 1960s and 1970s, to be waxing rather than waning against that of the United States, so some people in West Germany made an anticipatory adjustment of their own values and norms from a position close to that represented by the United States to a position closer to that represented by the Soviet Union. Might was taken for right. The clearest and most provocative statement of his argument is in *Kontinent* (German edition) 3/1983, pp. 6–17. For his earlier, more ambivalent discussion of the danger of relativisation and self-censorship on human rights see his *Die Menschenrechte zwischen Ost und West* (Köln: Verlag Wissenschaft und Politik, 1977). A later, more developed and outspoken argument is his *Die demokratische Weltrevolution. Warum sich die Freiheit durchsetzen wird* (Munich: Piper, 1987). Allowing for the provocative overstatement born of personal disillusionment, the argument nonetheless deserves to be noticed.

. . . different 'terms of business' . . . Bölling, *Die fernen Nachbarn*, p. 294.

. . . a 'Peace of Augsburg' . . . Gaus, *Deutschland*, p. 275, see also the reference on p. 282 to 'the believers of both confessions'.

. . . 'that time has passed by . . .' Bölling, *Die fernen Nachbarn*, p. 187 f.

. . . this particular history of the left . . . a first attempt to address this special history is Brigitte Seebacher-Brandt, *Die Linke und die Einheit* (Berlin: Siedler, 1991). Now see also Dieter Groh & Peter Brandt, *'Vaterlandslose Gesellen'. Sozialdemokratie und Nation, 1860–1990.* (Munich: Beck, 1992).

... **a distinctive history of journalism** ... A good case-study would be the book by journalists from *Die Zeit*: Theo Sommer, ed., *Reise ins andere Deutschland* (Reinbek: Rowohlt, 1986), an important example of the other hand working overtime. The papers of the Central Committee Secretary responsible for the press, Joachim Herrmann, ZPA: IV 2/2.037/58, contain remarkably detailed information on the preparations for, execution and subsequent evaluation of the visit. Here there is, for example, a letter sent by the chief editor of *Die Zeit*, Theo Sommer, to the head of the press department of the East German Foreign Ministry, Wolfgang Meyer. 'If I may say so,' Sommer writes, in a letter dated 31 January 1986, recalling his recent interview with Honecker, 'your Chairman of the Council of State does not need to take second place to Mr Gorbachev, so far as skilful dealing with Western journalists is concerned.' Sommer gave a retrospective justification of *Die Zeit*'s line in general, and this book in particular, in *Die Zeit*, 11 May 1990. But see also the honest and perceptive confessions of a former television correspondent in the GDR, Michael Schmitz, in *Die Zeit*, 14 February 1992.

... **a special history of scholarship** ... a sharp but perceptive first attempt at a critical analysis was made by Hartmut Jäckel in DA 10/1990, pp. 1557–65. An informative sketch and qualified defence of the GDR-studies of the 1970s and 1980s is given by Rüdiger Thomas in *Zeitschrift für Parlamentsfragen*, 1/1990, pp. 126–36. Critical remarks on the failure of West German contemporary historians to tackle the subject of the other German dictatorship at all are made by Wolfgang Schuller in FAZ, 18 March 1991.

A younger generation ... this argument is well and sympathetically described by Gert-Joachim Glaessner in Gert-Joachim Glaessner, ed., *Die DDR in der Ära Honecker. Politik, Kultur, Gesellschaft* (Opladen: Westdeutscher Verlag, 1988), pp. 111–19. The contributions to this Festschrift for Hartmut Zimmermann, one of the leading figures of the new, social-science orientation, give a good impression of its strengths and weaknesses. Christian Fenner makes some perceptive comments on the so-called *Immanenzansatz* in the *Jahrbuch Extremismus & Demokratie*, 3/1991, pp. 33–51.

Opening these schoolbooks ... all quotations from *Der Spiegel* 21/1990.

An associate of Adenauer's. ... Wilhelm G Grewe in conversation with the author, Bonn, 6 July 1991.

... **that older Germany** ... on this, see Garton Ash, *DDR*.

... **in a curious novella** ... Günter Gaus, *Wendewut* (Hamburg: Hoffmann 8 Campe, 1990). It must be said that the identity of the heroine, like much else in this book, is distinctly obscure.

... **described himself** ... Hans-Jürgen Schierbaum, Bonn, 16 March 1989.

... **strange bonds developed** ... see, for example, the account of the 'Leipzig circle' of those involved in negotiating the 'Church deals', in Geissel, *Unterhändler*, p. 350 and *passim*.

In a remarkable article ... in *Die Zeit*, 31 July 1987. But less than five years later, Schmidt wrote a short leading article in *Die Zeit*, 28 February 1992, in which he said that too much attention was being paid to the aged Erich Honecker. 'The fact that he was once the head of a dictatorship on German soil,' Schmidt wrote, 'should no longer suffice for this. He is now only a case — albeit an important one — for the German courts . . .' This little article was headed, 'Quite normal' — *Ganz normal*.

. . . **'the charge that the federal government . . .'** Schmidt, *Nachbarn*, p. 53.

'The suffering of partition . . .' *Bundestag Plenarprotokolle*, 10/228, p. 17684 (10 September 1986).

. . . *Vergangenheitsbewältigung* . . . the comparison was of course made many times, see, for example, the contribution by Ludwig Elm in DA, 7/1991, pp. 737–43, and the excellent article by Richard Schröder in FAZ, 16 February 1993.

. . . **to be made on the West German side . . .** It is hard to agree with Richard von Weizsäcker when, in the course of an eloquent speech about coming to terms with the history of East Germany, he describes the continuation of the debate about 'the West-West chapter of the past' — that is, presumably, including all the controversies about Ostpolitik — as 'otiose'. See his speech on receiving the Heine Prize, reprinted in *Bulletin*, 17 December 1991, pp. 1165–70, this on p. 1169.

This West-West debate had, however, already begun in the media, with innumerable revelations, personal declarations and polemics. A useful way in to the debate is Cora Stephan, ed., *Wir Kollaborateure. Der Westen und die deutschen Vergangenheiten* (Reinbek: Rowohlt, 1992), with a sharp, polemical introduction by the author.

This debate was closely linked to that about the role of the Protestant Church, and not just in the case of Stolpe. In a newspaper interview shortly before unification the widely respected East Berlin Bishop Forck said, referring to the policy of his Church: 'We worked for much too long in the hope of achieving a better socialism, of changing the representatives of the state. We erred.' FAZ, 24 September 1990. Similar remarks were made by the former bishop of Magdeburg, Bishop Krusche, in a retrospective survey of the twenty-one years of the Federation of Protestant Churches in the GDR, see the report in FAZ, 25 February 1991.

'We erred', says the East German churchman, who faced at first hand the agonising dilemmas of living under a dictatorship. Meanwhile the West German politicians who faced those dilemmas only indirectly, from the comfort of secure freedom, shouted to each other across the party lines: '*You* erred!' 'No, you got it wrong!' 'But so did you!'

One cannot, of course, expect politicians to behave like priests. But between the moving self-criticism of the priest and the maddening *tu quoques* of the politicians, perhaps the historians may tell us how it really was — provided the politicians give them access to the sources. Particularly important in this connection is the so-called *Enquete Kommission* set up by the Bundestag to examine the history and legacy of what it now referred to as the 'SED dictatorship'. Point 7 of its terms of reference requires it to look at German-German relations. See *Bundestag Drucksachen*, 12/2597, reprinted in DA, 7/1992, pp. 782–84.

Chapter V: Beyond the Oder

... **a seminal essay** ... Löwenthal, *Vom kalten Krieg*, pp. 2, 90.

... **markedly easier** ... Thus Haberl and Hecker, *Unfertige Nachbarschaften*, pp. v, 3 ff, class the Federal Republic's relations with Hungary, Romania, Bulgaria and — they add, very questionably — Yugoslavia, as 'unburdened' relationships. But their own chapter on unadjacent Yugoslavia notes that the wartime conflict did place a considerable burden on post-war relations (pp. 133–51).

It has been suggested ... ibid., p. 3 ff.

... **'the rule of odd and even** ...' Lewis Namier, *Vanished Supremacies. Essays on European History 1812–1918* (London: Hamish Hamilton, 1958), p. 170.

... **without formal treaties** ... for the short Communiqués on the opening of diplomatic relations with Romania (31 January 1967), and Bulgaria and Hungary (both 21 December 1973), see *Verträge*, pp. 63–4.

... **troubled historiography** ... one excellent recent book on this subject in English is Burleigh, *Ostforschung*, which concentrates mainly on the Third Reich period. Zernack, *Osteuropa* is a fine critical introduction to the discipline and problems of studying 'Eastern Europe' in German, with a bibliography up to the mid-1970s. There are important comments in Haberl and Hecker, *Unfertige Nachbarschaften*, which has a useful short bibliography including works published up to 1989. Stökl, *Osteuropa*, first published in 1967, is a magisterial introductory essay on a thousand years of German relations with Eastern Europe. The third edition (1982) includes a short essay on books published up to 1981. A very useful survey concentrating specifically on German settlement in East Central and Eastern Europe is Dralle, *Deutsche*.

Men and women of goodwill ... a notable example on the Polish side is the seminal essay by Jan Józef Lipski, 'Two fatherlands, two patriotisms', in *Kontinent* (German-language edition), No., 22, 1982, pp. 3–48. Lipski points out, to give one small but telling example, that the Polish words for roof (*dach*), brick (*cegła*), bricklayer (*murarz*), printer (*drukarz*), painter (*malarz*) and woodcarver (*snycerz*), all come directly from the German (*Dach, Ziegel, Maurer, Drucker, Maler, Schnitzer*).

... **the German-Polish relationship** ... there is no single book on 'Germans and Poles' to compare with the works of Wiskemann and Brügel on 'Czechs and Germans' (see below). Beside the general works mentioned above, Broszat, *Polenpolitik* remains an outstanding overview of German policy. A volume of essays by German and official Polish historians, very much in the spirit of 1970s détente, is Jacobsen, *Bundesrepublik-Volksrepublik*. Jacobsen, *Bonn-Warschau*, is an essential reference work, but the selection of documents clearly reflects the editors' 'détente from above' school. Both in the works edited by Jacobsen and in Haberl and Hecker, *Unfertige Nachbarschaften*, extensive reference is also made to the painful but interesting attempts of a German-Polish joint commission to work out recommendations for German and Polish school textbooks. Independent contributions from the Polish side are to be found in Kuwaczka, *Entspannung von*

Unten, and the special German-language edition of the Paris-based Polish quarterly *Kultura*, Autumn 1984, devoted to German-Polish relations.

... **Germans had ruled over Poles** ... Burleigh, *Ostforschung*, p. 3, rightly begins with this observation, arguing that this fact coloured German perceptions of the whole of Europe east of Germany.

'*Placet* ... quoted in Josef Homeyer, 'Deutsche und polnische Katholiken', *Die Politische Meinung*, January 1991, pp. 15–22, this on p. 15.

... **Czechs and Germans** ... there are several good works on this theme, with almost identical titles: Elizabeth Wiskemann, *Czechs and Germans* (2nd edition, London: Macmillan, 1967); J W Brügel, *Tschechen und Deutsche*, Vol. 1 (Munich: Nymphenburger Verlag, 1967), covering the period 1918–38, and published in an abridged but also revised English edition as *Czechoslovakia Before Munich* (Cambridge: Cambridge University Press, 1973); J W Brügel, *Tschechen und Deutsche* Vol. 2 (Munich: Nymphenburger Verlag, 1974), covering the period 1939–45; Ferdinand Seibt, *Deutschland und die Tschechen. Geschichte einer Nachbarschaft in der Mitte Europas* (Munich: List, 1974); Rudolf Hilf, *Deutsche und Tschechen. Bedeutung und Wandlungen einer Nachbarschaft in Mitteleuropa* (2nd edition, Opladen: Leske & Budrich, 1986); Jan Křen & ors, *Integration oder Ausgrenzung. Deutsche und Tschechen 1890–1945* (Bremen: Donnat & Temmen, 1986).

... **as Sebastian Haffner has written** ... see Sebastian Haffner, *Der Teufelspakt. Die Deutsch-russischen Beziehungen vom Ersten zum Zweiten Weltkrieg* (Zürich: Manesse, 1988), p. 5 and *passim*, and the review essay by Gordon A Craig, 'Dangerous Liaisons', in the *New York Review of Books*, 30 March 1989. On the pre-1945 relationship see also Walter Laqueur, *Russia and Germany. A Century of Conflict* (London: Weidenfeld & Nicolson, 1965).

... **to recall the spirit of Rapallo** ... with the exception of Germans on the pro-Soviet left, see, for example, Ulrike Horster-Philipps, ed., *Rapallo - Modell für Europa? Friedliche Koexistenz und internationale Sicherheit heute* (Köln: Pahl-Rugenstein, 1987). But see also an interview with Rudolf Bahro, 'Rapallo—why not?' in *Telos* 51, Spring 1982.

'**For the first time in their lives** ...' Norman Davies, *God's Playground. A History of Poland*, Vol. 2 (Oxford: Clarendon Press, 1981), p. 565.

'**One ought** ...' Golo Mann, *The History of Germany since 1789* (London: Penguin Books, 1974), p. 813.

... *Historikerstreit* ... the historians' debate already has its own extensive historiography. The early texts were collected in '*Historikerstreit*'. *Die Dokumentation der Kontroverse um die Einzigartigkeit der nationalsozialistischen Judenvernichtung* (Munich: Piper, 1987). The subject can be approached in English through the books by Charles S Maier, *The Unmasterable Past. History, Holocaust and German National Identity* (Cambridge, Mass.: Harvard University Press, 1988) and Richard J. Evans, *In Hitler's Shadow. West German Historians and the Attempt to Escape from the Nazi Past* (London: Tauris, 1989), and the article by Geoff Eley in *Past & Present*, No. 121, November 1988, pp. 171–208.

German historians at once documented . . . see the massive *Dokumentation der Vertreibung der Deutschen aus Ost-Mitteleuropa* edited by Theodor Schieder and others, and originally published in 1954 under the auspices of the Bundesministerium für Vertriebene. Deutscher Taschenbuch Verlag (Munich) issued a paperpack reprint in 1984. This was a scholarly and careful work: the point, however, is the selection of subject matter for first attention.

. . . **the prior horrors of German occupation** . . . thus Martin Broszat's *Nationalsozialistische Polenpolitik* was published in 1961. It is interesting to note that both Broszat and another outstanding West German liberal historian who has written on German-Polish relations, Hans-Ulrich Wehler, started their academic careers by working on the documentation of the expulsions under Theodor Schieder.

. . . **the Polish deportations** . . . see the discussion in Kuwaczka, *Entspannung von Unten*, pp. 69–71, and the article published under the pseudonym Stefan Krupiński in 1986 in *Kontakt* 1/1986, reprinted in Kuwaczka, *Entspannung von Unten*, pp. 229–46. It is significant that a Polish historian felt obliged, as late as 1986, to publish this article under a pseudonym. See also the excellent treatment of the whole period in the work of another Polish historian, Włodzimierz Borodziej, *Od Poczdamu do Szklarskiej Poręby. Polska w stosunkach międzynarodowych 1945–47* (London: Aneks, 1990).

. . . **by isolated, independent (indeed banned) Czech scholars** . . . Although there were the beginnings of a discussion in the 1960s, a more sustained discussion began only in 1978 with the essay by 'Danubius' (pseudonym of the Slovak historian J Mlynárik), 'Tézy o vysídlení Československých Nemcov' in *Svědectví*, 5–7, 1978, pp. 105–34. The whole debate is now well documented in Bohumil Černý & ors, eds, *Češi, Němci, Odsun. Diskuse Nezávislých Historiků* (Prague: Academia, 1990). See also the chapter by Eva Schmidt-Hartmann in Benz, *Vertreibung*, pp. 143–57.

. . . **as the historian Norman Davies has written** . . . in the *Independent*, 29 December 1987.

. . . **the Western allies wished to punish** . . . for a good introductory survey see Hermann Graml, *Die Allierten und die Teilung Deutschlands. Konflikte und Entscheidungen 1941–1948* (Hamburg: Fischer, 1985), but see also the still magisterial survey in John Wheeler-Bennett and Anthony Nicholls, *The Semblance of Peace. The Political Settlement After The Second World War* (London: Macmillan, 1972).

. . . **that some Polish leaders** . . . see Sara Meiklejohn Terry, *Poland's Place in Europe. General Sikorski and the Origin of the Oder-Neisse Line 1939–43* (Princeton: Princeton University Press, 1983). But see also the balanced and authoritative treatment by Piotr Wandycz, *Polish Diplomacy 1914–45. Aims and Achievements* (London: Orbis Books, 1988), which also has a very useful bibliographical essay.

. . . **Churchill** . . . **argued** . . . 'I am sorry about the Western Neisse . . .' Churchill wrote to his successor Clement Attlee on 3 August 1945, 'this was certainly not the fault of the British Delegation', see *Documents on British Policy Overseas*, Series 1, Vol. 1 (London: HMSO, 1984), p. 1278. In a powerful speech to the

House of Commons on 16 August 1945, his first as Leader of the Opposition, Churchill said 'I must put on record my own opinion that the provisional Western frontier agreed upon for Poland . . . is not a good augury for the future map of Europe.' In this same speech, referring to the fate of the Germans east of the Oder-Neisse line, he said 'it is not impossible that a tragedy on a prodigious scale is unfolding itself behind the iron curtain which at the moment divides Europe in twain'. *Hansard*, 5th Series, Vol. 413, p. 83. In his memoirs he claims to have had in mind at Potsdam 'to have a show-down at the end of the Conference, and, if necessary, to have a public break rather than allow anything beyond the Oder and the Eastern Neisse to be ceded to Poland'. Winston S Churchill, *The Second World War. Vol. VI: Triumph and Tragedy* (London: Cassell, 1954), p. 582. David Cecil rightly comments that this 'is magnificent, but it is not history'. See his article, 'Potsdam and its Legends', in *International Affairs* (London), July 1970, pp. 455–65, this on p. 456. Earlier in the same volume, explaining the basis of his position, Churchill writes: 'For the future peace of Europe here was a wrong beside which Alsace-Lorraine and the Danzig Corridor were trifles. One day the Germans would want their territory back, and the Poles would not be able to stop them.' ibid., p. 561.

. . . **it was Stalin's unbending insistence** . . . see Vojtech Mastny's masterly study, *Russia's Road to the Cold War. Diplomacy, Warfare and the Politics of Communism* (New York: Columbia University Press, 1979), and R C Raack, 'Stalin Fixes the Oder-Neisse Line', *Journal of Contemporary History*, Vol. 25, 1990, pp. 467–88, which shows how Stalin worked through his Polish puppets. A rich flow of material on this whole subject may be expected as the Soviet and East European archives reveal their hidden treasures.

. . . **almost all** . . . by conceding the small stretches of territory between the Molotov-Ribbentrop and the Curzon lines, Stalin managed to confer legitimacy on his claim, for the 'Curzon line' was the proposal not of a Soviet or Nazi but of a British foreign minister.

In one move . . . this is also the interpretation of Broszat, *Polenpolitik*, p. 314 ff.

. . . **the Soviet Union then devoted** . . . although there was some initial hesitation even on the Soviet side, and the 16 August 1945 Soviet-Polish Treaty actually left the question of the final delineation of the frontier line through East Prussia open until 'the final regulation of territorial questions by the peace settlement', see Lehmann, *Oder-Neisse*, p. 52 and *passim*.

. . . **'the final delimitation** . . .' see the English text in Grenville, *Treaties*, p. 36.

'The Socialist Unity Party regrets . . . quoted by Bingen, *Bonn-Warschau*, p. 10. On this see also Lehmann, *Oder-Neisse*, pp. 120–22, and the interesting discussion in Włodzimierz Borodziej, *Od Poczdamu do Szklarskiej Poręby. Polska w stosunkach międzynarodowych 1945–1947* (London: Aneks, 1990), pp. 290–314

. . . **'the state frontier between Germany and Poland'** . . . see the text in Grenville, *Treaties*, pp. 187–88. The German wording can be found in Jacobsen, *Bonn-Warschau*, pp. 72–73 and Fritsch-Bournazel, *Europa*, pp. 144–46.

Polish Lwów moved to German Breslau ... see the vivid discussion in Norman Davies, *God's Playground. A History of Poland*, Vol 2. (Oxford: Clarendon Press, 1981), pp. 512–14.

... **the sealing of Yalta** ... see Maresca, *Helsinki*, pp. 110–11, 212, Gromyko, *Memories*, p. 187. In his speech on the signature of the Final Act, Brezhnev described the conference as 'a necessary summing-up of the political outcome of the Second World War', quoted in Mastny, *Helsinki I*, pp. 87–88.

... **'forever'** ... see Zdeněk Mlynář, *Night Frost in Prague* (London: C Hurst & Co., 1980), pp. 239–40.

... **to 'regard as inviolable** ...' the text of the Final Act is conveniently reprinted in Maresca, *Helsinki*, pp. 248–305, this on p. 252.

... **a formula negotiated by Henry Kissinger** ... The remarkable story of how this formula was arrived at is told in Maresca, *Helsinki*, pp. 110–16.

... **'consider that their frontiers can be changed** ...' ibid., p. 251.

... **'regard as inviolable now and in the future** ...' *Verträge*, p. 14.

... **'have no territorial claims** ...' ibid., pp. 14, 22, 52.

... **as we have seen** ... see above, p. 71 f, and further references in the notes to those pages.

... **the 'Letter on German Unity'** ... *Verträge.*, p. 15.

... **'rights and responsibilities for Germany as a whole** ...' ibid., p. 16.

The Common Resolution ... ibid., pp. 66–7.

... **'so far as its territorial extent** ...' full text of the crucial 1973 verdict in *Zehn Jahre*, pp. 232–43, this on p. 237. In taking this position the Constitutional Court was, however, reaffirming what had clearly been the intention and undertanding of those who framed the Basic Law in 1949, see Lehmann, *Oder-Neisse*, pp. 145–47. One of the judges who delivered the 1973 verdict, Willi Geiger, emphasises the continuity of the Constitutional Court's position on this issue, pointing out that the Court, with a different membership, unconditionally reaffirmed it in a judgement in 1987. See Willi Geiger, 'Der Grundlagenvertrag und die Einheit Deutschlands', in Dieter Blumenwitz & Gottfried Zieger, eds, *40 Jahre Bundesrepublik Deutschland. Verantwortung für Deutschland* (Köln: Verlag Wissenschaft und Politik, 1989), pp. 53–64.

... **a suggestion by a leading German specialist** ... the specialist was Karl Kaiser, see the report in FAZ, 13 July 1989, the critical response by Wilhelm G Grewe in *Rheinischer Merkur*, 28 July 1989, Karl Kaiser's eloquent statement of his general argument in *Die Zeit*, 22 September 1989, and a further response by Wilhelm G Grewe in FAZ, 19 October 1989.

... **genuinely a territorial revisionist** ... see Schwarz, *Adenauer I*, pp. 945–96.

... **'Oder-Neisse, Eastern provinces** ...' quoted by Hans-Jakob Stehle in Josef

Foschepoth, ed., *Adenauer und die deutsche Frage* (Göttingen: Vandenhoeck & Rupprecht, 1988), p. 85. His source is given as a note by the journalist Fritz Sänger on a conversation with Adenauer on 30 August 1955. The remark was quoted by Karl Kaiser in his article in *Die Zeit*, 22 September 1989, and I am grateful to his assistant Klaus Becher for pointing me to the source.

... by the late 1950s ... A plan for German unification worked out by Adenauer's close associate Felix von Eckardt in September 1956 already envisaged a plebiscite in which the Germans in East and West Germany would be asked if they would be willing to accept 'certain sacrifices in the drawing of the eastern frontier' in return for reunification (of East and West Germany), see Schwarz, *Adenauer II*, pp. 321–23. The diplomatic trade-off of frontier recognition for reunification was also suggested by Wilhelm Grewe in a lecture in New York in November 1959, see Grewe, *Rückblenden*, pp. 419–20.

... following Byrnes' Stuttgart speech ... see Lehmann, *Oder-Neisse*, pp. 70, 78 ff.

... Kennedy and Macmillan as well as de Gaulle ... see Schwarz, *Adenauer II*, pp. 551–52. De Gaulle made his position unmistakeably clear in a famous press conference on 25 March 1959. Schwarz rightly points out that if Adenauer was under pressure on this issue from the German expellees in the Federal Republic, American presidents — particularly Democratic presidents — were under countervailing pressure from Polish émigrés in the United States.

... a diplomatic card ... Schwarz, *Adenauer II*, p. 687. Wilhelm Grewe to the author, Bonn, 6 July 1991.

... 'it is difficult for Germany's neighbours ...' Elizabeth Wiskemann, *Germany's Eastern Neighbours. Problems relating to the Oder-Neisse Line and the Czech Frontier Regions* (London: Oxford University Press, 1956), p. 112, hereafter Wiskemann, *Eastern Neighbours*.

... as Egon Bahr's closest legal adviser ... Antonius Eitel, in conversation with the author, Bonn, 1 July 1991. Eitel is the pseudonymous author of Zündorf, *Ostverträge*.

Alois Mertes ... argued ... see, for example, his comments recorded in *Politik und Kultur* (Berlin), 2/1981, pp. 20–38, especially pp. 32–33, and letter to the FAZ, 12 October 1982.

... the necessary starting-point ... the clearest statement is in his Memorandum for the leader of the CDU/CSU parliamentary party dated 20 August 1980. That the Basic Law did not require this to be a target was authoritatively confirmed by one of the judges who made the controversial Constitutional Court ruling of 1973, Willi Geiger, in *Neue Juristische Wochenschrift*, Heft 41, 1983, pp. 2302–04.

... Wilhelm Grewe ... a particularly clear and concise statement in his letter to the FAZ, 2 December 1983.

... an interesting exchange of letters ... in ACDP: I-403, 038/2. The exchange was initiated by Mertes, who was then Minister of State in the Foreign Ministry, and prompted by the Soviet compaign against German 're- vanchism'.

. . . 'too much effort' . . . letter of 13 July 1984, ibid.

The devil, replied Mertes . . . letter of 18 July 1984, ibid.

. . . the frontiers of 1937 as a target . . . even the Hupkas and Czajas would not say this explicitly in the 1970s and 1980s. But they fiercely insisted that the frontiers of 1937 were more than just a starting-point — see, for example, letter from Herbert Hupka to the FAZ, 30 July 1983 — and some of their followers were certainly less cautious. Thus, for example, a motion proposed by the Mainz-Bin- gen local group of the Federation of Expellees to that organisation's regional assembly (*Landesdelegiertentag*) on 7 March 1982 read as follows: 'The People's Republic of Poland has, in the last decades, proved itself in every respect incapable of administering the east German areas put under its control. The Federation of Expellees therefore calls on the victor powers to remove from Poland, even before peace treaty regulations, the administration of the German eastern territories as defined in the Potsdam resolutions.' It then went on to make a suggestion which curiously reflected the impact of Brandt's new Ostpolitik and the improvement in German-German relations: 'The Federation of Expellees,' so the draft resolution continued, 'further demands that in a first step to the unification of the divided German territories, the provinces currently under Polish administration should be subordinated and attached to the German Democratic Republic'! With the exception of this last sentence, the resolution was passed by the regional assembly, in Helmut Kohl's home territory, just before he became Chancellor — a vivid, if extreme, example of what he was up against. This curious document is in ACDP: 1403, 130/1.

. . . the 'Stuttgart Charter' . . . see Jacobsen, *Nachbarn*, pp. 232–33.

. . . Willy Brandt himself observed . . . in his contribution to Dieter Blumen- witz & ors, eds, *Konrad Adenauer und seine Zeit* (Stuttgart: Deutsche Verlags-An- stalt, 1976), Vol. 1, p. 107.

. . . a double integration . . . On this there is a large literature. A brief account is given by Dennis L Bark and David R Gress, *From Shadow to Substance 1945–1963 = A History of West Germany, Vol 1*, (Oxford: Blackwell, 1989), pp. 305–10. See also the chapters by Bauer, Wiesemann and Schillinger in Benz, *Vertreibung*. A useful account of the state of research is given by Arnold Sywottek in APZ, 15 December 1989, pp. 38–46. On the party-political side the most vivid impression is given by the narrative in Schwarz's biography of Adenauer.

An author who knew Helmut Kohl well . . . Peter Scholl-Latour in *Helmut Kohl. Fotografiert von Konrad R. Müller, mit einem Essay von Peter Scholl-Latour* (Bergisch-Gladbach: Gustav Lübbe Verlag, 1990), p. 32.

. . . Friedrich Zimmermann . . . in a speech to the Bavarian regional association of the Federation of Expellees on 29 January 1983, billed as presenting the policy of the new government. Zimmermann maintained his position, against a formal protest from the Polish government, which the minister ascribed to 'obdurate communists', see *Die Welt* 11 February 1983.

... **'Silesia remains ours'** ... Kohl had already addressed at least one meeting of expellees, in September 1984, in line with his conscious policy of active dialogue with them, see his speech reprinted in *Bulletin*, 5 September 1984, pp. 873–79. The planned motto became known at the end of 1984, provoking a whirlwind of media intention. The chairman of the Silesian *Landsmannschaft* (that is, organisation of Germans from that region), Herbert Hupka, observed: 'I cannot wholly understand the excitement ... — perhaps the language sounds too old-German, too Lutheran — nothing else is meant but that Silesia remains our homeland (*Heimat*), that Silesia remains our task, that we may and should not give up the claim to Silesia, historically, spiritually, culturally, morally and politically.' Interview on Bavarian Radio, 29 December 1984, quoted from BPA/KU I/2.1.85. Very reassuring. Matters were made still worse by a fantastic article in the Silesians' newspaper, *Der Schlesier* (25 January 1985), in which one Thomas Finke imagined West German troops sweeping forward to the Soviet frontier as a result of a 'New Ostpolitik' of the Federal Government, the goal of which was the destabilisation of the Soviet bloc. Only in Poland and Czechoslovakia, wrote Thomas Finke, in this charming fantasy, 'did parts of the armed forces put up resistance, which was, however, soon broken. The overwhelming majority of the population greeted the Germans as liberators.' Even Herbert Hupka felt compelled to distance himself from this article, pleading freedom of the press. After an icy public exchange of letters between Hupka and Kohl (the Chancellor's letter being printed in the *Bulletin*, 25 January 1985, pp. 69–70, a fairly unusual proceeding), and a clarifying statement in the Bundestag (also reprinted, unusually, in the *Bulletin*, 8 February 1985, pp. 121–23), the Silesians were prevailed upon to change the motto and the furore somewhat subsided.

In his speech ... reprinted in *Bulletin*, 20 June 1985, pp. 577–83. There also the following quotations.

... **a resolution of the Silesian association** ... the resolution dated from 2 March 1985, and was connected with the foregoing controversy.

'**... and not put it in question'** ... my own notes of the meeting, which I attended, record 'boos and whistles' at this point. Kohl had earlier used an almost identical formulation, referring to 'the territories beyond Poland's western frontier', see *Bulletin*, 28 February 1985, p. 200.

... **a banner** ... **torn down** ... author's observation. See also my report in the *Spectator*, 22 June 1985.

... **a 'political binding effect'** ... *Bundestag Plenarprotokolle*, 10/119, p. 8812 (6 February 1985). This statement, regarded at the time as an act of political courage, came following a visit by Volker Rühe to Poland, and at the height of the controversy about the Silesians' meeting. Karl Kaiser credits the Social Democrat jurist Claus Arndt with coining the concept, see Kaiser's article in *Die Zeit*, 22 September 1989.

... **an independent opinion survey** ... this was one of the fascinating series of surveys by Polish sociologists called simply 'Poles', see Garton Ash, *Uses*, p. 239, note 29.

. . . **a minister from the Christian Social Union** . . . this time the Finance Minister and Chairman of the CSU, Theo Waigel, once again at the Silesians' meeting, see reports in SZ and FAZ, both 3 July 1989. The FAZ's reporter noted that of some 100,000 people attending the whole festival, only some 5,000 bothered to come to hear Herr Waigel's speech. This was nonetheless rolled into the controversy about Karl Kaiser's comments (see above) to become the lead story in *Der Spiegel*, 29/1989.

. . . **'the Polish people should know . . .'** see *Umbruch*, pp. 75–6. This was the wording of the resolution proposed by CDU/CSU and FDP, see *Bundestag Drucksachen* 11/5589. The particular force of it was the commitment expressed in the formulation 'us Germans', implying that this would hold for Germans in a unified state as well. However, reflecting the painful compromises to be made within the ranks of the Christian Democrats, this passage was prefaced with the phrase 'For the Federal Republic of Germany it holds that . . .' On the argument inside the coalition see report in FAZ, 9 November 1989. The Greens proposed a much less qualified resolution, which said that the Oder-Neisse line as Poland's western frontier 'is inviolable for any German state authority', see *Bundestag Drucksachen*, 11/5591. The government resolution was supported by the Social Democrats. Four hundred votes were cast for the resolution, four against, and there were thirty-three abstentions.

'The Chancellor tried to calm my fears . . .' *Rok 1989. Bronisław Geremek Opowiada, Jacek Żakowski Pyta* (Warsaw: Plejada, 1990), pp. 327–28.

. . . **did not mention the frontiers** . . . see Kaiser, *Vereinigung*, p. 91.

. . . **the Chancellor . . . surprised and appalled** . . . see reports in FAZ, 3 March 1990, *Le Monde*, 4–5 March 1990, *Observer*, 4 March 1990. The result of this further flurry was another Bundestag resolution which paved the domestic political path for the agreement on the Oder-Neisse line in the '2 + 4' negotiations for German unity, and the final frontier treaty between united Germany and liberated Poland.

. . . **the other five (including Markus Meckel** . . .) this was clearly the impression of the Poles involved (Jerzy Sułek, Berlin, 11 May 1992). See also p. 353 f.

. . . **the final ratification of the final frontier treaty** . . . for the vote on 17 October 1991, see *Bundestag Plenarprotokolle*, 12/50, pp. 4098–99. At a meeting with Poland's first non-communist prime minister, Tadeusz Mazowiecki, in Frankfurt on the Oder in early November 1990, Kohl assured him that the frontier treaty could be signed already that month — a nice electoral gift to the presidential candidate Mazowiecki — and held out the prospect that it would be ratified, together with the 'neighbour' treaty, in February 1991. See report in FAZ, 9 November 1990 and *Bulletin*, 16 November 1990, pp. 1389–96, with text of the treaty signed on 14 November by foreign ministers Genscher and Skubiszewski. In fact, the negotiations on the second treaty lasted much longer, especially because of Bonn's insistence on detailing the rights of the German minority in Poland, see, for example, report in *Der Spiegel* 11/91. The texts on the signature of the 'neighbour' treaty in June 1991 are in *Bulletin*, 18 June 1991, pp. 541–56.

. . . **a retrospective conversation with the author** . . . Helmut Kohl, Bonn, 1 October 1991.

. . . **precisely as it ran** . . . A former head of the Bonn Foreign Ministry's legal department suggested in conversation with the author that Bonn might perhaps have tried for a slightly different interpretation of the Oder-Neisse line, closer to the original wording of the Potsdam Agreement. Since this suggested that the line run 'from the Baltic Sea immediately west of Swinamunde, and thence along the Oder river' it could be argued that the west bank of the Oder, including most of Stettin — now Szczecin — should have gone to Germany. The Görlitz Agreement, trying to square this vague provision with the line to the west of Szczecin that the Soviets had actually decided on, referred to 'the established and existing frontier running from the Baltic Sea along the line west of Swinoujscie and along the Odra river . . .'. (See Grenville, *Treaties*, pp. 36 & 188.) In fact there was a fierce border dispute between the GDR and Poland in the 1980s over the exact dividing line through the Szczecin harbour waters at the mouth of the Oder, after both sides had unilaterally extended their territorial waters to twelve miles. This dispute was only resolved, with a precise delineation of the line, in a treaty between the GDR and the People's Republic of Poland on 22 May 1989. See FAZ 24 May 1989. This line was then explicitly referred to in the treaty between united Germany and liberated Poland. One of the few lasting foreign policy acts of the GDR was thus to determine the exact line of the frontier between the Federal Republic and the Republic of Poland!

. . . **the price which Germany simply had to pay** . . . see the speech by Ottfried Hennig to the East Prussian *Landsmannschaft* (that is, organisation of the Germans from that region) in Bad Honnef on 8 September 1990. Hennig, a Parliamentary State Secretary in the Ministry for Intra-German Relations, there explains why he felt obliged to support the Chancellor on this point — because otherwise the reunification of East and West Germany would be impossible — but also felt obliged to resign his post as spokesman of the East Prussian organisation.

. . . **the basic outlines of the problem** . . . there is no satisfactory overall account of this issue. Beside the useful essays in Benz, *Vertreibung*, much essential information is given in the detailed research reports prepared for the German section of the Association for the Study of the World Refugee Problem, referred to here as *Aussiedler 1* and *Aussiedler 2*, and in the official publications of the Federal Ministry of the Interior. Most of the material on the remaining German minorities is to be found either in official publications or in newspaper and journal articles, but Schulz-Vobach, *Die Deutschen im Osten*, is a useful journalistic *tour d'horizon* reflecting the state of affairs in the mid- to late 1980s. Dralle, *Deutsche*, is good for the general background. Ingeborg Fleischauer & Benjamin Pinkus, *The*

Soviet Germans. Past and Present (London: Hurst, 1986), is invaluable on the history of the Germans in the Soviet Union up to the mid-1980s.

. . . and their replacement by settlers . . . see the brief but vivid description in Broszat, *Polenpolitik*, p. 286 ff. More detail in Martin Broszat, *Nationalsozialistische Polenpolitik* (Stuttgart: Deutsche Verlags-Anstalt, 1961).

. . . some four million . . . see the introduction by Hans Harmsen to *Aussiedler* 2, pp. 1–12, this on p. 3.

. . . *Germanissimi Germanorum* . . . On this community see also August Ludwig Schlözer, *Kritische Sammlungen zur Geschichte der Deutschen in Siebenbürgen*, (Vienna: Bohlau, 1979), a reprint of the original edition of 1795–97, and the review article by William C Dowling, 'Germanissimi Germanorum. Romania's Vanishing German Culture' in *East European Politics and Societies*, Vol. 5, No. 2, pp. 341–55.

. . . the remaining Germans within . . . **Poland** . . . for an introduction to this fiendishly intricate and delicate subject see the chapter by Gerhard Reichling in *Aussiedler 1*, pp. 9–56, and articles by Gotthold Rhode in APZ, B11–12/88, pp. 3–20 and Hans-Werner Rautenberg in APZ, B50/88, pp. 14–27. Christian Th. Stoll, *Die Deutschen im polnischen Herrschaftsbereich nach 1945* (Vienna: Österreichische Landsmannschaft, 1989 = *Eckart-Schriften* Heft 98) is a tendentious book, which nonetheless contains useful information.

. . . Upper Silesia . . . for the exceptionally complex history of this area see the introduction to Hugo Weczerka, ed., *Schlesien* (Stuttgart: Kröner, 1977 = *Handbuch der Historischen Stätten*), and Wiskemann, *Eastern Neighbours*, pp. 22–33.

. . . now turning one way, now the other . . . Interestingly enough, Helmut Schmidt reports Edward Gierek saying precisely this to him in Helsinki in 1975: 'We Upper Silesians were Poles when the Poles were doing well and Germans when you were doing well!' See Schmidt, *Nachbarn*, p. 481.

. . . the *Auslandsdeutsche* . . . very roughly 'Germans abroad'. On this see John Hiden, 'The Weimar Republic and the problem of the *Auslandsdeutsche*', in *Journal of Contemporary History*, 12/1977, pp. 273–89, and the same author's book, *The Baltic States and Weimar Ostpolitik* (Cambridge: Cambridge University Press, 1987), with bibliography.

. . . German foreign ministry support . . . on this see Norbert Krekeler, *Revisionsanspruch und geheime Ostpolitik der Weimarer Republik. Die Subventionierung der deutschen Minderheit in Polen 1919–33* (Stuttgart: Deutsche Verlags-Anstalt, 1973). He summarises some of the main points in his chapter in Benz, *Vertreibung*.

. . . the devil's grandmother . . . quoted by Rainer Salzmann in Dieter Blumenwitz & ors, eds, *Konrad Adenauer und seine Zeit*, Vol 2, (Stuttgart: Deutsche Verlags-Anstalt, 1976), p. 151. However in an article in *Die Zeit*, 1 January 1993, Karl-Heinz Jansen reports the conclusion of the historian Heinrich Meyer, on the basis of previously unpublished documents, that Adenauer might in fact have been able to get the prisoners-of-war home earlier. Another historical 'what would have happened if . . .'.

. . . significant improvements for the ethnic Germans . . . see the article by Barbara Dietz and Peter Hilkes in APZ, B50/1988, pp. 3–13, esp. p. 5.

. . . a second, extremely difficult round of negotiations . . . the best short account is given by Boris Meissner, who was very directly involved in them, see Meissner, *Moskau-Bonn*, pp. 27–30 and the documents indicated in the footnotes to those pages, with the actual agreement reprinted on pp. 370–72. The essential qualification for repatriation was to have possessed German citizenship on 21 June 1941.

The 1961 Bundestag initiative . . . explicitly linked . . . as one might expect from an initiative led by the Sudeten German Wenzel Jaksch. See the Jaksch report on the position of the Germans in the East, *Bundestag Drucksachen*, 3/2807, which was clearly linked to the more often quoted main 'Jaksch report', which is *Bundestag Drucksachen*, 3/2740.

. . . a measure of their success . . . see, for example, comments by the Interior Minister in *Bulletin*, 16 January 1979, p. 35, and by Chancellor Schmidt in *Bundestag Plenarprotokolle* 9/111, p. 6748 (9 September 1982).

. . . the official translation . . . *Basic Law of the Federal Republic of Germany* (Bonn: Press and Information Office of the Federal Government, 1977).

. . . two key categories . . . the following paragraph draws heavily on the authoritative commentary, Maunz-Dürig-Herzog, *Grundgesetz-Kommentar* (Munich: Beck, 1991). For this, as for many other legal references, I am grateful to Michael Mertes.

. . . guidelines . . . Friedland reception camp . . . the 1976 'Friedland guidelines' are reprinted in the 'working handbook' by a senior legal official: Liesner, *Aussiedler* pp. 66–77, but see also Liesner's introduction.

'A member of the German *Volk* . . .' ibid., p. 61.

. . . 'by his behaviour the consciousness and will . . .' ibid., p. 79.

. . . 'their overall behaviour . . .' ibid., p. 81.

. . . 'If the dominant influence . . .' ibid., p. 84.

. . . 'immediately before the beginning . . .' ibid., p. 82.

. . . 'they could not be expected . . .' ibid., p. 85.

. . . 'the concept of German stock . . .' ibid., p. 85.

. . . at the Friedland reception camp . . . A vivid description is given by Amity Shlaes in Chapter 1 of her *Germany. The Empire Within* (New York: Farrar Strauss, 1991). However, as will be clear from the above, she oversimplifies when she writes (p. 20) that 'In Germany blood is what counts, and the settlers are Germans because they are of German blood.'

... **entering them in group three or four of the so-called** *Volksliste* ... see, for example, Broszat, *Polenpolitik*, pp. 288–89. The *Volksliste* had four groups, of which the largest — and most problematic for West Germany — was Group 3. This contained persons described as Germans with 'ties to *Polentum*'. Some 1.7 million people were entered in this group alone between 1941 and 1944. Group 4, which contained only some 80,000, contained persons described as having 'gone up into *Polentum*' — that is, as an official of the Federal Interior Ministry nicely described it to me, 'Poles with blue eyes and blond hair'. Manfred Meissner, Bonn, 8 September 1989.

... **generally depended on a certification of Germanity** ... Manfred Meissner, Bonn, 25 March 1992. For the precise details, and exceptions, see Liesner, *Aussiedler*.

Question 15 of the questionnaire ... reprinted in Liesner, *Aussiedler*, p. 55. Those seeking recognition therefore sought evidence from such sources as the Berlin Document Center, the *Bundesarchiv*, and the so-called German Office for Informing the Next-of-kin of the Fallen of the former German Wehrmacht.

... **roughly half** ... Manfred Meissner, Bonn, 8 September 1989.

... **more German** ... in the sense of preserving national traditions, habits, even language lost in the commercialised, Americanised Federal Republic. This point was stressed in publications designed to win popular acceptance for the out-settlers, see for example the official free paper of the Federal Centre for Political Education, *PZ*, 56/1989, headlined '*Aussiedler ... Deutscher als wir ...*'.

... **not a family past in the Polish resistance** ... a first-hand observer told me of one applicant initially accepted, because he furnished evidence of having served in the *Wehrmacht*, but then definitively rejected, because it emerged that he had later fought with the Polish Army against the Germans.

... **could be bought on the black market** ... see reports in SZ, *Die Welt* and *Berliner Morgenpost* of 30 March 1988 and *Stuttgarter Zeitung* of 2 April 1988.

... **the Gomułka regime did permit** ... this included the founding, in April 1957, of a 'German Social-cultural Society'. See the valuable article by a leading West German historian of Poland, Gotthold Rhode, 'Die deutsch-polnischen Beziehungen von 1945 bis in die achtziger Jahre,' in APZ, B11–12/88, this on p. 14.

... **not in Upper Silesia** ... incredibly, a ban on the teaching of German in the voivodships of Opole and Katowice — that is, in Upper Silesia — was only lifted in September 1988. See the report by Stefan Dietrich in FAZ, 23 January 1989.

... **the Polish authorities at first maintained** ... for this and the following see Baring, *Machtwechsel*, pp. 482–87.

... **a so-called 'Information'** ... text in *Verträge*, pp. 27–29.

... **unpublished 'Confidential Notes'** ... see Baring, *Machtwechsel*, p. 484.

Following a long and emotional late-evening talk . . . see Link, *Ära Schmidt*, pp. 307–08, Bingen, *Bonn-Warschau*, pp. 26–29, Schmidt, *Nachbarn*, pp. 479 ff.

. . . a pension agreement . . . see *Verträge*, pp. 29–38. Bonn's main objective here was to ensure that Germans living in Poland who had payed their pension contributions to German pension funds in the *Reich* before 1945, would get a decent pension. But clearly the Polish side would not accept the direct payment by West Germany of pensions to people whose separate identity, as Germans, they anyway disputed. The compromise found was that West Germany would pay any Pole who came to live in the Federal Republic a regular state pension based on the years he had (notionally) contributed to a pension fund in Poland, and Poland would honour — at its regular state pension rates — the years for which people now living in Poland had previously paid into German pension funds. The results were threefold. First, a few tens of thousands of old people in the former German territories received a zloty pension which they might otherwise not have received. Secondly, the Gierek equipe pocketed a further DM 1.3 billion. Thirdly, any Pole coming to live permanently in the Federal Republic had a DM pension entitlement for the years he notionally contributed in Poland. Thus, for example, as the *Bild-Zeitung* hastened to point out, a Polish General (Leon Dubicki) who defected to West Germany shortly before martial law was declared in 1981 automatically received a pension larger than many ordinary West Germans. A detailed account of the agreements, looking particularly at their status in international law, is given by Dieter Blumenwitz in Dieter Blumenwitz and Gottfried Zieger, eds, *Menschenrechte und wirtschaftliche Gegenleistungen. Aspekte ihrer völkerrectlichen Verknüpfungen* (Köln: Verlag Wissenschaft und Politik, 1987), pp. 9–28.

. . . a DM 1 billion loan . . . see *Verträge*, pp. 38–40.

. . . 'on the basis of investigations . . .' ibid., p. 41.

. . . led by Franz Josef Strauss . . . see Bingen, *Bonn-Warschau*, p. 28; Link, *Ära Schmidt*, pp. 307–08; and, for Strauss's own colourful account, Strauss, *Erinnerungen*, pp. 458–66.

. . . further, quite humiliating public assurances . . . see *Verträge*, pp. 46–49. The then spokesman of the (Bonn) Foreign Ministry described these assurances as 'on the borderline of what can be reconciled with the concept of sovereignty', quoted in Bingen, *Bonn-Warschau*, p. 28.

The Jackson-Vanik amendment . . . on this see the detailed discussion in Kissinger, *Years of Upheaval*, pp. 250–55, 986–95, & 1252–53 (with the final text of the amendment).

In the case of Romania . . . see Kovrig, *Walls and Bridges*, esp. pp. 182–86.

So also with Romania . . . the best short account is given in the article by Anneli Ute Gabanyi in APZ, B50/88, pp. 28–39.

. . . cash being carried to the border . . . Günther van Well, Bonn, 8 July 1991.

. . . for the next five years . . . in 1988, Genscher began negotiations about raising the payment and accelerating the emigration programme, since the position of the German minority was held to have become intolerable, see the report by Olaf Ihlau in SZ, 4 August 1988.

... **cash for Germans** ... thus Werner Link: 'West German capital for Polish exit-liberalisation for German and German-stock citizens!' Link, *Ära Schmidt*, p. 307. See also the chapters by Schweitzer and Sułek in Jacobsen, *Deutschland-Polen*.

... **a personal declaration of friendship** ... Schmidt's remarkable *faible* for Edward Gierek is well documented. Klaus Bölling records him saying he would 'take him straight into the cabinet', and, on the night before martial law was declared, asking Erich Honecker whether he could not intervene with the Polish authorities on behalf of — Edward Gierek! See Bölling, *Die fernen Nachbarn*, p. 157.

... **'to advance the conditions'** ... *Verträge*, p. 38.

... **DM 290.5 million in interest subsidies** ... Link, *Ära Schmidt*, p. 308.

Alois Mertes estimated ... this came in an eight-page letter to a parliamentary colleague, Carl Otto Lenz, dated 14 December 1983, and widely publicised. All the following quotations are from a copy of the original letter in the Mertes file in the ACDP press archive.

... **that liberal-conservative interpretation** ... see above, pp. 224 f. The independent Polish specialist on German affairs, Artur Hajnicz, points out that the leader of the Silesian expellees, Herbert Hupka, 'instantly protested against the letter, which he had thoroughly perused and the intention behind which he understood'. See *Aussenpolitik* (English-language edition), I/89, p. 35.

Primate Glemp preached a sermon ... extracts in FAZ, 18 August 1984. Glemp attempted to undo some of the damage in an interview in *Die Zeit*, 13 June 1985.

'What Germans, what injury?' ... For this attitude he was, however, criticised in the independent, underground press. See, for example, an article in *CDN. Głos Wolnego Robotnika*, No. 85, December 1984.

The main reasons ... Manfred Meissner, Federal Ministry of the Interior, Bonn, 8 September 1989.

... **with renewed emphasis** ... as noted by Johann Georg Reissmüller in the FAZ, 16 May 1983, reprinted in Reissmüller, *Vergessene Hälfte*, pp. 118–21.

... **a net economic gain** ... see the article by Klaus Leciejewski in *Das Parlament*, 25 August 1989, and the Institut der deutschen Wirtschaft study reported in FAZ, 23 September 1989.

... **'Persons persecuted ...'** this is the official translation in *The Basic Law of the Federal Republic of Germany* (Bonn: Press and Information Office of the Federal Government, 1977). The German is actually simply and stronger: *'Politisch Verfolgte geniessen Asylrecht'*.

In practice ... detail and the following figures from Jürgen Haberland, Federal Ministry of the Interior, Bonn, 15 March 1989.

... some **200,000** ... this figure came from the Federal Republic's central register of foreigners. It did not include temporary visitors, those with dual citizenship, and, of course, those staying illegally.

... **a rough continuum of resentment** ... this emerges very clearly in the results of a survey in *Der Spiegel*, 16/1989.

... **less** *Volksdeutsche* **than** *Volkswagendeutsche* ... this is not, it must be emphasised, to deny the existence of a minority for whom the denial of cultural identity was a major motive for wishing to leave. See, for example, the article by Bronisław Tumilowicz in *Polityka*, 24 June 1989, and that by Hans Krump in *Die Welt*, 24 October 1987. But when Krump's article is subtitled 'More than a million Germans in Poland fight for their identity', it compounds the fateful confusion. There might be more than a million Germans *in the sense of the Basic Law* in Poland. What there certainly was not, however, was a million 'fighting for their identity'. On this see also Klaus Reiff, *Polen. Als deutscher Diplomat an der Weichsel* (Bonn: Dietz, 1990), p. 76 ff.

On the first visit by a President ... see Schulz-Vobach, *Die Deutschen im Osten*, p. 128 ff.

... **'the treatment of minorities** ...' press statement of the CDU/CSU parliamentary party, 1 September 1988.

... **to be understood as a signal** ... Volker Rühe, Bonn, 14 October 1988.

... **'Both sides must move** ...' quoted from BPA/KU I/08.08/88: Kohl, 0805-8/I.

... **a leading German banker** ... this was F Wilhelm Christians of the Deutsche Bank. See Christians's own account in SZ, 27 September 1989, and the article by Michel Tatu in *Le Monde*, 27 July 1990.

... **the young out-settlers** ... according to Federal Interior Ministry statistics, forty-three per cent of the out-settlers who came to the Federal Republic in 1988 were under twenty-five, while only four per cent were over sixty-five.

'Foreign trade ...' Ludwig Erhard, 'Die geistigen Grundlagen gesunden Aussenhandels,' 1953, quoted in Haftendorn, *Aussenpolitik*, p. 403.

At least one third ... the *Bonner Almanach 1987/88* (Bonn: Presse- und Informationsamt der Bundesregierung, 1987), p. 88, gives a figure of thirty-two per cent for 1985. In his chapter in Susan Stern, ed., *Meet United Germany* (Frankfurt: FAZ, 1991), p. 187, Norbert Walter, chief economist of the Deutsche Bank, says 'over one third'. Jürgen Bellers points out in *Liberal* 1/1989, p. 5, that if one includes the half-finished goods that go into the exports one can arrive at a figure of nearly fifty per cent.

... **one in five** ... this estimate for 1974/75, see Kreile, *Osthandel*, p. 165.

... **a 'trading state'** ... see Richard Rosecrance, *The Rise of the Trading State* (New York: Basic Books, 1986).

'The economy is our fate'... quoted by Otto Wolff von Amerongen in Hans-Dietrich Genscher, ed., *Nach vorn gedacht... Perspektiven deutscher Aussenpolitik* (Bonn: Bonn Aktuell, 1987), p. 113. Walter Rathenau's remark might also be translated as 'business is our fate'.

'You forget...' quoted in Van Oudenaren, *Détente*, p.259.

'We have all the raw materials...' Helmut Allardt, *Politik vor und hinter den Kulissen. Erfahrungen eines Diplomaten zwischen Ost und West* (Düsseldorf: Econ Verlag, 1979), p. 251.

... never more than seven and a half per cent... the figures are usefully collated in Table 3 of Haberl & Hecker, *Unfertige Nachbarschaften*, p. 272.

... more than nine per cent... ibid.

... Walter Scheel declared... speech of 18 May 1972 quoted in Meissner, *Moskau-Bonn*, pp. 1507–13, this on p. 1510.

'At present, economic exchange...' this famous Davos speech was on 1 February 1987. Quoted from Der Bundesminister des Auswärtigen, Mitteilung für die Presse No. 1022/87, this quotation on p. 42. The speech is now reprinted in Genscher, *Unterwegs*, pp. 139–50. As will be clear from the table in Haberl & Hecker, *Unfertige Nachbarschaften*, p. 272, this remarkably low percentage figure was achieved by excluding the Federal Republic's trade with both Yugoslavia and East Germany. Including those two, the figure for 1986 was actually 6.7 per cent.

... the distinctly abnormal German expansion... see M C Kaser and E A Radice, eds., *The Economic History of Eastern Europe 1919–1975* (Oxford: Clarendon Press, 1985), p. 436.

... three times more than the United States... see Table A.3 in Gordon, *Eroding Empire*, pp. 332–33, and Table II below.

... more dependent on it than any other Western state... see Table A.3 in Gordon, *Eroding Empire*, pp.332–33.

... as much as twenty per cent... Kreile, *Osthandel*, p. 173.

... an important 'lobby'... see Chapter 3 in Kreile, *Osthandel*, and the chapter by Arno Burzig in Haberl & Hecker, *Unfertige Nachbarschaften*. Because of the 'pioneer function' of economic ties for Ostpolitik as a whole, individual figures like the head of the Ost-Ausschuss der deutschen Wirtschaft, Otto Wolff von Amerongen, and the Chairman of the Deutsche Bank, F Wilhelm Christians, had an importance even beyond the lobbying 'weight' of the interests they represented. See Christians, *Wege*, Wolffs memoirs, *Der Weg nach Osten. Vierzig Jahre Brückenbau für die deutsche Wirtschaft* (Munich: Droemer Knaur, 1992), which unfortunately appeared too late to be used in the preperation of this edition.

... the number of jobs... see Stent, *Embargo to Ostpolitik*, p. 217.

... thirty per cent... figures from the Foreign Ministry.

... to increase the real economic interest as well... This is also the conclusion of Wörmann, *Osthandel*, pp. 269–70.

...**paints in his memoirs**... see Christians, *Wege*, esp. pp. 247–50.

'**For centuries**...' see Meissner, *Moskau-Bonn*, p. 1510.

...**an important original motive**... this point is stressed by Hanns-Dieter Jacobsen, Heinrich Machowski & Kalus Schröder, 'The Political and Economic Framework Conditions of East-West Relations', in *Aussenpolitik* (English-language edition), II/88, p. 139. See also the quotations in Wörmann, *Problem*, note 120, p. 215.

...**between a quarter and one third**... see Table A-12 in Gordon, *Eroding Empire*. The figure given for Czechoslovakia is actually more than one third: 35.9 per cent.

...**some forty per cent**... this estimate is given in the article by Andras Inotai in *Liberal* 4/1990, pp. 41–54, this on p. 41.

...**a quarter**... **no less than half**... ibid., p. 45.

...**joint ventures**... this figure was given by Béla Kádár, Hungary's Minister for International Economic Relations, in Reforms in the Foreign Economic Relations of Eastern Europe and the Soviet Union (New York: Economic Commission for Europe, 1991) p. 77.

...**some eight per cent**... a figure of 8.5 per cent is cited in *European Economy*, No. 45, December 1990, p. 154.

...**more than a quarter**... see Table 4.2 in Angela Stent, 'Technology Transfer to Eastern Europe. Paradoxes, Policies, Prospects', in William E Griffith, ed., *Central and Eastern Europe. The Opening Curtain?* (Boulder: Westview Press, 1989).

...**some eighteen per cent**... figures based on official Soviet statistics.

...**the largest single portion**... see Teltschik, *329 Tage*, p. 232.

...**a common general dilemma**... see my essay 'Reform or revolution?' in Garton Ash, *Uses*. The point is also stressed by William E. Griffith in the introductory chapter to William E Griffith, ed., *Central and Eastern Europe. The Opening Curtain?* (Boulder: Westview Press, 1989).

...**and the European Community in particular**... on this, see now the valuable book by Peter van Ham, *The EC, Eastern Europe and European Unity. Discord, Collaboration and Integration since 1947* (London: Pinter, 1993).

...**the question of how to use that economic power**... a lucid and stimulating introduction to the issues is Hanson, *Western Economic Statecraft*.

...**between Bonn and Washington**... On this there is an extensive literature, dating mainly from the mid-1980s. Wörmann, *Problem*, is a thorough and thoughtful treatment, as is the slightly earlier study by Hanns-Dieter Jacobsen, *Die Ost-West Wirtschaftsbeziehungen als Deutsch-Amerikanisches Problem* (Ebenhausen: Stiftung Wissenschaft und Politik, 1983). See also Stent, *Embargo to Ostpolitik* and the same author's chapter in William E Griffith, ed., *Central and Eastern Europe. The Opening Curtain?* (Boulder: Westview Press, 1989), pp. 74–101. On the American side, Jentleson, *Pipeline Politics*, contains a wealth of useful detail on issues far wider than just energy trade. See also the relevant chapters in Kovrig, *Walls and Bridges*, Gordon, *Eroding Empire*, van Oudenaren, *Détente*, and the chapters by Gary K Bertsch and Steve Elliott-Gower, and by Heinrich Vogel, in Gary K Bertsch & ors, eds, *After the Revolutions. East-West Trade and Technology Transfer in the 1990s* (Boulder: Westview Press, 1991).

... 'If you want grain ...' quoted in Kreile, *Osthandel*, p. 66.

Co-existence and Commerce ... Samuel Pisar, *Coexistence and Commerce. Guidelines for Transactions between East and West* (New York: McGraw-Hill, 1970). Giscard d'Estaing wrote a glowing Preface to the French edition. One might note that the book was largely written in a château Pisar rented from Giscard. Pisar records this, and Giscard's praise, in his autobiography, *Of Blood and Hope* (New York: Macmillan, 1982), pp. 186–88.

... the 'romantics of eastern trade' ... Otto Wolff von Amerongen, 'Aspekte des deutschen Osthandels', in *Aussenpolitik* 3/1970, pp. 143–48.

... including Franz Josef Strauss ... conversation with the author, Munich, February 1985.

... 'light-switch diplomacy' ... see Wörmann, *Problem*, pp. 47–48.

... Samuel P Huntington ... some of the thinking behind this approach is laid out in Huntington's important article, 'Trade, Techology and Leverage. Economic Diplomacy' in *Foreign Policy*, Fall 1978, pp. 63–80.

... Richard Perle ... see Jentleson, *Pipeline Politics*, esp. p. 19 ff, and Hanson, *Western Economic Statecraft*.

... a small set of sanctions ... see Hanson, *Western Economic Statecraft*, pp. 1, 41.

... a massive pipeline system ... on this, see the extensive discussion in Jentleson, *Pipeline Politics*, Wörmann, *Problem*, and the other general treatments listed above. The Deutsche Bank's leading expert in this field, Axel Lebahn, gives his account in *Aussenpolitik*, 3/1983, pp. 256–80.

'With equal insistence ...' Josef Joffe, *The Limited Partnership. Europe, the United States and the Burdens of Alliance* (Cambridge: Ballinger, 1987), p. 12.

... a 'tension-reducing role' ... in Hans-Dietrich Genscher, ed., *Nach vorn gedacht ... Perspektiven deutscher Aussenpolitik* (Bonn: Bonn Aktuell, 1987), p. 121.

'The Europeans have been trading ...' Helmut Schmidt, *A Grand Strategy for the West* (New Haven: Yale University Press, 1985), pp. 128–29.

'Mars must leave ...' quoted in *Der Spiegel* 1/1988.

. . . **as the historian Harold James points out** . . . see his very stimulating book *A German Identity 1770–1990* (London: Weidenfeld & Nicolson, 1989).

'In the West . . .' Jürgen Ruhfus, 'Die politische Dimension der Wirtschaftsbeziehungen zwischen Ost und West', *EA*, 1/1987, pp. 1–10. Ruhfus was then the *Staatssekretär des Auswärtigen Amtes*, that is, the top career official in the Foreign Ministry. He subsequently became Ambassador to Washington.

. . . **'helping Gorbachev to succeed'** . . . notably in his famous Davos speech of February 1987, reprinted in Genscher, *Unterwegs*, pp. 139–50.

. . . **the CoCom list** . . . on the Paris-based Co-ordinating Committee on export controls, which included representatives of Japan and all members of Nato except Iceland, see particularly the relevant chapters in Gary K Bertsch & ors, eds, *After the Revolutions. East-West Trade and Technology Transfer in the 1990s* (Boulder: Westview Press, 1991). Note, however, that dual-use or industrial-list items were not subjected to a blanket prohibition, but rather to case-by-case vetting.

What David Baldwin has called . . . see David Baldwin, *Economic Statecraft* (Princeton: Princeton University Press, 1985). Hanson, *Western Economic Statecraft*, takes the term from Baldwin.

As we have suggested earlier . . . see above p. 178 f.

. . . **George Kennan** . . . in his *Memoirs 1950–1963* (New York: Pantheon Books, 1983), p. 297.

Kissinger argued . . . see *Years of Upheaval*, pp. 25–51, 985–98.

. . . **as Philip Hanson has argued** . . . see Hanson, *Western Economic Statecraft*, p. 12 ff, 71 ff.

. . . **Adam Michnik told the author** . . . full text of the interview in *Encounter*, January 1985. Earlier in the same interview he observed that 'the Western sanctions against the Jaruzelski regime were generally seen as an act of solidarity with the Polish people and their aspirations'. One might note that similar sentiments were expressed by South African civil rights and opposition activists about Western economic sanctions against their country.

. . . **Neal Ascherson** . . . *Observer* (London), 6 August 1989.

. . . **Zbigniew Pelczynski** . . . communication to the author.

. . . **$35 billion** . . . **$18 billion** . . . see Table V.

. . . **advocated by the IMF or World Bank** . . . interestingly, this is sharply and concisely described by the GDR's Balance of Payments experts, Gerhard Schürer, Alexander Schalck and others, in their memorandum of 28 September 1989, see Przybylski, *Tatort 2*, pp. 358–63, this on p. 362.

. . . **what he called 'system-opening co-operation'** . . . see his speech reprinted in *Bulletin* 17 June 1987, pp. 525–29, and further discussion on p. 272 f.

A typical report from an East European visit . . . see, for example, Chancellor

Kohl on his visit to Prague in *Bundestag Plenarprotokolle*, 11/58, p. 3987 (4 February 1988).

... 'an increase of people-to-people contacts...' John F Kennedy, *The Strategy of Peace* (London: Hamish Hamilton, 1960), this quotation on p. 93, from a Senate speech on 21 August 1957.

'We need ... to seek forms ...' A revised and expanded German version of the Harvard speech was published as Willy Brandt, *Koexistenz — Zwang zum Wagnis* (Stuttgart: Deutsche Verlags-Anstalt, 1963). Brandt quoted this passage himself in his Tutzing speech on 15 July 1963, see *Dokumente*, IV/9, p. 567.

... implementing the détente half of ... Harmel ... see, for example, the observation by Horst Ehmke in *Bundestag Plenarprotokolle*, 10/228, p. 17718 (10 September 1986), and by Richard von Weizsäcker in *Bergedorfer Gesprächskreis* 84 (25 March 1988), p. 68.

... ideas of Helsinki ... among general works on Helsinki in English see particularly Mastny, *Helsinki I* and *Helsinki II*, Maresca, *Helsinki*, Davy, *Détente*, chapter 9 in Van Oudenaren, *Détente*, the relevant sections in Kovrig, *Walls and Bridges*.

Henry Kissinger, for example ... for the next two paragraphs see Maresca, *Helsinki*, esp. pp. 11, 45, 77 ff, 120 ff, 158 f, 215, Mastny, *Helsinki I*, p. 4, and Kissinger's own account in *White House Years* and *Years of Upheaval*.

'We sold it ...' quoted in Kovrig, *Walls and Bridges*, p. 123.

... historic purpose after the trauma of Vietnam ... a point made by Maresca, and very forcefully by Robert W Tucker, quoted in Mastny and Zielonka, *Human Rights and Security*, p.112,

... Congressional and independent initiatives ... the Congressional Commission on Security and Co-operation was established in 1976, largely on the initiative of Congresswoman Millicent Fenwick, see Maresca, *Helsinki*, p. 207. It played an important part in goading successive administrations. Arguably even more important was the independent New York-based Helsinki Watch committee, which was established in 1978, mainly as a response to the emergence of independent 'Helsinki monitors' in the Soviet Union and Eastern Europe. It was then mainly on the initiative of the New York Helsinki Watch that an International Helsinki Federation for Human Rights, with variously constituted European affiliates, was established in Vienna in 1982. See my article in the *Independent*, 18 April 1988.

American newspapers referred ... as recalled by Richard Davy in his perceptive chapter in Nils Andren and Karl E Birnbaum, eds, *Belgrade and Beyond. The CSCE Process in Perspective* (Alphen aan den Rijn: Sijthoff & Noordhoff, 1980), pp. 3–15, this on p. 5.

Robert Legvold has aptly observed ... quoted in Mastny, *Helsinki I*, p. 47.

... 'the favourite Soviet basket' ... thus the chapter heading in Mastny, *Helsinki I*, p. 121.

... to collate the whole vast forest ... An obvious, basic starting-point is the official Foreign Ministry publication, quoted here as *KSZE Dokumentation*. A companion volume, quoted here as *KSZE Dokumentation 1990/91*, covers developments until early 1991. A combination of documentation and analysis from the pages of *Europa-Archiv* is given in the three volumes edited by Hermann Volle and Wolfgang Wagner, *KSZE. Konferenz über Sicherheit und Zusammenarbeit in Europa* (Bonn: Verlag für Internationale Politik, 1976) — here quoted as Volle & Wagner, *KSZE* —; *Das Belgrader KSZE Folgetreffen* (Bonn: Verlag für Internationale Politik, 1978); and *Das Madrider KSZE Folgetreffen* (Bonn: Verlag für Internationale Politik, 1984). Many further official statements are then to be found in such standard sources as the *Bulletin*, the *Bundestag Plenarprotokolle*, *Bundestag Drucksachen*, *Texte*, *EA* etc.

... a virtually impossible task ... at least until the opening of the official papers of the major countries involved. What could be done now, however, is a systematic interviewing of the politicians and officials involved.

... feeding ... into the common approach ... this is stressed by Karl E Birnbaum and Ingo Peters in their very useful article on 'The CSCE. A Reassessment of its Role in the 1980s' in the *Review of International Studies* 16/1990, pp. 305–19.

... really came to life ... a point made strongly to the author by Günther van Well, Bonn, 8 July 1991. On co-operation between the nine see the article by Frans Alting von Geusau in Nils Andren and Karl E Birnbaum, *Belgrade and Beyond. The CSCE Process in Perspective* (Alphen aan den Rijn: Sijthoff & Noordhoff, 1980), pp. 17–26, Ferraris, *Report*, and the statements on behalf of the EC 9, and subsequently twelve, reprinted in *KSZE Dokumentation*.

... 'attempt to cover (*abdecken*) ...' quoted from the 10 April 1977 typescript version of the Marbella paper in AdsD: HS 002.

... 'The Federal Government had no orginal interest' ... quoted from a typescript, annotated in Schmidt's hand, in AdsD: HS 295. From the context in the file it would appear that this was in preparation for his trip to Helsinki, to sign the Final Act.

... essentially defensive goals ... this can be seen clearly in the article of early 1972 by the then State Secretary of the Foreign Ministry, Paul Frank, reprinted in Volle & Wagner, *KSZE*, pp. 41–47.

... 'throughout Europe' ... in German: *in ganz Europa*. See Maresca, *Helsinki*, p. 84, who recalls that this clause was also for some time known among delegates as the 'Andorra Clause'.

... Henry Kissinger negotiated on Germany's behalf ... this remarkable story is well told in Maresca, *Helsinki*, pp. 110–16. The final outcome hinged on the placing of a single comma.

... placed in the list of principles before ... see Volle & Wagner, *KSZE*, p. 94. Hermann von Richthofen, London, 3 March 1992.

... **Hans-Dietrich Genscher singled out** ... his speech of 25 July 1975 is reprinted in *KSZE Dokumentation*, pp. 303–15, for this see especially pp. 309–10.

... **following intensive internal discussions** ... Günther van Well recalls in particular a working party chaired by Ulrich Sahm. Günther van Well, Bonn, 8 July 1991.

... **'common rules of the game** ...' this and subsequent quotations from Brunner's article in EA 13/1973, reprinted in Volle & Wagner, *KSZE*, pp. 49–54.

... **now common to the main participants** ... see for example the statement by Harold Wilson at the Helsinki Conference: 'Détente means little if it is not reflected in the daily lives of our peoples. There is no reason why in 1975 Europeans should not be allowed to marry whom they want, hear and read what they want, travel abroad when and where they want, meet whom they want', quoted in Maresca, *Helsinki*, p. 154.

... **'a net of co-operation'** ... for this and following quotations see *KSZE Dokumentation*, pp. 303–15. See also the speech by Helmut Schmidt, reprinted there on pp. 316–20.

... **would explicitly berate** ... the precedent was set by the leader of the US delegation to the Belgrade review conference, Arther Goldberg, see the chapter by Richard Davy in Nils Andren and Karl E. Birnbaum, *Belgrade and Beyond. The CSCE Process in Perspective* (Alphen aan den Rijn: Sijthoff & Noordhoff, 1980), pp. 3–15. For a sample of intra-American debate about the wisdom of this approach see Mastny, *Helsinki I*, pp. 155–65.

... **'quiet diplomacy'** ... the view is eloquently expressed in Willy Brandt, *Menschenrechte misshandelt und missbraucht* (Reinbek: Rowohlt, 1987), especially pp. 89–101, where he makes it clear that this is a continuation of the line of 'small steps' developed in Berlin in the early 1960s. For a general discussion of this problem see Carola Stern, *Strategien für die Menschenrechte* (Hamburg: Fischer Taschenbuch, extended edition, 1983).

... **the German-American difference** ... see Kovrig, *Walls and Bridges*, p. 186 ff.

... **mapped out in basket two** ... for a highly critical account of the economic provisions of the Helsinki Final Act, see the article by Philip Hanson in *International Affairs* (London), 4/1985, pp. 619–29. The statements about economic relationships in the Helsinki Final Act, writes Hanson, 'are about as businesslike as the message in an average Christmas card'.

'Decisive is first of all ...' Weizsäcker, *Deutsche Geschichte*, p. 15.

... **on the subject of economic co-operation** ... on the Bonn conference on economic conference see *Bulletin*, 20 March 1990, pp. 285–88, and *Bulletin*, 19 April 1990, pp. 357–68. The concluding document is also reprinted in *KSZE Dokumentation 1990/91*, pp. 21–33. See also Mastny, *Helsinki II*, pp. 217–28, where the initially critical reaction of the United States to the West German proposal is noted.

...quietly to establish somewhat more autonomy... see, for example, Schmidt's comments in *Bergedorfer Gesprächskreis* 76 (17–18 December 1984), p. 20, and his article, 'Europa muss sich selbst behaupten', in *Die Zeit*, 28 November 1986. This was also seen as an objective of American Helsinki policy, Warren Zimmermann, Washington, 15 April 1987.

Schmidt sometimes presented himself... see Link, *Ära Schmidt*, p. 309.

...tacit co-operation with East Germany... the phrase 'tacit co-operation' comes from Karl E Birnbaum and Ingo Peters in *Review of International Studies*, 16/1990, p. 316, summarising the conclusions of a larger study.

...a concluding document... for a brief summary see my article in the *Independent*, 20 January 1989. The complete text is in *Bulletin*, 31 January 1989, pp. 77–105, and reprinted in *KSZE Dokumentation*, p. 189 ff.

...the greatest step forward... see Mastny, *Helsinki II*, esp. pp. 11–18, 85–144, and the chapter by William Korey in Mastny and Zielonka, *Human Rights and Security*, pp. 77–105.

...clearly spelled out at the time... ibid., pp. 89–90.

The German foreign minister tried to push... information from members of several delegations. See also *Financial Times*, 5 January 1989.

...the Joint Declaration signed by Helmut Kohl and Mikhail Gorbachev... text in *Bulletin*, 15 June 1989, pp. 542–44.

...'no one can have a greater interest...' speech of 25 July 1975, reprinted in *KSZE Dokumentation*, pp. 303–15, this on p. 303. The Foreign Minister quoted his own words in *Bundestag Plenarprotokolle*, 9/11, p. 6782 (9 September 1982).

'The comprehensive extension...' this in an interview in *Der Spiegel*, 24/1989.

...'through deepened co-operation...' *Bundestag Plenarprotokolle*, 11/49, p. 3435 (10 December 1987).

'Our policy is today in harmony...' speech on receiving the 'Thomas-Dehler-Medaille' in Munich, 3 January 1987, issued as: Der Bundesminister des Auswärtigen, Mitteilung für die Presse No. 1005/87.

'We do not want a technological division of Europe...' this in a speech at the Evangelische Akademie in Loccum on 20 September 1985, reprinted in *Bulletin*, 24 September 1985, pp. 889–93, this quotation on p. 892.

'Every jointly erected desulphurisation plant...' *Bundestag Plenarprotokolle*, 11/59, p. 4111 (5 February 1988)

...the Siemens computers...information to the author.

...the American handcuffs... Vladimir Bukovsky, *To Build a Castle. My Life as a Dissenter* (London: André Deutsch, 1978), p. 344.

'We all have only one alternative . . .' this in a speech to the Rotary Club in New York on 14 January 1971, *Bulletin*, 15 January 1971, pp. 25–28, the quotation on p. 27.

'The Federal Republic of Germany and . . .' *Bulletin*, 15 June 1989, p. 542.

. . . worse industrial pollution . . . see, for example, the map of sulphur dioxide levels in Keith Sword, ed., *The Times Guide to Eastern Europe* (Revised edition. London: Times Books, 1991), p. 280.

'. . . let us also direct attention to our common interests . . .' John F Kennedy, Commencement Address at American University in Washinton, 10 June 1963, in *Public Papers of the Presidents. John F Kennedy, 1963* (Washington, DC: US Government Printing Office), pp. 459–64, this quotation on p. 462. Compare also the comment by Chancellor Kiesinger in his 17 June 1967 speech to the Bundestag: 'We consider it to be a proven method first to seek areas that we can walk together, in order for the time being to put aside the great disagreements. This procedure, which is an important instrument in a policy of détente, has stood its test in the relations between states.' Quoted in Meissner, *Deutsche Ostpolitik*, p. 206.

. . . not so many French or British . . . a partial exception would be some French politicians in thinking about their relationship with West Germany. The underlying thought here was to anchor West Germany still more firmly against the temptations of eastward drift: interdependence as containment.

. . . the Kissingerite notion of the 'Gulliverisation' . . . Davy, *Détente*, p. 6.

. . . Klaus Ritter . . . see his article in EA, 15–16/1970, pp. 541–58, this on p. 558. Ritter was the long-time director of the *Stiftung Wissenschaft und Politik* in Ebenhausen.

. . . a speech to mark the fortieth anniversary of the Marshall Plan . . . delivered on 12 June 1987, and printed in *Bulletin*, 17 June 1987, pp. 525–29.

'We must find other "currencies" . . .' ibid., p. 528.

. . . 'under the sign of perestroika . . .' this speech, delivered on 27 October 1987, is reprinted in Theo Sommer, ed., *Perspektiven. Europa im 21. Jahrhundert* (Berlin: Argon, 1989), pp. 93–105.

. . . 'know that it's a matter of reforming their system . . .' ibid., p. 103.

'We too have our mistakes . . .' ibid., p. 104.

'Through our policy we don't want to change . . .' *Bergedorfer Gesprächskreis*, 84 (17–18 December 1988), p. 37.

'System-opening for me . . .' ibid., p. 38. The speaker was Dr Klaus Cantzler, a director of BASF responsible for dealings with East European countries.

. . . 'that is then system-opening co-operation . . .' ibid., p. 80. The speaker was Dr Friedbert Pflüger.

'I am inclined to believe . . .' this in the Preface to the English edition of *Eighteen Lectures on Industrial Society* (London: Weidenfeld & Nicolson, 1967), p. 13.

. . . 'is the result of a closed system . . .' *Bulletin*, 17 June 1987, p. 528.

. . . 'whoever recognises the social developments . . .' *Bundestag Plenarprotokolle*, 11/6, p. 293 (20 March 1987).

'The Conference on Security and Co-operation in Europe has . . .' this in a speech in Hamburg on 17 February 1989, printed in *Bulletin*, 22 February 1989, pp. 165–67, this quotation on p. 165.

'This attempt to pull over the divided Europe . . .' *Bundestag Plenarprotokolle*, 9/76, p. 4427 (14 January 1982).

. . . *auswärtige Kulturpolitik* . . . the best introduction to this aspect of West German foreign policy is the collection of essays and speeches by the veteran Foreign Ministry official in this field: Witte, *Kulturpolitik*.

. . . guidelines in 1970. . . . reprinted in *Vierzig Jahre*, pp. 230–33.

. . . as much as one third . . . figures from the Foreign Ministry.

Roughly half . . . Witte, *Kulturpolitik*, p. 233.

. . . *Sprachpolitik* . . . ibid., p. 233 f. See also the Preface by Hans-Dietrich Genscher to *Die Stellung der deutschen Sprache in der Welt. Bericht der Bundesregierung* (Bonn: Auswärtiges Amt, 1988). This official report was originally delivered to the Bundestag in 1985.

. . . 'decade of stagnation' . . . in a useful article specifically about Germany's cultural relations with her eastern neighbours in EA 7/1991, pp. 201–10, this on p. 201.

. . . only in 1988 . . . see the reports by Hans Schwab-Felisch in FAZ, 26 March 1988, and by Carl Gustaf Ströhm in *Christ und Welt/Rheinischer Merkur*, 11 March 1988. Ströhm there laments that 'Hungary — and especially the younger generation — lies under the spell of the English-American civilisation-, language-, music- and culture-offensive!'

. . . the official map of German cultural establishments . . . in *Vierzig Jahre*, Karte 14.

. . . more than nine million . . . *Die Stellung der deutschen Sprache in der Welt. Bericht der Bundesregierung* (Bonn: Auswärtiges Amt, 1988), p. 29.

. . . explosion of interest . . . on the state of German in Central and Eastern Europe see the series of articles in the Feuilleton of the FAZ, 7 March, 11 March, 25 April, 15 May and 13 June 1991. See also Joachim Born & Syvlia Dickgiesser, *Deutschsprachige Minderheiten. Ein Überblick über den Stand der Forschung für 27 Länder* (Mannheim: Institut für deutsche Sprache im Auftrag des Auswärtigen

Amtes, 1989). The Bundestag passed a resolution on 30 October 1990 supporting the promotion of German, particularly in Central and Eastern Europe, see EA 7/1991, p. 204.

... to remain ... a *lingua franca* ... in EA 7/1991, p. 204.

... 'Those who speak and understand German...' Witte, *Kulturpolitik*, p. 234.

... 'quangos' ... most of these are listed and briefly characterised in *Die Stellung der deutschen Sprache in der Welt. Bericht der Bundesregierung* (Bonn: Auswärtiges Amt, 1988).

... pioneering German-Polish projects ... The Bosch foundation started a major programme on German-Polish relations in the mid-1970s, see *Die Robert Bosch Stiftung und die deutsch-polnischen Beziehungen* (Stuttgart: Robert Bosch Stiftung, 1986). A notable element in this programme was also the support of publications and translations, including a small 'library' of translations from Polish literature, sponsored jointly with the Deutsches Polen-Institut (Darmstadt): the "Polnische Bibliothek" edited by Karl Dedecius and published by Suhrkamp.

... a large and increasing number ... thus a breakdown of Humboldt Research Fellowships granted in the years 1953 to 1990 shows that Poland had more than twice as many as any other European country, with Yugoslavia in second and Czechoslovakia in third place, *Alexander von Humboldt-Stiftung. Programm und Profil* (Bonn, 1991), p. 11. After noting the number of Polish visiting scholars the historian Gotthold Rhode observes 'it should be remembered that in the period of the Weimar Republic there was nothing remotely comparable'. See his article in APZ, B 11–12/1988, p. 15.

No Western country sent more tourists into the East ... In 1986, some 862,000 West Germans visited Hungary and 1.3 million visited Czechoslovakia. Nearly forty per cent of all Western visitors to Czechoslovakia in that year came from West Germany. Figures from *Press- und Informationsamt der Bundesregierung*, '*Deutsch-ungarische Beziehungen*' (Typescript, October 1987) and '*Die Beziehungen zwischen der tschechoslowakischen Sozialistischen Republik und der Bundesrepublik Deutschland* (Typescript, January 1988).

... than any other Western country ... Austria and Sweden, with no visa requirement for several East European countries, obviously let in *proportionately* more.

... more than 1.3 million ... figures supplied by the German Foreign Ministry. According to the Polish Interior Ministry, of 1.129 million Poles who travelled to Western countries in 1987, 405,000—that is, more than one in three—went to West Germany.

'It is important,' Kennedy had said ... this in his speech at the Free University in West Berlin on 26 June 1963, printed in *Public Papers of the Presidents. John F Kennedy, 1963* (Washington DC: US Government Printing Office), pp. 526–29, this quotation on p. 527.

... few Western societies were more open ... the exceptions are, once again Austria and Sweden.

... a minority also sought political asylum ... according to figures supplied to me by the Federal Interior Ministry, the figures for foreigners *officially registered* as resident in the Federal Republic as of 31 December 1988 included some 625,000 Yugoslavs, 200,000 Poles, 32,500 Czechs and Slovaks, 31,000 Hungarians, and 20,000 Romanians. These figures, from the *Ausländerzentralregister*, included those applying for asylum, but excluded people with dual citizenship.

... very few of them were actually sent back ... a 1966 resolution of the Conference of *Land* Interior Ministers determined that refugees from Warsaw Pact states could not be sent back against their will. This was modified by resolutions of 1985 and 1987, which raised the *possibility* of forcible repatriation to, for example, Poland or Hungary. Jürgen Haberland, Bonn, 15 March 1989.

... through the hard currency, goods or experience ... according to official Polish estimates, the total hard-currency remittances from all Poles living abroad in 1986 and 1987 was almost equal to the hard-currency trade surplus earned by the whole of the socialised sector. Estimate by the Ministry of Internal Trade and Services, quoted by Jacek Rostowski, 'The Decay of Socialism and the Growth of Private Enterprise in Poland', in Stanisław Gomułka & Antony Polonsky, eds, *Polish Paradoxes* (London: Routledge, 1990), pp. 198–223, this on p. 200. One can safely assume that a large part of this came from Poles working—legally or less so—in the Federal Republic.

... *na saksy* ... see under *Saksy* in W. Doroszewski, ed., *Słownik Języka Polskiego* (Warsaw, 1966), Vol. VIII, p. 16. There also a nice quotation from the work of the nineteenth-century novelist Władysław Reymont: 'Let those Germans come and see what they can do here ... I went *na saksy* for so many years that I've penetrated them.'

... an acceptance speech ... read on his behalf ... see FAZ, 16 October 1989, with the text of the speech on pp. 13–14. The texts are reprinted, in Czech and German, in Börsenverein des Deutschen Buchhandels, *Friedenspreis des Deutschen Buchhandels 1989: Václav Havel. Ansprache aus Anlass der Verleihung* (Frankfurt: Verlag der Buchhändler-Vereinigung, 1989). There also the following quotations. An English version of the speech can be found in the English-language edition of *Listy* 5/1989.

... 'a traffic accident on the road to détente' ... quoted by Pierre Hassner in Gordon, *Eroding Empire*, p. 197.

'That the Soviets found their way ...' Löwenthal, *Vom kalten Krieg*, p. 78.

... what the effect might be in the other direction ... see the illuminating discussion in Pierre Hassner, *Europe in the Age of Negotiation* (Beverley Hills: Sage, 1973 = Center for Strategic and International Studies, The Washington Papers, Vol. 1, No. 8), pp. 65–68.

'of all the Western states ...' Jacek Maziarski, 'My i Niemcy', *Poglądy* (Warsaw), 12/87, pp. 32–42, this quotation on p. 41.

... **not against the powers-that-be** ... a clear statement to this effect was made by Hans-Dietrich Genscher in *Bundestag Plenarprotokolle*, 10/149, p. 11150, 27 June 1985. See also the comment by Peter Bender in Böll, *Verantwortlich*, p. 32.

... **these independent East Central European intellectuals** ... for a general discussion see Garton Ash, *Uses*, and Garton Ash, *Solidarity*.

... **'the general idea of evolution in Eastern Europe** ...' quoted in Garton Ash, *Uses*, p. 174. See also János Kis, *Politics in Hungary. For a Democratic Alternative* (Highland Lakes, NJ: Atlantic Research and Publications/Columbia University Press, 1989).

... **'the power of the powerless'** ... see Václav Havel & ors, *The Power of the Powerless. Citizens against the state in Central-Eastern Europe* (London: Hutchinson, 1985).

... **Leszek Kołakowski's 'Theses on Hope and Hopelessness'** ... first published in *Kultura* (Paris), June 1971, and in English in *Survey* (London), Summer 1971.

... **'the New Evolutionism'** ... see Adam Michnik, *Letters from Prison and other Essays* (Berkeley: University of Califonia Press, 1985), pp. 135–48.

... **the Polish Workers' Defence Committee KOR** ... see Jan Józef Lipski, *KOR. A History of the Workers' Defense Committee in Poland, 1976–1981* (Berkeley: University of California Press, 1985).

... **to compel the ruling** *nomenklatura* ... It was, however, hoped that some of the more intelligent functionaries and leaders would support some, at least, of these reforms, out of enlightened self-interest. Arguably, this did happen to some extent in Hungary, and to a lesser degree in Poland, in 1988–89.

... **a strong civil society** ... there is now a large literature on the concept and significance of civil society in the East European context. For a classic statement see Ralf Dahrendorf, *Reflections on the Revolution in Europe* (London: Chatto & Windus, 1990). A useful collection is John Keane, ed., *Civil Society and the State* (London: Verso, 1988).

... **more fundamental goal** ... the crowds on the streets in the East German revolution of 1989 did not chant '*Wir sind die Menschen!*' They chanted '*Wir sind das Volk!*' and '*das Volk*' in this context comes close to the Polish or Czech sense of 'society': that is, the people getting together in spite of or against the so-called people's state.

... **it was better for him** ... The Soviet satirist Vladimir Voinovitch once said to me: 'you have *homo sovieticus* in the West too'. And then he told me of a distinguished Western visitor to Moscow who declined to meet with Sakharov on the grounds that this might harm Sakharov. 'What he really meant,' said Voinovitch, 'was that it would harm him, the Western visitor.'

... **détente could not survive** ... see above, pp. 94. But in a fragment of his diary from 29 October 1980, Zbigniew Brzezinski records: 'The Germans have told us at the Quad meeting that détente should not be the victim of such [Soviet] intervention [in Poland]: in other words,' Brzezinski goes on, 'the Germans are saying that in the event of a Soviet intervention the Germans would be prepared to continue with their East-West relationship. This was the best proof yet of the increasing Finlandisation of the Germans.' See *Orbis* (Philadelphia), Winter 1988, pp. 32–48, this on p. 34. A slightly different selection from this diary is given in the Polish edition of his memoirs, published as *Cztery Lata W Białym Domu* (London: Polonia, 1986), this on pp. 538–60. In an entry for 15 December 1980 he there records a disagreement between the Federal Republic on the one side and the United States, Britain and France on the other, about the imposition of sanctions against the Soviet Union in the event of a Soviet intervention. This, he writes, confirms his basic view about the Finlandisation of Germany.

... **Solidarity was, by its very nature** ... see Garton Ash, *Solidarity, passim*.

... **a 'result' of détente** ... see her article in *Die Zeit*, 29 August 1980. A similar argument was made by Kurt Becker in a leading article in the same issue.

... **causes of Solidarity** ... see Garton Ash, *Solidarity*, pp. 16–19, 34–36.

... **half million ... 4 million** ... these figures include private and 'business' visits. As with the statistics on German-German travel, the record is of visits rather than visitors. See Holzer, *Solidarität*, p. 75.

... **already borne some fruit** ... Willy Brandt formulated the claim quite cautiously. The 'normalisation' of external relations had, he said, removed the bogey of German revanchism, and perhaps made it easier 'to talk about reforms and debate. To this extent there is a certain connection, an indirect rather than a direct one'. Interview in *Die Welt*, 16 September 1980.

... **only 10.7 per cent** ... this was one of a remarkable series of sociological surveys entitled 'Poles '80, '81, '84 and subsequently '88. See Garton Ash, *Uses*, p. 239, note 29.

... **recognised by Polish activists** ... see, for example, Jan Józef Lipski, *KOR. A History of the Workers' Defense Committee in Poland, 1976–1981* (Berkeley: University of California Press, 1985), pp. 24–25; references in Peter Raina, *Political Opposition in Poland, 1954–1977* (London: Poets and Painters Press, 1978).

... **'without Helsinki ...'** Egon Bahr in conversation with Rainer Barzel in the *Magazin* of SZ, 27 September 1991.

... **'convention 87 ...'** see Garton Ash, *Solidarity*, pp. 46–7.

... **above all ... in the interpretation given it by the United States** ... See Garton Ash, *Solidarity*, p. 22. This is also the judgement of Holzer, *Solidarität*, p. 77 f.

... **the direct linkage** ... see, for example, the announcement by President Carter of new credits on his trip to Warsaw in 1977, as described in R F Leslie & ors, *The History of Poland since 1863* (Cambridge: Cambridge University Press, 1980), p. 438.

... **Klaus Reiff** ... see his *Polen. Als deutscher Diplomat an der Weichsel* (Bonn: Dietz, 1990), pp. 53–56.

... **'What would a German court say ...'** AdsD: Dep WB, BK 92, note dated 7 December 1970. Kovrig, *Walls and Bridges*, pp. 171–73, notes that in the early 1970s Senator Fulbright led a campaign to have Radio Free Europe and Radio Liberty closed down on the grounds that they were 'outworn relics of the Cold War'. Zbigniew Brzezinski, *Power and Principle. Memoirs of the National Security Adviser 1977–1981* (London; Weidenfeld & Nicolson, 1983), p. 293, recalls Helmut Schmidt complaining to him about RFE as a hindrance to détente.

... **clearly not envisaged** ... see the clear statement by Peter Bender in Böll, *Verantwortlich*, pp. 41–42.

... **one Western specialist** ... Alec Nove, quoted in Davy, *Détente*, p. 258.

... **too far too fast** ... Helmut Schmidt records himself saying in a private conversation with François Mitterrand on 13 January 1982 that Solidarity had wanted to press the process of change forward too fast, 'which had led to the recent reverse', see Schmidt, *Nachbarn*, p. 264. For a critical view of this judgement see Garton Ash, *Solidarity*, p. 297 ff.

... **some half billion D-Marks** ... Schmidt, *Nachbarn*, p. 259.

... **the latter stressed the risk** ... see, for example, comments by Brandt in *Bundestag Plenarprotokolle*, 9/49 (10 September 1981), p. 2753.

'Herr Honecker was as dismayed ...' recorded in the Bundespresseamt transcript, BPA — Nachrichtenabt., Ref. II R3, Rundf.-Ausw. Deutschland, DFS/13.12.81/12.55/he.

... **'that it was a mistake ...'** Bölling, *Die fernen Nachbarn*, p. 157. In his memoirs, Schmidt himself describes this as 'a not entirely happy choice of words', see Schmidt, *Nachbarn*, p. 74.

... **'I stand with all my heart ...'** *Bundestag Plenarprotokolle*, 9/74, p. 4289 (18 December 1981).

... **a high-level Polish defector** ... Colonel Ryszard Kukliński. See the interview with him, and additional material from Richard Pipes and Zbigniew Brzezinski, in *Orbis* (Philadelphia), Winter 1988. See also the discussion in Garton Ash, *Solidarity*, pp. 357–58.

An internal East German assessment ... draft of 30 December 1981, now in ZPA: IV 2/2.035/86.

... **a storm of political and publicistic argument** ... the best starting point is certainly Böll, *Verantwortlich*, although this collects contributions almost exclusively from left and centre authors. Also useful is the documentation by the independent, left-wing Berlin daily, *Die Tageszeitung* — the *taz* — which had consistently good and critical reporting on East Central Europe, and on German (especially SPD) policies towards it. See *Polen. "Euch den Winter, uns den*

Frühling" (Berlin: Taz-Verlag, 1982). Commentaries from the right and centre-right have not been so conveniently collected.

... **Herbert Wehner** ... Wehner's visit, which caused a considerable stir at the time, and the embrace of Jaruzelski, is briefly described in Klaus Reiff, *Polen. Als deutscher Diplomat an der Weichsel* (Bonn: Dietz, 1990), pp. 302–06. For Solidarity activists' dismay at this, and the visit of Karsten Voigt, see the report by Gert Baumgarten in *Der Tagesspiegel*, 17 February 1982. A copy of Wehner's letter to parliamentary colleagues, dated 15 February 1982, and the enclosed appeal from the Bolivian 'consulate in resistance' (with handwritten note: 'Dear Herr Wehner, heartfelt thanks for the support you are giving us ...'), is in the Wehner file in the press archive of the SPD.

... **also from French and Italian socialists** ... see the sharp criticism of the line taken by Willy Brandt as Chairman of the Socialist International, reported in *Der Spiegel*, 1/1982.

... **from Poles who had actually been locked up** ... see above, pp. 304–05.

... **and quite as emotionally** ... the emotion was directed notably against the American advocates of sanctions. Thus, for example, the leading Social Democrat Erhard Eppler, after suggesting that 'above all we must take Jaruzelski at his word,' argued: 'Whoever now imposes sanctions, does not make it easier for Jaruzelski to keep his word, but more difficult. Whoever decrees such sanctions from the USA, must be told a thing or two by Europeans: Firstly, if you please, Poland lies in Europe and is therefore mainly a matter for the Europeans.' Quoted from Böll, *Verantwortlich*, pp. 84–85.

... **'wishing success** ...' *Die Zeit*, 18 December 1981, p. 1.

... **'the highest priority** ...' Egon Bahr in *Vorwärts*, 21 January 1982, but see also many contributions to Böll, *Verantwortlich*.

... **'even more important** ...' *Vorwärts*, 24 December 1981.

... **'stability with a moderate continuation** ...' ibid.

... **'the Hungarian model'** ... interview in *Der Spiegel*, 1/1982, this on p. 24.

... **we have to think of our own German interests too** ... 'Is it presumptuous today to make clear that in this ethics of détente there were and are also German interests?' Freimut Duve in Böll, *Verantwortlich*, p. 75.

'In the GDR ...' Bölling, *Die fernen Nachbarn*, p. 121.

'Bonn depends on the Soviet Union ...' Hendrik Bussiek in Böll, *Verantwortlich*, p. 60.

... **Rakowski could not simply be assumed** ... although Marion Gräfin Dönhoff came close to it when she wrote, following Rakowski's visit to Bonn, of the satisfaction of people who ten years before could not have imagined 'that Bonn is the only capital in which *the Poles* seek help ...' (my italics), see *Verantwortlich*, p. 68, reprinting an article from *Die Zeit* of 22 January 1982.

'I shall very much follow ...' interview in *Der Spiegel*, 1/1982.

'When a freely-founded union ...' *Bundestag Plenarprotokolle*, 9/74, p. 4296 (18 December 1981).

When Franz Josef Strauss visited Poland ... This was part of a tour through East Central Europe in which, travelling ostensibly as a private tourist, Strauss nonetheless met political leaders including Jaruzelski and Honecker. In an interview with Radio Polonia, Strauss said: 'In Poland life had to be restored, that is, chaos had to be prevented. The fleeting impressions of a political tourist are that the situation has been consolidated ...', although he did go on to say that he still sensed worries among the people, who wanted 'bread, peace, freedom'. See the transcript published in *Die Welt*, 29 July 1983. Strauss was there just as martial law was lifted and argued that his remarks were aimed at encouraging Jaruzelski to take further positive steps, see the long report in *Bayernkurier*, 6 August 1983.

... major power ... most understanding ... of the less important Western states, Greece under Papandreou showed even more demonstrative understanding, and thereby also complicated the co-ordination of public postures in Nato and the EC.

... 'the renormalisation of political contacts' Berthold Johannes, 'Mittel-europa? Gesellschaftliche Grundlage der Entwicklung der Beziehungen zwischen der Bundesrepublik Deutschland und Polen', in *Frankreich – Europa – Weltpolitik. Festschrift für Gilbert Ziebura* (Opladen: Westdeutscher Verlag, 1989), pp. 227–36, this on p. 232.

... called off at twelve hours' notice ... see Radio Free Europe Research, Background Report 4, 15 January 1988. A third reason for the cancellation was the Polish authorities' refusal to grant a visa for the visit to a well-known right-wing journalist, the *Die Welt* commentator, Carl Gustaf Ströhm.

... not ... until January 1988 ... although he did make a short stop-over visit, en route from Helsinki to Sofia, in March 1985.

... very difficult negotiations ... see the authoritative but highly diplomatic account by the chief negotiator, Chancellor Kohl's foreign policy adviser, Horst Teltschik, in *Aussenpolitik* (English-language edition), 1/90, pp. 3–14. For background and further detail see Bingen, *Bonn-Warschau*, and Artur Hajnicz, 'Poland Within its Geopolitical Triangle' in *Aussenpolitik* (English-language edition), 1/89.

... more by good luck than by design ... ibid, p. 8. The Bonn government did, however, deliberately delay the visit in the summer of 1989, following Solidarity's success in the June elections.

... but not of course only West German ... a point made frequently and eloquently by the British political scientist George Schöpflin. See, for example, his trenchant 'Hungary: No Model for Reform' in *Soviet Analyst*, Vol. 12, No. 23 (23 November 1983), pp. 3–7. The British government was almost as fulsome as the Bonn government in the welcome it gave to Károly Grósz when he became party leader in 1988.

. . . a DM 1 billion loan . . . see reports in FAZ, 8 October 1987, SZ, 9 October 1987

. . . the communist Károly Grósz . . . in his case the label 'communist' may be justified, for, after the emergence of a multi-party landscape in Hungary, he remained as leader of the old Hungarian Socialist Workers' Party rather than joining the new Hungarian Socialist Party.

. . . a contribution to further 'reform' . . . see Bulletin, 14 October 1987, pp. 881–83.

'We spent two thirds . . .' This was quoted, without naming Németh, in an article by Joseph Fitchett in the *International Herald Tribune*, 24 March 1989, p. 2. Miklós Németh subsequently confirmed, in conversation with the author, that we was the speaker quoted, and that his view was that this loan had been substantially misused. He had said as much in the Hungarian parliament in December 1989 and also in conversation with West German leaders. Miklós Németh, Oxford, 22 January 1991.

. . . the record is also complex . . . in the following few paragraphs I draw heavily on my own experience in this field. In this connection I would like to thank all those I worked with in the Central and East European Publishing Project, the Jagiellonian Trust, the Fondation pour une Entraide Intellectuelle Européenne, the International Helsinki Federation for Human Rights and the Stefan Batory Trust.

. . . the German embassy had to ask the American embassy . . . information from the then American ambassador to Budapest, Mark Palmer.

The West German committee . . . largely decorative . . . This judgement might of course be disputed, not least by its chairperson, Annemarie Renger. A letter of 26 January 1984 from Annemarie Renger to a leading Christian Democratic member of the committee (and opponent of Ostpolitik) Werner Marx, now in ACDP: I-356-250, makes it clear that the founding of the German committee arose directly from the initiative of the International Helsinki Federation for Human Rights, in which the US Helsinki Watch group played the most dynamic part. The director of US Helsinki Watch, Jeri Laber, told the author, with regret, about the largely decorative role of the German committee. An even more critical verdict was given to the author by a disaffected former member of the German Helsinki committee, Martin Kriele (Leverkusen, 6 July 1991). In the Marx papers there is also a letter from Werner Marx to Martin Kriele, dated 27 February 1985, in which Marx writes that for at least eight months he has felt very unhappy to be the deputy chairman of a 'non-functioning association'. This in ACDP: I-356-250.

. . . George Soros . . . 'Open Society Fund had an endowment of $3 million a year from 1979 on. Most, but not all, of this amount was spent in Eastern Europe.

In later years I made additional contributions.' Letter from George Soros to the author, 30 April 1992.

... 'you cannot have democracy without...' quoted from his article in the *Independent*, 12 August 1991.

... the 'stability commandment'... thus Eberhard Schulz in Ehmke, *Zwanzig Jahre*, p. 219.

... Volker Rühe... see *Bundestag Plenarprotokolle* 11/106 (10 November 1988), p. 7289.

... 'the process of reform...' reprinted in *Bulletin*, 12 June 1989, pp. 530–35, this on p. 532. It is noteworthy — and was noted by members of Hungary's democratic opposition — that the guest of honour at this inaugural meeting of a liberal party foundation was a foreign policy functionary of the Hungarian Socialist Workers' Party.

... 'Not only the Social Democrats...' Hans-Peter Schwarz, 'Auf dem Weg zum post-kommunistischen Europa', in EA, 11/1989, pp. 319–30, this on p. 326.

'the blessing of a late birth'... see his speech in the Israeli Knesset in *Bulletin*, 2 February 1984, pp. 112–13. The phrase was originally coined by Günter Gaus, see his *Die Welt der Westdeutschen*. (Köln: Kiepenheuer & Witsch, 1986), pp. 111–12.

... that Adenauer had achieved with France and Israel... for this comparison, see, for example, his statement in *Bulletin*, 13 July 1989, p. 653, and *Bulletin*, 9 September 1991, p. 96.

Richard von Weizsäcker recalls... in conversation with the author, Bonn, 30 September 1991.

... their 1965 report... this seminal document is reprinted in *Dokumente* IV/2, pp. 869–97. It is ably discussed and set in context by Erwin Wilkens, *Vertreibung und Versöhnung. Die "Ostdenkschrift" als Beitrag zur deutschen Ostpolitik* (Hannover: Lutherhaus Verlag, 1986).

'We forgive and ask for forgiveness...' The text of this remarkable letter, which is in large part an essay on the relationship between Polish Catholicism and Polish nationalism in the run-up to the millennium celebrations of 1966, is reprinted in *Dokumente* IV/2, pp. 940–47, this on p. 947. On the background to it, see now the article by Piotr Madajczyk in VfZ, 40/2 (1992), pp. 223–40.

'We, too, ask to forget...' see the text of the German bishops' letter in *Dokumente* IV/2, pp. 973–76, this on p. 975.

... many individual writers... for example, Hansjakob Stehle, *Deutschlands Osten — Polens Westen?* (Frankfurt: Fischer, 1965).

... historians... Gotthold Rhode, a venerable German historian of Poland, notes that the first post-war German-Polish historians' meeting took place as early as October 1956. Significantly, all the Polish historians came from the emigration. See his article in APZ, B 11-12/88, p. 12.

. . . **young Social Democrats** . . . see the vivid short description in Bender, *Neue Ostpolitik*, p. 20.

. . . **'the immediate gain . . .'** This from a letter dated 9 December 1970, now in AdsD: Dep WB, BK6. Grass's letter of 25 November 1970 proposing that he, Siegfried Lenz and Marion Gräfin Dönhoff should accompany the Chancellor to Warsaw is in the same file. Marion Gräfin Dönhoff wrote on 7 December to explain why she could not bring herself to accompany him (BK4). On the same day Rudolf Augstein wrote to complain that he had not been included in the party whereas Henri Nannen of the rival *stern* had been (BK1). There was clearly some competition for the privilege of being allowed to be moved.

'. . . recognise morality as a political force' . . . quoted in Bender, *Neue Ostpolitik*, p. 179.

'We want to be a nation of good neighbours . . .' *Bundestag Plenarprotokolle*, 6/5, p. 34 (28 October 1969).

'The social-liberal coalition . . .' *Bundestag Plenarprotokolle*, 9/111, p. 6760 (9 September 1982).

'We lived until 1945 . . .' quoted in Kuwaczka, *Entspannung von Unten*, pp. 256–57.

. . . **the testimony of one unnamed German woman** . . . in Theodor Schieder & ors, eds, *Dokumentation der Vertreibung der Deutschen aus Ost-Mitteleuropa*, (Munich: Deutscher Taschenbuch Verlag, 1984 = Reprint of original 1954 edition), Vol. I/2, pp. 439–41.

. . . **Konrad Adenauer was restoring German 'honour'** . . . on this, see the vivid account in Schwarz, *Adenauer I*, pp. 897–906.

. . . **'In the relationship with Poland, too, . . .'** *Bundestag Plenarprotokolle*, 6/93, p. 5044 (28 January 1971).

. . . **right through the 1980s** . . . see Bingen, *Bonn-Warschau*, pp. 29–50, and, for the end of the 1980s, the excellent reports of Stefan Dietrich in the FAZ.

. . . **'An open letter to all Germans . . .'** see the special German-language issue of *Kultura* (Paris), Autumn 1984, pp. 80–83. Also reprinted in Kuwaczka, *Entspannung von Unten*, pp. 140–43.

. . . **unreconciled or unrepentant** . . . some of whom nonetheless also used the language of 'reconciliation'. See, for example, E von der Brahe, *Polen und Deutsche. Wie ist eine Versöhnung möglich?* (Lausanne: Kritik-Verlag, 1986), which, on inspection, argues that such a 'reconciliation' is only possible if the Poles give back West Prussia — that is, part of Poland since 1918! — to the Germans. It may fairly be objected that these were marginal voices. Yet the author found this work prominently displayed in a leading Bonn bookshop, together with a map showing

Germany in the frontiers of 1937. See also the correspondence columns of the FAZ, *passim*.

... 'terrible things ...' *Bulletin*, 13 July 1989, p. 653.

'The consequences of war and war crimes ...' *Bulletin*, 30 August 1989, p. 713. A detailed, sensitive and even more carefully balanced statement was issued on this occasion by a group of prominent Polish and German Catholics, *Für Freiheit, Gerechtigkeit und Frieden in Europa. Erklärung polnischer und deutscher Katholiken zum 1. September 1989* (Bonn: Zentralkomitee der deutschen Katholiken, 1989).

... the West German *Historikerstreit* ... see the references given above, p. 541.

... if one sought 'reconciliation' with the rulers ... interestingly enough, precisely this point was made by Franz Josef Strauss in opposing the ratification of the Warsaw Treaty. 'The question of reconciliation with Poland,' he declared in the ratification debate on 24 February 1972, '... which we very much want, goes far deeper than the superficial support for their present powerholders, who want recognition and economic support as a means to strengthen their system.' *Bundestag Plenarprotokolle*, 6/172, p. 9911. The fact that this argument was advanced by Franz Josef Strauss does not *ipso facto* make it false.

... 'take him straight into the cabinet' ... Bölling, *Die fernen Nachbarn*, p. 157. See also the perceptive observations by Schmidt's former speechwriter, Jochen Thies, *Helmut Schmidt's Rückzug von der Macht. Das Ende der Ära Schmidt aus nächster Nähe* (Stuttgart: Bonn Aktuell, 1988), pp. 122–24. Schmidt's own account of his relationship with Gierek is in *Nachbarn*, esp. pp. 479 ff and 508.

... on the election of a Polish Pope ... *Bulletin*, 19 October 1978, p. 1097.

... asking Erich Honecker to use his good offices ... Bölling, *Die fernen Nachbarn*, p. 157.

His 'specifically German motive' ... this and subsequent quotations from Schmidt, *Menschen und Mächte*, pp. 306–07.

... 'with all his heart' ... *Bundestag Plenarprotokolle*, 9/74, p. 4289 (18 December 1981).

... Kazimierz Wóycicki ... see his article 'Hass auf die Deutschen?' in *Kursbuch*, No. 81, September 1985, pp. 131–35, the quotation on pp. 134–35.

... these *Hitlerowcy* ... the post-war Polish term which applies roughly to all Germans who did Hitler's bidding, i.e. rather more than merely 'Hitlerites' or 'Nazis', but less than simply 'Germans'.

... 'everything' would be '*kaputt*' ... quoted in *Der Spiegel*, 1/1982.

... 'that it made me angry ...' in the special German-language issue of *Kultura* (Paris), Autumn, 1984, p. 42.

... an appeal to Willy Brandt ... ibid., pp. 48–49.

Willy Brandt did come to Poland . . . for an excellent account of this visit, and reactions to it, see the article by Harry Schleicher, 'Hoffnung auf das "moralische Kapital" ', in *Frankfurter Rundschau*, 20 December 1985. For an account sympathetic to Brandt see the article by Gerhard Hirschfeld, 'Der Besuch Brandts in Warschau galt dem Volk', in *Vorwärts*, 14 December 1985. For criticism from the Polish opposition see, for example, *Le Monde*, 10 December 1985, where the leading Solidarity adviser Bronisław Geremek is quoted as saying 'The reasoning of many German leaders is limited to their own interests, not those of Europe'; the letter from the veteran Polish socialist, Edward Lipiński, quoted in FAZ, 30 November 1985; the open letter from the Warsaw regional executive, *Tygodnik Mazowsze* No. 148 (reprinted in Kuwaczka, *Entspannung von Unten*, pp. 148–53), and the subsequent commentary in *Tygodnik Mazowsze*, Nos. 149 and 150.

. . . **nor even on that of the murdered Father Popiełuszko** . . . starting with a visit by the junior (British) Foreign Office minister, Malcolm Rifkind, in November 1984, it had by now become regular practice for official Western visitors to pay their respects at the grave of the martyred priest. There was thus no objective obstacle to Brandt doing the same. The ommission was finally made good by Brandt's successor, Hans-Jochen Vogel, on his visit in the autumn of 1987, when he also had a very direct encounter with leading Solidarity advisers. See the reports in *Der Spiegel*, 41/1987, and *Vorwärts*, 3 October 1987.

He declined an invitation . . . Bronisław Geremek recalls drafting the letter of invitation from Wałęsa, which was sent via an intermediary, who returned with a verbal answer. As Geremek recalls, the message given from Brandt — or on Brandt's behalf — was that it would not be possible for him to accept this invitation, and the very fact of extending it was to put him, Brandt, under unacceptable pressure! When Geremek raised the issue with Brandt on a subsequent encounter, Brandt's response included the argument that, instead of making the public gesture of going to Gdańsk he was able to make a private appeal to Jaruzelski to issue a visa for Geremek to come to the West. (Bronisław Geremek, Oxford, 1 May 1992.) This was entirely in line with the Brandt approach since the mid-1960s — quiet diplomacy for humane alleviations rather than public demands for human rights — but entirely at odds with the real requirements of Solidarity, for which the public symbolic politics were infinitely more important than any small, individual humanitarian concessions, which the Jaruzelski regime was generally only too happy to concede. On a charitable interpretation, Brandt was thus mistakenly applying an approach developed in an earlier period, and for different circumstances.

As reported in *Tygodnik Mazowsze*, No. 157, Brandt subsequently wrote to Wałęsa, explaining his actions.

A singular and revealing account of this episode is given in Hans Gerlach, *Europa braucht Polen. Begegnungen, Gespräche, Reflexionen* (Frankfurt: Fischer Taschenbuch Verlag, 1987), pp. 135–39. Gerlach emphasises that as 'a German of the war generation', he may be inclined to view Poland 'in too rosy a light' (p. 175). On this episode he recalls that Brandt 'talked freely of the pressures (*Pressionen*) which had he had been put under even before the journey. There was an "invitation" from Wałęsa, which was not one at all, so Brandt said. Allegedly Wałęsa and a former press spokesman (*sic*) of Solidarity, Masowiecki (*sic*), had expressed their dismay that the SPD chairman would not go to Danzig and that he had come to Poland at this time at all.' None of Brandt's critics, Gerlach continues, 'seemed to have spared even one thought for the connection between the ability to reform, that is, concretely, generosity towards enemies of the regime, and the normalisation of the situation internally and externally. So long as the Polish government had to fear, with some justification, open or concealed enemies, they could not release those political prisoners who were dangerous in their view. Should one arrest them again, with all the adverse attention at home and abroad, if they again used their freedom for agitation? This question was posed again and again, not only by people like Press Spokesman Urban, but also by Rakowski.' Gerlach's understanding for the cares of the gaolers is almost touching. The spirit of reconciliation moves in mysterious ways, its wonders to perform.

. . . **one of the most generous texts** . . . 'Two fatherlands, two patriotisms', Polish text in *Kultura* (Paris) 10/1981. German translation in the German-language edition of *Kontinent*, No. 22, July 1982, with an introduction by Gotthold Rhode.

West German historians exercised heroic patience . . . see, for example, the hilarious footnote polemics on the historical chapters in Jacobsen, *Bundesrepublik-Volksrepublik*.

'**Germans and Poles have found their way** . . .' *Bulletin*, 2 February 1982, p. 69.

'**People are often ahead of politics** . . .' *Bulletin*, 30 August 1989, p. 714.

. . . '**We need a breakthrough** . . .' *Trybuna Ludu*, 13 September 1989, p. 3.

. . . **cultural, scholarly and youth exchanges** . . . among these one should mention the regular series of German-Polish Forums held since 1977; the German Academic Exchange Service (DAAD) and the Alexander von Humboldt Foundation stipends that over the years brought hundreds of Polish scholars and intellectuals to the Federal Republic; the German-Polish Institute in Darmstadt, and the extensive German-Polish programme of the Robert Bosch Stiftung.

. . . **a 1981 survey of Warsaw schoolchildren** . . . reported in *German Politics and Society* (Harvard), No. 9, October 1986, p. 25.

. . . **a major survey in 1991** . . . see the report in *Der Spiegel*, 36/1991.

. . . **a pretty low opinion** . . . see, the survey report in *Der Spiegel* 47/1990, which shows both East and West Germans giving a negative sympathy rating for Poland. An Infratest survey conducted for the Rand corporation in the autumn of 1991 produced a similar negative sympathy rating, see the report by Ronald D Asmus in Rand Paper P-7767 (1992), this on p. 3. In a perceptive article in FAZ, 9 November 1989, at the time of Kohl's visit, Stefan Dietrich reports Polish survey results placing the Federal Republic second to last in a sympathy table of eighteen countries, with forty-four per cent of those asked in a poll by *Gazeta Wyborcza* regarded 'Germans' (West or East) with hostility or distaste. Clearly many caveats should be entered about these data, but the general impression they give was by no means at odds with everyday experience.

. . . **as one independent Polish writer put it** . . . Jacek Maziarski in *Poglądy* (Warsaw), p. 39.

. . . **the nationalism of the victim** . . . see Garton Ash, *Uses*, p. 121.

. . . **his long-delayed official visit** . . . for the main texts see *Bulletin*, 16 November 1989.

A state visit by Richard von Weizsäcker . . . in an interview with *Der Spiegel* 18/1990, von Weizsäcker described this as 'my most important task in my office in foreign relations'. But the trip, though successful, was in the event quite low-key.

. . . **the first time in 990 years** . . . Stefan Dietrich in FAZ, 27 April 1990. In the year 1000 AD, Emperor Otto III visited Gniezno to participate in the funeral celebrations of the martyr Wojtech/Adalbert.

. . . **'once and for all'** . . . see *Bundestag Plenarprotokolle*, 12/39, p. 3256 (6 September 1991).

. . . **'stepping out . . . from under the shadow . . .'** see extracts from his speech in January 1987, reprinted in *Frankfurter Rundschau*, 14 January 1987 and Strauss's own article in *Bayernkurier*, 17 January 1987, which appears to be an edited version of the speech. But see also the interview in *Die Welt*, 17 January 1987, where Strauss explains what he meant.

. . . **'only just beginning'** . . . Eduard Neumaier in *Rheinischer Merkur*, 10 November 1989.

Chapter VI: A Second Ostpolitik

. . . **the proper study of public opinion** . . . for a study which pays particular and expert attention to the evolution of public opinion with respect to German foreign policy, see Schweigler, *Grundlagen*.

. . . **'a second phase of Ostpolitik'** . . . see Moseleit, *Zweite Phase*, p. 1, note 2 and *passim*. Moseleit's book is a careful but highly favourable account, by someone who was actively engaged in the formulation of the party's new thinking. Moseleit himself prefers the label 'second phase of détente policy'. For the more casual but also more catching usage 'second Ostpolitik' see, for example, Peter Glotz in conversation with Eric Hobsbawm in *Marxism Today*, August 1987, p. 14, and Glotz's comments at a press conference following a meeting with Jan Fojtik in Prague, reproduced in the press service of the SPD, 14 April 1988 (318/88).

Karsten Voigt . . . **January 1980** . . . see Moseleit, *Zweite Phase*, p. 1, quoting from NG, 1/1980. In a retrospective conversation with the author (Bonn, 20 March 1992), Karsten Voigt himself stressed the importance of going back to 1980 to understand the party's second Ostpolitik.

...**what Horst Ehmke would call**... see his article in NG, 12/1987, pp. 1073–1080, this on p. 1073.

... **'the continuation of Ostpolitik ..** ' interview in *Zukunft*, 10 October 1986, pp. 8–9.

'... **the key to everything'**... Bahr, *Zum europäischen Frieden*, p. 35.

... **carried forward by a younger generation**... see Moseleit, *Zweite Phase*, p. 40, and *passim*.

... **clearly influenced by**... **movement**... on this see also the sharp observations in Baring, *Grössenwahn*, p. 78 ff and *passim*.

... **first 'ventured' to formulate**... Bahr, *Zum europäischen Frieden*, p. 23.

... **the Palme Commission report**... published in English as *Common Security. A programme for disarmament* (London: Pan Books, 1992).

... **the need for a 'security partnership'**... see the full text of Schmidt's speech in *SPD Parteitag. 19–23 April 1982, München. Protokoll* (Bonn: SPD Vorstand, 1982), pp. 126–65, this on p. 149.

Egon Bahr... **respectfully referred**... ibid., p. 310.

... **a specialist close to Bahr spelled out**... Dieter S. Lutz, *Security Partnership and/or Common Security? On the Origins and Development of a New Concept and on the Criticism and Reaction to it in the Federal Republic of Germany and the German Democratic Republic* (Hamburg: Institut für Friedensforschung und Sicherheitspolitik, 1986).

... **as Bahr himself wrote**... quoted in ibid., p. 5.

... **substantial elements of earlier Social Democratic plans**... a point well made by Stephen F Szabo in his article in *SAIS Review*, Summer-Fall 1987, pp. 51–62.

... **Protestant theologians**... see, for example, the works of Dorothee Sölle. For some samples from the Hamburg church congress of June 1981, see Baring, *Grössenwahn*, pp. 290–92.

... **security issues**... Moseleit, *Zweite Phase*, lists many of the publications in his extensive bibliography.

... **Andreas von Bülow**... specifically on this see the useful article by Heinz Brill in *Neue politische Literatur* 1/1986, pp. 82–91. The commission actually produced several papers, but the one that became known as the 'Bülow paper' and caused a furore was a typescript of September 1985, published in *Frankfurter Rundschau*, 13 & 14 September 1985.

... **'structural non-offensive capacity'**... a very useful introduction to this particular concept is the Friedrich-Ebert-Stiftung paper by Christian Krause, *Strukturelle Nichtangriffsfähigkeit im Rahmen europäischer Entspannungspolitik* (Bonn, January 1987).

Liberation from the Bomb . . . *Die Befreiung von der Bombe. Welfrieden, europäischer Weg und die Zukunft der Deutschen.* (Köln: Bund-Verlag, 1986).

Fear of the Friends . . . Oskar Lafontaine, *Angst vor den Freunden. Die Atomwaffenstrategie der Supermächte zerstört die Bündnisse* (Reinbek: Rowohlt, 1984).

The critical distance . . . **from the policies of the United States** . . . on this aspect, particularly, see the excellent article by Ronald D Asmus, 'The SPD's Second Ostpolitik with Perspectives from the USA' in *Aussenpolitik* (English-language edition) 4/1986, pp. 40–55.

. . . the **Selbstbehauptung Europas** . . . a party working group under the chairmanship of Horst Ehmke actually produced a document in January 1984 entitled *Programm für die Selbstbehauptung Europas*, see Moseleit, *Zweite Phase*, p. 46. For Ehmke's article based on this paper see EA, 7/1984, pp. 195–204.

. . . **coined** . . . **by Peter Bender** . . . see his book *Das Ende des ideologischen Zeitalters. Die Europäisierung Europas* (Berlin: Severin & Siedler, 1981).

. . . **'relative vassals** . . . ' quoted in Moseleit, *Zweite Phase*, p. 22.

. . . **Mitteleuropa** . . . on this see my article in *Daedalus*, Winter 1990, pp. 1–21 and the further references given there. As I note there, the word *Mitteleuropa* had, however, already appeared in the disarmament plans of the SPD in the 1950s — and notably in the '**Deutschlandplan**' of 1959. As noted above, Brandt listed '*MI*' — that is, on his own reading, *Mitteleuropa* — top of his list of 'hopes' in his talks with Brezhnev in August 1970, see above p. 75.

The pioneer . . . **Karl Schlögel** . . . see his *Die Mitte liegt ostwärts. Die Deutschen, der verlorene Osten und Mitteleuropa* (Berlin: Siedler, 1986), and his contribution to Spangenberg, *Mitteleuropa*, pp. 11–31.

. . . '**the proclamation** . . . ' this in Spangenberg, *Mitteleuropa*, p. 31. Schlögel here came out in favour of an 'antipolitical' revival of the concept, alluding to the notion of 'antipolitics' popularised by György Konrád.

'**The renaissance of Mitteleuropa** . . . ' in Spangenberg, *Mitteleuropa*, p. 87.

'**In the desire for détente** . . . ' ibid., p. 102.

'. . . **divided from the margins in** . . . ' ibid., p. 103.

'**We must win back Mitteleuropa** . . . ' NG 7/1986, p. 585. As chief editor of *Neue Gesellschaft/Frankfurter Hefte*, Glotz made it a forum for discussion on this theme.

'**Let us use the concept of Mitteleuropa** . . . ' in *Niemandsland* 2/1987, p. 127. There also the following quotations.

. . . **Eppler** . . . **leading an extensive exercise** . . . see Erhard Eppler, ed., *Grundwerte für ein neues Godesberger Programm. Die Texte der Grundwerte-Kommission der SPD* (Reinbek: Rowohlt, 1984).

. . . **nothing is more important than peace** . . . this formula seems to have emerged in the peace movement in response to a comment by Alexander Haig to the effect that there are things more important than peace. See the interview with Heinrich Albertz in Böll, *Verantwortlich*, pp. 18–24, esp. p. 20.

... 'lifting ideology onto the same level ...' quoted by Heinrich August Winkler in his contribution to Jürgen Maruhn & Manfred Wilke, eds, *Wohin treibt die SPD? Wende oder Kontinuität sozialdemokratischer Sicherheitspolitik* (Munich: Günter Olzog Verlag, 1984), p. 31. He gives his sources as *Vorwärts*, 20 October 1983.

... 'deideologisation' ... The notion was implicit in Peter Bender's title, *Das Ende des ideologischen Zeitalters*. Critics were charged with the heinous error of 'reideologisation', see the article by one such critic, Gesine Schwan, in *Rheinischer Merkur*, 20 July 1985. The 'end of ideology' had of course been proclaimed by Daniel Bell and others twenty years before.

... 'Peace is not everything ...' the 'government programme 1987–1990' is printed in the *Protokoll vom Wahlparteitag der SPD in Offenburg 25. Oktober 1986* (Bonn: SPD Vorstand, 1986), pp. 107–54, this on p. 145.

... originated from the Social Democratic side ... Moseleit, *Zweite Phase*, p. 25, suggests that it was first used by Rudolf von Thadden in 1981.

... 'Peace of Augsburg' ... Gaus, *Deutschland, p. 275.*

... 'Peace of Westphalia' ... thus Karsten Voigt in *Bundestag Plenarprotokolle*, 10/4, p. 135 (4 May 1983), 10/23, p. 1613 (16 September 1983), 10/35, p. 2449 (21 November 1983).

... the 'government programme' of 1983 ... printed in *SPD Wahlparteitag-Dortmund 21. Januar 1983. Protokoll* (Bonn: SPD Vorstand, 1983), pp. 161–92.

'Humankind ...' ibid., p. 88. There also the following quotations.

'never led Germany into a war' ... A carping historian might, however, point out that the SPD had, famously, voted funds for war in 1914.

'The peoples in the East-West conflict ...' the text of the resolution can be found in *Politik. Informationsdienst der SPD*, Nr. 8, September 1986. There also the following quotations.

... 'securing peace' ... *Protokoll vom Wahlparteitag der SPD in Offenburg 25. Oktober 1986* (Bonn: SPD Vorstand, 1986), pp. 145–53. There also the following quotations.

... legitimised and facilitated ... thus the report from the Soviet to the East German Party leadership on Willy Brandt's meeting with Gorbachev in May 1985 concludes by confirming the usefulness of increasing contacts with the Social Democrats 'as well as the possibility of actively involving the Social Democrats in the broad front of the struggle for preserving peace and banishing the danger of a new world war'. Quoted from the report ('Information') of 6 June 1985 in ZPA: IV 2/2.035/65.

... **supporting role** ... see also the pertinent observation of Moseleit, *Zweite Phase*, pp. 52–53.

... **ceremonious joint statements** ... the most ceremonious of these, a joint declaration with the Polish United Workers' Party on 'measures of mutual confidence-building', was published, with a joint preface signed by Brandt and Jaruzelski, on 25 November 1985. The joint group with the Hungarian Socialist Workers' Party produced a number of joint declarations, see for example the daily information service of the Social Democratic parliamentary party, 1845/1986, 533/1987.

... **vague joint proposals** ... see the statement of the joint working group led by Anatoly Dobrynin and Egon Bahr in the press service of the SPD, 13 October 1987 (842/87).

... **'many arguments...'** Soviet memorandum of 15 October 1984, now in ZPA: IV 2/2.035/65.

... **the great schism** ... see Carl E Schorske, *German Social Democracy 1905– 1917. The Development of the Great Schism* (New York: Harper Torchbook, 1972); Leszek Kołakowski, *Main Currents of Marxism* (Oxford: Clarendon Press, 1978), Volume 2; George Lichtheim, 'Social Democracy and Communism: 1918–1968' in *Studies in Comparative Communism*, Vol. 3, No. 1, January 1970, pp. 5–30. A very useful collection of documents is Weber, *Links*.

... **a Communist would tap furious polemics** ... this is recounted by Axel Eggebrecht, in his memoirs *Der halbe Weg. Zwischenbilanz einer Epoche* (Reinbek: Rowohlt, 1975), p. 273.

... **'demarcation resolution'** ... reprinted in Weber, *Links*, pp. 268–76.

... **drafted by Richard Löwenthal** ... In the 1930s, Löwenthal had himself been active in the *'Neu Beginnen'* group, which tried to join the efforts of Communists and Social Democrats against fascism.

... **amended** ... see the papers in AdsD: Dep WB, PV — *Theorie und Pro-grammdiskussion/Beschlusspapier "Sozialdemokratie und Kommunismus"*. Even here, however, there were tactical concerns, notably about the date of publication. Thus in the first draft of a letter to Löwenthal in early September 1970, Brandt wrote 'if the party board (*Vorstand*) were to deliver, at the same time as the evaluation of the [Moscow] treaty, such a clear statement against the system which rules in the lands of our treaty partners, this could be interpreted as an attempt to tread on the brake out of fear of one's own courage. This would be bound to hamper our negotiating chances.' On 5 September 1970 a milder and more elusive version of this letter was sent, with Brandt thus self-censoring his suggestion of self-censorship. Baring, *Machtwechsel*, pp. 357–58, records that the Party leadership nonetheless passed the resolution on 14 November 1970, but other sources give the date of the final resolution as 26 February 1971. This is confirmed by the wording, which refers to the Moscow and Warsaw treaties.

... **an 'exchange of speakers'** ... see Bender, *Neue Ostpolitik*, p. 132 and Hildebrand, *Von Erhard zur grossen Koalition*.

...reports of the Stasi's... see, for example, the reports of the Central Evaluation and Information Group (ZAIG) on popular reaction to the results of the November 1972 federal elections and to news of Brandt's resignation as Chancellor, MfS: Z4083 and Z4088.

'In my view...' this from the copy of Wehner's untitled memorandum, datelined Bad Godesberg, 2 December 1973, in AdsD: Dep WB, BK 75.

...the particular case of Honecker and Wehner... see above p. 199 and notes.

...a 'love-hate relationship'... Moseleit, *Zweite Phase*, p. 51.

...'now Ehmke and Bahr pose the same question...' Report of 29 January 1979 on the conversation of Erich Honecker and B. N. Ponomaryev on 26 January 1979 in ZPA: IV 2/2.035/56. There also the following quotations.

...on 2 November 1982... ZPA: JIV 2/2/1972.

...took over from Herbert Wehner... Hans-Jochen Vogel, Bonn, 18 March 1992.

At their second such meeting, in March 1984... On 14 March, and attended also by Wischnewski, Bahr, Voigt and the note-taker, Dieter Schröder. The establishment of the chemical weapons group seems not, however, to have been formally announced immediately following the Vogel-Honecker meeting. At its meeting on 29 May 1984, the Politburo discussed a report by Herbert Häber on the Social Democrats' Essen party congress, and approved a list of the measures to be pursued in relations with the SPD, of which this was the first. See point 5 and Appendix 4 to Protocol 22/84 in ZPA: JIV 2/2/2057. The deputy head of the Central Committee department for international relations, Manfred Uschner, who was to play a key role in the security policy working group, recalls starting work in the summer of 1984. Manfred Uschner, Berlin, 1 October 1992.

...a remarkable document... The Social Democrats published the document, together with the joint communiqué and a foreword by Karsten Voigt, based on his statement at the press conference in Bonn on 19 June 1985, in *Politik* 6/1985. The East German edition, including Axen's statement, was published as *Für Chemiewaffenfreie Zone in Europa. Gemeinsame politische Initiative der Sozialistischen Einheitspartei Deutschlands und der Sozialdemokratischen Partei Deutschlands* (Dresden: Verlag Zeit im Bild, n.d.).

...by the Communist Party of Czechoslovakia... see the joint statement reproduced in the press service of the SPD, 5 April 1988 (295/1988) and the commentary by Karsten Voigt in ibid., 296/1988.

...a cordial summit meeting... only a short report on this meeting is appended to the minutes of the Politburo meeting on 24 September 1985, in ZPA: JIV 2/2/2131. It should, however, clearly soon be possible to examine both the full record and that from the Brandt papers. (At the time of writing the author had access to the Brandt papers only up to 1981.)

...'in accordance with...' thus the wording of the Joint Communiqué of 21

October 1986, printed together with the text and preface by Egon Bahr in *Politik*, 19/1986. There also the following quotations. The East German version, with Axen's statement at the press conference, was published as *Für Atomwaffenfreien Korridor in Mitteleuropa. Gemeinsame politische Initiative der Sozialistischen Einheitspartei Deutschlands und der Sozialdemokratischen Partei Deutschlands* (Dresden: Verlag Zeit im Bild, n.d.).

... 'questions from the SPD ...' Uschner, *Ostpolitik*, p. 137.

... would generally fly ... Manfred Uschner, Berlin, 1 October 1992.

In his commentary, Bahr ... *Politik*, 19/1986.

... for a 'zone of trust and security' ... *Politik*, 6/1988. Also published in ND, 8 July 1988.

... the Soviet answers ... the Soviet comments on Bahr's questions at the working group meeting, in Bonn on 27 January 1988, are now in ZPA: IV 2/2.035/60.

... 'social scientists' ... In his book *Wie Feuer und Wasser. Sind Ost und West friedensfähig?* (Reinbek: Rowohlt, 1988), p. 13, Erhard Eppler talks of 'almost two years' of cautious exploration. See also Häber's report of 17 October 1983 on a trip, 9–16 October 1983, in ZPA: JIV 2/10.02/13. One should note that it was the East German 'social scientist' Otto Reinhold who had been charged with main responsibility for relations with the SPD already in the Politburo resolution of 2 November 1982.

... the summer of 1984 ... this was one of the steps approved by the Politburo in its meeting of 22 May 1984, see the record and appendix 4 in ZPA: JIV 2/2/2057.

... delicately pitched ... Moseleit, *Zweite Phase*, p. 63 ff.

... on the Scharmützelsee ... Erhard Eppler, *Wie Feuer und Wasser. Sind Ost und West friedensfähig?* (Reinbek: Rowohlt, 1988), p. 98 f. See also the recollections of Carl-Christian Kaiser in *Die Zeit*, 21 August 1992.

... 'six theses on the relations ...' published in the daily press service of the SPD, 17 March 1986.

... its party congress to coincide ... on this, see the very useful summary by B V Flow in Radio Free Europe Research Background Report, 87/1986. Strictly speaking, the anniversary was on 22 April while the congress finished on the 21st.

For the first time ... see report in FAZ, 18 April 1986.

... now merely 'non-communists' ... Otto Reinhold in *Horizont*, 4/1986.

... their common paper ... published in *Politik* 3/1987 and ND, 28 August 1987.

Gesine Schwan ... see her article in FAZ, 23 September 1987. Egon Bahr responded in FAZ, 2 October 1987. See also the sharply contrasting commentaries of Gerd Bucerius and Marion Gräfin Dönhoff in *Die Zeit*, 11 September 1987.

'**if it really happens** . . .' . . . 'there is . . .' Erhard Eppler, *Wie Feuer und Wasser. Sind Ost und West friedensfähig?* (Reinbek: Rowohlt, 1988), pp. 77, 83.

. . . **spokespersons for Western democracy** . . . ibid., p. 100 f.

Richard Löwenthal . . . see his article in *Die Welt*, 2 September 1987.

. . . **a rare argument** . . . Egon Krenz, Berlin, 29 September 1992. Karl Seidel, Berlin, 30 September 1992. Kurt Hager, Berlin, 8 May 1992. Seidel, who was present to answer any detailed questions about preparations for Honecker's trip to West Germany, recalls Krenz — in the chair in Honecker's absence — ending the discussion with a comment to the effect that 'Erich wants it'. Here one also sees clearly the limitations of the Politburo minutes as a source, for in the minutes of the meetings on 18 August and 26 August there is no record of any such disagreement. ZPA: JIV 2/2/2235 and 2236. Rolf Reissig gives a slightly different account of how the paper was pushed through in *Berliner Zeitung*, 27 August 1992.

Kurt Hager, soon publicly qualified . . . see his speech reprinted in ND, 28 October 1987. On the reception and argument inside the SED see the useful article by Rüdiger Thomas in *DDR-Report*, 1/1988, p. 14 ff. *Der Spiegel*, 51/1987, reported an internal Party '*Information*', circulated to regional Party headquarters, which also gave a highly restrictive interpretation of the paper.

'**There were, if you like** . . .' Kurt Hager, Berlin, 8 May 1992. But if Reissig was a Social Democrat, then only in private or by Hager's definition. Egon Krenz says most emphatically that few if any traces of the 'social democrat' were visible at the time. Egon Krenz, Berlin, 29 September 1992.

. . . **sharply contrasting testimonies** . . . thus Manfred Uschner (Berlin, 1 October 1992) recalls lecturing to fascinated audiences even in a Party organisation of the frontier troops. Karl Seidel (Berlin, 30 September 1992), by contrast, recalls very little — and if anything rather critical — discussion in his Party organisation in the Foreign Ministry. Kurt Hager (Berlin, 8 May 1992) believed it had very little impact in the Party, but Egon Krenz (Berlin, 29 September 1992) believed it made a great impact. This is clearly a subject for further detailed research.

A September 1987 report . . . the eight-page report dated 24 September 1987 is in MfS: Z4230.

. . . **Protestant Church** . . . More critically, Hans-Jürgen Fischbeck in conversation with Thomas Meyer and Rolf Reissig in *Berliner Zeitung*, 27 August 1992.

A small group . . . this included Gert Weisskirchen and Jürgen Schmude.

. . . **Gert Weisskirchen, himself says** . . . Gert Weisskirchen, Bonn, 24 June 1992. See also his interview in TAZ, 21 February 1992, and his article in DA, 5/1992, pp. 526–30.

Eppler . . . genuinely affronted . . . this was also the impression of Carl–Christian Kaiser, see his article in *Die Zeit*, 21 August 1992.

'Those who refuse internal dialogue . . .' The statement is reprinted, together with Reinhold's response, in DA, 6/1989, pp. 713–16, this on p. 715.

. . . the traditional 17 June speech . . . see *Bundestag Plenarprotokolle*, 11. Wahlperiode [special session], pp. 11296–303 (17 June 1989).

. . . 'GDR-consciousness . . .' ibid., p.11299.

. . . 'neither side can prevent the other . . .' ibid., p.11300. The speech is reprinted in Erhard Eppler, *Reden auf die Republik. Deutschlandpolitische Texte 1952–1990* (Munich: Chr. Kaiser, 1990), pp. 31–46.

. . . 'We are pushing for . . .' typescript of Lafontaine's opening remarks at the 'Saarbrücken Conversation', 7 June 1989. It should, however, be pointed out that Lafontaine went on to warn against these conversations becoming a sort of *Friedenskumpanei* (i.e. ganging up in the name of peace), and against covering up the different views about democracy and the violations of human rights. Moreover, his guest, Egon Krenz (Berlin, 29 September 1992) recalls Lafontaine being quite tough and outspoken in his demands in private talks.

. . . extremely confused . . . some of the debate can be followed in the extensive collection of press cuttings in *Deutschland 1989*, Vol. 24.

'Nothing can be changed . . .' quoted in *Die Welt*, 30 August 1989. See also report in FAZ, 30 August 1989. Earlier in the year, Horst Ehmke had reacted critically to the founding of a social democratic party in Slovenia, see the report in FAZ, 30 March 1989.

. . . 'Wandel durch Anbiederung . . .' *Bundestag Plenarprotokolle*, 11/156, pp.11723–733 (5 September 1989).

. . . Norbert Gansel . . . see his article in *Frankfurter Rundschau*, 13 September 1989.

. . . after Horst Ehmke let it be known . . . this is clear from an urgent message from the GDR's Permanent Representation in Bonn dated 12 September (1691/89), in which Ehmke's travel plan includes a formal meeting with Manfred Stolpe, and 'for the evening he points to a personal meeting with Bohley'. This in ZPA: IV 2/2.035/81. Extracts from the speech that Ehmke proposed to deliver are printed in FAZ, 18 September 1989.

From now on, contacts with the Churches and opposition . . . see report in FAZ, 20 September 1989.

. . . Bahr called for a stabilisation . . . TAZ, 30 September 1989.

. . . reforms leading to a third way . . . thus, explicitly, in ZDF's *Kennzeichen D* programme on 30 September 1989, transcript in BPA/KÜ I/31.08.89.

. . . 'a different GDR' . . . see his interview in *Der Spiegel*, 42/1989.

The people of the GDR . . . *Bergedorfer Gesprächskreis* 88 (6–7 September 1989), p. 62.

. . . **'homeopathic changes . . .'** this in a radio interview on 8 October 1989, transcript in BPA/KU I/09.10.89.

. . . **'there's a principle that applies . . .'** ibid.

. . . **of a** *new* **unification** (*Neuvereinigung*) . . . see the report of his conversation with a group of schoolchildren in FAZ, 6 Mai 1989.

'that which arbitrarily divides . . .' *Bundestag Plenarprotokolle* 11/150, p. 11193 (16 June 1989).

. . . **'how and how far . . .'** *Bild*, 21 September 1989.

. . . **discreetly let it be known** . . . see *dpa* agency report, 18 October 1989.

. . . **'now what belongs together . . .'** this famous phrase is to be found in the text of his speech before the Schöneberg City Hall on 10 November 1989 as printed in Willy Brandt, *". . . was zusammengehört", Reden zu Deutschland* (Bonn: Dietz, 1990), pp. 37–41. It is interesting to note that Brandt referred in the previous sentence to the 'division of Europe, Germany and Berlin' and went on to say that what was growing together was 'the parts of Europe'. However, he seems in fact to have used the phrase earlier in the day in off-the-cuff remarks at the Schöneberg City Hall.

. . . **then rallied at their party conference in Berlin** . . . see *Protokoll vom Programm-Parteitag. Berlin, 18.–20.12.1989* (Bonn: SPD Vorstand, 1990), *passim*.

Had not Willy Brandt met with Tadeusz Mazowiecki . . . on this, see above, pp.306 and Notes. See also the article by an anonymous Solidarity representative in NG 6/1986, responding to Horst Ehmke's article in NG 11/1985.

. . . **Vogel with Solidarity advisers** . . . see reports in *Der Spiegel*, 41/1987 and *Vorwärts*, 3 October 1987. Several eye-witnesses report that this was a very difficult meeting.

. . . **Erich Mielke reported to the Politburo** . . . copy in ZPA: IV 2/2.035/81.

. . . **Gerd Poppe** . . . Bonn, 18 March 1992.

As Egon Bahr himself observed . . . see his interview in *Die Zeit*, 13 March 1992.

. . . **a first, simple answer** . . . ibid. So also Hans-Jochen Vogel, Bonn, 18 March 1992.

. . . **the 'governmental' or 'statist' tradition** . . . thus, for example, Gert Weisskirchen in TAZ, 21 February 1992, and in conversation with the author, Bonn, 24 June 1992. Somewhat surprisingly, Karsten Voigt (Bonn, 29 February 1988 and 20 March 1992) also identified this 'etatist' line, but suggested that he himself belonged to a different, reform and freedom-oriented line.

. . . **Metternich of the left** . . . to which charge Bahr himself once replied: 'Oh no. But even if it were true: Metternich achieved fifty years of peace in Europe. That was also not bad.' *Abendzeitung*, 24 November 1989.

. . . **as the external dimension of détente** . . . Horst Ehmke to a seminar of the Friedrich-Ebert-Stiftung in Bonn, 12/13 March 1988 (typescript), p. 6, referring back to his own contribution to the 1,000th volume of the Edition Suhrkamp edited by Jürgen Habermas in 1979. This seminar was a venture in dialogue with advocates of 'détente from below' from the Western left and peace movement, and with oppositionists from Eastern Europe, as Ehmke himself notes in *Vorwärts*, 20 August 1988. His article was in response to a powerful critique of the SPD's lack of support for the East European opposition by Sibylle Plogstedt in *Vorwärts*, 13 August 1988.

Karsten Voigt pinned his hopes . . . Karsten Voigt, Bonn, 20 March 1992.

'by our not . . .' This on the ARD programme entitled 'Als Erich auf dem roten Teppich stand . . .', 30 April 1992. He made the same argument in one of his most considered retrospective statements, a lecture in Dresden on 16 February 1992, circulated by the SPD Press Service, 85/92.

. . . **original documents from the Party archives** . . . See note on p. 526. The most important sources available for research on this particular topic were the papers of the office of Hermann Axen (*Büro Axen*), the minutes and working papers of the Politburo, and some other holdings in the internal archive of the Politburo.

Extracts from some of the documents from the *Büro Axen* appeared in an article by Christian von Ditfurth in *Der Spiegel*, 35/1992. A promised book-length treatment of this subject by von Ditfurth was not available when this chapter was written.

. . . **a few from the SPD side** . . . As this book was finished, the leadership of the SPD was still considering a request from the author for permission to examine the relevant documents. However, as already mentioned, Hans-Jochen Vogel took an exemplary initiative by making available to the author the records of his own regular annual meetings with Erich Honecker.

. . . **Egon Bahr and Erich Honecker on 5 September 1986** . . . this and the documentation of the following developments are in ZPA: IV 2/2.035/89 (with some related material in IV 2/2.035/78). There the following quotations.

. . . **the possibility of a tendentious record** . . . The record is signed by Hermann Axen, 8 September 1986.

. . . **fine-sounding (yet in fact still vague)** . . . for what would 'full respect' of GDR citizenship in practice have meant? After all, the right of a GDR citizen to remain a GDR citizen, travel (if they could) as a GDR citizen, and return to the GDR as a GDR citizen *if they wanted to* was already fully respected by the Bonn government.

. . . **evening television news** . . . that is, the '*Tagesthemen*' on 18 September. The West German official transcript (BPA/Ku I/19.9.86) has a virtually identical wording. An excellent account of the effect of the announcement is given in *Neue Zürcher Zeitung*, 20 September 1986.

. . . 'the policy of the GDR . . .' record of a conversation with Axen in Berlin, 6 April 1987, now in ZPA: IV 2/2.035/79. The note-taker was probably Günter Rettner.

. . . 'however it was the SPD's view . . .' record of the conversation on 15 April 1987 in ZPA: IV 2/2.035/79.

. . . 'more firmly under control . . .' But he really need not have worried. Just 9 days earlier, on 6 April 1987, Erich Mielke had sent out an additional executive instruction (*Durchführungsbestimmung*) to the basic service order of 1975, covering the control of Western visitors. This additional instruction was concerned specifically with the control of what it also referred to as 'polit-tourism', which it interpreted as being in the interests of Bonn's 'contact policy'. *2. Durchführungsbestimmung zur Dienstanweisung Nr. 3/75*, MfS Nr. 20187 (no new archival signature).

. . . records of his annual conversations . . . photocopies in the author's possession.

. . . seventeen pages of them . . . record of the conversation on 25 May 1989, typescript, p. 12.

. . . a cautious defence of Ronald Reagan . . . record of the conversation on 28 May 1983, typescript, p. 13.

'Dr Vogel replied . . .' record of the conversation on 15 May 1987, typescript, p. 17.

. . . near the end of the talk . . . ibid., p. 19.

. . . the East German record . . . in ZPA: JIV 2/2/2220.

. . . 'the administration slipped unprepared . . .' record of the conversation on 29 April 1988, typescript, p. 10.

. . . 'The Social Democrats didn't want . . .' ibid.

The East German version . . . see the record (*Niederschrift*) of the conversation in the Hubertusstock on 29 April 1988 in ZPA: IV 2/2.035/80, this on p. 12. This may have been written by Günter Rettner or by Honecker's State Secretary in the Council of State, Frank-Joachim Herrmann. The usually reliable Karl Seidel did not attend this particular meeting.

. . . Oskar Lafontaine, Klaus von Dohnanyi and Klaus Wedemaier . . . see the minute (*Notiz*) of the conversation on 23 October 1987 in ZPA: IV 2/2.035/79, also for the following quotations. The minute was probably written by Günter Rettner.

'Personally, Comrade Rettner continued . . .' report by Günter Rettner dated 12 December 1987 of his talks in West Germany on 9–11 December 1987, in ZPA: IV 2/2.035/79. Rettner had taken over from Herbert Häber (who had retired 'on health grounds') as head of what was now euphemistically called the Central Committee Department for International Politics and Economics (IPW). Like the Institute of the same name, this — the West Department by another name — was essentially concerned with West Germany. Regrettably, Rettner declined to talk to the author.

...profound confidence in E. Honecker... as evidence, Lafontaine also pointed to his article on the occasion of Honecker's 75th birthday, in *Der Spiegel*, 35/1987.

Receiving Rettner again five months later... report by Günter Rettner dated 16 May 1988 of a conversation with O. Lafontaine in Saarbrücken on 13 May 1988, in ZPA: IV 2/2.035/80.

...'note on a confidential [piece of] information...' dated 8 July 1988, this is now in ZPA: IV 2/2.035/80.

...hotly disputed... for some reactions see the article by Christian von Ditfurth in *Der Spiegel*, 35/1992. In conversation with the author (Berlin, 1 October 1992), Manfred Uschner suggested that the note — which is unsigned — may have been made, on Axen's instructions, by a diplomat at the GDR's Permanent Representation in Bonn who was also present at the lunch. Tendentious though the note may be, Uschner's own recollection is that Voigt did definitely speak of a possible expulsion.

In August 1988, Lafontaine... record (*Niederschrift*) of the conversation between Honecker and Lafontaine in the Hubertusstock, 18 August 1988, in ZPA: IV 2/2.035/80. On the atmosphere of these meetings between the fellow Saarländers, the East German note-taker, Karl Seidel, head of the Foreign Ministry department responsible for dealing with West Germany, comments: 'all that was lacking was the fraternal kiss'. Karl Seidel, Berlin, 30 September 1992.

...a tense exchange... in ZPA: IV 2/2.035/81.

...the Politburo agreed... the directive is in ibid., the actual Politburo decision in the minutes of the meeting on 8th August in ZPA: JIV 2/2/2340.

...an urgent message... in ZPA: IV 2/2.035/81. Lafontaine also sent his suggestions for defusing the situation, through an emissary, Hans-Peter Weber, despatched to talk to Günter Rettner in Berlin on 18 August 1989. According to Rettner's report of 21 August 1989 (in the same file) Lafontaine even suggested that the state government of the Saarland was considering not giving West German passports to East Germans who were visiting the Saarland and wanted them for trips to France and Luxembourg! According to Rettner's report, Lafontaine's emissary also made the helpful suggestion that East Germans who had taken refuge in the Federal Republic's Permanent Representation should be allowed by the East German authorities to leave the building with an assurance that they would not be prosecuted, while Honecker should give a private undertaking that they would then be allowed to leave East Germany 'after a longer period'. It must be emphasised, however, that this is a report of an emissary's report of Lafontaine's views, and both Lafontaine and the emissary in question dismissed it as false. See also the article by Christian von Ditfurth in *Der Spiegel*, 35/1992.

. . . a copy, courtesy of the Stasi . . . in ZPA: IV 2/2.035/81, this comes attached to one of Mielke's confidential '*Information*' sheets, on SPD contacts with Church and opposition groups in East Germany.

. . . scholars and journalists also frequently indulged . . . see above p. 211 and Note on p. 538.

. . . *kameradschaftlich* . . . Erich Honecker, Berlin-Moabit, 27 November 1992.

. . . a note prepared for Hans-Jochen Vogel . . . Note of 15 June 1990, final balance in the field 'Humanitarian help/GDR'. Copy kindly made available to the author by Dr Vogel.

'There is much to be said . . .' '*Trotz allem — hilfreich. Das Streitkultur-Papier von SPD und SED. Fünf Jahre danach. Eine Stellungnahme der Grundwertekom-mission*' (Typescript, August 1992), reprinted in DA, 10/1992, pp. 1100–08. See also the article by Gode Japs in the same issue, pp. 1011–14.

. . . 'security is the key to everything' Bahr, *Zum europäischen Frieden*, p.35.

. . . 'you expected everything . . .' *Die Zeit*, 9 February 1990.

'My real mistake was . . .' in *Die Zeit*, 13 March 1992.

'There have been, if you like . . .' this in the radio interview on 8 October 1989 already quoted, transcript in BPA/KU I/09.10.89. In an article in *Die Zeit*, 24 November 1989, the first of what were to be many sallies in defence of his SPD-SED paper, Erhard Eppler cited Willy Brandt to the effect that 'reform' was no longer an adequate word to describe what was now happening between the Bug and the Elbe. 'Reforms,' wrote Eppler, 'are changes or adjustments inside a power-system'.

. . . the breakthrough of the Leipzig demonstration . . . see above, p. 345.

. . . the illusions of the Prague Spring . . . It is interesting to find a foreign policy aide to the Social Democratic parliamentary party, Jutta Tiedke, taking the Prague Spring as a model for change in Eastern Europe as late as summer 1988. See her article in NG, 8/1988, pp. 712–17. Horst Ehmke told the author (Bonn, 19 April 1988) that he had nightly to defend the Social Democrats' Ostpolitik to his Czech wife. Ehmke could rightly claim consistency for his own approach; the question is, however, whether the consistent approach was right.

The Berlin programme . . . *Grundsatzprogramm der Sozialdemokratischen Partei Deutschlands* (Bonn: SPD Vorstand, 1990). There all the following quotations.

. . . a *Sonderbewusstsein* . . . see Karl-Dietrich Bracher, *Die totalitäre Erfarhrung* (Munich: Piper, 1987), p.91 ff. See also the contribution by Kurt Sontheimer in the Festschrift for Bracher (to whom he attributes the term): Funke, *Demokratie und Diktatur*, pp. 35–45.

. . . 'in a large part of the young generation . . .' in *Partisan Review*, 2/1984, pp. 183–198, this on p. 190. Alas, Löwenthal's own article quoted above (*Die Welt*, 2 September 1987) showed old-age symptoms of the youthful disorder he himself had analysed.

Martin Gutzeit recalls . . . Berlin, 29 June 1992.

Chapter VII: German Unification

. . . **329 days** . . . thus Teltschik, *329 Tage.*

. . . **as Peter Pulzer has suggested** . . . in a verbal contribution to a seminar by Catherine McArdle Kelleher at All Souls College, Oxford.

. . . **published sources** . . . the best single collection of the most important documents is in the last three volumes of *Texte*: III/7, 8a and 8b. The Foreign Ministry's *Umbruch* and the companion volume *Deutsche Aussenpolitik 1990/91. Auf dem Weg zu einer europäischen Friedensordnung. Eine Dokumentation* (Bonn: Auswärtiges Amt, 1991) provide some useful additional material on the diplomacy of unification, and Volker Gransow and Konrad H Jarausch, *Die deutsche Vereinigung. Dokumente zu Bürgerbewegung, Annäherung und Beitritt* (Köln: Wissenschaft und Politik, 1991) includes an interesting variety of less official documents. Among the already innumerable accounts of German unification, useful introductory surveys include Kaiser, *Vereinigung*, Jesse & Mitter, *Einheit*, and, in English, Szabo, *Diplomacy* and Grosser, *Unification*. Elizabeth Pond, *Beyond the Wall. Germany's Road to Unification* (Washington: Brookings for Twentieth Century Fund, 1993) appeared too late to be used in the preparation of this chapter.

. . . **writes Michael Wolffsohn** . . . in his contribution to Jesse & Mitter, *Einheit*, pp. 142–62, this on p. 142.

. . . **literally an iron curtain** . . . see Horn, *Erinnerungen*, p. 293.

. . . **more direct and conspiratorial means** . . . this, what one might call the 'hidden hand' theory, was of course the subject of endless speculation, especially among former Politburo members, concerning the role of the KGB, Markus Wolf, Hans Modrow and so forth. A fairly sober treatment of this aspect in English is Jeffrey Gedmin, *The Hidden Hand. Gorbachev and the Collapse of East Germany* (Washington: AEI Press, 1992).

'It began in the Caucasus' . . . Hans Klein, *Es begann im Kaukasus. Der entscheidende Schritt in die Einheit Deutschlands* (Berlin: Ullstein, 1991).

. . . **'refolution'** . . . see my articles 'Refolution: The Springtime of Two Nations' in *The New York Review of Books*, 15 June 1989, and 'Refolution in Hungary and Poland', *The New York Review of Books*, 17 August 1989.

. . . **Albert Hirschman's terms** . . . Albert O Hirschman, *Exit, Voice and Loyalty. Responses to Decline in Firms, Organisations and States* (Cambridge: Harvard University Press, 1970). Hirschman discusses the applicability of his own theory to what happened in the GDR in an article in *World Politics*, Vol. 45, No. 2, January 1993, pp. 173–202.

. . . **'who comes too late . . .'** It is not clear whether he ever said precisely this. A letter in FAZ, 5 December 1991, suggests that what he actually said in public, in a spontaneous response to journalists, was 'it is dangerous for him who does not react to life'. His own official speech was extremely cautious, see *Texte* III/7, pp. 275–77.

What he said in private to the East German leadership was 'if we remain behind, life punishes us straightaway', but the immediate context was a discussion of the situation in the Soviet Union itself. See the record of his meeting with the Politburo on 7 October 1989, printed in Mittag, *Preis*, pp. 359–84. Several Politburo members told the author that they understood the remark to apply mainly to the Soviet Union.

In the protocol of his immediately preceding personal conversation with Honecker, Gorbachev is recorded as saying: 'E Honecker and the Party should seize the initiative, otherwise demagogues could suggest other ideas. From his own experience he knew that one should not come too late. He had very much liked E Honecker's speech [i.e. at the banquet the night before] because it said honestly and correctly what had to be done.' See the record (*Niederschrift*) in ZPA: IV 2/2.035/60. Here he clearly was applying the thought to the GDR. Interestingly, Honecker underlined the immediately preceding and the immediately following sentences, but not this one key sentence ('From his own experience . . .').

. . . **a German revolution . . .** witness countless speeches, headlines, book titles etc. A good first introduction to the subject in English is now Gert-Joachim Glaessner and Ian Wallace, eds, *The German Revolution of 1989. Causes and Consequences* (Oxford: Berg, 1992).

. . . **'the turn within the turn' . . .** see, for example, Meuschel, *Legitimation*, p. 318 ff, and Eckhard Jesse in Jesse & Mitter, *Einheit*, p. 118 and note.

According to a transcript . . . published in *Der Spiegel*, 48/1990. The news magazine maliciously published this mildly embarrassing document on the eve of the all-German election on 2 December 1991.

. . . **Chancellor Kohl's 'ten point programme'** . . . see *Texte* III/7, pp. 426–33.

. . . **partly a response . . . partly prompted . . . partly designed** . . . Teltschik, *329 Tage*, pp. 42 f, 48 f, 55 f. Horst Teltschik, Bonn, 12 July 1991. Helmut Kohl, Bonn, 1 October 1991.

. . . **real and very emotional breakthrough** . . . Wolfgang Bergsdorf at a seminar in St Antony's College, Oxford, reproduced in an edited version in Grosser, *Unification*, pp. 88–106, this on p. 91. Helmut Kohl, Bonn, 1 October 1991. Teltschik, *329 Tage*, p. 87 ff.

. . . **Round Table(s)** . . . for one eyewitness account see Uwe Thayssen, *Der Runde Tisch. Oder: Wo blieb das Volk. Der Weg der DDR in die Demokratie* (Opladen: Westdeutscher Verlag, 1990). He summarises his argument in Grosser, *Unification*, pp. 72–87.

... '**dual power**' ... the term is used by Gert-Joachim Glaessner, *Der Schwierige Weg zur Demokratie. Vom Ende der DDR zur deutschen Einheit* (Opladen: Westdeutscher Verlag, 1991), p. 89 ff.

... **proclaiming his own commitment** ... see *Texte* III/8a, p. 49 f.

Just three weeks before ... ibid., p. 13 f.

... **nearly 350,000** ... Teltschik, *329 Tage*, p. 103, records Wolfgang Schäuble's report to the cabinet on 10 January, with a total of 343,854 registered as having come permanently as 'over-settlers' from the GDR, in 1989. In his entry for 12 February (p. 144) he records a rate of around 3,000 a day. See also the article by Hartmut Wendt in DA, 4/1991, pp. 386–95, especially the tables on p. 393.

... *Bleibt daheim!* ... see the interesting collection by Helmut Herles & Ewald Rose, eds, *Parlaments-Szenen einer deutschen Revolution. Bundestag und Volkskammer im November 1989* (Bonn: Bouvier, 1990), this on p. 26.

... **had himself fled** ... see his own account in Wolfgang Mischnick, *Von Dresden nach Bonn. Erlebnisse — jetzt aufgeschrieben* (Stuttgart: Deutsche Verlags-Anstalt, 1991), p. 249 f.

... **if we don't take the DM** ... thus Teltschik, *329 Tage*, p. 129, and countless other examples.

... **negotiated by Wolfgang Schäuble** ... see Wolfgang Schäuble, *Der Vertrag. Wie ich über die deutsche Einheit verhandelte* (Stuttgart: Deutsche Verlags-Anstalt, 1991).

... **understanding/agreement/support** ... In the debate about the wording of the CDU's Wiesbaden resolution in 1988, the words used were first *Einverständnis* (agreement), then, in the final version, *Verständnis* (understanding) and *Unterstützung* (support), see above, p. 446–47. The German word used most often after unification was *Einvernehmen*, meaning general all-round agreement. In an article explicitly making the comparison with 1871, Wolfgang Bergsdorf writes of 'the agreement and support of all Europeans', *German Comments*, No. 26, April 1992, pp. 35–41, this on p. 41.

... **Bronisław Geremek** ... *Rok 1989. Bronisław Geremek Opowiada, Jacek Żakowski Pyta* (Warsaw: Plejada, 1990), p. 328.

... '**perhaps two and a half**' ... Hans-Dietrich Genscher, Bonn, 23 June 1992.

... **the American side of the story** ... beside the invaluable Szabo, *Diplomacy*, useful accounts are given by Elizabeth Pond, *After the Wall. American Policy toward Germany* (New York: Priority Press Publications, 1990) and Alexander Moens, 'American diplomacy and German unification' in *Survival*, Vol. XXXIII, No. 6, November/December 1991, pp. 531–45. See also Oberdorfer, *Turn* and Beschloss & Talbott, *Highest Levels*. Important details of the American role can also be gleaned from Teltschik, *329 Tage*.

... **Vernon Walters** ... Wolfgang Schäuble (Bonn, 17 March 1992) recalls Walters telling him on his arrival in Bonn in the late spring of 1989 that he would see German unification in his period as ambassador. Walters' memoirs will clearly be an important source.

... **Francis Fukuyama** ... Szabo, *Diplomacy*, p. 12.

... **instrumental in winning** ... ibid., pp. 24, 58 ff. See also the article by Elizabeth Pond in EA 21/1992, pp. 619–30.

... **the Nine Assurances** ... ibid., pp. 61–62, 86.

... **'see to it that no harm comes** ...' in his speech to a Central Committee plenum on 9 December, see Freedman, *Europe Transformed*, pp. 384–91, this on p. 385. Teltschik, *329 Tage*, p. 85, notes that Gorbachev subsequently wrote to Kohl emphasising this position 'in language tougher than the Central Committee speech'.

... **'quite impossible'** ... quoted from an interview on ARD television on 6 March in Teltschik, *329 Tage*, p. 168.

... **domestic political consumption** ... Gorbachev told François Mitterand in December 1989 that if Germany were to be reunited there would be a two-line announcement the next day, saying that a marshal had taken his place. He was exaggerating — but exaggerating a real danger, as the coup of August 1991 showed. ibid., p. 109.

... **matchless supremacy** ... in talking to Kohl in Moscow on 15 July, Gorbachev described the Party congress, in allusion to John Reed, as eleven days that shook the world, Teltschik, *329 Tage*, p. 325. Without this success in consolidating his power inside the system, it is very doubtful if he could have risked making such concessions as he did over German unification.

... **the published day-by-day account** ... Horst Teltschik emphasises, in response to a query from the author, that while the published version is closely based on his notes made at the time, and original documents, it only contains about half of his original rough diary.

... **a message** ... from Shevardnadze ... Teltschik, *329 Tage*, p. 100 ff.

... **52,000 tonnes of canned beef** ... ibid., p. 114.

... **an important and very specific signal** ... thus, also, Helmut Kohl, Bonn, 1 October 1991.

... **shape the last decade** ... Teltschik, *329 Tage*, p. 139.

According to Teltschik's Russian counterpart ... this in the lecture by Anatoly Chernyaev, printed in Gabriel Garodetsky, ed., *Soviet Foreign Policy, 1917–1992. A Retrospective* (London: Frank Cass, forthcoming). Chernyaev's direct quotations may be compared with the indirect quotations in Teltschik, *329 Tage*, p. 140.

... **a suggestion made** ... Boris Meissner ... ibid., p. 192.

... **'in the Bismarckian spirit'** ... ibid., p. 206.

... Shevardnadze directly confirmed ... ibid., p. 218 ff.

... a secret mission ... ibid., p. 230 ff.

While James Baker discussed ... ibid., p. 241 f.

Writing to Gorbachev ... ibid., p. 244.

... 'chess move' ... ibid., p. 325.

... the edited and then retranslated Russian record ... this in *Gipfelgespräche*, pp. 161–77. Note that this is a retranslation from the Russian record, which is presumably based on Chernyaev's notes, and perhaps those of the Russian interpreter. The account in Teltschik, *329 Tage*, is based on Teltschik's own notes, which he checked with those of the German interpreter, but unfortunately not quoted verbatim.

... 'we must turn to Europe ...' *Gipfelgespräche.*, p. 171.

... exchanging 'non-paper' drafts ... ibid., pp. 171–72.

... 'on the former territory ...' ibid., p. 175.

'The sovereignty of united Germany ...' ibid., p. 175.

... the security conditions ... summarised by Kohl in eight points on 16 July, and in ten on 17 July, see the statements to the press reprinted in EA 18/1990, pp. D480–90.

... 'Stavrapallo' ... The *Economist*, 21 July 1990. However, this article attributed the coinage to an East German official, and argued that the agreements did *not* add up to a Rapallo.

'We have acted ...' Gorbachev at the joint press conference on 16 July, EA, 18/1990, p. D481.

... eleven men in three capitals ... Szabo, *Diplomacy*, pp. 17 and 117 f.

'But,' he continued, ... *Gipfelgespräche*, p. 173.

'Genscher is mainly concerned ...' Teltschik, *329 Tage*, p. 339. This entry is perhaps not wholly without a touch of inter-departmental malice.

... diplomatic tactics ... for one observer's account of how the Polish Foreign Minister was actually treated at the Paris meeting see Ulrich Albrecht, *Die Abwicklung der DDR. Die "2+4 Verhandlungen". Ein Insider-Bericht* (Opladen: Westdeutscher Verlag, 1992), pp. 101–16. This and Szabo, *Diplomacy*, p. 72 ff make it clear that the Bush administration was rather impatient of Warsaw's specific diplomatic stance. Szabo quotes an American lawyer involved describing the Polish border issue as 'small potatoes'.

... 'sympathy' but ... Teltschik, *329 Tage*, p. 237

... the emotional decision ... 'Georgian games' Valentin Falin, Hamburg, 14 May 1992. Horst Teltschik (Bonn, 12 July 1991) notes that Falin was present at the Moscow meeting with Kohl in February, but no longer in the Caucasus. Clearly, the Georgian had won this particular game. This interpretation is confirmed by Falin's then deputy (and subsequently Gorbachev's spokesman) Andrei Grachev (Oxford, 24 January 1992).

. . . **haggled hard on the telephone** . . . Teltschik, *329 Tage*, pp. 359–62.

. . . **no less than four** . . . see Chancellor Kohl's statement on 12 September, in *Texte* III/8b, pp. 688–91. Negotiation of all four treaties only began after the Caucasus and Paris meetings in mid-July.

. . . **a last-minute British objection** . . . this concerned the possibility of Nato forces carrying out manoeuvres in East Germany. See FAZ, 14 September 1990, and the resulting *Protokollnotiz* in *Texte* III/8b, p. 678.

. . . **'the historic changes** . . .' text in *Texte* III/8b, pp. 672–78.

. . . **'Treaty on good-neighbourliness** . . .' text in *Texte* III/8b, pp. 851–59.

. . . **'finally to have done with the past** . . .' *mit der Vergangenheit endgültig abzuschliessen.*

. . . **'on several transitional measures'** . . . text in *Texte* III/8b, pp. 795–801.

. . . **terms on which the Soviet troops** . . . text in ibid., pp. 802–44.

. . . **'on the development of a comprehensive co-operation** . . .' see *Bundesgesetzblatt*, 1991, Teil 1, pp. 798–809.

Gorbachev concluded . . . text in *Texte* III/8b, pp. 848–51, this on p. 851.

. . . **Genscher would argue** . . . Hans-Dietrich Genscher, Bonn, 23 June 1992.

In July 1987, Gorbachev had said . . . see above p. 108.

In January 1989, Erich Honecker . . . this statement, made partly in response to criticism of the Wall at the Vienna Helsinki review conference, is reprinted in *Texte* III/8b, pp. 24–25, from ND, 20 January 1989.

. . . **Reiner Kunze** . . . in *Die Zeit*, 5 October 1990.

Chapter VIII: Findings

. . . **the most constructive answer** . . . Michael Stürmer in a seminar at St Antony's College, Oxford, 24 February 1989.

. . . **Vertrauenskapital** . . . see, for example, his Preface to *Deutsche Aussenpolitik 1990/91. Auf dem Weg zu einer europäischen Friedensordnung. Eine Dokumentation* (Bonn: Auswärtiges Amt, 1991), p. 7.

. . . **'the more European** . . . this in a speech in the National Library in Vienna on 14 September 1989, Der Bundesminister des Auswärtigen, Mitteilung fur die Presse Nr. 1134/89.

... **happily acknowledge** ... see the references on p. 441–42 above.

As with Stresemann ... I draw here on the work of my colleague Jonathan Wright, of Christ Church, Oxford, who is preparing a new biography of Stresemann. For further references see the note on p. 442 above.

... **an ongoing debate** ... a very useful introduction to the terms and assumptions of the debate within the academic subject of International Relations is Martin Hollis & Steven Smith, *Explaining and Understanding International Relations* (Oxford: Clarendon Press, 1990). The debate was much stimulated, particularly in the United States, by the end of the Cold War. See successive contributions to the journal *International Security*.

... **'complex interdependence'** ... thus Robert O Keohane & Joseph S Nye, *Power and Interdependence. World Politics in Transition* (Boston: Little, Brown, 1977).

... **Feindbilder** ... thus in June 1989 the West German Foreign Ministry actually organised a colloquium on the analysis and dismantling of enemy-images, and the resulting booklet went into a second edition in 1991 'on account of the strong demand'. See *Abbau von Feindbildern* (2nd edition, Bonn: Auswärtiges Amt, 1991).

In this rhetorical world ... on this see also Schwarz, *Gezähmten Deutschen, passim*.

... **more concretely directed** ... notable in this connection, beside the extensive public record, is a note made by Alois Mertes on 23 August 1983, summarising a conversation with Kohl. 'It was a political task of historic dimensions,' Mertes summarised Kohl's view, 'that the FR Germany should make a new attempt in the direction of European unification.' After noting that Kohl preferred the word 'unification' to the technocratic 'integration', Mertes continued: 'the revitalisation of national reunification must be joined by the revitalisation of European unification — both in line with Western ideas of personal human rights and national self-determination'. Note of 23 August 1983, in ACDP: I-403, A-000.

... **and cared as deeply** ... in his opening speech to the first sitting of the first freely elected Bundestag of united Germany, Brandt made a point of saying that the fulfilment of his political life would be the day when not just Germany but Europe was one. See *Bulletin*, 21 December 1990, pp. 1545–49, this on p. 1549.

When Helmut Schmidt says ... Schmidt, *Menschen und Mächte*, p. 11.

... **'for all the importance ...'** letter of 31 May 1976, quoted from the copy in AdsD: Dep EB, 409.

Vladimir Semyonov ... Köln, 21 March 1992.

... **paid fulsome tribute** ... *Texte* III/8b, p. 849.

... **'my friend Ronald Reagan'** ... quoted in the *Daily Telegraph*, 5 May 1992.

... **Pope John Paul II** ... quoted in *Der Spiegel*, 11/1992.

In outward discourse ... classic examples in the speeches on the day of German unity, 3 October 1990, reprinted in *Texte* III/8b, p. 698 ff.

... *Helsinkipolitik* ... see for example the interview in *Die Welt*, 7 February 1992.

... **'human rights motor'** ... this in his speech on receiving the Heine Prize on 13 December 1991, reprinted in *Bulletin*, 17 December 1991, pp. 1165–70, this on p. 1169.

... **'the favourable atmosphere** ...' Charter 77 Document No. 31, 1986, message to the participants of the Conference on Security and Co-operation in Vienna.

... **an internal memorandum** ... a copy of this memorandum, entitled 'Towards a new conception of Soviet-Central/East European Relations' (typescript, 26 pages) was kindly given me by Dr Marina Pavlova-Silvanskaya. Translation from the Russian by Tina Podplatnik.

... **the economic components of power** ... See the interesting reflections in Susan Strange, *States and Markets* (Pinter: London, 1988), and Joseph S Nye, *Bound to Lead. The Changing Nature of American Power* (New York: Basic Books, 1990).

... **at least since Ranke** ... see Hedley Bull, *The Anarchical Society. A Study of Order in World Politics* (London: Macmillan, 1977), p. 201 ff, and Martin Wight, *Power Politics* (Leicester: Leicester University Press, 1978), pp. 41–53, 295 f.

... **Paul Kennedy** ... *The Rise and Fall of the Great Powers. Economic Change and Military Conflict from 1500 to 2000* (New York: Random House, 1988). It is interesting to note how relatively little attention is paid specifically to the Federal Republic in Kennedy's last speculative chapter.

... **Bishop of East Berlin** ... Bishop Forck, quoted in FAZ, 23 April 1988.

... **'Whether Warsaw or Prague** ...' Brandt, *Erinnerungen*, p. 224.

... **Gyula Horn records** ... Horn, *Erinnerungen*, p. 308 ff.

According to Németh's recollection ... Miklós Németh, Oxford, 22 January 1991. See also Grosser, *Unification*, p. 9.

... **DM 1 billion** ... actually DM 500 million federal guarantees, and DM 250 million each from Baden-Württemberg and Bavaria. See report in FAZ, 9 October 1989.

'Do you realise ...' Horn, *Erinnerungen*, p. 322.

'The Germans ...' Dominique Moïsi, Jacques Rupnik, *Le Nouveau Continent. Plaidoyer pour une Europe renaissante* (Paris: Calmann-Lévy, 1991), p. 134.

... **an 'exemplary' or 'model' character** ... see, for example, the remarks by Hans-Dietrich Genscher in *Bundestag Plenarprotokolle* 9/49, pp. 2767–69.

... **a short leading article** ... *Die Zeit*, 10 August 1984. Volker Rühe had earlier talked of the two German states developing 'a German model for a real détente across the dividing system frontiers' in the INF deployment debate, see *Bundestag Plenarprotokolle*, 10/36, p. 2515 (22 November 1983). In his 1987 state of the nation address, Kohl referred to the hope of developing 'an exemplary co-operation' between the two states, see *Bundestag Plenarprotokolle*, 11/33, p. 2162 (15 October 1987).

... **one analyst has noted** ... Michael Wolffsohn, in EA, 7/1991, p. 211 ff, and in a lecture at St Antony's College, Oxford, 1 March 1991.

... *sterben für Danzig* ... Günter Gaus at a seminar in the Free University, West Berlin, 4 February 1987.

... *mourir pour Dantzig* ... this in his speech (read in his enforced absence) to mark the centenary of Marc Bloch. Quoted in Carole Fink, *Marc Bloch. A Life in History* (Cambridge: Cambridge University Press, 1989), p. 344.

... **his greatest satisfaction** ... thus already in a letter to Bruno Kreisky dated 1 November 1971, in AdsD: Dep WB, BK11.

... **Eugen Gerstenmaier** ... see his *Streit und Friede hat seine Zeit. Ein Lebensbericht* (Frankfurt: Propyläen, 1981), p. 422.

... **order** ... **an important value** ... see Hedley Bull, *The Anarchical Society. A Study of Order in World Politics* (London: Macmillan, 1977), p. 96 f and *passim*.

... *'Vous aimez l'ordre ...'* Thomas Mann, *Der Zauberberg*. The French philosopher André Gorz said something similar in an interview in *Der Spiegel*, 4/1982.

... **identification** ... **less complete** ... At the end of his 1989 *Erinnerungen*, p. 500, Brandt said the real satisfaction of his life was to have contributed to the fact that the name of Germany, the concept of peace *and the prospect of European freedom* are 'thought [of] together'. But this was more true of peace than of freedom.

... **'vulnerable to blackmail'** ... *Bergedorfer Gesprächskreis* 91 (7–8 October 1990), p. 16.

... **this getting on with all sides** ... the author has described Genscherism, in jest, as the attempt to have friendly relations with heaven, a deepening partnership with the earth, but also fruitful co-operation with hell.

... **patience was the strongest weapon** ... quoted by Klaus Gotto in his article 'Der Realist als Visionär', in *Die Politische Meinung*, Nr. 249, 1990, p. 6.

... **'German patriots in European responsibility'** ... Brandt, *Erinnerungen*, p. 331.

... **'reunification of Europe'** ... in Lutz, *Bahr*, pp. 249–51, Carl-Friedrich von Weizsäcker recalls an article he wrote in 1956 in which he argued that the reunification of Germany could only come as a consequence of the reunification of Europe, and if the reunification of Europe did not happen in the next three decades there would be war. 'Was I right?', he asks.

... **'under which we've lived quite happily'** ... see above, p. 2.

Epilogue: European Answers

In 1965, Konrad Adenauer ... Konrad Adenauer, *Erinnerungen 1945–1953* (Stuttgart: Deutsche Verlags-Anstalt, 1965), p. 13.

... *Historikerstreit* ... see the references given above, p. 541.

... *Literaturstreit* ... this began in 1990 with the publication of Christa Wolf's *Was bleibt?*, and raged in the feuilleton sections of the FAZ, *Die Zeit* and other journals. The issues are briefly discussed in English by J H Reid in *The New Germany. Volume 1: Divided or United by a Common European Culture?* (Glasgow: Goethe Institut, 1992), with further references.

... **agree with E H Carr** ... *What is History?* (London: Penguin, 1964), p. 108.

... **old books** ... see, for example, J A R Marriott, *The Eastern Question. An Historical Study in European Diplomacy* (Oxford: Clarendon Press, 1917; 4th edition, 1940), R. W. Seton-Watson, *Disraeli, Gladstone and the Eastern Question* (London: Macmillan, 1935; reprinted by Frank Cass & Co., 1971).

They'll come again ... from 'Tiananmen' in the song-cycle 'Out of the East'.

... **Kinkel, visited China** ... quotations are from *Der Spiegel*, 46/1992, *Die Zeit*, 6 November 1992, FAZ, 3 November 1992. See also the interview with Kinkel in *Rheinischer Merkur*, 6 November 1992. Obviously stung by the criticism, the Foreign Ministry let it be known in early 1993 that Kinkel's quiet diplomcy had resulted in the release of four human rights campaigners, FAZ, 2 February 1993. Once again, the echo of Ostpolitik is very strong. It was also suggested that there might be an official or semi-official German-Chinese symposium on human rights.

... **'equipped not with more power ...'** speech of 30 November 1990, reprinted in *Bulletin*, 5 December 1990, pp. 1485–89, this on p. 1485.

... **a new superpower** ... Antje Vollmer, quoted by Horst Teltschik in his own reflections on this subject in *German Comments*, 21/1991.

... **'world power against its will'** ... Christian Hacke, *Weltmacht wider Willen. Die Aussenpolitik der Bundesrepublik Deutschland* (Stuttgart: Klett-Cotta, 1988).

... **a new great power** ... thus Gregor Schöllgen, *Die Macht in der Mitte Europas. Stationen deutscher Aussenpolitik von Friedrich dem Grossen bis zur Gegenwart* (Munich: Beck, 1992), pp. 169, 177, 182.

... **a political scientist** ... Ludger Kühnhardt, in his inaugural lecture in the Albert-Ludwigs-Universität Freiburg, 27 November 1991, typescript, p. 16.

... 'we in West and Central Europe' ... quoted in *Der Spiegel*, 37/1991.

A leading contemporary historian ... Baring, *Deutschland*, p. 9.

A television newscaster ... this in the course of the ARD '*Tagesthemen*', 2 July 1991.

Another analyst recalled ... Reinhard Stuth in *Aussenpolitik* (English-language edition), 1/92, pp. 22–32, this on p. 22.

In an interview on Austrian television ... ORF, 27 March 1991.

... 'the Western powers' ... Johann Georg Reissmüller in FAZ, 11 January 1993. In German, he referred to them as *die westlichen Mächte* but also once as *die Westmächte*, the term previously used for the Western occupying powers in Germany and Berlin.

In a great symbolic decision ... see Helmut Herles, ed., *Die Hauptstadt-Debatte. Der Stenographische Bericht des Bundestages* (Bonn Berlin [!]: Bouvier, 1991).

... the predictions of the economists ... see, for example, Leslie Lipschitz & Donogh McDonald, ed., *German Unification. Economic Issues* (Washington: IMF Occasional Paper No. 75, 1990).

... tied to a certain level ... of prosperity ... for a stimulating general discussion of the connections between prosperity and democracy, see Samuel P Huntington, *The Third Wave. Democratisation in the Late Twentieth Century* (Norman: University of Oklahoma Press, 1991).

... it just might face such a test ... the general point has of course been made many times, but for the specific concern see, for example, the interview with Ralf Dahrendorf in *Der Spiegel*, 3/1993.

... Bundesbank ... A very striking critical analysis of the conduct of Bundesbank policy in 1992, by Ulrich Cartellieri, a director of the Deutsche Bank, is given in *Die Zeit*, 26 February 1993. Despite its somewhat sensational sub-title, David Marsh, *The Bundesbank. The Bank that Rules Europe* (London: Mandarin, 1993) is an excellent introduction.

... projected budget deficits ... the official projections in February 1993 were: DM 132.5 billion for 1993, DM 108 billion for 1994, DM 100 billion for 1995, and a mere DM 75 billion or 1996. These were the total budget deficits, that is, including federal, state, local government and the special funds for German unity. Information from the Federal Chancellery.

... total public debt ... The official projection in February 1993 was DM 1,504.5 billion. Again, this included federal, state and local government debt, and the inherited debts of the former GDR. Information from the Federal Chancellery. Writing in *Die Zeit*, 13 November 1992, Helmut Schmidt found it instructive to spell the figure out, thus: DM 1,500,000,000,000.

... some of the largest armed forces in Europe ... since most of the military powers in the world were engaged in intense discussion of how and how far to cut their conventional forces, no figures are reliable. According to *The Military Balance 1992–1993* (London: Brassey's for the IISS, 1992) the total armed forces of Germany in mid-1992 were 447,000, compared with 431,700 for France and 293,500 for Britain (although the British army was of course a professional, not a conscript army). For very crude comparison: the United States had 1,913,750 on active service, and some 2 million in reserve, Russia some 2,720,000 on active service, and some 3 million in reserve, Turkey had a conscript army of 560,300, with more than 1 million reserves. The July 1992 final agreement of the negotiations on conventional force numbers in Europe (begun in Vienna in January 1989 — see above, p.265), set targets for 'land-based military personnel' (that is, army and air force) *in Europe* of 1,450,000 for Russia, 530,000 for Turkey, 450,000 for Ukraine, 345,000 for Germany, 325,000 for France, 315,000 for Italy, 260,000 for Britain, and 250,000 for the United States. See *Bulletin*, 17 July 1992, pp. 753–59. However, in early 1993 it appeared that leading Nato states might actually cut their forces still further, although perhaps at the same time making them more professional. See, for example, report by Michael Binyon in *The Times*, 10 February 1993.

. . . **more than $6,500 million** . . . this figure is given in a valuable article by Ronald Asmus, 'Germany and America: Partners in leadership?', in *Survival*, Vol. XXXIII, No. 6, November/December 1991, pp. 546–66, this on pp. 554–55. According to the official US government figures, this was 12.2 per cent of the financial contributions, compared to 18.7 per cent from Japan.

. . . **attractiveness** . . . magnetism . . . Joseph S Nye has tagged this 'soft power', see his *Bound to Lead. The Changing Nature of American Power* (New York: Basic Books, 1990), pp. 31–32.

. . . **'too big to play no role . . .'** see above, p. 54 and the corresponding note.

. . . **Henry Kissinger** . . . in conversation with the author, Berlin, 29 June 1991.

'Germany has become a normal state . . .' quoted from *Bergedorfer Gesprächskreis* 91 (7–8 October 1990), p. 16.

. . . **'normalisation' of German foreign policy** . . . this in a speech on 5 October 1992, devoted to the 'guiding principles of the foreign policy of united Germany', reprinted in *Bulletin*, 7 October 1992, pp. 1011–15.

. . . **it was argued** . . . notably in the FAZ. As the path to the new Ostpolitik was beaten by 'published opinion' in the 1960s, notably in the Hamburg journals of the centre-left, above all *Die Zeit* and *Der Spiegel*, so it now seemed possible that the path to some of the new directions of German foreign policy was again being beaten by 'published opinion', but this time perhaps more of the centre-right, and above all by the FAZ. For the arguments for and against Bonn and Berlin see Alois Rummel, ed., *Bonn. Sinnbild deutscher Demokratie* (Bonn: Bouvier, 1990) and Helmut Herles, ed., *Die Hauptstadt-Debatte. Der Stenographische Bericht des Bundestags* (Bonn Berlin [!]: Bouvier, 1991).

. . . **by intellectuals of the centre-left** . . . Jürgen Habermas went so far to define the idea that Germany was again 'normal' as the 'second life-lie of the

Federal Republic'. According to Habermas, the first life-lie had not been (as Willy Brandt had suggested) that of *re*unification, but rather the claim in the Adenauer that 'we are all democrats'. See *Die Zeit*, 11 December 1992. See also the article by Peter Glotz in NG, 9/1991, pp. 823–26.

... **Hans-Peter Schwarz** ... *Rheinischer Merkur*, 7 September 1990.

... **Nietzsche's famous dictum** ... in *Jenseits von Gut und Böse*, §. 244.

'Germany is our fatherland ...' this in his government declaration of 30 January 1991, published as *Deutschlands Einheit vollenden. Die Einheit Europas gestalten. Dem Frieden der Welt dienen. Regierungspolitik 1991–1994* (Bonn: Presse- und Informationsamt der Bundesregierung, 1991), p. 78.

... **'the political unification** ...' ibid., p. 86.

'The *Staatsräson* of a united Germany ...' Wolfgang Bergsdorf in Grosser, *Unification*, p. 106.

... **amended in December 1992** ... report and text in FAZ, 3 December 1992. But note that as this book went to press these changes were being challenged in the Federal Constitutional Court.

'Maastricht,' said President von Weizsäcker ... article in FAZ, 13 April 1992, also reprinted in *Bulletin*, 15 April 1992, pp. 385–86.

... **'European century'** ... speech in honour of the President of Bulgaria, 2 September 1991, reprinted in *Bulletin*, 10 September 1991, pp. 769–70.

... **General Naumann, said** ... interview on ZDF, 6 October 1991.

... **'German and European** ...' speech of 20 December 1990, reprinted in *Bulletin*, 21 December 1990, pp. 1545–49.

... **asked by a weekly newspaper** ... *Rheinischer Merkur*, 28 December 1990.

... **'no single national, German** ...' quoted from the transcript of the Berlin Colloquium convened by Lord Weidenfeld, Berlin and Potsdam, 28–30 June 1991, this on p. 83.

... **'does not want more power** ...' *Kanzler-Kinderfest-Zeitung*, 26 June 1991.

As Henry Kissinger observed ... *White House Years*, pp. 410–11.

... **talking to students in Hamburg** ... Thomas Mann, *Schriften zur Politik* (Frankfurt: Suhrkamp, 1973), pp. 204–206.

... **J P Stern wrote** ... see his *The Heart of Europe. Essays on Literature and Ideology* (Oxford: Blackwell, 1992), p. 3.

'The evil Germany ...' this in his lecture on 'Germany and the Germans', reprinted in Thomas Mann, *Schriften zur Politik* (Frankfurt: Suhrkamp, 1973), pp. 162–183.

'There are a number of things ...' William Hazlitt, 'On Cant and Hypocrisy', in *Sketches and Essays* (Oxford: Oxford University Press, 1902), this on p.26.

. . . a value in itself . . . see his celebrated essay 'A Kidnapped West or Culture Bows Out' in *Granta* 11, pp. 95–118.

. . . '*qui parle Europe a tort* . . .' this was a marginal comment on a letter from the Russian Chancellor, Gorchakev, in November 1876, see Johannes Lepsivs & ors, eds, *Die Grosse Politik der Europäischen Kabinette 1871–1914* (Vol. 2, Berlin: Deutsche Verlagsgesellschaft für Politik und Geschichte, 1922) No. 255, p. 87.

Thomas Mann . . . an Oxford audience . . . this in a lecture for the Goethe anniversary celebrations, 'Goethe and Democracy', reprinted in Thomas Mann, *Goethes Laufbahn als Schriftsteller. Zwölf Essays und Reden* (Frankfurt: Fischer Taschenbuch, 1982), pp. 283–308, this on p. 285.

. . . wild Irish and Spanish . . . the Irish reference was an article by Conor Cruise O'Brien in *The Times*, 31 October 1989, the Spanish, a book published in Germany: Heleno Saña, *Das vierte Reich. Deutschlands später Sieg* (Hamburg: Rasch & Röhring, 1990).

. . . 'which is bound to democratic . . .' quoted from text in FAZ, 3 December 1992.

'At the end of this decade . . .' this in his New Year's speech for 1992, printed in *Bulletin*, 3 January 1992, pp. 1–2.

'Now we must put Europe . . .' *Die Zeit*, 21 September 1990.

. . . the values of the West . . . easier to define . . . which is not, of course, to suggest that they are *easy* to define. Interestingly, at their Malta meeting in December 1989, Gorbachev, Yakovlev, Bush and Baker had a little discussion about whether 'Western values' are actually *Western* values, or just 'democratic', 'humanist' or 'all-human' ones. See *Gipfelgespräche*, p. 128 f.

. . . done extremely well out of the EC . . . a stimulating discussion of this is the article by Andrei S Markovits and Simon Reich in *German Politics and Society*, Issue 23, Summer 1991, pp. 1–20.

Chancellor Kohl declared that . . . see his lecture at St Antony's College, Oxford, on 11 November 1992, published as Helmut Kohl, *United Germany in a Uniting Europe* (Oxford: St Antony's College & the Konrad Adenauer Foundation, n.d.), this on p. 2. German text in *Bulletin*, 25 November 1992, pp. 1141–45, this on p. 1141.

. . . aggregated the sacred egoisms . . . interestingly, Kohl himself hinted at this point in the same lecture, ibid., p. 9. In German text, p. 1144.

. . . the aim of German foreign policy . . . this at the second Berlin Colloquium convened by Lord Weidenfeld, 26–28 June 1992.

Helmut Kohl saw . . . a European roof . . . Helmut Kohl, Bonn, 1 October 1991.

. . . Mitterrand expanded on his vision . . . Teltschik, *329 Tage*, p. 208.

. . . **scribbled by Churchill for Adenauer** . . . see Konrad Adenauer, *Erinnerungen 1945–1953* (Stuttgart: Deutsche Verlags-Anstalt, 1987), p. 512.

. . . **concentric** . . . the image of concentric circles had first been given wide currency by an article by two advisers to Chancellor Kohl, Michael Mertes and Norbert Prill, in FAZ, 19 July 1989. It is reprinted in Michael Mertes & ors, *Europa ohne Kommunismus. Zusammenhänge, Aufgaben, Perspektiven* (Bonn: Europa Union Verlag, 1990).

. . . **European Communities** . . . then still really in the plural. Readers will recall that the European Coal and Steel Community, Euratom and the European Economic Community were only merged in 1967.

. . . **Kohl once described Mainz** . . . this in welcoming George Bush to the Rheingoldhalle in Mainz on 31 May 1989, see *Vierzig Jahre*, p. 586.

When Mitterrand launched . . . in Prague, 12–14 June 1991. The author was one of those invited to participate in this curious event.

. . . **a large map** . . . the map was a rather ingenious design showing Europe as the yellow foliage of a tree emerging from a blue tree trunk. The shade of yellow in the further eastern parts was, however, somewhat lighter — perhaps the Czech input to the design?

Josef Joffe summed it up . . . this also at the Berlin Colloquium, 26–28 June 1992.

Kohl identified two great tasks . . . speech to the International Bertelsmann Forum, 3 April 1992, printed in *Bulletin*, pp. 353–56, this on p. 353.

. . . *Kleineuropa* as *Kerneuropa* . . . for a stimulating treatment of these issues see Ludger Kühnhardt, *Europäische Union und föderale Idee. Europapolitik in der Umbruchzeit* (Munich: Beck, 1993 = *Schriftenreihe des Bundeskanzleramtes*, Band 14). Interesting remarks can also be found in Peter van Ham, *The EC, Eastern Europe and European Unity. Discord, Collaboration and Integration since 1947* (London: Pinter, 1993).

. . . **'Ostpolitik mark-two'** . . . The *Economist*, 29 February 1992.

. . . **'a moving moment'** . . . this and the following quotations from Kohl's statement in the Bundestag on 4 September 1991, reprinted in *Bulletin*, 5 September 1991, pp. 749–752.

. . . **the dramatic headline figures** . . . in September 1992, the government spokesman announced that some DM 80 billion had been provided since the end of 1989. But of this, more than DM 19 billion was directly related to unification (see the chapter on unification above), more than DM 17 billion was exports from the former GDR which had been paid for in transferable roubles, more than DM 28 billion was for export credit guarantees, and DM 2.9 billion costs for financing oil and natural gas investment projects. Figures taken from the overview provided in *Report from the Federal Republic of Germany*, 118/92.

. . . **in terms of direct grants and aid** . . . the point is made by Ronald Asmus in *Survival*, Vol. XXXIII, No. 6, November/December 1991, pp. 546–66, this on p. 560.

... **Kohl agreed with Yeltsin** ... report in FAZ, 17 December 1992.

... **Hans-Dietrich Genscher called** ... in *Welt am Sonntag*, 10 January 1992.

... **an** *Ukrainepolitik* ... on Foreign Minister Kinkel's first visit to Ukraine, see reports in FAZ, 17 February 1993.

... **Yugoslavia** ... this deserves a longer treatment. A good short discussion is given by Harald Müller in Stares, *New Germany*, pp. 150–54.

... **according to a credible source** ... private information to the author

... **proceeded to do so itself** ... see the statement by the government spokesman on 19 December 1991, printed in *Bulletin*, 21 December 1991, p. 1183.

... **public and especially published opinion** ... Germany also now had its equivalent of the 'ethnic lobbies' in the United States: in this case, some half a million Croats. See again Harald Müller in Stares, *New Germany*, p. 153. It is interesting to find that (in more general terms) Genscher mentioned the influence of this lobby in a speech calling for 'self-determination' for the Yugoslav republics, reprinted in *Das Parlament*, 15/22 November 1991.

... **250,000 refugees.** ... figures from the UN High Commissioner for Refugees and Federal Interior Ministry

... **Helsinki process** ... **golden bridge** ... see the Foreign Ministry documentation, *Deutsche Aussenpolitik 1990/91. Auf dem Weg zu einer europäischen Friedensordnung* (Bonn: Auswärtiges Amt, 1991). Dieter Kastrup, Bonn, 18 March 1992.

... **'Visegrád three'** ... this referred to the Visegrád Declaration following the trilateral Polish-Hungarian-Czechoslovak summit at Visegrád in February 1991.

... **the bilateral treaties** ... the texts of these are conveniently collected in EA, 10/1992, pp. D369–402, with that with Poland in EA, 13/1991, pp. D310 ff.

... **a Polish quality newspaper** ... leading article in *Obserwator codzienny*, 14 February 1992.

... **the negotiation** ... **with Czechoslovakia** ... Harald Müller in Stares, *New Germany*, pp. 148–50, once again gives a useful succinct account, and further references. Jiří Gruša, Bonn, 20 March 1991.

... **'see a future ...'** thus in his speech of 4 September 1991, *Bulletin*, 5 September 1991, p. 750.

... **the numbers of out-settlers from Poland** ... see Table IX.

... **as Hans Magnus Enzensberger** ... see his *Die Grosse Wanderung. 33 Markierungen* (Frankfurt: Suhrkamp, 1992), pp. 25–27.

... **the total numbers** ... figures and detailed explanation from the Federal Ministry of the Interior.

. . . **agreement was reached** . . . this paragraph is based on the text of the so-called 'asylum compromise' of 6 December 1992. The final law and administrative solutions might therefore be somewhat different.

. . . **European burden-sharing** . . . the phrase *eine europäische Lastenverteilung* actually appeared in the text of the 'asylum compromise'.

. . . **'the *völkisch* worm'** . . . this in FAZ Magazin, 29 January 1993.

'That only those . . .' ibid.

. . . **Richard Schröder** . . . see his article in *Die Zeit*, 22 January 1993.

. . . **state-nation** . . . that is, one in which belonging to the nation is defined by being a citizen of the state, rather than vice versa. The classic example is, of course, the United States. To some extent, however, this is also true of Britain. 'British nationals', in the language of the Home Office, are actually English, Scottish, Welsh, Irish, and now also often of Asian or Caribbean descent, heritage and tradition. But this is not for a moment to underestimate the immense difficulty of combining a heterogeneous 'multi-cultural' society with a strong, democratic state and the rule of (one) law, as the Rushdie affair in Britain and countless examples in the contemporary United States go to show. In the relative success of these examples of state-nations there clearly has been a strong element of homogenisation by one dominant culture, one language, one set of institutions and traditions: English, the flag and the constitution in the United States; English, parliament and the monarchy in Britain. Eugen Weber's study of 'Peasants into Frenchman' shows how there is a real sense in which in France, too, the state created the nation, rather than vice versa.

. . . **not so restrained** . . . see, for example, the reports in *Der Spiegel* 24/1991 and 45/1992. The former report is sensationally entitled 'We want *Anschluss*'. However, the actual quotation in the text is 'we want to join Europe, to join progress' (*wir wollen Anschluss an Europa, Anschluss an den Fortschritt*).

Hartmut Koschyk . . . see his article in *German Comments* No. 26, April 1992, pp. 19–25, this on p. 25.

. . . **investment** . . . figures given by specialists at a conference organised by the Konrad Adenauer Foundation in Oxford, July 1992. In response to an enquiry from the author in April 1993, the German Foreign Ministry gave a significantly lower estimate: 37 per cent for the Czech Republic, 20 per cent for Poland, 18 per cent for Hungary.

. . . **Andrzej Szczypiorski** . . . quoted in Baring, *Deutschland*, pp. 103–04.

'Nothing might do greater harm . . .' Wiskemann, *Eastern Neighbours*, p. 295.

. . . **'the good traditions . . .'** see the treaty texts in EA, 13/1991, D310 ff, and EA, 10/1992, D369–402.

. . . **German studies** . . . poisoned chalice . . . see Burleigh, *Ostforschung*, passim.

... the territory of political science ... interesting discussion on the state of Soviet and East European studies in the Federal Republic could be found in the journal *Osteuropa*.

... 'the German-settled or German-permeated ...' quoted from the publisher's brochure for this *Deutsche Geschichte im Osten Europas. Eine Bilanz in 10 Bänden* (Siedler Verlag).

... 'again the hegemonial power ... leading power' Baring, *Deutschland*, p. 83.

... 'regaining her traditional role' ... ibid., p. 84.

'Bohemia and Moravia ...' ibid., p. 92.

'supremacy' ... 'key role' ... 'of course ...' ibid., pp. 105–06.

... 'cautiously and yet energetically ..' ibid., p. 106.

... 'colonisation task ...' ibid., p. 70.

... 'these, if you like, common territories' ... ibid., p. 40.

As early as 1988 ... see the report in *Frankfurter Rundschau*, 13 September 1989 and the interview with Christians in SZ, 27 September 1989. By Christians' own account, he first raised the subject in talks with the Soviet prime minister Nikolai Ryzhkov and Eduard Shevardnadze in March 1988. In this interview, he also supported the idea of resettling in the Kaliningrad region some of the ethnic Germans from other areas of the (then still) Soviet Union. In his preface to Christians, *Wege*, August Count von Kageneck summarises the basic idea of his friend Christians' proposal for the 'Baltic region K' (*Ostseeregion K*) as being to combine 'Russian workforce and German organisational talent' (quotation on p. 14).

... 'A Task called Königsberg' ... FAZ, 26 September 1992. There the following quotations.

Writing in *Die Zeit* ... 15 November 1991.

... 'One day the Germans ...' Winston S Churchill, *The Second World War. Volume VI: Triumph and Tragedy* (London: Cassell, 1954), p. 561.

... 'a good chunk of Silesia ...' this in *Die Zeit*, 9 February 1990.

... 'Centre of Lower Silesia' ... *Financial Times*, 26 October 1992.

'To be sure,' he replied ... the story is told in an 'Editorial' by Johannes Hampel in *Politische Studien*, Nr. 284, November/December 1985.

'Our time,' he wrote ... the message was addressed to the Socialist International, on his retirement from the Presidency. Text in FAZ, 16 September 1992.

... what the historian Fritz Stern has called ... this now well-known observation was made as part of the attempt by several historians, including the author of this book, to clarify what actually happened at a seminar of specialists on Germany convened by Mrs Thatcher at the Prime Minister's country residence of Chequers in March 1990. These are usefully reprinted, together with a number of other interesting observations by other historians, in Udo Wengst, ed., *Historiker betrachten Deutschland. Beiträge zum Vereinigungsprozess und zur Hauptstadtdiskussion (Februar 1990–Juni 1991)* (Bonn Berlin: Bouvier, 1992), with Stern's on pp. 139–43.

... **had also to look south** ... this is, however, definitely not to say that any of Germany's West European partners (or eastern neighbours) would be happy with the 'European division of labour' suggested at the end of Christians, *Wege*, p. 250, with Britons responsible for looking after 'the American cousins, the French and Italians for the African neighbours, Spaniards and Portuguese for their descendants in Latin America, and the Germans for Central and Eastern Europe'!

... **lacked the 'internationalist élite'** ... thus Robert Gerald Livingston in *Foreign Policy*, No. 87, Summer 1992, pp. 157–74, this on p. 172.

'I have the impression ...' interview in *Die Zeit — Magazin*, 17 July 1992.

... **in an inaugural lecture** ... Ludger Kühnhardt, inaugural lecture in the Albert-Ludwigs-Universität, Freiburg, 27 November 1991, typescript, this on p. 18.

Chronology

This chronology includes events that were relevant to the development of German Ostpolitik, of East-West relations in Europe more generally, and of the European Community. The terms 'Federal Republic' and 'West Germany' are used interchangeably, as are the terms 'GDR' and 'East Germany'. The label 'German-German' is applied, for the period 1970 to 1990, to talks or agreements between East Germany and West Germany, including those relating to West Berlin. Where reference is made to 'German-Soviet', 'German-Hungarian' etc, the word 'German' refers to the Federal Republic.

1945

4–11 February	Yalta Conference.
17 July–12 August	Potsdam Conference.
13 August	Russian agreement to final protocol of European Advisory Commission on division of Germany into occupation zones and Berlin into sectors.

1946

22 April	Forced merger of Social Democrats (SPD) with Communists (KPD) in Soviet occupation zone to form SED.

1948

24 June	Start of Soviet blockade of Berlin.

1949

25 January	Comecon founded.
4 April	Nato founded.
12 May	End of the Berlin blockade.
23 May	Basic Law of the Federal Republic of Germany promulgated: Founding of West Germany.
14 August	First election to Bundestag.
15 September	Konrad Adenauer elected first Chancellor.

21 September	Occupation statute for West Germany comes into force.
7 October	Constitution of the German Democratic Republic promulgated: Founding of East Germany.

1950

6 July	GDR recognises Oder-Neisse line: 'Görlitz Agreement'.
8 July	Federal Republic becomes associate member of Council of Europe.
5 August	Charter of the Germans expelled from Eastern and East Central Europe: 'Stuttgart Charter'.

1951

15 March	Establishment of the *Auswärtiges Amt*, the West German Foreign Ministry.
18 April	Founding of the European Coal and Steel Community.
20 September	Interzonal Trade Agreement between West and East German authorities.

1952

10 March	Soviet Union offers Western allies terms for a peace treaty with Germany: the 'Stalin Note'.
26 May	Signature in Bonn of *Deutschlandvertrag* (or 'General Treaty') with Western allies, linked to:
27 May	Signature of European Defence Community Treaty in Paris.
14 August	Federal Republic becomes member of IMF and World Bank.

1953

5 March	Death of Stalin.
17 June	Popular rising in East Germany.

1954

25 January–18 February	Berlin Conference of the foreign ministers of the Four Powers.
30 August	French National Assembly rejects European Defence Community.
23 October	Signature of 'Paris Treaties' including revised version of 1952 *Deutschlandvertrag*, linked to West German membership in Nato and West European Union.

1955

25 January	Soviet Union declares itself no longer in a state of war with Germany.
5 May	Paris Treaties come into force: the Federal Republic's 'Day of Sovereignty'.
9 May	Federal Republic accepted into Nato.
14 May	Founding of Warsaw Pact, including GDR.
15 May	State Treaty gives Austria independence on condition of neutrality.
17–23 July	Geneva Conference.
9–14 September	Adenauer in Moscow. Diplomatic relations established between Federal Republic and Soviet Union.
17–20 September	GDR premier Otto Grotewohl in Moscow. GDR given greater 'sovereignty'.
8–9 December	Introduction of so-called 'Hallstein Doctrine' in West German foreign policy.

1956

18 January	Creation of National People's Army out of Garrisoned People's Police in the GDR.
14–25 February	20th congress of the Communist Party of the Soviet Union: 'De-Stalinisation'.
19 March	General conscription introduced in the Federal Republic.
October–November	'Polish October' and Hungarian Revolution. Soviet invasion of Hungary.

1957

25 March	Signature of Rome Treaties (EEC and Euratom).
2 October	Polish Foreign Minister Adam Rapacki announces at the UN his plan for nuclear weapon-free zone in Central Europe: the 'Rapacki Plan'.
19 October	Federal Republic breaks diplomatic relations with Yugoslavia on basis of 'Hallstein Doctrine'.

1958

19 March	In conversation with the Soviet Ambassador to Bonn, Konrad Adenauer suggests an 'Austrian solution' for the GDR.
25 April	German-Soviet Trade Agreement, and agreement on repatriation of German citizens from the Soviet Union, signed during vist of Soviet deputy prime minister Mikoyan to Bonn.
10–27 November	Khrushchev's Berlin Ultimatum: Soviet Union

demands status of demilitarised Free City for West Berlin.

1959

10 January	Soviet proposal for a peace treaty with two German states.
18 March	SPD *Deutschlandplan.*
20 March	FDP *Deutschlandplan.*
May–August	Geneva Conference of foreign ministers of Four Powers, attended by delegations from Federal Republic and GDR. Western allies propose 'Herter Plan' for German unification.
13–15 November	SPD agrees 'Godesberg Programme'.

1960

30 June	In a Bundestag speech by Herbert Wehner, SPD expresses acceptance of the Federal Republic's integration in Nato and EEC as basis for future policy.
31 December	Signature of German-Soviet Trade Agreement in Bonn.

1961

14 June	All-party Bundestag resolution (based on so-called 'Jaksch reports') urges more active West German Ostpolitik.
13 August	GDR begins construction of Berlin Wall.
7 November	Konrad Adenauer elected Chancellor for fourth time. Gerhard Schröder (CDU) is new Foreign Minister.

1962

28 February	Publication of the Tübingen Memorandum by eight leading West German Protestants, suggesting abandonment of Hallstein Doctrine and recognition of the Oder-Neisse line.
22 March	Wolfgang Schollwer's first working paper on the Deutschlandpolitik of the Free Democrats.
6 June	Adenauer suggests to Soviet Union a ten-year 'truce' on the German Question.
17 August	Peter Fechter bleeds to death at the foot of the Berlin Wall.
October	Cuban missile crisis.
18 December	Federal Republic joins Nato pipeline embargo, breaking contracts with Soviet Union.

1963

22 January	Adenauer and de Gaulle sign Treaty on Franco-German Co-operation: the 'Élysée Treaty'.
7 March	West Germany agrees opening of trade missions with Poland.
11 March	Willy Brandt forms social-liberal (SPD-FDP) coalition government in West Berlin.
10 June	Kennedy proclaims 'strategy of peace' at American University in Washington.
23–26 June	Kennedy in Berlin delivers Free University lecture applying the 'strategy of peace' to Germany and city hall speech: *Ich bin ein Berliner*.
15 July	Willy Brandt and Egon Bahr speak at Evangelical Academy in Tutzing. Bahr's 'Tutzing speech' proclaims *Wandel durch Annäherung*.
15–16 October	Adenauer resigns after fourteen years as Chancellor. Ludwig Erhard elected to succeed him.
17 October	West Germany agrees opening of trade missions with Romania.
10 November	West Germany agrees opening of trade missions with Hungary.
17 December	First 'permit agreement' between West Berlin city government and East German authorities, allows West Berliners to visit relatives in East Berlin for Christmas and New Year holidays.

1964

6 March	West Germany agrees opening of trade missions with Bulgaria.
12 June	Treaty of Friendship, Co-operation and Mutual Assistance between Soviet Union and GDR.
14 October	Fall of Khrushchev. Leonid Brezhnev is new party leader, Alexei Kosygin is prime minister.
25 November	Introduction of compulsory exchange of hard currency for West German visitors to the GDR.

1965

8 April	Treaty on the fusion of European Coal and Steel Community, EEC and Euratom into single EC (effective 1 July 1967).
15 October	Memorandum of the Protestant Church in Germany (EKD) on 'the situation of the expellees and the relationship of the German people to its eastern neighbours'.

18 November	Message of the Polish Catholic bishops to their German counterparts: 'we forgive and ask for forgiveness'.

1966

25 March	Federal Republic sends 'Peace Note' to all states, including those in Eastern Europe, but not the GDR.
21 June–1 July	De Gaulle in Russia.
29 June	SED calls off proposed 'exchange of speakers' with SPD.
4–6 July	Bucharest Declaration of Warsaw Pact.
6 October	End of 'permit agreements' in Berlin, leaving only 'hardship post' for urgent family matters.
1 December	Grand Coalition (CDU/CSU-SPD) government formed in Bonn, with Kurt-Georg Kiesinger (CDU) as Chancellor and Willy Brandt (SPD) as Foreign Minister and Deputy Chancellor.
13 December	Chancellor Kiesinger's government declaration.

1967

31 January	Federal Republic opens diplomatic relations with Romania.
8–10 February	Warsaw Pact foreign ministers agree not to open diplomatic ties with the Federal Republic until it recognises the GDR: the 'Ulbricht Doctrine'.
3 March	Wolfgang Schollwer (FDP) produces another working paper proposing a major change in Deutschlandpolitik.
15 March	Poland signs friendship treaty with GDR.
17 March	Czechoslovakia signs friendship treaty with GDR.
12 April	Chancellor Kiesinger's government declaration on Deutschlandpolitik.
24–26 April	Karlovy Vary (Karlsbad) Conference of European communist parties.
18 May	Hungary signs friendship treaty with GDR.
May–September	Exchange of letters between Chancellor Kiesinger and GDR Prime Minister Willi Stoph.
17 June	Chancellor Kiesinger's speech on the 'day of German unity'.
3 August	Federal Republic agrees opening of trade missions with Czechoslovakia.
7 September	Bulgaria signs friendship treaty with GDR.

1967 *continued*

12 October	Beginning of diplomatic exchanges between Bonn and Moscow on possible renunciation-of-force agreements.
November	Egon Bahr becomes head of planning staff in West German Foreign Office.
6–12 December	De Gaulle in Poland.
14 December	Nato agrees Harmel report.

1968

29–31 January	FDP party conference elects Walter Scheel as party leader.
31 January	Diplomatic relations with Yugoslavia restored, puncturing 'Hallstein Doctrine'.
11 March	Chancellor Kiesinger delivers first annual 'Report on the state of the nation in divided Germany'.
17–21 March	SPD party conference in Nuremberg.
March–April	Repression of student protests in Poland. Anti-semitic campaign and purge.
11 June	GDR imposes visa obligation for travellers in transit between West Berlin and West Germany.
25 June	Nato proposes mutual balanced force reductions: the 'Reykjavik signal'.
11 July	Soviet Union breaks off talks on renunciation-of-force agreement with Federal Republic.
21 August	Warsaw Pact invasion of Czechoslovakia. End of 'Prague Spring'.

1969

20 January	Beginning of Nixon administration in USA, with Henry Kissinger as National Security Advisor.
2 March	Clashes between Soviet and Chinese border troops on the Ussuri.
17 March	Budapest Appeal of Warsaw Pact.
28 April	Soviet Foreign Trade Minister visits Hanover Trade Fair, and meets West German Economics Minister. Announcement of first German-Soviet natural gas pipeline deal since 1962 embargo.
10 June	Federation of Protestant Churches in the GDR begins its work.
3 July	Soviet Union and Federal Republic resume diplomatic exchanges on renunciation-of-force agreements.
24–25 July	FDP leader Walter Scheel in Moscow, with a delegation including Hans-Dietrich Genscher.

20–23 August	SPD parliamentary leader Helmut Schmidt with a delegation in Moscow.
12 September	Soviet diplomatic notes to Western allies suggesting negotiations about Berlin, and to the Bonn government suggesting negotiations in Moscow on renunciation-of-force agreement.
28 September	Elections to 6th Bundestag. CDU/CSU win 242 seats, SPD 224, FDP 30, thus giving SPD and FDP the chance to form a coalition with a majority of twelve.
21 October	Willy Brandt forms social-liberal (SPD-FDP) coalition government, with Walter Scheel as Foreign Minister.
28 October	Chancellor Brandt's government declaration.
17 November	USA and Soviet Union begin preliminary talks on strategic arms limitation (SALT).
28 November	Federal Republic accedes to Nuclear Non-Proliferation Treaty.
1–2 December	EC summit in The Hague. Resolutions on economic and currency union and foreign policy co-operation.
18 December	In a letter to Federal President Heinemann, Walter Ulbricht proposes negotiations on opening relations between the GDR and the Federal Republic.

1970

30 January	Egon Bahr begins talks in Moscow with Soviet Foreign Minister Andrei Gromyko.
1 February	Signature in Essen of German-Soviet natural gas pipeline agreement.
5 February	Ferdinand Duckwitz begins talks in Warsaw with Polish Deputy Foreign Minister.
19 March	Willy Brandt meets GDR Prime Minister Willi Stoph in Erfurt, East Germany.
26 March	Beginning of four-power negotiations on Berlin.
16 April	Beginning of Soviet-American SALT talks.
21 May	Willy Brandt and GDR Prime Minister Willi Stoph meet in Kassel, West Germany. Brandt offers his '20 Points'.
26–27 May	Nato meeting in Rome reviews state of bi- and multilateral East-West negotiations.
1 July	Confidential 'Bahr-paper' summarising results of German-Soviet talks is published in German press.

1970 *continued*

26 July–7 August	Walter Scheel negotiates final details of Moscow Treaty.
12 August	Signature of Moscow Treaty. Scheel hands Gromyko 'Letter on German Unity'.
3–13 November	Walter Scheel negotiates final form of Warsaw Treaty and 'Information' on German minority in Poland.
19 November	First meeting of EC foreign ministers for European Political Co-operation (EPC), in Munich.
27 November	Opening of German-German negotiations between Egon Bahr and State Secretary Michael Kohl.
7 December	Signature of Warsaw Treaty. Willy Brandt kneels at the memorial to the heroes of the Warsaw ghetto.
20 December	Strikes and protest demonstrations in Poland's Baltic ports lead to resignation of Party leader Władysław Gomułka. He is succeeded by Edward Gierek.

1971

26 February	Social Democrats pass 'demarcation resolution', defining their differences with Communism.
3 May	Walter Ulbricht replaced by Erich Honecker as East German party leader.
15–19 June	8th party congress of the SED.
3 September	Signature of Quadripartite Agreement on Berlin.
16–18 September	Brandt meets Brezhnev at Oreanda in the Crimea.
30 September	German-German agreement on post and telephone links, complementing Quadripartite Agreement on Berlin.
20 October	Brandt awarded Nobel Peace Prize.
17 December	German-German Transit Agreement, complementing Quadripartite Agreement on Berlin.

1972

23 February	Beginning of Bundestag debates on the Moscow and Warsaw treaties.
29 March	For the first time in nearly six years ordinary West Berliners are allowed to visit East Berlin.
23 April	SPD-FDP coalition loses majority in Bundestag.
27 April	Failure in Bundestag of Christian Democrats' 'constructive vote of no confidence' against Chancellor Brandt.
17 May	Bundestag ratifies Moscow and Warsaw treaties. 'Common Resolution' of CDU/CSU with SPD and FDP.

22–30 May	Nixon visits Soviet Union. Signature of SALT I arms control treaty.
26 May	Signature of German-German Traffic Treaty.
15 June	Egon Bahr and GDR State Secretary Michael Kohl begin talks on a general framework treaty between GDR and Federal Republic.
5 July	German-Soviet Agreement on Trade and Economic Co-operation.
July	Further German-Soviet natural gas pipeline agreement signed in Düsseldorf.
19 November	Elections to 7th Bundestag. SPD win 225 seats, FDP 41, giving them a majority of thirty-six over CDU/CSU, who have 230 seats.
21 November	United States and Soviet Union begin preliminary talks for SALT II treaty.
22 November	Representatives of all European states (except Albania), the Soviet Union, the United States and Canada begin preliminary talks in Helsinki for a Conference on Security and Co-operation in Europe (CSCE).
12 December	Willy Brandt re-elected Chancellor, continuing social-liberal (SPD-FDP) coalition government.
21 December	Signature of Treaty on the Bases of Relations between Federal Republic and GDR.

1973

1 January	Britain, Ireland and Denmark become members of the EC.
31 January	Beginning of preliminary talks on Mutual Balanced Force Reductions (MBFR). Establishment of a German-German Frontier Commission.
23 April	Henry Kissinger proclaims his 'Year of Europe'.
11 May	Bundestag ratifies Basic Treaty with GDR, and legislates for Federal Republic to join the UN.
18–22 May	Brezhnev on state visit to the Federal Republic. New agreements on economic, technical and industrial co-operation and on cultural exchange.
28 May	Bavarian state government appeals to Federal Constitutional Court to test constitutionality of Basic Treaty with the GDR.
31 May	Erich Honecker receives the parliamentary leaders of the Social and Free Democrats, Herbert Wehner and Wolfgang Mischnick.
18–25 June	Brezhnev in the United States.

1973 *continued*

21 June	German-German Treaty on the Bases of Relations comes into force.
3–8 July	Opening in Helsinki of Conference on Security and Co-operation in Europe.
31 July	Federal Constitutional Court declares Treaty on the Bases of Relations with the GDR is compatible with the Federal Republic's Basic Law.
18 September	Federal Republic and GDR become members of the UN.
25 September	United States and Soviet Union begin SALT II arms control talks in Geneva.
18–20 October	Scheel in Poland.
30 October	MBFR talks begin in Vienna.
15 November	GDR doubles compulsory exchange of hard currency for West German and other Western visitors.
11 December	Prague Treaty signed. Diplomatic relations established between the Federal Republic and Czechoslovakia.
21 December	Federal Republic opens diplomatic relations with Hungary and Bulgaria.

1974

18 January	German-Soviet Economic Commission produces further accord on long-term co-operation.
2 May	Federal Republic and GDR open 'Permanent Representations' in their respective capitals.
6 May	Resignation of Chancellor Brandt, after the exposure of an East German spy in his office.
15 May	Walter Scheel elected Federal President.
16 May	Helmut Schmidt elected Chancellor in succession to Willy Brandt. Hans-Dietrich Genscher becomes Foreign Minister in succession to Walter Scheel.
20 June	Bundestag ratifies Prague Treaty.
27 June–3 July	Nixon meets Brezhnev in Moscow and Yalta.
7 October	Changes to GDR constitution on 25th anniversary of the state's founding. Reference to united Germany removed and GDR proclaimed 'for ever and irrevocably allied' with the Soviet Union.
26 October	GDR announces reduction of compulsory exchange for West German and other Western visitors from 15 November.
28–31 October	Chancellor Schmidt and Foreign Minister Gen-

	scher in Moscow. Signature of third German-Soviet natural gas pipeline agreement.
1 November	German-Polish agreement on economic, industrial and technological co-operation.
11 November	German-Hungarian agreement on economic, industrial and technological co-operation.
23–24 November	President Ford meets Brezhnev in Vladivostok.
9–10 December	At a conference in Paris, EC heads of government agree to meet three times a year, together with their foreign ministers: the 'European Council'.
11–12 December	Signature of agreements between West Berlin and GDR agencies on the disposal of West Berlin's rubbish and sewage in the GDR.

1975

22 January	German-Czechoslovak agreement on economic, industrial and technological co-operation.
10–11 March	First meeting of EC's 'European Council', in Dublin.
14 May	German-Bulgarian agreement on economic, industrial and technological co-operation.
30 July–1 August	Ceremonial signature in Helsinki of concluding document of Conference on Security and Co-operation in Europe (CSCE): 'Helsinki Final Act'. Chancellor Schmidt has bilateral talks with Leonid Brezhnev, Edward Gierek and Erich Honecker.
22–30 September	CDU leader Helmut Kohl in Soviet Union.
7 October	New treaty of friendship, co-operation and mutual assistance between GDR and Soviet Union.
9–10 October	Genscher in Poland. Signature of agreements on a credit, pensions and accident insurance, and a protocol on emigration possibilities for the German minority.
10–16 November	President Scheel on state visit to Soviet Union.
24–28 November	Bulgarian Party leader Todor Zhivkov on state visit to Federal Republic.
19 December	German-German agreement on transit arrangements between West Berlin and the rest of West Germany. Federal Republic will pay annual lump-sum for 'transit fees', plus further sums for improvements to rail and motorway links.

1976

7 January	Publication of Tindemans report on further moves towards a 'European Union' of the EC.

1976 *continued*

January	First 'Parliamentary Symposium' of representatives of the Bundestag and Supreme Soviet.
19 February	Bundestag ratifies new agreements with Poland.
30 March	German-German agreement on postal and telephone links.
18–22 May	9th party congress of the SED.
8–12 June	Polish communist party leader Edward Gierek visits Federal Republic.
June	Workers' protests in Poland precipitated by food price rises. Violent repression in Radom and Ursus.
September	Formation of Workers' Defence Committee (KOR) in Poland.
3 October	Elections to 8th Bundestag. SPD wins 214 seats, FDP 39, giving majority of ten over CDU/CSU which have 243.
16 November	Balladeer Wolf Biermann deprived of his GDR citizenship during a tour in the Federal Republic.
15 December	Helmut Schmidt re-elected Chancellor.

1977

1 January	Charter 77 declaration in Czechoslovakia.
27–28 May	Schmidt in Yugoslavia.
13–15 June	Genscher in Soviet Union.
4–7 July	Hungarian Communist Party leader János Kádár visits Federal Republic.
4 October	Opening of CSCE follow-up conference in Belgrade.
28 October	Chancellor Schmidt's speech on Western security needs at International Institute for Strategic Studies (IISS) in London.
21–25 November	Schmidt in Poland.

1978

1 January	After five-year transitional period, Britain, Ireland and Denmark formally become full members of the EC.
6–7 January	Schmidt in Romania.
9 March	End of Belgrade CSCE follow-up meeting with further concluding document.
10–13 April	Visit of Czechoslovak Communist Party leader and head of state, Gustáv Husák, to Federal Republic.

4–7 May	Brezhnev in Federal Republic. Joint Declaration. Agreement on development of economic and industrial co-operation.
16–17 July	Summit of world's leading industrial countries (G7) in Bonn.
16 October	Cardinal Karol Wojtyła, Archbishop of Kraków, elected Pope John Paul II.
4–5 December	EC's European Council meets in Brussels. Agreement to introduce European Monetary System.

1979

5–6 January	Guadeloupe summit conference of Presidents Carter and Giscard d'Estaing, Prime Minister Callaghan and Chancellor Schmidt.
2–4 May	Schmidt in Bulgaria.
23 May	Karl Carstens elected Federal President.
2–10 June	Pope John Paul II visits Poland.
10 June	First direct elections to EC's European Parliament.
18 June	Carter and Brezhnev sign SALT II arms control agreement in Vienna.
21–24 November	Gromyko in Bonn.
12 December	Nato's 'double-track' decision to offer negotiations on intermediate-range nuclear forces (INF) with the Soviet Union, but to deploy new intermediate-range nuclear missiles in Western Europe from 1983 if these negotiations are unsuccessful.
27 December	Soviet invasion of Afghanistan.

1980

4 January	President Carter announces sanctions against Soviet Union, interrupts ratification of SALT II treaty, and threatens boycott of Moscow Olympics.
15 May	West Germany joins boycott of Moscow Olympics.
19 May	Giscard d'Estaing meets Brezhnev in Wilanów, near Warsaw.
12–13 June	EC's European Council in Venice.
22–23 June	G7 summit in Venice.
30 June–1 July	Schmidt and Genscher in Moscow.
10–12 August	Bundestag delegation in Soviet Union on tenth anniversary of Moscow Treaty.
22 August	Cancellation of planned meeting between Schmidt and GDR leader Erich Honecker on account of strike wave in Poland.

1980 *continued*

31 August	Signature of Gdańsk Agreement permits founding of Independent Self-Governing Trades Union 'Solidarity'.
5 October	Elections to 9th Bundestag. SPD win 218 seats and FDP 53, thus having a majority of 61 over CDU/CSU, who together have 226.
9 October	GDR announces increase in compulsory exchange for West German and other Western visitors.
13 October	Erich Honecker's 'Gera speech'.
17 October	Beginning of Geneva talks between Soviet and American representatives on intermediate-range nuclear forces (INF).
5 November	Helmut Schmidt re-elected as Chancellor.
12 November	Opening of CSCE follow-up conference in Madrid.

1981

1 January	Greece becomes tenth member of the EC.
20 January	Ronald Reagan sworn in as US President.
11 June	Richard von Weizsäcker elected Governing Mayor of Berlin.
29 June	Willy Brandt meets Brezhnev in Moscow.
10 October	Mass demonstration in Bonn against Nato double-track decision.
20 November	Signature in Essen of agreement between a German-led consortium and the Soviet foreign trade organisation on new natural gas pipeline to, and supplies from, Siberia.
22–25 November	Brezhnev in Bonn.
30 November	United States and Soviet Union resume talks on intermediate-range nuclear forces (INF) in Geneva.
11–13 December	Schmidt visits GDR. Summit meeting with Honecker at the Werbellinsee.
13 December	General Jaruzelski declares 'state of war' in Poland.
29 December	President Reagan announces sanctions against the Soviet Union as response to the declaration of martial law in Poland.

1982

5 January	Schmidt in America for talks with Reagan.
19–23 April	SPD party conference in Munich. Establishment of working group on 'new strategies' chaired by Egon Bahr.
May	Publication of Palme Commission report.

16 July	American and Soviet negotiators' informal 'walk in the woods' produces possible compromise formula on intermediate-range nuclear forces not accepted by their governments.
17 September	Social-liberal coalition ended with resignation of four FDP ministers.
20 September	German-German agreement on youth exchanges.
1 October	Schmidt deposed as Chancellor by a constructive vote of no-confidence, and succeeded by Helmut Kohl, who will lead a conservative-liberal (CDU/CSU-FDP) coalition government.
12–13 October	German-Soviet economic commission meets in Bonn.
November	Brezhnev dies, succeeded as Party leader by Yuri Andropov.
31 December	'State of war' in Poland is 'suspended'.

1983

16–19 January	Gromyko visits Federal Republic.
6 March	Elections to 10th Bundestag. CDU/CSU win 244 seats, FDP 34 seats, thus giving the conservative-liberal coalition a majority of 58 over the SPD, with 193 seats, and the Greens, with 27.
23 March	President Reagan announces Strategic Defense Initiative (SDI) research programme.
29 April	Honecker postpones his planned visit to West Germany.
28 May	SPD parliamentary leader Hans-Jochen Vogel has first of a series of annual meetings with Erich Honecker, in the GDR.
16–23 June	Pope's second visit to Poland.
29 June	Federal Government guarantees a DM 1 billion credit to the GDR, organised by Franz Josef Strauss.
4–7 July	Kohl and Genscher in Moscow.
15 July	End of Madrid CSCE review conference.
22 July	'State of war' in Poland is 'lifted'.
July	Franz Josef Strauss visits Czechoslovakia, Poland and the GDR.
1 September	In a joint letter on the anniversary of the outbreak of the Second World War, the Protestant Churches in West and East Germany appeal to the leaders of both German states to work within their alliances for arms reductions, especially in the Geneva negotiations on intermediate-range nuclear forces. Peace movement blockade of American military depot in

1983 *continued*

	West Germany. A South Korean jumbo jet is shot down by Soviet forces.
15 September	Richard von Weizsäcker, as Governing Mayor of (West) Berlin, meets Erich Honecker in East Berlin.
5 October	Lech Wałęsa awarded Nobel Peace Prize.
10 October	East German media publish letter from Honecker appealing to Chancellor Kohl not to go ahead with the deployment of new American nuclear missiles.
10 November	GDR celebrates Luther's 500th birthday.
10–16 November	German-Soviet economic commission meets in Moscow, chaired by Federal Economics Minister Otto Graf Lambsdorff.
18 November	SPD special party conference in Cologne votes by 583 votes to 14 (with three abstentions) against deployment of new American medium-range missiles in the Federal Republic.
22 November	Bundestag votes by 286 votes to 226 (with one abstention) for deployment of new American medium-range missiles in the Federal Republic, in line with Nato's double-track decision of December 1979.
23 November	Soviet delegation breaks off INF negotiations in Geneva.
24 November	Honecker tells his Central Committee the GDR should aim to 'limit the damage' done by the Bundestag decision.

1984

9 February	Bundestag Common Resolution of CDU/CSU, FDP, and SPD on Deutschlandpolitik.
9–13 February	Andropov dies. Kohl and Honecker meet for the first time at his funeral. Konstantin Chernenko succeeds him, and has talks with Kohl.
14 March	At their annual meeting, Erich Honecker and Hans-Jochen Vogel agree to establish joint SED-SPD working group on a chemical weapon-free zone.
17–21 May	SPD Essen party conference. Resolution on security policy incorporating 'new strategies'.
20–22 May	Genscher in Moscow.
27 June	A total of fifty-five East Germans take refuge in West Germany's Permanent Representation in East

	Berlin, hoping thereby to leave East Germany for the West.
1 July	Richard von Weizsäcker becomes Federal President.
25 July	Federal Government guarantees a DM 950 million credit for the GDR.
17 August	At a meeting in the Kremlin, the Soviet leadership express to Erich Honecker and his delegation their disapproval of his proposed visit to West Germany.
4 September	GDR announces the postponement of Honecker's visit to West Germany.
20 September	SPD and SED begin talks on a chemical weapon-free zone in Central Europe.
19 October	Father Jerzy Popiełuszko abducted and murdered by functionaries of the Polish secret police.
21 November	Last-minute cancellation of Genscher's planned visit to Poland.

1985

20 January	Ronald Reagan installed for second term as US President.
21–22 January	German-Soviet economic commission meets in Bonn.
10 March	Death of Chernenko.
12 March	Mikhail Gorbachev succeeds Chernenko as Party leader. Kohl meets Gorbachev and Honecker at Chernenko's funeral.
22–29 March	Lothar Späth visits Soviet Union in his capacity as president of the Bundesrat.
March	Resumption of American-Soviet arms control talks in Geneva.
18 April	Gorbachev receives F Wilhelm Christians, head of the Deutsche Bank.
8 May	Richard von Weizsäcker's speech on fortieth anniversary of the end of the Second World War in Europe.
16 May	Hans-Jochen Vogel meets Erich Honecker.
May	Willy Brandt meets Gorbachev in Moscow.
6 June	Herbert Wehner visits Erich Honecker.
14–16 June	Chancellor Kohl addresses meeting of expellees from Silesia.
May–June	Gdańsk trial of Solidarity leaders, Władysław Frasyniuk, Bogdan Lis, Adam Michnik.

1985 *continued*

19 June	SPD-SED draft treaty on chemical weapon-free zone in Central Europe.
2 July	Eduard Shevardnadze succeeds Andrei Gromyko as Soviet Foreign Minister. Gromyko becomes State President.
7 September	SPD defence specialist Andreas von Bülow publishes paper envisaging superpower disengagement and militia defence for West Germany by the year 2000: 'Bülow paper'.
8–11 September	Johannes Rau, Social Democrat prime minister of North Rhine Westphalia, visits Soviet Union and meets Gorbachev.
18 September	Willy Brandt, Egon Bahr and Günter Gaus visit Erich Honecker. Agreement to form joint working group on a nuclear weapon-free corridor.
19–21 November	First Reagan-Gorbachev summit meeting, in Geneva.
November	SPD joint declaration with Polish United Workers' Party on confidence-building measures in Europe.
29 Nov–5 December	Bundestag delegation visits Soviet Union.
7–8 December	Willy Brandt in Warsaw for fifteenth anniversary of Warsaw Treaty. Meets Jaruzelski but not Wałęsa.

1986

1 January	Spain and Portugal join the EC.
25 February	27th congress of Communist Party of the Soviet Union.
2–8 April	German-Soviet economic commission meets in Moscow.
17–21 April	11th Party congress of the SED.
22 April	40th anniversary of forced merger of Social Democrats with Communists to form SED.
26 April	Disastrous accident at nuclear power plant in Chernobyl, Ukraine.
6 May	German-German cultural agreement signed.
28 May	Gorbachev addresses top-level internal conference of Soviet foreign ministry. Hans-Jochen Vogel meets Erich Honecker in GDR.
25 June	Johannes Rau, prime minister of North Rhine Westphalia and probable Social Democrat candidate for Chancellor, in Soviet Union. Received by Gorbachev.

20–22 July	Genscher in Moscow, agrees with Gorbachev to 'open a new page' in German-Soviet relations.
25–29 August	Nuremberg party conference of SPD. Johannes Rau confirmed as the party's candidate for Chancellor.
11 September	Amnesty in Poland, includes virtually all political prisoners.
21–22 September	Conclusion of Stockholm Conference on Confidence- and Security-building Measures and Disarmament in Europe.
September–October	First German-German town-twinning agreement, between Saarlouis and Eisenhüttenstadt, is signed and ratified.
11–12 October	Second Reagan-Gorbachev summit meeting, in Reykjavik.
21 October	SPD-SED joint declaration on a nuclear weapon-free corridor in Central Europe.
4 November	CSCE review conference opens in Vienna.
10–11 November	At a meeting in Moscow, Gorbachev communicates in general terms to East European Party leaders a new and more permissive Soviet line towards them.
19 December	Soviet Union announces release of Andrei Sakharov from internal exile.

1987

January	Beginning of 750th anniversary celebrations in Berlin (East) and Berlin (West).
25 January	Elections to 11th Bundestag. CDU/CSU win 223 seats, FDP 34 seats, giving them a majority of 29 over the SPD, with 186 seats, and the Greens, with 42.
27 January	In a speech to the Central Committee of the Soviet Communist Party, Gorbachev demands the 'democratisation' of party and society.
25 March	Willy Brandt resigns as SPD party chairman.
15 May	Hans-Jochen Vogel meets Erich Honecker at Werbellinsee.
28 May	Matthias Rust flies his Cessna 172 to Moscow, landing on Red Square.
8 June	East German police clash with young East Germans on the Eastern side of the Brandenburg Gate.
8–14 June	Pope's third visit to Poland.
12 June	President Reagan speaks on the Western side of the Brandenburg Gate, calling on Gorbachev to open the gate and tear down the Berlin Wall.

1987 *continued*

14 June	Special party conference of the SPD elects Hans-Jochen Vogel as party chairman.
1 July	EC's Single European Act comes into force.
6–11 July	President von Weizsäcker in Moscow, together with Foreign Minister Genscher. Restatement of intent to 'open a new page' in German-Soviet relations.
26 August	Bonn government increases 'welcome money' for visiting East Germans from DM 30 to DM 100 a year.
27 August	Publication of SPD-SED Joint Paper on ideological argument and common security.
7–11 September	Erich Honecker makes his long-delayed official visit to the Federal Republic.
October	SPD joint statement with Communist Party of the Soviet Union on 'disarmament for development'.
25 November	State Security Service (Stasi) search of premises of the Zion Church in East Berlin, followed by further measures against dissident groups.
7–8 December	Third Reagan-Gorbachev summit meeting in Washington. Signature of treaty between the United States and the Soviet Union on the elimination of their intermediate-range and short-range missiles: the 'INF Treaty'.
28–31 December	Franz Josef Strauss flies himself to Moscow, and is received by Gorbachev.

1988

17 January	In East Berlin, an official demonstration in memory of Rosa Luxemburg and Karl Liebknecht is joined by unofficial demonstrators, many of whom are arrested.
17–19 January	Soviet Foreign Minister Eduard Shevardnadze in Bonn.
7–11 February	Lothar Späth, prime minister of Baden-Württemberg, in Soviet Union.
10 March	A West German cultural institute is opened in Budapest.
21–24 March	Rita Süssmuth visits Moscow as chairwoman of the CDU Womens' Union.
5 April	Joint declaration of the SPD, SED and Czechoslovak Communist Party, proposing a chemical weapon-free zone in Central Europe.
29 April	SPD chairman Hans-Jochen Vogel meets Erich Honecker for further talks.

April–May	Strikes in Poland, including major Solidarity strongholds such as the Lenin shipyard.
May	János Kádár resigns as Hungarian party leader.
11 May	German-Soviet economic commission meets in Moscow.
29 May–1 June	Fourth Reagan-Gorbachev summit meeting, in Moscow.
13–15 June	Wiesbaden party conference of CDU passes extensive resolution on foreign policy and Deutschland-politik.
23 June	At a Church congress (*Kirchentag*) in Halle, Wittenberg pastor Friedrich Schorlemmer presents twenty theses for social and political renewal.
25 June	EC and Comecon open official relations.
28–31 June	19th conference (not congress) of Communist Party of the Soviet Union.
7 July	Hermann Axen for the SED and Egon Bahr for the SPD present joint proposal for a 'zone of trust and security in Central Europe'.
31 August	Wave of strikes in Poland leads to meeting between General Czesław Kiszczak and Lech Wałęsa. First formal discussion of Round Table talks with Solidarity.
30 Aug–2 September	SPD party conference in Münster.
1 October	Gorbachev becomes state President as well as Party leader.
24–27 October	Kohl in Moscow.
7 December	Gorbachev addresses the UN: principles of freedom of choice and renunciation of force. Gorbachev meets with Reagan and his successor George Bush.

1989

15 January	Vienna CSCE review conference ends with detailed provisions in concluding document.
16–18 January	Plenum of Central Committee of Polish United Workers' Party concludes with agreement in principle to relegalisation of Solidarity.
2 February	End of the sixteen-year long MBFR talks in Vienna.
6 February	Round Table talks begin in Poland.
10–11 February	Central Committee of Hungarian Socialist Workers' Party discusses reassessment of 1956 revolution and endorses the idea of a multi-party system.

1989 *continued*

21 February	Václav Havel sentenced to nine months' imprisonment.
19 March	Beginning of new talks on conventional force reductions, between Nato and Warsaw Pact, and on security and confidence-building measures, between all CSCE participant states; both in Vienna.
5 April	Polish Round Table talks conclude with agreement leading to relegalisation of Solidarity and semi-free elections to parliament.
6–7 April	German-Soviet economic commission meets in Bonn.
17 April	Legal (re)registration of Solidarity.
2 May	Hungary begins to dismantle the 'iron curtain' along its frontier with Austria.
7 May	Local elections in the GDR. Independent monitors point to rigging of the results.
12 May	In Texas, President Bush speaks of going 'beyond containment' in relations with the Soviet Union.
22 May	GDR and Poland sign treaty agreeing the exact frontier line across the Oder estuary.
29–30 May	Nato's fortieth anniversary summit, in Brussels.
4 June	First round of Polish parliamentary elections. Massacre on Tiananmen Square in Beijing.
12–15 June	Gorbachev in West Germany. German-Soviet Joint Declaration: the 'Bonn Declaration'.
13 June	Round Table talks begin in Hungary.
16 June	Ceremonial reburial of Imre Nagy and his associates in Budapest.
18 June	Second round of Polish parliamentary elections give Solidarity-led opposition all seats available to it in lower house (thirty-five per cent) and 99 out of 100 in the new upper house. In the EC, direct elections to the European Parliament.
6 July	Gorbachev addresses Council of Europe in Strasbourg.
7–8 July	Warsaw Pact meeting in Bucharest ends with declaration rejecting interference in the internal affairs of any state.
9–12 July	President Bush visits Poland and Hungary.
19 July	General Jaruzelski elected President of Poland.
July–August	Growing number of East Germans escape via Hungary to Austria, or take refuge in the West German missions in East Berlin, Budapest and Prague.

24 August	Veteran Solidarity adviser Tadeusz Mazowiecki is appointed Polish Prime Minister.
25 August	Hungarian Prime Minister Miklós Németh and Foreign Minister Gyula Horn visit West Germany for talks with Chancellor Kohl and Foreign Minister Genscher.
26 August	Initiative to found a social democratic party in the GDR.
9–11 September	Announcement of the founding of the New Forum opposition movement in the GDR.
10–11 September	Hungary announces the opening of its frontier to Austria for East Germans, at midnight on the 11th. From now until the end of October some 50,000 will leave by this route.
21–22 September	Shevardnadze meets with Bush in Washington and visits James Baker on his ranch in Wyoming.
25 September	Thousands in protest demonstration in Leipzig.
30 September	Some 6,000 East Germans who had taken refuge in the West German embassy in Prague are given permission to leave for the West in special trains, which pass through East Germany.
2 October	Some 15,000 in protest demonstration in Leipzig.
1–5 October	Some 1,500 East Germans who had taken refuge in the West German embassy in Warsaw are allowed to leave for the West.
4–5 October	A further 7,600 East Germans who had taken refuge in the West German embassy in Prague are allowed to leave for the West, in special trains which pass through East Germany.
5 October	Gorbachev arrives in East Berlin to take part in the GDR's fortieth anniversary celebrations. He warns against 'coming too late'.
7 October	On fortieth anniversary of the founding of the GDR, East German security forces break up demonstrations for reform in several East German cities. Founding of a Social Democratic Party in the GDR.
9 October	Some 70,000 demonstrate in Leipzig. Security forces gather, but do not intervene.
10 October	Hungarian Socialist Workers' Party dissolved, Hungarian Socialist Party succeeds it.
15 October	Václav Havel is unable to travel to Frankfurt to receive the Peace Prize of the German Book Trade.
16 October	More than 100,000 join in the now regular 'Monday demo' in Leipzig.

1989 *continued*

18 October	Erich Honecker resigns, succeeded by Egon Krenz.
23 October	Proclamation of the new Hungarian Republic in Budapest. Some 300,000 East Germans demonstrate in Leipzig.
28 October	Demonstrations in Prague to mark the seventy-first anniversary of the founding of independent Czechoslovakia are broken up by police.
30 October	More than 300,000 demonstrate in Leipzig.
4 November	Massive demonstration in East Berlin (estimates up to 1 million). Thousands more East Germans leave via Czechoslovakia.
6 November	Massive demonstration in Leipzig (estimates up to 500,000).
8 November	Bundestag resolution on Poland's western frontier.
9 November	Opening of the Berlin Wall.
9–14 November	Kohl visit to Poland, interrupted to return to Berlin to mark the opening of the Wall.
10 November	Resignation of Bulgarian party leader Todor Zhivkov.
13 November	Hans Modrow appointed Prime Minister of the GDR.
16 November	Hungary applies to join Council of Europe.
17 November	In Prague, police repression of a demonstration to mark the anniversary of the death of a student killed by the Nazis sparks what will be called the 'velvet revolution'. In East Berlin, the Modrow government proposes 'treaty community' with West Germany.
18 November	EC leaders meet in Paris to discuss response to developments in Eastern Europe.
20 November	Calls for unity as well as democracy at the regular Leipzig 'Monday demo'.
28 November	Kohl offers his '10-Point Programme' to overcome the division of Germany and Europe.
2–3 December	Bush-Gorbachev meeting in Malta.
3 December	Egon Krenz resigns as party leader, together with the whole Politburo and Central Committee.
6 December	Mitterrand meets Gorbachev in Kiev. Egon Krenz also resigns his state offices.
7 December	Round Table talks start in East Germany.
9 December	EC summit in Strasbourg reaffirms German right to unity through self-determination.
10 December	President Gustáv Husák swears in new Czechoslovak federal government, dominated by non-Communists, and then resigns as President. In

Sofia, more than 50,000 people join in a pro-democracy demonstration organised by the newly-founded Union of Democratic Forces.

16 December	Special conference of the CDU in the GDR ends with commitment to unity. Lothar de Maizière elected chairman.
16–18 December	Kohl in Hungary.
19 December	Kohl in Dresden, greeted by large crowds demonstrating for unity. Agreement with East German Prime Minister Hans Modrow on moves towards a 'treaty community' of the two German states.
18–20 December	Special party conference of the SPD in Berlin votes for confederation between the two German states and passes new basic programme, replacing the Godesberg programme of 1959.
20–21 December	President Mitterrand pays a state visit to the GDR. He is the first and last head of state from one of the three Western Allies ever to do so.
21 December	In Bucharest, pro-Ceauşescu demonstration turns into anti-Ceauşescu demonstration.
22 December	Opening of the Brandenburg Gate.
24 December	Visa-free travel to the GDR for West Germans and West Berliners.
25 December	Alexander Dubček elected president of the Czechoslovak federal parliament. Nicolae and Elena Ceauşescu are executed.
29 December	Václav Havel elected President of Czechoslovakia.
30 December	Polish parliament changes the name of the state to Republic of Poland, and passes package of laws to begin economic transformation according to the 'Balcerowicz plan'.

1990

11 January	Gorbachev visits Vilnius, attempting to stop the movement to independence.
28 January	East German prime minister Modrow and the Round Table agree that Volkskammer elections should be brought forward to 18 March.
30 January	Modrow in Moscow for talks with Gorbachev.
1 February	Modrow presents plan for 'Germany, united fatherland'.
7 February	Bonn government forms cabinet committee called 'German unity' and agrees in principle to proceed with talks on German monetary union.

1990 *continued*

8–10 February	James Baker in Moscow, discussing, among other things, the '2 + 4' modality for talks on German unification.
10–11 February	Kohl and Genscher in Moscow. Gorbachev gives green light for unification of Germany.
12–14 February	'2 + 4' formula for negotiations on the external aspects of German unification is announced at Ottawa 'open skies' meeting.
13–14 February	Modrow in Bonn.
24–25 February	Kohl and Bush meet in Camp David.
2 March	Kohl appears to make signature of frontier treaty with Poland conditional on Polish undertakings on the reparation and German minority issues.
8 March	Bundestag resolution on the Polish frontier.
11 March	Lithuanian parliament votes to 're-establish' independence.
15 March	Gorbachev gains powers of an executive President.
18 March	Elections to the Volkskammer in the GDR. The Alliance for Germany, with the CDU as its leading member, gains 193 seats, the SPD 87 seats, with the former SED, now called the Party for Democratic Socialism, in third place with 65 seats.
19 March–11 April	CSCE conference on economic co-operation in Bonn.
9 April	Meeting in Bratislava of leaders of Czechoslovakia, Hungary and Poland, to discuss trilateral co-operation.
12 April	Lothar de Maizière forms coalition government in East Berlin. He declares his government to be in favour of joining the Federal Republic by way of Article 23 of its Basic Law.
18 April	Mitterand and Kohl send joint message to current President of the European Council of the EC, proposing an inter-governmental conference on 'political union' of the existing EC, as well as that already planned on economic and monetary union.
21 April	EC foreign ministers, meeting in Dublin, agree outline plans for the former GDR to join the EC when it joins the Federal Republic.
28 April	EC Dublin summit.
2–5 May	President von Weizsäcker on state visit to Poland.
5 May	First 2 + 4 meeting, in Bonn.

14 May	Kohl's foreign policy adviser Horst Teltschik takes bankers on secret mission to Moscow.
18 May	Federal Republic and GDR sign Treaty on Monetary, Economic and Social Union.
30 May–3 June	Bush-Gorbachev summit in Washington and Camp David.
5–8 June	Kohl meets Bush.
17 June	Joint session of Bundestag and Volkskammer to commemorate 17 June 1953 rising in East Germany.
21 June	Bundestag and Volkskammer ratify Treaty on Monetary, Economic and Social Union, and pass resolutions on the Polish frontier.
22 June	Second 2 + 4 meeting, in East Berlin.
1 July	German Monetary, Economic and Social Union comes into force. The DM comes to East Germany.
5–6 July	Nato's London summit.
1–13 July	28th congress of the Communist Party of the Soviet Union.
9–11 July	Houston summit of the G7.
14–16 July	Kohl and Genscher in Moscow and the Caucasus. Crucial agreements on the external aspects of German unification, with united Germany in Nato.
17 July	Third 2 + 4 meeting, in Paris. Discussion of the Polish frontier issue with the Polish foreign minister.
2 August	Treaty on all-German elections. Iraq invades Kuwait.
3 August	Árpád Göncz elected President of Hungary.
23 August	Volkskammer votes for the GDR to join the Federal Republic by Article 23 of the Basic Law on 3 October.
31 August	Signature of Unification Treaty between the Federal Republic and the GDR.
8 September	Bush and Gorbachev meet in Helsinki.
11–12 September	Fourth 2 + 4 meeting, in Moscow. Signature of the Final Treaty with Respect to Germany — the '2 + 4 treaty'.
13 September	Genscher and Shevardnadze initial bilateral German-Soviet friendship treaty.
17 September	EC Council of Ministers agrees measures for the accession of the former GDR to the EC on 3 October.
1 October	Formal declaration of the suspension of four-power rights in Germany.
3 October	The Day of German Unity. GDR joins the Federal Republic.

1990 *continued*

9 October	German-Soviet agreement on 'transitional measures'.
12 October	German-Soviet treaty on the arrangements for remaining Soviet troops and their planned withdrawal.
9 November	On the first anniversary of the opening of the Berlin Wall, Kohl and Gorbachev sign the German-Soviet friendship treaty and a further treaty on economic co-operation, in Bonn.
14 November	Signature of German-Polish frontier treaty.
19 November	Twenty-two member states of Nato and Warsaw Pact sign common declaration.
19–21 November	CSCE summit in Paris. Launch of the Paris Charter for a New Europe.
2 December	First all-German election to the Bundestag. In the resulting 12th Bundestag, the CDU/CSU have 319 seats and the FDP have 79 seats, giving the centre-right coalition government a majority of 134 over the SPD, with 239 seats, and the Bündnis '90/Greens (8) and PDS/LL (17).
9 December	Lech Wałęsa is elected President of Poland.
15 December	Beginning of EC's inter-governmental conferences on economic, monetary and political union.
20 December	First meeting of the all-German Bundestag. Shevardnadze resigns as Soviet Foreign Minister, warning of the danger of dictatorship.
20–21 December	EC begins negotiations with Czechoslovakia, Hungary and Poland on new association agreements.

1991

13 January	'Bloody Sunday' in Vilnius. Some fifteen Lithuanians killed following action by Soviet forces.
15 February	Visegrád Declaration of Hungary, Poland and Czechoslovakia.
25 February	Warsaw Pact agrees to dissolve its military structures on 1 April.
4 March	Supreme Soviet ratifies 2 + 4 treaty, together with the accompanying German-Soviet treaties.
13 March	Erich Honecker is transported by the Soviet military to the Soviet Union.
15 March	The Soviet ambassador to Bonn hands over the Soviet ratification document on the 2 + 4 treaty.
12–14 June	In Prague, President Mitterrand attempts to launch his European Confederation.

17 June	Signature of German-Polish treaty on good-neighbourliness and friendly co-operation.
19–20 June	CSCE Council of Foreign Ministers meets under Genscher's chairmanship in Berlin.
20 June	Bundestag votes that Berlin should remain the capital and become the seat of government of the Federal Republic.
25 June	Croatia and Slovenia declare their independence.
29 July–1 August	Bush-Gorbachev summit in Moscow. Signature of START treaty.
19–21 August	Attempted coup in Soviet Union.
28 August	Germany restores diplomatic relations with the Baltic states.
9 October	Signature of German-Bulgarian treaty on friendly co-operation and partnership.
18 October	Bundestag ratifies frontier and 'neighbour' treaties with Poland.
14 November	Bundestag passes law on the 'Stasi' papers, opening them for carefully regulated use from the beginning of 1992.
11–12 December	EC's Maastricht summit and treaty.
16 December	Signature of so-called 'Europe' agreements between the EC and Poland, Hungary and Czechoslovakia. Under pressure from Germany, EC foreign ministers agree to recognise former Yugoslav republics on 15 January, if certain conditions are met.
19 December	Bonn government announces that it is going ahead with the recognition of Slovenia and Croatia, as previously promised, before Christmas.
25 December	Gorbachev resigns as President, marking the effective end of the Soviet Union.
1992	
6 February	Signature of German-Hungarian treaty on friendly co-operation and partnership.
27 February	Signature of treaty on good-neighbourliness and friendly co-operation between Germany and the Czech and Slovak Federative Republic.
21 April	Signature of German-Romanian treaty on friendly co-operation and partnership.
18 May	Hans-Dietrich Genscher retires after eighteen years as German Foreign Minister. He is succeeded by Klaus Kinkel.
9 October	Death of Willy Brandt.

Maps

643

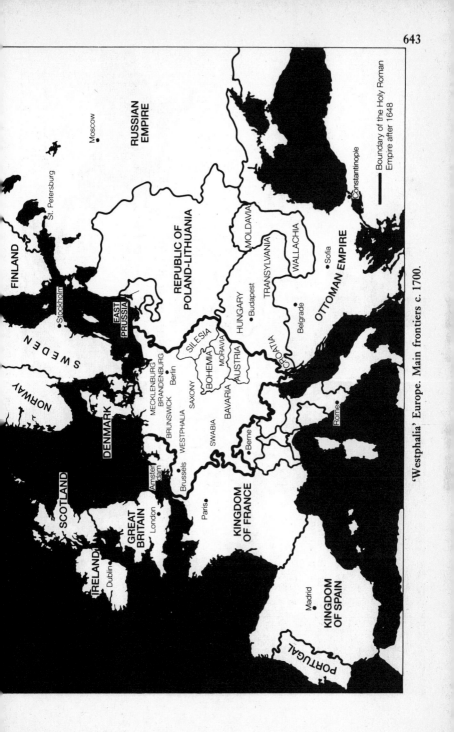

'Westphalia' Europe. Main frontiers c. 1700.

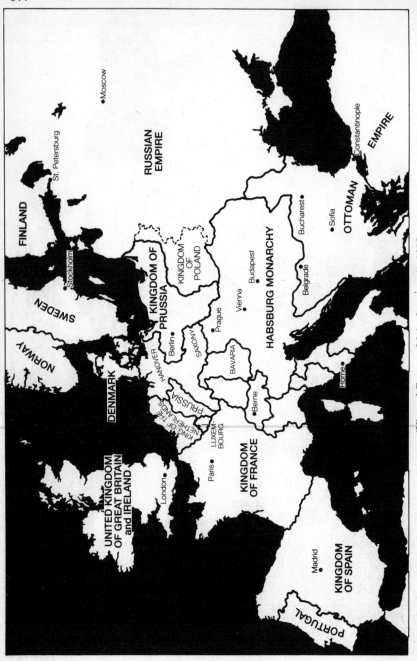

'Vienna' Europe. Main frontiers in 1815.

Europe after the first unification of Germany. Main frontiers in 1890.

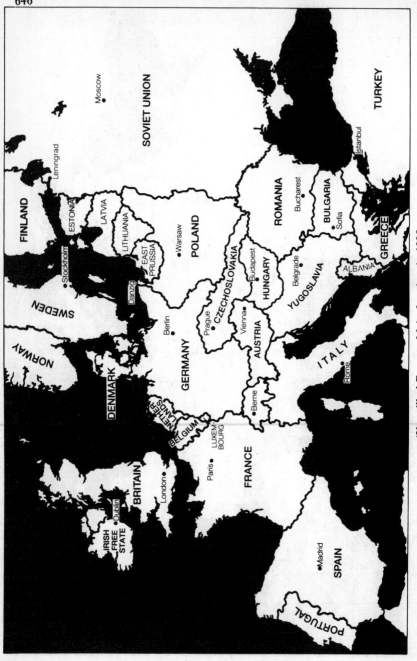

'Versailles' Europe. Main frontiers in 1925.

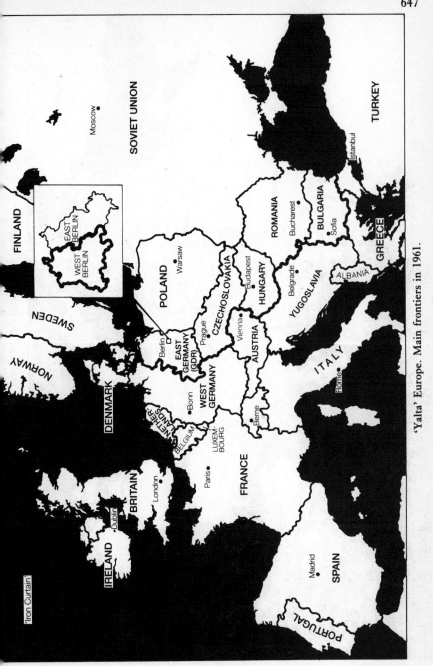

'Yalta' Europe. Main frontiers in 1961.

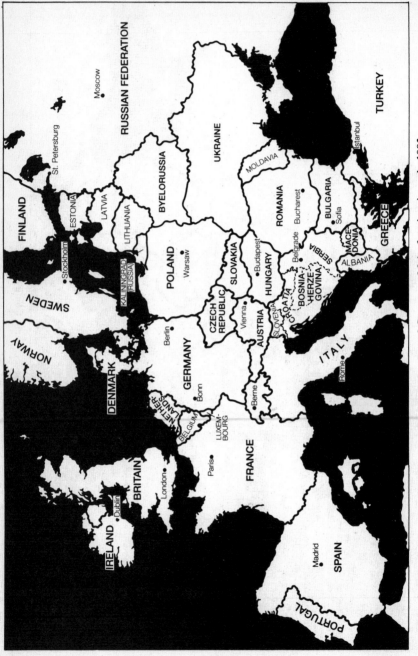

Europe after the second unification of Germany. Main frontiers in early 1993.

Tables and Graphs

I. ESTIMATED PER CAPITA GROSS NATIONAL PRODUCT OF SELECTED EUROPEAN STATES IN 1937 AND 1980

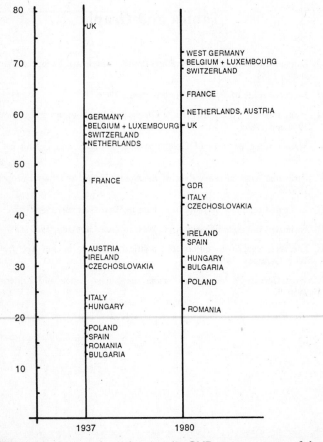

	1937	1980
80	UK	
70		WEST GERMANY / BELGIUM + LUXEMBOURG / SWITZERLAND
		FRANCE
60	GERMANY / BELGIUM + LUXEMBOURG / SWITZERLAND / NETHERLANDS	NETHERLANDS, AUSTRIA / UK
50	FRANCE	
		GDR / ITALY / CZECHOSLOVAKIA
40		
		IRELAND / SPAIN
30	AUSTRIA / IRELAND / CZECHOSLOVAKIA	HUNGARY / BULGARIA / POLAND
	ITALY / HUNGARY	
20	POLAND / SPAIN / ROMANIA / BULGARIA	ROMANIA
10		

NOTE: This table shows estimated per capita GNP as a percentage of that in the USA. It is based on the work of the Hungarian scholar Eva Ehrlich. Individual entries seem questionable (for example, both the relatively low 1937 position for Czechoslovakia and its relatively high position in 1980) but the overall picture of the economic division of Europe emerges quite clearly.

SOURCE: Adapted from the article by Paul Marer in William E. Griffith, ed., *Central and Eastern Europe: The opening curtain?* (Boulder: Westview Press, 1989).

II. EASTWARD TRADE OF SELECTED WESTERN STATES
(millions of US dollars)

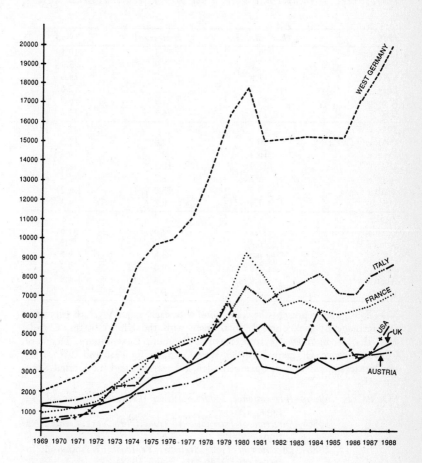

NOTE: This table shows volume of trade with the Soviet Union, Bulgaria, Czechoslovakia, Hungary, Poland and Romania.

SOURCE: Comtrade Data Bank, United Nations. Calculations by Jerzy Lisiecki.

III. MAIN WESTERN TRADING PARTNERS OF CZECHOSLOVAKIA, HUNGARY AND POLAND IN 1936, 1956 & 1986
(percentage of total trade with a set of Western industrial states)

1936	Czechoslovakia	Hungary	Poland
Germany	29.7	31.5	19.4
France	7.9	1.9	5.9
UK	11.6	9.0	24.4
Italy	1.7	13.5	2.6
Austria	10.4	21.9	6.9
US	11.7	4.9	12.5
1956			
Germany (West)	20.7	22.0	17.6
France	10.3	9.3	10.3
UK	11.9	10.3	18.0
Italy	5.2	8.3	2.4
Austria	9.6	15.0	8.2
US	1.4	0.8	4.3
1986			
Germany (West)	37.2	32.0	31.6
France	6.4	5.2	7.2
UK	6.0	4.8	9.7
Italy	7.9	9.0	7.7
Austria	12.0	17.6	6.8
US	3.2	6.7	5.5

NOTE: Figures represent the trade done with each major Western partner as a percentage of the country's total trade with the Unites States, Canada, Australia, Japan, New Zealand, Austria, Belgium, Luxembourg, Denmark, Finland, France, Germany (in 1936; West Germany for 1956 and 1986), Italy, the Netherlands, Norway, Spain, Sweden, Switzerland and the United Kingdom.

SOURCES: 1936—International Trade Statistics (Geneva: League of Nations, 1937)

1956—Direction of International Trade (New York: United Nations, 1960)

1986—Direction of Trade Statistics Yearbook (Washington: International Monetary Fund, 1989)

IV. MAIN TRADING PARTNERS OF CZECHOSLOVAKIA, HUNGARY AND POLAND IN 1991 & 1992
(shares in total exports and imports in per cent)

| | Czechoslovakia | | | | Hungary | | | | Poland | | | |
| | Exports | | Imports | | Exports | | Imports | | Exports | | Imports | |
	1991	1992	1991	1992	1991	1992	1991	1992	1991	1992	1991	1992
Soviet Union	19.6	10.9	29.9	24.6	13.4	13.1	15.3	16.9	11.0	5.5	14.1	8.5
Czechoslovakia	—	—	—	—	2.2	2.7	4.1	4.3	4.6	3.8	3.3	3.2
Hungary	4.3	4.4	1.9	1.6	—	—	—	—	0.7	..	0.9	..
Poland	7.3	4.7	4.7	3.6	2.1	1.3	1.9	1.6	—	—	—	—
Germany	25.2	30.6	21.5	24.7	26.9	27.7	21.4	23.5	29.4	31.3	26.5	23.9
Austria	5.8	7.4	8.4	9.3	10.8	10.7	13.3	14.4	4.5	3.2	6.3	4.5
Italy	4.5	5.7	3.4	4.9	7.6	9.5	7.2	6.3	4.1	5.5	4.5	6.9
France	2.4	2.9	2.5	4.0	2.9	3.2	2.7	3.1	3.8	3.6	3.6	4.4
UK	1.9	2.2	2.0	2.2	2.0	2.0	2.5	2.9	7.1	4.3	4.0	6.6
USA	1.0	1.6	1.9	4.3	3.2	3.2	2.6	2.9	2.5	2.3	2.3	3.4
Japan	0.6	0.8	1.2	1.7	1.7	0.9	2.7	2.4	0.6	0.5	1.6	2.1

NOTE: Whereas until 1989 these countries' trade inside Comecon and that with the West was measured in different and strictly non-comparable units of account, for 1991 and 1992 it is possible to get an all-round picture. For 1992 it is, of course, the former Soviet Union.

SOURCE: Calculations by Dariusz Rosati, United Nations Economic Commission for Europe, on the basis of national statistics.

V. ESTIMATED HARD CURRENCY DEBT OF THE SOVIET UNION AND EAST EUROPEAN STATES
(billions of US dollars)

	1975	1980	1984	1985	1986	1987	1988	1989
Bulgaria								
gross	2.6	3.5	2.8	3.2	4.7	6.1	8.2	9.2
net	2.3	2.7	1.4	1.2	3.3	5.1	6.4	8.0
Czechoslovakia								
gross	1.1	6.9	4.7	4.6	5.6	6.7	7.3	7.9
net	0.8	5.6	3.7	3.6	4.4	5.1	5.6	5.7
GDR								
gross	5.2	13.8	11.7	13.2	15.6	18.6	19.8	20.6
net	3.5	11.8	7.2	6.9	8.2	9.7	10.3	11.1
Hungary								
gross	3.9	9.1	11.0	14.0	16.9	19.6	19.6	20.6
net	2.0	7.7	9.4	11.7	14.8	18.1	18.2	19.4
Poland								
gross	8.4	24.1	26.5	29.3	33.5	39.2	39.2	40.8
net	7.7	23.5	24.9	27.7	31.8	36.2	35.6	36.9
Romania								
gross	2.9	9.6	7.2	6.6	6.4	5.7	2.9	0.6
net	2.4	9.3	6.6	6.2	5.8	4.4	2.1	-1.2
Eastern Europe								
gross	24.2	67.0	63.9	71.0	82.7	96.0	97.0	99.7
net	18.8	60.5	53.2	57.4	68.1	78.4	78.2	79.9
Soviet Union								
gross	10.6	23.5	21.4	25.2	30.5	40.2	46.8	52.4
net	7.5	14.9	10.1	12.1	15.6	26.1	31.4	37.7
Comecon								
gross	34.8	90.5	85.3	96.1	113.1	136.2	143.7	152.1
net	26.3	75.5	63.3	69.5	83.8	104.5	109.7	117.6

NOTE: These figures are Western estimates based on officially reported data. In the case of the GDR, in particular, internal figures that became available after unification indicate that these estimates understated the net debt. The table nevertheless gives a sense of orders of magnitude.

SOURCE: Adapted from Vienna Institute for Comparative Economic Studies, *Comecon Data 1990* (London: Macmillan, 1991).

VI. ESTIMATED NUMBER OF VISITS FROM EAST TO WEST GERMANY, 1962–89 *(in thousands)*

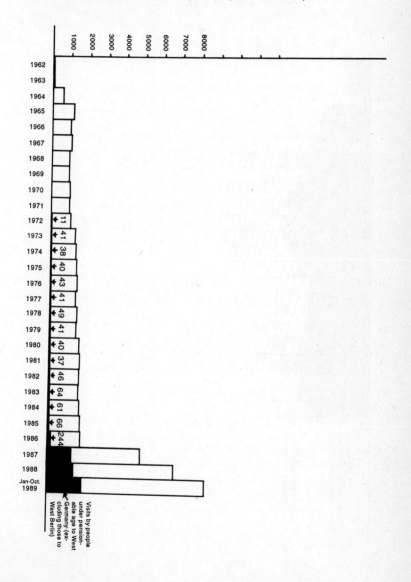

656

VII. ESTIMATED NUMBER OF VISITS FROM WEST TO EAST GERMANY, 1967–89 *(in thousands)*

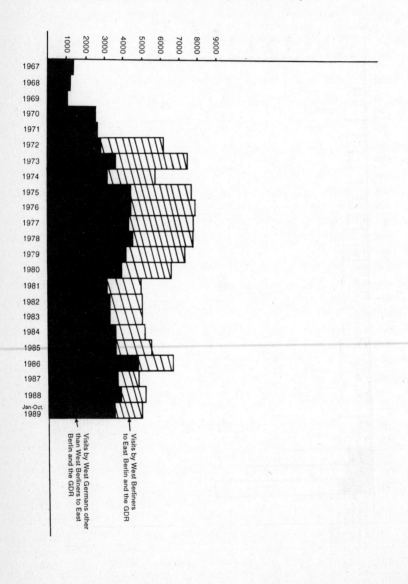

NOTES TO TABLES VI AND VII: The data on German-German travel are frustratingly incomplete. For a start, the records show the estimated total number of *visits*, but not the exact number of *visitors*. Moreover, just at the moment when the travel figures from East to West were soaring, the West German Ministry for Intra-German Relations changed its methodology. Whereas for the period up until 1986 it had collated information from frontier controls, supplemented by other sources, for the years 1987 to 1989 it relied mainly on a large-scale survey conducted by *Infratest Kommunikationsfor-schung*, based on interviews with West Germans. The resulting figures, starting with a pilot survey in 1986, suggested that there were actually more visits from East to West than had previously been thought, but less from West to East. So far as travel from East to West is concerned, one cannot therefore definitely say what part of the increase from 1986 to 1987 is due to a more permissive East German travel policy, and what to the change of methodology. Somewhere in the the East German archives there are presumably the precise East German figures, which would supplant all these. Note also that both tables deliberately give the figures only up to the end of October 1989, since the opening of the Berlin Wall obviously changed the picture completely.

On TABLE VI, note that the small black column, which gives the crucial figure of visits by people under pensionable age, allowed out of East Germany under the rubric of 'urgent family matters', does *not* include visits to West Berlin, only those to the rest of West Germany. The total number of such visits can therefore be assumed to have been larger.

On TABLE VII, note that in the earlier years some West Berliners were allowed to visit East Berlin by special permit (*Passierschein*). But the numbers were so small—some 60,000 a year from 1967 to 1969—that they would not show up on the scale on which this table is drawn.

SOURCES: For the period up to 1986: *Zahlenspiegel*. For the years 1987–89: author's estimates based on the 1987, 1988 and 1989 *DDR-Reisebarometer* of *Infratest Kommunikationsforschung* (Munich), supplemented by publications of the Ministry for Intra-German Relations and published East German figures.

VIII. ESCAPEES, LEGAL 'OVER-SETTLERS' AND POLITICAL PRISONERS 'BOUGHT FREE' FROM EAST TO WEST GERMANY, 1961–1989

	Total	Legal 'Over-Settlers'	%	Escaped via other countries	%	Escaped across the German-German frontier	%	Prisoners 'bought free'	%
1961	51 624		0.0	43 117	83.5	8 507	16,5		
1962	21 356	4 615	21.6	10 980	51.4	5 761	27,0		
1963	42 632	29 665	69.6	9 267	21.7	3 692	8,7	8	0.0
1964	41 873	30 012	71.7	7 826	18.7	3 155	7,5	880	2.1
1965	29 552	17 666	59.8	8 397	28.4	2 329	7.9	1 160	3.9
1966	24 131	15 675	65.0	6 320	26.2	1 736	7.2	400	1.7
1967	19 578	13 188	67.4	4 637	23.7	1 203	6.1	550	2.8
1968	16 036	11 134	69.4	3 067	19.1	1 135	7.1	700	4.4
1969	16 975	11 702	68.9	3 230	19.0	1 193	7.0	850	5.0
1970	17 519	12 472	71.2	3 246	18.5	901	5.1	900	5.1
1971	17 408	11 565	66.4	3 611	20.7	832	4.8	1 400	8.0
1972	17 164	11 627	67.7	3 562	20.8	1 245	7.3	730	4.3
1973	15 189	8 667	57.1	4 050	26.7	1 842	12.1	630	4.1
1974	13 252	7 928	59.8	3 255	24.6	969	7.3	1 100	8.3
1975	16 285	10 274	63.1	4 188	25.7	673	4.1	1 150	7.1
1976	15 168	10 058	66.3	3 010	19.8	610	4.0	1 490	9.8
1977	12 078	8 041	66.6	1 846	15.3	721	6.0	1 470	12.2
1978	12 117	8 271	68.3	1 905	15.7	461	3.8	1 480	12.2
1979	12 515	9 003	71.9	2 149	17.2	463	3.7	900	7.2
1980	12 763	8 775	68.8	2 683	21.0	424	3.3	881	6.9
1981	15 433	11 093	71.9	2 602	16.9	298	1.9	1 440	9.3
1982	13 208	9 113	69.0	2 282	17.3	283	2.1	1 530	11.6

	Total	Legal 'Over-Settlers'	%	Escaped via other countries	%	Escaped across the German-German frontier	%	Prisoners 'bought free'	%
1983	11 343	7 729	68.2	2 259	19.9	228	2.0	1 127	9.9
1984	40 974	34 982	85.4	3 459	8.4	192	0.5	2 341	5.7
1985	24 912	18 752	75.3	3 324	13.3	160	0.7	2 676	10.7
1986	26 178	19 982	76.3	4 450	17.0	210	0.8	1 536	5.9
1987	18 958	11 459	60.4	5 964	31.5	288	1.5	1 247	6.6
1988	39 845	29 033	72.9	9 129	22.9	589	1.5	1 094	2.7
1961–88	616 066	382 481	62.1	163 815	26.6	40 100	6.5	29 670	4.8
1989	343,85	325,054			17,073			1,727	

NOTE: Legal 'over-settlers' are those who left with the permission of the East German authorities. For 1989, the distinction between escapes across the German-German frontier and those via other countries can apparently no longer be drawn. Some of those counted as 'over-settlers' for 1989 would in earlier years have been counted as escapees.

SOURCE: FAZ, 21 October 1989, based on figures from the *Bundesausgleich-amt*. Figures for 1989 from the *Bundesverwaltungsamt*.

IX. WEST GERMANY'S 'OUT-SETTLERS' FROM THE SOVIET UNION AND EASTERN EUROPE, 1950–92

	1950	1951	1952	1953	1954	1955	1956	1957	1958	1959	1960
Soviet Union	0	1,721	63	0	18	154	1,016	923	4,122	5,563	3,272
Poland	31,761	10,791	194	147	664	860	15,674	98,290	117,550	16,252	7,739
Czecho-slovakia	13,308	3,524	146	63	128	184	954	762	692	600	1,394
Hungary	3	157	30	15	43	98	160	2,193	1,194	507	319
Romania	13	1,031	26	15	8	44	176	384	1,383	374	2,124
Yugoslavia	179	3,668	3,407	7,972	9,481	11,839	7,314	5,130	4,703	3,819	3,308
Other areas	1,901	175	182	84	50	23	8	8	11	21	15
Total	47,165	21,067	4,048	8,296	10,392	13,202	25,302	107,690	129,655	27,136	18,171
Via third countries	332	3,698	9,321	7,114	5,032	2,586	6,043	6,256	2,573	1,314	998
Grand Total	47,497	24,765	13,369	15,410	15,424	15,788	31,345	113,946	132,228	28,450	19,169

	1961	1962	1963	1964	1965	1966	1967	1968	1969	1970	1971
Soviet Union	345	894	209	234	366	1,245	1,092	598	316	342	1,145
Poland	9,303	9,657	9,522	13,611	14,644	17,315	10,856	8,435	9,536	5,624	25,241
Czecho-slovakia	1,207	1,228	973	2,712	3,210	5,925	11,628	11,854	15,602	4,702	2,337
Hungary	194	264	286	387	724	608	316	303	414	517	519
Romania	3,303	1,675	1,321	818	2,715	609	440	614	2,675	6,519	2,848
Yugoslavia	2,053	2,003	2,543	2,331	2,195	2,078	1,881	1,391	1,325	1,372	1,159
Other areas	9	12	15	6	13	33	14	6	5	9	23
Total	16,414	15,733	14,869	20,099	23,867	27,813	26,227	23,201	29,873	19,085	33.272
Via third countries	747	682	614	743	475	380	248	196	166	359	365
Grand Total	17,161	16,415	15,483	20,842	24,342	28,193	26,475	23,397	30,039	19,444	33,637

	1972	1973	1974	1975	1976	1977	1978	1979	1980	1981	1982
Soviet Union	3,420	4,493	6,541	5,985	9,704	9,274	8,455	7,226	6,954	3,773	2,071
Poland	13,482	8,903	7,825	7,040	29,364	32,857	36,102	36,274	26,637	50,983	30,355
Czecho-slovakia	894	525	378	516	849	612	904	1,058	1,733	1,629	1,776
Hungary	520	440	423	277	233	189	269	370	591	667	589
Romania	4,374	7,577	8,484	5,077	3,766	10,989	12,120	9,663	15,767	12,031	12,972
Yugoslavia	884	783	646	419	313	237	202	190	287	234	213
Other areas	6	11	18	15	19	5	9	21	15	19	16
Total	23,580	22,732	24,315	19,329	44,248	54,163	58,061	54,802	51,984	69,336	47,992
Via third countries	315	331	192	328	154	88	62	85	87	119	178
Grand Total	23,895	23,063	24,507	19,657	44,402	54,251	58,123	54,887	52,071	69,455	48,170

	1983	1984	1985	1986	1987	1988	1989	1990	1991	1992	1950 to 1992
Soviet Union	1,447	913	460	753	14,488	47,572	98,134	147,950	147,320	195,576	746,147
Poland	19,121	17,455	22,075	27,188	48,423	140,226	250,340	133,872	40,129	17,742	1,430,059
Czecho-slovakia	1,176	963	757	882	835	949	2,027	1,708	927	460	104,691
Hungary	458	286	485	584	581	763	1,618	1,336	952	354	21,236
Romania	15,501	16,553	14,924	13,130	13,994	12,902	23,387	111,150	32,178	16,146	401,800
Yugoslavia	137	190	191	182	156	223	1,469	961	450	199	89,717
Other areas	4	26	13	10	21	10	67	90	18	12	3,048
Total	37,844	36,386	38,905	42,729	78,498	202,645	377,042	397,067	221,974	230,489	2,796,698
Via third countries	81	73	63	59	25	28	13	6	21	76	52.626
Grand Total	37,925	36,459	33,968	42,788	78,523	202,673	377,055	397,073	221,995	230,565	2,849,324

NOTE: For the complicated definition of 'out-settlers' see the section 'Compatriots' in Chapter Five. For 1992, it is of course 'former Soviet Union' and 'former Yugoslavia'.

SOURCE: Federal Ministry of the Interior.

Acknowledgements

For permission to consult all or part of their papers in the archives, I am indebted to the late Willy Brandt, to Helmut Schmidt and Egon Bahr, to the heirs of the late Alois Mertes and Werner Marx, to Wolfgang Schollwer, and, in his capacity as chairman of the Free Democrats, to Hans-Dietrich Genscher. Invaluable assistance was then given me by the archivists of the *Archiv der sozialen Demokratie*, notably Frau Gertrud Lenz for the Brandt papers, Herr Christoph Stamm for the Schmidt papers and Frau Barbara Richter for the Bahr papers; by those of the *Archiv fur Christlich-Demokratische Politik*, notably Dr Günter Buchstab, Frau Kessler and Herr Dietmar Haak; and of the *Archiv des Deutschen Liberalismus*, led by Dr Monika Fassbender.

I owe a special debt of gratitude to the archivists of the *Zentrales Parteiarchiv* in East Berlin, notably Dr Inge Pardon, Frau Räuber, Frau Gräfe and the invariably cheerful Herr Muller and Herr Lange, all of whom made special efforts to facilitate my work during a difficult period of transition for that archive. Equally, I thank particularly Dr Hubertus Knabe for facilitating my access to the archives of the former Ministry for State Security, now under the so-called *Gauck-Behörde*, and Herr Förster and Frau Schulz for their detailed assistance.

Dr Hans-Jochen Vogel gave an example to his colleagues (in all parties) by making available to me his own records of his talks with Erich Honecker, so that these could be compared with those in the *Zentrales Parteiarchiv*. This was of course a valuable test of the veracity of those East German records.

The *Zentrales Dokumentationssystem* of the *Bundespresseamt* gave me invaluable assistance in tracking down the press and media reports which are so much the bread and butter of contemporary politics. I thank Professor Wolfgang Bergsdorf for opening the door to this wonderful resource, and Frau Anna Maria Kuppe for producing swift and meticulously researched answers to my often obscure queries. Equally helpful was the press archive of the SPD, which made available its rich files and tireless photocopier.

At a later stage in the work, the *Auswärtiges Amt* answered a number of detailed queries which could not readily be answered elsewhere. I am grateful to Dr Dieter Kastrup, the State Secretary of the *Auswärtiges Amt*, for suggesting this, and to Dr Martin Ney for organising the responses. The staffs of *Gesamtdeutsches Institut*, when it still existed, of the library of the ZI6 at the Free University of Berlin, of the Bundestag library and of the *Bundeszentrale für Politische Bildung* — there particularly Herr Rüdiger Thomas — were consistently helpful in providing books and information.

The many historical witnesses to whom I spoke provided one of the richest sources for this book. Their names appear at the appropriate places in the Notes, but I would like to thank them all for giving me their time and their selected memories. In addition, I would like to thank the following for their valuable help in discussing particular aspects or pursuing specific queries: Professor Egon Bahr, Dr Peter Bender, Dr Lev Bezymensky, Dr Brigitte Seebacher-Brandt, Dr Günter Buchstab, Lord Bullock, Richard Davy, Herr Roland Freudenstein, Herr Karl-Wilhelm Fricke, Professor Gabriel Gorodetsky, Dr Klaus Gotto, Professor Philip Hanson, Dr Hans-Jürgen Heimsoeth, Professor Sir Michael Howard, Professor Harold James, Professor Karl Kaiser, Dr Axel Lebahn, Professor Werner Link, Herr Manfred Meissner, Dr Sigrid Meuschel, Dr Marina Pavlova-Silvanskaya, Dr Jerzy Lisiecki, Dr Zbigniew Pelczynski, Dr Peter Siebenmorgen, Dr Wolfgang Stock, Herr Horst Teltschik, Dr Jochen Thies, Dr Armin Volze, Craig P Whitney, Professor Heinrich-August Winkler, Dr Stefan Wolle, Dr Jonathan Wright, Professor Hartmut Zimmermann.

Work on this book has been supported above all by extremely generous funding from the Ford Foundation, first for a research project based at St Antony's College, Oxford, then for a Senior Research Fellowship at that College. I should like to thank particularly Enid Schoettle and subsequently Shep Forman and Paul Balaran. At a later stage, the research was supported by the European Cultural Foundation, one of the few genuinely European foundations that exist, and my thanks there go especially to Franz Alting von Geusau and Raymond Georis. Further funding was provided by the Nuffield Foundation, by the Cyril Foster Fund at Oxford, and, at the last, by the Modern History Faculty of Oxford University. I am grateful to them all.

The very earliest drafts of the first part of this book were written during my time as a Fellow at the Woodrow Wilson International Center for Scholars in Washington DC, and I thank in particular the then director, James Billington, and the head of the West European Program, Michael Haltzel, for their assistance and support. A short stay at the *Stiftung Wissenschaft und Politik* in Ebenhausen, on the kind invitation of the Director, Professor Michael Stürmer, enabled me to discuss my ideas with the specialists there and to pursue some additional sources. A visiting fellowship at the Vienna *Institut für die Wissenschaften vom Menschen*, which has itself made a significant contribution to reducing the intellectual division of Europe, gave me an opportunity to discuss my ideas with Austrian and East Central European colleagues. I am grateful to Krzysztof Michalski for this opportunity.

The largest part of this book was, however, written in Oxford. I owe much to the wider community of scholars in the University, particularly to those in German and East European history, European politics and International Relations, and to the students who ask good questions.

The institution to which this book owes most of all is St Antony's College. It would, I think, be impossible to find a better place to pursue such a project. Virtually all my colleagues have provided a stimulus of one sort or another. For their assistance on particular points, I would like to thank specifically Andrew Walter, Alex Pravda, Anne Deighton, Archie Brown and Michael Kaser. I am especially grateful to Tony Nicholls, the Director of the European Studies Centre, who not only presided over many interesting seminars on related themes but also read and commented expertly on the whole typescript. The College librarians, Rosamund Campbell and Hilary Maddicott, have been unfailingly helpful and cheerful. Caroline Henderson gave me stalwart secretarial help in the early years, as did Anna Lever in the later ones.

I have been most fortunate in my research assistants, starting with John Connelly in Washington, and continuing in Oxford with Mark Smith, John Laughland, Tina Podplatnik, Frank Müller, Nikolas Gvosdev and, last but by no means least, Danuta Garton Ash. Their help was both invaluable and enjoyable.

Sir Julian Bullard, Pierre Hassner and Fritz Stern read the typescript, and greatly enriched it by their comments both at this and earlier points. I am much in their debt.

At the last editing stage, my publishers, David Godwin of Jonathan Cape and Jason Epstein of Random House, and my editor, Euan Cameron, encouraged the author and improved the text.

My final, very special thanks go to four friends who have, in their different ways, accompanied and shaped this book from its earliest days.

Werner Krätschell was for the first part of the writing still shut in behind the Berlin Wall, in Pankow. For the second part, he was free to visit his godson in Oxford at the drop of a hat. I have thought of him and his family often while working on what for most readers is history, but for them has been life.

Arnulf Baring, who crucially sharpened the definition of the subject at an early stage, has influenced me by the example of his own writing of contemporary history, by his encouragement, and, most of all, by his characteristic, restless and provocative questioning.

Michael Mertes has sustained a truly wonderful flow of information, ideas, suggestions and advice, by post, fax and telephone, culminating in an immensely helpful commentary on the complete typescript.

Ralf Dahrendorf has quite simply been godfather to this book, not just institutionally, as Warden of St Antony's, but even more intellectually and personally, informing, questioning, encouraging, sharpening at every step, with a unique perspective which is both German, British and, after all, European.

Index

Important terms such as Cold War, détente, Deutschlandpolitik, Europe (East, West and Central), Germany (West, East and united), Ostpolitik, socialism and the West have not been included in the following index since they appear so frequently throughout the book. Only the main text has been indexed.

678

678

THE MAGIC LANTERN

The Revolution of '89
Witnessed in Warsaw, Budapest, Berlin and Prague

"A wonderful combination of first-class reporting, brilliant political analysis and reflection."
—*The New York Times Book Review*

The Magic Lantern is one of those rare books that define a historic moment, written by a brilliant witness who was also a participant in epochal events. Whether covering Poland's first free parliamentary elections—in which Solidarity found itself in the position of trying to limit the scope of its victory—or sitting in at the meetings of an unlikely coalition of bohemian intellectuals and Catholic clerics orchestrating the liberation of Czechoslovakia, Garton Ash writes with enormous sympathy and power.

In this book, Garton Ash creates a stunningly evocative portrait of the revolutions that swept Communism from Central Europe in 1989 and whose after-effects will continue to shape events for years to come.

CURRENT AFFAIRS / HISTORY / 0-679-74048-1

THE USES OF ADVERSITY

Essays on the Fate of Central Europe

"[Garton Ash's] own involvement in these events, intellectual and emotional, is of such intensity that he can speak, in a sense, from the inside as well as from the outside."
—George F. Kennan, *New York Review of Books*

"This collection will endure because it depicts so exactly, and often presciently, the region on the brink of its most dramatic political transformation since the early years of the Cold War."
—*Wilson Quarterly*

POLITICAL SCIENCE / 0-679-73199-7

using it was wrong. Reaching into his pocket, Jeremy handed over a set of keys hanging on a large red key chain.

"Thank you," said Lissa. "And where is it parked?"

"Down the street," he said dreamily. "At the corner. By Brown." Four blocks away.

"Thank you," she repeated, backing up. "As soon as we leave, I want you to go back to studying. Forget you ever saw us tonight."

He nodded obligingly. I got the impression he would have walked off a cliff for her right then if she'd asked. All humans were susceptible to compulsion, but Jeremy appeared weaker than most. That came in handy right now.

"Come on," I told her. "We've got to move."

We stepped outside, heading toward the corner he'd named. I was still dizzy from the bite and kept stumbling, unable to move as quickly as I wanted. Lissa had to catch hold of me a few times to stop me from falling. All the time, that anxiety rushed into me from her mind. I tried my best to ignore it; I had my own fears to deal with.

"Rose . . . what are we going to do if they catch us?" she whispered.

"They won't," I said fiercely. "I won't let them."

"But if they've found us—"

"They found us before. They didn't catch us then. We'll just drive over to the train station and go to L.A. They'll lose the trail."

I made it sound simple. I always did, even though there

was nothing simple about being on the run from the people we'd grown up with. We'd been doing it for two years, hiding wherever we could and just trying to finish high school. Our senior year had just started, and living on a college campus had seemed safe. We were so close to freedom.

She said nothing more, and I felt her faith in me surge up once more. This was the way it had always been between us. I was the one who took action, who made sure things happened— sometimes recklessly so. She was the more reasonable one, the one who thought things out and researched them extensively before acting. Both styles had their uses, but at the moment, recklessness was called for. We didn't have time to hesitate.

Lissa and I had been best friends ever since kindergarten, when our teacher had paired us together for writing lessons. Forcing five-year-olds to spell *Vasilisa Dragomir* and *Rosemarie Hathaway* was beyond cruel, and we'd—or rather, I'd—responded appropriately. I'd chucked my book at our teacher and called her a fascist bastard. I hadn't known what those words meant, but I'd known how to hit a moving target.

Lissa and I had been inseparable ever since.

"Do you hear that?" she asked suddenly.

It took me a few seconds to pick up what her sharper senses already had. Footsteps, moving fast. I grimaced. We had two more blocks to go.

"We've got to run for it," I said, catching hold of her arm.

"But you can't—"

"Run."

It took every ounce of my willpower not to pass out on the sidewalk. My body didn't want to run after losing blood or while still metabolizing the effects of her saliva. But I ordered my muscles to stop their bitching and clung to Lissa as our feet pounded against the concrete. Normally I could have outrun her without any extra effort—particularly since she was barefoot—but tonight, she was all that held me upright.

The pursuing footsteps grew louder, closer. Black stars danced before my eyes. Ahead of us, I could make out Jeremy's green Honda. Oh God, if we could just make it—

Ten feet from the car, a man stepped directly into our path. We came to a screeching halt, and I jerked Lissa back by her arm. It was *him*, the guy I'd seen across the street watching me. He was older than us, maybe mid-twenties, and as tall as I'd figured, probably six-six or six-seven. And under different circumstances—say, when he wasn't holding up our desperate escape—I would have thought he was hot. Shoulder-length brown hair, tied back in a short ponytail. Dark brown eyes. A long brown coat—a duster, I thought it was called.

But his hotness was irrelevant now. He was only an obstacle keeping Lissa and me away from the car and our freedom. The footsteps behind us slowed, and I knew our pursuers had caught up. Off to the sides, I detected more movement, more people closing in. God. They'd sent almost a dozen guardians to retrieve us. I couldn't believe it. The queen herself didn't travel with that many.

Panicked and not entirely in control of my higher reasoning, I acted out of instinct. I pressed up to Lissa, keeping her behind me and away from the man who appeared to be the leader.

"Leave her alone," I growled. "Don't touch her."

His face was unreadable, but he held out his hands in what was apparently supposed to be some sort of calming gesture, like I was a rabid animal he was planning to sedate.

"I'm not going to—"

He took a step forward. Too close.

I attacked him, leaping out in an offensive maneuver I hadn't used in two years, not since Lissa and I had run away. The move was stupid, another reaction born of instinct and fear. And it was hopeless. He was a skilled guardian, not a novice who hadn't finished his training. He also wasn't weak and on the verge of passing out.

And man, was he fast. I'd forgotten how fast guardians could be, how they could move and strike like cobras. He knocked me off as though brushing away a fly, and his hands slammed into me and sent me backwards. I don't think he meant to strike that hard—probably just intended to keep me away—but my lack of coordination interfered with my ability to respond. Unable to catch my footing, I started to fall, heading straight toward the sidewalk at a twisted angle, hip-first. It was going to hurt. A *lot*.

Only it didn't.

Just as quickly as he'd blocked me, the man reached out and caught my arm, keeping me upright. When I'd steadied myself, I noticed he was staring at me—or, more precisely, at my neck. Still disoriented, I didn't get it right away. Then, slowly, my free hand reached up to the side of my throat and lightly touched the wound Lissa had made earlier. When I pulled my fingers back, I saw slick, dark blood on my skin. Embarrassed, I shook my hair so that it fell forward around my face. My hair was thick and long and completely covered my neck. I'd grown it out for precisely this reason.

The guy's dark eyes lingered on the now-covered bite a moment longer and then met mine. I returned his look defiantly and quickly jerked out of his hold. He let me go, though I knew he could have restrained me all night if he'd wanted. Fighting the nauseating dizziness, I backed toward Lissa again, bracing myself for another attack. Suddenly, her hand caught hold of mine. "Rose," she said quietly. "Don't."

Her words had no effect on me at first, but calming thoughts gradually began to settle in my mind, coming across through the bond. It wasn't exactly compulsion—she wouldn't use that on me—but it was effectual, as was the fact that we were hopelessly outnumbered and outclassed. Even I knew struggling would be pointless. The tension left my body, and I sagged in defeat.

Sensing my resignation, the man stepped forward, turning his attention to Lissa. His face was calm. He swept her a bow and managed to look graceful doing it, which surprised me considering his height. "My name is Dimitri Belikov," he said. I could hear a faint Russian accent. "I've come to take you back to St. Vladimir's Academy, Princess."

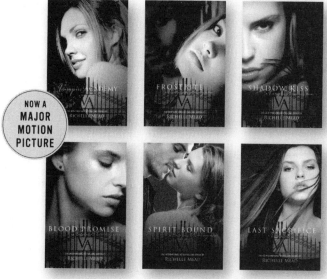